Cerberus MC Collection 6

Marie James

Colton

Drew

Jinx

Colton

Copyright

Colton: Cerberus MC Book 14
Copyright © 2020 Marie James
Editing by Marie James Betas & Ms. K Edits
EBooks are not transferrable. All rights are reserved. No part of this book may be used or reproduced in any manner without written permission, except in the case of brief quotations embodied in critical articles and reviews. The unauthorized reproduction or distribution of this copyrighted work is illegal. No part of this book may be scanned, uploaded, or distributed via the Internet or any other means, electronic or print, without the publisher's permission.
This book is a work of fiction. The names, characters, places, and incidents are products of the writer's imagination or have been used fictitiously and are not to be construed as real. Any resemblance to persons, living or dead, actual events, locale, or organizations is entirely coincidental.

Synopsis

Detective Colton Matthews has experienced a lot in the last ten years.
Promotions.
Divorce.
Single-dad life.
His work life is as full of surprises as his home life.
But nothing prepared him for *her*.
Saying yes to the favor asked of the Cerberus MC was a no-brainer.
He's a good guy, helping other good guys.
How hard would it be to allow Sophia, Dominic Anderson's daughter, to shadow him for a few months to complete a college credit and keep things professional?
The short answer...
Impossible.
Especially when his job puts her in danger.

Chapter 1

Colton

"That's correct," I sigh, head bent over my keyboard, eyes squeezed shut as if it will help to stave off the irritation of having to deal with this for a third time. "I submitted my request two weeks ago."

"We can't find it, Detective Matthews. You'll have to submit it again." The voice on the other end of the line seems just as annoyed as I'm feeling.

Mondays suck.

Pinching the bridge of my nose, I take another deep breath. The first ten didn't help, and this one doesn't seem like it's going to either.

"That's the same thing I was told last week, so I submitted the request again. Is there a supervisor I can speak with?"

"Hold, please."

Ridiculous elevator music fills the line as my eyes dart to the growing stack of cases on my desk. Farmington isn't a huge town, so every questionable death lands in front of me. I contemplate taking a vacation, but I know the work will only be waiting for me when I return.

"Hey."

My eyes snap up to the doorway. I've only been at work for twenty minutes, but I'm still not capable of reflecting back the grin that's being aimed at me.

I raise an eyebrow when my chief doesn't immediately open his mouth to speak.

"What's up?"

"Don't forget you have Professor Wesley from that community college coming today."

How could I forget?

The answer is simple, I have a million other things to worry about than entertaining the idea of speaking to a bunch of gore-hungry college students about police work. They don't want to know a damn thing about the ins and outs of the job. Of course their questions start off simple, but they always end with wanting to know about the gruesome side of the job. I blame television for desensitizing today's youth.

"Tell me that isn't today."

"It is," Chief Monahan confirms as he looks down at his watch. "She should be here any minute."

"Thanks," I mumble, holding up a finger when the music stops and someone comes back on the line.

"Detective Matthews?"

"Still here," I mutter because her voice is filled with the hopefulness that I've hung up the phone while waiting.

"I've found your request for those documents. I'll start processing it now."

"Will it be expedited due to the delay?"

Light from the outer room fills my office when Monahan walks away.

"Did the precinct pay for the rush fee?" My eyes narrow.

"No, but the initial request was made over two weeks ago."

"Without the correct fees applied, it will be five business days."

"Perfect." It's anything but perfect, but the request is for a cold case I've been dabbling with for the last six months. Another week, honestly, won't make a difference.

"The requested documents will be ready for pickup next Monday."

My lip twitches, the agitation I've felt since my alarm went off this morning coming to a head.

"Thank you," I tell the clerk before dropping the phone back on the receiver.

If my first thirty minutes at work is a reflection of how today is going to go, I may need that vacation after all. With my eyes closed, I roll my head around on my shoulders, but the back-and-forth motion doesn't alleviate the stress that's been building nonstop since I graduated from the academy fourteen years ago.

"Looks like you could use a massage."

My eyes snap open, but before I can open my mouth to tell the interloper to fuck off, I notice her smile.

Yes, it's the first thing I see, but I'm a cop, so the ability to take in the full picture in the blink of an eye is a skill I honed many, many years ago.

Mysterious dark eyes, haloed by long lashes, watch me. A slender neck leads to a regretfully fully buttoned blouse. The no doubt sexy curve of her breasts is hidden behind a suit jacket. The soft flare of her hips is covered by a pencil skirt that flirts at the top of her knees. Her tan skin glistens, which should be an anomaly considering the harsh florescent lights.

She's utter perfection. Younger than I would think a college professor would be, but what the hell do I know? There's so much cosmetic stuff on the market these days, fifty is the new thirty-five. Going by that math, I'd say this woman may look no older than twenty-five, but she's probably about ten years older—same age as me.

Suddenly, helping this woman out with her class seems like the best idea my chief has ever tossed my way. When her smile widens, I understand completely. As a married man, Monahan probably didn't want the trouble that would come with this woman. Not that he would cheat, the man is as loyal as they come, but this woman is clearly meant for sin.

"May I have a seat?"

I blink up at her, my brain refusing to come back online.

"What?"

"A seat?" She points a perfectly manicured nail at the chair in front of my desk.

"Oh, yeah." I stand like a starstruck idiot and point.

She chuckles, and it makes me wonder if she gets this reaction all the time. I wouldn't doubt it. I see crazy stuff nearly every day, and I'm certain this is the first time my brain has been fried by a good-looking woman.

"Monahan reminded me this morning you'd be here."

Her brow furrows, and I give myself an internal pat on the back. It's the only way I can think to regain some power, to let her know I may be acting like a fool now, but that I haven't been waiting around for her to show up.

"Who?"

"Chief Monahan," I clarify.

She gives me a small smile as she lowers a leather computer bag beside the chair at her feet.

"I'll be honest, I don't know Chief Monahan very well. I think I've only met him once."

"Great guy," I say as I settle back in my chair. "Surprised you wanted to meet with me instead of him."

"I'm not very interested in the administrative side of the department, Detective Matthews."

Is her voice actually as sultry as it sounds when she says my name, or has it just been too long since I've had a woman under me?

I clear my throat, the office being no place to even contemplate the things that seem to want to infiltrate my head right now.

"What exactly are you interested in?"

I lean back in my office chair, finding it strange that I'm being weird about where my hands are situated. Clasping them together, I settle them on my lap, but then realize I look like a teen trying to hide an erection, so I curl my fingers around the armrests. The woman is smoking hot, but I'm a grown-ass man in control of my damn body.

Then she shifts, lifting her leg slightly to cross it over her other, and my hands go right back to my lap.

Clearing my throat, I scoot further under my desk.

"You seem a little out of sorts." She bends, the top buttons on her blouse stretching and sadly holding when she reaches into her laptop bag. "Is it because it's Monday or does every day on the job stress you out?"

My brain doesn't come back online again until she straightens in her chair with a notebook on her lap and a pen in her hand.

"Some days are better than others."

"You make it sound like all days have some degree of bad."

"I'm a homicide detective," I remind her. "Every day is bad for someone."

Her smile drops from her pretty face when she takes in the gravity of my words.

"You don't seem as rabid for information. Are the students in your class the same?"

I'm probably not the first person she's approached to speak to her class. Most criminal justice programs are smaller, and the students take the majority of the classes offered. I imagine recycling the same guest speakers would get boring.

"I guess like with any class, the personalities range from disinterested to rabid as you called it." She lifts the end of her pen to her mouth, her plump lips pursing against it, and I'm fascinated at the sight.

I can't concentrate, not even a little.

"I have a pretty full schedule today. Maybe we should get together over dinner to discuss the finer details?" I keep my focus on her mouth, praying she's savvy enough to understand my hesitation to continue a discussion in my office.

"Dinner?" My skin heats when her gaze focuses on my own mouth. "It's not even nine yet. We could get so much done between now and then."

"We could," I agree. "But I have to work."

"Won't you be tired by the end of your shift?"

"I have a very good feeling my energy level won't be an issue."

"No?" That fucking pen teases her lower lip, and the erection I was certain I could keep at bay is throbbing behind the zipper of my slacks.

I lower my voice. "Not a chance. We could meet at Wright's, the little diner off Main. Say six o'clock?"

"For dinner?"

"Yes."

"Seems like a waste of time." Her eyes lift to mine, sparkling with mischief and desire. "Wouldn't the Hampton Inn be better?"

"Get right to the point?" I tease.

"Is there any other way?"

"We'll have to discuss your class, eventually."

"It can wait another day, or we could chat while you're recharging."

"You assume you'll wear me out."

"I know I will." Perfect teeth dig into her lower lip, and although I've never done it before, I have the sudden urge to feign illness and leave for the day.

I shift in my seat, and she gives me a knowing look.

"Besides," she leans closer, "are you really going to get anything done with a hard co—"

"Matthews!"

Guiltily, I snap my head up, and I want to unleash a territorial growl when Detective Haden Gaffey smiles down at my visitor.

"What?" I snap, but he ignores me.

"Are you serious?" Gaffey asks the woman opposite of me as he draws closer. "I didn't know I'd be seeing your beautiful face today."

"Haden," the professor says with an easy smile.

I nearly come unglued like a psycho when she stands and his arms automatically go around her waist.

"You look amazing. How's your dad?"

"He's good. Staying busy with work. You know how it is."

I release a breath I didn't know I was holding when she steps back, putting a couple feet of distance between them.

Gaffey has been on the police force for almost twenty years, and he was one of my training officers when I was first hired. I've always respected the hell out of the man, and it's shocking I was ready to chew his face off when he first walked in here.

"Don't let this one give you a hard time," Gaffey says, hitching his thumb over his shoulder in my direction.

Oh, I have a hard time for her alright.

She grins at me. "I can handle him."

"Yeah?" Gaffey laughs. "I don't imagine it'll be too bad working with him. I don't think there's a man alive that would want to get on the wrong side of your dad."

She rolls her eyes, making her appear much younger than her attire is hinting at.

"It's good to see you, Soph." Gaffey turns in my direction. "That professor from the college is waiting in the lobby for you."

He walks away, but my eyes snap to the woman in front of me.

Chapter 2

Sophia

"Soph?"

I roll my lips between my teeth to keep a grin from taking over my face.

When I first saw this man months ago at the clubhouse, I knew I wanted to see him again. As a soon-to-be-graduating criminal justice major, I had the perfect in.

Detective Colton Matthews stares at me, confused.

I'm not surprised.

I could tell he thought I was someone else mere seconds after I darkened his office door.

He didn't look at me like a charity case, like I was a favor he was doing for my dad.

And I reveled in it.

Then his eyes swept down my body as he took stock of each and every one of my features. That has never happened in this town. Of course I get checked out, I'm young and decent looking. I work out often, so my body type appeals to some people, but the fact that he didn't care who I was when he noticed me standing there meant he in fact didn't know who I was.

The flirting got out of hand. The suggestions got cruder, and if we weren't interrupted by Haden, I imagine we'd be sliding into his car and heading for a nice quiet hotel room.

But, just my luck, I've been figured out.

"Soph?" he repeats after another long pause.

I know his brain must be working ninety to nothing, trying to figure out who exactly I am and going back over our entire conversation word for word as he prepares for the defense against the inappropriate topic we discussed.

"Sophia Anderson," I say as I hold my hand out for him to shake.

"Anderson?"

"Yes." I drop my hand when he makes it clear he isn't going to offer his.

"Dominic Anderson's daughter?"

"Correct." I straighten my suit jacket, growing mildly uncomfortable now that the ruse is over. "I'm here for my internship."

"You were supposed to be here at the beginning of the semester. I expected you in January, not mid-March."

"I had another class I had to finish before I could leave campus." I settle back into the chair across from his desk. "I emailed to let you know I'd be here today."

"Emailed?" His head tilts as his throat works on a swallow. He drops back into his seat, hands shaking the computer mouse to bring his system to life. He focuses on the screen for a long moment before looking back in my direction. "You emailed yesterday."

"Correct." Heat pinks my cheeks, and I hate that he's making me feel like a damn child so soon after our sexual banter mere moments ago.

"That's not very responsible."

"I apologize." The back of my throat burns, but I straighten my back, keeping my eyes locked on the side of his face.

He can't even look at me right now, and I'm certain I've ruined everything. I don't have another internship lined up, and I'm lucky my professor is even allowing this to count as the full credit I need when she didn't have to be so gracious. If I get tossed out of here, I won't graduate on time.

"And you're late because you had to make up another class? Was that also because you flaked on those responsibilities?"

My lips quiver, and I know if I open my mouth to talk about the situation I was in before the holidays last year, I'll cry. There's nothing more cliché than a college girl shedding tears when put on the spot, so I refuse.

I blink at him, mouth clamped closed. Something over my shoulder catches his eye.

He clears his throat and stands from his chair. I mimic his actions. Giving myself permission to break eye contact, I reach down for my computer bag before facing him again.

"I have to meet this professor." He waves his hand, cupping his fingers to someone across the room.

"Do I need to leave?"

His eyes find mine once again, and even though there's still a desk and several feet separating us, I feel small in his presence. Even with respectable three-inch heels on, I feel like he could overpower me if he wanted to, and it's not just his size that intimidates—it's the entire package, the look in his eyes, the way his jaw clenches as he assesses me.

"No, but you will need to change."

"I didn't bring—" My mouth snaps closed when he shifts his weight. "I'll figure it out."

I follow him out of his office, skirting around a middle-aged woman with graying hair.

"Professor Wesley, good morning. Please, have a seat."

The woman greets him cordially. I turn back around to offer a whispered apology, but he closes the door in my face before I can open my mouth.

Deciding to stick around even though I want to run and beg my dad to fix my mistake, I walk out of the police station and head to my car. Dropping my computer bag in the trunk, I mentally go over my options. I can drive back to my parents' house, or I can wear the gym clothes I brought this morning for my evening workout. It'll take well over an hour to go home, get changed, and make it back here. I opt to wear the workout clothes. Besides, I already messed up royally today, so it's not like my apparel could make things worse.

"Things seemed tense in there."

I grimace as I pull the gym bag from the backseat. When I straighten to find Haden standing a few feet away, I want to run through every excuse in the book, but lying to a cop hasn't worked out so far for me today. Yet, the truth isn't an option either. I decide on half and half.

"He wasn't happy with my attire." I shrug. "So, it looks like I'm going to be spending the day in workout gear."

"Can't really chase a perp in heels, Soph."

My eyes widen with the prospect of getting to do some real police work on my first day at interning.

"Really? Think I'll get to tackle a criminal?"

"No." He shakes his head, a genuine smile playing at his lips. "You don't get to rough up perps. Do you honestly think your dad would let you be here if he thought you were in any danger?"

"True." I shrug because arguing with my dad's friend about being a grown woman and able to make my own life choices will only fall on deaf ears.

"Is there a bathroom inside?"

"Let me show you to the women's locker room."

I follow Haden as he opens a side door with an ID card, and less than a minute later, he's standing outside of a heavy door.

"I'll wait here while you change and show you how to get back to Matthews' office."

I make quick work of changing, stashing my gym bag, now filled with the skirt from my business suit I ridiculously thought would make me look more professional. Although I'm sure I look ridiculous, I knew I couldn't spend the day in leggings and a sports bra, so I've kept on the blouse and jacket of my suit, and only replaced my skirt and heels with black leggings and sneakers. I blame police procedural dramas on television for making me think I could do police work in a damn suit and heels.

Haden is on his phone when I exit the locker room, but I follow him when he starts walking. Once we're back in the main office area, he points his finger across the room to a row of four chairs. He gives me a quick wave before disappearing.

My fingers drum on the top of my thighs as I wait for Detective Matthews to exit his office. He can stay in there all day as far as I'm concerned. I figure the longer he's talking to that woman, the better the chance of him not sending me away the second he's done.

"Have you been helped?" I look up to find a handsome man in uniform grinning down at me.

"Hi," I squeak.

"Did you need some help?"

My mouth opens to ask him if he could help with the Detective Matthews situation, but I close it with the ridiculous thought.

"I'm Officer Dillon Ramshaw."

I take his warm hand when he offers it. "Sophia Anderson."

"If you haven't checked in at the front desk, no one will know that you're here." His smile is sweet, his eyes a little more roving than they'd need to be if he only approached me with the purpose of helping.

"I'm waiting for Detective Matthews."

His face falls immediately. "I'm sorry."

I give him a grin of my own at the sincerity in his voice. "Is he a jerk or something?"

His head tilts slightly to the left, confusion apparent on his handsome face. "Are you here about a death?"

"Internship," I answer, barely restraining a mumble about it being over before it even began.

"Ah." His smile returns. "Glad it's not because you've lost someone. He's not a jerk. He's actually a great guy. A little too serious most days, but he works his ass off."

"That's good to know."

"Fuck off, Ramshaw."

Dillon doesn't cringe at Detective Matthews command, and I guess that speaks to the truth he claimed a minute ago about him being a great guy.

"It was nice to meet you, Sophia Anderson."

"You, too, Dillon."

Officer Ramshaw nods at Matthews before strutting away, his hands resting on his utility belt like I've seen many police officers do in the movies.

"Need a napkin for the drool on your chin?"

I narrow my eyes as I stand, trying to get on even ground with Matthews, but I'm now in sneakers, making me even shorter than I was when we first met.

"Jealous?" My throat works on a rough swallow as regret swarms like angry bees in my gut. My mouth—Dad has warned me for years—will be the thing that gets me into trouble every time.

"No reason to be jealous over a boy wanting to—"

"Do the same things to me you wanted to do earlier?" I interrupt, my inability to keep my damn mouth shut continuing.

He crowds my space but somehow still manages not to touch me. I have to crane my head up to keep my eyes locked on his.

"We'll both forget that conversation took place."

Yeah, is that even possible?

"That is if you want to still do this internship."

"It is," I confirm, because the next couple of months are all that stands between me and the rest of my adult life.

"Good. Now let's go. We were expected at a scene ten minutes ago."

Chapter 3

Colton

I'm contemplating my life choices as we leave the police station.

But deep down, I know why I didn't send her away once I realized who she was. Flirting with her, although wildly inappropriate now that it's clear she isn't a college professor, was fun.

Denying that she's sexy as hell, despite knowing she can't be a day over twenty-two, would be useless. Every man in the vicinity is trying to catch her eye, including Ramshaw. He's a decent guy, but sniffing around Dominic Anderson's daughter isn't a very smart thing to do.

Everyone in town knows any female connected to the Cerberus MC is off-limits. We don't even have to be warned. We just all somehow know.

I've always had my concerns about the motorcycle club on the outskirts of town. They're mostly private, only offering bits and pieces of information. Of course, they're extremely active in the community. They help with fundraisers, and I know Monahan could call them for help and they'd show up at any time of day or night, but El Chapo had the respect of the citizens in his community, and we all know that drug dealer wasn't a good guy.

Women in Farmington find their mysterious demeanors attractive, like they're the holy grail of what men should be like. To me, their high level of privacy is suspicious.

"It's locked," Sophia says on the other side of the glass, and I look through the passenger door, wondering when I climbed inside the car and sat down.

I hit the unlock button and wait for her to climb inside.

The fabric of her athletic leggings draw tighter on her thighs, and I try to refocus my attention on something that doesn't have the potential to end with me buried in a shallow desert grave, because honestly, is there a legitimate biker club in existence that is a hundred percent on the right side of the law?

"Detective Matthews?"

I loosen the death grip I have on the steering wheel before looking over at her. She's kept the top part of her outfit on, the thin white fabric hinting at the delicate outline of her bra, and I snap my eyes straight forward again.

"Call me Colton."

"Colton," she repeats, letting the sound play on her tongue.

Big damn mistake.

I clear my throat.

"We're heading across town. A neighbor reported a foul smell, and patrol discovered a deceased person when they went for a wellness check."

"Okay." In my periphery, I see her snapping her seatbelt in place, and it reminds me I need to have mine on as well.

I'm going to have to call Dominic and tell him this just isn't going to work. I can't even climb in the car and head out on a call without getting distracted. My damn job is dangerous, and I don't want to get hurt. I sure as hell don't want to be responsible for this girl—*woman*, my mind reminds me—and her safety.

Maybe I can find someone else in the office that would be willing to take her off my hands. As I put the car in gear and roll out of the parking lot, my mind thinks of Gaffey, but then I remember how I felt when he put his hands on her, and I know that shit won't fly. Granted, he's old enough to be her dad and has worked long enough in the community to know to keep away from her, but Sophia is beyond gorgeous and a temptation to any man that gets hard for the opposite sex.

"Was it back there?" I look at Sophia to see her hitching her thumb over her shoulder.

A quick look in the rearview mirror proves that I can't handle much more of this. The flashing lights of two police cruisers are behind us because I just fucking drove right past the scene we're responding to.

"I want to park on the opposite side of the street," I lie as I pull into an empty driveway and turn around.

A tiny grin plays on her lips as I pull up across the street from the house in question and put the car in park.

"Do you want to stay in the car or come inside?"

I don't know why I'm giving her an option. I know exactly what we're going to be facing in there, and I'd bet there's no quicker way to get her out of my hair than insisting on her tagging along, but for some reason I want to protect her.

"I want to go inside."

"You're sure?" She nods, her eyes looking past my shoulder to take in the activity going on behind me. "There's a dead person in there."

"Correct."

"Have you seen a dead person before?"

"My aunt died when I was twelve."

"Murdered?" I feel a rush of sadness wash over me at the thought of this woman suffering with such a loss.

"Heart failure. She died in her sleep."

This is getting eerily familiar.

"The person in that house probably died in their sleep," I warn, not wanting to trigger her.

"Okay."

"Days ago," I amend.

Her eyes finally meet mine.

"It's cold at night, so the heat in the house has been on. The neighbors called because of the smell."

"Okay."

"You can stay in the car," I offer again.

"Is that where you want me?" There's no sexual inflection to her question, but that doesn't mean that my body knows the difference.

My body wants you under me, a million miles away from the stench of death.

"You're welcome to come inside. I just wanted to warn you, give you a heads-up about what you're going to be walking in on."

"I appreciate that."

She opens her car door when I open mine, and heaven help me, I wait at the front of the car for her to catch up to me. I should regret letting her walk a foot or so ahead of me because my eyes seem to have a mind of their own.

Why in the hell did I have her change her clothes? No skin on her legs is exposed like it was in the skirt, but the leggings peeking out from under the suit jacket are so tight I can't be sure she's wearing underwear.

Jesus, fuck, I'm so screwed.

"Matthews."

I try my best not to frown when I lift my eyes to see Gaffey standing on the front stoop.

"Hey, kiddo."

Sophia gives him a little wave, her jaw clenching with the nickname. It's clear she doesn't like to be seen as a child, and even though I feel the need to correct him because my own thoughts would be illegal if she were an actual kid, I keep my own mouth closed. Demanding he see her as a woman would be showing my hand, and that's the last thing I need.

"It's pretty gruesome in there. Sure you don't want to stay outside?"

"I can handle it." I wish the bravado in her voice would hold up when she's inside, but I know it won't.

"Same as always?" Gaffey asks me. "Ten?"

"Make it twenty," I counter with false faith before turning my attention back to Sophia. "Put gloves on and cover your shoes with those."

I point at the crime scene tech who's holding the supplies, taking my own after she grabs hers. I watch her nose scrunch when a uniformed officer opens the front door. He looks green in the gills, but thankfully he has the wherewithal to get to the other side of his cruiser before losing his breakfast on the asphalt.

"Ready?" I ask Sophia once we're in the proper gear, giving her one more out before we go inside.

"Ready."

Gaffey opens the front door with a flourish, stepping inside quickly as we follow him.

Sophia clears her throat the second we're fully inside, and both Gaffey and I watch her face for signs of getting sick. The smell is god-awful, and I don't know that there's a worse smell in the world than decaying flesh, but she has wide eyes as she looks around the room.

"The deceased is in the master bedroom. Right this way," Gaffey says as he starts to walk down the hallway, sadness hunching his shoulders a little.

Sophia is sandwiched between us as we walk down the narrow hallway, but I don't hear gagging noises come from her as we draw closer to the scene.

"Details?" I ask a uniformed officer as we enter the room.

"Margaret Hanson, seventy-eight. Lives alone. No sign of forced entry. Officers first on the scene had to access the home through a window. Medication in the bathroom indicates she had both heart and kidney problems."

I look over to find Sophia writing all the details in a small notebook. Sweat is beading at her temples, but she doesn't look like she's going to be sick.

"What do you see?" I ask her.

She looks around the room, taking in not only the bed where the deceased is but also looking at the floor, the position of the covers, and the items on the bedside table.

"It all looks... normal."

"She was also on hospice," the original reporting officer adds.

"Natural causes?" Sophia asks, her eyes finding mine.

Before I can answer, the officer who got sick a few minutes ago reappears in the doorway to the room, looking just as ill as he did on his way out earlier.

"Her son is here," he says, his hand covering his mouth.

"I'll be with him in a minute. Why don't you go back outside and wait with him?"

The officer nods, grateful for the reprieve before spinning around and hauling ass out of the house.

"That saliva that's pooling on your tongue is the first sign you're going to puke," Gaffey whispers, and I have to shake my head when I look over to see him leaning in close to whisper in Sophia's ear. The fucker is trying to psych her out. "Can't spit at a scene and swallowing it makes you want to gag."

"Natural causes?" Sophia asks again, ignoring Gaffey.

"Probably," I tell her. "The medical examiner will take all the information we provide and decide if an autopsy is required."

"And the smell of rotting flesh..." Gaffey makes a gagging sound, but Sophia just slowly blinks in his direction. "Do you want some Vicks for your nose?"

"Good cops don't use stuff in their noses. Sometimes the smells coming from the scene can provide hints to the situation the eyes can't see," she says.

My lip twitches, but I manage not to smile.

"Damnit," he mutters as he reaches into his pocket.

"Let's go talk to the family," I say, holding my hand out so Sophia can leave the room first.

"She didn't even flinch," Gaffey complains as he slaps a twenty-dollar bill into my palm.

"She's a badass," I tease, but as I head outside to deliver the bad news, I realize the absolute truth in my words.

Chapter 4

Sophia

"Don't make those gagging noises," I whisper, my throat threatening to close up.

"Really? You're the one going on and on about the smoking hot cop that's old enough to be your dad."

"He's in his mid-thirties. That's not old enough to be my dad."

"Well, he's old enough to be *my* dad."

"Not quite," I argue. "Plus, stop thinking about his age. He's sexy as hell."

Izzy makes another gagging noise, and I nearly lose my dinner.

Keeping it together at that scene earlier was quite possibly the hardest thing I've ever done. When Gaffey started taunting me like he wanted me to get sick, I knew I couldn't cave. I couldn't be a joke or the laughingstock, even though they didn't make fun of the other officer who couldn't handle it.

I wanted to prove something to them, and I think I did. Detective Matthews—Colton as he prefers—was different when we left. His attitude, although not completely gone, was a little more muted than it was before we arrived.

"So, your first dead body, huh?"

It doesn't surprise me that my friend would rather talk about a crime scene than anything resembling romance or sex.

"Really, Izzy?" I shake my head, grinning down at her smiling face on the Facetime video. "I can't talk about it just yet."

Izzy is Hound's daughter, and although I grew up with Gigi, Hound's woman, I'm closer to the former. She's finishing her college semester in Albuquerque, and I already miss her even though we saw each other over spring break last week.

"Let's talk about Colton." I give her a wide smile, batting my eyelashes cartoonishly as I lean back against my headboard.

"Colton? First name basis, must be serious," she deadpans.

I huff a laugh at her lack of enthusiasm. "Iz! He's got muscles for days. His five o'clock shadow would make angels weep."

"He sounds old."

"He's majestic and so tall."

"You're short," she reminds me. "Everyone is tall to you."

"Can you just hop on the Colton-Matthews-is-the-sexiest-man-alive train with me for ten minutes?"

If she doesn't approve of my crush, then there's no sense in even mentioning what happened during the case of mistaken identity first thing this morning.

"Choo-choo." She smiles as she pumps her arm up and down like a train conductor.

"Better." I grin into the camera.

"Are you going to keep flirting with him? Because that may make things weird while you're working together."

"I—" I snap my jaw closed because we've promised each other we'd always be honest. We get too many half-truths from the people in our lives under the auspices of protecting us. "I probably shouldn't. I have to graduate on time."

"True. Plus, you're used to being around hot guys. He's no different."

I couldn't even explain my attraction to Colton out loud without sounding like a fawning teen. Yeah, the man is possibly the hottest creature I've ever seen, but there's just something else about him that makes me want to inch in closer to him, to crawl inside his head and figure out what he's thinking.

"Professional," I muse.

"I think that's best. I know there are a couple guys on campus who are going to miss you."

"That part of my life is over," I explain.

"Over? Like dating?"

"Dating college guys," I clarify.

"Who else will you date? And don't tell me Detective Colton Matthews because he's not an option."

"I'll have to date, eventually."

"Not in Farmington you won't."

"He's going to have to let me date eventually," I argue.

"When you're thirty, like Jasmine."

God, she's right. My older sister didn't introduce a man to my dad until she was out of her twenties. She led a wild life, going to sex clubs and having a good time, much like I've done for the last four years at college, but I don't want to have to move away to find a life. My family is here in Farmington. It's where I want to work, and where I want to eventually raise a family.

"I'm not going back to college boys."

"You mean boys your age?"

We both laugh because it's true. I'm not quite twenty-two, but boys my age no longer appeal to me, and this isn't new information since meeting Colton. I haven't really wanted drunken parties and fumbling boys for a while now.

"College boys are terrible at sex."

Izzy clears her throat.

"Like they seriously can't even find the clit."

She chokes on nothing, and I grin watching her cheeks pink up in embarrassment.

I don't have a lot of experience, but she has even less. I'm not sure she's even lost her virginity yet.

I'd ask, but she'd give me the runaround. I don't know how she was born to very young parents and still has all of these hang-ups about sex.

Me, on the other hand, I'm what she likes to call devilish, but really it's mostly all talk. I'm not a virgin, having given that prize drunkenly away at a frat party to a douche named Chad. He didn't stick around, but that's on me because *Chad*, really? Enough said. My dalliances since haven't been anything to write home about. Nonetheless, I'm mostly all talk. The bravado I managed to hold onto in Colton's office was all talk, much like my complaints on college boys being bad at sex. I don't really know how to please a man either, but at least I'm willing to try.

Footfalls in the hall draw my attention.

"And the blush was on sale too. You should check them out online," I'm saying when my bedroom door swings open.

I look over to see my dad as Izzy speaks without missing a beat. "But what about the foundation because mine is almost out. Figure I should grab both while I'm there. Do you have any coupons?"

Code for *how long is this going to take*.

"I have one in my email I'm not going to use. I'll send it over to you. Tell Dad, hi." I turn my phone around so Izzy can wave at my father who even nearly twenty-two years later still doesn't knock on my bedroom door.

"Hi, Mr. Anderson."

"Call me, Dom, Izzy. How many times do I have to tell you?"

Izzy laughs, but doesn't speak to him again. "I have to study for that political science test. I'll be waiting on the coupon."

Code for *call me when he leaves, we aren't done discussing this*.

"Bye. I'll send it over shortly."

Code for *as soon as I can get rid of him, I'll call you back*.

We end the call, and I give my dad all of my attention.

I love this man. Honestly, he's my hero. He kissed every scratch, held me when my sister, Jasmine's, dog died, but he hasn't let me experience much life outside of the clubhouse and school. I blame his twenty years in the Marine Corps, along with his work with Cerberus for being overprotective. He does it out of love, but it's smothering.

That's why I need the internship with Colton to work out because once I graduate, I'll be able to get a real job and have the ability to move out. Besides, he needs to put more focus on my sister and what she's doing rather than sticking his nose in my business. So I have a crush on an older guy. Jasmine is living with two men, as in they're all three in a relationship.

My dad didn't want me driving to work alone this morning, but he hardly blinked an eye at her news. Granted, she's over thirty, but get your priorities straight, man. This is Farmington, and nothing seriously bad ever happens here.

"Mom mentioned you needed different clothes for work." Dad holds up a bag I'm only now noticing. "I talked with Monahan and he's going to have some shirts for you tomorrow."

"Thanks, Dad." I take the bag and pull out several pairs of khaki-colored utility pants, running my fingers over the waffle-like texture of the fabric.

"I honestly don't see the need for those type of pants. It's not like office work on fraud cases really require it."

"Fraud cases? Dad, really? I saw my first dead body today. It was absolutely disgusting, and the smell nearly made me puke, but I didn't."

"Dead body?" He inches closer as if he has the ability to protect me now, after the fact. His fingers shove into his pocket. "Matthews works fraud."

"He's a homicide detective," I correct.

"Is that so?" His voice has an edge to it I haven't heard since he caught me sneaking back into the house late one night and tried to convince him I was at a study group.

"Yes." I straighten my spine, worried that he's going to do something to compromise my internship. "And I want to keep working there. I only have two months left of school. If you do something to make me lose my internship, I'll never forgive you."

He frowns. "That's a little dramatic don't you think? I'm just going to see if I can get you moved to a department that isn't going to give you nightmares."

"Dad!" I hiss, but he spins around and leaves the room.

I follow him, unwilling to just let him plow through another situation in my life.

"Do not call the police station."

"Police station?" Mom asks when we make it into the kitchen. "Do we need to go to the panic room?"

I know there's a safe room in their closet, but we've never had to use it once since I've been born.

Mom smiles at me, and I have to roll my eyes. She tries to be on my side, knowing that keeping us locked down will only cause problems later in life. *They have to experience things*, she argued once, but her defense fell on deaf ears.

"He's trying to ruin my life," I whine.

She turns back around, continuing to wash vegetables in the sink. "Is that so, or are you being dramatic?"

Okay, so neither my dad nor I are perfect.

"He's upset that I'm interning with the homicide detective."

That news is enough to make her turn off the water and dry her hands.

"He's going to force me to work with the fraud guy."

"Matthews is supposed to be the fraud guy," Dad argues, but at least his phone is back in his damn pocket.

"Matthews? Isn't he that cute detective working with Jinx and Rocker?"

"He's working with Simone Murphy," I correct, knowing that much from the gossip around the clubhouse.

The situation is more complicated, but the gist is that Simone killed her abusive ex and is now pregnant with either Jinx or Rocker's baby. I don't know if paternity has been determined yet.

"Cute?" Dad asks, focusing on his wife.

The rumble of his voice is a challenging hint at foreplay, and as much as I want to cringe and crawl away, I have to stand my ground on this one. Growing up with parents with mass amounts of sexually charged energy has been both a blessing and a curse. A blessing because it showed Jasmine and I exactly what we should aim for—a man that only has sights for one woman and doesn't have a problem showing her how he feels. The curse because they're my parents. So seriously... gross.

"Mom!" I groan when she starts to bite her lip with her eyes on my dad. "Can you get it under control for a few minutes? Tell him not to call the station to rearrange my internship."

"Don't rearrange her internship," my mother says.

"She saw a damn dead body today," Dad argues, and this is one of the few times I want him more concerned about the chance of getting my mom naked than focused on me.

I shudder and refocus on my dad.

"Really?" Mom's voice grows softer, and I can tell she's looking at me, but I can't face her right now.

The man outside of that house this morning was devastated, and it didn't matter that he was grown and had adult children of his own. Losing a parent can't be easy at any age.

Emotion clogs my throat with the memory because there's just something heartbreaking about seeing a man cry.

"Are you okay?"

She inches closer to me, arms out as if she wants to wrap me in a hug.

"I'm fine." I step away, putting the kitchen island between us.

I'll break down if she touches me, and I have to be stronger than that if I want Dad to take me seriously.

"I know you want to protect her from everything in the world, but you also raised her to think independently and not to rely on anyone." Mom is speaking to Dad now so I let some of the tension in my shoulders fall. "You can't change that opinion now that she's finally doing it."

I'm both happy and sad with her words because I know it's part truth, part jab. I'm standing here arguing about my freedom of choice, but I also needed new clothes to wear to work. Instead of going to the store and getting them myself, I called my mom to fix the dilemma. Apparently, I have one foot in and one foot out, and gaining my own autonomy isn't possible this way.

Chapter 5

Colton

I was awake before the alarm clock went off this morning, drinking coffee in the kitchen before the sun even thought about starting the day. It has nothing to do with being eager to go to work, and nothing to do with getting to spend another day with Sophia Anderson.

I can't have those thoughts.

They're not allowed.

I can't think about the way her flowery scent filled the car yesterday or predicting what she's going to wear to work today.

Nope.

None of that is allowed.

Shouldn't even be in my head.

So that definitely means I should stop thinking about her mouth.

I shouldn't have spent my morning shower concocting ways to get in her space today.

I should probably erase all curiosities about what her hair would feel like sifting through my fingertips.

And I sure as shit shouldn't speculate the types of sounds she'd make when I—

My ringing phone startles me, making me wonder how I got halfway to work without a single memory of even pulling out of my driveway.

"Matthews," I snap after answering the call through my truck's Bluetooth.

"Sophia was ecstatic about her first day working with you."

I nearly rear end the car in front of me as it slows for a red light.

"That so?"

Great, man. Way to sound casual. I swallow wondering if he heard the crack in my voice.

Silence fills the cab of the truck, but I wait him out.

"Something you need to tell me?"

Aw fuck. Surely, she didn't go home and tell him every damn thing.

"Sophia handled herself very well yesterday. I won a twenty-dollar bet."

More silence.

"You should be proud of her."

Silence.

I clamp my jaw closed, pressing on the gas a little too hard when the light turns green and the car behind me honks.

I'm not going to say another damn word. I'm a cop for fuck's sake. I know exactly what he's doing. This shit isn't going to work on me.

"That's not what I'm talking about."

I return the silence when he doesn't elaborate.

Why does it feel like an admission of guilt? Would this man understand if he knew I thought she was someone else?

And the thoughts you had about her after her identity was revealed?

The tires on my truck screech when I pull up to the police station, the pressure from my brakes too much for the situation. One of the patrol officers looks my way, but I wave off his concern.

"You're no longer working fraud."

"I've been on homicide for the last year."

"You didn't tell me that when we talked in November."

"You didn't ask."

A rush of air comes through the line, and I can't determine if it's a growl of anger or a chuckle. I don't know enough about the man to make an educated guess either.

"I've worked the Simone Murphy case. I thought you knew that."

"I thought you were just helping out with that."

"Nope. All deaths land on my desk."

He grows silent once again, and as much as I want to wait him out again, I just can't seem to manage it.

"The case yesterday was an elderly woman who died in her sleep. The horrific part was she was there for a couple of days. Sophia didn't even blink."

It makes me wonder what her childhood was like that a decaying body didn't cause more of a reaction.

"She's strong, even one of the beat cops got sick… twice."

"She's a great kid."

I do my best to ignore the skeevy feeling his declaration causes, but I don't really see her as a kid. I mean, how could I? Other than her father and other family members, I don't think there's a man alive that wouldn't give her a second glance, and that makes my jaw ache with tension at the thought of her at the MC clubhouse.

"Let me know if she starts to cause problems."

I'm certain this man isn't interested in hearing about the perpetual hard-on she's going to cause for the next couple of months.

"Will do," I assure him before hanging up.

I sit in the truck a little longer, questioning my sanity because although I wanted to move her to a different division yesterday, I can't imagine doing that now.

Telling by the questions she asked about the case yesterday, she's intelligent. She caught on amazingly fast with the system we used after offering to help type up my handwritten notes. She didn't flirt or mention our introductions.

I mean, it didn't stop my eyes from taking her in or my thoughts from speeding out the front door of the police station and landing in a dark room at the Hampton Inn, but at least I can keep my distance if she doesn't hint at wanting to hook up.

I walk into the building, eyes assessing, seeing who's here, and although I'm nearly an hour early, I find Sophia in my office looking through the paperback version of this year's traffic code.

"Interesting reading?" I ask, slipping around my desk and placing my coffee cup near my computer monitor.

"Not really." She closes the book before looking up at me.

Her hair isn't in a tight knot on the back of her head like it was yesterday. For all the sexy librarian vibes I got yesterday, make that tenfold for the head cheerleader thoughts the ponytail is giving me right now. I dated a head cheerleader once, and she managed to change my entire life trajectory.

Won't be making that mistake again.

Not that Sophia was a cheerleader at any point in her life. Just after the ten-minute call with her dad, I can't picture the man letting her put on a short skirt and bounce around for hundreds of men in the stands, but hell if I can't get lost in the imagery.

"What is it?" Her grin is casual with no hints of the seduction the woman used yesterday morning.

"Were you a cheerleader in high school? College?"

Her head snaps back a little. "What? No."

"Think cheerleading is dumb?" I break eye contact, wiggling my mouse to wake up my computer.

"Too much work. Do you know how much time cheerleaders spend training? Yeah, that's not for me."

I keep my eyes on my screen. I'm not disappointed so much as remembering what she said yesterday about falling behind in her classes. Despite her enthusiasm yesterday, I expect her to lose interest in this internship quickly. Maybe she's good at putting on a front, but if there's one thing I know, it's that people who aren't willing to accept any level of responsibility don't stick around for long.

The grass is always greener after all.

"I'm going to go get a coffee refill." Sophia places the traffic code on the corner of my desk before standing. "Can I get you anything?"

"Nope," I say without looking in her direction.

"Be right back."

But she doesn't come right back. I sit in my office for twenty minutes before going to look for her. I don't know what I was expecting to find, but her in the breakroom surrounded by smiling, horny cops isn't too much of a surprise.

I stand off to the side for a few minutes watching the interactions, and it gives me the opportunity to get a good look at her. She isn't in a sexy, little pencil skirt or athletic leggings. Today, she's got on khaki utility pants, much like the guys in the criminal investigation division wear. Those aren't the issue, nor is it really what's causing all the dogs on the force to come sniffing around. I mean, it may contribute, but I haven't seen her from the back yet.

What's drawing all the attention—or at least mine anyway—is the tight, sweat-wicking fabric of her shirt. It may be department issued, with the Farmington PD logo just above her left breast, but there isn't a soul I've met that could pull it off the way she is right now. Let me just say, if she had lace on her bra, the men standing close to her would be able to count the eyelets in the pattern.

"Yeah, I get off at seven this evening," Dresden says as I walk closer. "But we could definitely see about a ride-along later in the week."

Sophia catches sight of me over the man's shoulder, and instantly I can tell her genuine smile—the one she's giving me—versus the polite one she's been giving Dresden.

"How's Emily and the baby, Pete? Little Ava is what, two weeks old now?"

Dresden spins, giving me a lethal look. "Four weeks, tomorrow."

Without another word, Dresden begins to walk away. Several of the other guys, many loitering but not brave enough to approach her, begin shouting comments about him being a dick and how his wife deserves better.

"Really?" Sophia asks as she begins to follow me back to my office. "He's married with a newborn?"

"Men are dogs," I respond automatically. "You're twenty-two, you should know that by now."

"In three months."

"Hmm?" I plop back down in my office chair, already exhausted when the day is just getting started. Tossing and turning last night isn't doing me any favors today.

"I'll be twenty-two in three months. How many of those guys out there are married?" She takes the seat across from me, but she ignores the traffic code on the corner of my desk.

"Most of them, either that or they're divorced." I study her when she frowns. "Dresden's marriage won't last either but I wouldn't suggest getting in the middle of it right now."

"I wouldn't," she snaps, sounding offended. "So, there's a high divorce rate among police officers?"

I can't stop the snort that leaves my nose. "The first thing the training officer told my class during the academy was to get the first marriage out of the way."

"Really?" Her cute little nose scrunches up as if she's disgusted.

"I take it your parents are still together?"

"Aren't yours?"

"Well, yeah, but my dad isn't a cop."

She nods, conceding the fact, but she still looks curious. "How old are you?"

"Old enough."

"Yet acting twelve with that response." She leans back in her chair, arms crossed over her stomach, and fuck, that damn shirt is going to be the death of me.

"Thirty-five, and before you have the chance to ask, I was divorced before I was old enough to even go into the police academy."

I turn my attention back to the stack of cases on my desk, shuffling through them until I find the one that needs to be worked on today.

"What?"

"We have everything we need to clear this case today, but I'd like you to look through it and see if there's anything that catches your eye." I offer her the folder, effectively shutting down whatever questions she could want to ask next.

I keep my work and personal life separate for a reason, and I don't plan on changing that anytime soon.

"A drunk driving accident?" she asks, but her eyes keep scanning the file. "Isn't this open and shut? The man blew a point two-nine at the scene. By the time he got to the hospital for the blood draw it was even higher. Oh God. The entire family?" Emotion clogs her throat, but for some reason it calms me.

I lost sleep last night questioning her lack of response to the scene with the elderly woman yesterday.

"The mother, father, and their four-year-old son," I confirm. "They were on their way back from a playdate."

"This is awful."

"The worst. Ramshaw was the first on the scene. He's a stronger man than me."

"Was he able to hold it together?"

I shake my head, dropping my eyes to my desk when she looks up at me. Man, people hurting kids. It's just something I have serious trouble dealing with.

"He worked the scene. Gave the breathalyzer. Handcuffed the man. Made sure to transport the drunk driver to the hospital to get everything we would need to make sure he's locked away for a long time."

"Isn't that what he's supposed to do?" I nod. "But not what you would've done?"

I lift my eyes to hers. "I would have unloaded both my magazines into him."

She looks back down to the folder, brushing a tear off her cheek. There was no judgment, no disappointment on her face before she broke eye contact.

"He's twenty," she gasps.

"In his statement, he said he was too scared to call someone for a ride. Since he's underage, he knew his parents would lose their shit about him drinking. He decided to take the chance."

"My dad would be livid if I called home drunk and needed a ride home," she whispers. "But I still wouldn't get behind the wheel of a car. How selfish."

"Who would you call?" I ask.

"Anyone but Dad." She looks up, winking at me, and the sadness filling the office fades away. "Who would you have called?"

"If I were that young and in trouble?" She nods. "My dad. It wouldn't be the first time he had to bail me out of a life changing situation. Do you drink often?"

It's a college student's rite of passage, right? I mean, I wouldn't know because my college courses were taken several years after high school graduation, and responsibilities kept me from living that type of life.

"Not really. I mean, I can have a couple beers at the clubhouse, but there's always a bed to crash in or someone able to take me back home."

A bed to crash in. Why does that sentence bring up a little green monster?

"I can't get drunk."

"Never? Didn't you go away for college?"

"Albuquerque," she confirms. "And what Daddy doesn't know, doesn't hurt him."

Another wink.

Another erection I'm going to have to talk down before I can stand from this desk.

"If you're ever in the situation and need a ride, you can always call me."

"I don't have your number."

I pull a pen from the cup on my desk and scribble out my number before offering her the slip of paper. That was the first step I made on my journey to ruin this girl's life.

Chapter 6

Sophia

"You've been a huge help these last couple of weeks."

I give Colton a weak smile.

"Seriously. My desk is nearly cleaned off, and that's thanks to you."

"Most of those cases just needed to be typed up and submitted to records," I remind him.

"And now you know my greatest weakness."

"Follow through?" I tease, but snap my mouth closed when I realize how provocative it sounded.

He coughs a laugh into his hand. "Yeah."

"What happens next?" I ask, tilting my face toward the window but still unable to take a full breath.

The man smells amazing, always does. I even find myself sniffing my clothes when I get home to see if by chance it's somehow permeated my own clothes. I come up empty-handed every time, but it doesn't stop me from checking.

I've been doing this internship for the last three weeks, and I've managed to stop biting my lip when he walks by. Some days, I can even carry on a conversation without staring at his mouth. Twice this week alone, he was able to get up and leave his office and I didn't follow him with my eyes all the way out the door, but I'm feeling exceptionally weak where he's concerned today. Maybe it was the dream I had last night or the haircut he got after work yesterday, but he's managed to land right back on my radar, and I'm struggling.

Hitting the button for the window, I lean my head a little further away, hoping for a breath of fresh air that isn't tinged with the spicy scent of his cologne.

"Hot?"

Burning up.

"Struggling a little today," I confess, but then think better of telling the full truth. "That last scene was a bit much."

"Worse than the SIDS case we worked on Tuesday?"

"Somehow," I answer, rolling my head on the back of the seat to look at him. "I don't think there was much more the parents could've done for that baby."

I cried so much Tuesday night that layers of makeup couldn't hide my puffy eyes the next day. I clear my throat, knowing the tears will start back up if I let myself focus on that family's loss.

"I understand. Someone could've helped that young woman today. It was clear by the track marks on her arms and the filth she was living in that today wasn't her first time to shoot heroin."

"Exactly," I whisper, emotion clogging my throat. "How many people saw her and didn't help? Had her parents done anything to try to get her clean?"

"Both good questions," he answers. "We're heading to her mother's house now, and I can tell you by the address given that there's a good chance the answer is going to be that she didn't get help because her parents aren't able to help themselves. Many addicts also have family members that are also on drugs. Not all, mind you, but some."

"And this woman we're going to go see?"

"Has had numerous arrests for drug possession. Has been to prison more than once because of them."

"That's sad."

"It's a vicious cycle, and some people are wound so tight up in it that no amount of help will set them free."

"She was only seventeen."

"Heartbreaking," he mutters, and it makes me want to go home and reach out to Landon.

Dustin "Kid" Andrews' son is the youngest one around, not counting Gigi's daughter, and he had to have known this girl. Farmington isn't an overly large community.

"Here?" I ask when Colton pulls into the back part of a parking lot.

I can't handle this right now. Leaving that crack house with the sight of that girl's vomit-covered blue lips is burned into my brain, and I need to keep myself busy to keep from thinking about it.

"I want you to look at this."

I barely register the brush of his hand on my leg when he reaches for the lock on the glovebox, but the sensation skates up my leg anyway. Maybe it's the proximity of him that's frying my brain, or my need to always be tough and strong around him. I don't know what it is, but I'm grateful it's Friday and I have two days Colton-free to get my head back on straight.

He reaches into the glovebox, shuffling the papers around until he pulls his hand free.

"A pamphlet?" I ask when he lays the tri-fold paper in my lap without touching me further. "Notifying next of kin?"

I look at the dull, faded information sheet, briefly going through the bullet points of the best practices when notifying someone that a person they love is deceased.

"Really?" I look up at him to find a faraway look in his eyes. "This is the training a cop gets to help tell a mother that her daughter is never coming home again? That she'll never see her smile or hear her laugh ever again."

"Sophia."

"No," I snap. "This is ridiculous. A child is gone and the department hands this to someone, expecting them to deliver the worst news a person is ever going to hear."

I freeze when he brushes his fingers under my eyes and they come away wet.

"Fuck," I mutter, untucking my shirt and lifting the hem of it to dry my face.

He reaches past me again, grabbing a few fast-food napkins from the glovebox and shoving them my way. "This is better, put your shirt down."

I don't even have the strength right now to feel embarrassed that I may have just flashed this man the bottom curve of my bra-covered breasts. I mean, who even cares at this point.

"That pamphlet is a guideline, a reminder that even when giving bad news, we have to be diligent and observant. Not all notifications are simple and straight forward. Sometimes we're walking into a situation where the person being notified already knows what happened because they were the perp." I stiffen at his words. "Notifications never get easier, and there's nothing on that card that can prepare you for the grief a person feels, but it's helpful to look at so that the officer is cognizant that they have a job to do."

I flip the pamphlet over, feeling a little better for the hotline numbers on the back for police officers to call. First responders see so much brutality and pain. It's no wonder they burnout quickly, commit suicide, and have trust issues. They're dealing with some of the worst situations the world can dream up. Take today for example. Three hours ago, we were in the office going through cases and debating our equality staunch stances on *The Office* versus *New Girl*—I'm team Zoey Deschanel all the way—when we were called out to work the case of a dead seventeen-year-old overdose victim. It's like zero to a hundred in the blink of an eye, and although I've only been helping out for a few weeks, it's already taking its toll on me.

"Soph?"

I pull my eyes from the paper in my hands to look at him.

"If this is too much for you—"

"I'm fine." His jaw clenches.

"You don't have to be strong in front of me."

If only that were true.

"So, we're looking at the situation from the outside, assessing the entire scene as if it were an open investigation?" I ask, changing the subject because I've been vulnerable enough for one day. Hell, to last a lifetime as far as I'm concerned.

"It's good practice. The narcotics team will help with this investigation to see if they can get any leads to dealers, but I don't expect them to get far. The house has been abandoned for years. People have been squatting in there. You saw the condition of the place. I wouldn't doubt that they could pull over a hundred different DNA samples from that carpet."

I cringe at the reminder. That young girl died in solid filth on a threadbare mattress, all alone.

"Are you ready?"

"I'm just observing, right?"

"Of course. I'll do all the talking."

I shove the pamphlet back in the glovebox, wipe my face with the napkins one more time, and focus my attention out through the windshield. When I take a deep breath, I'm once again overwhelmed with the rich scent of him, only this time I breathe in deeply and hold that part of him in my lungs.

Too soon, less than three minutes to be exact, we're pulling up in front of a rundown duplex with boarded-up windows.

"Someone lives here?" I ask, nose to the glass, but still uncertain about getting out of the car.

"Destiny's mother does. Well, it's her last known address." He opens his car door, but my hand hesitates on my door handle. "You can stay in the car if you want."

Instead of taking him up on his offer, I shove open my door. He gives a quick grin, and I can tell he's impressed with my resiliency. What he doesn't know is tonight will be another night I cry myself to sleep, all the while being grateful for the life I've been allowed to live, including my overprotective, overbearing dad who I can see now has only ever wanted what's best for me by keeping me safe and protecting me from the ugliness that seems to be infecting the world.

"Keep your eyes open," he reminds me as we make our way up the cracked concrete walkway.

His hand goes to my back to steady me when I catch the toe of my boot on the uneven terrain.

"Careful."

"Sorry," I mutter.

"You good?"

Before I can answer, the door on the right of the duplex swings open, the screen door hitting the side of the house with a loud crack.

"Matthews," the woman standing in the doorway grunts as we approach.

I don't make a sound when he steps in front of me. Any other day I might get mad, but this is a neighborhood I was never allowed in, and although at the time I thought my parents were being elitist jerks, I can see clearly they had their reasons.

A car alarm goes off down the street, inciting several unruly dogs to begin barking, but the woman in front of us doesn't blink an eye or look in the direction of the noise. No one else opens their doors, no curtains flutter from curiosity within. I don't imagine someone calling for help would draw much attention, and definitely not someone willing to offer a helping hand.

"Doris," Colton says as we draw closer. He stops several feet away, and I use the opportunity to take in all the information that I can.

This woman doesn't seem nervous, but more annoyed that we're interrupting her day. Her fingers flex in and out several times before she lifts a hand to scratch at an already irritated spot on her arm.

"Who's the new trainee? She looks a little young to be a detective."

"I'm here to talk about Destiny, Doris."

"She took off again. I told social services last week I didn't know where that damn girl is. You know they're trying to take me to court because she isn't going to school. I told that lady that she refuses to go, and the last time I tried to make her, she hit me in the face. Did social services tell you that? I'm not going to jail over her again."

"Doris—"

"Ever since she took off with Hershel, she's been a different kid." Her jaw works back and forth between her words, and it doesn't take a rocket scientist to deduce this woman has had her own struggles with drugs. Although not as filthy as we found her deceased daughter, it's clear it's been a couple of days since she's seen the inside of a shower. It makes me wonder if she has running water, another thing I've always taken for granted.

"Doris—"

"I won't. I'm not going to jail!" she screeches, her bony arms crossing over her chest with defiance.

"Police were called out to the abandoned house over on the hill."

Doris swallows, and I can see it in her eyes when she realizes why we're here. We don't even have to say the words, and this woman is already cycling through the stages of grief.

Tears burn the backs of my eyes because despite all that's going on, this woman has lost a child.

"She's dead?" Her chin quivers heavily.

"She is. An overdose is suspected, but it'll take some time before toxicology comes back."

"Was Hershel there?"

"She was alone in the house, Doris. Someone called into the anonymous tip line."

Tears roll down Doris's cheeks, but she doesn't crumple the way I believed she would at the news. Her affect is a little flat, but it's clear she's hurting.

"Gone? She's gone?"

"Yes, ma'am. I'm so sorry for your loss. Detective Winston will probably be by in the next week or so. He's going to have some questions about who she's been hanging out with."

"I'm not telling him shit," she snaps.

Colton nods his head in understanding before reaching into his shirt pocket for a business card. "There's a number for a grief hotline on the back, Doris. Call them if you need someone to talk to."

She snaps the card out of his hand, ignoring it when it flutters to the ground.

"Did she have any money on her?"

My head snaps in her direction, but it's the clench in Colton's strong jaw that garners most of my attention.

"She didn't have any possessions on her, Doris."

"Personal effects can be picked up at the coroner's office, right?"

There's no talking sense into this woman, and it's clear this isn't her first notification.

"Yes, ma'am. Give them a couple days, and you can pick up anything she had."

We turn to leave. Colton crowds me but not a single part of his body brushes mine as we walk back to the car, and it sucks because I feel like I need some form of comfort after today. I don't know that I have the strength to do this all over again on Monday.

Chapter 7

Colton

"Sometimes those are harder to deal with than brutal murders," I say after sitting in the car for ten minutes outside of the station.

Sophia is still looking out the side window, making no move to get out of the car.

"She didn't care."

"She cared," I counter. "She's just too far gone to feel the real pain of her loss. She may spend the next two years with a needle in her arm to keep from feeling that pain."

"Denial," she whispers.

"Addict," I argue. "It's much worse."

"That girl deserved much better."

"Doris deserves better, too."

"I don't see it."

She hasn't looked at me once since we walked back to our car, leaving Doris to deal with her grief the only way she knew how.

"Destiny was a toddler the first time I dealt with her mother. Doris was drunk one night at a bar in town and left her kid in the car. Destiny was never one to stay still, and someone called it in that they found a kid walking down the road in the middle of the night. My partner at the time wasn't surprised. He knew exactly who the kid was and who she belonged to. We drove straight to the bar after making sure the kid was safe with social services."

I have to look out my window to get a better handle on my own anger. There are so many situations I wish were different in my career as a police officer.

"They gave her back to her mother?"

"There are circumstances. Years ago, Doris worked very hard to comply with the courts."

"Circumstances?" She finally jerks her head in my direction, and the hatred for what she saw today is so much better than the tears she cried in the parking lot earlier.

"Not everyone gets to grow up in a two-parent household with love."

She blinks at me. "I won't be shamed for having a healthy childhood."

I want to ask her if she really did, but I can tell by the look in her eyes that the man that raised her kept her safe. The experiences we've faced in this job together has opened her eyes to the terrible things that are possible so close to home.

Over the last couple of weeks, the wondering I had going on about what really happens at the Cerberus MC clubhouse has been laid to rest. Her reaction at the very first crime scene was a hundred percent bravado, and it wouldn't surprise me if I found out later that she went home and got sick more than once.

"I'm glad you had a healthy childhood." I grip the steering wheel because that pressure under my palms is the only thing keeping me from reaching for her and brushing my fingertips down the side of her face. "Doris didn't have a good childhood."

"Neither did Destiny," she counters. "Hell, that girl probably didn't have a childhood at all."

"Doris was raped by her father from the time she was seven years old until she ran away at fifteen. She was pregnant with Destiny when she left."

"What?" A trembling hand lifts to cover her mouth, but it doesn't stop the anguished sob from escaping.

"There are circumstances all over this community. Nothing is cut and dry. Everyone has a story, some worse than others. You'll learn if you work in the criminal justice field long enough that every situation is different. Some people make it out of shitty situations, and some people are born with no chance at all. Sometimes horrible things happen to good people. But most importantly, you'll come to understand that most often, there's no rhyme or reason. You saw two families change this week with the loss of a child. Two families that will never be the same, and no matter the individual situation, two mothers will close their eyes tonight with another piece of their soul missing."

"But some people make it out," she whispers, holding on to the good, and that's one of the things I admire most about this woman.

"Yes." I open my mouth to share a little more truth, but she doesn't need to know that the ones like us that grow up in homes where we were loved tend to have the most compassion for those who didn't. It's the ones who pulled themselves out of shitty situations, most often, that have less than stellar attitudes about those still stuck by their circumstances. Maybe it's because they made it out, they stop seeing excuses the same way. I don't know what it is, but everyone deals with police work differently.

"I'm just glad it's the weeks' end."

Glassy eyes blink up at me, and my mouth opens before I think. I don't want her going home for two days with all of this heaviness weighing on her. She'll soon find out that each day in this job, a little piece of you is plucked away and never returned. She's too young to be jaded by the evils in the world.

"What are you doing this evening?"

"Besides going home and hugging my mom and dad?" She chuckles, the sound sullen and humorless.

"What about dinner?"

"Mom usually leaves me a plate in the oven."

I smile at her confession even though her cheeks pink.

"I know how to cook, and I was on my own for almost four years at college. I mean, I was in a dorm, but I'm not a spoiled brat who can't take care of myself."

I press a hand to her arm to get her attention and stop her rambling, but pull it away before she can read it as anything else. God, I want my hands all over her. I clear my throat.

"My mom still brings over meals, and I'm thirty-five. I'm pretty sure I have enough casseroles in my freezer to survive a zombie apocalypse."

She grins at me, but the smile I saw earlier today in my office is still absent.

"Will you join me?"

"For what?"

I chuckle, shaking my head and looking out my window after realizing the way I asked about dinner wasn't taken as the invitation it was meant to be.

"Will you have dinner with me?"

Her eyes widen, and more of her beautiful smile takes over her face.

"I mean as a reward for going back into the office and helping me wrap a few things up?"

"Of course there's a catch."

"I'm not on call this weekend, but I'll end up at my desk tomorrow morning if I leave stuff undone."

"Really?" She licks her lips, and I'm snared by the action. "Last week I helped close out a case that was lost under a pile for the last four months."

"See." I hold my hands up in offering. "I need your help."

"I'll warn you, I eat a lot."

I laugh again. "I know. I've seen your lunch orders. Come on."

I slide out of the car, making sure to grab my gear since I'll leave the vehicle here for the weekend, and head inside before she has the chance to change her mind.

***

"Please don't tell me you're counting calories."

I glare at Sophia as she looks down at her plate of pasta, her mouth working back and forth.

"What? No." She leans across the table, lowering her head as if she's going to tell me a secret. "But would it be rude to ask for more cheese?"

I laugh, but then she winks at me and the sound dies on my lips.

I know she isn't flirting. She's been nothing but professional. The last couple of weeks have been easygoing when I would've put money on the chance of it being difficult to be around her.

I mean, some days it isn't easy, and those are the days she wears her hair down around her shoulders, and I spend the entire shift trying to keep from reaching out to touch her brown locks.

Today is one of those days. Her grin is enticing, but add in the soft waves flowing around her face and shoulders, and I can now see that inviting her out while not working in an official capacity may have been a mistake.

"Do you really want more cheese?" I ask when my brain decides to finally come back online.

"Of course not." Those are her words, but her eyes dart around the restaurant.

We eat in silence for the next couple of minutes, and her cheeks flame red when the waiter stops by to check on us and I ask for more cheese. She must not be too upset because her eyes go wide and it takes forever to tell him that's enough when the grater starts working.

"This is so good," she mumbles, her mouth half full as she shovels more linguini into her pretty mouth.

"The best," I say, but I'm only partially talking about the meal. "Tell me about growing up at the clubhouse."

"I didn't," she says, covering her mouth with her cloth napkin as she finishes chewing. "My mom and dad never lived on the property. They have a house out on the lake."

"But you spent a lot of time there?"

"We were there all the time. We still spend a lot of time there."

"And there are a lot of men around?" Jesus, why did I ask that fucking question? "I mean the guys that work for Kincaid."

"Diego is my uncle." She narrows her eyes, ready to defend him the second my mouth opens to offer something inflammatory.

"Everyone at the station loves him. He helps the community a ton."

"I had thousands of community service hours by the time I graduated."

If that's the case, I'm surprised I never saw her until she walked into my office, but my homelife the last decade and a half hasn't really left much time for extracurriculars.

"And you hated it?"

"Not even close. I spent a lot of time at the animal shelter. Sunday afternoons we spent many hours at the assisted-living home. I've done my fair share of time at the library. That wasn't my favorite. It was normally only visited by old stuffy people. Most kids my age get all of their information from the internet."

"True," I agree, knowing all too well.

We reach for our glasses of water at the same time, the backs of our hands brushing. She smiles. I return it, lifting the cold water to my mouth while trying to talk myself out of turning it over and dumping it on my head so it can cool me down.

I should've sat across from her instead of right beside her, but who was I to argue with the hostess when she placed our menus on the connecting corner of the table?

"I told you a little about my parents. What about yours? What are they like besides forcing home-cooked meals on you?"

I watch her eyes, and they light up as she waits for me to talk about my own family. She genuinely wants to know. We aren't just sharing small talk while getting through dinner. This is new for me. My normal outings that look similar to this are a rush to eat because both parties already knew how the date was going to end. Hell, many times, the meal was skipped.

A waste of time, as Sophia said to me in my office that first day.

But we aren't wasting time right now, and no matter how badly I want tonight to end like the other dates I've had over the last decade, I know that isn't where this night is going. It can't, and I have to remind myself of that more often than I should.

"My parents are the most loving, supportive people I know. They only live a couple miles from my house, and I see them several times a week. We have dinner together on the weekend when I'm not working."

"So tomorrow?"

"Probably Sunday. They're both retired, and Saturdays are their time away from each other. Mom visits friends, and Dad pretends to know something about golf."

She laughs, twirling her fork in her pasta as she watches my face.

"Tell me about college. I didn't get the leave-home-and-go-crazy experience."

A frown takes over her pretty features.

"I didn't mean anything by it. Sorry, I—"

"No, it's okay." She takes a fortifying breath as she lowers her fork to her plate. "Remember I told you about falling behind in school?"

I nod because I was once again wrong about her work ethic. The woman is a machine in the office. Sometimes, I have to force her out with excuses of checking on a case just to get her to take a breather.

"Last year—" Her jaw snaps shut as her eyes narrow at me. "If you breathe a word about this to my dad, I'll never forgive you."

She points a finger, tapping me in the chest, and I would grin at her intimidation tactic if her face wasn't so serious.

"I'm not friends with your father, Sophia, but even if I was, I wouldn't share your secrets."

No, I'd hold them inside of me so that way I knew more about you than someone else—a treasure I'd appreciate until my last dying breath.

"I had trouble at school last year. A stalker."

I grip the edge of the table, ready to bundle her up, encase her in bubble wrap and drive all the way to Albuquerque without her breathing another single detail. I'd hunt that fucker down and—

"The school handled the situation as best they could, but he stayed right on the side of legal in his creepiness. I was afraid to leave my room, and although I tried to keep up with my schoolwork from inside my dorm, it was just hard with upper level classes, and impossible with the science lab I'd registered for. I had to spend the first half of this semester working through those labs again for credit." She refocuses on her plate, head hung in misery, and I barely keep my finger from crooking under her chin to make her look up at me. "I'm lucky the teacher let me do the labs that way and the dean over the program is letting me shove a full semester of internship into these last couple of months. I would've had to stay another semester."

"You mean you would've had to spend an entire semester following me around?" She lifts her head grinning. "You did get lucky."

"Maybe." Her eyes sparkle, and I have to look away before I mistake the look for something more than it is.

"You didn't tell your dad?" She shakes her head. "Afraid he'd hurt him?"

"I could say my dad would probably kill him then laugh it off as a joke, but I honestly don't know what he'd do to him." I wouldn't blame the man. "I do know what he'd do to me, and I wasn't about to be locked down. I was lucky to go away to college, and it was a subject of contention for a very long time. My senior year of high school was almost ruined by it. I didn't want to be forced to transfer or do online classes from my gilded tower."

"Cerberus is very protective?" I deduce.

"I'm surprised someone hasn't already tracked my phone tonight." She doesn't laugh. "But I'll be even more surprised if we walk outside and there isn't a row of motorcycles waiting to escort me home."

"Seems smothering. Did you let them know where you were?"

"I did. I texted my mom. She told me to have a good time. She's not as strict as my dad despite having grown up in... circumstances."

She gives me a weak smile, and her statement makes me want to dig a little deeper into her life, but I won't do that. Unless I suspect she's in an unsafe situation, I want all of her secrets whispered from her perfect mouth, not discovered from digging into her family's history.

"So no wild parties at school?"

"My freshman year grades were compromised from having a little too much fun, but after I had to retake a math class, I knew I had to calm down. So really just a wild second semester."

"Not a first semester?"

She grins and opens her purse when the waiter drops the check off. I wave her off and pull out my wallet, handing him my card before she can argue. She still pulls a twenty out and drops it on the table.

"For the tip," she explains, and I know there's no sense in arguing. It also won't stop me from tipping the young man myself.

"So, no partying the first semester?" I ask again.

"I was so sheltered growing up. It took that first semester, and my dormmate's incessant begging for me to finally cave and attend a party. After that, I was hooked. I wanted to party every weekend. Thursday night to early Sunday morning you could find me on frat row or at one of the bars playing pool and darts. I was a hellion. Bad things could've happened. Last year was proof of that, but thankfully, I stayed safe."

"Did he hurt you?"

"David?"

"Is that his name? Your stalker?"

She sits back in her seat, and until this moment, I didn't realize just how close we were to each other.

"He didn't hurt me. He texted, called, emailed, slid notes under my door. Gifts were delivered. I didn't return his affections, blew him off once at a party not knowing he was the same guy spamming my school email. I caught him one day trying to slip a package under my door, and I called campus security."

"What was in the package?"

She watches my face, biting the inside of her lip, and it's clear she doesn't want to tell me. I may have to backpedal on the declaration of learning all of her secrets from her own lips.

"A manifesto."

"What?"

"Yeah. So the police said it was like two hundred handwritten pages of his declaration of love and a lot of messed up plans about our future. Until that day I saw him standing outside of my dorm, I wouldn't even have been able to pull him out of a police lineup. He was that unmemorable."

"What happened to him?"

"I didn't read the document he was trying to slide under my door, but it freaked the administration enough to expel him from school."

"Has he contacted you since then?"

Her eyes dart across the room. "He hasn't, but can we talk about something else?"

"Sophia," I reach for her, but she pulls her hand away before I can make contact.

"I should go. Can you give me a ride back to my car?"

"Of course." I stand, pressing my hand against her lower back as we walk out together.

"No motorcycles." She laughs as we step outside, but there's no real humor in her voice.

I open the passenger side of my truck for her but give her space. If she's thinking about that creepy fucker and the liberties he took while pursuing her, the last thing I want to do is make her see some relation between him and me.

I'm mentally berating myself all the way back to the police station parking lot because I wanted tonight to be different, a way to get her mind off the shit day she had, but I failed epically at that.

This is why I don't fucking date.

I can never turn the detective in me off. I want all the facts, all the details, I want to know if she's safe. What that asshole is doing now. Will he come after her again?

She made me promise not to talk to her dad, but fuck, what if she's still in danger? Can he protect her if he doesn't know she needs protecting?

"I had a good time tonight," she says as I pull into the parking lot, lining my truck up beside her car.

"Me too," I tell her, wondering what I can say to get a redo, a chance to make things right before she's gone for the next two days.

Chapter 8

Sophia

I fiddle with my fingers in my lap, making no attempt to get out of his truck. We were in this very situation a couple of hours ago, and once again, it seems like neither one of us want the night to end.

I'm stuck on wondering if this was a date, but he's probably counting down the minutes until my crazy-attracting ass gets out of his truck, all the while regretting asking me to dinner in the first place.

It felt like a date up until I ruined it with my damn stalker story, but the warmth of his hand on my back as we left the restaurant didn't feel like him pulling away.

He opened the truck door for me, waiting for me to put my seatbelt on before closing me inside—gentlemanly things. Things I've seen my dad and the other men in Cerberus do for their women.

Maybe I'm delusional. Maybe I'm like David and only a few more interactions away from writing my own manifesto about my future with Detective Matthews.

I laugh at the possibility.

"Penny for your thoughts?"

"Did you do this on purpose?" I ask, pointing to my car out of the passenger window.

"How do you want me to answer that?"

"Honestly."

"Then yes. It's dark outside, and despite this being city property with probably no less than a half a dozen cops in the near vicinity, crime can still happen."

"It's something my dad would do," I explain with a grin. "Something the guys he works with would do."

"Then I think I like your dad and the Cerberus guys because there's never anything wrong with making sure a pretty girl is safe. Hold tight, and I'll come around."

Without turning the truck off, he climbs out. My eyes follow him all the way around the front of the truck as the headlights reflect off the gun on his hip.

"Do you want me to start it for you?" he asks when he opens up my door.

"I can do it," I tell him, reaching into my purse to grab my key fob.

I crank the car as I climb out of his truck, but for some reason he doesn't take a step back to give me room.

I'm not upset in the least by the fact that he's so close. I was sure I'd ruined the evening and non-date with my horror story, but he's still close.

Not a date.

Not a date.

Not a date.

I chant in my head because it seems I need the constant reminder with him standing right in front of me.

He lifts his hand, pushing back a lock of hair the wind has blown in my face. His hand lingers, his warm palm resting against my cheek.

Before I have the chance to lean into the touch, he clears his throat and takes a step back.

Although I blink up at him, the moment is gone.

I won't press the issue. Today has been too much already, and a rejection from him is just one more thing I'll be forced to stew over for the next two days. Damn if I don't have enough to think about already.

"I'll see you on Monday." I give him a quick smile before stepping around him and climbing into my car.

He stands in the parking lot, staring after me as I pull away, and even though I tell myself I won't, my eyes are locked on the sight of him in the rearview mirror until the night swallows him up.

I can't go home. I'm too raw, too confused about what's going on, feeling too disjointed to see my loving mom and dad sending each other secret looks they think no one else around them can see.

So I don't go home. I head straight to the gas station on the corner and grab a six-pack of tiny wines. Classy as hell I know, but honestly, if no one is around to see you moping with gas station wine, then did it even really happen?

On my way back through town, I drive by the police station, a sinking feeling in my gut when I see his truck is no longer there. Maybe I had it in my head to follow him home, but I spent an hour tonight regurgitating my story about someone creeping on me so it doesn't seem like the best idea. Plus, he's a great detective and would probably spot me before he got out of the damn parking lot.

With that plan thankfully foiled, I head to the park instead. It's dark, so it should be deserted but even if it's not, I anticipate late-night teens up to no good scattering like roaches when my headlights pull into the parking lot.

I don't think about tomorrow when I park my car. I don't worry about what Monday is going to look like, not only the work but the awkwardness that's sure to be there when I have to see Colton again.

I worry about nothing other than finding the perfect playlist on my phone—locking my doors because safety—and twisting off the top of my blush wine.

The first bottle goes down cold, the aftertaste washed away by the second. By the third, I'm bouncing my head to the music, drumming my fingers on the steering wheel as if I joined the band myself. When I twist the top off the fifth one, I can't remember drinking the fourth one, but I'm committed. Exhaustion fills my bones as I sip the sixth, and my eyes won't seem to stay open enough for me to finish it.

My phone dings, the sound echoing around me due to being connect through my car's Bluetooth.

I frown down at the message, but my fingers work quickly with the lie to my dad about staying at a friend's house tonight. I should ask him to come get me, but I don't.

Judgment from him is the very last thing I need tonight. I need a fluffy blanket, a pillow, and warm strong hands all over my body.

Colton's face flashes in my mind of course, but that's a ship that's never going to sail. Nope, that boat is stuck in the slip, dry docked from drought along with my underused pu—

My phone chimes again, and I'm hit with a rush of guilt with my dad wishing me a good night. I groan. I shouldn't have to lie. I don't actually have to lie, and I don't know why I did.

I fire off a text because I have to let someone know where I am.

If I go missing, it's because I have to sleep in my car at the park. I'm not going to risk killing a family of three.

The text goes unanswered, but I'm not surprised. There's no reason for him to respond. Colton has already had to deal with me for like fifty hours this week. I shouldn't be bothering him on his weekend off, anyway. We're not friends. He's sort of my boss.

I could text Griffin, Lawson, or even Cannon. There's no shortage of people I could reach out to at eleven on a Friday night. There's a good chance not a single person I know is already in bed, but my arms are heavy, much like my eyes. Even my soul seems burdened by the week and sleeping right here won't be all that bad. Yeah, I know I'll probably have to mainline Aleve in the morning, and I'll certainly have to explain to my parents why I'm coming home in my work clothes, but I can deal with all of that in the morn—

I squeal like I've just spotted Jason Voorhees with a knife when someone knocks on my window. I cringe away and lift a hand when a megawatt light is shined right in my eyes.

"Open the door," the criminal snaps after trying the handle and getting nowhere. "Sophia, open the damn door."

I know I read somewhere that most people are murdered by people they know, and I have a choice to make. Put the car in drive and risk killing someone, or take the chance with a murderer.

My hand reaches for the gearshift, but then the image of that four-year-old little boy from the drunk driving case sneaks back into memory. I crack the window instead.

"May I help you?"

A husky chuckle fills my ears, and I inwardly wonder if Ted Bundy had such a sexy laugh. If he did, then I completely understand why women jumped at the chance to spend a little time with him.

I smack my forehead with my palm, groaning in pain with the contact. What a fucked up thing to joke about even mentally. The man was a sex offender and serial killer. I once again blame television, and more specifically, Zac Efron for making crazy look so damn appealing.

"Are you drunk?"

"Buzzed," I argue, squinting my eyes but still unable to see well, even though the light is no longer pointed directly at my face. "Too intoxicated to drive."

My phone rings, but I decline the call from Izzy, too invested in the conversation with this stranger to whine to my best friend about Colton fucking Matthews.

"Should I take you to the station?" he asks as he reaches inside the car to hit the door unlock button.

"Fire station?" I muse. "Firefighters are hot."

I snort, an unladylike sound, but the alcohol swimming in my bloodstream tells me it was a cute sound.

The guy chuckles as he opens the door. "And here I thought you had a thing for cops."

I take his hand when he offers it to me, and damn if my eyes are broken because here stands Colton Matthews. Think of the devil and he shall appear.

"I'm not the devil, Sophia." I roll my lips between my teeth because I had no idea I said that last part out loud. Hold on. How much have I said out loud?

"I'm guessing nearly everything you think you thought since I arrived. And if you're taking notes, I think Mark Harmon played a much better Ted than Zac Efron."

"And the sexy laugh part?" I ask, hoping against hope I didn't say that out loud.

"The part about Bundy having a sexy laugh or the fact that you think I have a sexy laugh?"

Kill me now.

"No can do. I work homicide, and I'm off this weekend, remember? Conflict of interest. Let me grab your things and I can see about getting you home."

"I can't go home. I lied to my dad about staying at a friend's house," I explain in a rush as Colton leans me against the car so he can turn off my car and grab my personal belongings. "And I can't leave my car here. It'll end up on blocks."

"We'll drop your keys off at the station so one of the guys can swing by and grab it."

"You're impounding my car?" I scoff, the jerk of my head overexaggerated. "For drinking in my car? Seems a little harsh, don't you think?"

He stands to look at me, his hands full of my belongings. "You are so fucking cute."

I blow a strand of hair from out of my face, but he doesn't take the hint to push it behind my ear. I mean I know his hands are full, but he's missing out on a pretty intense kiss. If he'd only get a couple inches closer, I could seal the damn deal.

"I have no doubt the kiss would be intense, Sophia." He leans in close enough that I can feel his warm minty breath on my lips. "But I don't kiss drunk girls."

"Let's make a deal?" I bargain. "How about when I say stuff out loud, and it's clear I meant to think them, why don't you be a gentleman and keep your mouth shut?"

"Deal," he agrees. "Now get in my truck."

He's so damn bossy. It makes me wonder how bossy he would be in bed. Like would he smack my ass to get my attention or maybe wrap his sexy fingers around my throat?

"Jesus, Soph. Just get in the damn truck." He groans when I look over my shoulder at him.

"Did I—"

"Just get in the damn truck."

Chapter 9

Colton

She's asleep before I can even get back in my truck after securing her car. She doesn't stir when I call one of the guys at the station to grab her car from the park, or when we swing by the station to drop off her keys.

She's snoring softly at the last red light in town, and sawing logs by the time I pull up in my driveway.

Taking her home will be something I already regret, but some of the things in my past I initially saw as a mistake have turned into some of the best things about my life. I'm crossing my fingers that tonight will end up being one of those things as well.

"No regrets," I mutter to myself as I climb out of my truck and walk around to open the passenger side door.

She jolts when I scoop her up in my arms, but she settles back into my embrace quickly. The flowery scent of her skin was once something I looked forward to, but it's a whole other story this close. Especially after realizing as I walk her inside my house that it's concentrated more on the spot under her ear than near her shoulder. I now crave the ambrosia covering her skin. God, what this woman is doing to me.

The lights in the house are still on. I was moments from heading to bed when I got her text, but hadn't made it as far as turning the television off and shutting everything down. I contemplate letting her sleep on the couch, but that's not something I'm going to want to explain in the morning, so like a fool, I carry her to my own damn bed.

I make excuses in my head as I carry her down the hallway, but the simple truth is, I want her in my bed. I want the scent of her skin on my sheets. I want to close my eyes tonight with thoughts of her in my space, the intimacy of it will live inside my brain for eternity.

"I wanted to kiss you," she whispers, her eyes still closed when I settle her on the mattress.

"I know, baby." God, I want that, too.

I grind my back teeth together. She's supposed to be speaking her truths out loud, not me.

"Where am I?" Her words are soft, filled with sleepiness, and she probably won't remember them in the morning. I can only pray she doesn't wake up with regret for calling me.

"You're at my house, Sophia. I'm going to leave the bathroom light on in case you need to get up. I'm going to lock the bedroom door from the inside, so you'll have to call out for me if you need me."

"Thank y—"

She doesn't even get the second word out completely before her body relaxes entirely into my sheets. I tug the comforter up around her shoulders after tugging off her boots. I don't remove another stitch of clothing. I tuck her sock-covered feet under the blanket and leave the room, locking her inside like I promised.

Grabbing blankets and a spare pillow out of the hall closet, I head back to the living room, turning out lights and checking locks on the way.

This isn't even close to how I pictured my night going, and I'm glad I was too lazy to get off the couch and grab the bottle of whiskey I had been salivating over after getting home from eating dinner. I mean, I would've found a way to get to Sophia safely, but I'm just glad I was able to manage it without witnesses. The gossip at a police station is worse than the nurse's station at a hospital, and that's saying something. Those hens cackle incessantly.

I spend the first ten minutes on the couch regretting my decision to purchase a sectional that curves because sleeping in a u-shape isn't fun. After conceding to a crick in my neck in the recliner, I watch the hallway, waiting to see if she's going to need me.

I only saw a six-pack of mini wine bottles, of which I disposed of in the park trash, but that doesn't mean she didn't drink more and discard the empty containers before I got there. I seethe at the idea of her being alone in that park. The crime rate isn't high in that area, but anything could happen at any time.

Resisting the urge to curl up outside the bedroom door, I let my eyes close, but my senses are on full alert. I locked the door so she'll feel safe, but my heart pounds with thoughts of her needing me and not being able to get to her.

I tell myself that she's a grown woman, not a sick child, but it doesn't do much to calm the irrational fear. My fingers are tapping on my chest in arrhythmic anxiety, but I hold steady.

Would she freak if I jimmied the lock open and slept in the bed beside her?

If I did that, would I be able to keep to the far side of the bed, or would I wake up with my arms wrapped around her?

I know the answer to that question no matter how much I want to deny the truth. It's nearly impossible to keep from touching her during the daylight hours when we're awake. Keeping my distance while sleeping wouldn't happen. With the rising sun, I'd have her cocooned in my arms.

I roll my head on my shoulders with the image I've conjured of her soft breath ghosting over my bare chest. Because, of course, I'd only be wearing a pair of boxers.

Jesus, I have to stop.

Shaking my head, I open my eyes, but staring at the sliver of light between the front curtains from the streetlight outside doesn't deter my focus.

When the dog from down the street starts barking, I'm out of the recliner with my nose to the window's glass. The noise gives me an excuse to move, but my reasoning isn't sane. That dog barks every night at the same time when his owner comes home from his second-shift job. I could set my watch by it, but tonight things seem different. Sophia is in my home, intoxicated and vulnerable, and my sense of protection is at an all-time high.

After the dog settles, I slowly make my way down the hall. My ear to the door allows me to hear the soft snores coming from inside, but instead of backing away, I let a smile take over my face as I stand and listen for several long minutes.

"This is stupid," I mutter, but it takes another minute before I pull my face away and head back into the living room.

With determination, I flop back down in the recliner, pull the thin blanket up to my chin, and close my eyes.

I helped a friend out this evening and nothing more. I would've done the same for nearly everyone down at the station had they needed help. Granted, I probably wouldn't have brought them home, but she was adamant about not letting her dad know what was going on. I now know that's because she doesn't want to disappoint him, not out of fear. I don't have a daughter, but I can't say that I'd do things much differently if I did. Dominic was given this precious gift, and he's spent his life protecting it. I've only known her for a few weeks and I have this incessant urge to behave exactly the same way.

Maybe tomorrow will be different. Maybe tomorrow I'll be able to take a long look in the mirror and be able to convince myself that worrying about Sophia isn't my place. She has men in her life—namely her father, uncle, and probably every other man at the Cerberus clubhouse—that are looking out for her.

I just have to make it until the sun rises, and the day will look completely different. Things always seem dire in the middle of the night.

With my eyes squeezed shut, I start the backward countdown from a thousand.

Only it takes me doing it four times before I'm finally able to fall asleep.

Chapter 10

Sophia

The mild headache I wake with is a better outcome than I deserve.

The scent of Colton under my head is a reward I didn't earn with truthfulness.

It doesn't stop me from burying my head deeper to take the spiciness of his cologne into my lungs, but hey, I've always been a little selfish. Admitting you have a problem is the first step, right?

And my problem is Detective Colton Matthews. What started as a little harmless flirtation that first day has somehow morphed into a longing that has taken over nearly every waking thought, and although many of those thoughts—like the ones I'm having now—lean toward the sexual side of things, I also think about everyday things, like drinking coffee together or watching the sun rise. More than once, I've let myself envision what he would look like cooking a meal or doing yardwork.

I punch the pillow under my head, because I know none of that stuff can happen. Dating a man thirteen years older than me? Never going to happen, especially not after acting so irresponsibly last night. What grown man wants to be responsible for a woman who gets drunk in her car at the park?

My intention last night was to just get a break from everything going on, including Colton. I didn't park my car with the hopes that I would end up in his bed. Yet, here I am. I'm moments away from having to do the walk of shame when I haven't reaped any of the rewards. There's no beard-burn marking my skin. My muscles don't ache from overuse.

All I have is a worsening headache and shame.

In an attempt to prolong the inevitable, I regretfully climb out of his bed. I hate the sight of unruffled sheets on the far side. Although I hoped he'd climb in bed with me, I never expected him to. And hope, like most often, is fruitless.

The bathroom is inviting when I step inside, and without a second thought, I strip down and climb in the shower, moaning with relief when the hot water pounds on my back. Tension I didn't know I was holding onto leaves my muscles slowly, and the water is running cold by the time I turn it off.

His towels are soft, something I'd never expect from a bachelor, and I take my time drying off, pausing periodically to breathe in the scent of my skin that is now coated with his fragrance from his body wash. Putting on my clothes from yesterday isn't going to happen. Just the sight of them piled on the floor makes me think about the horror of responding to the scene where a young woman was found dead.

Honestly, I'm no longer thinking about escape, not after spending more time in his space. If anything, I never want to leave. I push down thoughts of consequences and open Colton's closet door, selecting a dark button-down shirt before grabbing the top pair of boxers from his drawer.

I feel like a temptress as I roll the boxers up so they stay on my hips and can't help biting my lip when I take a look at myself in the bathroom mirror. After rinsing my mouth with mouthwash, I gather as much courage as I can muster and leave the room.

I won't do any kind of begging with Colton, but maybe voicing my thoughts to him would help. Maybe if he knew how I felt, things would be different. Maybe if I let him catch me watching him, he would understand how much I desire him. There's only one way to find out, and I'm determined to leave this house today with every one of my cards on the table. Rejection would suck, but at least I can go home knowing how he wants to proceed.

I mastered the art of sneaking around by the time I was twelve, not that I ever got past my dad without him knowing, so I traverse the hallway on the tips of my toes. Pausing just inside of the tidy living room, I take a moment to watch Colton. Asleep in the recliner, he looks incredibly uncomfortable. Having sunk down during the night, his long legs extend past the end of the chair, bare feet hanging out of the end of the blanket.

Guilt swims in my gut. The man worked hard this week, and my antics have relegated him to a horrible night of sleep. I could spend all day watching him, trying to ignore the urge to wake him up with a kiss and insist he go climb in his bed while I make him breakfast, but a noise in the other room distracts me.

Tilting my head, I wait for the noise again, thinking maybe he has a dog or something, but silence surrounds me. Curiosity gets the better of me, my heart pounding with the unknown as I turn in the direction of the sound I heard. I don't find a hungry puppy sniffing around looking for breakfast, but the sight before me does make me pause.

Vibrating back muscles disappear into a pair of low-slung jeans as the man in the kitchen dances to a song playing through a pair of Bluetooth headphones. I don't make apologies and back away and maybe looking back later, I can still use the excuse that my brain is muddled by alcohol. Instead, I stand there and watch, an impressed smile on my lips. This man is tall, the hint of a shadow on his jaw when he turns slightly to grab something from the cabinet.

He's attractive. I'll give him that, but he's got nothing on the man in the other room.

Is he a roommate? Colton didn't offer up much about his homelife, and he seemed reluctant to answer the questions I had about his family last night.

The man turns around, startling for a brief second before a wide smile spreads across his handsome face. Mischievous eyes skate up and down my body from my bare legs to the top of my messy head. He nods in appreciation, and I easily determine he's related to Colton. Not only are the facial features strikingly similar, but he's behaving exactly the same way Colton did when he first saw me. He pulls his headphones from his ears as the flirtatious look on his face grows.

"Good morning."

He's definitely a younger brother, possibly a cousin.

"Morning." Nerves force me to shift from one foot to the other as I weigh the benefits of using this guy to make Colton jealous. Nothing forces a man's hand like competition, but Colton doesn't really seem like the type of man who's willing to fight over a woman.

"I didn't know we had an overnight guest." His eyes continue to rove over the length of me, and I can tell when he notices the pucker of my nipples.

The guy is good-looking, but I'm not aroused by the sight of him. If anything, it's the proximity of the man in the living room that's got my blood heated this morning, but I don't make a move to cover my chest. I'm not indecent. He can't really see anything due to the dark nature of the shirt I chose, but it doesn't stop the man from getting his fill.

"Is there coffee?"

He clears his throat, eyes snapping to mine instead of remaining on my chest.

"Y-yeah, let me get you a cup," he stammers, which is adorable, as he reaches into the cabinet. I don't bother hiding a smile at the sight of his back muscles flexing.

I'm not desperate for attention, but I also won't deny feeling like a queen when I feel his eyes follow me across the room. He steps away so I can pour a cup of coffee, and I know if I look over my shoulder, I'm going to find him still watching me.

Only when I look, teeth digging into my bottom lip because of the power I feel it gives me, I find Colton leaning against the doorframe with his arms crossed over his chest, a messy head of hair, and his sexy mouth in a playful smirk.

"What's going on in here?" he asks before I can muster up an explanation.

"Dad!" the other man yelps. "You scared the shit out of me!"

My eyes widen as they sweep between the two. "D-dad?"

Not a chance.

Nope.

No way.

I attempt to swallow the lump in my throat, but it doesn't budge.

Instead of answering, Colton's eyes sweep down my legs, and I feel like a pervert knowing it looks like I'm not wearing anything under his shirt. Hell, embarrassment heats my cheeks at having the audacity to wear his clothes at all.

When his eyes make it up to my chest, my breasts betray me by growing heavy, nipples furling even more than they were in the cool room. With shaking hands, I grasp the fabric and pull it away from my skin.

"I thought he was your brother. You have a son?" I look over at the young man, who now that I think about it looks younger than he did at first sight. I feel gross.

The guy stares at me, his eyes now staying on my face instead of drinking me in like he was before Colton appeared. I want to shift on my feet. No, I want to run away, but I'm not ten, and I know the problem won't disappear when I leave the room.

"No way," I argue, pausing for them to start laughing and let me in on the joke. "You're too young."

The kid swallows, but it's clear he's deferring the conversation to Colton.

"Rick, why don't you take the trash cans down," Colton instructs, his eyes never leaving mine.

"The trash doesn't run until Monday," Rick argues.

"Now, Rick."

The kid grumbles under his breath, but he disappears, the front door opening and closing less than a minute later.

"I swear to God, I thought he was your brother." My throat is thick with emotions I don't have the time to analyze, and the backs of my eyes burn with unshed tears.

"And that would make you coming out here half-naked okay?"

"I have on your boxers," I assure him, pulling up the hem of the shirt so he can see I'm telling the truth.

His eyes flare, a sharp intake of breath whistling from his nose. He pushes away from the doorframe, inching closer, and it forces me to take a step back.

"I feel like a pervert," I admit.

"He's seen more on Netflix," Colton whispers, his eyes still on my legs. I drop the shirt, letting the fabric kiss the tops of my thighs. "He's not some protected baby."

"I'm s-sorry," I stammer, blinking with shame when his eyes meet mine.

"He's a lucky boy," he continues as he draws closer.

My butt is now against the counter, and even though he's still several feet away, I feel like a caged animal.

"I would've given a year's worth of allowance at his age to walk into the kitchen and find you grinning at me."

My fingers tangle in the fabric of the shirt, nervousness winning out over anything else. Is this where he throws me out? Tells me he never wants to see me again because I was creeping on his teenage son.

"He looks older," I justify. "He has a beard."

"He has stubble because he hasn't shaved in a month." Colton lifts his hand to his own chin. "He hit puberty earlier than most. He had a mustache at thirteen."

"His name is Rick?" I ask, not knowing what else to say.

"Yes."

"Mother?" I look around the kitchen, noticing the lived-in feel of the space. The curtains have lemons on them, and there's a spoon rest on the stove for shit's sake. Tears threaten to fall. "Does she live here? Are you still with her?"

This isn't a bachelor pad. Men don't have seat cushions on dining room chairs, do they?

"I'm not a home-wrecker," I whisper, the very first tear falling from my eye.

No wonder he stopped the flirting that very first day.

God, dinner last night? I let myself believe it was a damn date.

Jesus, what's wrong with me?

Me?

What about him?

I stand to my full height, my false bravery betrayed by the fingers still twisting in the shirt.

Oh God, *his shirt*.

"I'm not married," he says, his body now mere inches from mine. "Only Rick and I live here."

"Where's his mother?"

He shrugs but doesn't offer up any more information.

"How old is he?"

"Sixteen." My brow scrunches together, and he must see that I'm trying to do the math in my head. "Conceived at eighteen, born at nineteen. We were twenty when she decided she no longer wanted to be a mother or a wife."

This is the divorce he mentioned. My heart cracks for him as a man, but splits wide open for their son to not have a mother.

"How did I not know you were a single dad?"

He licks his lips, and it leaves me distracted.

"You are single, right?"

"Can you put the shirt down, Sophia? It's a little distracting."

I gasp when I look down to not only find my fingers tangled in the shirt but also that they're only about an inch or so away from his crotch.

"Shit," I hiss and release the shirt.

His chuckle washes over me, but I nearly stop breathing when I look up and see the heat burning in his eyes.

Chapter 11

Colton

Did she even realize her fingers brushed the front of my jeans?

I didn't miss it. The split-second touch has my blood singing in my veins, but she looks like she's about to cry.

I want to wipe away the single tear that's rolling down her cheek but that would be a mistake.

Bringing her here was a mistake.

Having her in my home is a mistake because I'm seconds away from scooping her up and carrying her back to my bedroom.

"You didn't tell me about him," she whispers, her head hanging down, denying me the sight of her gorgeous brown eyes.

"I'm surprised he hasn't been by the station since you started your internship."

The conversation is casual when I'm feeling anything but inside. Rick stayed with a friend last night, and I didn't expect him home so early.

"I didn't know he was so young." Finally, her eyes lift to mine, shrouded with unease. "I thought he was your brother."

"Were you trying to make me jealous?"

The prospect of it makes me thicken further with possession.

"I thought about it."

"That's not very nice, Sophia. Jealous men seldomly act with reason."

I'm not in competition with my teenage son in the least, but a sick sense of ownership fills me when she bites her lip without answering.

"Almost kissing me and backing away isn't very nice either."

Is she talking about last night or now? Because the urge took over my body in both instances.

"You want to be kissed?"

Her eyes dart away when she refuses to answer.

"Look at me."

She hesitates, taking several long breaths before turning her face toward me.

"I shouldn't want to kiss you," I whisper.

"But you do?"

My tongue wets my lips.

Fuck yeah, I do. "I can't."

"But you want to?"

Kissing her would make so many fantasies come true. My lips on hers, finally knowing what her tongue felt like against mine, is what my dreams have been made of for weeks. Could we cross that line and come out the other end unscathed? My guess is no.

"I can't," I repeat.

"Why not?" She looks so innocent, reminding me of just why I've backed off the countless times I've wanted to be this close to her.

I'm thirty-five with a teenage son. My baggage has baggage. She has her whole life ahead of her. The weight on my shoulders has no business getting close to her. It would be such a disservice to be that selfish.

"It's just a kiss," she barters. "Just one little—"

"No, Sophia. It wouldn't be just a kiss."

Her breath hitches, her eyes wide and blinking.

Can't she understand that one kiss would turn into two and then three? Seconds would tick by and the sun would set tonight with her in my bed and in my arms. Surely she can understand that my lips on hers would only be the beginning of a train wreck both of us would be powerless to stop?

"I want all of that," she says, as if she's capable of reading my mind.

There are parts of me that beg me to change my mind, mostly the areas below my neck, and I falter when I realize the muscle pounding behind my ribcage has somehow gotten involved.

When did things shift from just wanting to be inside of her to wanting to stand beside her, to wanting to be a part of her life in and out of the bedroom?

It's this realization that forces me to take a step, the foot now between us seeming like a wide chasm of indecision.

I don't know that walking away from her is possible, but I have to try. We're in totally different places in life, and I come with a nearly grown child.

I don't know what it is about her that makes the entire situation different. I've been with women since Rick's mother left, but not one of them tempted me the way she does. Not one of those women made me pause and want to think about the future.

It's not because she's beautiful, I've known beautiful women before.

Is it because the age difference is a little taboo? Maybe because she's off-limits according to the unspoken decree set out by her father's club? Because we work together and that means I should keep my distance?

Even with knowing all of that, do I *have* to stay away?

A rush of breath leaves my lips as she watches me.

Yes, I do, because I've got intentions of trapping her in a life with me, and just sex won't work. Just one kiss isn't possible. One of anything with her would just be a fool's errand.

"Sophia, I think—"

"Is it because of how I acted with Rick? I swear I—"

"I'm not mad about that," I assure her, my feet itching to step near her again.

I'm obsessed with her lips, the soft pillows twitching as I watch them. My cock is full and throbbing, and that's the power this woman has over me. One look, one hint of her mouth on mine and I'm ready to bury myself inside of her.

"But you are mad?"

Fucking furious. Exceedingly irritated at the compromises I'm making in my head.

"You've done nothing wrong, but this needs to—"

"Dad, look who came for a visit."

I don't even have to turn around to look when Rick talks. There are only two people in the world who come in this house aside from Rick's friends.

"Fuck," I mutter, willing my heavy cock to deflate.

"Colton?"

Yep, that's about all it takes. Slowly, I turn around, giving my parents a weak smile, hoping they can't see the agitation at being interrupted even though it couldn't have come at a better time.

I block their view of Sophia, not because I'm ashamed of her being in my home, but to save her the unease of meeting them while half-dressed.

"Mom. Dad. How lovely to see you this morning."

Mom cocks an eyebrow. Dad huffs a laugh, and for the first time in my life I feel like a teenage boy getting caught doing something wrong.

And that's saying something because I had to confess to them that I was going to be a father four months before high school graduation.

Chapter 12

Sophia

Parents?

Parents!

Only me. I swear, if there is something else that could go wrong today, it will.

I'm in Colton's button-down shirt, a pair of his rolled up boxers, and it looks like we're having a fucking family reunion in the kitchen. I haven't even had coffee yet, and I've managed to sort of flirt with his teenage son—cringe—and get caught by the man's parents half-naked.

If this were some late-night sitcom, I'd squeal like a trapped pig and run away, but as established earlier, the situation doesn't disappear when you leave the room.

Peeking around Colton's massive shoulder, I see his mother, a beautiful woman with his same warm brown eyes, standing with a stoic look on her face. His dad, on the other hand, is grinning, throwing me a silly wink when I make eye contact with him. Is every man in this family a hopeless flirt?

Rick is leaning against the doorframe looking so much like his dad that I want to gag at the memory of thinking of him in any other way.

Colton turns so he can swipe his gaze back and forth between his parents and me. If there were cheesy music playing in the background, I'd swear I was standing on the set of that television show I thought about earlier.

No one is saying anything, and I don't know if they're just at a loss for words or if they're deferring to me.

What I do know is that I hate the spotlight, and my face is absolutely on fire.

We were seconds away from kissing for the first time. I'm certain of it. I could tell he was debating the merits of it, but the scale was beginning to tip in my favor, and now this!

"Dad's friend stayed the night last night," Rick helpfully offers.

Colton clears his throat, and I'm once again near tears.

"Sophia, these are my parents, Franklin and Sally Matthews. Mom and Dad, meet Sophia Anderson."

I give them a little wave, glued in this spot and unable to offer my hand to shake. They both say good morning, and I don't get the vibe that they think I'm being rude. His dad, thankfully, keeps his eyes on mine. I can't say the same for Rick.

Colton crosses the room and leans over to whisper something in Rick's ear, making the boy turn around and leave the room.

"Mom and Dad, we'll join you in the living room shortly."

They both turn but his mom looks over her shoulder, watching me as she walks away.

"You said they play golf and visit friends on Saturday," I hiss, but Colton holds up his hand to silence me.

"She's gorgeous," I hear his mother whisper. "A little young, but absolutely gorgeous. I need more grandbabies."

I only thought my skin was on fire before. What's hotter than fire? That's where I'm at right now.

Grandbabies?

What. The. Actual. Fuck?

"Do you think she's related to those Anderson bikers?" his father questions before their voices trail off into the other room.

My hackles go up, and it's not lost on me that I'm half-naked in this man's kitchen and have no right to question others' opinions, but my family is a hotspot for me.

It's clear Colton's trying to hide a smile when he turns back around to face me.

"Still want that kiss now?"

I swallow, backing away because my head is swimming with a million and one questions. He gives me an almost imperceptible nod of understanding.

"There are more appropriate clothes waiting for you on my bed." And now I know what he whispered to his son.

I scurry past him, not even looking in the direction of his parents when I run by the living room.

Rick is leaving his dad's room when I try to enter. His eyes trail down my legs once again.

"Not a chance, buddy," I snap before stepping into the room and closing the door.

Much to my horror, Colton's more appropriate clothing includes a pair of sweats and a Farmington High t-shirt. Nothing says I'm too young for him like replicated clothing that I wore only a few years ago.

In no position to argue, I change, leaving his boxers on out of spite. I don't linger in his room because I don't want to appear even more rude than I know I already look. As I make my way down the hall toward the living room, I pray Colton will offer to take me to get my car. My earlier interaction with Rick seems even more skeevy considering what I was wearing. I don't imagine they'll care that I came out first thing this morning thinking Colton and I were alone in the house.

The end of the hallway opens up to the sight of all four Matthews sitting in various places with coffee in their hands. Well, Rick is drinking a glass of milk because he's a fucking child.

My stomach turns as I look around the room. The only spot left to sit is between Colton and Rick, but I don't have the nerves for that right now. Colton pats the spot with an open hand. I eye the front door before looking back at him, and I don't miss the challenging look in his eyes. Does he think I can't handle spending time with his family?

I mean, I don't know that I'll survive it, but I've never been one to back down from a challenge.

I cross the room, a small smile playing on my lips and take a seat. Colton doesn't open his mouth to begin a conversation, and neither does anyone else.

Silence swirls around us, and I see everyone smiling. It's as if I've stepped into the middle of a family joke, and I'm the only one who doesn't know the punchline.

"Would you like a cup of coffee?" Colton whispers low in my ear.

Goosebumps travel down my arm, and the question feels more intimate than it should with three other people in the room.

"I'm fine," I assure him, but he doesn't inch back, doesn't put distance between us.

A drop of sweat forms between my shoulder blades, trickling down my spine.

"How do you know our son?" his dad asks, and everyone in the room seems invested in my answer.

"We met at the police station." His mom tilts her head, and I realize I haven't offered enough information. I can't tell if she thinks he arrested me or something. "I'm working an internship there."

"You're still in college?" Mrs. Matthews asks.

I answer her honestly, trying not to give too much information while at the same time attempting not to seem evasive.

Colton doesn't offer anything up, and why should he? They aren't interrogating him. I'm the one under the spotlight. Rick eventually wanders off, but I'm stuck in the living room answering a million questions. They don't ask relationship questions but rather only personal questions, starting with school and family before ending with goals. By the time they stand to leave, I feel like I've sat through an interview for the damn FBI.

"We would love to have you over tomorrow evening for family dinner," his mom says before they step out onto the front porch.

Looks like I got the job, I think.

I give her a noncommittal answer, but it seems like enough for her as she waves goodbye.

Within minutes of his parents pulling out of the driveway, I'm back in his truck on my way to pick up my car from the police station.

Conversation is limited, as in nonexistent. He asked if I needed a bag for my dirty laundry before we left the house and hasn't said much since. I climbed into the truck while he was getting his wallet just so I wouldn't have to put either of us through the awkwardness of him opening my door for me.

My hand is clutching the door handle as we pull into the parking lot at the station. He parks the same way he did last night after dinner, but in the light of day it feels more like a quicker way to get rid of me.

"Thank you for helping me last night," I mutter before climbing out of the truck.

In my hurry to get away, I leave the bag of clothes in the floorboard of his truck, but I'd rather buy an entirely new wardrobe than go back for them. I don't cry on the way home, and I'm relieved my parents are nowhere to be found as I lock myself in my room.

Monday is going to be the worst, and I'm already thinking of what to say when I call in sick.

Chapter 13

Colton

I'm not well rested. I'm not bright-eyed and ready to get the week started. I don't arrive early, overcome with eagerness to see Sophia.

I drag my sleepy ass into work ten minutes late, exhausted from three nights with limited sleep.

Sophia isn't in my office when I open the door and a pang of loss hits me in the chest, but I don't deserve the right to go look for her. I last half an hour alone in my office before I tell myself I'm emerging to get a cup of coffee. Distracted, I left mine sitting on the counter at home. I fire off a text to Rick to make sure he checks to be sure the pot is turned off before heading to school because I can't remember if I did or not. He texts back with some bullshit about me being a senile old man. I'd normally argue with him, but I'm not feeling it this morning.

It's a blessing that Sophia isn't surrounded by cops this morning when I find her working quietly in the corner. I think I'll lose my shit if I have to witness another blowhard hitting on her.

She doesn't look up at me when I cross the room or when I make more noise than necessary while getting a cup of coffee, and for some reason I walk out of there and back to my office without opening my mouth either.

The day drags by, filled with paperwork and phone calls, absent of Sophia's pretty face, and by lunchtime I'm itching to just talk to her, wishing things could be like they were before dinner Friday night. Things shifted, and I'm not liking the outcome. This is what I expected would happen if I slept with her, knowing she wouldn't be very happy with me when I told her we couldn't be anything more, but I didn't even reap the reward of spending the night with her, and I'm suffering the punishment like I did.

I work through lunch, not wanting to submit anyone else to my surly ass attitude, and it's nearly three in the afternoon before my door swings wide. I open my mouth to yell at the person interrupting me, but it's Sophia walking in with a pile of folders.

"Soph," I say, the one syllable sounding more like a plea than I intended.

She doesn't even look at me as she drops the files on my desk.

"Please," I beg, reaching for her wrist before she can turn and walk away.

She freezes, her eyes glued to the contact on her skin.

I keep my hold on her as I stand and join her on the other side of my desk, only releasing her long enough to close the office door. She's glaring at me when I turn back around.

"Can we talk about it?"

"About what?" I love the way she cocks her hip out to the side, but I don't think she'll find it funny that I think she's cute right now. "I'm working. That's why I'm here, remember?"

"About Saturday morning—"

Before I can apologize, she closes the distance between the two of us, pressing her lips to mine. Shocked, I stand frozen, eyes open and blinking down at her. Her eyes flutter for a brief second, but she pulls back almost immediately.

Being the brave woman I've come to admire, she doesn't look away from me. She doesn't hang her head in embarrassment at my inaction.

"You're too young," I say, clearing my throat when the words sound like a lie even to my own ears. "We have to keep things professional."

"And that's what's wrong with Saturday morning," she hisses through her teeth, that fiery attitude I've only seen a couple of times coming out. "You tell me I'm too young, but you're the one who acted like an adolescent boy in front of your parents. You're the one playing around, and I'm too fucking mature for games."

She sidles around me, flying out of my office without another word. She doesn't slam the door behind her when she leaves, and without that final act, things seem left unfinished.

My cell phone rings before I even have the chance to settle back in my desk and overthink all the ways I've fucked up in the last month. The last thing I need as a distraction is a female murder victim with three bullet holes in her chest and a boyfriend that seems to have fled the scene.

***

"Tell me what you see."

Sophia looks around the small home, taking in every inch of the mess made. I don't miss the fact that her eyes avoid the woman's body crumpled near the entryway to the kitchen.

"Chaos," she answers.

"What else?"

"A man lives here."

"How do you know?"

"There are three pairs of men's shoes near the door. The jacket hanging on the hook is too large for her. There's a pile of men's belongings on the front porch."

"What do you think happened?"

"She tried to kick him out. He wasn't happy, and he killed her."

"The boyfriend's name is Dennis Milton," Ramshaw says as he joins us in the room.

His eyes are on the notebook in his hands. Mine are on Sophia.

"Penny was on the phone with 911 when she was shot. She was deceased by the time officers made it to the location."

Sophia flinches with the news. Sometimes it only takes minutes for the unthinkable to occur.

"Dispatch heard them arguing. There were four gunshots, only three hitting the victim. One went wide. Peterson found the other bullet lodged in the bottom cabinet in the kitchen."

"He continued to shoot her as she fell," Sophia deduces.

"There's a BOLO out for Milton's late model Ford Ranger," Ramshaw continues. "He left his wallet on the nightstand in the bedroom, so I don't imagine he has much money with him. He's limited on what he can do. A unit has already been sent to his mother's house across town."

"Thank you," I tell Ramshaw who nods at both of us before backing away.

We continue to work the scene, Sophia taking notes and writing down everything I say out loud. I'm grateful I have better control over my thoughts than she did intoxicated on Friday night because I'm awash with thoughts of her and regrets for my actions. This isn't the time or the place to have that conversation.

We stand out of the way as the crime scene guy takes photos of nearly everything in the house. Having too much is always better than not having enough. Within an hour of us being on scene, a call comes in that the unit sent to Milton's mother's house was able to locate him. After a short standoff, Dennis Milton surrendered and is currently in custody on his way to the police station.

Sophia follows me to the car without a word, and I know that her sullenness is from a combination of what happened earlier in the office and knowing that another life is gone all too soon.

Interrogating suspects never gets easier. Facing evil drains me each and every time I'm tasked with doing it. Procedure sates that Sophia, not a licensed peace officer, can't be in the room with us, but Monahan has given her permission to watch on the other side of the two-way glass. She hasn't witnessed this part of the process yet. She's halfway through her internship, and with any luck, she won't have the opportunity again. We've had too many deaths recently, and the entire department is long overdue for a break from it.

I'm nervous as I enter the room, folder in hand and come face-to-face with Dennis Milton for the first time. I've interviewed hundreds of people in my time on the Farmington Police Force, hundreds of times with people in the other room, but my nerves are on edge knowing that she's on the other side of the glass at my back.

She may see things differently after today. She may have preconceived notions from watching television about what it's really like in an interrogation room, but everyone interviews differently. Hell, each interview is different.

I can only hope she'll still respect me when today is done.

Chapter 14

Sophia

Rubbing the outside of my arm, I watch through the glass as Colton enters the interrogation room.

"Hey, Milton."

How is his voice so calm after leaving the crime scene?

"I bet you've had better days."

Milton doesn't look up from the table to engage with him as Colton informs him that the interview is being recorded. He states the guy's name, the date, and the location of the interview. He even mentions that Milton is handcuffed on his right wrist to the table and the brand of handcuffs being used.

"He's one of the best interviewers we have," Chief Monahan says as he joins me in the room. "His tactics are a little strange, just thought I'd warn you."

"Women, am I right?" Colton asks, and my hackles go up.

"She fucking kicked me out, man. I pay goddamn rent on that place. She didn't have any right."

"Legally, that's your place, too," Colton agrees. "I know I'd be pissed if I came home and saw all of my shit sitting on the front porch."

"She did that shit while I was in the garage changing the oil in *her* fucking car."

"Really?" Colton sounds angry by proxy by the way this murderer was treated. "That's pretty fucked up."

"The fucked up part is that chick she was mad about wasn't even worth it, but the bitch wouldn't listen. Bad sex shouldn't fucking count, man. It was one mistake, and she just went apeshit on me."

Milton throws his hands up in disgust, the one handcuffed only moving a few inches. I flinch with the action, but Colton doesn't budge an inch.

"She hit you?" I could choke Colton right now. Blaming the victim? Not on my watch.

"Easy," Monahan says, his hand on my arm, and I realize I took a step closer to the glass. "Just watch."

"Hit me?" Milton scoffs. "The bitch wouldn't dare."

"So you were just pissed when you shot her?"

Milton doesn't backpedal. He doesn't open his mouth and ask for an attorney. He grins. The man fucking grins, and if I didn't know that he was a murderer, I could see how Penny found him attractive. Surely she was able to see the malice in his eyes.

"She called the cops."

"I'm a cop," Colton reminds him.

"You're just doing your job. She knew better. She knows not to get other people involved in our business."

"Now she's dead."

"And I'd kill her again if I had a chance."

"She's fucking dead, man. You killed her."

"I loved her, too."

Misplaced sobs fill the room, and instead of Colton standing and leaving the room, having gotten the confession, he grabs a box of tissue from the side table and slides it in Milton's direction. The man takes a couple, dabbing the tears from his eyes, and I've seen enough.

My phone buzzes in my pocket and since I told myself I was no longer going to work past the parameters of my internship, I let Monahan know I'll be back to the station tomorrow morning and leave.

I give a hundred percent while I'm there, but I can no longer stick around. Colton wants professionalism. He said as much in his office earlier when I tried to kiss him, so professionalism is what he's going to get. That means no more long hours. No more helping after five o'clock. No more dinners with low lighting. No more drunken texts or kitchen confessions. No sleeping at his house or showering in his home. No conversations with his parents or awkward interactions with his son.

I'll come in, work, and leave. We won't see each other in public. I won't watch him from across the room. Hell, I won't even work in his office anymore. The corner in the breakroom is noisy, but I'll make it work. I only have a month left anyway.

I can't face my parents, so I take the turn toward the clubhouse. There's always something going on there, and if not, the indoor pool is always a fun time. When I pull into the parking lot, I see my dad's SUV near the front door, so I turn right back around and leave the property.

I feel raw, like there's an open wound in my chest which I know is crazy. I know it doesn't make sense for Colton's earlier rejection to hit me so hard, but here I am, miserable and wanting to vent.

Izzy has been distant lately, and I know she won't be in the mood to listen to me complain about losing a guy I never even had, so calling her isn't an option. The idea of going back to the station pulls at me, but I resist, wondering how long I'll last before I cave.

I choose the gym instead, needing to release all of my frustrations. The kickboxing class is packed and twenty minutes in when I arrive, so I don't join them. I hate when class is interrupted, and I wouldn't do that to anyone else. The room with all the treadmills is steaming, thick with the perspiration and humid breaths of the after-work crowd. The machine weight room is packed with meatheads chatting about protein powder and the proper weight increase for back day. The free weight room is filled with men and women alike posing in the mirror. The hallway leading back to the treadmill room is housing four teenage girls filming a *Tik Tok*, and as I begrudgingly climb on a treadmill, I'm regretting even coming here to begin with.

I run hard and fast, giving everything I've got, but my mind still wanders. The last month has drained me, and as much as I'd like to mentally blame Colton, I know the numerous crime scenes have also had an impact. Seeing a dead body is one thing, and I honestly think I can handle that part of the job, but it's the backstory, the flimsy reasoning for the loss of a life that is stealing bits and pieces of me.

Dad told me working in this field wasn't going to be a good fit for me, but I dug in my heels. I don't like being told *no* or *you shouldn't do that*. I changed my major to criminal justice from sports medicine after one simple conversation over an episode of *Brooklyn Nine-Nine* of all things. Police work looked fun, and I voiced that opinion. Dad grew more serious than I've ever seen him, reminding me that the real world isn't like what we were watching. Of course, I knew it wasn't, although hilarious, that show is completely ridiculous. But, he told me no, and I wasn't going to let him stop me.

And look at me now, running on a treadmill, so frustrated I feel like crying because bad things are happening to people and there isn't a damn thing I can do about it.

Hot tears mix with the sweat running down my face, and I nearly jump to the ceiling when a hand taps me on the shoulder. I look over without thinking, nearly losing my footing. Cannon wrinkles his brow, pulling the emergency key from the machine.

"Hey. What are you doing here?" I ask stupidly because it's a damn gym. I already know what he's doing here.

With another frown, he pulls the headphones from my ears. "Are you okay?"

I look around the room to find no less than half a dozen people glaring at me like I ruined their night. I let Cannon guide me from the room, and by the grace of God, the teens are no longer dancing at the end of the hall.

"Take this." He offers me a bottle of water, and I chug it.

"Where's Rivet?"

"Working. They left late last night."

"And my dad?"

"With them in South America. Wanna explain why you're trying to kill yourself in there?"

I try to hand him back the half-empty bottle, but he waves it off.

"Bad day at work?"

"Is that the answer or are you asking me?"

"Are you always this annoying?"

"Yes," he deadpans as I unscrew the cap of the water and take another drink. "And you know it. Tell me what's wrong. Boy problems?"

I sputter, spraying water on the commercial grade carpet at our feet. "Definitely not *boy* problems."

"So what then?"

"Any chance you'll just leave it alone?"

He crosses his arms over his chest. "None, now spill."

"Have you ever made a choice in life and realize it was the wrong one?"

"Many times. Every woman before Rivet was a mistake."

I make a gagging noise. "I'm talking about like work or school, not sex."

He winks at me, but there's no sexual vibe to it. The man is madly in love with his woman, and even though I thought I had a crush on him in years' past, there's none of those feelings lingering around at all. If my face wasn't already flushed from running, I know he'd be able to see how embarrassed I am for trying to kiss him that one time.

"I thought I'd be living in Denver after graduation."

"You're not going?"

He graduates next month just like I do, his degree coming from San Diego. He's one of the ones who met the love of his life and changed his path to line up better with hers. This last year of his has been spent doing classes online.

"I'm working for Cerberus, and I don't see that as a step down, more like a step to the left. I'm working in my field of choice, and every night, well most nights, I get to lay my head down beside Rivet's. I'm a happy fucking man."

"That's good." I focus on my hands.

"But it's clear you're doubting your own choices?"

"Clear, huh?" I huff a humorless laugh. "I don't think I can do the criminal justice field. I've seen more dead bodies, dead kids, and people dead inside from loss. I'm just not cut out for it."

I don't mention that I want to stay in Farmington and at the same time keep my distance from Colton, which is impossible because even if I got a job working for the Sheriff's Department instead of the PD, we'll still end up crossing paths.

"Then do something different."

I lift my eyes, glaring at him.

"It's not that simple. I'm a damn month from graduation, Cannon." I drop to the floor, pressing my back against the wall. He follows and takes a seat beside me.

"Maybe it is. Have you considered academia?"

"I don't want to be a teacher."

"Not even college?"

"And follow in Jasmine's footsteps?"

"There's nothing wrong with being a teacher. Cerberus is filled with them. It's a respectable profession."

"It's safe," I argue. "I want to be a badass."

He laughs at this, but it's not in a mocking tone. "If you think I'm going to spew some shit about gender roles, you're mistaken. Rivet kicks ass as some commando chick and I sit behind a desk, but you can always be a badass teacher, someone who changes people's lives. You can make a difference."

"Yeah," I agree, but I know he's given me something to think about.

"Now, get off your lazy ass and let's go lift some weights. You can't be a badass with such skinny arms."

Laughing, I follow him downstairs to the weight room with a little portion of the burden lifted from my shoulders.

Chapter 15

Colton

No matter the amount of conviction I had when I told Sophia we could only be in a professional relationship, I regret every word I uttered that day in my office.

There hasn't been any flirting or secret smiles.

There are no jokes.

There has been no extra time. She arrives within minutes of her responsibilities in the mornings and leaves promptly at five in the evening.

She doesn't look over her shoulder to make sure she's doing something right.

She doesn't sit at my desk and eat lunch.

We don't argue about opinions on television shows, something we always found middle ground on.

Nope, none of that. It's all business, all the time.

I haven't caught her eyes on me or a single salacious look on her pretty face.

I also haven't caught her talking to the patrol officers either, which has been a blessing. If she ignored me and then turned around and handed her attention so readily to others, I'd probably go insane.

Once again it's Friday, the weekend looming over me like a dark cloud. In two weeks, she graduates, and that means she only has eight more days in the office. What happens after that is anyone's guess. That's a lie. What happens is, she walks away and never looks back. She hasn't asked Monahan about the police academy or if there were office jobs available. I know because I asked him. She hasn't mentioned her after-internship plans with me because we hardly talk. If we aren't discussing a crime scene, her lips are closed.

She's polite but distant. She's not rude, but she's no longer the peppy girl that walked into my office six weeks ago either. Some of her light is gone, and I don't know if that's solely because of me or if some of the blame can land at the feet of the cases we've been working.

This week has been brutal, but after working all night, the suspect was arrested, a full confession was gained, and another case is closed. Everyone at the station is exhausted, but there are smiles all the way around. Even Sophia's lips tilt up a little when Monahan congratulates her on the work she's done. She was instrumental in helping to solve the case, noticing a few discrepancies at the scene on Monday and voicing her opinion about them. Her reasoning was wrong, but it helped get me on the right track, and I wouldn't have been able to do that if it wasn't for her.

"So first round on me?" Gaffey asks the room.

Several readily agree, but I already know Sophia's answer. Each time we close a case, I ask her to dinner to celebrate, and each time she turns me down. She doesn't even give me an excuse like she did the first two times. Her simple no is all I get these days.

"No thank you," she says when Gaffey turns his attention to her.

"You sure?"

"I'm sure." Her eyes meet mine for the briefest second before she turns her attention to Monahan. "Do you mind if I cut out of here a little earlier today?"

"Sure thing, kiddo. Thanks for your help this week. Have a great weekend."

My eyes track her across the room, feet nailed to the floor when she enters my office to get her things. With everyone around, I don't even consider following her, but my eyes follow her until she's clear of the building.

"What about you, Matthews?" Gaffey slaps me on the back. "Wanna join us at *Jake's* for a couple beers."

"Naw, man. Not tonight. I still have some shit to wrap up. Have a good time though."

I leave my colleagues in the front office and head back to my own workspace, shuffling shit on my desk until their laughs and congratulations die off. I lied to my fellow detective. I don't have a damn thing to do tonight, or all weekend for that matter. Sophia has spent so much time working and avoiding me that my desk is completely cleared. Other than the cold case I've been working on the last couple of months, I have nothing left to do.

Leaving my office, I turn off the light and head to my truck. Maybe Rick will be around tonight and we can hang out. That idea is ruined before I get to my truck by a text letting me know he's staying with a friend tonight. Maybe a couple beers with the guys from the station isn't such a bad idea.

Knowing we're low on a few things at the house, I swing by the grocery store before heading in that direction. Hell, with Rick occupied, maybe tonight would be a good night to head up to Durango. There's a little bar there that's always proven to be good for picking up a woman. Just the thought of crawling into a bed and losing myself for a couple of hours with someone other than Sophia makes my stomach turn.

Yep, well and truly fucked.

Once inside the grocery store, the task of grabbing a few things feels like more energy than I have to waste, but I skirt around people shopping and indiscriminately shove things in the damn cart. The good thing about teenage boys is that they can make a meal from practically anything so it doesn't really matter what I end up carrying home. Rick will eat it.

"Detective," I hear from behind me, and I cringe before turning around.

It isn't an angry citizen or someone I've arrested in the past. It's worse.

"Mr. Anderson," I say, holding my hand out.

"Dominic, please. This is my wife, Makayla."

I shake her hand as well. I've never met this man before, but I know Kincaid and they look so much alike it's uncanny. I've also looked him up in the system, just to verify a few things, and I've seen his driver's license photo.

"How's work?"

I scan Dominic's eyes, wondering exactly what he's wanting to hear from me. I give him the answer I pray he's looking for.

"Good. Sophia has been such a big help. There are many people in the office who are going to miss her after the end of next week."

"You should come to her graduation party next Saturday," Makayla offers.

"I—"

"Seven in the evening at the clubhouse," she continues.

Would declining be a red flag? A mentor would go to help a student celebrate, right?

"That would be nice. Should I bring a dish?"

"We've got it covered," Dominic answers for his wife.

Silence settles around us, and I grow uncomfortable. Is this what Sophia felt like in front of my parents? If so, shit, I can see why it pissed her off so much.

"She's going to make an amazing detective one day," I say to fill the weirdness surrounding us.

"Thankfully we don't have to worry about that for a few more years," Makayla says, a soft hand on Dominic's chest as she looks up at him.

"Sophia is planning to go to graduate school for her master's degree before deciding on a career path," Dominic explains.

"She mentioned maybe teaching college," Makayla adds.

"She'd make an amazing teacher," I agree.

"Well, we better get going. See you at the clubhouse Saturday after next."

I raise my hand for a little wave, and despite feeling like I handled myself well, I can see in Dominic's eyes that I'm not fooling him. He knows something is off where Sophia and I are concerned. I hover around the produce section, watching and waiting for them to leave before deserting my shopping cart and getting out of there.

The bar and a few drinks with the guys is sounding like a great idea right about now. Sitting at home thinking about a girl that doesn't want to be thought about is ridiculous.

Knowing how my night is going to end up, I drive home, park my truck, and order an Uber to *Jake's*. I'll be in no condition to drive once I'm done trying to drink her out of my mind.

Once I step inside *Jake's*, my eyes automatically dart to the tables in the far corner. I clock at least five guys I know are linked to Cerberus, and wouldn't doubt if there were more on the dance floor, but I don't see Sophia with them.

Gaffey yells my name from the other side of the bar, holding up a beer in one hand and an empty shot glass in the other.

"Glad you could make it!" He slaps my back when I approach. "Grab a shot."

I pick one up from the table, tossing it back without asking what it is first. Rookie mistake.

"Fuck," I sputter, lifting the back of my hand to my mouth in a failed attempt to stave off the burn.

"Everclear," Gaffey hisses on a laugh. "No sense in wasting time tonight."

Haden is a good guy, but sometimes the job makes life nearly impossible to live without kicking back every once in a while. I don't see his wife around, but if he's here, she can't be far.

A waitress brings another round of beers and shots for the table, and I don't waste time drinking them down. I'm smiling at a couple dancing to the side when I start on my third round, knowing I'm going to be the dad that will end up calling my child tonight for a drunken ride home. I don't think Rick will mind even though he's staying at a friend's house. Hell, he used the running errands excuse for reasoning when he begged for his own vehicle. I don't think the hand-me-down Ford 150 was what he had his sights on, but the kid never complained.

"Hey!" I grin, looking over at one of the newer patrol officers that joined us. "How?"

"Excuse me?" I ask, nearly screaming over the loud music.

I move around Gaffey who has found his wife and slide in next to the guy trying to get my attention. Like all friendly drunks in a bar, he slings his arm around my shoulder like we're best friends. I don't even know this guy's name, but I go with it because I haven't thought about Sophia in at least half an hour.

Well, I guess I just fucked that streak up.

"What?" I ask again when he settles against me.

"How can you spend five days a week around that hot piece of ass and not spend half the day fucking her over your desk?"

I take a step back, letting his arm fall away from me. I could punch this guy in the mouth for saying shit like that. The protective part of me wants to lay his ass out. The drunk part of me wants to tell him it's been hell to spend time with her. I don't do either of those things, opting to just glare at him instead.

"I mean, look!"

I follow the point of his finger and fucking sure enough, there's Sophia. She's not dressed for the bar. She's in her work clothes just like everyone else at our table. Twenty feet away, she's smiling and laughing while playing darts with Ramshaw.

A hand that's moments away from sporting five broken fingers rests on her hip as she tosses the dart at the board, laughing when she misses the thing completely. Ramshaw, being the laid back decent guy that I know he is, doesn't seem irritated that his partner is going to make them lose the game. Of course he's not. He's as fucking charmed by her as every other person in the damn office, myself included.

My mind wanders back to the time she confessed about thinking of making me jealous in my kitchen, and I know this isn't one of those times. I don't catch her looking at me once as I stand there and stare holes in the back of her head. Another ten minutes go by without her looking around at all. There's a good chance she doesn't even know that I'm here being tortured just by her presence and the distance between us.

Leaning in close to Ramshaw's ear, she tells him something before walking toward the back of the bar. He watches her walk away, and hell, so do I.

I can't believe she's here after turning down the offer to come at the office. Did she do it because she didn't want to be near me? Did she simply get bored and change her mind?

I need answers to these questions, and it seems Ramshaw has thought of a few things he needs to tell her too because he's making his way across the bar toward the restrooms as well.

Not on my fucking watch.

"Nope," I tell him with a hand against his chest when he tries to walk by.

"I need to piss," he snaps.

"You can wait until she comes out or you can piss outside."

His eyes dart between mine but decides against arguing. I know he was planning to corner her in the hallway. I don't think he has ill intentions with Sophia, but kisses are easily stolen in private. I'll be damned if he's going to get something that belongs to me.

Chapter 16

Sophia

Cold water from the faucet doesn't take the edge off the trembling in my hands, and I don't think anything will. Ignoring Colton at the station isn't easy, but it's manageable since I can leave his office and work in the breakroom. Ignoring him after realizing he's here at *Jake's* was nearly impossible even with Dillon's distracting game of darts. I'm an excellent dart player, largely in part because I grew up around a bunch of bikers with a dart board on the wall of the clubhouse. You wouldn't know that from watching me play tonight, though.

I blame Colton. Hell, I blame Colton for nearly everything these days.

Bad hair day? Colton.

The flat tire I had on the way to work Tuesday? Colton.

The new dart holes in the wall tonight? Colton.

Everything is his fault, even the flush in my cheeks, heavy breathing, and the knot in my stomach each time I think about walking out of this bar tonight and not cutting my eyes in his direction.

The distance I've put between us the last couple of weeks has been harder than I ever anticipated, and my resolve is breaking quickly.

I watch my eyes in the restroom mirror, knowing that dark circles are hidden under a layer of makeup. I've seriously wondered if I'm losing my mind because it doesn't make sense. I've had crushes before. I've been attracted to guys at school that turned me down or didn't show any interest. I'm not new to rejection, although it doesn't happen very often. That's more on college guys' lack of being very selective, but pressing my mouth to Colton's only for him to look down at me like I violated him hit harder than I ever thought it could.

Arguments in my head are a constant whisper.

If the man doesn't want you, Sophia, move on.

It's that simple.

But I'm finding that it isn't simple at all.

I growl in frustration, turning the tap off and drying my hands.

So what that he's here, probably less than a hundred feet away? I've been coming to this bar for years, long before I was legally able to belly up to the bar. He doesn't own the space, and I shouldn't let his presence deter my evening.

With a straightened spine and head held high, I walk out of the restroom, ready to join Ramshaw back at the dart board.

The false bravado lasts all of ten seconds, because the man infiltrating my mind on a constant rotation is standing in the hall, leaning up against the wall, looking more perfect than I ever remember him being. Is it the soft lighting? The mysterious shadows hiding part of his handsome face? A combination of the two?

Who the hell knows, but my skin tingles and my heart beats faster with just the sight of him.

He watches me the same way I watch him, long seconds ticking between us with neither speaking a word.

Having him across the room in the bar was one thing, something I could eventually distance myself from. Him in front of me, expectant eyes waiting for something? I swallow thickly, a swarm of emotion hitting me right in the chest and look away.

"Goodnight," I whisper before turning to walk away.

"Sophia." His hand brushes my arm, and that single touch has the ability to stop me in my tracks.

My mouth is dry, and I've lost the ability to speak without my words revealing the pain I've been feeling for weeks. I close my eyes, just breathing in his proximity, hating the pain it causes me.

Is this what obsession feels like? It must be, and I hate it, hate every single thing about it.

"Look at me," he pleads.

"I can't." It's true. Even him being this close to me is painful, and the bad thing about it is, I've done this to myself. I've let my mind fixate on this man, knowing from day one that there could never be anything between us. He has his own set of morals guiding him, and if he doesn't want to be with a younger woman, then who the hell am I to try to tempt and tease him into something? Maybe I did violate him that day in the office. Maybe I misread his cues. Maybe he wasn't looking at me in his kitchen that day with desire. Maybe it was disappointment or disgust and I just read it wrong.

"Sophia."

With his hand on my hip, he turns me to face him, but my gaze lingers on his shoes. Why can't he just let me walk by? He doesn't have to tell me again he doesn't want me. He's made it very clear time and time again. Doing it again when I didn't seek out validation is just cruel.

I hold on to that emotion, because every other one I'm feeling would end with tears on my face. My cheek twitches when I look up at him, but he's too close, his deep blue eyes too searching for me to hide a single thing from him. Reading people is his job, and I feel like he can see right through me.

"I miss you." The scent of whiskey on his breath isn't completely off-putting, but it's knowing he wouldn't be standing in this hallway with me had he not been drinking that makes me want to dart away.

"Please," I whisper, and I don't know exactly what I need.

Please feel the same way when you wake up sober?

Please release me from this hold you have on me?

Please make me yours?

"My sheets no longer smell like you." His nose sweeping down the side of my neck is like a lightning bolt to my spine, but he ignores my whimper. "God, how I want to feel you under me, whispering my name."

Other than his hot hand on my hip and his face buried in my hair, he doesn't touch me. He doesn't push his hips against me to prove his attraction, and it feels like another form of manipulation.

My body doesn't care. My heart is pounding, thighs itching for me to rub them together, mind telling me to step further into his space, but his grip tightens on my waist, preventing me from moving.

"I'm so hard for you. I want to spend hours stroking inside of you. I want your teeth marks in my shoulder from pushing into you just a little too deep." I rake my tongue between my teeth just to feel the pressure. "I'm always hard for you. Every day at the station. Every time I see you or you walk by."

"Colton." My fingers tangle in the front of his shirt, and I can't decide if the best course of action is to push him away or pull him closer.

"I hate the weekends when I don't get to see you. I hate knowing that after next week, I may never get to see you again."

His words are a crushing blow. I've been both looking forward to and dreading the end of my internship.

"I need you."

"Stop." I decide pushing him away is best. "No more fucking games."

He blinks down at me, but I refuse to guess what he's thinking. I'm not willing to take the chance of him getting what he wants while horny and drunk only to backpedal with regret tomorrow.

"Soph." He steps in closer, but I spin away from him.

"No more, Colton."

My back is no longer straight, my head no longer held high when I walk out of the back hallway. Defeated, I skirt past Ramshaw and head straight for the tables where I know I'll be safe. Colton may want me in the moment, but there isn't a man in this bar that's willing to go through half a dozen scary bikers to get laid.

Jinx nods at me when I pass to sit in the empty seat against the wall before continuing his conversation with Rocker, both of them here because Simone is tending bar tonight. I take an offered beer, but spend the next half hour peeling the label rather than drinking it. I want to leave, but the three beers in my system keep my ass planted on the bar stool. It doesn't appear anyone is ready to head out, and that means I'm stuck until they are. Just because my night is ruined doesn't mean I'm going to do the same for someone else.

"Everything okay?"

"Yes," I answer Cannon. "Having a good night?"

"Always a good night," he answers, drawing Rivet closer to his side.

I tried kissing this man when they were in the middle of figuring what they meant to each other. Of course I didn't know that was going on because they were keeping their private lives private, but not once has she looked at me with jealousy. It's something I've always been grateful for. Drama at the clubhouse isn't an anomaly, but I've never wanted to be in the middle of it. As I watch her look up at Cannon like he's the best thing on the planet, I realize she isn't jealous because I was never competition for her. I don't know if it's because she's so sure about herself or if she knows I'm just not good enough to be loved by anyone.

And of course I blame Colton for the self-deprecating attitude because I never felt this way before him.

I swipe the now label-less bottle from the table in front of me and turn the thing up.

Chapter 17

Colton

"What are you doing?"

"What do you mean?" Mom asks, once again looking around me to the driveway.

Rick chuckles and walks past us into the house.

"Just you two today?"

I frown. "Like always. Expecting someone else?"

She shrugs, turning her disappointed face around and following my son into the house. "More like hoping."

"Did he bring her?" Dad calls from the kitchen.

Instead of going in there to face an inquisition, I take my ass to the living room and turn on the television.

"They're talking about Sophia," Rick helpfully offers as he plops down beside me with a soda in his hand.

"I know who they're talking about," I mutter.

They pulled this shit the Sunday after they met her at my house, as well as every family meal after. I knew it was coming, and for the first time since high school, I thought about not showing up today.

"Just you two?" Dad asks, walking into the living room, wiping his hands on a dish towel.

"Don't sound so disappointed." I don't pull my eyes from the television. The car insurance commercial is more interesting than a repeat of this conversation.

"Lunch is in five minutes. We expected you sooner," Dad goads, but he isn't going to get a rise out of me.

I may not have stayed home to avoid this, but I've been coming later and later each week in an attempt to lessen the time spent with them, wondering why I once again showed up alone.

"Better go wash up," Rick says, slapping my thigh and deserting me with my old man.

Ten minutes later, because Dad's time management skills aren't the best, we're settling around the dining room table with a full spread in front of us.

"Nice," Rick says, rubbing his hands together like he's never seen food before in his life and he's overwhelmed with the selection.

"Are you feeding him regularly?" Mom asks as my son reaches for a bowl of mashed potatoes.

"Every meal is like this." Rick piles the potatoes high before reaching for the platter of baked chicken. "He probably has worms or something."

My son is no longer affected by our joking. Like clockwork, this also happens every week. We all smile, watching him load his plate up. At thirty-five, I know he'll be my only child and as the only grandchild, neither my parents nor myself take this young man for granted.

"Did Sophia have other plans today?" Mom asks with a smile as she passes the potatoes to me.

"I don't know what Sophia's plans were today, Mother."

She scoffs at the formal designation, but she either doesn't take the hint that I don't want to have this conversation yet again or she doesn't care.

"We liked her," Dad offers.

"I know."

"She seems very smart."

I take a deep breath. "She is."

"Very mature—"

"She's twenty-one."

"—for her age," Mom continues. "Twenty-one?"

My eyes lift to hers. "Yes. She's still in college."

"I thought she was in a graduate program."

"Nope, undergrad." Maybe this will be enough to put an end to these conversations.

"Her age really isn't an issue," Dad adds.

"But she's probably not ready for something serious," Mom interjects.

"I'm not ready for something serious," I mutter around a mouthful of potatoes.

"She's definitely not ready to be a mom to a teenage son."

Rick chuckles before muttering, "MILF," under his breath.

I kick him under the table, giving him a glare that he knows translates to a conversation we'll be having later. His head drops, eyes back to focusing on scooping food into his mouth.

"She's too young for all of that," I tell my parents.

"Some would argue that nineteen was too young to become a father, but you did an amazing job with Rick."

My mom smiles at me before looking at my son.

"I am kind of perfect, Dad."

I narrow my eyes at him. My parents affection for the kid is in no short supply.

"Keep it up and you'll be on the roof cleaning gutters when we get home," I threaten, aiming my fork in his direction to get my point across.

"So it's just sex then?"

I sputter around a bite of green beans and glare at my mom.

Rick wheezes, clearly choking on his own food, but at this point in the conversation, it's every man for himself. Dad claps Rick on the back, but his eyes stay on me, expectant and waiting for an answer.

Geez, it's like sophomore year all over again. That time I snuck a girl in my bedroom for a make-out session—didn't even make it to third base, if anyone is wondering—and I spent four hours at this very table having the dreaded birds-and-bees talk a year too late.

"I haven't had sex with her," I inform them, uncaring that my son is sitting at the table with me.

As a young father, I've never kept anything hidden from him, and now is no different. I don't flaunt sexual relationships in front of him, but I also don't hide the fact that I've had relations since he was born. Not even my parents preach the no sex before marriage, so a conversation about sex isn't exactly taboo in this household.

"She was half-naked in your clothes."

I glare at Dad, begging him to get Mom to stop talking, but there's a smile that says *no way, I'm just as curious for the answer* playing on his lips.

"She wasn't half-naked," I argue. "She had boxers on under the shirt."

"Your boxers?" Mom continues. "I'm not a prude. I don't care that—"

"I didn't sleep with her," I snap, taking a deep breath to calm down. Not because I'm honestly upset with them, but because of the regret I've been plagued with for the last several weeks. My behavior at the bar the night before last was atrocious, and the anxiety I feel having to go to work tomorrow and once again apologize has left me with minimal tolerance today. "She had been drinking. She called for a ride and didn't want to go home. I let her stay at my place."

"In your bed," Dad clarifies, and it's official, I'll be skipping family brunch next week.

"If you recall the blanket and pillow on the recliner, you can deduce yourselves that I slept there, not in the bed with her."

"You two looked cozy in the kitchen when we walked in."

I clench the edge of the table, knowing that getting up and storming out would not be a very good example for my son.

"Dad struck out," the little traitor says. "I bet I have a better chance with her."

Mom gasps and Dad chuckles when I lift the bread roll from the edge of my plate and throw it at his head. He ducks, and it misses him, of course, but the message is clear. He smiles around a bite of potatoes, and I can't help the twitch of humor in my own mouth.

The kid is right. I struck out. Big time. What I thought was best doesn't seem to be working out the way I had hoped. Wanting her has never been the issue. My desire for Sophia Anderson has only grown since the first time she walked into my office looking like a naughty professor. It's knowing her life would become something she never pictured if we were to make that leap.

Mom is also right, she isn't ready to be a mother to a teenage son, and that's exactly what would happen if things grew serious between us. I'd never ask that of her. Most importantly, I'd never bring a woman into my son's life only to have her leave when she got bored. We've already been hurt like that once, and I won't let it happen again.

"We work together," I say after a long silence. "That's it. We haven't gotten together, and we aren't going to be getting together."

"That's a shame," Mom whispers, but I think she can see that the conversation is getting to me.

"Can we talk about something else?"

"Of course," Dad agrees. "Rick, let's talk about those videos I saw on Tik Tak."

Rick groans, and it's my turn to laugh.

"It's *Tik Tok*, Gramps. We've been over this."

The spotlight stays on my son for the rest of the day, and when we finally leave because we're doing the gutters today, I have a smile on my face. There's still a chance I'll skip next week's family meal, but at least I got a little reprieve today.

"The gutters? Really, Dad?" Rick whines an hour later when I tell him to get the ladder out of the garage.

"I'll get the highest parts," I say, not flinching when he complains again. "But you'll be in big trouble if I ever hear you say another derogatory word about any woman again. Shit like you said at dinner should never leave your mouth, not in front of me, your grandparents, or your friends. I raised you to have more respect than that."

"She's hot as fuck, Dad. People should know."

"People know, Rick." I grind my teeth together. "Everyone who looks at her knows, but being disrespectful isn't going to cut it. Keep that shit to yourself."

"Yes, sir," he mutters before walking toward the garage.

My words from the other night slam into me like a tsunami.

I'm so hard for you. I want to spend hours stroking inside of you. I want your teeth marks in my shoulder from pushing into you just a little too deep. I'm always hard for you. Every day at the station. Every time I see you or you walk by.

God, I hope he turns into a better man than me.

Chapter 18

Sophia

"That's all I have for now. Be safe."

Patrol officers scatter after Monahan ends the beginning-of-shift briefing. Several hover near the coffee pot, waiting to fill up their travel mugs before hitting the streets, and I hang back in the corner of the room like I have been doing every morning for the last couple of weeks.

Ramshaw winks at me before leaving the room. Thankfully, he doesn't ask me why I disappeared Friday evening. I was drunk before Cannon finally gave me a ride back to my house, and both Saturday and Sunday were spent with a hangover. Not my finest moment. Even Dad kept his distance, which was a blessing.

Since helping Colton clear his caseload, I've been asked to help a couple of the other detectives at the station, and I'm happy for the distraction. I'm not going out on calls, but paperwork is a never-ending thing for police. At least helping them type notes and submit reports keeps them on the streets and helping those that need them.

Colton was late once again this morning, sneaking into the briefing mere minutes before it was over. I try to keep my eyes on the folder in front of me, but my other senses track him across the room, picking up bits and pieces of conversation he's having with Gaffey.

All too soon, he leaves the breakroom, and I'm left feeling equal parts relieved and saddened. We need to have a conversation about what happened Friday night, but I just don't have the stomach for it today, or any day in the near future for that matter.

My work, the laundry list of things to get done handed to me by Chief Monahan this morning, ends too quickly. I don't know if he's only giving bits and pieces of the work to me to keep me from getting overwhelmed or he just doesn't realize how efficient I've become with my tasks since starting my internship.

It's not even noon and I'm done. To buy more time in my effort to avoid Colton, I head to the mailroom. I catch the woman who works in here leaving with a quick smile, and I want to hang my head in defeat. My intention to keep busy has been thwarted by her own efficiency. I grab Gaffey's mail, as well as Colton's and head out. Haden isn't in his office when I drop his off, so I head back to the breakroom to sort through Colton's. Strangely, detectives, as well as some patrol officers, get all sorts of weird mail, and I've wondered more than once if some people working here aren't using the police station as their permanent address. I toss several clothing magazines in the trash before opening a simply addressed letter, frowning at the sloppy handwriting before even reading the words. Inmates from the jail are known to spend their time writing letters to arresting officers, the chief, and often times, probation officers, something I learned early on after a conversation with people at a crime scene.

My head tilts, eyes scanning the letter, but then it hits me exactly what it is that I'm holding in my hand. Threats aren't new, but I've never seen a letter written with such graphic terms. The letter goes into the heinous ways he's going to torture Colton if his demands aren't met. I don't know what the person wants because I don't get that far without having to look away.

On trembling legs, I leave the rest of Colton's mail on the table and head straight to his office. I don't bother knocking on his door, and it takes more than one try to get the doorknob to work in my shaking hand.

"Sophia?" Colton looks up from his computer screen, concern drawing his brows together. "What's wrong?"

Unable to answer him, I shove the paper in his direction. At first, he doesn't take it, keeping his eyes on me and trying to assess the situation.

"L-look," I beg. "It's bad."

"Lay it on the desk," he advises, but he doesn't reach for it. "Was there anything else in the envelope? Did it feel gritty or damp?"

"No," I tell him. "Just the one piece of paper."

I pull my hand back once the letter lands on his desk.

"Don't do that," he instructs, reaching for me when I try to lift my trembling hand to my face. "You'll need to wash your hands."

"It's f-fine. There was nothing on the paper."

"Can't be too sure."

Only now do I realize he's holding my hand, and I hate the way the warmth of his touch has a calming effect. It only makes me want to be closer to him, to take more from him than he's willing to offer.

"You're shaking." His grip on my hand tightens.

Looking up at him, I have the urge to touch his face, but I know I can't. Not only is there a concern for what might be on my hands, but he doesn't want that from me.

"Come here."

I don't resist when he pulls me to his chest. Instinctively, my arms go around his back, tangling in the fabric of his shirt as he holds me close.

"It's nothing," he assures me. "We get these all the time."

"He said he's going to kill you, your family, and your dog."

"I don't have a dog, Sophia."

"But you have a family." The memories of the scenes we've worked and the devastation those people had in their eyes with the loss of a child, I can't imagine that same fate for him.

"He doesn't have a clue about my family, baby."

I cling to him tighter.

"Shh, I've got you."

It sounds like a promise, and God, how I wish it were true. I tremble even more, my knees threatening to give out. I feel like such a child right now. I've gone to and assisted on several deaths in the last six weeks, but at the moment, I feel the most vulnerable. Maybe it's because it's my own life in turmoil right now and I don't have the ability to close my eyes and distance myself from it, or maybe it's simply his proximity and finally being in his arms.

I open my mouth to beg him to feel the same way right now while he's sober that he felt Friday night, but a sob comes out instead.

"Baby," he whispers, his face buried in my hair. "Everything is fine."

He couldn't be more wrong.

Fine is subjective. Yeah, nothing may come from the letter. His family may not be in real danger, but I'm not fine. I haven't been *fine* for a very long time.

"I miss you, too," I confess, the admission coming easier since he isn't looking into my tear-soaked eyes.

He holds me tighter, the embrace transitioning from comforting to something a little more carnal.

"All of those things you mentioned at *Jake's*, I want those, too."

More than I could even admit out loud.

Fingers tangle in my hair, his hips moving closer until his entire body is pressed against mine. The stiff length of him presses against my lower belly, and it takes all of my strength not to moan his name.

The threatening letter forgotten, I move my hips only slightly.

"Sophia." The grip in my hair tightens as he tugs, my face coming away from his chest to look up into his eyes.

His teeth dig into his lower lip as he assesses my face. I know my makeup is smeared, cheeks stained with tears, but he's looking at me like I'm the most beautiful woman in the world. It's the same way he looked when I first walked out of the restroom at *Jake's*.

"Are you sure?" he whispers, and all I can do is nod. "If you're not—"

"Matthews, I need—"

We both freeze, and even though my back is to the door, I know that Chief Monahan just caught us in an embrace.

"In my office, Matthews. Now."

I watch silently as Colton pulls on a pair of gloves, picks the letter up off his desk on the corner, and leaves. He doesn't look back or say a word to assure me that everything is going to be fine. If anything, he looks relieved to be walking away.

I wipe angry fingers at the renewed tears on my face, uncaring of what could be on my hands. It can't hurt me any more than I'm hurting right now.

Once my face is dried, I head straight back to my little corner of the breakroom, although I don't know how long I'll be here. I may very well be minutes away from getting shown the damn door. Monahan walked in on a private moment, one that had no business happening at the police station. He's the boss. The one that approved my internship, and he's also the man that can easily yank it right out from under me a week and a half before graduation.

C

Chapter 19

Colton

My heart is pounding more than it did when I had to sit my parents down to tell them that I got a girl pregnant after a drunken bad decision, but I'll face this the exact same way. I haven't backed down or made excuses for a bad decision in my life.

She's not a bad decision.

And yet, I somehow managed to take advantage of her while she was upset.

"Fuck," I mumble as I step into Monahan's office.

"Close the door." He doesn't move from his leaning position against the front of his desk. "Have a seat."

With my gloved hands, I place the letter that upset Sophia on the corner of a side table and do as he asks. I respect the hell out of this man, and since I know I deserve a dressing down, I'm gonna sit here and fucking take it. Hopefully, it doesn't end in the request for my gun and badge.

"We have a no fraternization policy."

"We do." Not that anyone follows it. Two of the women in dispatch are dating the same damn patrol officer, and it makes for some really intense investigations some days.

"Sophia Anderson was required to complete the same paperwork with human resources as if she were being hired for a permanent position with the department."

"Okay." I didn't know that, but it makes total sense. We deal with some pretty serious stuff up here.

"You can't start something with her while she's working here."

I don't miss the fact that he doesn't say never.

"Her father wouldn't be very happy to know you were taking advantage of his daughter while she was trying to finish her school year."

"I'm not taking advantage of her, Chief."

Yet, only moments ago I was berating myself for feeling like I did.

"So it's a mutual thing?"

"There's no *thing*, Chief."

"I've been a cop for as long as you've been alive, son. I know what I saw. She's out of here in less than two weeks. You're going to need to hit the brakes on it until she's out of here."

"Chief." He holds his hand up to silence me, and my jaw snaps shut.

"I have to admit, I'm a little disappointed because I want that girl working here. She's the best intern we've ever had. I can't employ her, knowing you're having a relationship with her." His eyes narrow. "Just how far have you taken things with her."

I glare back at him, my agitation at not being able to explain getting the best of me. "Are you asking as my boss or as her father's friend?"

He pauses, clearly deciding which direction he wants to go. "Both."

I huff a laugh. No middle ground, I see.

"I'm supervising her while she does her internship, as I was told to do."

"And your supervision requires daily hugs?" He scoffs. "You're not fooling me, Matthews. I'm old and married, but I still know a gorgeous woman when I see one."

"I'm not—"

"And lying is only going to piss me off more."

I twist my jaw, taking slow breaths through my nose and releasing them out of my mouth. "May I speak?"

His arms cross in front of his chest, and it's a clear sign he isn't going to be very receptive of anything I say. It almost makes me wish I was guilty of what he's accusing me of. At least it would make everything worth it.

"Sophia goes through my mail. It's one of the things she offered to do so I could focus more of my time and energy clearing cases. Which, I might add, has happened at an astonishing rate the last six weeks." I point to the letter I dropped on the side table, but his assessing eyes stay on me. "She freaked out when she opened one envelope and found that letter. I haven't read the entire thing, but I scanned it on the walk from my office. It's graphic, extremely detailed about how I'm going to die and how my entire family, including my dog, is going to be tortured."

"You don't have a dog," Monahan says, and it brings a smile to my face. I have more in common with this man than I want to admit.

"I know. Sophia didn't know that." It's my first lie since I walked in here. "She was terrified, shaking, and crying."

Okay, so she wasn't crying until I pulled her to my chest, but he'll never know the true sequence of events.

"I've been thinking for weeks that she wasn't ready to just be thrown into the type of cases I work. Most patrol officers don't see the kind of stuff she's been dealing with while working with me. It's too much for her. I don't know what tipped the scale today, but she was nearly inconsolable. I hugged her. It was a comforting move, and I think her father would be okay with that."

Another lie. Dominic Anderson would never be okay with me having my hands on his daughter for any reason.

"I wondered the same thing before I put her with you." Monahan finally drops his arms, the guarded stance slowly fading away. He circles his desk before falling into his office chair. "I made the assumption that she was just as strong as the man who raised her, but it's clear I fucked up."

"I don't think it was the letter on its own, but it just came at the right time."

"We need to distance her from the cases."

"What?" I snap my eyes back to him. "No."

I've had enough distance from her, all of it emotional. I won't survive actual physical distance.

"Your objection makes my mind go right back to my original way of thinking."

Jesus, fuck. I can't win.

"She has seven days after today. I think if you pull her from my cases now, she's going to think she's done something wrong."

"She hasn't," he agrees. "But I don't want the girl losing sleep over the shit she's seeing in the field."

He was probably more focused on my arms around her when he came in my office, but I know if she turned around to face him, he would've seen the darkness under her eyes. Like he said, he's been doing this job for a long time. I don't know if those smudges are there because of me or the job. Would it make me a complete asshole if it made me feel slightly better if she was losing sleep over me the way I have been with her?

Probably.

"Seven more days, Chief. She's planning to go to grad school. I think she made up her mind on her own that she isn't ready for this line of work."

His hand rubs at the stubble forming on his chin as he thinks about it.

"She can help work scenes with you if you get called out, but I don't want her spending much time with the victims. You're right about most cops having the shit she's seen spread out over years and years. I think she's just been too close to a bunch of bad shit at too high of a rate." He points toward the letter I brought in here. "Ease her fears by arresting the fucker who mailed that fucking letter first."

"You got it, Chief."

I stand from the chair and turn around to grab the letter.

"And, Matthews?" I turn to face him again. "I don't doubt anything you told me in here today, but I'm not a damn fool either. There was more than comfort in your eyes earlier. Seven more days until she's out of here. Keep your fucking hands off of her at least that damn long, would you?"

"Yes, sir."

"And even after," he continues when I have my back to him, "you better be a hundred percent sure that whatever is going on between the two of you is worth sacrificing the connection this community has with the Cerberus MC. Fucking around with one of the princesses could sever ties we've spent decades building."

Well, fuck.

Sophia isn't in my office when I return, and it only takes me five minutes and a quick conversation with Gaffey to discover she went home because she wasn't feeling well. It's probably for the best.

Her words mix with the chief's warning in my head as I read the sent letter over and over and over. The dick that wrote the letter wants his brother released from jail. Of course Dennis Milton, the man who shot his girlfriend three times in the chest has a crazy brother that thinks threats will get him released. Just another fucking day in the office as far as I'm concerned. Since the idiot all but signed his own name to the damn thing, it doesn't take long to get a warrant from a judge to have him arrested. I hand the task off to a patrol unit because I know I'll strangle the fucker for scaring Sophia. That little pesky fact and that technically I'm considered a victim in the case, which makes me being the arresting officer a conflict of interest.

Unbidden and like always, my thoughts drift back to thoughts of her. From the warning Monahan gave me, I know he thinks whatever I would start with Sophia wouldn't be worth it in the long run, but as much as I want to know what she sounds like in bed, as much as I want to know the exact shade of her nipples and the way the inside of her thighs taste like, I also want to know a million other non-sexual things.

I want to know how she likes her steak cooked and if she prefers warm showers over hot showers. Does she like ranch salad dressing or does she have more exotic tastes like a poppy seed vinaigrette? Would she smile or be a sore loser if Rick beat her at *Monopoly*? Does she prefer the beach over the mountains? Would she stick around when things got tough?

I swallow, emotion rising up my throat, at the memory of dream-Sophia smiling up at me with our newborn daughter in her arms.

Would it be worth it?

If she were in a position in her life to share those things with me, then I know without a shadow of a doubt that Sophia Anderson would be worth every single second of my life.

Chapter 20

Sophia

"We're waiting for the arson investigator," the fireman says, his eyes still on the smoldering building in front of us. "I can't give the official word, but I've been on the job for thirty years and I can tell you there's no way this isn't an arson case."

"We have three deceased on the second floor," the voice on the radio on his turnout jacket says. "We're still working on clearing the third."

"I need you to stay back," Colton says as he walks toward the building. "It's dangerous."

"If it's dangerous for me," I say, snagging his shoulder before he can get away from me, "then it's dangerous for you, too."

"It's too dangerous for both of you. No one goes in until we're sure of the structural stability," the fireman says, his eyebrow going up when something inside of the structure collapses. "See?"

An echo of voices come over the radio, letting the fireman know they're all safe and giving technical details for what's happening inside.

"Wait in the car with me?" Colton offers when I cross my arms over my chest, making it clear I'm not going anywhere if he's planning to work this scene.

We both concede, the heat from the sun as well as the fire becoming a little too much for comfort.

It's the middle of May, and I'm three days, including today, away from ending my internship with the Farmington Police Department. Technically, I'm done. My final grades, including the one for my internship posted last night. The writeups from both Colton and Chief Monahan complimentary enough to earn me an A.

And honestly, it was difficult to show up to the station today because the last week has been much like the weeks prior. Despite the connection I know we shared in his office, Colton has kept his distance. I haven't pursued anything either because it was clear with the way he avoided me the next day that he no longer felt what I presumed he was feeling.

Since I already have a pit in my stomach as my last days draws closer, I knew I couldn't stay away and spend these last couple of days with him. He's attending my graduation party at the clubhouse on Saturday, and I've cried myself to sleep several times knowing that may be the last time I'll see him.

The air conditioner runs in the car, but it doesn't stop sweat from beading between my shoulder blades. It has more to do with the words I want to say to him rather than heat that's causing the reaction, but I just don't know where to start. I know I need to lay it all out before my last day, but sitting in a car while waiting for the death investigation of at least three people makes it seem disrespectful.

Instead of talking, I watch the firefighters work the scene, still having to put out small fires popping up in hotspots.

"I always thought firefighters and cops hated each other."

Colton chuckles. "It's more of a brotherly competition than true hatred, like a school rivalry."

And there he goes breaking down information in a juvenile way to remind me of our age difference once again.

"Detectives get more animosity from patrol officers than we ever get from the fire department."

"Hmm."

I can feel his eyes on the side of my face, but I can't look in his direction. Terror keeps me from opening my mouth. Everything he says is true. There's a nearly thirteen-year difference between our ages. To most that would make him too old. He has a nearly grown son for heaven's sake. I still live at home with my parents, and I'm more than likely not even done with college. If I pursue my master's degree, I'll still be in college by the time Rick goes into college. Having a son and a girlfriend in college at the same time? What man wants that? What could he possibly see in me other than sexual release? What in the world do I have to offer a man like him?

Nothing.

That's the simple answer, but I can still sense his eyes on me, as if he's waiting expectantly for me to say something to him.

"When I showed up to your office that first day, I really thought things were going to be different." I roll my head on the back of the seat and finally look at him.

His eyes dart to my mouth, but that's not a new thing. I never doubted his sexual attraction to me, he's just more able to keep his desires in check than the college boys I've been with were.

"I did, too." His words are soft as I blink up at him. "I was certain you were going to get in the way or flake on me by Friday. You've legitimately become an amazing addition to our department the last two months."

Not even close to what I was thinking would happen that first week. A noise outside of the car draws his attention, and we both watch as the firefighters continue their work.

"I was certain I'd fuck you by the end of the week."

My heart stops with my vocal confession. Colton's hands grip the steering wheel tighter, his knuckles turning white from the pressure.

"That so?" he asks after a long silence, but he doesn't look at me.

"You were disappointed when you found out who I was."

"I was," he agrees, and it hurts a little more than I thought it would. "I was also hard as fuck the second you darkened my door. I spent the first five minutes of our conversation wondering if I actually had it in me to fuck someone in my office."

"You wonder that often?"

He turns his head, fiery eyes meeting mine, and I feel his embrace even though he isn't touching me.

"Not once until the day you showed up."

I swallow. "And since then?"

"Every fucking day."

He doesn't break eye contact, and his gaze doesn't drift from mine.

"Why are we avoiding each other if it's what we both want?"

"Is it what you want?" His eyes dart between mine. "You want to be a quick fuck on my desk?"

"No." My eyes burn with the implication. "I want it long and hard. Deep. Fast."

"Jesus Christ, Sophia." He pulls his eyes away, adjusting himself in his slacks.

"We've been dancing around each other for the last two months. In your kitchen. At *Jake's*."

"You think I don't fucking know that?" He sounds angry, but I don't get the feeling that he's mad at me. He's not blaming me for the attraction, and if I had to guess, I'd bet he blames himself fully. According to him, he's the adult after all. He's the one who should be able to control himself, no matter the slipups he's had recently. And that's exactly what *Jake's* was, a mistake, something he can blame on alcohol and correct by not drinking when I'm near.

"Are we really just going to walk away from each other at the end of the week and pretend we haven't been getting ourselves off with the thoughts of each other?"

His eyes squeeze shut, and it's the best confession he can give me. At least I'm not the only one. At least he shares some mutual obsession about me.

"I respect your father too much to cross that line with you."

"You don't even know my father."

"The department respects him too much," he amends.

"I'm a grown woman."

"I'm very well aware."

"I get to make decisions about my life without having to consult my parents."

"I'm a parent," he says as if I need reminding, his head swiveling back toward me. Gone is the needy look in his eyes, having been replaced with desolation and loss. "I have to think about Rick."

"I would never cross a line with him. I told you—"

"The thought didn't even cross my mind, Sophia. I want you to know that, but his happiness and stability is my number one concern. I can't bring another woman into our lives only for her to leave."

"You were heartbroken when she left," I whisper.

"I think kids deserve two parents."

"You loved her."

"I—" His hands scrape over the top of his head before falling right back to the steering wheel, and I can't help but wonder if his grip there is so he's not tempted to reach for me. "I should have. A man should love his wife."

"But you didn't?"

"We were young. I wasn't in a relationship with her when we hooked up. When she came to me three months later to tell me she was pregnant, if felt like the right thing to do even though neither one of us really wanted it."

"Your parents were okay with you marrying so young?" I know my dad would be very vocal if the situation happened in our family.

"No, but we were both eighteen. They didn't really have a say. I wanted to give Rick what I had growing up, two parents in a happy home. She was gone before I knew that love, not marriage, was the foundation for that. Failure was inevitable."

"I'm not her."

"You don't know that."

I want to grab a handful of his hair and shake it until he sees reasoning. "I would never walk away from a child, Colton."

He nods as if he understands, but it doesn't seem to change his mind. It's not only age keeping us apart. His mind is so warped from Rick's mother leaving and deserting them both that I don't think there's a thing I can say to convince him otherwise.

His relationship with her was over before it began, and it seems it's the same for us.

"I would never hurt you like that," I vow.

His eyes meet mine, and all the walls he's put up over the last couple of months fade away. He's no longer hiding a single piece of himself, and the sight makes my chin quiver with unleashed emotion.

"I'd never give you the chance."

And the shutters go back into place.

"Okay." I nod in understanding. "I won't beg you, no matter how much my body wants you, how much I throb for you, or how much time I've spent at night thinking about you and what your touch on my skin would feel like. I won't waste another second of your time trying to convince you that I'm worth the risk."

Before I start to cry, I open the car door and get out.

I approach the fireman we were speaking with earlier.

"I have a few questions about burn patterns in arson cases." I pull my little notebook and pen out of my pocket. "I was hoping you could share a little of your expertise."

"Sure thing," he says before going into a long description of accelerants.

I may only have a few days left in my internship, but I plan to learn everything I can until I'm done.

Since I already know what a broken heart feels like, I might as well add arson investigation on top of the pile.

The rest of the shift is uneventful, and even though I didn't get very close, I know it's going to take several washes for the scent of smoke to leave my clothes.

My phone rings on the way home, and despite what I'm feeling where Colton is involved, I smile when I see Izzy's name on my dash.

"Hey!" I say when the call connects, hoping she can't hear the waver in my voice.

"Are you sitting down?"

"I mean, technically. I'm driving. What's up?"

"Park somewhere."

"I'm almost home."

"Do not go home yet."

I pull my foot from the gas and slow down. "You're scaring me."

"I'm scared myself. Tell me when you park."

Silence fills my car as I drive, a million horrible scenarios coming at me in flashes.

"Parked," I say as I pull into a gas station and park around the back so I'm out of the way of traffic. "Fucking talk, Izzy."

She sighs instead.

"Is everything okay?"

"Not really." A sob escapes her throat. "I'm pregnant."

And that wasn't even at the top of the list of things I conjured.

"Wh-what?"

"My dad is going to kill me."

"He won't." Hound doesn't have a leg to stand on. He got Gigi pregnant at nineteen.

"I didn't even know you lost your virginity."

"It was—" Another sob. "That same night."

"You got pregnant by the guy you lost your virginity to? Fuck, bad sex and a baby. Talk about a double whammy."

"It wasn't bad sex!" she screams, and my eyes widen at her hysterical response.

"Okay, sorry," I mutter. "What did the baby daddy say?"

Silence.

"Izzy?"

Silence.

"Isabella Roze Montoya, you better tell me everything."

And she does. She tells me about meeting this guy, how they hit it off, how charming he was, how they spent some time together. It sounds like a fairy tale—a girl meeting the man of her dreams—but then she admits, she never got his first name, oddly only his last, and even if she did, she doesn't want him to know about the baby. She knows more, and for some reason she doesn't feel comfortable talking about it right now. I'll get the truth out of her eventually because there are red flags all over this situation, but she's distraught and not willing to open up fully.

"What are you going to do?"

"I don't know," she whispers. "I just don't know."

Chapter 21

Colton

The easy smile on her pretty face forces one on mine. I'm standing off to the side of her little going away party at the office, and due to the in-and-out nature of law enforcement, it's been going on for nearly two hours, patrol officers and other detectives stopping in when they get a break from duty.

I'm not the only one she's charmed with her quick wit, intelligence, and work ethic. Everyone, from patrol and dispatch to Ethel, the woman who works part time in the mailroom, has a quick smile and some small token or gift for her last day. The cake Monahan's wife made, as well as the small spread of finger foods has been destroyed.

Both Ramshaw and that douche Dresden offer to carry her with them on a patrol shift. She turns Dresden down cold, giving him a look scathing enough that I don't think the man will ever approach her again. Ramshaw doesn't get the same treatment, and he walks away with a wide grin on his face, winking at me in victory as he leaves to do final paperwork before he gets off shift. I wonder if it was the jogging leggings with the hidden gun holster he bought for her that tipped the scale in his favor.

The small box in my back pocket burns my skin, but I don't want to give her the gift in front of everyone else. She's less than an hour away from being free and clear of the police department, and I'm hoping to get just a few minutes of her time alone before she walks out of here for good.

Unable to watch everyone fawn over her without approaching her myself, I edge out of the room. Her purse is still in my office, so I know she'll have to come in here eventually. The wait—forty-five minutes to be exact—is spent with me staring at the blank screen of my computer. Cases are cleared, and with any luck, I can make it through the weekend without getting called out, but that's highly unlikely.

She doesn't look surprised to see me in my office, but she doesn't speak when she reaches for her purse on the shelf either. My throat feels like it's going to close up.

"Sophia," I say, standing and coming around my desk to be near her.

"It was nice working with you, Detective Matthews."

A harsh breath slips past my lips at the formality. I step around her and close the door, turning back around to find her back ramrod stiff, eyes looking over my shoulder. If it weren't for the trembling grip she has on the strap of her purse, I'd think she was indifferent.

"I got this for you." I pull the box from my back pocket, frowning down at the rumpled state of it.

"I didn't expect a gift from you." Her tone suggests that she doesn't even want it.

"Please take it," I beg when she doesn't reach for it.

Courtesy wins out as she places her purse in the chair in front of my desk and clasps the box.

"Thank you." Her bottom lip trembles when she pulls the lid off, revealing the tiny charm hanging from a delicate chain.

"It's—"

"Saint Michael, Patron Saint of Police." She smiles weakly down at the necklace. "It's beautiful. Thank you."

"To keep you safe while you finish school."

"I won't go back until the spring. I missed the deadline for the fall application."

"What are your plans for—" I shake my head. It's none of my business. "Never mind."

She smiles softly. "I should…"

"Yeah."

I don't think I can watch her walk out of here. I know she's going to be in town, even longer now since her college plans have been delayed, but it feels like a forever goodbye. I didn't even have to get this woman in my bed for her to break my heart. I'm such a damn fool.

"Thank you for everything." She offers her hand, but it's too formal, too impersonal, and I pull her against my chest for a hug, my nose immediately diving into her fragrant hair.

I plan to let her go, but five seconds later, I'm still clinging to her. Another five go by, and I know it's time to step back, but I feel her fingers curl into my clothes, making me hold her tighter.

Can I watch her walk away without having gotten a real taste of her mouth? God, I was a fool that day I pushed her away, and I've been a fool every damn day since.

She breaks the contact like I knew she would, her eyes sparkling with tears. Without hesitation, I reach up and wipe them away with my thumbs, my body stepping into her rather than giving her the distance I know we both need.

"Colton?"

"Just one?" I ask, swallowing as I focus on her mouth. "One kiss. A good luck, a congratulations, thanks for helping me out the last two months—an I'm going to miss you kiss. Just one?"

She blinks up at me, her eyes searching. "Just one?"

I nod.

"Can you make it a good one? One I'll remember for the rest of my life?"

God, I could only hope I'll stay in her memory.

I tilt her chin, pausing for the briefest of seconds before my lips meet hers.

The first sweep is soft, a prelude to what we're both wanting. I can't rush this. If one is all we're going to get, I want it to be the best kiss she'll ever have. When asked thirty years from now who made her the most breathless, I want my face in her mind.

My hands leave her face when I press my lips to hers the second time, one gripping her low on her back, drawing her even closer to me, the other tangled in her hair at her nape.

She hums her approval when I nip at her bottom lip, the action making it easy to slip my tongue inside. A million butterflies take flight in my stomach, their wings flapping in a way I've never felt once in my life. It's more than arousal, more than need, more than that tingle in my spine telling me we'd be amazing in bed together.

It's lov—

Damnit! I can't even think of the word in my head because my heart is already halfway to breaking with the loss of her, and she's still in my arms.

I spin the two of us, her tongue sweeping over mine, and press her against my office door. Her amazing tits throb against my chest with each ragged breath she takes, small whimpers escaping her mouth when I push my hips against her. I'm solid, an iron pipe in my slacks, but that isn't what this is about.

I change the angle, delving deeper into her mouth, wanting to crawl inside of her and build a home. When I can no longer resist licking down the column of her neck, I break the kiss and take a step back. Her pink tongue skates over her swollen lips, and the sight is enough to make me groan.

I notice the tremble in my hand when I push a lock of her hair behind her ear.

Without thought, my thumb traces her bottom lip.

"Goodbye," I whisper as I open my office door and then walk away.

Chapter 22

Sophia

I built my college graduation up more than I should have. Instead of it being this huge shining moment, it was hours of sitting and pretending to pay attention while waiting for the entire thing to just be over with.

Tonight is different. Tonight is going to be fun. I have just the right amount of alcohol in my system to smile at everything, and just enough to feel bold at the sight of Colton Matthews standing across the room. He doesn't look uneasy in the clubhouse, but I don't miss the way his eyes roam around the room, taking everything but me in.

I have no doubt he knows where I'm at and would track me across the room if I got up and walked somewhere else. I could go and flirt with the new guys Cerberus hired, but I don't have it in me to waste my time. I told him more than once, I wasn't looking to play games with him. Hell, I was prepared to walk away and count the loss of him as a lesson learned then...

"One kiss. A good luck, a congratulations, thanks for helping me out the last two months—an I'm going to miss you kiss. Just one?"

There's not even half a chance I can stay away from him now because that kiss was the kiss. The one that will make everyone after pale in comparison. The one that will haunt my dreams until I get another. There's no walking away after that.

I told him a week and a half ago that I wouldn't beg, but hell that was before knowing what his tongue felt like against mine. Then, I was strong and determined. Now, I'm an addict, and like the letdown after that first taste of heroin, my skin is itching for the next hit.

I pressed a cordial kiss to his cheek when I greeted him upon arrival but begging him to get me out of here at the time didn't happen. There were too many people watching, too many people without an ounce of alcohol in their systems for me to make my move that early in the night.

With confidence, I pull out my phone and shoot off a text.

Me: *Still turned on by that kiss.*

I turn my phone over in my lap when Izzy shifts beside me.

"Look." I nudge my head in the direction of Delilah and Ivy. They're both fawning over Simone's little boy. "No one around here gets upset about babies."

"Hush," she snaps, looking around the room to make sure no one overheard me.

I watch as Colton pulls his phone from his pocket, but he doesn't send a text back before stuffing it right back in his jeans.

That fucker.

Picking up my phone, I fire off another text. Go big or go home, right?

Me: My pussy is so wet for you.

His head tilts halfway in my direction but he catches himself before looking at me fully. There's a warning there, I just know it, but I'm no longer going to listen to the voice in my head telling me it'll be better if I walk away.

"Who are you texting?" Izzy whispers near my ear.

"Hush," I hiss. "Mind your own business."

"My own business?" She huffs. "Pot. Kettle. Daddy? Really, Soph, aren't you a little old to have Dom's phone number in your phone like that?"

I turn my phone over just as it buzzes in my hand. Then it buzzes again, and again, and again. Izzy is still in my face, so I turn my phone over and hold it comically close to my nose. Before I read the texts, I make a quick scan of the room. Mom and Dad are nuzzling each other like teens during prom. Other than Izzy, no one else is around that I'm worried about.

Daddy: Stop.
Daddy: Please don't do this to me.
Daddy: Fuck.
Daddy: And how am I supposed to explain an erection to your father?

I bite my lips to stave off a smile, my eyes taking in every inch of his massive body. The way he pressed me into his office wall Thursday comes to mind, and I know the man has the strength to pick me up, fuck me hard and not even break a sweat.

"Really?" Izzy squeals. "That's who you're texting?"

"Shhh," I snap.

"Your dad will kill you and him."

Maybe... maybe not.

"You have to try these!" My sister Jasmine sits down on the other side of Izzy, attempting to pass a cheeseburger slider to me, but I'm only hungry for one thing right now.

I ignore her, shooting off another text.

Me: I have a few ideas on how we can solve that problem.

"Oh, God," Izzy groans. In my peripheral vision, I see her hand clutch her stomach. A second later, she's covering her mouth like she's going to be sick and running for the hallway.

"Oh no," Rocker hisses from the sofa only a couple of feet away.

"What's wrong with her?" Hound asks, concerned about his oldest daughter as he walks across the room holding Amelia's tiny hand as she toddles beside him.

"How far along is she?" Simone blurts, and my eyes have to look like saucers.

"Excuse me?" Hound snaps.

My eyes dart around the room—everything but this conversation suddenly more interesting than the glare I know I'm getting from Hound.

"What did you say?" Hound demands again.

"It's the meat. I mean I could be wrong, but the smell of meat makes me sick," Simone explains.

"You're pregnant, too?" I ask, the question slipping out before I can stop it. I slap my hand over my mouth, but the damage is already done.

"She isn't," Hound argues, his head shaking back and forth like saying the words will make them true. "She's too young."

"She's the same age as I was when we got pregnant with Amelia," Gigi says, looking at her husband with a bored expression.

Did Izzy confide in her, too? She doesn't look exactly surprised by the news.

I watch in horror as Hound looks around the room trying to figure out who he's going to kill for touching his daughter. Little does he know the man will never step foot in this clubhouse. Izzy has no interest in tracking down the guy who got her pregnant, and I doubt Hound will ever be able to get the truth out of her.

"No fucking way, man!" Apollo, one of the new Cerberus members says, holding his arms up near his head in mock surrender. "I haven't touched her!"

Ignoring the man's declaration, I watch as Apollo's face turns white when Hound begins to cross the room.

A phone rings, but most people are waiting to see if blood is going to be shed on the clubhouse floor. Like I said, there's always drama around here.

"That's not fucking possible," Lawson hisses, his drink falling to the floor at his feet when he surges up from the couch. "I'll be there."

Lawson is ignoring the mess at his feet and staring down at his phone like it's a bomb ready to explode.

"What's going on?" Delilah asks, her hand clamping on her husband's arm.

"Drew," he whispers, and the entire room goes silent.

Tears instantly burn the backs of my eyes. Drew, Lawson's younger half-brother, is working for the New Mexico State Police. He's only been on the job for a couple of months. Fuck, he's still training to be a cop.

"No. Please, no," I gasp, my lungs refusing to fill completely with air.

Several others around me are having the same reaction.

"No, no," Lawson says, lifting his head and looking around the room. "He hasn't been hurt. Well, not yet, but when I get my hands on him—"

"Then what?" Lawson's dad asks as he steps in closer.

Lawson looks up, despair in his eyes. "He's been arrested by the police."

"Arrested by the police?" Someone scoffs on the other side of the room, and I think it's Cannon, but I can't pull my eyes away from Lawson. "He *is* the police."

"This seems familiar," Griffin mutters, having had his own run-in with law enforcement awhile back. "What's he been picked up for?"

Lawson doesn't pull his eyes from his dad when he answers, "Homicide."

The room erupts in chaos. Even Hound has stopped his pursuit of Apollo.

Questions fly, ones Lawson can't answer, before people start piling out. Kincaid, my Dad, Kid, Snatch, and several other men shuffle a traumatized Lawson and Delilah into the conference room, closing the door with a thunderous bang.

Ivy moves into action, Simone climbing off the couch to help clean up. I'm a robot as I move around the room collecting plates and trash.

"This is your party. You shouldn't be helping." My sister clutches my forearm, pulling the trash bag from my fist. Without even looking, she hangs it out to the side for Tug to take. He presses a kiss to her temple before walking away and picking up where I left off.

When she steps away, my eyes dart around the room. Only I find Colton's back as he heads for the front door instead of spotting him across the room where he was moments ago. Does he really think he can just walk out of here and leave me behind? That is not on the agenda for tonight.

Chapter 23

Colton

I couldn't even imagine getting the news this club just got hit with, and no matter how curious I am, it's not my business. It didn't happen in my jurisdiction because I would've gotten the call about a homicide long before family and friends were notified of a suspect's arrest.

I pull my phone out of my pocket as I leave, just to make sure I didn't miss something while trying to will my dick to deflate after Sophia's damn filthy texts. She's a different level of distraction than I've ever known.

Nope. Nothing. I breathe a sigh of relief. I hope I never have to work a case against a fellow officer, and I'm doubly glad I'm not having to work a case against a man under the protection of the Cerberus MC.

Cool air hits me in the face as I step outside, a sharp relief to the warmth that was filling my cheeks inside the clubhouse. I could blame the abundance of people in the large room, but I know it's the thoughts of that damn temptress in there that's making me warm from head to toe. Hell, even after watching a group of people horrified with bad news, my cock is still semi-interested in what Sophia was offering via text message.

"Detective Matthews!"

I keep walking, knowing if I stop and face her, I'll end up making a huge mistake—one I won't be able to argue against if her dad walks out of the clubhouse.

"Colton!" she snaps when I reach for the door of my truck.

"Go back inside, Sophia."

She shoves me from behind, the surprise of it making me stumble more than the force she's able to manage.

"Turn around." The command makes my cock throb—not because I like being bossed around but from the gall of thinking she can tell me what to do. "I need answers."

"I thought we said just one—"

Jesus, if she tempts me tonight, I won't be able to walk away.

"Not that." My heart deflates. "I need to know what's going on with Drew."

"I don't know anything. It didn't happen here."

"I know, but you're a cop. Use some of that professional courtesy we talked about before and find out."

"From the sounds of it, it's still an open investigation. I can't call the department he's working for and ask for information."

"The State Police," she corrects.

"Especially them," I mutter. "You know how this goes, Sophia. We've worked several cases together from start to finish. If it happened in the last twenty-four hours, there's a good chance the information isn't even in their system. Those men are having to work a case against one of their own, and I can't get involved in that. It could bring heat down on my department."

"Okay." She hangs her head in disappointment, but I know she knows I'm right.

I open the truck door, ready to tell her goodnight although I don't want to, but she shoves past me and climbs across the driver's seat, settling her sexy ass body against the passenger window.

If she leaves here tonight with me, she won't be going home. I know her father already suspects something with the way he glared at me when she pressed her hot, little lips to my cheek in greeting when I arrived. Of course, her mother just smiled at the two of us, but her look was knowing as well. I could be on a damn hitlist already, and I've only been here an hour and a half.

"What are you doing?" I try to hide the smile at her brazen attitude, but it's impossible.

All she does is smile at me.

"How much have you had to drink?"

"Why? Are you wanting to take advantage?"

This little devil.

"Sophia," I warn.

"Yes, Daddy?" She giggles, but her words make my face screw up. "I have you in my phone as Daddy."

I cringe even further. I never considered the woman having daddy issues as reasoning for being attracted to me. "That's disturbing."

"I didn't want my friend to be suspicious," she explains. "Take me home with you, Colton."

Done resisting, done hesitating, I climb in the truck and crank it. A second later, we're leaving Cerberus' property and heading toward my house.

She hums along to the radio, watching out the window rather than engaging me in conversation. Is it possible she's as nervous as I am right now? My heart is racing, sweat dampens my temples, and it's worse than the ten minutes right before I lost my virginity, and I was only nervous then because I didn't know what to expect.

Now, I know how amazing sex can be. I have no doubt sex with Sophia is going to be out of this world, but I'm still freaking out, more from wondering what happens after than from anticipation.

"The light is green," she whispers when I get entranced at the sight of her running her finger back and forth, back and forth over the bottom hem of her dress.

"Right," I say, darting my eyes forward so I don't get us both killed in a traffic accident.

She chuckles, but I only manage a quick look in her direction before focusing back on the road ahead of us.

"What?"

I grin when she laughs again.

"Why are you so nervous?"

"Is it that obvious?"

"You're strumming your fingers on the steering wheel. You have beads of sweat rolling down your neck. Your back is as stiff as a board."

"Very observant, detective."

She laughs even louder at that. "I learned from the best."

"You've been the perfect pupil."

"I bet there are a million more things you can teach me."

Her voice takes on a sultry tone, and my dick takes notice before my brain can even catch up, making me wish I made a checklist of the things I want to do with her tonight.

"Rick isn't home tonight?" she asks when I make the turn into my neighborhood.

"Staying with a friend," I assure her.

In the drive, I put the truck in park, but don't turn off the ignition.

Her legs, tan in the moonlight and a stark contrast to the light color of her dress, hold every ounce of my attention. I haven't seen them bare since that day in my kitchen, and what a damn shame that is. They're perfect, deserving of attention.

"If we go inside—"

"I know," she interrupts, her eyes finding mine in the dim light.

We both knew what was going to happen when I drove away from the clubhouse, but I'm giving her one last chance, one more opportunity to walk away. I can't make her promises. I don't have a crystal ball able to tell me what tomorrow is going to look like for us.

Maybe it's a casual sex thing. Maybe I don't have to worry about Rick getting hurt because she'll only come around when he's gone. Maybe it'll be a one-time thing because we'll find out we aren't even close to being sexually compatible.

I shake my head, answering every one of those questions in an instant. There's nothing casual about what's been stewing between the two of us. Rick will hurt because I'll be hurting if she walks away. There's no way I'll spend only one night inside of this woman.

"What will tomorrow look like?" she asks as if reading my mind. Her fingers tangle in the hem of her dress, but she keeps her eyes locked on mine.

I bite my lip before answering, knowing it could be a moment of truth for us. If she wants something different, I may have to be the one to walk away.

"You mean after I wake you with my cock inside of you?" She swallows, getting distracted with the possibilities.

"Is this a one-time thing?"

"It can't be, Sophia. Nor is it casual. I can't do no-strings attached with you."

"You're sure?"

"A hundred percent. If that's not what you want, I can take you home."

Her eyes flutter as she looks at me. "I'm right where I want to be."

Chapter 24

Sophia

Not casual.

I think I hesitated for so long because this was my top fear.

I'm not afraid of what my family will think or the possible backlash of dating an older man. My mom is younger than my dad. My entire life I've witnessed what love should look like. Does that mean I have daddy positivity rather than daddy issues because of my childhood? Maybe.

"Are we going to sit here all night?" I whisper when his eyes focus on my mouth but he makes no move to get out of the truck.

"If we go inside—" he repeats.

"I know," I assure him once again.

"A lot has happened tonight. Your graduation party was ended abruptly because of the phone call Lawson got, and you—"

"I want to go inside with you."

He scrapes his hands down his face, refocusing on his front door. "Maybe we could—"

"If you don't want me inside—"

His groan is feral, the sound of a trapped beast demanding to be released.

"Inside is what I've wanted for the last two months."

My throat works on a swallow.

"Okay." I open my door and step out, waiting at the front of his truck for him to climb out.

He locks up the truck, stepping around me on the sidewalk. He doesn't touch me, doesn't brush my hip or press his hand to my back. I ache for his touch, ache for reassurance that he wasn't making empty promises just moments before.

With a trembling hand, he unlocks his front door, stepping away so I can enter first. Instead of sweeping me into his arms, he turns off the alarm system, flipping on lights as he walks deeper into his home.

"Colton?"

"Would you like something to drink?"

I watch him, his nerves on full display as he starts to pace.

"Are you nervous?" I aim for serious, but the question is laced with humor.

I don't think I've ever been moments away from stripping naked and the man I was getting naked for was turning shy.

"I wouldn't call it nerves."

I clasp his trembling hand.

"We can watch a movie—"

He huffs, his fingers tangling with mine. "I want to watch you come."

And those words light me up from the inside.

"Yeah?"

His teeth dig into his bottom lip. "I want your legs shaking. I want my name on your lips. I want to be inside of you so deep, you feel me in your soul."

How can I tell him he's already there?

"And you want that right here in the entryway?"

"My bed. I need you in my bed."

I squeal with delight when he scoops me up in his arms.

His lips are on mine, his tongue seeking, searching, licking my consent right out of my mouth.

Our hands are a blur, my dress hitting the soft carpet with a whisper the second we step inside his bedroom. The hiss of his zipper echoes around us, churning the atmosphere around us until we're both frenzied.

"Let me." He reaches behind me to unclasp my bra, the lace and satin tickling my skin as it falls away. "I'm one lucky man."

My cheeks heat, the anticipation of finally being with him, like this, is better than anything my mind could've conjured.

"You're beautiful when you blush." His fingers sweep over my face, trailing down my neck before tracing the curve of my collarbone.

"You're still dressed," I pout, my fingers inching toward his open fly.

He steps away, a mischievous look in his eyes. "And you're not completely naked."

His eyes flare when I dip my thumbs into the side of my panties and work them down my thighs. I know the second he sees the evidence of my desire. His eyelids lower, the pink tip of his tongue licking at the curve of his bottom lip. His reactions to me are the best aphrodisiac, making me want him more than I've ever wanted someone in my life.

"Now I am," I tease, standing there trying to look like a goddess when in fact I have no idea what to do with my hands.

When I lift them to my breasts, teasing the points of my nipples, I know I made the right choice. "Are you hard for me?"

In answer, he fists his cock, his hand sliding behind the open zipper of his jeans to grip it over the dark fabric of his briefs.

"So fucking hard. I need you in my mouth."

"This?" I cup the bottom swell of my right breast and hold it up as if I'm offering it to him.

He's not disappointed, his eyes zooming in on my hand.

"All of it." His eyes sweep my body. "Get on my bed, Sophia. I want your scent all over it."

I back away slowly, not willing to take my eyes off of him for a second. When his comforter brushes my thighs, I place my hands behind me and inch my way to the center of his bed.

"No," I tell him when he moves to climb on. "No clothes in this bed."

His grin is magnetic, and mine falls away when his shirt drops to the floor. I'm salivating when he shoves his jeans down. By the time his boxer briefs disappear, I'm breathless, panting in an attempt to pull enough oxygen in my lungs to function.

"I—shit—you're gorgeous."

His thick cock bobs freely as he moves, and I don't know where to focus as my eyes dart from his muscular thighs to the ridges lining his torso. His pecs flex as he climbs on the bed, but his mouth is a tempting focal point as well.

"Are you still with me?"

"I'm right here."

"You seem distracted."

"I am," I confess. "You're a lot to take in."

"So complimentary," he teases, his nose tracing the curve of my calf. "I'm distracted, too."

"Mmm."

"Where do you want my mouth?" He punctuates his question with a nip to my inner thigh.

"All over."

"Here?" His mouth teases my hip.

I nod, unable to form words. For a flash of a second, I feel like I should be embarrassed with how turned on I am. I know he can see my arousal. There's no way to hide the way my body is responding to him, preparing for him. Have I ever been this turned on in my life? That would be a no, and God, does this man make me want to do this every damn day of my existence.

"What about here?" His lips tickle the flesh just below my belly button.

"Lower," I pant, feeling his lips turn up into a smile against my overly sensitive skin.

"Here?" His breath ghosts over where I need him the most, his mouth once again on my inner thigh.

"Is this how you want to play it?"

His eyes meet mine, mouth still on my leg.

"I want to savor you. I want to spend the entire night worshipping your body."

"I want your mouth on my pussy," I counter, loving the way his eyes flare with my filthy declaration.

Perfect teeth dig into his bottom lip once again, and I can tell he's trying to hide a smile. It pulls one from my own mouth.

"But savor away," I tell him as my fingers trace over my breast, inching lower. His eyes find mine when I circle my belly button and aim lower. "Don't mind me."

His head pulls back mere inches as my wandering fingers skate over my clit. It takes sheer determination not to buck my hips with the first brush over it.

"Jesus, look at you." He gasps when I dip my fingers into my arousal before teasing my clit once again.

I'm seconds away from coming, a blink away from screwing my eyes tight and moaning with release.

"Does it feel good?"

"So good. You'd feel better."

"My fingers? Or my—"

His mouth is on me, his tongue tangling with the tips of my fingers, and I'm lost in him. Lost in the sensation of his heated mouth. Lost in the perfection of finally having him like this.

I'm just lost. My hand falls away, but doesn't stay near my hip for long. When he groans against me, my back bows, arching off the bed to the point of pain. Strong arms hold me against his mouth, and as I come, he laps at me, the incessant movement of his tongue making me tremble and flutter like I've never done before.

I chant his name until my throat is raw, and only after I seize a final time does he back away. Wetness coats his mouth and chin, and the grin on his face is reminiscent of a man who has just gotten everything he's ever wanted.

My eyes burn, the threat of tears making it impossible to speak.

"You're amazing."

I nod like a fool, hoping he understands that I think the same of him.

"I don't know what to do with you."

Love me forever.

I don't speak the words, but it's exactly what I want from him.

I want his love and affection. I want to wake each morning in his arms. I want to spend Saturday afternoons arguing about what to watch on television. I want to spend early mornings making love as the sun comes up.

"My turn," I finally manage after long moments of looking into each other's eyes.

He must be distracted because it takes minimal effort to get him on his back with his head against the headboard.

"Not gonna happen, gorgeous." His hands cling to my shoulders when I start to lower my mouth to the trail of hair below his navel.

"I want to return the favor."

"No."

My head snaps back, unsure of the direction he's taking.

"I want your cock in my mouth."

"And I want the first time I come with you to be deep inside your pussy." He angles his head to the side table. "Grab a condom."

His patience is commendable as I lean to the side to grab the unopened box of condoms from the drawer. My hands shake as I open it, trembling comically as I tear one from the strip. His hands trace the outer curve of my hips, making me insane with need.

"Let me," he says with his hand out, palm up.

I don't give him the condom once I have the wrapper removed. If he thinks he has the upper hand here, he's mistaken.

His teeth dig into his bottom lip when I touch him the first time, my free hand sliding down the length of him. He moans in need, and if I weren't straddling his thighs, I might have missed the way his muscles tighten under me.

"Deep breaths," I taunt as I tease the sensitive spot under his cockhead.

"Sophia," he warns when my thumb swirls in his precum. "Put the condom on, or I'm going to flip you over and fuck you bare."

He groans again when my thighs clench at the threat. We need a very long discussion before we get to that point, but it's a tantalizing offer either way.

More for my own mercy than his, I roll the condom down the length of him. His mouth is parted, breath slow and purposeful as I lift up on my knees and position him at my entrance.

We've both waited for this moment, but as much as I want to revel in it, my body demands more.

"Yes," he hisses, his fingers gripping my hips as I slide down. His body rolls under me, and we're both equally giving and taking at this moment. "Perfection."

"That sounds," I moan as I lift my weight and lower again, "so sexy."

"That sound means I'm not going to last," he warns. "That sound—God, you feel so fucking good."

"I knew," I gasp. "How did I know it would feel this good?"

Soon, talking isn't possible. Soon, my legs are shaking so hard, I can no longer get my legs to work. Soon, I'm trembling harder than I did the first time, my body convulsing around him in appreciation.

And soon, he's following me over the edge like he'd been waiting for me to whisper his name.

Chapter 25

Colton

I wake when the first hint of morning makes itself known, and a dozen things come into focus. I could focus on the warmth of her body against mine, or the softness of her hair brushing my arm. I could fixate on the way she let me keep my arms wrapped around her all night, or the way she has stayed slick between her milky thighs even after we fell to the mattress drained of energy from hours of fixating on each other.

But it's the soft snores that make me smile.

That and the erection that's been pressed against her ass for the last ten minutes. It only takes a few seconds for my fingers to brush the strip of condoms we stashed under the pillow and work it over my tired cock. I'm drained. We're both probably dehydrated, but you wouldn't be able to convince my lower half that we need a break.

My fingers find her wet as I split her folds and explore. The snores stop, replaced with a groan of pleasure, and it's all the permission I need to lift her thigh and position myself. Just like every time last night, sliding inside of her is a heaven I never thought I'd experience. Experiencing it over and over? I must have some very good karma saved up because never in my wildest dreams...

"You awake?" I whisper in her ear, my hips moving back and forth.

"Mmm," is her only response.

Well, that isn't entirely true. She lifts her leg, moving it back and over the top of mine, opening herself up in the most delicious way. My fingers tease her, skirting around her clit without actually touching it. I know if I do, she'll come, and even though that's the end goal, feeling her clench around me will set me off like a choreographed explosion, and I want to relish in the experience just a few moments longer.

"Feel good?"

"Always," she pants. "So good."

I've always considered sex functional, a quick way to release endorphins and better my mood, but with her, it's a whole event. It's not entirely about the outcome. I don't want inside of her just to get off. Our orgasms are the culmination, but not necessarily the main focus.

"Jesus, baby. Roll your hips."

She responds by gripping the arm I have wrapped around her, arching her back, and swiveling her perfect hips. She whimpers as she fucks herself on my cock, and I try my best not to mark her skin with fingertip-sized bruises.

"My clit," she begs. "Make me come."

Fuck, I thought she'd never ask.

I reposition our bodies with her stomach flat on the mattress and me behind her. I slam into her, sawing back and forth when I really want to take things slowly as my fingers make maddening circles on her clit.

"Higher," I urge, my hand smacking the globe of her ass, and her back arches like she was made to take me this way.

She screams my name, and I know I'll hear the echo of it every night when I close my eyes.

I grunt my release at the first whisper of her body rippling around mine, and my fingers don't stop moving between her legs until she squeals and pulls away.

"Join me in the shower?" I press my lips to her back, planting kisses along her spine.

"Hot water," she instructs as I climb off the bed.

I spend a few lingering minutes just watching her before turning around to do her bidding. The water scalds my skin, but she never joins me, and I'm not surprised to find her snoring gently when I walk back into my bedroom with water droplets still on my skin and a towel tight around my waist.

The sight of her naked, collapsed exactly where I left her before the shower is enough to rejuvenate my dick, but we both need a break and some breakfast. After throwing on some sweats and a t-shirt, I press my lips to her shoulder blade before covering her body with the comforter.

"I'm telling you, man, she's the hottest girl I've ever seen."

"I believe you."

"Tits like you've never seen."

"Really, Rick? And just how many sets of tits have you seen?"

I stop near the threshold to the living room. I swear teenage boys have a one-track mind.

An uneasy laugh slips from my son, but he doesn't answer the question.

"Exactly, and quit talking like that, dude. It's seriously fucking disrespectful."

I recognize Landon Andrew's voice, and I knew I liked this kid for a reason.

"Seriously?" Rick continues. "You stare at every female you pass."

"I'm trying to do better," Landon mutters.

"Sounds like you've had another conversation with your dad."

I narrow my eyes at this. After knowing what I know about the Cerberus MC, it's clear those men have raised good kids, but teen boys are a different breed. What they say and do in front of parents and how they act when they think no one is looking can be two different things.

"I had a... reaction."

"A reaction?" Rick questions. "Like a rash or something?"

A slap rings out. "No, you idiot. Like at the pool. I got hard."

"How hard?" I tilt my head to hear better.

"Quit looking at my crotch, fucker."

Rick laughs.

"I'll just say it was noticeable. People noticed. It was embarrassing."

"I imagine."

"So when are you going to talk about the argument you had with Seth?"

"I'm not fucking talking about it," Rick hisses.

My stomach grumbling reminds me why I left Sophia alone in my bed, so I cough to make myself known before walking out of the hallway.

"Hey, Dad," Rick mumbles.

"Hey, Mr. Matthews."

"Colton," I remind the kid with a quick grin. Most kids pretend to be respectful in the face of adults, but after listening in to part of their conversation, it's clear this young man is being genuine.

The boys are sitting on either sides of the couch. The television is on, volume low.

"You guys hungry? I was gonna make breakfast."

"For us, or your friend?"

"Are you hungry or not?" I repeat as I turn in the direction of the kitchen.

Rick either isn't aware of Landon and Sophia's connection or he doesn't care. I don't think her being here at the same time as Landon is a big deal, but her coming out with no warning wouldn't be fair to either of them. I have no clue how she wants to handle this situation even though I know last night and this morning wasn't a fluke. She's going to be spending more time here, and Landon comes over often enough that their paths are eventually going to cross. First thing on a Saturday morning without knowing exactly what the boys heard from my room earlier probably isn't the perfect time though.

"Pancakes and eggs?" I ask as I open the fridge.

I know I have an awkward conversation coming with Dominic, but with any luck, I won't have to have it today.

"You don't have to cook for us Mr. Matt—Colton."

"He doesn't speak for me," Rick says with a smile as he slides past to get into the fridge. "What about bacon?"

He places the unopened package of meat near the stove before taking a long swig of orange juice from the container.

"Get a glass, you heathen," I chide, but all he does is smile and take another drink.

"Juice?" he asks his friend when there's only a little left in the jug.

"No way, man. I'm not getting anywhere near where your mouth has been."

Rick shrugs before polishing off the juice.

I make quick work of the food, insisting they take their plates to Rick's room to eat.

"Is it because you don't want your girlfriend checking me out again?" Rick says as he reaches for his plate.

"Go, Rick."

"Maybe next time keep it down. I didn't get a wink of sleep last night. You know a growing boy needs his sleep."

Landon's cheeks flush, and he avoids eye contact with me. It makes me wonder if he has ever had conversations with his parents like this.

Rick is cackling like a lunatic as he walks out of the room.

Landon stumbles on the threshold, plate in hand. "He's joking. We stayed at Aaron's house last night."

The redness in his face as he walks away tells me that they were here long enough to bear audible witness to what Sophia and I did this morning.

And that's another consideration we need to discuss. Having an active sex life is healthy, and I plan to spend as much time inside of her as she allows, but we have to keep in mind that Rick and his friends could be lurking around at any moment.

I'm pouring coffee into two mugs on a tray when Sophia walks into the room. Her hair is a mess, face marked with lines from the pillow, but it's her soft knowing smile that makes everything come into focus.

"I was bringing you breakfast," I say softly as she walks to me, pressing her chest against my body.

Without hesitation, I place the coffee pot back on the machine and wrap my arms around her.

This is how it should've been that first night she was here, and I want to kick myself for not doing this sooner. I press my nose into her hair, inhaling the scent of the two of us.

My cock, although exhausted from the time we've spent together, jerks in my sweats. She chuckles like it's exactly what she expected, but she doesn't make a move to take things further. I'm equal parts relieved and flustered.

"Can't get enough of you," I confess, my face still buried in her hair.

"Want to join me in the shower?"

"Need me to wash your back?" I tease.

"Yeah." Her fingers slide under my shirt, and I never thought the brush of fingers on my spine could be sexual, but here we are. "I'm feeling extra dirty this morning."

I hold her tighter, imagining what my cum would look like striped across her tits, mixing with soap suds.

"What about breakfast?"

"I'm not—"

Her stomach loudly interrupts, grumbling its displeasure.

"I made pancakes, eggs, and bacon."

"Are you trying to spoil me?"

"Is it working?"

"I don't think I ever want to leave."

Her fingers dig in deeper, emphasizing her confession.

"Mmm," I groan against the top of her head. Her hair tickles my nose, but it's not enough of an irritation to make me release my hold on her. "I like the sound of that."

"Is breakfast in bed still an option?"

"If we take this to my room, I don't know that pancakes are still going to be on the menu."

"I thought you wanted to eat," she says as she takes a step back.

My eyes burn into hers. "Oh, I'll be eating if we go back to bed."

White teeth dig into her lower lip, and I can see she's weighing the possibilities. I might have to gag her to keep her quiet, but going the rest of the day without being inside of her again, even with the boys here isn't an option.

That reminds me...

"Rick isn't alone this morning. He brought—"

As if thoughts of him caused him to appear, Sophia turns around and comes face-to-face with Landon.

Well, shit.

Chapter 26

Sophia

I never understood what people really meant when they said they were frozen in place. I grew up with a dad whose number one favorite thing was interrogating his daughters. I learned from an early age to at least attempt to talk my way out of trouble, but seeing Dustin and Khloe's son standing in Colton's kitchen, all I can manage is staring at him, praying with each blink of my eyes that he disappears.

At least I'm not half-naked like I was the first time I met Colton's parents, but the mop on my head and the ill-fitting clothes I grabbed out of Colton's drawer are as good as any flashing sign of what I've been up to.

I don't know what to say, but starting a conversation with *when two adult people love each other* doesn't seem like the best idea either. First off, I haven't even had that conversation with Colton and second, there's really nothing I can say that won't make it back to the clubhouse in the next damn hour.

Landon doesn't look surprised to see me here, and it makes me wonder how many conversations Rick has had with him about me.

"Morning," I say stupidly as all three of us stare at each other.

"Morning," Landon replies, a small smile tugging up the corners of his mouth as he looks between Colton and me.

I can already see his mind working on ways to blackmail me with this newly discovered situation.

"This isn't—"

"This is exactly what it looks like," I counter, not wanting to make things worse with Colton trying to lie for us.

We're adults, and we can both do what we want with each other without having to worry about the sensibilities of a boy whose eyes bug out of his head anytime a female walks by. If he wants to make a bigger deal out of this than it is, I'll just bring up what a couple of the girls were talking about last night at the graduation party. Apparently, being a teenage boy and unable to control yourself in public is a very hard and embarrassing thing to struggle with.

"I didn't—"

I hold my hand up to stop Landon, and his jaw snaps closed. "Can I speak with Landon alone?"

Colton looks down at me, unease filling his dark blue eyes, and I have no idea what he's worried about. It isn't like Landon is going to hurt me or try to blackmail me, even though I'm not above offering him cold hard cash to keep his adolescent mouth closed until I'm ready to disclose this situation to my parents and every other person at the clubhouse. Lord knows once the match is lit, the information will blaze through there like flames kissing the edge of a dry field.

"Are you sure?" Colton looks at me like Landon doesn't exist, and I love that he's concerned for me.

"I'll be fine. Just need to have a little chat with my buddy." Colton nods before backing away, and until the cool air of the kitchen hits my back, I don't realize he's been plastered against me this whole time. "Don't forget the food. I know how hungry you get."

Colton snorts before wrapping his big hands around the handles of the tray and walking out of the room.

"Crazy seeing you here," Landon says after Colton's bedroom door closes.

"Don't start with me."

"What would Dominic say?" He winks. "Didn't know you had a thing for older men."

"He's not that much older than me," I argue.

"You're closer in age to Ricky than you are Colton."

I narrow my eyes at him as he crosses his arms over his chest and leans against the doorframe. What is it about men in this house doing that?

"Rick is a child. Colton isn't. So your reasoning doesn't make sense."

"I see." He nods his head as if he understands, but that little annoying smile is still on his face.

"What do you want?"

"What do you mean?"

"I guess you want something for your silence?"

His brow furrows.

"No."

"And is this you playing hardball?"

"What?"

"What. Do. You. Want?"

"For what?"

"In exchange for your silence."

He stands, growing taller than I remember him being, but the action doesn't have an imposing feel to it.

"I don't want your money or favors."

I throw my hands in the air in irritation. "Then what?"

"Nothing, Sophia. I don't want anything."

"Because nothing will keep you from running back to the clubhouse to blab?"

"Blab? I'm not a fuc—" His mouth snaps closed. "I'm not a kid. I'm not going to run off and tattle on you."

"Because you expect the same courtesy if I see you doing something wrong?"

"Who hurt you?"

"What?" The question makes me take a step back, only the counter is there, and I don't remember moving since we started talking.

"I'm not going to blackmail you. I'm not going to expect anything for my silence. This isn't my business."

"Really?" Surely he isn't that damn mature. He's only sixteen, and teens are notoriously looking for a way to benefit from every situation.

"Really. Do you know how many weekends I'm over here?"

"I have no clue." I cross my own arms over my chest because I'm feeling oddly vulnerable right now. There are a million things I don't know about Colton, and it chafes a little that this kid may know more than I do.

"A lot," he clarifies. "Not once have I walked in here and seen a smile so big on Colton's face, or a morning where he isn't shuffling to get out the door to go to work."

"Really?"

"He comes out of his room with a wide smile on his face, relaxed in sweats, and I tell you what, it looks good on him. If you're the reason he's different this morning, then I say more power to the two of you. He's an incredible man. He's an awesome dad. Rick, although he doesn't know when to shut his mouth sometimes, is one of my best friends. He's someone Mom and Dad approve of because he was raised the way we were. Do you know how hard that is to find these days? And that man raised him alone. That in itself shows his character. You could do worse than Colton Matthews."

"So you were just giving me shit about our age difference?"

Landon shrugs, and it seems like an incredibly simple action with the mature words that just came out of his mouth. "You're both adults."

"We are," I confirm.

"Do you love him?"

Jesus, talk about coming out with the big guns.

"Because I don't think he's going to let you go. He's too much like Dad, too much like Dominic. I've never seen a woman over here, just like I've never seen him look at someone the way I saw him look at you. I sure as hell hope you're in it for the long haul, because it's clear that man is."

"How are you only sixteen?"

He grins at this. "You forget my birthday is in a few weeks. Seventeen and completely legal."

"Can't vote until you're eighteen," I remind him.

He winks at me. "Legal to consent."

I don't even try to stop the chuckle that escapes my throat. The boy thinks he's God's gift to women.

"Would it be weird if I asked you about Rick?"

"Depends."

"Do I need to worry about him, like hitting on me? I don't want to come between him and his dad, but I also don't want to be uncomfortable around here either."

I expect reassurance, a quick answer, but that isn't what I get. Landon looks away, thinking about my question for a long moment before answering.

"Rick is complicated, but I can guarantee he's a hundred percent talk. If he flirts, just ignore him and he'll stop. Pretty soon, you'll figure out that he only does it when he has an audience. He's a great guy, but he feels the need to put on a show."

"He'll grow out of it." That may actually be a lie because I've met dozens of guys—adults honestly—that have never grown out of peacocking for the benefit of others.

"Hopefully."

"So, we're good here? I don't have to worry about getting plowed over the next time I go to the clubhouse?"

"Your secret is safe with me," he says.

"It's not that it's a secret. We're going to tell people, but we just have to do it in our own time."

"And I understand needing to figure things out before opening a door that may never close again."

Sadness fills his eyes, but he turns away before I can question him.

"True," I agree.

"Just be careful."

"I don't think he'll break my heart."

His eyes find mine again, the sadness still there and heartbreaking. His phone chirps with a text, but he only glances at it before finding my eyes again.

"I'm not worried about your heart. It's different getting involved with a family than dating a single guy."

"I know." And I do. It's something that has always been a consideration since finding out about Rick.

"Okay," he whispers before walking away.

He doesn't head down the hall toward Rick's room. Instead, he walks out the front door, not even saying goodbye to his friend. I have to trust that he isn't going to run off and speak about what he saw today, but that assurance doesn't calm the feelings swimming around in my gut.

Colton isn't in his bedroom when I go look for him, but I find him and Rick with their heads bent together talking. I don't know what to do. Should I interrupt them? Walk away?

Maybe this is yet another conversation I need to have with Colton. So much is happening so fast, and it's becoming almost too much to deal with at one time. My feet urge me to the front door but taking off without explaining isn't the mature way to handle things. That's done with talking and uncomfortable discussions.

I fire off a text to Izzy, wondering what happened after I left the clubhouse. It doesn't take long for her to respond that her dad is livid.

Izzy: When I told him I was pregnant, I thought he was going to blow a gasket.
Me: He'll come around.

Izzy: Maybe, I'm not so sure. He left last night pissed off and hasn't come home.

Me: Maybe he's helping with the Drew situation?

I don't believe it as I type it. Whatever is going on with Drew would be handled with closed ranks, and as much as Hound is part of the Cerberus group, he's not in the core circle which includes my dad, Uncle Diego, Rob, Jaxon and Morrison, and Dustin–Landon's dad.

Izzy: Did you hear what happened?
Me: I haven't.

Is it selfish of me for spending time with Colton rather than sticking around to get the latest news on Drew? Suddenly, I feel like an irresponsible jerk.

Izzy: I only know what I read online because no one is talking, but from what I saw, Drew went apeshit on some guy at a scene and killed him.

I can sympathize with Drew because there have been times while I was working with Colton that I wanted to bloody my knuckles on someone who had no respect for human life.

Me: Wow.
Izzy: Yeah.
Me: Did you ever meet him?

I've only ever seen Drew two or three times in the last couple years, and one of those times was during his short stay with Jaxon and Rob before his paternal grandparents came for him. They moved him to New England and I think he's only been back once since.

Izzy: Nope.

I drop my phone when the bedroom door opens, and the look in Colton's eyes tell me that he's no longer in the mood for breakfast.

I don't feel that way either. There's too much going on, too many things between us that we need to hash out. The sex has been great, amazing even, but if we want this to work between us, we need to sit down and talk it all out.

"I—can I just hold you?"

I nod my agreement, needing his touch as much as it seems he needs mine.

Chapter 27

Colton

The entire day since Sophia left has been insanely weird.

She didn't talk much after Landon left, and I can't help but wonder if he said something that made her change her mind. She let me hold her in the bed but despite our physical closeness, I could feel her pulling away.

Does people knowing about us make her uneasy?

I want to call Dominic and tell him everything, but that seems like an incredibly selfish thing to do considering everything that family is going through right now. I know Sophia isn't related by blood to Lawson and his brother, but the MC is as close as I've ever seen a biological family.

Me: Missing you already.

She left mere hours ago but the time and miles of distance seems like an eternity and worlds apart.

Maybe it's the unknown that's making me question everything that's happened. My body doesn't regret a thing. The time we spent, the ways we came together could never be a mistake, but that isn't keeping my head from jumbling everything up.

"I thought you had plans," I tell Rick as he walks into the room, collapsing beside me on the sofa.

"Canceled," he huffs, eyes straight ahead on the news playing on television.

"I thought it would take a catastrophe to cancel a teenager's plans."

"Or someone being charged with murder."

That makes me pause.

"We stayed at Aaron's house last night. Landon just found out what was going on with one of the guys linked to the club."

"I see." How do I talk to my son about this?

As a detective, I'm inclined to lean toward commending the arresting officers for being strong enough to arrest one of their own, but my experience tells me that nothing is as black-and-white as most want to believe. There are always extenuating circumstances with every case.

"Do you have any details?"

"I was hoping you'd have some."

"I don't know much. Drew O'Neil works for the state police. He responded to a call and someone ended up dead. The state police are keeping things close to the chest right now."

"Murder?"

"Technically, it's only classified as a homicide right now. It hasn't even been twenty-four hours. There's a good chance he hasn't been formally charged yet."

"Sucks," he mutters, lifting his feet to the coffee table. "Everyone has been ordered to the clubhouse. It's like they're closing ranks or something."

"I imagine the situation is rocking everyone involved."

"Landon isn't involved, and if he's the type of guy to defend a bad cop, I don't know what to think about that."

"Drew's arrest doesn't necessarily make him a bad cop."

"If he wasn't guilty, he wouldn't have been arrested."

"That's not how it works, Rick."

I've never had long conversations with my son about my job. Not only does he seem disinterested in police work, I think he's a little scared to know full details about how dangerous it can actually be.

"The police arrest on probable cause. It's up to a judge and jury to decide guilt." I turn the volume on the television down all the way. "What we know is someone is dead and someone was arrested for it. We have to wait for more details before passing judgment."

"That's nearly impossible."

"It is," I agree.

"It sucks."

"It sucks that your plans were canceled or—"

"It sucks that my best friend is going through something, and I can't be there for him."

"I'm sorry your plans were canceled, but I'm actually glad you're here."

He groans, sinking further into the sofa. "Please tell me we aren't having a sex talk."

"Not exactly." I smile at his reluctance. "I do want to talk about Sophia."

His mouth turns up in a grin, but the smile doesn't reach his eyes. There are a lot of things I know this young man needs to speak with me about. Many, I won't push the issue on because I know those conversations need to happen at his own pace, but I can't let Sophia be a subject that festers.

"How do you feel about her spending more time over here?"

He shrugs.

"I need a real answer."

"She's smoking hot, Dad. It's not exactly a hardship to have her around."

I take a deep breath, holding it in my lungs before releasing it on a whoosh. I'm not agitated or frustrated, but it's clear he's deflecting. I just have to figure out which parts are causing him concern.

"I find her extremely attractive as well."

He snorts, his eyes still focused on the television even though I know he doesn't have an ounce of interest in the evening news.

"I'm going to be spending a lot of time with her." God willing. "I need you to tell me if you start feeling neglected."

He snorts again. "Neglected? Come on, Dad. I'm nearly seventeen. I'm not going to complain about less attention. If anything, I'm going to love it."

"And that's another thing I worry about."

"I'm responsible," he grumbles.

"I know."

We haven't exactly struggled as I raised him because my parents were always around to help, but I tried my best not to lean on them too much. I've never looked at Rick like a burden or a mistake. His arrival just catapulted me into adulthood quicker than I had planned.

"This is a new situation for all of us."

"I never told you not to date."

"But the fact remains that I haven't had anything serious with a woman in a very long time. It's as new for me as it is for you."

"You've been alone too long. I just want you to be happy."

Would he find it weird if I hugged him right now? I stay sitting with my ass firmly planted on the couch, not wanting to ruin the moment.

"I'm happy when I'm with her."

"I've noticed." He chuckles, eyeing me from the side.

"I want you to know I've never been unhappy. Raising you has been my primary focus all of these years. I honestly never thought I'd get a chance at being happy with someone romantically."

It's been no secret that love and true affection weren't in the cards where his mother was concerned. I've been as honest with him as his age and maturity level allowed when he had questions. My parents don't bad mouth her, but we never put her on a pedestal she didn't earn either.

"Sophia isn't my mom," he whispers, more pain in his voice than I think he even realizes.

I can't imagine growing up without a mother, and although we haven't talked much about her in recent years, I know he feels the loss of something he can never remember having. Landon's parents are still together. So are Aaron's. He seeks out friends that have two-parent households. I like to think he does that because he was also raised in a healthy environment, not that I believe for a second that a single-parent household has a negative impact. I've proven that it can be just as healthy, sometimes healthier than sharing a life with someone who doesn't want to be there.

His mother walking away from her responsibilities is a blessing I count daily. Some people aren't meant to stick around. I'm just glad she made that decision early on instead of after he was old enough to remember her.

"I know she isn't," I answer before I spend too much time getting lost in my own head. "And I don't think she has any aspirations of bossing you around."

"A hot stepmom? Sign me up." He winks at me, and all I can do is shake my head.

"And that mess needs to stop. I don't want her uncomfortable."

"Did she say something?" He finally looks at me, frowning as he waits for my answer. "I've just been joking."

"She hasn't, and I don't think it bothers her much, but maybe stop while you're ahead?"

"Sure thing," he agrees quickly. "Is she coming over tonight?"

I look down at my dark phone, knowing if I check it again, it's not going to magically make a text appear. She hasn't responded to my text from earlier, and I'm still wondering if I played too many cards too quickly.

"Not tonight, I don't think. She's part of those people that are circling the wagons right now just like Landon."

Our conversation begins to shift, going from Sophia to Rick's last couple of weeks in school. He's a bright kid, never having really struggled with school until the last two years. He claims to have been distracted but doesn't go into detail. He assures me he's going to pass all his classes without needing summer school like last year. I make sure before he gets off the couch to go to bed that he knows how proud I am of him.

He shrugs off the praise like he always has, like he's got secrets he believes will make me change my mind.

My heart is heavy and my bed is empty by the time I lock the house down and turn off all the lights. Only the soft thump of music coming from Rick's room can be heard as I close myself in my own bedroom.

Waking up high on a cloud and going to bed filled with the unknown is draining. I check my phone one last time before lying down, deciding it's best to send her a final text telling her goodnight.

That one goes unanswered too.

Chapter 28

Sophia

A quiet house has never bothered me. A quiet clubhouse is a whole other story.

Half the team, including my mom and dad are in Albuquerque dealing with the Drew situation, and the other half of the team have a job in South America. Tensions are always high when Cerberus is out of town on a mission, but the atmosphere for most of the day before they departed was rife with stress no one was openly speaking about.

Those of us left behind know there's a lot going on, but no one seemed willing to talk about it. I learned as a child not to ask many questions, not that they would've been answered, and even as an adult, I'm left in the dark more often than not.

Izzy and I have taken up residence in the only room left empty, but even her soft breaths as she sleeps don't calm my nerves.

The text messages Colton sent draw all of my attention even with my phone dark and on the bedside table. He misses me, and I miss him, but listening to Landon tell me to be careful with him and Rick hit me in the chest like a tanker truck.

I want to think I'm doing the right thing, but I haven't stuck with anything in my life long-term except for school, and had I gotten bored, I don't know that I would've graduated.

Opening my life up to Colton means also opening up to Rick. They're a package deal, something I didn't know in the beginning when I let myself fantasize about an older man. I'm not uneasy with him having a son. You can't really expect someone to have no history, but it's the future I'm worried about.

Can I love a man who loves someone so fiercely? Would my love even compare to that or his love for me?

I'm selfish. I know that. I'm fickle. I can admit to that as well, but those two traits have no business in a relationship with a man with a child, no matter how nearly grown the young man is.

Rick will always come first, and I know that's how it should be. What I can't stop asking myself is if I'll be okay with that. Will I be okay with being the second choice? What if Rick and I don't agree on something? Will Colton side with him because it's his son, even if he's wrong?

I have a million questions, but the one thing that's keeping my eyes wide open when I should be sleeping is knowing that no matter the answers to any of them, I've fallen for that man. I can't see myself carrying on with my life without him being there with me. I don't want to walk away not knowing the kind of future we should have.

Mom always told me loving a kid was different from loving others when I asked her how she had enough love for me when she would've given all of her love to Jasmine, who is technically her half-sister. At the time, she told me something about her heart growing to hold more love, and I remember watching her as she smiled at me, Jasmine or my dad, waiting to see her chest open up to accommodate all the love that was filling her because it was always on her face, in her words, and in her actions.

As I got older, I understood what she was talking about, and how that love wasn't a physical thing, but an ability to love many people that came into my life without sacrificing those feelings for others.

Like getting hit by a lightning bolt, I sit straight up in bed. Colton could love me as much as he loves his son. It's a different love, a different spot in his chest, and I know there's room there. I love many people, and I know there's a whole section of my soul that belongs to him.

With shaking hands, I scoop up my phone, shove my feet into my sandals, and walk out of the room. I'm met with eerie silence in the living room of the clubhouse, but determination keeps my feet moving. The drive to Colton's house seems to take forever despite the fact that it's the middle of the night and hardly anyone is driving around.

The power driving me across town leaves me anxious when I pull into his driveway. All the doubts I had earlier come crashing back. I'm able to get out of the car and to his front door by sheer will alone. My feet tell me to turn and run, that if I leave now, I'll be safe. If I leave now, I won't risk my heart getting broken, I won't somehow break Colton's or Rick's heart.

My eyes are burning, tears threatening to fall when I lift my hand and knock. I know my knuckle doesn't hit the wood hard enough to wake anyone, and I think that's another subconscious way for me to say I was here and tried without actually facing him.

Then the damn door opens.

Colton stands in front of me, hair ruffled, sleep in his eyes, and his gun held down at his side.

"Soph? What are you doing here?"

He takes a step back, disappearing inside before coming back to the door empty-handed.

"Expecting trouble?" I tease, but there's no humor in my voice.

"You're trouble," he whispers, his eyes a little glazed and focused on my lips.

It would be so easy to step into him, let him make me forget about all the things I've been worried about, but the problems wouldn't disappear though. My concern would be just as viable tomorrow as they are right now. Going inside, getting another taste of him, another night in his arms will only make things worse if we don't work out. I feel a little manic standing here. My legs want to move, but at the same time, I'm rooted in place. I want to wrap my arms around him, but they hang heavily at my sides.

The tears I thought I'd be strong enough to keep from falling have begun to crest my lashes and are rolling down my cheeks.

"Please," he says, and I don't know what he wants.

The pain on his faces makes my heart clench in my chest.

"Please don't do this to me." Anguish distorts his handsome face as he takes a step back, much of his profile lost in the shadows.

"I don't know how to explain what I'm feeling." I lick at the tears flowing over my lips. "It's a crushing weight, but at the same time when I'm with you, I feel free."

I have to concentrate not to lower my eyes to my hands even though I want to look away from him. I feel more exposed than I ever have, and instinct tells me to hide.

"Is it love? Do I love you?"

He clears his throat but doesn't speak.

"Is that selfish? I don't want to hurt you or Rick. Is wanting you selfish? It would probably be easier to walk away."

"I'd be devastated if you did." He takes a step closer, his handsome blue eyes darting between mine.

"Why?" I manage.

"Because I love you, too."

"I'm terrified of what that means," I confess.

"Me too."

I want his hands on me. I want to be in his arms. I want the assurance that whatever life throws at us, we'll make it because we're stronger when we're side by side.

"You love me?" I ask, because I'll never get tired of hearing it.

"I love you."

Tingles cover every inch of my skin as butterflies take flight in my stomach.

Was all the worry for nothing? I have no doubt we'll hit snags as we traverse our new relationship, but can happiness really come this easily?

"Are you going to stand out there all night?" he asks, a glint of devious intent in his eyes.

"Is Rick home?"

"He is, but you're welcome here any time."

"I don't want to make things weird for your son."

"We spent the better part of the evening discussing you."

"And you still want me in your home?" I chuckle, trying to add some humor, but he doesn't laugh at my half attempt at a joke.

"I love you, Sophia." *Will I ever get tired of hearing him say that?* "Of course I talked with Rick. He's a part of my life, and I wanted to make sure he was aware that you're going to be a part of it too."

"He's okay with me being here?"

"More than okay. Do I have to pick you up and carry you? My bed is calling my name."

"Tired?"

He doesn't answer, and when I squeal when he steps close and picks me up, I know I've probably awoken the neighbors.

"Am I going to have to gag you?" he asks as he urges my legs around his waist so he can carry me inside.

I can't answer him because our lips crash together. With me still in his arms, he locks the front door, grabs his firearm and walks us in the direction of his room.

"Can't wait to get you naked," I breathe against his lips, his cock already thickening against my center.

"Ah! Gross. Get a room."

I stiffen at the sound of Rick at my back.

"And maybe keep the squealing to a minimum?"

Colton laughs, his head buried in my throat as Rick closes his bedroom door. Music, louder than decent at this time of night, filters out, and for a split second I feel sorry for the kid. My parents are very affectionate with each other, and I remember nights when my skin would crawl, knowing what they were doing in their room because they were being too loud.

"I'm going to buy him noise canceling headphones," I vow as Colton carries us into his room.

"He has them, but I'm sure he would appreciate the gesture."

I bounce on the bed with a squeal, covering my mouth and eyeing the front wall of the room. Rick's bedroom is across the hall, and I don't think I've even been happier about one room not sharing a wall with another in my life.

Colton deposits his gun in the bedside drawer before turning his attention back to me.

"Maybe we should just cuddle," I offer, even though my body is humming with need.

Being a responsible adult in charge of others means sometimes forfeiting what you want for what's appropriate.

"Not a fucking chance," Colton says as he shoves his sweats down his legs.

How have I only now noticed that he answered the door without a shirt? Dark chest hair calls to me, and I want to feel the soft brush of it on my lips. I didn't get enough of it last night. I don't know that I'll ever get enough of it.

"Get naked," he insists, but I watch distracted as he produces a condom and rolls it down his very eager and ready cock.

"He'll hear us," I argue, but my hands are already working open the buttons on my jeans.

"We'll be quiet."

Apparently, I'm not moving fast enough because he climbs on the bed with me, removing my shirt and staring down in awe at my tits.

"No bra?"

"I was in bed when I decided to come here," I explain, my needy fingers getting tangled in my panties in my bid to shove them down my legs.

Being the helpful guy that he is, Colton lowers his body, using his mouth to get them free.

"Oh God!" I hiss when he licks up my center on the way back up my body.

"That gag is sounding like a good idea."

"Your fault," I pant when he presses his hands into the mattress near my head and leans in to kiss me. "Shouldn't feel so good."

"I'll never touch you without bringing you pleasure."

"I can't be quiet," I warn as he lines himself up with an expert swivel of his hips.

"I'll go slow," he promises, but even as he fills me inch by slow delicate inch, I moan his name loud enough to wake the dead.

Chapter 29

Colton

"Are you sure you don't need more cheese?"

Sophia flips me the bird over her shoulder before grabbing another handful of cheese and sprinkling it over the omelet she's cooking.

Seeing her in my kitchen, although wearing more clothes than I'd like, is like a dream come true.

My throat still wants to seize at the memory of why I thought she showed up last night, and I know I'm one lucky motherfucker for it to turn into a confession of love rather than her ripping my heart out on my front porch at two in the morning.

"Eventually, you're going to have to worry about cholesterol," I warn with a smile on my face.

"Don't listen to the old man," Rick says on a yawn as he enters the room. "Not everyone is going to end up on Lipitor."

Sophia chuckles, tossing Rick a quick smile before turning back to the stove.

"Want an omelet?" she asks as she plates the one she's working on. I grin at her as she hands me the cheesy dish. "How's your life insurance?"

"Trying to get rid of me already?"

Rick watches us, his head volleying back and forth as we banter.

"Death by eggs?"

"Death by cheese," I tell her with a wink, pressing my lips to her cheek before she can step away.

I take a deliberate bite before pretending to choke and grabbing at my heart.

"Adults are weird," Rick mutters as he reaches in the fridge. "We're out of juice."

"You guzzled it all yesterday," I remind him. "It's on the list. I'll grab some this evening."

Knowing I'll forget, Rick pulls the magnetic marker from the fridge and jots it down on the list.

"Omelet?" Sophia asks again.

"Whole eggs or egg whites?"

"Whole. Unless you only want whites."

"Whole is fine," Rick says with a grin, and I already know where this is going. I didn't figure he'd test her so early on, but I guess he wouldn't be my kid if he didn't break someone in right out of the gate. "But can you dice my meat smaller? Is that ham? I prefer turkey and tiny crumbles of bacon. And make sure it only has an ounce and a half of bell peppers, and a teaspoon of onion because I don't want bad breath all day. Also, can you pick all the Colby out of that cheese blend? It doesn't fit my macros."

Sophia doesn't even look at me, her eyes darting between my son and the ingredients on the counter.

"I can leave something in or take something out. If you want to measure everything out to your specifications, I'll be happy to toss that mess in the pan when you're done."

With a hand on her hip, she watches him, waiting for his answer.

"Loads of meat, no veggies. As much cheese as you can add in."

She narrows her eyes, waiting to see if it's another test.

"Perfect," she says after a long beat.

When she turns back to the stove, he gives me a thumbs up as he walks closer.

I grin at his antics.

"Why is she cooking?" he whispers as he takes a seat at the kitchen bar to my right.

"She wanted to."

"That looks incredible." He motions his head toward my plate. "Can I have a bite?"

"No," I hiss, smacking his hand with the back of my fork when he reaches for a piece of bacon on my plate. "Wait for your own."

"She's going to spit in my food after what I just did."

"She won't," I promise, but we both keep a vigilant eye on her until she hands over his plate.

He finishes his before she can get the eggs cracked for her own.

We don't speak as we watch her cooking in our kitchen.

"You're happy," he says, breaking the silence.

"Extremely," I confirm.

"I don't mean to ruin your day." He looks up at Sophia as she sets her plate on the bar across from where we're sitting. "I imagine Sophia will be joining us for dinner?"

I tense as I watch her reaction, but since she's uninformed what Rick is talking about, she simply grins at him.

"Do you have special instructions? Maybe you want spaghetti but only with pureed sauce, and let me guess, can I pick out all the parsley because anything green doesn't fit in your macros?" She smiles around a cheesy bite of omelet.

"No. You don't have to worry about cooking anything. My grandmother prepares the entire meal."

Her eyes find mine, and she begins to choke.

I glare at my son as I rush around the bar and clap her on the back.

"You okay?" I ask when she's finally drawing in ragged breaths, and I'm certain she doesn't need the Heimlich maneuver.

"D-Dinner?" she sputters. "With your parents?"

"We go every Sunday when Dad isn't working," Rick says with an innocent smile. "They've been expecting you to show up with us for weeks."

Sophia's head swivels on her shoulders until she's glaring at me.

"What?" I back away, wondering if now would be the time to call in a priest for an exorcist. "You were here when they invited you the first time."

"I thought they were just being polite."

"My mother would never invite someone to sit down at her table if she didn't want them there."

"They saw me in your shirt," she whisper-hisses. "I was half-naked in this very kitchen. I thought they didn't want to seem rude."

Rick laughs, making the situation worse.

"I figured they invited all the women they've caught you with."

"They haven't—"

"Dad doesn't have women over." He smiles widely. "You're the first."

"The only," I clarify. "I don't bring women home."

"You only brought me home because I was drunk."

"Rick, can you go to your room?"

"I thought this was a family discussion." I could strangle this damn boy.

"You weren't drunk last night, and yet here you are," I remind her, my voice growing low, intent clear in my eyes.

What started as a mild shock about an invitation to dinner is somehow transforming into a situation that's going to turn graphic very soon.

Rick clears his throat, giving us both a wide berth as he places his plate in the sink. He thanks Sophia for breakfast before hauling ass out of the kitchen.

"You don't look like you want to discuss dinner any longer."

"Was that the goal? You know I like it when you argue with me."

"You do?"

Okay, maybe she didn't know, but the tent in my sweats is physical proof of my words.

"Are you saying you don't want to join us? I'm not going to force you, but I'd like to have you there."

"You don't think that's moving too fast?"

"They wanted you there weeks ago. I wanted you there weeks ago. Things aren't moving fast enough if you ask me."

"Really?"

"My parents were very impressed with you."

"They spent less than an hour with me, and they grilled me the entire time."

"The inquisition will only continue if you join us this evening."

"Are you trying to deter me from going?"

"I don't want you blindsided."

"Don't you think it's weird? You haven't met my parents."

"I met your parents at the grocery store the night I cornered you at the bar."

My cock thickens even further at the memory of being pressed against her, my drunken confessions slipping past loose lips.

"You don't think it will be weird?"

"It's been weird for weeks," I tell her truthfully. "They ask about you every Sunday. Mom won't shut up about it."

"I'd like to go, if you're okay with it."

"I want you there," I whisper against her lips, my fingers tangling in the oversized t-shirt of mine she insisted on wearing before we left my room earlier.

"I don't have anything to wear. I'll need to go home to change."

"You can wear what you have on."

"Not funny." She smacks my chest her hand lingering over my heart.

"It wouldn't be the first time they saw you in my clothes."

She tweaks my nipple, finding it shockingly quickly over my own shirt.

I hiss in pain but don't release her. "Too soon?"

"Are you sure they don't want me over there just to try to run me off?"

"I'm certain. They wouldn't tell me they liked you if they didn't. My parents aren't fake people. They speak their minds, and this time when talking about you, it was something I needed to listen to."

"Are you telling me your parents helped you decide to be with me?"

"They encouraged it, but I knew it was inevitable. Walking away while loving you wasn't ever going to happen."

"Is that so?"

She grins, her gorgeous eyes sparkling the way they have every time I've confessed my feelings for her.

"I'm going to be a nervous wreck."

"I know a way to solve that problem before we even leave the house."

With my words, she takes several steps back, making my arms fall to my sides.

"Nope."

"What do you mean, nope?"

She holds her hands up when I reach for her again. I look around the room, making sure my son isn't creeping around since teens are so damn light on their feet these days.

"I know the perfect way to relax you before spending several hours with my parents."

"Is it yoga?" I shake my head as she backs further away from me. "Is it a nap?"

"It's orgasms," I offer, instead of her wasting another minute with ridiculous guesses.

"Tempting." She smiles as she taps her finger over her lips, but I can tell by the shifty way she's acting that it isn't going to happen.

"We can nap," I offer.

"And you won't try anything when we lie down in the bed?"

Finally having backed up enough, I have her caged to the countertop with my hips. The steel rod in my sweats answers for me.

"I don't think it'll work."

"Only one way to find out."

"We should nap on the couch."

"We aren't napping." I fling her over my shoulder, delighted in her squeal. Thankfully, Rick doesn't come out of his room this time as I carry her down the hall. Come to find out it takes orgasms *and* a nap to get her fully relaxed.

Chapter 30

Sophia

"You promised you were relaxed."

I refuse to look over at Colton on the drive to his parents' house.

"I was," I hiss, my fingers tangling in my lap. "I look ridiculous."

Thankfully, Rick decided to drive himself earlier so he's not a witness to me freaking out.

"You're adorable."

"I shouldn't be adorable. You're like twenty years older than me. I should look refined."

"Baby, I don't want you to ever look refined, and there's less than thirteen years between us."

I can't even bask in the sentiment of his words because I'm sitting in the passenger seat of the truck wearing a pair of Rick's athletic leggings and a baggy t-shirt.

"Just swing by my house."

"We're already late."

"That's your fault."

He chuckles. "You're the greedy one."

"I didn't know I had to choose."

The fact is I was exhausted after the orgasms and the nap was a necessity. What I didn't think to do was set an alarm giving me enough time to get home and get changed.

"I smell like you," I hiss, lifting the shirt to my nose. "Your mom is going to know what we've been doing."

"You're an adult."

"Doesn't make it any less embarrassing. Is she going to question why I'm wearing Rick's clothes or why my skin smells like you?" I swivel my head in his direction, and I don't think the vibrant smile on his face has waned in hours.

"My parents know I have sex, Sophia."

I wish I could say the same thing. "Mine don't."

The truck jerks, his foot sliding off the gas and hitting the brakes.

"Yeah, I mean go ahead and live it up. It's a big joke that I'm going to dinner with your parents mere hours after screaming your name while coming on your face. At least they know you have sex, seeing as you have a son and all." My smile turns teasing to something akin to devilry. "My dad probably still thinks I'm a virgin, but don't worry, I'll make sure you're nice and relaxed before we sit down to a meal with him."

He doesn't find my wink comical.

"Wait," he says as I reach for the door handle when he pulls up outside of a lovely one-story home with light blue shutters, and flower boxes on the windows.

"What are you saying?"

"You'll be the first guy I bring home." Maybe my shrug is a little dismissive of the situation, but this man normally has nerves of steel. Is he anxious about meeting my father as more than my internship training officer?

Instead of looking at me, his eyes settle on Rick's truck parked in front of the house.

"They're going to get suspicious if we just keep sitting out here."

"You weren't a virgin."

"Neither were you."

"Your dad didn't meet the man you gave that to?"

I cringe. "Yeah, that's a no. I barely knew him. No way I'd bring him home."

"Oh."

Is that disappointment?

"Look, we both have histories, but I'm not going to sit here and let you think I'm some innocent girl without experience. I mean, I don't have twenty years' worth like some people." I side-eye him, hoping he'll take the jab as a joke. "I haven't taken guys home because I haven't ever found a man worth the trouble until you."

"Trouble?"

"Do you really think that my dad is just going to smile at you, shake your hand, and welcome you into his home?"

"That's what my parents are going to do for you."

He frowns when the shifting of the front curtains draws both of our attention.

"My dad is different. I think being a father to girls is different. Combine that with twenty years in the Marine Corps and another twenty-plus years working for Cerberus, and he's not the most trusting man, especially when it comes to his girls. Max and Tug still get stared down on occasion by him, and they've vowed to cherish her until the day they die. He did, however, invite you to the graduation party—"

"Because he didn't know I wanted to blow my load on your perfect tits," he mutters.

"Don't bring that up during the first dinner with him, and maybe you'll survive to see another day. But my point is, he respects you. If he didn't, he wouldn't have extended the invitation."

"It wasn't the first time I went to the clubhouse."

"I know." I grin, remembering seeing him there months and months ago. His handsome face and that badge on his hip made me grateful I'd gone against my parents' wishes and started working on a degree in criminal justice because it led to the opportunity to do the internship with him. "I saw your handsome face and tight ass last year while you were working Simone Murphy's case. That's the day I decided I wanted to work at the police department for my internship."

He grins, the thoughts of trouble with my dad falling away. "No kidding?"

"I had fantasies about you long before walking into your office that day."

"You're worried about what my parents will think of your clothes." His fingers brush down my face, folding my bottom lip down in the most seductive way. "How are we going to explain my rock-hard cock?"

"Whatever takes the pressure off of me." I press a quick kiss to his lips and hop out of the truck before he can grab me and demand more of my mouth.

"You're playing with fire," he hisses as he catches up to me at the front of the truck.

In a second flat, my back presses to the grill of his truck, the heat from the engine running combined with the bright May sun nearly enough to make me squirm.

"Am I?" I tease.

His fingers tangle in my hair, hips pressed against mine. Damn, this man makes me forget my head.

"Do I need to turn the hose on you two?"

I freeze, my cheeks heating at the baritone voice coming from the front porch.

"They kept me up all night last night," Rick says from somewhere inside.

My eyes widen as I look up at Colton. "I'm going to kill your son."

"I'll help you hide the body," he mutters, adjusting himself with one hand as much as he can while clasping mine with the other.

Mrs. Matthews chuckles, and his dad winks at me as we walk up.

"Ah, young love. I remember those days." I don't deny her words as I step closer. Her arms are out, and I know I won't be able to get out of a hug. I allow this woman, who has only met me once, to wrap her arms around me, and other than my own parents, it may possibly be the best hug I've ever had.

"I'm so glad you're here," she tells me, turning in my arms and keeping her arm around my waist. "I hope you like chicken fried steak."

"Good to see you, too, Mom," Colton mutters as he walks in behind us.

"She's just giving you a minute to calm yourself, son," I hear his dad say, and my cheeks heat even more.

"You have a lovely home, Mrs. Matthews."

"Sally, please, and it would be lovelier if I could get these young men in my life over to repaint the front porch. I asked ages ago, but I doubt it'll ever get done."

"You asked last week, Mom, and the paint you insisted I get is on backorder. Don't try to make me sound like a jerk in front of my girlfriend."

I bite the inside of my lip to keep from reacting. I want to laugh at the easy banter between him and his parents. Even Rick seems comfortable enough to joke around with them. I also want to squeal and jump into his arms for calling me his girlfriend in front of them.

"I'll let it slide this time," Sally says as she directs me to take a seat in the living room. "So, it's official?"

"Official?" Colton asks confused. Bless his nearly geriatric heart.

"They haven't posted it on Facebook or anything yet," Rick mutters.

"I don't have Facebook." Colton looks at me. "Do you?"

"Are you telling me you don't know?" I tease back.

If he's wanted me as long as he claims, then I know he's looked, probably more than once just to be sure.

"We don't have Facebook," Colton confirms. "But yes, we're together."

His mother releases the squeal I was able to hold on to.

"They kept me up—"

"You'll clean the gutters," Colton threatens, and comically Rick slams his mouth shut, winking at me much the same teasingly way his grandad did on my walk of shame up the sidewalk.

"No social media?" Sally asks, and I shake my head. "At all? Even I like to get lost in a little *Tik Tok* every now and then."

"You mean you like to watch half-naked men swing their junk around in gray sweats," Mr. Matthews corrects.

Sally waves her hand dismissively at her husband as Rick scrunches his nose as he pulls out his phone.

"What are you doing?" Colton asks, making me wonder if they have a no-electronics rule on Sundays. This is just another question I need to ask. Honestly, I need to start writing them down because I get distracted while we're alone and they're really starting to pile up.

"Making my accounts private."

"If you're making obscene—"

"Dad," Rick groans. "I'm not. Stop."

Both of the grandparents laugh, and I feel bad for the kid with all the adults in his life picking on him, but then I remember the stunt he pulled with the omelets at breakfast and I realize very quickly he came by it naturally.

My fear of being around his family fades quickly.

"Not even Instagram?" Sally asks, still fixated that I'm a woman in my twenties and not spending hours a day on social media platforms.

"Nope. According to my dad, they're one of the easiest ways to hack your information. It's hard to keep secrets when you practically sign your life away through a company's terms of service without even reading them."

Rick drops his phone in disgust causing everyone in the room to laugh.

"Got something to hide, Ricky?"

Rick isn't laughing as he ignore his grandfather's question.

"And you're related to Diego, the man that runs the Cerberus MC?"

"He's my uncle."

"And that makes Dominic—"

"My dad."

I give both of them a weak smile. We didn't talk about much else other than school that first time I met them. It seems they're diving in deeper this time around, and although Colton warned me they would, it doesn't make it any easier to sit here and answer the questions as they're rapid fired at me.

"Incredible men," Mr. Matthews says with a little awe in his voice.

"Incredible women," Sally adds. "Emmalyn and Khloe both took classes with me when I first started teaching at the community college."

"Small world," I manage.

Maybe Landon isn't the only one I have to worry about spilling the beans. I have to be concerned about everyone who knows about me and Colton slipping up and mentioning it to any one of the thirty or so people I know closely linked to the club. We're going to have to make a game plan to talk to my parents quickly because this isn't going to stay off the radar for much longer.

The conversation comes easy, and just as Colton said, his parents really seem to like me, not that I've ever had a problem with people disliking me, but their approval means the world. I couldn't imagine being in a relationship that the people closest to him didn't agree with. It gets us one step closer to fully being together, and as much of a hard time as I give Colton about my dad, I know he'll be okay with us being together. It may not happen instantaneously, but eventually he'll be able to tell how much I love this man, and he'll come around.

Chapter 31

Colton

"Yes, I can," Sophia says, her lips turning down in a frown that makes me want to kiss it away.

She a temptress of the greatest extremes. There haven't been many days I didn't get out of bed ready to head to the station. My job, although heartbreaking at times, serves a purpose. Rick and that purpose is what has driven me for as long as I can remember.

But now there's a naked woman in my bed, tempting me to stay home and make good on the promises we've whispered over and over to each other this weekend.

"You can't," I argue. "You signed the same damn paperwork I did. There's a no fraternization policy in place."

"It's stupid."

"It's supposed to make things safer at work, less drama." I pull an undershirt over my head, loving the way she seems disappointed with each article I cover my body with. "And before you argue about no one knowing, Monahan already suspects something is going on."

"Does he not know about what's going on with the two women in dispatch?"

"I don't know, but you coming to work with me isn't possible, and it's a bad idea even if the policy wasn't in place."

"Have a hard time concentrating?"

"You know I do. I don't know how I got anything done the last couple of months with you around."

Her mouth hangs open, disbelief on her face. "I'm a professional. I think I can go to work with you and keep my hands to myself for a couple hours."

"I can't say the same," I mutter, reaching into the closet for a pair of slacks. This makes her happy, and I love everything about the grin spreading across her face. "I think we'd spend the day either locked away in my office or down some dark alley."

"I can't even tell you the number of times I pictured myself riding you in the car."

"And saying shit like that is why I'm going to be late for work."

I'm hard as stone, but that's not a new thing around her. Leaving for work knowing she's here, naked between my sheets, is what's causing the problem today.

"You can't blame me. I'm not doing anything to keep you here."

She moans a low throaty sound, and my hand freezes on my zipper.

"What are you doing?"

"Nothing." The sheets move the smallest fraction.

"Where are your hands?"

Rolling her lips between her teeth, she shrugs. "Don't mind me."

"Sophia," I warn, gripping the edge of the comforter and tugging on it slowly.

I'm in complete awe of her gorgeous body, of every sexy inch that's revealed. She doesn't stop what she's doing, the sheet finally pulling away to expose her fingers working over her delicate flesh.

"It feels so good," she whispers.

"Yeah?"

She nods. "Do you like what you see?"

"Fucking love it." My mouth is dry, and I can think of one way to moisten my lips, but getting an inch closer to her would mean explaining my tardiness to my superiors. "Dip them inside."

She does, and the slickness of her arousal makes me ache.

"Jesus, that's perfect. So pink."

"Swollen. I'm so tight, so sensitive from the last couple of days."

"Sore?"

"Tender in the most delicious way."

I lick at my dry lips, reaching into my boxers and stroking my cock. I may not have time to taste her or slide my cock inside of her, but I won't get a damn thing done if I don't take care of myself.

"Let me see," she begs.

The pleading tone of her voice makes my balls tighten, the threat of release imminent. I pull my cock out, my hand working the length of it with expert strokes.

"Small, soft circles," I whisper. "Imagine it's my tongue. God, I love seeing you like this."

She whimpers, obeying my words even though I know she wants to be rougher. My girl likes it hard and fast, and most days that would work for me too, but this morning I want her to burn with the same desperation I'm going to feel the entire time we're apart today.

"Are you close?" Her eyes focus on my working hand. She doesn't answer, but I've become an expert on reading her body these last couple of days. Her stomach muscles flutter, breasts tipped with hard points, and her breath is coming out in short, labored bursts. "I'm going to come so fucking hard."

And it's true, but I'm waiting for her, needing her to tip over the edge before I allow the same relief for myself.

"Colton," she sighs, and I'm fucking done.

Her fingers move faster, her thighs tensing as her eyes flutter closed.

"Watch," I hiss as I take a few steps closer to the bed.

I paint stripes of cum over her bare stomach, groaning with soul-deep pleasure at the way I mark her skin.

Her teeth dig into her lower lip as she pulls her trembling fingers from her pussy, swirling the glistening tips in the mess I made of her.

"Put them in your mou—"

I don't even have to utter the words because her hand is already moving, eyes lighting up with mischievousness as she licks us both away.

"This is going to be the longest day of my life," I complain as I tuck myself away, my hand finally managing to get the zipper all the way up this time. I already know the hours between now and getting back to her are going to drag.

"Are you going to kiss me goodbye?" Her still sleepy face looks up at me.

I couldn't walk away from her right now if I had a gun pointed at my head, so I bend at the waist, groaning at the taste of us on her tongue. It seems filthy and scandalous, but somehow perfect all at the same time. Is this what perfection looks like?

Like I haven't been laid in years, my cock threatens to harden with a jerk.

I cup her cheek, locking my eyes with her when I pull back a few inches.

"I love you."

"I love you, too." The four words aren't just a confession. They sound like a promise, and that's what I'll take when I leave. That's what will make me hold steady throughout the day.

"I won't linger too long, but I'm going to get a shower before I leave."

"I want you here."

"I'll be here when you get back, but I have to go home and get clothes. Maybe pack a bag if you want me to stay over again."

Would it be too soon to tell her I never want her to leave, that lying in this bed even one night alone would be a nightmare?

"I want you here. I want your clothes in the closet, your soaps and bodywash cluttering the bathroom. I want you marking my space and making it your own."

She angles her head to take my lips again.

"We need to talk about how we're going to tell my dad. A couple of nights away from home is one thing, but practically moving in without speaking to him wouldn't end well."

My parents know about us and telling them was no big deal to me, so I don't really understand why my heart kicks so hard at thoughts of telling her dad.

"We have a lot to talk about," I confirm. "This evening?"

She nods. "I'll be here when you get off work."

"There's a spare key hanging on the rack in the kitchen. Rick probably won't get home until after me. He hangs out with friends right after school."

"I'll make sure I'm fully clothed just in case."

I want to ease her mind about my son, but since he hasn't opened up to me about what's going on in his life, it feels like a violation to speak about those things with others.

With one more press of my mouth to hers, I say my goodbyes, my legs heavy as I leave her in my bed.

I make it out the front door and into my truck by sheer will alone, keeping my eyes out the front windshield instead of glancing back at my home.

I'm only going to work, but it's getting back to that part of my life without her that's a struggle. Not to mention the strange feeling I have in my gut that things are going to change soon. Realistically I know they will, but the acid burning deep inside of me feels like a warning that those changes may not be for the best.

I'm not able to hyperfocus on conversations we'll have this evening because I get called out mere minutes after settling behind my desk to check emails.

After clearing the scene—another overdose—I'm able to fire off a few texts to Sophia. It doesn't take long for things to turn sexual, and I'm praying as I look down at a picture of her naked breasts that this never changes. I hope we're just as hot for each other in ten years as we are now.

I explain I have to work and she's making that nearly impossible with images of her perfect tits on my phone, but that doesn't stop the disappointment I feel when she stops texting back.

Chapter 32

Sophia

Being alone in his house should be weird. Nothing is familiar except the scent of our skin on his sheets, but I find that I'm comfortable here. It's not like visiting a distant relative and worrying about being caught looking too long at something that doesn't belong to me.

I don't worry about getting in trouble for picking up and inspecting the framed pictures on the mantel, but I do make a mental note to get more of Rick and Colton together. Like I imagine any busy, single father would, the pictures are more plentiful when Rick was younger, tapering down as he got older. They need more physical proof of their lives, and that's one thing I know I can help with.

I grin at the most recent picture, one of Sally and Franklin with Colton and Rick. Rick doesn't look pleased to be in what can only be described as an ugly Christmas sweater, but what makes it hilarious is the fact that they're all wearing the same one, the only difference being the bow on Sally's wool reindeer head.

What makes it perfect is that we have a picture almost identical to this at my house, only it's my dad with discomfort-filled eyes. As a career Marine in matching footie pajamas, I think he was a very good sport, but there's seldom a time when he tells Mom no if she has an idea.

I could walk around this house all day long and learn a million things about the men that live here, but I also have a ton of things to get done if I want to be back by the time Colton gets off work. I don't want to miss a single second with him.

I can't fully regret the nap I took after my shower because the bed was too inviting to pass up. Colton didn't seem disappointed with the pictures I sent to him either. My dad would lock me away if he found out I sent digital images. I know Colton wouldn't share them, but there's always the risk of someone else getting their hands on his phone.

My nipples bead against the soft t-shirt I'm wearing, reminding me that I still need to get clothes from home as well as check on Izzy. Her entire world has been turned upside down, and I know she was still working out a way to tell her dad about the baby when her truth was spilled long before she was ready.

Keeping on the t-shirt and sweats I took from Colton's drawer, I slide my feet back into my sandals. I start a running list in my mind for all the things I need to grab. Colton may regret offering up closet space after I return. If this is where we both want me to be, then I'm going to need some comforts from home. I grin as I grab the spare key from the kitchen and swirl it on to my own key chain. I wonder how he's going to feel about my fluffy robe and the worn slippers I like to wear on the weekends. I add long pajamas to my list, remembering that there's someone else in this house besides my guy.

I'm light on my feet, filled with utter happiness when I open the front door, only to have that elation blasted away when a masked man grips my face in a gloved hand and shoves me back inside.

I falter. Even after all the training and conversations I had growing up about what to do, my mind can't decide whether to run or stay and fight. Either option seems viable, so why do I just stumble back in shock, as if the masked man will lift the bottom of the mask and reveal himself as Colton.

I know it isn't him in the split second my brain tries to catch up to the situation. He doesn't smell the same. This man's build is smaller in size and rounder in the middle.

I can evaluate all of that, but as I fall on my ass in the entryway, crying out from the pain the impact causes in my tailbone, I still haven't figured out what to do next.

"Please don't hurt me."

I scurry back, my fingers not keeping up with my legs, which makes me land flat on my back, head bouncing off the hard wood under me.

Oh Jesus. Being on the ground is the worst position to be in. He's not as big as Colton, but he's still bigger than me, and basic physics say that he can overpower me easily.

He's going to rape me. It's the very first thought that hits me in the chest as he slams the front door closed and stands over me. The sound echoes around me making me realize I lost the opportunity to scream for help. I attempt to anyway, throwing my head back and yelling at the top of my lungs.

It doesn't take long for him to swing out, clocking me in the cheek to shut me up. Fire burns my face with the hit, my hands instinctively reaching up to cover the wound.

"Shut the fuck up, bitch," he seethes, spittle falling from his lips onto my face.

I kick and scream, bite and claw at him when he picks me up off the ground with a tight grip on my shoulders, and I want to berate myself for worrying about the bruises he's going to leave behind when I know things are probably going to get much, much worse.

I'm thrashing in his arms, unable to hear his threats as he drags me into the kitchen. I try to stomp his foot and get my leg high enough to kick him the balls. I know there's a good chance I'm going to die today, many home invasions end exactly like that, but being raped and then dying seems like too much to go through. If I can hurt that part of him, maybe the death will be quick. At this point, it's the best I can hope for.

It's mid-afternoon, and Colton won't be home for hours. According to him, Rick won't be home until even later, and I see that as a blessing, praying that Colton comes home before his son. I don't want Rick walking in to discover what this man has done to me. No child should have to live with those images in their head.

Tears leak down my cheeks as I'm thrown into a dining room chair with little care.

"Enough," he hisses, producing a length of rope from his pocket. "Keep that shit up and I'll slit your fucking throat."

The threat is enough to make me freeze, even though I know the outcome will still be dire. Maybe talking some sense into him will help, although deep down I know this man came here on a mission, and trying to reason with someone who is brave enough to break into a detective's house isn't going to work.

"This is a cop's house," I say, hoping that maybe it was chosen at random and the threat of extra vigilance at catching him will be enough to get him to leave.

"I fucking know that." My skin burns under the rope as he ties my hands behind the chair. "Detective Colton Matthews is the whole reason I'm here."

"Kincaid is my uncle."

His eyes find mine, a knowing look in the bloodshot depths.

"That so?"

I nod, allowing myself hope that the threat of my family will be enough to make him walk right back out of here.

"I bet they'd be willing to do just about anything to see you safely out of this?"

I swallow, my mouth going so dry, my lips begin to ache.

"Wh-What do you want from Colton?"

"I ask the fucking questions." He hits me again right over the same spot the first blow landed, and it makes my vision go blurry.

I want to sob. I want to hang my head and beg for my life. I want Colton to have never left for work because I know without a doubt that I wouldn't be sitting here in pain. He'd keep me safe. He'd give his own life to protect mine.

And that makes me pause because he has a son. Rick needs his father. Surviving without me is possible, losing that kid isn't.

My spine stiffens, resolve making me as brave as possible in this situation.

"When does he get off work?"

I keep my mouth closed.

"How many guns does he have in the house?"

I still refuse to answer him, squeezing my eyes closed and flinching when he lifts his hand to hit me again. The blow doesn't come, and when I open my eyes, I see him pacing back and forth in the entryway, hands tugging at the top of the ski mask like he wants to pull it off.

He mumbles to himself, but his words are too low for me to understand. I would bet money that this man is either mentally unstable—I mean you kind of have to be to break into someone's house—or he's on drugs.

The latter is confirmed when he pulls a baggie from his pocket before bending over the dining room table. With a dirty card he pulls from his wallet, the man cuts lines of what looks like cocaine before snorting them one after the other.

Now, I don't have any experience with drugs, but four lines in less than a minute seems a little extreme. Is he revving himself up to hurt me more? Is he trying to distance himself from the acts he's about to commit?

As he pours more powder on the table, my entire body begins to tremble uncontrollably. The best outcome would be that he overdoses before Colton gets home. I could handle looking at him seizing on the floor and foaming out of his mouth. The compassion and circumstances Colton reminded me to always be cognizant of while working a case are nowhere to be found in my current situation. I don't care what this man has been through. I don't care who hurt him or what injustices he thinks he's owed retribution for. I know he's here because of a case Colton worked. That was clear when he admitted to knowing whose house this was with Colton's full name and position with the police department.

It's retaliation, and I'm caught right in the damn middle. If I do survive this, I can't see this being a winning point to get my parents over to the side of accepting that we're together.

After he's done snorting the powder, he pulls a disgusting bandana from his pocket, wrapping it around my face and forcing my mouth to open up around it before he ties it at the base of my skull. I fight him as much as I can, but the combativeness is futile. The fabric is tight inside my mouth making my jaw ache almost instantly.

The drugs only make the man pace faster, his movements jerky as frustrated hands swing around.

I'm trying to convince myself that things could be a lot worse when the front doorknob turns. The masked man produces a gun I didn't know he had and points it in that direction.

My heart sinks when Rick and Landon step into the house. Terror fills their eyes, but neither turns to run. A look of defiance crosses Landon's young face when he spots me tied up across the room, and I just know that it's going to be that stubbornness that's going to get him hurt.

Chapter 33

Colton

Today has been the longest day in history. Three calls, endless paperwork, and more than one patrol officer asking about Sophia kept my body busy, but my mind has managed to stay at home with her.

My cock is rock hard with anticipation from her texts, my fingers twitching to smack her perfect little ass for not responding to my last four texts as I pull into the driveway.

She didn't message back when I let her know I was going to be later than I'd originally promised before leaving this morning, and I'm nearly certain the burgers I picked up for us on the way home will get cold on the counter while I spend an hour or so showing her just how much I missed her.

My hand lingers on the door handle inside my truck when I look at the front of my house. It's dark outside already, and my front porch light isn't on. There's no warm glow making the front of my home inviting, and the sight of darkness at my door makes my pulse ramp up. The light is always on. I never wanted Rick to come home to darkness, plus it's a safety feature. As a cop, I also know the porch light is often dismantled by criminals. Common courtesy makes people open their front door when someone knocks, and that invitation into a home goes up when the person inside can't see who is ringing the doorbell, despite knowing it could end badly.

Fear begins to swallow all reasoning as I climb out of the truck, making sure to close the door without making a sound. I feel like a fool as I creep along the side of my house but instinct tells me something is off. Sophia's car is in the driveway, and Rick's is right behind it, which forced me to park a ways up the street.

I hope to look inside and get a good laugh. Maybe the bulb I installed a few months ago was bad, and it burned out too fast. Crazier things have happened.

But I can't take that chance. Dread washes over me when I peek through the curtains outside of the dining room. Sophia, tied to a chair and gagged, has fat tears rolling down bruised cheeks as her eyes dart across the room. Someone has hurt her. I left her here in my home where I thought she was safe, and she's been hurt. Anger laced with fear makes me sweep my eyes down her body. She's clothed, but there's no telling what hell she's been put through or how long she's been at the mercy of those wanting to cause her harm.

My world implodes even more when I see that Rick and Landon are also tied side by side on the floor near her feet. All eyes are across the room, but I can't see who the perpetrator is.

I'm unable to categorize the violation I feel knowing that someone is in my house hurting the people I love most in this world. My hands itch to pull my gun from the holster and blow the motherfucker away, but instinct keeps me moving to get more information. I need to know who is inside and how many people there could possibly be.

Because I'm obsessed with safety and privacy, there isn't another window in the house that leads to more information. Every curtain is pulled tightly closed, and even though I can see one shadow pacing back and forth, I can't be certain that there aren't others inside. I'm forced to head back to my truck, my hands trembling with helplessness as I reach for my phone.

I immediately turn the thing to vibrate because I don't want a call or text to notify those in the house if I go back to the window.

Before I can pull up Monahan's contact information, the damn thing rings in my hand.

"Hello," I answer with hope. "Dominic?"

"Sophia isn't answering her phone."

All hope that he may know about this situation fades away.

"She's ah—"

"Do you know where she is?"

I don't have time to work through why he would be calling me to find her. I don't think that Sophia would've had that conversation without me, but it doesn't matter right now.

"She's at my house—"

"That so?"

"Listen, I'm not going into that right now. There's an assailant holding her, my son, and Landon Andrews hostage. Well, fuck. I don't know if it's a hostage situation, but I just got home and all three are tied up."

"Excuse me?"

"I don't know how many or why they're here, but I need help."

I can hear activity on the other end of the line, and after a few muffled words, it sounds like a herd of elephants moving. The thundering sound reignites the hope that had so easily faded away moments ago.

"Can you get a visual on them?"

"I can't see who has her. I can tell at least one guy is inside, but that's it."

"I need fifteen minutes," Dominic says before he grunts out more commands to those around him.

"I don't have fucking fifteen minutes. I can't risk them being hurt."

"My fucking daughter is in that goddamned house. You'll give me fifteen fucking minutes before you go in there half-cocked and getting someone killed."

"Did you miss the part where my son is trapped inside as well?" I seethe. "I would never do anything to put any of them in danger."

"Fifteen minutes," he grunts before the line goes dead.

My fingers move over the screen of my phone, and thankfully Monahan answers on the first ring. He listens to all the information I have with a calmness I wish I could possess before telling me he's going to get SWAT here as soon as he can. He gives me the same instruction to stand down that Dominic did, and it makes me want to spit fire.

Although I've had training, we haven't had many hostage situations in my time with the police department. Most situations even close to this, the victims are already dead, and we're tasked with getting the perp out alive. Nine times out of ten they either end with suicide or forcing an officer's hand to shoot them.

Knowing the statistics makes it even harder to stand in the street doing nothing.

Dominic somehow manages to make it with his team in ten minutes, and I'm in awe of them as they walk up stealthily in full combat gear. At the police department, we move as quickly as possible but it's clear they're an efficient group.

I don't question the tactical weapons strapped to their chests, but I want to curl in on myself with the way Dominic is looking at me. I've only seen the man a couple of times in person, but it doesn't take an expert to recognize the disappointment in his eyes.

"Only one?" Dominic asks as he steps in beside me, his eyes darting to the house like he can't stand the sight of me.

"That I could see."

Dominic makes a quick hand gesture and a bearded man darts off toward the house. I want to yell, to make the man stop in his tracks. I can't stand and watch as someone else takes a risk that will make my world crumble around me, but the man beside me clamps a hand on my shoulder before I can move.

"There isn't a better sharpshooter within a thousand miles. Let Shadow work."

I feel impotent, utterly helpless as we wait, but long minutes go by without a sound. There's no gunshot. There's no screaming coming from inside. Only the sound of the wind blowing through nearby trees and an occasional dog bark interrupts the atmosphere around us.

"Were there injuries? Could you see all of them?"

I turn to look at Dustin "Kid" Andrews, and although I know he's feeling the same riot of emotions threatening to drag me to my knees on the asphalt, he seems put together and confident in his buddy's ability to save those inside. I wish I shared his certainty.

"I could see Sophia and the boys. They're tied up. She's gagged. She's got bruises on her face like she's been hit, but I didn't see any of that on the boys." I keep my eyes on Dustin instead of turning my attention to Dominic when I continue, "She's been there since I left this morning. The boys wouldn't have gotten there until after school got out. I don't know if they came straight here."

"They did," Dustin confirms, and I focus on his news rather than the growl that emits from deep in Dominic's chest. "I tracked Landon here just before four."

It doesn't surprise me that he would keep that close of tabs on his kid, but knowing Sophia could've been in this house alone with him for hours makes my gut turn sour.

"She texted me just after one. She hasn't texted me since."

"Did her text seem unusual?"

I look back to Dominic.

"No."

"What was the text?"

I take a step back, wondering if he's willing to wrestle my phone from me. I'm in no position to make my confessions now, and I'd never betray Sophia's trust. She wouldn't want her father digging through our text thread.

"She wasn't upset. There was no hidden message. If I thought for a minute there was danger, I would've been here sooner," I explain, hoping he takes it at face value.

She did stop texting me abruptly, but that was only after I insisted I needed to work without distractions. I'll know better next time. If there is a next time.

"One guy," Shadow says, coming back without me noticing. "He along with all three captives are in the east side of the home. There's enough of a crack in the curtains that I can get a shot."

Why the fuck didn't he do it before coming back? Every second they spend inside increases the chances for any one of them to be hurt.

"Go," I urge with a hiss. "Do it."

"We have to wait—thank fuck. Finally."

We watch as the SWAT team pulls up down the street. Monahan isn't far behind in his personal SUV.

I stand to the side as my Chief discusses the situation with Dominic and his men.

"We can't respond the same way we normally would." I jolt at the sound of Dustin's voice beside me. "It's taking everything I have not to run in there, guns blazing and take that fucker down, but I know this situation will be remedied very quickly. They're all going to be okay."

I open my mouth to ask what level of okay he's talking about because alive and okay are two different things. There's no telling the trauma those three have already endured, and we're all out here standing around and doing nothing.

"My guys are all mic'd up. Shadow can let you know what frequency," Dominic says, standing near Monahan as the department's team waits for instruction.

"We need to open a line of communication. We may be able to settle this without bloodshed if we know what he wants."

"We don't even know who it is," I spit, my legs telling me to take care of this shit myself.

"That's why you need to call. I bet he'll pick up if he sees it's you," Monahan assures me.

"Since they're all in danger because of you," Dominic adds, and I know without a doubt, this man will never be happy with me being with his daughter.

And it may not even matter how he feels. I don't see Sophia walking out of that house and into my arms. She's going to blame me as much as her father is.

Chapter 34

Sophia

"Your family?" the guy spits into my phone. "I don't give a shit about your fucking family!"

It's been ringing and beeping with texts for hours, but he didn't answer it until now. He ran out of drugs over thirty minutes ago, and his level of agitation has tripled. Thankfully, he hasn't hit me again, but he was rough when tying up the guys.

I want to reassure them they'll be okay, but I can't muster enough energy for the lie. The gag in my mouth prevents me from speaking, so I opt to look at them, hoping my eyes tell them not to worry.

I watch as a tear rolls down Landon's cheek, the gag in his mouth catching the liquid. Rick leans in closer to him, resting his head on his shoulder, and even though we're living through hell right now, I can appreciate the closeness they share. I look away, not wanting to violate their moment, but the only other thing to look at is the angry man who's yelling into my phone.

He's either talking to Colton or my dad. Either would be a mistake to piss off, but knowing that someone knows that we're in here brings a sense of relief, although I can't help but wonder if it's a false security. Either man would gladly die to make sure we're safe. I pray that whoever it is keeps a calm head on their shoulders.

With frustrated hands, the man finally rips the ski mask off of his head, and it only makes me tremble even more. Not only is he showing his face which is a clear sign he knows he's not going to get away with what he's doing, but I recognize him.

Dennis Milton, the man who killed his girlfriend because she tried to kick him out of their house after she caught him cheating is the man pacing in front of me. How is he out of jail? Colton got a confession from him weeks ago. His case is open and shut. Murderers don't get to post bond, do they? And even if they had the chance, it should've been set so high, he'd never have the ability to afford walking out of jail while he waits for court.

"I already fucking told you what I want!" Milton pulls the phone from his mouth, shouting down at him with malice. "I want my brother out of jail!"

His brother?

Only now do I begin to see the differences. The man in front of us has lighter colored hair and a small scar near his lip that Dennis Milton didn't have during his arrest and interrogation. They're twins if I had to guess.

"Don't talk to me about impossibilities. Just bring him here!"

The pacing continues, his free hand opening and closing repeatedly. I don't know why he chose now to answer the phone, but I can sense that things are going to come to a head very quickly.

I was never called out with Colton to a hostage situation, so I have no clue what the protocol is. I do know that after looking out the window a few minutes ago, that he closed the curtain up tighter than it was prior. I know that he's purposely walking behind us instead of between us and the street.

All of this is concerning, but I also know that Colton wouldn't hide this situation from the police department or my dad. If we have any luck at all, both groups are outside working out a way to put an end to this situation.

I nudge Landon with my foot, angling my head back. He reads it like I knew he would scooting closer to me and keying Rick in on doing it too. We shift closer together, making a smaller target, or if things go down like I think they will, we're a small obstruction to whomever may need to take down Milton.

"Because I want to fucking kill him!" the guy roars into the phone. "He killed Penny. I can't let him get away with it."

He listens, his face sweaty from all the walking around and no doubt the drugs, shaking his head to whatever is being said on the other end of the line.

"No. I have no interest in that fucking kind of justice. I'll take care of it myself. Bring him here. I'll save the taxpayers a ton of fucking money."

He stiffens, his eyes sweeping over the three of us.

"You're not in any place to threaten me, motherfucker. If I don't get what I want, you won't see them alive again."

Both boys are trembling against my own shaking legs. He's made numerous threats since he arrived, but they were mostly random mumbled thoughts. We have all of his attention right now, and the anger in his eyes tells me he has a point to prove and things are going to end badly.

"I loved her. I took a step back. She wanted Dennis. No one ever wants me, but I loved her enough that I wanted to see her happy." A tear rolls down his cheek.

The sight of it makes me whimper. He's beginning to break and not in a good way. He no longer feels any hope.

"He took the most beautiful thing in the world away from me, and if you don't give me what I want, I'm going to do the same to you."

He doesn't even bother hanging up before throwing the phone against the wall where it shatters into a dozen pieces. He's effectively broken any further line of communication.

I want to close my eyes to what I know is coming. The police rarely give in to demands, and if they do, it's only because it somehow gives them the upper hand. Regardless of who is in this house, the Farmington Police would never, and I mean never, let a murderer out of jail so his brother could kill him. It doesn't work that way. I know this, and telling by the shaking going on near my legs, the guys know this too. Milton must be too high from hours of snorting drugs to realize the truth of the situation. Hopefully he keeps believing they'll give in so it gives the police and possibly my dad the chance to rectify this situation before it goes to shit.

"He loves you." He's looking at me with irritation. "And a man who loves a woman that much will do anything to protect her. Do you love him?"

I don't know if he's referring to Colton or my dad, but the answer is still the same.

I nod my head trying to speak and tell him that I do love him, but the gag only allows for muffled sounds.

"A man with both his woman and his son threatened is more likely to get shit done."

Ah, so it was Colton on the phone.

He sniffs, the back of his hand swiping at his running nose.

I can't recall how long it takes an addict to come down and need another fix, but I hope the guys act fast because even though this man has been doing enough drugs to keep a small city high for days, I don't think he's going to keep it together much longer.

"Do you know how hard it's been to look at myself in the mirror?"

I don't bother attempting to answer him as he walks to the mirror hanging on the far wall. Despite his words, he stares at his reflection as if he'll be able to get all of his answers from the man staring back.

"I have his face. I've always been nicer. I'd never hit a woman the way he hit Penny."

He must have memory failure because my face still throbs from his repeated blows.

"Yet, she chose him. They always choose him." He spins to face me. "What is it about abusive men that makes women keep crawling back? Do you like it when men talk down to you? Do you think you can change them?"

I shake my head as he steps closer, hating the way Landon and Rick attempt to stay in front of me. I don't want them to protect me. I need to be the one protecting them.

"Answer me!" he roars.

But how can I? I don't understand women like that because I've never been in that situation, and explaining the psychology of women who stay in abusive relationships would not only be lost on his drug-addled mind, but it's impossible to do so with a fucking gag in my mouth.

I whimper, turning my head to the side when he lifts his hand once again, only this time it isn't his fist he's threatening me with. The gun in his hand is unsteady, but he's close enough to hit his mark without much effort.

I plead with my eyes, but it's clear he's no longer seeing me. I'm not Sophia, Colton's girlfriend. I'm Penny, the woman who broke his heart by making the wrong choice in brothers.

"You didn't have to die. We would've been so happy together." His words come out broken and filled with palpable pain, but I have no doubt Penny's life would've been ruined with either one of them. She may not have been hit, although his actions tonight make me doubt that, but being in a relationship with an addict brings its own set of problems.

"Don't worry," he whispers, lowering the gun and cupping the side of my face with his free hand. "When the night is over, we'll finally be together."

Chapter 35

Colton

I feel like I've been struck with an invisible blow when the call ends. I tried to keep my cool, but the man is threatening my entire fucking world. Losing either of them would destroy me. Losing both of them is a tragedy I'll never come back from.

For some reason, it's in this moment that the many conversations I've had with Sophia while working come back to me. I told her compassion is fleeting. I explained that people are put in impossible situations. Sometimes, it's because of a mental break. At other times, it's because they've been struck so hard by loss that they see no other way out. It seldomly entails actual psycho or sociopathic reasons. There are mitigating circumstances that put Sophia and Rick in this man's path tonight, but I can't muster an ounce of that compassion. I can't see being satisfied with any other outcome than this man being carried away from here in a fucking body bag.

"He closed the curtain," Shadow says, his voice coming over the mic. "I no longer have a shot. Get with Max and tell him to get us ears inside."

It's mere minutes before the conversation inside is transmitting. Max, a guy I'm guessing that works for Cerberus, was able to tap into Landon's phone. The muffled words are hard to hear because the phone is in his pocket, but the dangerousness of the situation comes across loud and clear.

"He's insane," Monahan says after hearing the way he's talking to Sophia. "Like clinically. Did you know about the link between him and Penny?"

"We knew he had a twin. That came out in the investigation. Both brothers have spent a little time in jail. Roger, the man inside, has a few possession charges. He was picked up for a drunk and disorderly a couple months ago, but we didn't dig enough into his life to find out he was in love with his brother's girl," I explain.

"Probably not something he talked to anyone about," Dominic says, giving me a small concession.

"Obviously, we can't give him what he wants," Monahan says out loud even though we all know it.

Unintelligible garbles come through the tap in Landon's phone followed by sobs. Dominic is slowly losing his cool. The ice-man stature he arrived with has been slowly melting away, and now I can see he's just as worried as I've felt since I pulled up and noticed the front porch light out.

"I love her. My son is inside. Another young man I'm responsible for is sitting beside the both of them," I tell anyone standing close enough to hear. "We have to fucking do something. He's devolving and shit is going to go down sooner rather than later."

Dominic's jaw twitches at my confession, but he refuses to look in my direction. It's clear he blames me. Hell, I blame me. If it weren't for my involvement in the case, this wouldn't be happening. No matter how much the reasonable part of my brain tries to tell me that this situation could happen at any point to any officer over the course of their career, this isn't happening years ago to someone else. It's happening to me.

I'm to blame.

"Peterson is an excellent shot. If we can get him in the hous—"

"Shadow is better," Dominic interrupts. "Let my guys handle this, Chief."

Monahan shakes his head. "This is Farmington jurisdiction."

"You're going to let that come into play here?" Dominic hisses, and I bet he's seconds away from wrapping his hands around my boss's throat. "We don't have time to spend measuring our dicks out here. Shadow has decades of experience. He's not some cowboy wanting a little piece of the glory. Sophia and Landon are just as much family to him as they are to us, and even if they weren't, he'd protect all three of them with his own life. That's an oath he took."

"My guy took an oath, too, and he's not a fucking cowboy looking for glory," Monahan argues.

"When was the last time he had to pull his gun or the trigger on a man in his scope? When was the last time he had to sneak into a building and take out a suspect? This month? This year? At any point in his career?" Dominic points in the direction of the house, and I know he's indicating Shadow who's been out of sight for a while. "Shadow did that shit three weeks ago. I'm not saying your guy is bad. I'm saying my guy is better."

Dominic has a point, and although I don't know Shadow, my confidence in his abilities grows with each word that comes out of his mouth.

"He can get in there and take that fucker out without the mice in the wall knowing he's in there," Dominic continues. "We can end this shit in seconds."

I don't have mice, but I understand the sentiment.

Monahan looks from Dominic to the SWAT team waiting on his orders. Peterson is the one to finally step forward, the heaviness of his gear a different sight than when he's on normal patrol.

"He's got a point. I'm not a coward, and I'm confident in my skills, but my training is no fucking match for that other guy's experience. It doesn't even compare."

Dominic nods at him, knowing it takes a real man to step up and say that, especially coming from a cop. We all carry this inflated sense of worth and bravado. Yeah, we scare as easily as the next guy, but it's dangerous to show that in our line of work. Most cops walk around acting like they're bulletproof all the while knowing they'll be the first to take lethal gunfire if shit goes down. It's a very tenuous line to straddle.

"If this goes bad," Monahan mutters, "it's my ass on the line."

"The longer we wait, the higher the chance," Dominic says, his stance as strong as it was when he first arrived.

"Have your guy handle it," Monahan finally concedes, and I know it takes a good man to act with what he knows is best rather than letting protocol control his decisions.

The Farmington SWAT team moves back as Dominic issues commands into the mic. I know they'll step back in if given the command, but they seem okay with letting the Cerberus team take the lead.

"They're going to be fine," Dustin says at my side. "I trust that man with my life."

I nod my head, knowing I have to trust him with mine as well. My arms tremble, muscles needing to do something to burn off the extra energy I can't seem to get rid of, but I stand as stock still as Dominic does. He's got a lot to lose here tonight as well, but I don't think I'll ever be as calm in situations like this.

Maybe it's his years of experience or his assuredness in his guy's skills. Maybe it's a combination of both, but I bet deep in his soul, he's screaming as loud as I am.

The insane man in my house represents everything that's wrong with the world. Turning grief and anger into acts of violence won't solve a damn thing here tonight. Coming here, no doubt prepared to die, from what we heard him saying to Sophia, was his plan all along, and if Shadow doesn't move fast this bad situation is going to quickly turn to tragedy.

"Colton," Dominic hisses, and I snap out of my racing thoughts and look at him. "Best point of entrance?"

"The master bedroom on the west side of the house is furthest from where they are. Less chance of being heard."

He nods at me, relaying that information.

"I hope this was the right fucking choice," Monahan says as he rests a reassuring hand on my shoulder.

I don't know if the touch is meant to calm me or keep me in place so Shadow can get the job done.

"Me too," I whisper. "Me fucking, too."

Chapter 36

Sophia

I don't realize how calming this guy's pacing was until he stops. He looks at his empty wrist as if there would normally be a watch there. People planning to die sometimes take things off and leave them behind, either just to prepare or because they want to leave tokens and sentimental things behind. People planning to jump to their deaths remove their glasses, and it can be argued they do that so they don't see the fall coming or because it's what they do every night before they go to sleep.

The coked-out man on the other side of the room seems resolved, calming completely until he's standing directly in front of me.

"They aren't going to bring Dennis here."

"They will," I argue, even though I know he can't understand my words. "They will."

I can't stop the sobs from escaping, no matter how hard it is to breathe. My throat is dry and agitated from having the gag in my mouth, and I find it strange that's what I choose to focus on seconds before I die.

I scream when splatter hits my face wanting to die quickly knowing he's shot one of the boys first. They didn't deserve this. Neither boy got the chance to live. None of us will. Heaviness weighs me down, and honestly it's a lot more peaceful than I thought it would be.

An odd sense of calm washes over me. I was loved. It may not have been for long, but I was raised by wonderful parents. I have the best sister and friends anyone could ask for, and Colton loved me. I know he did. So I guess technically, I've had it all.

But then realization slaps me in the face. I won't get to walk down the aisle toward the man of my dreams or have a real job. I'll never know what it's like to feel a child move inside of me. There's so much I'm going to miss.

"Soph, open your eyes. Are you okay?"

A swarm of people surround us, but it doesn't stop the screaming when I watch another masked man roll the dead guy off my lap.

"Look at me." I can't. I just can't. "Sophia Anderson, open your eyes."

That voice. I know that voice. It assured me everything would be okay when I had nightmares. That voice chastised me when I got caught swimming in the lake alone when I was five. That voice promised to protect me forever.

"Daddy?" Dark eyes, exactly like mine, are inches from my face, and rough, loving hands cup my cheeks.

I don't know why I called him that. I haven't called him anything other than dad for a long time. Maybe it's the memories flooding me from my childhood or him following through on so many promises.

"It's gonna be okay, baby. Look at me." Tears stain my cheeks, and he wipes them away with a gentle thumb. "Are you hurt anywhere?"

"The boys," I whimper. "The boys."

"They're fine. Look." Dad shifts out of the way so I can see Dustin with his arms wrapped around Landon. Colton is clinging to a sobbing Rick, his eyes focused on me over his shoulder. "Hold tight. It's over. It's over, baby. You're safe."

My dad isn't one to waste words, but it seems the situation calls for it, and I know the repetition is to reassure me. I would gamble that he's in need of reassurance as well. He flips open a knife, making easy work of the ropes holding me in place, but before I can stand, he sweeps me up in his muscled arms and carries me out of the house.

"Dad, put me down. I can walk."

He doesn't listen as his legs carry me away from the house.

"Dad!" I snap. "Put me down."

He freezes, his eyes finding mine, but he doesn't open his mouth to argue as he lowers my feet to the ground.

"I can't leave you here."

"I have to stay."

"There's a dead body in the house, Sophia. Let me take you home where it's safe."

"The guy is dead. I'm no longer in danger."

"You'll always be in danger."

I don't know if he means with Colton or in life in general. Knowing my dad and the caution he raised me with, he means the latter.

"I love him."

Confessions right after a traumatic event when everything is heightened can be taken seriously, right?

His eyes search mine and I don't know if he's trying to determine if I'm speaking the truth or if he's giving me a chance to change my mind.

"Please?" The one word asks a million questions.

Please let me love him.

Please be okay with my choice.

Please don't hate me because of the choices I've made.

Please remember what it was like when you fell in love with Mom.

I don't know how many questions his simple nod answers, but my feet are moving the second he does it.

I don't hesitate running back into the house where the man who terrorized me lies dead on the carpet in a pool of blood. I don't give the police and Cerberus guys milling around a second glance. The moment Colton and Rick are in sight, I rush to them and wrap my arms around them both.

They envelop me in an embrace, both of them clinging to me. I sob from fear and relief, from knowing how close I came to losing this. God, I don't think I'll ever be able to let them go. Warm tears combine with mine, and I look up to see utter devastation written all over Colton's face.

"Shh," I say, pressing a shaking finger to his lips before he can speak.

I know what he's going to say, but warnings against loving him isn't something I can take right now.

"We're fine. We're safe."

"I'm smothered," Rick jokes as he takes a step back, but the evidence of his own fear continues to pour from his eyes.

He notices me looking at him and quickly wipes his eyes.

"I'm going to stay with Landon tonight."

"Like hell—"

"I think that's a great idea. He'll be safe on Cerberus property," Dustin says as he steps up to us, clearing his throat. "I imagine you two are going to need some time alone."

My cheeks flame. Telling your dad you love someone is worlds away from one of the guys on his team, a man that helped raise me, hinting at anything sexual in nature.

"Landon needs me," Rick argues, his eyes now pleading with his dad to understand.

I know Colton has the same suspicions as I do when he gives his son a simple nod. Rick groans when Colton wraps his arms around him one last time, squeezing him to his chest, but as much noise as Rick is making, I don't miss the fact that he holds his dad even tighter.

"Be safe," Colton whispers. "Call me if you need me."

"I will, Dad." Rick walks out of the house with Landon and Dustin.

Colton wraps his arms around me once again, and there's so much emotion between us, it's as if we can both just forget about the dead guy ten feet away and the people walking around.

"We're standing in the middle of an active crime scene," I mutter against his chest, reluctant to ever let go of him again.

"You have to give a statement."

I know I do. I've been on the other side of this situation before, but having lived it makes each one of those scenes I went to with him seem different. Being the victim sucks, and although I know I may never get this night out of my head, I hope I can move past it.

"He's the one that sent that letter."

"A warrant was signed that day, and people have been actively looking for him, but a man who doesn't want to be found can easily avoid detection."

My fears, something I tried to convince myself were an overreaction, are justified.

"Look at me." Colton takes a step back, holding my face in gentle palms as he looks me in the eye. "I took that situation seriously. I did everything I could to track him down and bring him in. I don't want you to think tonight happened because I thought it was no big deal."

"I know." I nod my head, hoping the action combined with my words are enough for him.

As much as Colton complained about being distracted with me around, the man did damn fine police work. Downtime was nearly nonexistent where he was concerned, and I think that was a lot of his appeal. Maybe it's another one of those traits from my dad—that daddy positivity—that made him attractive to me. I know a good man when I see one because I was raised around a dozen of them growing up in Cerberus.

"Can she give her statement in the morning?" Colton asks over my shoulder, and I turn, meeting the eyes of Chief Monahan.

"First thing," Monahan confirms. "So that means you need to pack a bag and get out of here. I'll make sure crime scene cleanup is scheduled for when we're done."

I don't know how but I manage to fall asleep nearly seconds after Colton drives away from his house. I wake as he lifts me out of the seat.

"Where are we?" I whisper against his warm, firm chest.

"Hampton Inn."

A laugh escapes my lips, and I can feel his chest moving up and down with his own silent laughter.

"Talk about full circle."

He presses his lips against the top of my head before releasing me so I can stand.

"I don't want to lose you, but—"

"You won't."

"I'll understand if this was too much for you. Did he hurt you?"

I angle my face to the light. Gentle fingers brush over the tender spots on my face.

"Did he try to—"

"No. Nothing like that. He didn't. I don't think it was ever his intention. Don't even get that mess in your head. I'm fine."

"I can't stop thinking about the way I saw you tied up and in pain."

I press my mouth to his, effectively shutting him up. We have a lot to talk about, but none of those conversations need to happen tonight.

"I love you. Tonight. Tomorrow. In fifty years and every single day in between. That's all that matters right now."

"You're an amazing woman. You know that, right?"

I smile up at him, cherishing the heat of his body and the security of his arms around me.

"You know there's always a chance of getting hurt if you're involved with me."

"Are you going to hurt me?"

"I'd die before that ever happens."

"And that's why you're stuck with me."

It's his turn to lower his mouth to mine, the kissing staying just on this side of public lewdness.

"Take me upstairs so I can sleep in your arms?"

I squeal in delight when he once again sweeps me off my feet. I press my nose to the column of his neck, and will every bad thought from my head. There's no place for any of it while we're holding each other.

Chapter 37

Colton

"Even after everything you've seen and done as a cop, you're still nervous about this?"

I side-eye Sophia, unable to fully appreciate the humor in her tone.

"You put your life in danger every day," she reminds me.

"Are you saying my life is in danger?"

She shrugs, her eyes pointed toward the house. "Not necessarily."

"That isn't a no."

"I mean, he already knows, right? He's had time to work through things."

"He's had less than twelve hours," I remind her.

"He processes things quickly. It's imperative in his line of work."

"How many times is the man going to be told his daughter is in love?"

"Hopefully only twice." She winks at me, her teeth digging into her bottom lip to keep from smiling.

"Twice?" That hits me wrong.

"At least you're only one guy. Jasmine had to have this conversation, and I don't imagine it was easy to tell my dad that she was in love with two guys at the same time. Well, Dad actually walked in on her with both of them, so the conversation went a little differently."

"Jesus, Sophia. Really?"

"No joke. It was the talk of the clubhouse for a while."

"No." I shake my head, hands running over the top of my head. "Are you really talking about your sister's three-way minutes before I have to face your father?"

"Does that turn you on?"

"No," I say truthfully. "I'll never share you. Ever. But that sultry tone in your voice makes me want to choke you with my dick."

"Is that so?" She turns her body toward me, her hand falling to my thigh.

I push it away like it's burning me, and in a way, I guess it is. I think I'll always run hot for this woman, but now is not the time and in her parents' driveway is definitely not the place.

"Is this how the day is going to go?"

She licks her lips. "If you're lucky."

"Not that. Damn it, woman. Can you get control of yourself?"

"I thought you liked me out of control. This morning when I—"

"Stop!" I can't help the laugh that slips out. "You're maddening."

"Is your cock hard."

"You know it is," I grumble. "I don't want to be disrespectful."

"We can do this another time."

"You saw the curtains flutter when we pulled up. They know we're here. I don't want to have to explain leaving."

"I'm sure they saw us on the camera monitors before the curtains fluttered."

My eyes dart around. If there are cameras, they're well-hidden because I don't see them.

"There are cameras?" I shift in my seat, willing my cock to deflate.

"Of course there are cameras."

"Are you purposely trying to psych me up for this?"

She shrugs again. "You think better on your feet when your adrenaline is up."

"I'm nervous," I confess.

"And that isn't going to help."

I follow her eyes, watching with trepidation as an SUV pulls up beside us. Sophia's sister and two men climb out, all three giving us a little wave before going inside the house.

"Great. Now we have an audience."

"You'll be fine, champ." She smacks my chest like a teammate and climbs out.

I manage to catch up with her at the front of the truck, clasping her hand like a lifeline.

Laughter hits me when we step inside the house, but once the front door closes us in, the sound drops away.

Sophia's sister is standing in the center of the living room with a man on either side of her. Her eyes are shining as they dart between Sophia and me, but she doesn't speak. I wouldn't be surprised if there's popcorn in the damn microwave with the way they're all looking at us. It seems we're the entertainment for the day.

"Kingston," one of the guys says as he steps forward with his hand out.

"Max," the other says in introduction, offering his hand as well. "It won't be as bad as you're thinking. I promise."

"Our situation was bad," Kingston adds with a sly grin. "At least you have clothes on."

Both Sophia and Jasmine laugh like it's funny I'm moments away from facing the firing squad.

"Colton," booms from the other side of the room.

"Just don't lie about anything. He'll know," Max hisses before they all make a hasty exit.

"Hey, Dad," my girl says as Dominic crosses the room. He presses his lips to her temple, but his eyes never leave mine. "Go easy on him."

She smacks his chest, much the same like she did mine before climbing out of the truck, then that beautiful traitor walks away.

She. Walks. Away!

She leaves me alone in the room that may soon end up a crime scene.

I swallow, trying to convince myself this is no big deal. We're both adults. We've done nothing wrong. I love her for heaven's sake. All of that should count for something, but what the hell do I know? I don't have a daughter.

"Sir," I say, holding my hand out to him.

He looks down at the offering, his eyes scrunching just a bit in the corners, but he takes my hand, albeit squeezing too hard for comfort.

"Have a seat." He sweeps his hand in the direction of the couch, but even as I lower myself to the sofa, I'm wondering if requesting to stay standing is an option. "You seem nervous."

My eyes dart toward movement, and I see the entire damn family watching from the other room. There isn't popcorn, but Max is eating handfuls of cereal from the box, his eyes glued on us, so it's practically the same thing.

"A little," I admit because I was told not to lie. He's an expert in his field, so there's no doubt he can see the flop of sweat forming on my brow.

"Never sat down and had a conversation with a girl's dad before?"

"No."

"Because you only use women?"

My eyes meet his, anger swimming in my gut. Is that the type of man he thinks I am?

"You have a son."

"And my ex-wife was raised without a father. Her mother wasn't around much either."

"Your parents are still married?"

"Happily."

"Any issue with us meeting them?"

"None."

"Are you going to keep giving me single word answers?"

"If you keep asking single word questions."

His lip twitches, and for the life of me, I can't tell if he thinks it's funny or if he's preparing to attack.

"You love my little girl."

"With all my heart."

"What are your intentions?"

We're really doing this? I thought this only happened in the movies.

I lift my eyes from him, landing on Sophia in the kitchen. She's positively gorgeous, radiant even.

"I'm going to spend the rest of my life making her happy."

"And if she doesn't want that?"

The warning is clear in his voice.

"Then I guess I'll be walking away with a broken heart."

"You'd give up so easily?"

This feels like a trap.

"I would never do what Milton did last night, but I figure if I work hard every day to keep her, she's more likely to stay. She loves me, too, and I cherish that like a gift." I meet his eyes. "If she changes her mind, I'll have to accept that. I may never be whole again, but I also have a son to worry about."

He nods in understanding. "But you haven't had a serious relationship in years."

"I know how to treat a woman right, sir. I was raised by an incredible man and raised in a household full of love. I may be a single father, but Rick was also raised in a household full of love."

"What happens when she leaves for school?"

I swallow, not wanting to think about her being gone, but we discussed this last night.

"I'll wait for her. I spend as much of my free time going to see her. We'll make it work, but she mentioned last night that she wanted to stay in town and complete the degree online."

He sits back on the sofa, crossing his ankle over the opposite knee. I'm not an expert on his emotions, but I think he's happy with this news.

"I'll support whatever decision she makes. I know I've lived a lot of my life already, and she needs the opportunity to do the same."

"And if she gets pregnant?"

This makes me pause, but there's no way to hide the smile. "We're safe."

Did I just admit to sleeping with this man's daughter? I mean, surely he knows it's happened or is going to happen, but confessing it out loud is weird for everyone.

"Safe?"

"I plan to marry her, sir. If she wants babies, I'll give her a dozen."

"Are you asking permission?"

"No."

His eyes narrow again.

"I won't let anyone stand between us. Absolutely no one, and I don't mean that as any form of disrespect. Your blessing would be nice, though. I don't want her thinking she has to choose."

"I would never put her in that position. I want her happy."

I look over his shoulder once again, meeting Sophia's eyes. I want to touch her skin and have her pressed against me. She's only across the room, and I miss her already. Her delicate features soften even further with my eyes on her, and if I wasn't so entranced, I'd find it comical the way Kingston's eyes dart back and forth between us like he's afraid he's going to miss something.

"I'm happy if she's happy."

"I'll spend every second of my life making sure she is."

"I understand the appeal. Makayla is a bit younger than I am, but if you don't stop looking at my daughter like you're undressing her with your eyes, I may have to punch you in the nose."

I wink at Sophia before refocusing on Dominic.

"I also understand what it's like to take on the responsibilities of another kid," he says, leaving that hanging in the air.

"Rick and Sophia get along very well."

"I'm not happy you guys hid what was going on."

"It's very new," I explain. "The attraction was there, but nothing umm... happened until after the graduation party. I didn't abuse my power or use her internship in a negative way. I've loved her long before I—" I have to look away, my hand immediately going to the back of my neck. "The physical relationship hasn't been going on very long. It's new. Very new. Like days. Just a couple days. Day three. This is day three."

Did someone turn up the heat to make me sweat on purpose? Why am I rambling? I feel like a suspect, only it's my own volition that's keeping me here rather than steel cuffs chained to a table.

"Are you done interrogating him?" Relief washes over me as Sophia steps up to us, but then she sits on my lap, wrapping her arms around my shoulders. "Everyone is ready for brunch."

I don't know if I should push her off my lap because Dominic is watching us like he's assessing the situation and taking notes, but on instinct, my arms go around her as well.

Dominic nods once before standing up and heading into the kitchen.

"Jesus," I hiss, keeping my voice as low as I can manage. "That was intense."

"I think you passed the test," she whispers, pressing her lips to my jaw.

We could be in the middle of a battlefield and that one simple action would calm me.

"I was willing to fight him for you." It's mostly the truth. The man is a massive brick wall, and I'm sure even at his age he could kill me with his bare hands. "I would've probably died, but you're worth it."

She chuckles, her nose resting against my neck.

"You may still get your chance. We haven't told him I'm moving in with you yet."

Chapter 38

Sophia
Several Months Later

"It's weird."

I look across the room, unable to deny his words. My parents and his parents are chatting with Uncle Diego and Aunt Emmalyn. They're all smiling and joking with one another.

"It's a little strange," I admit.

"My dad is wearing jeans, Sophia. And a pair of fucking combat boots."

I roll my lips between my teeth to keep from smiling. "Think he'll buy a Harley next?"

"My mom would never allow it."

"I overheard her telling Khloe that she always wanted to feel the wind in her hair."

He snaps his face in my direction. "Seriously? What have we done?"

"Besides falling in love and bringing two families together?"

His gaze focuses on my lips, and a very familiar warmth fills my blood. We're insatiable when we're together, unable to keep our hands to ourselves. It's always our biggest concern when we go out in public. Getting handsy at the clubhouse isn't an option, but it doesn't stop the desire from pooling in my stomach.

"You've got to stop looking at me like that," I warn. "Do you want to end up in the empty bedroom again?"

He nods his head slowly, and the temptation is real.

"Stop." I swat at him, causing him to laugh.

"You guys are disgusting," Izzy groans beside us. "Can't you turn it off even for a few hours?"

I release Colton's hand to turn my attention to my best friend. She shifts her weight on the sofa, grimacing. It's clear she isn't comfortable.

"What's wrong?" I press my hand to her round belly. "Feeling a little left out?"

"How can I feel left out when I'm right in the middle of your foreplay?"

"Maybe you just need to get laid."

Her nose scrunches up, and Colton chuckles. He's long given up telling me to keep my ideas in my head. Training him has been so easy.

"Umm..." She points to her very pregnant belly. "No one wants to touch me."

"You'd be surprised," Jasmine interjects. "There are many men attracted to pregnant women."

"True," Gigi adds. "There are all types of fetishes out there."

Izzy looks around the room, and I know she's checking the location of her dad. He knows she's pregnant and accepted it long ago, but he'll never be a man okay with discussing sex so openly with his daughter. Gigi, her stepmother who is only a few years older than her, has no qualms about it.

"I'm uncomfortable," Apollo says as he stands from the sofa.

"Only because Hound still thinks you're the one that got her pregnant," Max teases.

Apollo's eyes widen as he stares down at Izzy. "I thought you cleared that up."

I grin as he looks down at her belly before walking away.

"He'd definitely scratch that itch for you," I murmur.

"Not ever going to happen," my best friend says, but when her eyes follow him all the way across the room, it makes me wonder if she believes her own words.

"Self-love isn't bad either," Gigi says when the group grows silent.

Leave it to her to say something like that.

"My orgasms are always stronger when I'm pregnant." Gigi presses a soft hand to her tiny bump.

"I'm not discussing this with you," Izzy snaps with mild disgust. She grunts when she tries to stand up, the roundness of her belly making it hard to gain leverage to get off the couch.

Like the good friend I am, I push on her back to help even though I don't want her disappearing right now. We both just started our online programs. She's trying to finish up as many hours as she can before the baby arrives, and I'm in my first semester of graduate school. I spend most of my free time with Colton, and she's been withdrawing more and more.

I make a mental note to spend more time with her.

"Don't go," I whisper, my hand clinging to hers, but all she does is stare down at me like I have two heads.

"I have to pee. Wanna come with me?"

"That's another popular fetish," Gigi offers out of nowhere.

Several people chuckle, making Izzy scrunch her nose again. The woman is becoming an expert on the action.

The front door opens before she can walk away, and of course everyone in the room turns their heads.

Lawson walks in beaming, a wide smile on his handsome face. Behind him is Drew, who has been in lock-up for the last couple of months while waiting for things to play out after his arrest. I haven't had many interactions with the man, but the agitated look on his face as he steps inside is new. From what I remember of him, he was always smiling, always joking. He is the comic relief in contrast to Lawson who tends to be the more serious brother.

"That's Drew," I whisper to Colton who turns his head to look.

We've had many conversations about what happened with him, but I had no clue he'd be coming back here. All of his family, other than Lawson, is in New England.

"Oh," Izzy whispers, and I smile because no matter how sour Drew looks, he's just as good-looking as his older brother.

Maybe her luck is looking up?

Drew's eyes dart around the room, taking in the scene like I would expect any trained cop would do, but then his eyes land on Izzy and he freezes. She shifts on her feet when his eyes sweep down the length of her. Tension fills the room when he stares at her belly.

I expect questions. I expect emotions from both of them.

What I don't expect is for Drew to turn around without a word and walk back out the front door.

Drew

Copyright

Drew: Cerberus MC Book 15
Copyright © 2020 Marie James
Editing by Marie James Betas & Ms. K Edits
EBooks are not transferrable. All rights are reserved. No part of this book may be used or reproduced in any manner without written permission, except in the case of brief quotations embodied in critical articles and reviews. The unauthorized reproduction or distribution of this copyrighted work is illegal. No part of this book may be scanned, uploaded, or distributed via the Internet or any other means, electronic or print, without the publisher's permission.
This book is a work of fiction. The names, characters, places, and incidents are products of the writer's imagination or have been used fictitiously and are not to be construed as real. Any resemblance to persons, living or dead, actual events, locale, or organizations is entirely coincidental.

Synopsis

Falling for a girl I just met was never in my plans.

We had one night together, and most days I convince myself that she was an apparition—something I made up in my mind to get me through the hard days.

Then I found her again.

Only she wasn't happy and smiling, giving me a hard time like she did the day we met.
She was broken... unseeing eyes no longer filled with life.
She was gone because of another person's disregard for human life.

That night devastated me—transformed me from a person who upheld the law to a man that broke it.

My life was ruined, and all I had to fall back on was the Cerberus MC. Returning to the clubhouse breathed new life and determination into me.

Prologue

Isabella

"Here you go, Izzy."

"Thank you," I tell the waitress as she places the plate of food on the table in front of me.

My empty stomach is even more enthusiastic, growling at the scents wafting up from the plate.

She chuckles as she walks away, but I'm too hungry to feel an ounce of embarrassment.

I dig in, barely cutting the pancakes into manageable bites before shoveling them into my mouth.

Why I left campus before grabbing something to eat is beyond me. I've been traveling back and forth from college in Albuquerque to where my dad lives in Farmington, New Mexico for years, and I always manage to forget to eat. Maybe it's why the staff at this small family-owned diner know me by name.

Pancakes are a simple thing, mere batter honestly, but covered in butter and thick, sticky syrup makes them a masterpiece. I'll fight anyone that wants to argue. The bacon here is cut thick and crisped to perfection. I groan in appreciation, thankful for the thin crowd tonight.

"I was thinking of getting a burger, but you're making those pancakes sound like they're the best thing you've ever had in your mouth."

Looking up, I freeze, uncaring there's a dribble of syrup threatening to drop from my bottom lip. I'm no stranger to good-looking men, or men who approach me with some slick pickup line laced with sexual innuendo. I'm a college student, after all. Guys on campus think they're God's gift to women, and we should be so lucky to get a little alone time with them.

Think being the operative word when it comes to those guys at school.

There's a good chance this man standing beside my table is *actually* God's gift.

His military haircut, shaved close on the sides and just a little longer on top, combined with bright blue eyes makes him handsome. The muscles peeking out from under his shirt to showcase thick biceps have the ability to make me lose my breath, but the uniform, the gun belt, the badge displayed proudly on his chest make him devastatingly gorgeous.

I blame my dad, a man who's fiercely loyal and honorable, for my attraction to protective men. Being safe is a huge turn-on for me, and this man looks like he has those abilities in spades.

"Are they good?" His lip lifts in the corner, and as a woman who normally hates a smirk, this man is quickly making me change my mind.

"Hi," I squeak stupidly, my brain unable to answer his actual questions.

His smile widens, and I can tell by the knowing look that he realizes I'm already putty in his hands.

It should alarm me, should make me stop to think, but I don't. Hell, with him looking down at me, I can't.

Dad would be so disappointed.

Even the Devil was beautiful in God's eyes.

Although Dad isn't very religious, he's told me those words as a warning more than once. Translation—stay away from handsome men, they're the ones who will bring you the most grief.

"May I join you?"

Blinking up at him, I don't answer, too enthralled by watching his lips move each time he talks.

"May I?" he repeats, pointing to the empty part of the booth across from me.

Somehow, I manage to nod my head, pulling a rumbling chuckle from deep inside of him.

"You've got—" I'm frozen as he lifts his hand to my mouth, using a single finger to wipe away the syrup clinging to my lip.

It's like he's lit a fire inside of me, and when he draws that sticky finger to his own mouth, licking away the syrup, I'm certain I melt into a puddle right there.

Is this even real life? Do creatures this gorgeous even exist?

When the waitress approaches, she manages to take his order for a plate of his own pancakes, even though it's clear she's just as enamored.

Strong, thick fingers tap the tabletop as he watches me. It feels more like an undressing than scrutiny, as if while sitting here, he's stripping each item of clothing from my body. I feel the cool air of the diner on my overheated skin, feel the brush of his fingertips down my side, tracing each rib even though we aren't touching.

My mind is warning me of danger while my body is itchy and eager for anything he could suggest.

"You're quiet. Are you nervous?"

I manage to shake my head.

"So no warrants then?"

I grin back at him. "No. I never get into trouble."

"That's a shame. I was hoping to frisk you."

Oh. I like the flirting.

"Wouldn't a female State Police Officer be the one to do that?"

He licks his lips before speaking again, and I swear he's torturing me on purpose.

"Most people would just call me a cop, without specifying which department."

"That's silly. It's on your patch."

I've been trained to look at patches for years now. After my dad joined the Cerberus MC a couple of years ago, I'm constantly around people who have them on their clothing.

I toy with my fork, twisting the tines in the fluffy pancakes, trying to figure out a way to get our conversation back to his frisking comment and hating that we've gone so far off course.

"O'Neil," he says, his hand reaching across the table.

"Megan," I lie, placing my hand in his.

Using a fake name isn't unusual to me. Dad taught me to be diligent, and the less people know about you, the harder it is for them to track you and hurt you.

Expecting him to shake it, he throws me off-kilter when he lifts my hand and presses warm lips to the back of it.

"Aren't you charming," I whisper as he lowers our hands.

"And you're gorgeous." He doesn't release my hand, and I find it strange that it doesn't feel at all weird to be holding the hand of a man I just met.

"Thank you."

"Are you from around here, Megan?"

"Yes." It's not really a lie. Around here is subjective, and since I live in New Mexico, it's mostly truthful. Besides, ask vague questions, and you'll get vague answers.

"Here you go, sweetheart." The waitress lingers even after placing the plate of pancakes in front of him, but he never pulls his eyes from me.

This man is good at what he's doing. Does it make me a fool for falling for it?

People are supposed to have fun, have wild nights when they're in college, right? I can't help but wonder what a little time spent alone with this man would look like.

"Your food is going to get cold," he says, releasing my hand so he can begin his own meal.

He groans with the first bite, and if I sounded anything like he just did, then I know why he approached me. The sound is pure sex, decadent sin and arousing.

He licks away the syrup on his lips before I can open my mouth to offer doing it for him, but the little wink he shoots my way tells me he knows the suggestion is there.

"H-How long have you been a police officer?" I manage only by focusing on the plate in front of me rather than his handsome face.

"Not long. Less than a year. I'm still doing my field training." Like every other man I know, he shovels food in his mouth and still manages to grin while he chews.

"Where's your partner then?"

"He's working on a personal project right now," he says after taking a sip of coffee. "What about you?"

"I'm not a cop." I barely refrain from smacking my forehead at the stupid response. "I'm a college student."

And if it weren't for my best friend Sophia managing to get behind in her classes, I wouldn't even be alone right now. We normally drive back home for spring break together, but she's been delayed.

I don't know if being alone right now is a good or bad thing.

"And your major?"

"Elementary education." His smile grows, and I feel my own lips mirroring his. "Why the big smile?"

"Most of the guys I work with are married to teachers. It seems it's like the American dream."

"Police officers and teachers?" He nods. "I think people who are focused on helping others, although in much different capacities, are drawn to those same types of people."

"I'm definitely drawn to you, Megan."

I hate the sound of my fake name coming from his lips, but I'm committed to it and not going to confess now.

"What's your first name, O'Neil?"

He shakes his head.

"Too personal?"

"Oh, I want to get personal with you."

And an expert at avoidance. Figures.

"It was nice meeting you," I say after wiping my mouth and pulling cash from my purse to leave on the table. "Be safe."

He doesn't try to stop me when I stand, and although he's gorgeous and a protector, did I honestly think we'd have some type of love match?

His job is dangerous.

Cops are notorious, unfortunately, for cheating on their significant others.

This man won't even tell me his first name.

All clear signs to cut my losses and get out of here.

The walk into the diner didn't unnerve me at all, but leaving now that it's dark outside makes me realize I parked a little too far out for comfort. My dad's voice is in my head as I slip my keys between my fingers in case I need them for protection.

The fact that a New Mexico State Police Officer is thirty yards away inside the diner doesn't ease all of my fears. I'm well aware that bad things can happen right under people's noses with them being none the wiser.

"Megan!"

I freeze, the new voice somehow already familiar.

"Let me walk you to your car."

I don't turn to face him, but when he makes it to my side, I fall into step with him. The warm hand he places flat on my back sends shivers down my spine even though I'm no longer scared in the darkness.

When we approach my car, the only light comes from the parts of the moon not covered in clouds, and I feel reckless. I feel like I don't want the night to end even though he has a job to do, and I'm expected at the Cerberus clubhouse in two hours.

When I turn around to face him, he doesn't step back. His fingers trail down my face, pushing a lock of hair from my cheek.

"You should park closer. It's not safe—"

I lift up on my toes and press my mouth to his. He doesn't pull back, doesn't tell me I'm being inappropriate.

He does none of that. When I lick at his lower lip, he groans, pulls me to his chest, and opens his mouth to sweep his tongue across mine.

Tonight, by far, will be the craziest thing I've ever done in my life.

Prologue

Drew
Several Months Later

"Really?" I grin, keeping my eyes on the road as my field training officer, Warren, tells me the good news.

"Seriously, and I owe my thanks to you."

I chuckle. "Dude, I didn't have anything to do with knocking your wife up."

"Asshole," he mutters, but there's still humor in his voice. "It happened that night I went home."

That night.

He doesn't even have to give me details to make me recall what I was doing that night.

That night I dropped Warren off in front of his house after his wife texted that she was ovulating.

I cringe now, just like I did then with the memory, but apparently he's an oversharer.

That night, I was instructed to grab something to eat and stay out of trouble while he took care of business.

That night, I met Megan.

That night, she kissed me under the moonlight.

That night, I did something I thought I'd never do and took her right on the hood of her car in the parking lot of a diner.

I scrub my hand down my face. I was in full-damned uniform, gun belt still around my waist as I—

Nope. Not revisiting what happened. Chubbing up with Warren riding shotgun can't happen. I save those thoughts and memories for when I'm alone. That night has haunted my mind, infiltrated my dreams, and have been the images I've been getting myself off with for months.

Megan broke me.

Or maybe it was the experience, the knowing we were doing something wild and crazy, something illegal that could make me lose my badge that is such a turn-on. Whatever it is, I can't let go of the memory. Can't see another girl with long brown hair and pretty hazel eyes without thinking it's her. More than once, I've tapped a woman on the shoulder only to be disappointed when she turns around.

"Seriously, though. Thank you. We find out in a couple weeks what we're having, but man, I'm just happy she's finally pregnant. We've been trying for the last year. Now we can have regular sex and it doesn't feel like a job."

"How many times have I told you the details of your sex life don't interest—"

Dispatch interrupts with a call, giving the location and not much else in regard to details about a two-person collision on U.S. Route 550 North.

"It's that time of night," Warren mutters after responding to dispatch about being en route. "Plus graduations, and kids going home for summer break."

As I drive to the scene, lights flashing and siren blaring, lead settles in my gut, as if there's a dark cloud over me. I'm not an intuitive person. Most of the skills I have that are useful as a police officer have been part of my training.

Before we're able to get close enough to park and assist, before my eyes can register the smoke billowing from a mangled blue car, before I can even get my seatbelt off, I know this night is going to change me forever.

"You get the car. I'll get the truck," Warren tells me, his calm voice a stark contrast to the pounding happening in my chest.

Ambulance sirens are distant, and I can't tell how far away they are as I approach the driver's side door of the wrecked car, its familiarity threatening to bring my lunch back up.

Then I see the brown hair, tangled and matted with blood.

"I can't get her out," a man yells, his voice frantic.

"Sir, step aside," I somehow manage.

Graduation. Kids going home for summer break.

Warren's words echo in my head as I lean into the vehicle to assess the situation.

A shattered windshield. A crumpled dash. No seatbelt. A broken girl.

"I'm a college student. Elementary education."

That's what she told me *that night*. I can hear the words as if Megan is standing right beside me.

"Ma'am," I say, my voice lower than it should be, too filled with emotion for the job that's expected of me. "Can you hear me?"

Her face tilts the slightest bit, but her gorgeous hazel eyes don't open.

"Megan," I snap a little louder. "Open your eyes, baby. Let me know you're going to be okay."

I clasp her hands in mine as her eyes flutter weakly. The shadows in the car are too dark for me to see them clearly, but I know what they look like. I memorized them *that night*.

The cut on her face seems superficial, although it's bleeding. Keeping a hold of her hand, I scan down her body to assess for other injuries. The steering wheel pressed to her chest and the spider-webbed windshield are both concerning, but a ragged breath draws my eyes back to her face.

"Help me," she gasps.

"I'm here. We're going to get you out of here."

The minuscule amount of grasp she had on my hand disappears, and the tension in her body eases. Her flushed skin turns ashen so quickly it's as if someone waved a wand from her hairline to her neck, taking all her coloring along with it.

She's gone.

This isn't the first fatality accident scene I've responded to. Objectively, I know she's dead.

I know I'll never speak to her again.

I know I'm going to have to notify her family of their loss.

I know she'll never be a teacher.

I know I'll never get to brush my mouth against hers, again.

I know I'll regret not getting her number that night, but at the time, I didn't realize just how obsessed with her I'd become, how she'd manage to take over my thoughts.

I know all of this, but accepting it seems like an impossibility.

"Move." I'm shoved out of the way, seconds from clocking some asshole in the face when I realize it's the paramedics finally arriving to help.

In stunned shock, I stand to the side watching as they take vitals, watching as one guy shakes his head with a frown, watching as they pull a blanket out and drape the side of her car with it.

"O'Neil! A little help?"

Warren is standing in front of a frowning man of about fifty, but all that registers is his flailing arms as he points at his truck. My feet move on their own, carrying me toward my training officer and the man involved in the accident. His face is bleeding, a cut on his forehead leaving streaks of red down his pale, ashen cheek. Bloodshot blue eyes dart all over the place as if he can't seem to focus on any one thing.

"The truck will be towed," Warren is explaining as I join them.

"It's fine to drive. I'm not paying towing and impound fees." I hear the words, but it's the alcohol on his breath that tells me all I need to know.

"You're going to jail," Warren says. "You caused this accident."

"A fucking fender bender," the man counters. "I have fucking insurance."

"She's dead," I mumble. "She's fucking dead!"

Most people claim they black out when they go into a rage, that they just snap and don't realize what they're doing.

That isn't the case for me.

When I charge this piece of shit, I feel the power in my legs moving me forward. I feel the scratch of his shirt under one palm and the slam of my knuckles against his face. I feel the spittle leaving his mouth and landing on my cheek when I make impact. I feel his boots skid against mine as he goes down. I feel the heave of his chest when we both land on the ground. I feel each blow to his face as I rain down my own judgement on this man.

What I don't feel is Warren tugging on me. I don't hear him cussing and telling me to calm down. I don't feel the other men required to drag me away.

All those things were caught on our body cams. Not only will I get to see what happened that night, reliving it over and over, so will a jury of my peers.

Chapter 1

Isabella
Several Months Later

"I'm telling you. It's not going to happen that way for me."

My best friend Sophia snuggles closer to her boyfriend, a frown marking her pretty face. "I'm sure my dad would be mad if I got pregnant, but he'd come around, eventually."

"My dad isn't the problem. My mother will never accept this baby."

My hand flutters protectively over my huge belly.

"Didn't your mom have you even younger?"

"Seventeen," I confirm. "But I was supposed to learn from her mistakes, not make the same ones."

"You're grown," Sophia reminds me. "Graduated college and everything."

I nod, agreeing with her, but this isn't the first time I've had this conversation with her. My mother is sticking to her guns. She won't accept my phone calls and definitely doesn't want anything to do with news on the baby. It's as if she believes if she ignores the entire situation, it'll go completely away.

In a way, it has. I'm living with my dad now. His house is finally finished, and although he didn't anticipate his daughter getting pregnant, he had a room ready for me when I came home with the news.

Came home with the news isn't exactly how it went down. I told my best friend and she let it slip many months ago. It just so happens everyone was around, including my dad and my stepmother. The craziest part, aside from getting pregnant from a one-night stand that happened in a parking lot on my Toyota Corolla—a story I fully plan to lie about when my child is old enough to start asking questions—my stepmother is also pregnant.

Dad and Gigi's story is about as wild as the one I'm keeping close to my chest. I can't even trust Sophia with the details. It's not that I feel shame, but yeah, getting pregnant by a guy whose first name I don't even know? Not really the things fairy tales are made of, you know?

Back to Dad and Gigi. Georgia Anderson is not only just a few years older than me, she's also the daughter of Diego "Kincaid" Anderson, the Cerberus MC president.

When Dad told me he was joining an MC, my head went straight to guns, drugs, using women and hurting people—all the things television has portrayed motorcycle clubs to be. Cerberus is nothing like that. If the bad MCs are one-percenters on one end of the spectrum, Cerberus is on the opposite. My dad, as well as all the other members, are good guys, all retired Marines, all working together to help people who have been sex trafficked. Their job repeatedly takes them out of the country, putting them in harm's way, but over the decades, the MC has managed to build a family, a group of people willing to go above and beyond for anyone welcomed into the fold.

Dad, working for Kincaid, somehow got Gigi on his radar, and as fuzzy as the details surrounding that situation are, I prefer to keep them that way. Those two are like horny teenagers, and I doubt they care that they aren't fooling anyone with side-eyes and whispered comments. When I first visited, they were a little more closeted about their bedroom lives, but as I've gotten older, they either aren't hiding it as much or I'm now understanding what certain looks can lead to.

I got those looks once—eyes drilling into me with suggestion and wishes. I run my hand back over my belly. Those looks are how I'm in this situation.

"She'll come around," Sophia assures me, and I just nod my head in agreement.

Sophia's dad, Dominic, is Kincaid's brother and although he works with the MC, he's never officially joined. He's the only one around here without a leather cut, but that doesn't make him any less imposing when he's in a room.

Sophia is of the opinion that things will work out, and eventually my mother will open her eyes and accept this baby. Sophia also comes from an intact family. Her mother and father still so much in love, they're literally making goo-goo eyes at each other across the room right now. She has an older sister that is involved with two men. Actually, Jasmine, Max, and Tug are a triad, all loving each other equally. So it's no surprise her dad didn't really bat an eye when she came forward not long ago and confessed her love for her intern-training officer, Colton Matthews, despite their age difference. Hell, I think Sophia's parents are nearly twenty years or so apart in age. Colton has a teenage son, who come to find out was already sort of a Cerberus family member already because Dustin's—one of the other original members—son, Landon, is best friends with him.

We're just one big happy family and growing more every day it seems.

Apollo, one of the newest Cerberus members to join the ranks, squeezes my hand. We've become good friends, growing close during the time my dad wanted to murder him because he thought Apollo was the man who got me pregnant. Although I haven't explained my situation to my dad, I assured him his assumptions were wrong.

"You okay?" he whispers as Sophia and Colton strike up a conversation about how weird it is for Colton's parents to be here at the clubhouse.

"I'm fine."

"You're squirming."

"The baby is sitting weird." I straighten my back, but it doesn't alleviate the ache.

"Are you going to be sick?"

I shake my head. God bless this man for being such a good friend. This pregnancy has been brutal. Morning sickness started before the test came back positive, and I'm sure I haven't had but a handful of vomit-free days since.

"I don't think so."

His lip twitches, and not for the first time, I wonder why I can't be attracted to him, why I can't see this man as more than a friend. He'd take care of me, a promise he made months ago when he confessed his own feelings for me. He took the news of me not seeing him that way on the chin like a champ, and not once has he faltered in his friendship. It still leaves me wondering if he isn't holding out for me to change my mind, but it's the reason I pull my hand from his and place it in my lap. Things that I didn't analyze before, the touching, hand holding, the kiss on the cheek goodnight are all things I have to avoid now. These are the things I think are confusing him into thinking there's the possibility of being something more.

"Let me know if you need anything." Apollo pats my leg before twisting to talk to one of the other guys over his shoulder.

When I look back at my best friend and see the way she's looking at Colton, I should avert my eyes, but they're so in love. They can't keep their hands, mouths, or eyes off each other, regardless that both of their parents are on the other side of the room.

With eyes focused on each other's mouths, I feel my own body grow warm.

"You've got to stop looking at me like that," Sophia whispers loud enough for me to hear. "Do you want to end up in the empty bedroom again?"

Colton nods his head slowly, and I have to clamp my lips between my teeth to keep from smiling. They've been in and out of that empty room more than once today. Maybe I'm jealous. Maybe I wish I had what they have. Maybe I'm just hungry or need a nap. Maybe it's gas making my heart pound.

"Stop," Sophia says as she swats at his chest.

"You guys are disgusting," I groan. "Can't you turn it off even for a few hours?"

Sophia shifts her weight to give me more of her attention.

"What's wrong?" She presses her hand to my round belly. "Feeling a little left out?"

"How can I feel left out when I'm right in the middle of your foreplay?" I mutter.

"Maybe you just need to get laid." Ah, my best friend, always the problem solver.

"Umm..." I point to my belly. "No one wants to touch me."

"You'd be surprised," Jasmine interjects. "There are many men attracted to pregnant women."

"True," Gigi adds. "There are all types of fetishes out there."

I want to cringe with this information coming from my stepmom, but I can remember a time when the "adults" wouldn't have these conversations in front of me. Cerberus members may ride motorcycles and kick ass for a living, but respecting women is an expectation they insist on at all times. Sharing sexualized information with teenagers didn't happen. I lived in the dark, learning many things from the internet rather than having actual conversations with the people in this club. How strange it was to find out most of them are into some pretty kinky stuff.

I look around the room for Dad, knowing that if Gigi is here sharing her wealth of knowledge that he can't be too far behind.

Gigi smiles at me, her hand going to the roundness of her own belly. Dad doesn't want me involved in conversations like this one, but Gigi has no problems sharing too much.

"I'm uncomfortable," Apollo says as he stands from the sofa.

"Only because Hound still thinks you're the one that got her pregnant," Max teases, his fingers running up and down Jasmine's arm until goose pimples appear.

Is it foreplay, or am I as hard up as Sophia insists I am?

Apollo's eyes widen as he stares down at me. "I thought you cleared that up."

I don't say a word because he knows better. His eyes dart down to my belly before he walks away.

"He'd definitely scratch that itch for you," Sophia says.

"Not ever going to happen," I counter, but I don't stop my eyes as they track him across the room. My fear is he's all too ready to jump into the role of being a dad and taking care of me. I love him like a friend, but us together will never happen.

"Self-love isn't bad either," Gigi says when the group grows silent. "My orgasms are always stronger when I'm pregnant." *Jesus Christ. Why didn't I get up and leave an hour ago?*

"I'm not discussing this with you," I snap at my stepmom. I swear, she says stuff like that just to embarrass me. If my dad were around, I'd say she was earning one of those spankings I have to cover my head with my pillow at night to keep from overhearing.

Not wanting to stick around to hear anyone, I try to stand, but my belly makes it nearly impossible to get up without help.

Sophia notices, giving me a gentle push on my back so I can stand

"Don't go," Sophia whispers with my hand in hers.

She knows how uncomfortable I get when everyone starts talking about sex and stuff. I blame being sheltered for so long, but recently it has more to do with missing out, with knowing I can track O'Neil down if I really wanted to.

"I have to pee. Wanna come with me?" I ask Sophia.

"That's another popular fetish," Gigi offers out of nowhere.

Several people chuckle, and I scrunch my nose. Most days it would be funny, but today I'm just not feeling it.

Chapter 2

Drew

"We're meeting Delilah at the clubhouse," Lawson says as he steers his truck around the curve of the road.

I know what's coming up. Although it's daylight now, I'll never forget where my entire world exploded.

I'll never forget where a girl I couldn't get off my mind drew her last breath, where I beat a man into a coma that took his life three days later.

Where my field training officer had to handcuff me for aggravated assault charges that would later be enhanced to homicide when the drunk driver succumbed to the injuries I caused.

Where I was stripped of my gun and my shield, having everything I worked for taken away from me.

I close my eyes as we get closer, knowing I'll be unable to stay sane if I see the scorched road left behind from the wreckage.

"Did you hear me?"

I nod. "Meeting Delilah back at the clubhouse."

"Everyone is excited to see you," my older brother says, and I don't doubt they are.

I'm like an animal in a cage. I bet loads of people will be around to see what a real-life murderer looks like, what a man who has nothing left to live for looks like before he crumbles to ash.

I can't say I'm excited to see anyone. Until I was jailed for my crimes several months ago, I led a mostly private life. I lived alone, and other than work, I didn't socialize much. Being a cop doesn't lend much trust to those people around you.

That solitary life changed in the blink of an eye. Sleeping alone in a two-bedroom home became sleeping in a room with a group of men, all criminals, all waiting for the next opportunity to get their own brand of vengeance out on a cop. Showering and taking care of bathroom needs became a group event, and I don't know if I'll ever recover from those demoralizing situations.

"I'm glad you're coming home. It shouldn't have taken so long to get you out."

There's so much to unpack with his words.

Home no longer exists, not at Cerberus, not back home in New England where my mother's family couldn't be bothered to get involved when I ended up with my wrists in cuffs.

Four months in jail was literally hell, spent looking over my shoulder and getting the shit kicked out of me because I used to have a badge on my chest. Didn't those men realize I'm just as much a felon now as they are?

Doesn't my brother understand that my reprieve from incarceration is going to be short lived?

I'm going to prison for what I did that night, and most of me has accepted it. The only thing that will keep me from going to prison is ending up in a box six feet under, and as much as I hate to think about it, that may be the better option. There's so much brutality in jail, I can only imagine prison will be worse.

The bruising on my ribs from the last jail brawl serves as a constant reminder that things are bad in lockup. The best I could hope for would be being placed in solitary confinement, and while I may make it out of prison with my life, my sanity will be gone.

"Four months is a long time. Are you sure you're okay?"

I huff a humorless laugh. Lawson and I are close. Well, at least we used to be. High school, college, and the police academy got in the way a lot, and despite the efforts he's put in to visit, write, and have attorneys work on my case, staying close to him has been a struggle.

"I'm not okay," I confess.

"You'll be exonerated, Drew. Your attorney—"

"I'm guilty." I turn my head to look at him, grateful when I open my eyes that we've passed that horrific spot on the highway. "I won't be exonerated. I won't get my badge back. I'm going to prison. If I can accept that, then you need to as well."

"There were extenuating circumstances."

Doesn't he know there are always extenuating circumstances? Adrenaline is always running. Someone is always hurt. Someone is always doing something wrong. Always. With every call. With every response. With every action we take while on duty.

They took my badge. They took my gun. They took my freedom.

They won't take my integrity.

Lying, sneaking, and being manipulative is something that he never would've stood for before. We grew up with a mother who had more interest in drugs and men than her sons. Somehow, Lawson held on to his honor the best he could while his friends and those around us sank into criminal activity. He got into trouble, landed on a juvenile probation officer's caseload in Texas, but he made sure to keep me out of those things. He protected me, kept me safe, and I repay all of that by killing a man.

"The judge released you," Lawson adds after a long moment of silence. "That's saying something."

"What the judge was saying is he doesn't want the country liable for my death when the other inmates beat me to death. It's not an opinion about my guilt or innocence."

"But he's—"

"Please, Lawson," I interrupt. "I'm exhausted."

He doesn't say another word as we drive toward Farmington. I couldn't go back to the house I was renting. Lawson and the guys packed my things and took them to a storage unit at Cerberus. I didn't think I was going to get out, but they didn't listen when I told them to just donate everything.

A condition of my bond is that I have to stay with my brother. Several other guys from the MC were listed as supervisors of my care, making me feel like the bad kid on an outing from a treatment center, my freedom fake and filled with so many stipulations it's like not having any freedom at all.

Lawson sighs more than once, and as much as I want to open my mouth and tell him every single detail of why I did what I did, I just can't. None of it seems real to me.

Megan Barnes died on U.S. Route 550 just over four months ago—three months after I met her at a local diner.

She told me she was a student. She lied. She dropped out of community college after half of a semester.

She told me she was going to be a teacher. She lied. Megan Barnes was a barista at a coffee shop.

I didn't ask if she was single, but I was floored when her husband came to visit me in jail, thanking me for doing something he wished he was there to do himself.

Knowing the lies, knowing she wasn't as pure and pristine as I convinced myself she was, I still feel this connection to that girl. The one who made me see stars, made me want things in life I hadn't considered until then. The woman who moaned my name in this breathy way that still has the ability to make my breathing hitch when I think about it.

The woman who looked me in the eye and begged me to help her seconds before taking her last breath.

The woman who even knowing what I know now has the ability to make me act in the very same way I did that night if given the chance.

And that's where the guilt comes from.

That's where I check my integrity.

I can admit my wrongdoing.

I know murder is wrong.

Joel Green, the man I beat until his face was unrecognizable that night, deserved his day in court. He deserved a fair trial, not the judge, jury, and executioner I turned myself into that night. He didn't deserve to go from drunk and upset about his truck to being on life support from blunt force head trauma.

I took all of that from him, the way my freedom has been taken away from me.

As true as all of that is, I wonder why I still want to open my mouth and explain away the unexplainable. Why I want my brother to look at me and possibly understand just what was going through my head that night.

He's married to the woman of his dreams. He's right in the middle of his happily ever after while my world is shattering.

Would he have acted the same way? Does it even compare?

He and Delilah love each other. They've said vows before God and their families.

It's not the same. I didn't love Megan Barnes. I slept with her. She said her own vows, had her own husband.

Turning my head until I'm looking out the passenger-side window, I try my best to go back to *that night*, the one where I saw a pretty girl in a diner and flirted. Back to the night where nothing mattered but pancakes and the taste of syrup on her lips when she kissed me. Back to the feel of her warm skin against my palm when I lifted her leg higher, when I pushed inside of her deeper.

But those images have faded, disappeared, and have been replaced with unseeing eyes, blood-stained skin, and a *help me* that went unanswered.

"The girls set up your bedroom," Lawson says as the terrain becomes familiar. "You have your own bathroom."

We're only a few miles away from Cerberus property, and even though I should feel relief at knowing I'm going to get some time to myself soon, I still hate the idea of being released. It's only going to make it that much harder when I have to go back.

"The house is over there, but I promised Delilah, I would meet her here." Instead of turning left off the road toward the four newly built houses, Lawson turns right into the Cerberus MC parking lot. A huge grin fills his face as he looks toward the front door. "Ah. There she is now."

Lawson drove in yesterday for my court hearing this morning. I told him it was fruitless to keep coming into Albuquerque since we've already had several bond hearings, but I'm grateful he stuck with it. I don't know that I would've been released if there wasn't someone there willing to stand up and agree to babysit me.

I try to smile at the sight of my sister-in-law, but I can't even muster a fake one. I don't have much to smile for these days and faking it takes too much energy.

"Come on," Lawson says as he climbs out of the truck.

I've been back here a handful of times for short visits, so it's familiar, but I still feel like I don't belong. This is my brother's family, not mine. Not once have they made me feel unwelcome, but forming attachments has never been easy for me. That's why the connections I felt with Meg—

"Drew!" Delilah barely stops long enough to brush a kiss on Lawson's cheek before she's running in my direction. "So good to see you!"

Before that night, I would've wrapped her in a hug, swirled her around, and made a joke about stealing her away from my brother, but I'm no longer that man. That man died the night Megan did.

"Good to see you, Delilah." I pat her back, ignoring her frown when she steps away. "How are Jaxon and Rob?"

"Good," she answers, her manners always on point, but she's not impressed with my lack of enthusiasm.

Jaxon is Lawson's biological father, a man he didn't meet until he was nearly grown. Our mother, a woman who used to hang out at the Cerberus clubhouse, got pregnant and took off. The man never knew he had a son, and our mom didn't disclose his identity until she was on her death bed. We came to New Mexico so Lawson could give him a piece of his mind, only he ended up giving a piece of his heart away instead. Delilah and her twin brother Samson were adopted by Jaxon and Rob, two of the original Cerberus members. I left to live with my father's family shortly after arriving but Lawson stayed behind and managed to fall in love. Their story is more complicated than that, but you can't tell by their smiling faces that they'd have it any other way.

"Ready to go inside?" Delilah wraps her arms around my brother's waist, and he doesn't miss the opportunity to hold her tight and press his lips to the top of her head.

No. "Sure."

Lawson walks toward the front of the clubhouse, once again making small talk I can't be bothered to pay attention to. I can hear the smile in his voice even with his back to me. He hasn't always been so optimistic, but I guess having an amazing woman will do that to a man. I follow along, trying not to feel bitter about my own brother and the life he's been allowed.

Chatter fills my ears the second the door opens. This place has always been lively—Cerberus members mingling with the adult children of several members. That chatter stops as if someone flipped a switch and powered down the sound. I knew I was going to be on display, and as much as I hate being here, I figured getting it done while everyone is around meant only doing it once instead of twenty different times as I ran into individual people.

I look around the room, making eye contact with several of the men who showed up to support me in various stages of my proceedings, but then my eyes snag on a pretty brunette.

This time, blinking doesn't make her fade away. Blinking doesn't turn her from the girl I've wanted to see since that night at the diner into someone I've mistaken for her.

She's there, standing in the middle of the room as gorgeous as she was the first time I saw her moaning around a decadent bite of pancakes. Her dark hair is longer now, hazel eyes wide with surprise, not unseeing and empty like last time. Her hands cling to her body, her swollen belly covered by trembling fingers.

I've truly fucking lost my mind, and if that's the case, I refuse to have several dozen people witness it.

On unsteady feet, I turn around and walk right back out the door.

Chapter 3

Isabella

"That's Drew."

Sophia whispered those words with humor in her voice when the front door opened.

I couldn't argue with her because he never told me his first name.

Drew O'Neil.

I feel like a fool.

Lawson's brother is a cop, works for New Mexico State Police.

I should say worked because he was arrested several months ago. It's all anyone has really talked about lately even though most details have been kept behind sealed lips.

Dad went to Albuquerque more than once to help with his case. I don't know how he could help because he wouldn't tell me anything when I asked.

I never put two and two together. Never once considered that the father of my child was Lawson's brother.

My hands clutch my belly, seeming too small to protect it from the fallout we both may be facing.

Drew walked out minutes ago, but I'm still standing in the middle of the room staring at the open front door. I can feel everyone's eyes on me, can hear the echo of whispers, the questions everyone are dying to ask.

"Isabella." I know that tone, and nothing good comes from my father using it.

I can't even look at him, and I don't know if it's shame or embarrassment, but my neck heats, no doubt turning red under everyone's scrutiny.

"Honey?" I look down to see Sophia's concerned eyes blinking up at me. "Is that—is he the...?"

I squeeze her hand, hoping she understands this isn't something I can talk about right now, and sure as hell won't be having this conversation in front of every single Cerberus member, their spouses and every person connected to them.

I always loved having so many people around, getting to know each and every person connected to the club. Most people gather for holidays and birthdays. Cerberus gets together every chance they can.

Tonight is no exception, only I'm the one right in the middle of the drama that always seems to hit this place. It's not Jasmine disclosing her love for two men, or Rivet admitting in front of everyone that she and Cannon—the goofball of the group—are together.

This is the second time I've been the center of the drama—the first being when Sophia let it slip I was pregnant in the first place—and last time the drama was interrupted by the phone call that Drew had been arrested.

"I'll kill him!" my dad roars.

The man has always paid way too much attention, and I'm not refuting Sophia's question. The man has put it together, and that doesn't bode well for everyone involved.

"Stop," Lawson hisses, his chest against Dad's.

"You need to calm down," Jaxon insists, his hand going to one of Dad's shoulders as Kincaid draws even closer.

"What is happening right now?" Delilah asks, confusion drawing her brows in as she looks around the room.

"Oh, Izzy. Way to go," Gigi whispers at my side. "That is going to be one good-looking baby."

I look around meeting Jasmine's eyes. Despite the age difference, she's always there for me, always the first I look to when something goes wrong.

Sadness fills her features, and I don't know if it's because I've managed to disappoint her or if she doesn't have a solution.

Dad is fuming, his face red as his eyes stay focused on the front door Drew disappeared through. He reacted the same way when he found out I was pregnant. He went after Apollo that night just because the new Cerberus member and I had a conversation in the kitchen. We talked about crackers and ginger ale, and although I never verbally confessed I was pregnant to Apollo then, I think he made the correct assumption.

Max wasn't wrong earlier when he was joking about Dad still thinking Apollo was the father even though I've been adamant that he isn't. Dad finding this out now about Drew is like getting that initial news all over again.

"Dad," I say, crossing the room and placing my hand on his chest. "You need to calm down."

"Is he—" he swallows a growl. "Did he get you pregnant?"

I stand a little taller. "I'm not having this conversation with you right now."

His eyes search mine, and I know even without the words, he can see my truth there. He's still mad, but he stops pushing against the guys who are keeping him from going after Drew.

"Are you going to go talk to him?"

I turn to look at Lawson, wondering why there's hope I haven't seen in months in his eyes. Everyone has put on a good face around here, but the strain of Drew's arrest has affected many people—Lawson and Delilah in particular. They haven't openly spoken about the strain of being apart while Lawson is out of town dealing with Drew's case, but it's clear in the way they interact with each other. They've both been quieter, less engaging. Some nights, everyone gets together and they don't come from across the street to socialize.

"Should I?"

"I don't know if that's a good idea," Delilah says, holding on to her husband's arm. "He's upset. I don't want him to—"

"He's not going to hurt her," Lawson snaps, the words coming out gritty from between his teeth.

Clearly that's part of the contention between the two. Lawson has faith that his brother is a good man, and possibly Delilah is looking at surface facts. I can't be the judge either way because I've been kept in the dark and working on my master's program, getting as much work done as I can before the baby is born.

"Go talk to him," Lawson urges again.

With a queasy stomach and trembling legs, I step outside on the front porch and close the door behind me. Dad is livid, but he knows I have to do this on my own. I had more faith in my ability until I was out here alone. I don't see a shadow walking across the road to Lawson's house, so that tells me that he didn't go that direction.

The darkness around the clubhouse doesn't scare me. I know how protected I am here, that there isn't a person around willing to mess with the men of the Cerberus MC or the women they have sworn to protect, but there's something in the air that makes my feet not want to work properly. Maybe it's knowing I'm fixing to come face-to-face with a man I never thought I'd see again, a man I didn't want to have to explain that night to.

I mean, seriously, what woman in her right mind sleeps with a guy she doesn't know? What kind of woman hands over her virginity without so much as a whimper?

Me, apparently, but he doesn't know that. More than likely, to him, I was a good time, a thrill while he was waiting for his partner to take care of whatever personal project he was working on that night.

And getting pregnant? Isn't that just the scab on a wound he didn't even know he had?

I didn't have expectations. I don't keep myself up at night with all the what could've beens.

I decided the second those two lines showed up that I could do this on my own, but not having this conversation isn't something I can avoid, not with him walking in here like a ghost from my past.

A noise on the side of the clubhouse draws my attention, forcing my feet to move in that direction.

I don't know much about this man, but I know he was charming the night we met, gentle when I needed him to be while we were up against my car, caring in the way he kissed me and how his hands fluttered over my skin like our meeting meant more to him than he could describe with words. But Delilah's unease has now become my own. I don't know him, and the man has been charged with beating another man to death. I know what he's capable of, and that is almost enough to make me turn around.

Then I hear a sob, a shuddering rush of air like an animal wounded and in need of help.

"Drew," I whisper when his hunched form comes in to view.

When he turns, I expect to see the same look of disbelief on his face, which is there in part, but it's the tears flowing down his cheeks that have me reaching for this man.

He's swift in his movement, coming to stand directly in front of me. One of his hands clamps the back of my neck, the other at my waist as he presses his forehead to mine.

"I wanted to. I just couldn't. I didn't get there in time. I should've never let you leave that night. Should've begged you to stay with me before you got in your car."

His rambling makes no sense, but that doesn't stop the urge to comfort him.

"I should've opened my mouth and said all the crazy things that were in my head. Should've told you that what we shared was special, that the connection I had to you was something I never felt before. I've thought about you every fucking day." His head draws back a few inches, those bright blue eyes that once looked at me with mirth now filled with pain and sorrow. "But you have to go, baby. You have to stay out of my head, stay out of my dreams. The torture is just too much. If I could change things, I would. If I could've saved you, if I could've gotten there... I'd give anything to go back. If I had never let you walk away, maybe you would've been somewhere else that night."

"Drew, what are you—"

"Please. I need you to go."

I blink up at him, confused by what he's saying but still feeling that same pull to him I felt that night. I brush my lips against his, my own tears now rolling down my face.

He jerks back, his face a mask of shock and confusion.

"You're real?"

He pulls his hands away, looking down at them as if he's just now realizing he was touching me.

I shake my head. "Of course I'm real."

"You died—" He takes another step away from me. "Megan, you died that night."

I hate that I lied to him. I hate a lot of things, but the regret from not being truthful to him that night hits me in the chest. I don't know what he's talking about or what he believes, but I get a sick feeling in my gut that whatever happened is somehow my fault.

"My name isn't Megan," I confess. "That's the name I use at parties when I don't want the people around me to know who I really am."

He's still confused, eyes still roving up and down my body, not spending extra time on any particular part. It's as if he thinks if he blinks or looks away, I'm going to disappear.

"My name is Isabella, Izzy. My dad works for Cerberus. Hound? Do you know Jameson Rawley?"

"You were there that night."

"At the diner. Yes. We met that night." Is there a history of schizophrenia in his family? This is something I didn't consider when deciding not to seek him out after finding out I was pregnant.

"Not at the diner! Fuck!" he roars. "In the car. You were in the car, in the wreck. You begged me to help you, but I was too late. You fucking died right in front of my eyes. I saw you in that car, saw your blood, saw your matted dark hair."

He reaches for the locks over my shoulder but draws his hand away at the last second.

"Megan died that night."

"I'm not Megan."

"Is everything okay?"

I don't look over my shoulder with Lawson's question. Drew doesn't look away from my face but doesn't open his mouth to say another word either.

He begins to rock back and forth on his feet as if he can't decide between running away or losing control. Lawson must feel the change in the air because he comes around me, putting his body between mine and his brother's.

"I ruined my fucking life for you!"

The angry words make me clutch my belly as I take a few steps back. Getting away, protecting myself and this child becomes my only priority. I know from experience that you can't talk sense into someone as upset as Drew is right now. I walk away not knowing if I'll ever get another chance to speak with him again.

Chapter 4

Drew

I'm losing her again.

She's fading away, her silky hair flowing in the breeze.

I need her. I need to chase after her, to touch her skin, to hold on to her for just a little while longer.

It can't be real. She can't be real. Have I really fallen so far that my mind is breaking?

"Megan!" I yell, but strong arms wrap around me, preventing me from chasing after her.

"That's Izzy," my brother hisses in my ear. "Hound's daughter."

She said the same, but that still doesn't explain why she's here. I spin, punching the brick of the clubhouse wall. Maybe pain will make me snap out of whatever delusion I'm having. Maybe pain will wake me up from this nightmare, and I'll find myself snoozing in the passenger seat of Lawson's truck. I lost time while he was driving, and this has to be why.

I'm not at the Cerberus clubhouse.

I'm asleep, reliving something I've wanted for months—seeing her face again, feeling the warmth of her skin. God, this isn't the first time I pictured her, but making up a swollen belly, letting myself imagine a universe where we have a child together?

Jesus, how fucked up is my head?

My feet are moving, and before I know it, we're standing on an unfamiliar front porch.

"Let's get inside. Maybe it's low blood sugar. We should've stopped to grab something to eat on the way here. Are you hungry?"

I manage to shake my head, and thankfully my brother doesn't push the issue.

Low blood sugar. What a ridiculous notion for seeing ghosts and feeling warm skin, but nightmares aren't like reality. Nightmares take the form of the things we can't have, the things we regret most.

Lawson clings to me, guiding me up the stairs, and as much as I want to pull away, as much as I need to be alone right now, I know I won't make it without his help.

"I don't want this," I mutter, eyes on my feet as they take each stair cautiously.

"Do you want to go back across the street?"

I want nothing more, but I don't know that my fractured mind could handle seeing her again.

"I want a bed and a stiff drink."

"You can't—"

"I know."

Even in my nightmare I can't get relief from the rules and regulations the judge set forth before allowing me to bond out.

"Is she... is that your baby?"

"You saw it too?"

I look over at him, an all too familiar frown on his face.

"She's pregnant."

"The girl I was with died. Megan died."

"She isn't Megan."

"Nothing makes sense," I confess as he opens a door at the end of the hallway.

"You just need sleep."

I need so much more than sleep, but there's no real reason to argue the point with him.

He releases me, stepping away and further into the bedroom as I linger in the doorway.

"We had all of your things brought here."

A familiar comforter is spread out on the bed, the lamp on the side table the one from my house back in Albuquerque.

"We figured that comforts from home would make it easier to be here."

He couldn't have been more wrong. I don't want reminders of what I had, what I lost that night.

"Thank you," I say instead, because how could he have known?

"Your furniture is in storage along with several other boxes. The room is only so big, but if you need anything that's missing, just let me know and I'll get it for you."

"This is fine."

My back molars grind together, a way to keep my mouth shut. He's only helping, doing what he thinks is best, but it's all futile, a waste of time and energy because I'll be gone again shortly, either in a grave or in the New Mexico State Prison system where I'll also end up in a grave. The results are the same no matter which avenue is taken.

And somehow, that thought comforts me. Knowing it'll all be over soon calms something inside of me, making the worry seem less extraordinary.

"Drew, I... fuck..." Lawson's hand scrapes over the top of his head, and I don't say a word.

I don't offer an out because I'm just as lost as he seems.

"Do you want to talk about it?"

I hitch my shoulders. "Nothing makes sense. I can't talk about something that I can't get right in my head."

"Megan Barnes died that night, Drew. Hound's daughter, Izzy isn't her. Have you gotten them confused? Do they look alike?"

I look at him, but can't seem to get my head on straight enough to explain.

No one knows about that night I shared with the woman at the diner, but if what he's saying is true—if Izzy's proclamation is true—the girl who died in the crash and the woman I spent time with aren't the same person.

"I just need some time to work through it all."

"Did you hurt—"

"Killed Lawson." My jaw ticks while I glare at him. "I killed that man."

"Did you do it because you thought it was Izzy?"

"I need some time," I repeat.

"If you did, that changes things. It—"

"It changes nothing."

"But—"

"I'm going to bed," I snap, walking toward the open en suite door.

"I'll see you in the morning."

Different emotions—shame, confusion, disappointment, heartache—hit me in the chest one after the other.

Did I mess up so completely that I killed a man because I thought he hurt someone I imagined finding and making a life with?

Would I have acted the same way, done the same thing for a stranger, if it were clear when I approached that car that it wasn't Megan—Izzy?

I blamed a bad memory for minor color difference in cars, for the wreckage being a Camry instead of the Corolla I pressed that woman to in the parking lot.

I blamed time for the shade difference and length of her hair, for the tiny tattoo on the girl's wrist, one I didn't notice that night in the parking lot.

My mind registered so many differences, but I shoved them all down, seeing what I wanted to see rather than keeping a straight head.

The lies she told that night make more sense now. They weren't lies at all. The woman in the car and the woman in the diner aren't the same.

One is still dead and one is across the street, potentially pregnant with my child.

I'm sick to my stomach over the relief I feel that's accompanying the enlightenment.

Fuck, am I glad that woman didn't die? Does that mean I'm happy the other one did?

No.

I shake my head to rid it of those thoughts. She didn't deserve to die, didn't deserve to use her last breath begging for help from a man that had none to offer.

She's alive. The woman that infiltrated my thoughts long before that night on the highway is alive.

I have the chance to see her again, talk to her, get to know more about her. This would be my own fairy tale if I hadn't ruined my entire life.

Pregnant with my baby?

Please, God, let it be someone else's child. I'm in no position to be a father, in no way good enough to deserve something like that. No child should be raised with a dad in prison.

I have a million questions, half of which I don't think I want the answers to. In order to prevent myself from running across the street and demanding all the truths from her, I strip down and climb into the shower, first taking the punishment of freezing water over my body before turning it so hot that it scalds my skin. What other ways can I repent for the choices I made?

I don't even know what will happen next. All I know is staying away from that woman will be the only thing that will keep me sane.

Chapter 5

Isabella

I thought I was ready to handle this situation until the knock hit my door. All night I formulated what parts I would share and which ones I'd keep to myself. Honestly, I'm grown and I don't owe anyone in this house an explanation, but I know I'm going to give one anyway.

Hiding the facts of this pregnancy wasn't easy, but it's impossible now.

"Come in."

Dressed in his normal jeans and t-shirt, Dad opens the door, choosing to lean against the doorframe rather than coming fully into the room.

He's closed off, probably mad, and not impressed with the news that came to light last night.

"I can make a lot of assumptions, Iz, but I'd prefer to get the truth."

"Okay." I drop my eyes to my hands, doing my best to keep them from clutching my pregnant belly.

"Can you start at the beginning?"

"I stopped at the diner in Cuba, the one with those fluffy pancakes."

He doesn't engage, doesn't smile at the reminder that we stopped there together on the way to get into my dorm at college freshman year.

"It was spring break. I met him there. He was flirty and charming." I drop my eyes, unable to say the next part while looking at him. "I got pregnant."

He grunts, an unhappy sound from deep in his chest. "So flirting these days turns into unprotected sex?"

"I didn't know that he didn't wear a condom."

I knew after we were done, but I was so wrapped up in him, I didn't consider the consequences.

"Didn't know? How is that even possible? We've had more than one conversation about being safe."

"I hadn't ever—" I snap my mouth closed.

"Hadn't ever..." He growls again, this time the sound closer as he pushes away from the doorframe. "Are you telling me that you gave up your virginity to a man you just met?"

If he's angry now, I can't imagine how he'd react if he knew exactly how it went down.

"Don't," I hiss, somehow finding my backbone. "I'm a grown woman. I make my own choices. If I recall, you knocked Gigi up the first night you met her in a back alley outside of a strip club, so don't act all high and mighty right now."

"How did—"

"She likes to overshare, Dad." I straighten my back and look up at him. "I don't regret that night. I don't regret this baby. But if you have a problem with it, then I don't have to stick around."

"That's not my intention, Izzy."

He holds his hand out to me, but I refuse to take it. Pain flashes in his eyes as he lowers it back down to his side.

"It's not a perfect situation."

"You kept all of this to yourself. I asked more than once who the father was. I nearly put Apollo in the ground for it."

"And I told you I don't lie to you. When you asked if Apollo was the father, I told you the truth. That night with him was wild, a whirlwind of chaos. I'm not proud to say I never got his first name. His last name was on his uniform, but I never put two and two together. I didn't know that this baby's father was Lawson's brother until he walked into the clubhouse last night."

"And he didn't know about the baby?"

"Wasn't it obvious?"

Dad takes a step back, a stumbling sort of shuffle as if he'd been hit in the chest with a bullet. "You weren't going to tell him."

It's not a question, but I feel obligated to answer, anyway. This is where most of my guilt comes from.

"I wasn't. I didn't figure a man who... I didn't think he'd want to be a dad."

"That's not your decision to make. How could you do that, take that choice away from him after you know what I went through with your mother, how much time I lost with you?"

Tears burn the backs of my eyes.

"You could've tracked him down. Hell, you knew his last name and where he worked. It would've been simple, and if you were having trouble, Max can locate anyone."

"I know."

And I considered all of that, but a man who has sex with a girl on the hood of her car didn't seem like the type of man to step up to the plate, and watching his face turn from that flirty smirk he had that night into pure disgust wasn't something I could handle. I knew what the outcome would be, so I made the choice to avoid the pain of his rejection.

"And what were you going to tell that son of yours when he asks questions?"

"I hadn't gotten that far."

"Being a parent is about selflessness, Iz. The child has a right to know. Drew had a right to know."

The stubborn side of me wants to argue that he does know now, so there's no point in being mad about it, but I know what I did wasn't the best course of action.

"I'm just... fuck, Isabella, I'm disappointed in you."

Without another word, he turns around and leaves my room. Mere seconds later, the front door opens and slams closed. Hearing Amelia crying and calling for her daddy downstairs makes my stomach turn. He hurt her feelings by walking out, and I caused that.

Queasiness forces me from the bed, but I go to the window for fresh air rather than the bathroom to puke. I'm so tired of being sick, of feeling horrible every day, but I wouldn't change it. Nothing about how my father just acted is enough for me to regret this baby.

I was shocked when I found out I was pregnant. I questioned everything about my life, but with time came acceptance, and now I'm excited. I told myself I'd be a good mother, better than the one I was given, but Dad's words come back to me.

Drew had a right to know.

And boy is Dad right.

My mom took off with me and married another man, one that could support her current lifestyle, one my Marine father would never be able to provide. At seventeen, he joined the Corps to do everything he could to take care of my mom and me. She repaid him by disappearing. Dad never set eyes on me until I was four, and although we eventually started writing each other back and forth through my nanny, I didn't meet him in person until I was a teenager.

Dad is right. I was going to do the very same thing to Drew that was done to him. He despises my mother for what she did, and I have no doubt that he'll never be able to look at me with kindness again.

With breaths in through my nose and out through my mouth, I lift the window to get some fresh air into the room. I already know I'm going to be sick, but right now, I can't tell if it's the baby or disappointment that's going to force me to my knees in the bathroom.

All thoughts of nausea vanish when I look across to Lawson and Delilah's house. Of course they're right next door, the houses having been built at nearly the exact same time.

And there stands Drew, shirtless and frowning, the skin of his torso marked with horrific bruises.

He's looking in this direction, but it's as if he doesn't see me, like he's looking through me.

I want to go over there, insist he tell me what happened that would leave such brutal marks on his skin. My legs ache with the need, but I'm frozen in place, thinking back to last night and his insistence that he thought I was dead, begging me to leave him alone because he just couldn't handle seeing me.

I press my fingers to the window glass, an olive branch of sorts to let him know I'm here, but instead of offering the same, he turns and walks away, disappearing into an area of the room I can't see.

Dad's mad, Lawson's mad, it's clear Drew is mad.

And I deserve it. I kept a secret I wasn't supposed to keep.

My ringing phone startles me enough to rip a yelp from my throat, but the name flashing on the screen was just as expected as Dad's visit to my room this morning.

"Hey," I say when I answer.

"We have a lot to talk about," Sophia begins. "Are you ready to talk?"

"Not really," I mutter.

"But you will if I ask the right questions?"

"I've got nothing to hide," I confess.

"Drew is the father?"

"Yes."

She chuckles. "Don't give me too much information or anything."

I remain silent, and when she speaks again, her tone is different, taking on a more serious edge.

"What are you going to do?"

"Have a baby."

"Iz." It's a warning. "Are you going to talk to him?"

"I don't think he wants to talk to me."

I'm not going to explain what happened outside the clubhouse last night. His confusion and anger isn't anyone's business, and I understand Lawson well enough to know he won't discuss it with anyone unless he feels they really need the information. He may tell Delilah and probably Jaxon and Rob, but this isn't going to be a topic of discussion around the Cerberus clubhouse living room.

"You have less than three months before that baby gets here. You need to talk with him."

"And what, give him a choice? Is it really even a choice? The man may go to prison."

"The Cerberus men won't let that happen."

"I know you were raised with those men, and they can do no wrong in your eyes, but they don't control the judicial system in New Mexico. Drew O'Neil has been charged with homicide, and there's a good chance he'll land in prison for it. Your degree is in criminal justice. You should know that better than I do."

"He's still owed a conversation."

"Are you going to jump on me for not seeking him out, too? I already got it from Dad today. I don't need a second round."

"You were wrong."

"I know."

"I thought you told him. You let me believe the dad knew and didn't want anything to do with the baby."

"I was avoiding this conversation," I murmur.

"It was wrong."

"I know," I hiss. "But is it wrong because the dad is Drew or because it's innately wrong? What if the guy wasn't a cop? What if he was a drug dealer? Would you still have the same opinion?"

"Now you're just trying to justify your wrong actions."

Leave it to my best friend to tell it straight. I should be grateful to have someone like her in my life, but right now I just want to hang up on her and bury my head in my pillows.

"It's done. I can't change my choices."
"But you still need to go over there and talk to him."
"And if he tells me to get lost, that he's not interested?"
"Then you have your answer, but he deserves the choice."
"I'll talk to him," I concede.
"Today?"
"Eventually," I offer. "Right now I need to shower and probably throw up."
I hang up the phone before she can try to argue about my timeframe choices.

Chapter 6

Drew

Seeing her even after hours of coming to terms with the truth is like a knife to the gut. I can't make reality mesh with what I've thought for the last several months.

I walk away from the window because seeing her, seeing that hand raised for me is too much to handle.

Pacing doesn't help.

Questioning my next steps doesn't bring any answers.

I've seen a lot of things, been through more before I graduated high school than most kids will experience in a lifetime. When my mother died, I felt guilty for the possibility of a different life. Lawson found his in Delilah and I was able to have everything I never knew I could ask for when I moved to the East Coast with my Aunt Kathy and Uncle Pete. I had a home, a loving family, food and shelter, all things I needed but never fully had as a small child.

But before I lived with them, I saw death and destruction. I witnessed what many boys without a father did, saw their choices, the way their hands were forced. I stood to the side while crimes were committed, while young boys hurt others because they weren't taught that life was valuable.

By the time I left New Mexico, after only spending a short time here with Lawson's family, I knew I wanted to be a cop. I wanted to make a difference. I needed to be a light in the darkness for those that couldn't see a way out. I chose the New Mexico State Police because it brought me closer to my brother, the man who despite his own upbringing became a man who garnered respect, a man who could hold his head proud and know that he makes a difference in the world.

And less than a year on the job brings me to now, a murderer heading to prison.

I guess getting out of the old neighborhood, graduating with good grades from a nice school on the East Coast means nothing. The degree I earned through fast tracking before the police academy means nothing. I'll never work as a cop. I'll never be able to put my education to use. I'll never be able to look back and know I've helped even a single person do better in life. I didn't have time to make a difference. I acted without thought and ended up right where I was always meant to be. There is no escape, no reprieve from my past.

I jolt with the knock on my door, but it's not surprising that Lawson isn't going to let me sit up here and wallow in my choices. He's the good brother, the one actually capable of helping. But when I tug the bedroom door open to tell him I'm a lost cause, it's not him.

Izzy blinks up at me, her hazel eyes greener today than amber colored.

"I umm..."

My heart pounds in my chest. The need to pull her against me, to once again make sure she's real is a struggle.

Keeping my gaze on her face is impossible, and I eventually look at her swollen stomach.

"I'm not really in the mood for company."

She frowns, but doesn't get the hint to turn around and leave.

Her fingers caress her belly, and mine itch to do the same. It only serves to make me even angrier, even more confused and simultaneously, I take a step back and bite my tongue to keep from spewing all the hateful words I feel like I'm deserved.

"The baby is yours," she says, stepping inside my room and closing the door.

There goes the hopes I had last night that this was another man's situation to deal with.

"Were you ever going to tell me?"

"No." She blinks as if she's trying to keep tears at bay. "I never expected to see you again."

"That's pretty fucked up, don't you think?" I move further away, sitting down roughly on the edge of the bed when my legs hit the mattress.

I anticipated her answer, but that doesn't make it any easier to deal with at the moment.

"The same night we met, I let you make lo... we fucked on the hood of my car."

I cringe at her choice of words. I knew then she deserved better than what I did, and it's not easier to stomach it now.

"I didn't figure you'd be interested in having a baby with a woman charmed so easily."

Is she calling herself a whore? I know what she gave me that night, and not once since have I thought about her in a negative way. I can't tell her any of that, though. I don't know where we stand, but I know what my future looks like. Offering any type of hope—not that she's interested in what I can or can't offer—would be pointless. She could be here to tell me she doesn't want me around, that raising our baby with a felon dad involved isn't going to happen. Can I really blame her if that's the case?

"I never wanted to be a father." The words are true. I grew up disappointed, and I didn't want the same for my own children.

"You don't have to be one now." Her tone is flat, unemotional, and although we're talking about serious, life-altering things, I don't get the impression that she's saying it to induce guilt.

"Does your dad know?"

I got out of the clubhouse so fast last night that I didn't speak to another person but Lawson, but my behavior when I saw her doesn't leave much room for question.

"He does," she confirms.

"So you're forcing my hand?"

"No one is telling you to step up. If you don't want to be a dad, then don't."

"That's not—"

"I'd rather you stay away than sticking around just to save face. Your son deserves better than that."

There are no tears on her face when she turns around and leaves. There was no anger or malice in her voice—plain, simple truth, resignation is all that registers. She doesn't even slam the front door when she leaves.

I think that hits me harder than I could've ever imagined. She literally doesn't care if I'm around or not.

I drop my head into my hands, my shoulders burdened under the weight of the decisions I have to make.

***

"I grabbed strawberry jam at the store," Lawson says as he places a couple of loaded down reusable grocery bags on the center island. "Delilah only eats grape."

"Thanks," I mutter, refusing to tell him that I haven't been able to stomach peanut butter and jelly sandwiches since we left Texas years ago after our mom died.

Choices were slim as far as food was concerned growing up, and when I was able to make my own selections, I left many of the things we ate back then in the dust. If I never set my eyes on a pack of ramen noodles again in my life, it would be too soon.

"We're going to grill out tonight, but anything in the fridge or pantry is up for grabs."

"I just came to get some water."

"You need to eat."

My jaw flexes, the urge to tell him to get off my ass strong, but I know he'd act this way even if he hadn't just picked me up outside of the jail with my meager belongings in a clear trash bag.

"Like steaks and burgers?" I ask, offering him an olive branch.

I don't have to make his life miserable or insult his generosity just because I'm an asshole going through a ton of shit.

"Jinx would call them best burgers. Kincaid will do the steaks. Delilah is already across the street helping to get things ready." He has his back to me as he's putting away groceries. "You're coming, right?"

I don't miss the insistence in his voice. I'm not supposed to be left alone, and although the judge didn't have an issue with me staying at Lawson's house while he's at work, it's Saturday and the shop is closed.

"I'll be there."

"I saw Izzy over here earlier."

"You just saw her, huh? Come on, Law, if you have a question just ask it. Stop fucking around."

"One, you'll remember to watch that mouth when we head across the street. Kincaid and the guys have your back with everything that's going on, but they're not going to tolerate that kind of language."

"Kincaid cusses more than I do," I argue. I've witnessed some extremely heated conversations between him and the first attorney I hired. That man was fired and replaced with one Cerberus approved of. The suggested tactics for my case weren't much different, but the presentation was the change. Kincaid didn't take very kindly to the first attorney saying, *"He's fucked."*

"He doesn't talk like that in front of women, and you'll be expected to do the same."

"And two?"

"You've got to stop being this angry, surly bastard. I know what you're facing, and although I'm hoping for a different outcome than the one you're resigned yourself to, you're free right now. You get to go across the street and swim in the pool if you don't mind your nuts shriveling because honestly, it got too damn cold last night. You get to sit down with amazing people and enjoy a meal."

Take away the circumstances that brought me to Farmington in the first place, and all of that sounds like heaven. Well, maybe minus the cold-ass pool part.

"Okay."

"Okay? Just that easy?"

"I'll try not to be an asshole. I'll watch my mouth. I'll eat the food."

"Now back to Izzy."

I groan, turning around and walking into the panty. Maybe PB&J doesn't sound so bad right now. Talking with a mouthful of peanut butter is nearly impossible after all.

"She was here. I know she was because I opened the door for her when she knocked. What did she have to say?"

"She confirmed I'm the father."

Strong arms wrap around me from the back.

"That's awesome, man. You're going to have a son."

Izzy used the word son earlier, but it didn't hit me until just now.

A lump forms in my throat so large, I can't form the words to tell my brother that being in this entire situation is my worst damned nightmare.

Chapter 7

Isabella

"They're nuts," I mutter, but a smile is spread across my face watching some of the guys playing around in the pool.

"They're manly men, showcasing that even a little cold water won't keep them from having fun," Sophia clarifies.

"I'm a manly man," Colton argues.

"Sure you are, sweetheart." She pats his chest in a comically placating way, making the others around us laugh. "But Rick and Landon are clearly more manly."

I watch the teens splashing around after the volleyball they've been hitting back and forth across the net.

"I'm just glad it's a clear day," Delilah says, her eyes closed, face tilted up to the sky.

I grin but turn my head away when Lawson's eyes get trapped to the front of her bikini top.

"It's almost too hot," Gigi complains even though a smile is on her face watching Amelia play with Kincaid.

Dad hasn't said a word to me since this morning, and I'd wager he's purposely keeping his distance. Gigi doesn't seem fazed by it, used to his moods by now.

If Lawson is here, that means there's a good chance that Drew is lurking around. I refuse to scan the group of people to find him. Everyone from Cerberus is here. I overheard that their orders will be pulling them away first thing in the morning, so they're trying to have a little fun before their responsibilities kick back in.

"Hey, baby girl."

My smile feels fake and I pray it doesn't look that way when I glance at Jinx, one of the Cerberus guys bent over Simone's belly.

"Would you stop?" Rocker says, swatting at his best friend to get him away from his woman.

"What?" Jinx looks genuinely confused. "I've always talked to her belly that way."

"When it was *your* baby in there. This one is mine. Get lost."

How those three—Simone, Jinx, and Rocker—have managed to remain so close in a situation that would've torn many others apart is beyond me. She has two men in her life willing to protect her, her son, and the little boy growing in her belly, and I can't even make eye contact with Drew without wanting to strangle him.

Or kiss him.

God, how many times have I thought about kissing him since he walked into the clubhouse last night? I think a million would be lowballing the guess.

"Hey."

I squeal when cold water drips over my legs and stomach, but a genuine smile is on my face when I look up and see Apollo drying himself with a towel.

"Having fun with the manly men?" I tease as he sits on the edge of my lounger.

"Always."

"And your nuts?" Cannon asks. He's always been the one skating on the edge of the rules Cerberus has lain out for everyone.

"My nuts are perfectly fine."

"Because Izzy keeps them in her purse?"

The smile drops from Apollo's mouth, and I can tell he's gearing up to argue. He looks down at me instead when I place my hand on his.

Cannon hisses when Rivet, the only female member of Cerberus, pinches him. They stare at each other having a conversation without words before Cannon offers, "It's just a joke, man. Sorry."

Apollo ignores him, leaning in close to whisper in my ear. His hand is on my stomach, an intimate gesture that never bothered me before.

"My nuts wouldn't fit in your purse." He presses cold lips to my cheek.

I should be focused on him, should be paying attention to my friend and those around me, but it's then that my eyes find Drew's on the other side of the pool.

He's in cargo shorts and a t-shirt, a stark contrast to the uniform he was wearing the night I met him, but the leisurely look does nothing to detract from his handsomeness. His jaw is tense, fingers nearly crushing the can of soda in his huge hand.

Apollo, noticing my attention is elsewhere, swivels slightly to look over his shoulder. "We still need to have a conversation about him."

I nod, an instinctual reaction to appease him.

"Soon, Izzy."

"Okay," I agree.

At this point, I should just hold a damn conference with everyone here, tell them all my secrets and get it over with.

"Izzy?" Cold fingers brush my skin, making me pull my eyes from Drew's glare to look at Apollo. "Him being here now doesn't change things for me."

Oh, God. Was he lying when he agreed to being only friends? What kind of drama is this going to cause? Will I ever catch a break?

Maybe moving out on my own and coming here less would be best. That might work for my sanity, but I know the baby will have a better life sticking closer to family. Running from my problems isn't an option. I know my dad wouldn't let it happen, and I have no doubt Apollo would chase after me as well. Drew? Who knows what he would do if I left. He'd probably be relieved that his mistakes were no longer right in front of his face.

"Can we talk?" Drew asks.

Apollo releases my chin, a low growl coming from his thick chest.

"I'll catch you later?"

"Sure," I tell him.

Then the man presses another cold kiss to my cheek, his hand running over the exposed skin of my belly. Several guys chuckle at Apollo's display, but I don't have time to evaluate the entire situation.

I knew a bikini was a bad idea, but none of my other bathing suits fit.

"Izzy," Drew hisses. "A moment alone?"

"Okay," I tell him, trying my best to get out of the lounger without help.

It's impossible, but when Drew reaches down and takes one hand while using his other at my lower back, I don't regret that Sophia, the one who normally helps me stand, is too entranced by Colton to notice.

The second I'm on my feet; however, he releases me and steps back, like someone would do after bumping into a stranger on the street.

As we walk toward the back door of the clubhouse, I attempt to stiffen my resolve, try to tamp down the anger that has been slowly building since this morning and his declaration that he never wanted to be a father.

I don't know why I expected anything different. That very reasoning is why I didn't plan to seek him out with the news of my pregnancy in the first place, and this high horse he's on right now is enough to make me shove him in the pool despite the frigid water.

Knowing people will be in and out of the kitchen, I lead us to the hallway.

"Yes?" I ask, turning around to face him.

I attempt to cross my arms under my breasts, but my stomach gets in the way, so I drop them to my sides.

His eyes flare watching the movements, but they stay on my chest when I lower my arms.

Goosebumps form on my skin, and as much as I want to blame the wet spot on my suit from contact with Apollo's damp swim trunks, I know it's his eyes on me once again that makes it appear.

"Drew," I whisper, and it seems to snap him out of whatever trance he was in.

"You let him touch you."

"Apollo? He's my friend."

"And that's my baby."

"And what's your point?" I snap.

"I don't like seeing another man touch you."

"You don't own me. One night definitely doesn't grant you any rights where I'm concerned, even if I am pregnant with your child. Apollo is just a friend." I step closer, hating that he steps away from me.

What was I expecting? For him to hold his ground and wrap his arms around me once I got close enough? Maybe that's what I wanted, even in my angry state.

"You never wanted to be a dad? Well, I never wanted to be a single mother either. I'm not one of those women that's going to fight for independence and turn away every man interested in me just off principle. So either step up or step out of the way. I'm not going to be alone forever."

"I didn't..." His mouth hinges open and closed, but he doesn't speak.

"If love is in the cards for me, I'm not going to snub my nose at it, Drew. I deserve to be loved and so does this baby."

With the threat of tears clogging my throat, I spin around and walk away from him. Rejoining the get-together outside isn't an option. Dad will take one look at my face and would then run the possibility of being arrested for knocking Drew's lights out. I don't know why I let that man get me so riled up. It's fine, albeit a little heartbreaking, if he doesn't want to be involved in the baby's life, but I'll be damned if he's going to stay in the shadows and only poke his head out when he thinks another viable candidate is sniffing around.

"You okay?" Relief washes over me when I see Apollo standing in the living room.

I knew he wouldn't be far.

"I think I need to go lie down."

"What did he say to you?"

"Nothing. This isn't about him. I'm tired."

"He's jealous of me."

He has nothing to be jealous of, and that rubs me more wrong than anything. I could understand him being upset if I had feelings for another man, but getting angry at a guy that doesn't have a chance? Ridiculous.

"I'm not discussing this with you right now."

"Do you ever plan to talk to me about it?"

"I'm going to go lie down," I repeat.

"I'll walk you."

Apollo's warm capable hand presses to my lower back and the touch is comforting. Apollo is comfort and help and reassurance. He's friendly and willing to put in the time.

Why can't I feel something more than platonic love for this man? He's handsome and generous. He's genuine, but has never once looked at me with the type of charismatic smile Drew gave me the night we met.

Allowing him into my life, letting him love this baby and love me like I insisted to Drew I deserved would be so easy, seamless really, but I see the love Gigi and Dad have. I've witnessed my best friend fall in love. I've watched everyone around me with their significant others, and I want that too. Apollo deserves someone willing to look at him the way Diego still looks at Emmalyn even after decades.

"Thank you," I tell him when he helps me down the front steps. "When you go back, will you let everyone know where I am? Dad will worry."

"I can text him. I'd rather not leave you alone."

"I'll be fine."

"We can cuddle like we did a few weeks ago."

I smile. "I fell asleep, you cuddled me."

"It was nice."

I pause before climbing the steps to my front porch and turn to face him. Placing a soft hand on his bare chest, I want to comfort him, but then he covers mine with his own, and he looks so damn hopeful it makes me feel like a jerk.

"Apollo," I sigh, pulling my hand away. "We're friends."

"I know." He gives me a weak smile.

"We're only ever going to be friends."

"I want to help you raise your son."

"And I want a romance worthy of a love story." I didn't know it was what I needed until the words left my mouth, but as they meet his ears, I know every syllable is true. "True love doesn't start with let me help you with that kid."

"It does." He claps both of my hands in his, excitement filling his eyes. "My grandad was in the Navy. He met a woman who had four kids, and he offered that to her. They were married for over forty years before he died. I don't care if love comes later. We'll get there."

"Do you love me?" He opens his mouth, but I shush him. "Really love me, Apollo?"

He swallows. "I'll get there."

"I don't want to lose you as a friend, but you need to understand, friends is all we'll ever be. I don't *want we'll get there*. I deserve more. You deserve more."

I lift up on my tiptoes and press a kiss to his cheek. He's reluctant to release my hand, but he doesn't say a word as I climb the steps to the house and disappear inside.

Chapter 8

Drew

"Crap," Lawson hisses as he wipes at his eyes with back of his hand. "That one is stout."

I chuckle, taking a drink of my soda and wishing it were a damn beer. "Don't tell me Mrs. Pierson's chili is what's going to bring you to your knees."

"I think she made it with ghost peppers," he says reaching for the can in my hand. "I won't be able to judge the others because I no longer have taste buds. You can do it. Here taste this."

I hold my nearly empty hands up, refusing to take the bowl of chili from him. "Not a chance. I hate spicy food."

He coughs a little before turning the soda up and draining it. The grimace never leaves his face. "You're a man now. I thought you'd get over that with age."

"Getting over not liking my mouth being on fire isn't a thing. How is it working for you?"

"I'm considering taking up your stance on it."

I laugh, a sound that seems to be coming easier these days. I've been back in Farmington for a little over a week, but although I'm here at the community chili cookoff and fundraiser, I'd prefer to be nearly any place but here.

Families swarm around, children running and laughing, dragging colorful balloons behind them. Cerberus members are milling about, smiling and interacting with everyone, their leather cuts not a deterrent in this situation. I've always known the MC was involved in the community, but it's eye opening to see them in action.

Most of the men that are paired up stick close to their women, not taking their eyes from the beauties for a second. They see a lot in their lives and aren't willing to risk their safety at an event like this. Most people would call it possessiveness, and from the way I've seen a few of the men eyeball some guys willing to risk a second look, that may play a part, but I also recognize it as hypervigilance. Some would consider it a bad thing, being too alert to the point of obsessive, but these men handle themselves well. They manage to carry on conversations, something I've struggled with since arriving and noticing Izzy on the other side of the park.

Thankfully, both Hound and Dominic, Izzy's best friend's dad, are keeping close to her.

That asshole, Apollo, is also extra attentive to her as always. Just the sight of him makes me want to be violent. I know he's a good guy. I know he'd never hurt her. Kincaid doesn't hire people like that. But even though I told her I never wanted to be a dad, even though I've kept my distance since she told me to step aside in the hallway last weekend, I can't help my own sense of possessiveness I feel for her.

I felt it the night I met her, and every second since. When I thought she died, I wanted to strangle Megan's husband when he showed up to thank me, and none of it makes sense.

I don't do possessive. I never did. I watched my mother struggle with it, being controlled by the men coming in and out of her life. I didn't want to be that guy. I didn't want to get so wrapped up in a woman that I lost my head over her.

Yet, as I watch Izzy from forty yards away, I want to shove my fist into the face of the man grinning and talking to her.

"That's Landon," Lawson says, finally able to speak without hissing air over his burning tongue. "Kid's son."

"That man?" I don't point, but rather angle my head. "In the blue shirt?"

"He's only seventeen, not really a man."

I could remind him just how much of a man he thought he was at that age, but I hold my tongue.

"What the hell are they feeding him?" I can calm down now knowing that there's no way a kid would have a chance with her.

"Who knows, but the boy is a beast. Kills it every year on the baseball field."

"Where is he headed after high school? Marines?"

Lawson chuckles. "I don't know him well, but from what I hear, he plans to get as far away from Farmington as possible, and has no interest in following in his father's footsteps. Griffin is the only one of the original members' sons that went into the military."

"Oh." I don't know what else I can say. I'm not exactly an asshole, but hearing the life stories of everyone connected to the club doesn't interest me if they aren't somehow directly linked to Izzy.

"Izzy and Apollo aren't together?"

Lawson is silent for so long, I have to pull my eyes from the man offering a red sno-cone to Izzy.

"Well?"

"No, they aren't together. Just friends. I don't think Apollo is happy about it, but according to Delilah who has talked with Izzy's best friend, Sophia, I don't think the man is willing to give up on her just yet."

"But you don't know for sure?"

He shrugs. "Hound thought he was the baby's father for the longest time."

"Is that right?"

"He's very protective of her. Most men wouldn't get within a couple of feet of that girl with all the warnings he's issued about her. Apollo is the first one to brave his wrath to get to know her."

"He hasn't said a word to me," I confess.

I figure he's trying to psych me out, get me agitated enough to come talk to him. I respect the man. He's one of the ones who stood up in court and told the judge he'd be responsible for me at my first denied bond hearing, but I don't owe him an explanation. Izzy is grown and made her own decisions that night.

"He will," Lawson says, and it sounds like an ominous promise. "Have you met Colton Matthews?"

My brother smiles, extending his hand as the tall man walks up with a smiling Sophia on his arm.

"Colton, this is my brother, Drew."

I shake the man's hand and nod at Sophia whose eyes are darting between me and the guy. He looks a little old for her being at least ten years or so older, but who am I to judge.

"Did you ever get involved in events like this?" Colton asks, his eyes roving over the crowd dispersed with several uniformed officers.

"We should have them more often," Sophia interjects. "This is the first time I've seen this one in full uniform."

Her hand runs the length of Colton's shirt, stopping barely above his gun belt. The move is blatantly sexual, and although it pulls an uncomfortable chuckle from Lawson, Colton rolls his eyes as if he's used to her acting this way.

"No, sir," I answer. "I wasn't with the department long enough."

"Ah." Colton cringes and I feel bad for his embarrassment. "Sor—"

"You know who else loves a man in uniform?" Sophia smiles. "Izzy, but I guess you already know that, huh?"

My cheeks flame, not with embarrassment or shame this time but anger.

"Sophia," Colton hisses as Lawson shifts back and forth on his feet.

"What?" she asks, genuinely confused before turning back to look at me. "Oh shit. I didn't mean... fuck, Drew."

She cups her hand over her mouth, and as she tries to blink away tears forming in her eyes, I know she didn't mean to be insulting by bringing up the fact that I'll never wear another uniform, but the words hit their mark.

I clench my jaw as Colton guides her away.

"That one doesn't think before she speaks," Lawson explains.

"It's fine." It isn't. "I think I'm ready to head back to the house."

"Ah, well, Delilah has promised to stick around for cleanup, but I bet I can find someone that's ready to get out of here."

He knows I need to leave, knows I can't stomach being here, and thankfully it doesn't seem like he's going to argue about me being left at the house alone.

I stand by myself for ten minutes before he returns. While waiting, I can't even look in Izzy's direction.

"I found you a ride."

My mood sours even further when I turn in the direction of Lawson's voice to see Hound and Gigi walking up. Their little girl is fast asleep in a stroller, pouty lips stained pink from a sno-cone.

"Perfect," I say with a half-hearted smile, not entirely certain this man wouldn't kill me in front of his wife and child and dump my body in the desert.

Thankfully, Gigi climbs into the passenger seat while Hound straps his little girl into the back beside me. He must not distrust me too much if he's willing to leave me back here with his child.

The drive feels simple—just a ride home—until I notice Hound taking glances in my direction in the rearview. Unease fills me from top to bottom on the ten-minute drive that lasts a millennium.

Once we arrive back to the property, Gigi climbs out and grabs the kid from the back seat.

"You have a beautiful daughter," I say, feeling like I can't get out until he gives me permission. He hasn't budged an inch since he turned the truck off, so neither have I.

"I have two beautiful daughters," he corrects.

"Yes, sir."

"I was pissed when I thought Apollo got Izzy pregnant." What can I say to something like that? "But after watching your ass for the last week, I can't help but wonder if it wouldn't have been better for her if he were the father."

That cuts like a fucking dull knife.

"Are you going to man up or bow out?"

His eyes are once again on mine, and I hold his gaze. I respect this man, but this really isn't his place.

Then I take a breath and proverbially step back to assess the situation. How would I react if the tables were turned, if it were my unwed daughter?

"That might have been better. Apollo being the father that is."

"Because he's a better man than you?"

"Because he's not a felon. Because he's not going to prison for murder. Because she's safe with him."

"Is she not safe with you? Do you hurt women, Drew?"

I narrow my eyes. "Of course not."

"You're hurting my daughter every single damned day."

"She won't even talk to me."

"Because you've tried so many times?"

He's got me there. I've avoided the clubhouse since that day in the hallway. Hell, I've avoided my bedroom window in fear of seeing disappointment on her beautiful face.

"I'm going to prison, man." I break eye contact to scrub my hands over the top of my head.

I have felt like crying a hundred times since this mess started, but it isn't until right now that I feel like I'm not going to be able to stop them.

"The situation isn't ideal, but that boy deserves to know his father. You aren't in prison now. You can be involved. She can bring him to visit—"

"Not a fucking chance," I snap, anger replacing the sad emotions that threatened just seconds ago. "My son will never see me like that."

My mom did that shit with my dad. The man was sentenced to prison for drugs, having enough in his possession that he'll probably never see the light of day outside of those walls again. Hell, he could be dead now for all I know. My aunt and uncle took me in, but they'd disowned him long before that. Although I've tried to block it out, I can still picture the way I felt seeing my dad dressed in a prison uniform, his neck and half his face covered in sloppy tattoos. Thankfully, the visits didn't last past my sixth birthday. Mom found a new man by then and couldn't be bothered to take me any longer. I've been bitter about being subjected to those terrifying experiences rather than the loss of them.

"And that's what makes you an amazing man."

"I'm not."

"You fucked up that night. Hit that guy too many times. The outcome was dire. The consequences suck, Drew, but you're not going to prison forever. You're going to have to face this eventually."

"What should I do, huh? Ask her to wait for me? Tell her I don't want her to move on?"

It's his turn for narrowed eyes. "I said you need to be involved in the kid's life. I'm not telling you to date my daughter. You're not worthy of her yet."

"Yet?" I shake my head, confused.

"Any man worth her love wouldn't spend his hours holed up in a bedroom because he's got some shit to work through. A man worthy of Isabella Montoya would spend every free second he had making her feel loved. He'd be the man helping her rise from the sofa, the one holding her hair when she gets sick because this pregnancy has been hard on her. That man would be the one to make sure she's taking her vitamins and making her doctor's appointments. Right now that man is Apollo."

I grind my damn teeth together.

"But Apollo is leaving on Monday for work, and she's going to need someone."

He opens the truck door and climbs out, leaving me inside and more confused than I've ever been in my life. Did he tell me to fuck off or step up?

Chapter 9

Isabella

"It's only preseason but they treat it like the damn World Series," Sophia explains as Landon and Rick walk through the clubhouse, arrowing for the kitchen. Both boys are filthy and wreak from practice.

"Do they always smell like that?" I scrunch my nose, but it isn't enough. I fight the urge to cover my mouth with my hand.

"Always," she says with a chuckle. It doesn't seem like the stench bothers her much, but there's a real possibility I'm going to get sick.

"They smell like—"

"Goats," she interrupts. "Like a pasture full of goats. Where is everyone?"

The clubhouse is practically silent, only a few of the original members hanging around. I followed Gigi over here after Dad left for work this afternoon, and couldn't be bothered to get off the couch when she went back across the street.

"Venezuela, I think."

"And have you spoken with—"

"I haven't."

"You said you would."

We had a conversation days ago, and Sophia insisted that I try to have a civil conversation with Drew, but I just haven't mustered up enough nerve. The man only seems to sneer at me when I'm around, so forgive me for not jumping at the chance to do that while he's close to me.

"I was going to the other day at the park but he left."

"That was my fault."

"You have no filter."

Sophia called me later that night in tears because she was insensitive about the situation Drew is in and opened her big, fat mouth. Everyone else around here is used to it, and we take no offense when she speaks before thinking, but Drew hasn't been around as long. He doesn't know the nuances of everyone's personality.

"Ah crap. I know I need to apologize, but I didn't think it would be so soon," my best friend says as she watches out the window.

"Is he coming here?"

"Yep, and Lawson, too. What are you doing?" Sophia cocks an eyebrow at me.

I still my hands from where they started checking my hair to determine how bad the flyaways are. Getting sick nearly every day doesn't lend much enthusiasm for caring what I look like.

"Are you primping for him?"

"No."

"Liar." Her grins widens. "I know I have a man, but he's hot as hell. Describe to me in fine detail how those biceps feel under your fingers."

Amazing.

"I'm not talking about that with you."

"I told you about the time Colton—"

"You overshared. It's different."

"Gigi tells me all sorts of things."

I nearly gag. "About my dad?"

She pulls her face back. "I—well I guess—gross. I wasn't even seeing it that way."

"Yeah, gross." I chuckle as I smack her arm with the back of my hand.

"Ladies, how are you today?" The voice belongs to Lawson, but even if Sophia didn't tell me Drew was with him, I'd still feel the air charge around me.

"Good," Sophia responds quickly with mirth in her voice.

"Fine," I mumble.

"There's my man," Sophia says with a squeal, her eyes still outside.

I grab her arm when she goes to leave, giving her the *I will murder you if you leave me* look. She either ignores it or doesn't read what I'm trying to say with facial expressions alone.

"Good to see you guys." My best friend deserts me. She gets up and walks outside.

"Delilah needs some Cajun seasoning," Lawson says. "Is there any over here?"

"In the cabinet to the left of the stove," I say, watching in horror as Lawson walks in that direction while Drew lingers.

Is he waiting for his brother to be out of earshot before saying something snippy to me? We've spoken twice since he held me outside the first night he showed up. Neither time went very well.

He doesn't say a word as he sits on the opposite end of the sofa I'm on, leaving the cushion Sophia abandoned between us.

I get a reprieve when Landon and Rick come out of the kitchen with plates piled high with food. Sitting here in silence would be rude. It would force me to open my mouth, and that's the last thing I want to do since I know exactly what I'd be getting from another conversation with Drew.

"For you," Landon says, pulling a can of root beer from the pocket of his athletic pants and handing it me.

"Thanks." This sweet kid didn't even ask me if I wanted one.

The boys take seats on the other couch, Landon reaching for the remote and turning on some sports channel as they settle in. I'm grateful for them being around, but it doesn't make me any less aware that Drew is mere feet from me.

He's said so many hateful things. I've returned those hateful things with bitterness of my own, but my body knows what he's capable of. My body has felt his touch, tasted his lips. She's threatening to betray me.

I clear my throat as I open the can of soda, taking a sip long enough to make my tongue burn from the carbonation.

My hands are shaking, I notice when I focus my attention on the can, but when I lean forward to place the can on the table, Drew reaches out and takes it from me. Using one of the coasters on the table, he places the drink down.

"Thank you," I mutter loud enough for him to hear over the boys arguing about some professional ball player.

"He graduated from Lindell," Rick snaps. "He's fu—freaking amazing."

My lip twitches with the correction. Do the people at the clubhouse not know that ninety-eight percent of boys and men don't curb their foul mouths around women any longer? After being around high school boys, coming here was an eye opening experience. I've never met men so respectful.

"We can't stay long."

My eyes snap up finding Colton and Sophia walking toward us. Sophia looks like the cat that ate the canary, whereas Colton looks a little irritated. I know Sophia, and she has something up her damn sleeve. Her man doesn't seem as ready to get involved in whatever scheme she's running right now.

"Hey, Dad," Rick says around a mouthful of sandwich.

Colton rolls his eyes in that *boys are disgusting but you gotta love* them sort of way.

"Drew, can you scoot? It'll be easier for us to sit."

"Sit on the other couch," I hiss at Sophia, but Drew is already lifting his butt from the sofa and repositioning it on the cushion in the center.

"Thanks," my friend says, sticking her tongue out at me like a child when Drew refocuses on the television.

Colton takes a seat with a sigh, his arms immediately reaching up to Sophia. When she settles on his lap in a way that makes Drew shift a few more inches in my direction, I'm seconds away from getting up and moving. There are a handful of couches in this area because a lot of people live here. The choice to sit where she's selected is intentional, but this isn't a joke. Whatever is going on between Drew and me isn't a game. I'm pregnant and he's been charged with homicide. This isn't a high school crush with the end result being an invitation to flipping prom.

For an eternity, everyone around me engages in conversation while I sit in silence, wanting a drink from my root beer but unwilling to lean forward and get it. Doing so runs the risk of Drew grabbing it, and if his fingers brushed mine once again the rein I have on my control would snap.

I learn a lot about Lindell University and how both Landon and Rick hope to go there. Apparently, Lindell is one of the best schools for producing professional athletes in numerous sports, baseball being one of them.

I try, and fail, to hold back a yawn, drawing Drew's attention.

"Tired?" he asks.

If I wanted to focus on him, I could say he's concerned, but I know better. What I don't understand is why he's still sitting here after Lawson grabbed the canister of seasoning and went back across the street nearly an hour ago.

"Izzy is the queen of naps," Sophia helpfully adds, making me sound like a lazy bum.

"Growing a baby is hard work," Colton says in my defense, and I give him a weak smile of gratitude.

"I can walk you back," Drew offers, and it makes me want to stay on this damn couch forever.

"That's so sweet of you, Drew." I'm going to strangle my best friend the second we're alone.

"Okay," I agree, taking a long moment to prepare myself to stand.

"Let me help." As agile as he proved himself to be the night we met, Drew is off the sofa and standing with his hand out in the next breath.

"Thanks," I mumble as I take his proffered hand and stand. Internally, I praise myself for being able to do so without the grunt that usually accompanies such effort.

Sophia winks at me as I turn to leave, so I don't even say a word to her as I walk toward the front door of the clubhouse.

"You kids have fun," comes her gleeful goodbye.

I mutter a curse under my breath as we step outside, and it's only now that I realize Drew isn't only still holding my hand, but the heat of his other is at my back.

I'm losing my mind by the time we make it to the road and have gone completely insane by the time we're at the porch of my house. I want to lean into him, want him to say sweet things. I want that mischievous smirk he gave when he caught me moaning erotically around a mouthful of pancakes. I want to hear him grunt in my ear the way he did when he pushed inside of me the very first time. I want to hear him say, *"Come for me,"* the way he demanded it that night.

I won't get any of those things, not tonight and probably never again. My wants have to now take second place behind my needs for the baby, and Drew's attitude this last week isn't one that makes me want to fight for him being around in our son's life.

"Have a good nap," he says, pressing his lips to my temple before walking across the lot to Lawson's house.

I blink at his back until he disappears inside, my phone ringing causing me to jump.

"What?" I snap when I answer and climb the front porch steps into my own house.

"What are you doing?" Sophia hisses. "That wasn't a kiss! Follow that man and jump his bones. Girl, you need it."

"Sophia," I hear Colton warn in the background.

"This is bigger than just getting off, and I did that once. Look where it got me." I turn to face the clubhouse across the street, knowing she's watching me out the window. I point to my belly, flip her the bird, and then I hang up on her before walking into the house.

Trudging up the stairs, I silence my phone when it begins to ring again. The bed is inviting, the fluffy pillows and soft blanket calling to me, but the window across the room has more pull.

To my surprise, I find Drew standing at his window. He doesn't look away, or look through me this time. When I turn around to climb into my bed, I'm more confused than I've ever been.

Chapter 10

Drew

"A lot on your mind?" Lawson asks as he wipes his hands on a shop towel.

"Always," I mutter.

Helping around his shop hasn't been as satisfying as he made it sound. I wanted to get my mind off of everything, take a little break from the constant echo in my head, but although we're busy, it's still solitary work. Even the music blasting in the shop isn't enough to distract me.

Any man worth her love wouldn't spend his hours holed up in a bedroom because he's got some shit to work through. A man worthy of Isabella Montoya would spend every free second he had making her feel loved. He'd be the man helping her rise from the sofa, the one holding her hair when she gets sick because this pregnancy has been hard on her. That man would be the one to make sure she's taking her vitamins and making her doctor's appointments. Right now that man is Apollo.

I've played the conversation with Hound over and over in my head.

He doesn't think I'm worthy.

I know I'm not worthy of her.

But I want to be.

As much as I hate the situation, I know Izzy is the woman I couldn't get out of my head long before Warren and I pulled up at that accident scene. I fantasized about her, got myself off to memories of her. I wanted to be a part of her life. I wanted her body, her mouth, her moans in my ear, but I also pictured coming home to her, watching her work on lesson plans and grading papers. My fantasies weren't all sexual. In my mind, I was already building a life with her, regretting not getting her phone number.

I let myself live in a dream world in the parking lot that night. I didn't want to break the perfection of the night by asking for too much, and I also didn't realize she'd still be on my mind months later.

"Want to talk about it?"

I roll my eyes. "Sure, Dr. Phil, pull up a chair."

"That's not a bad idea."

"I'm not going on a fucking talk show, man."

He chuckles. "Not a talk show, but I don't think talking to someone is a bad idea."

"Like a shrink?" I scoff when he nods. "No way. Plus, there will be plenty of time for that in prison."

He frowns, but at least this time he doesn't open his mouth with the false hope he's been holding onto for months.

"There's an amazing doctor down at the medical complex. She's helped several people from the clubhouse."

"I'll consider it," I lie, just to get him off my back.

"That's all I can ask," he says as he looks down at his watch. "Let's get home, all of this stuff can wait."

There's an extra shuffle in his step as we lock up the shop and head to his truck.

"You're pretty excited."

He stifles his grin by biting his lower lip as he unlocks the truck.

"Does that look on your face mean I need to make myself scarce once we get back to the house?"

He busies himself climbing in the cab, turning on the air conditioner, and making sure the radio is on a station he likes.

"What? Are you avoiding a conversation with me?" I tease. "I thought that was my job."

"We're, umm... Delilah, she's..." His hand grips the back of his neck, his cheeks turning pink.

"You're trying to have a baby and she's ovulating?"

His head snaps back, a combination of confusion and shock on his face. "What would you know about that?"

"Is it true?"

He grins, his lips wide and eyes shining.

"Yeah. How did you know?"

"Warren, my training officer was going through the same thing. He said it was a lot of work. Said the sex got boring, more like a job."

I focus on the conversation I had with Warren that night rather than how it ended.

"Delilah is..." He clears his throat. "Making love to my wife would never be work."

It's my turn to look away.

"So I'll make myself scarce tonight."

"Shit, man. I'm not trying to kick you out of the house."

"It's your house," I remind him. "Besides, I can find something to do. Just stop at that gas station."

He pulls in and doesn't say a word as I climb out.

Once inside, I bypass the energy drinks, knowing if I drink one this late in the day, I'll get even less sleep than I anticipate getting tonight. The sight of the same root beer Izzy was drinking the other day catches my eye, and I stare at it in the cold case so long, another customer has to reach around me to grab a drink for themselves.

"Sorry," I mutter as she scoffs before walking away.

After the discussion with Lawson about his evening plans, I figured I'd go to the clubhouse. Most of the Cerberus guys were still out in the field, so it would be mostly quiet, and if I got lucky, Izzy would be over there.

But the root beer has me making different plans.

I leave the soda in the case and head back to the truck, going around to the driver's side window instead of climbing inside.

Lawson's brow furls as he rolls down the window. "Forget your wallet?"

He reaches for his own.

"No. Do you know what kind of candy Izzy likes?"

"Izzy?" He shakes his head. "Why would I know that?"

"Right." It was a dumb question, so I turn back around and go into the store once again.

With a root beer in hand, I stare down at the racks of candy.

Is she a chocolate kind of girl? If so, does she like white, dark, or the milk chocolate variety?

Does she like hard candy?

Does she even like candy at all?

I turn around, facing the racks with chips and pretzels.

Why does there have to be so many damn options?

My cell phone dings with a text, and I pull it from my pocket.

Lawson: Reese's

My brother the lifesaver.

I ignore the thoughts of wondering how he got that information, knowing how fast gossip burns through the Cerberus community and turn my attention back to the orange and black packages. Knowing her favorite candy only leaves me with every other question I had before.

Not wanting to make a mistake, I grab one of every kind, struggling not to drop them as I walk to the cashier.

"Hell of a sweet tooth you got there, darlin'," the female cashier says with a wink.

I look down at the dozen or so packages and back up at her but don't say a word.

I almost open my mouth to tell her my girl is pregnant, but Izzy isn't my girl.

After paying, she tosses the drink and the ridiculous amount of candy into a plastic bag before looking over my shoulder to help the next customer.

Lawson laughs when I climb inside and place the full bag between us while I pull on my seatbelt.

"Trying to give her gestational diabetes?" he asks as he pulls back out onto the road.

"What?" I look down at the bag, finding my attempt at a kind gesture as offensive now.

"It's a joke, Drew. She'll think it's sweet."

"I just want—"

"You don't have to explain yourself to me."

"Does she have any complications?" I ask, realizing I don't know anything about her or the pregnancy.

Hound mentioned she'd been sick a lot, but aren't women always nauseous while pregnant? Mom made sure to make us feel bad for the way she felt while she was pregnant with us as often as she possibly could. She used it as a guilt trip, making us bend to her will for the sacrifices she made to bring us into this world.

Shit, now Izzy is doing the same thing for a child with a no-count dad with a bad attitude. Women really are the stronger gender, aren't they?

"I don't think so. Her morning sickness has stuck around a lot longer than Gigi's and Simone's, though."

"Delilah tell you all of this?"

He shrugs. "Mostly I just listen when everyone talks. We all spend a lot of time together. Having our own baby is important to us. My ears tend to perk up when everyone is discussing babies and kids. I don't want to miss anything."

"You're going to be an amazing dad."

"You are too." He keeps his eyes forward, but I know my brother well enough to know that he means it. He doesn't say it as a courtesy. I just wish I could feel as confident about myself.

"Think I have time to grab a quick shower before you jump on your wife?" I ask as he pulls up to the house.

"I think I can hold off," he jokes. "Just don't take all day."

He may be joking, but I rush inside, flying up the stairs to get clean. It has more to do with excitement about seeing Izzy than needing to escape.

The anticipation turns to nerves fifteen minutes later when I'm crossing Lawson's yard to Hound's. Her dad isn't home, and I can't help but wonder if I'm crossing a line by going to visit her. He urged me to be better, to spend more time with her for the baby's sake, so it's that knowledge that keeps my feet moving once I reach the porch.

Mere seconds after my knuckles meet the wood of the front door, it's tugged open.

"Drew," Gigi says with a familiar smirk.

This woman is devious. She was years ago as a teenager when we first met, and it seems even motherhood hasn't been enough to make her change.

"Nice to see you." Her eyes dart to the bag in my hand. "Is that for me?"

"For Izzy. Is she home?"

"She's in the living room."

Gigi doesn't move from the doorway as I look around her.

"May I come in?" I finally ask when it's clear she's waiting for something.

"Oh, of course." She steps to the side, and I wouldn't be surprised to discover that she's purposely trying to make me more nervous than I already am. It seems everyone around here finds this situation comical. First it was Sophia and her desperate need for the spot on the couch at the clubhouse and now Gigi is following me through the house with a grin on her face like she's about to see a show she's been waiting to catch the season finale of.

"Hey," I say the second Izzy comes into sight.

She squeaks in the cutest way, her eyes blinking much like they did the day I approached her in the diner. The only thing that's missing is a dollop of syrup dripping from her pouty lips.

"I umm..." I turn to look toward Gigi who is still lingering nearby.

Thankfully, she catches the hint and turns to walk out. "No sex in the living room, kids."

I shake my head, but Izzy looks mortified when I turn back in her direction.

"Does she not know you're more of a fan of outdoor sex?"

I could kick my own ass right now.

Izzy's eyes widen, but she doesn't say a word.

"Sorry, that wasn't appropriate. I grabbed this while I was at the store."

Like a crazy person, I shove the bag in her direction.

She takes it with a flat smile.

"I showered before coming over." Like that's important information. Cringing, I continue, "What I mean is, the soda may be warm. I can get you some ice."

"This is very kind of you," she says, but she sets the bag on the side table.

"What are you watching?" Could I be anymore awkward?

"*Graceland*," she answers but the show is paused, the name on the screen, and I feel even more like an idiot.

She presses play, but I can't concentrate on the television, not while her bare legs are tucked under her. Is she even wearing anything but a t-shirt? Jesus, now is not the time to get hard.

"You're acting weird," she says as if she can read my thoughts.

"Yeah," I agree, pulling my eyes from her exposed skin to look at the television.

"I've been wondering where that filthy smirk of yours went."

"A lot has happened since that night," I remind her.

"I miss him," she whispers.

I should open my mouth to tell her she doesn't even know that man, but I understand the sentiment because I miss him, too.

"I was wanting—"

Gigi sneezes in the other room, closer than I realized she was, making it obvious that she's hovering around and being nosy.

"Can we talk?"

"Sure," she answers immediately, giving me some hope she's open to spending more time with me.

"Somewhere a little more private?"

Her eyes drift to my lips, and fuck that is not what I came over here for.

"My room?"

"No!" I snap, hating the way her head jerks back. "I don't think that's a good idea."

Her in a room with a bed? I imagine the next conversation with her dad after that wouldn't be as civil.

She nods, grunting as she tries to stand. "We can go outside."

I help her off the couch, my eyes focusing on her legs and the tiny shorts she's wearing.

"Do you need to go change?"

"Is there something wrong with what I'm wearing?" Her hands flutter down her stomach, straightening her shirt.

"N-Nothing," I stammer. "It's fine."

Like I was able to do days ago, I keep her hand in mind and press the other to her lower back. Touching her this way, something much more civilized than I want is my own form of punishment.

"Come on," she says, noticing my feet locked in place. "I know where we can go."

Chapter 11

Isabella

"Where are we going?" he asks, my hand still in his as we make our way across the street.

"Nervous," I tease because I just have to.

I saw the glimpses he made my way moments ago, saw the way his eyes trailed down my body. It was reminiscent of the way he looked at me that first night, and I want that again. This surly man, the one who doesn't smile and doesn't joke isn't the man I want around.

He made a grand gesture this evening, bringing me a bag of my favorite candy and soda to drink. He's trying, either to be a part of my life or the baby's life, and I have to open myself up to that. I told him to step up or get out of the way and maybe this is how he plans to do the former.

"We could've just stayed on the porch."

"And Gigi would have her ear to the door or window."

"I don't think it's safe to be sneaking around the side of the clubhouse." His eyes dart left to right as we cross under the front porch light of the clubhouse on our way to the back of the property.

"Max knew we were here the second we crossed the road. I wouldn't be surprised if we didn't trigger part of his system the moment we opened my front door," I explain. "We're safe. No one is going to jump out and demand to know why we're here."

"Doesn't seem like there's much privacy," he says.

"We wouldn't be on camera back in my room."

I stop in my tracks, waiting for him to make a decision. He wanted to go up there just as much as I did when I made the suggestion.

"This is fine." He tugs my hand to move us forward again. "Isn't it a little chilly?"

His eyes track down to my bare legs.

"You aren't wearing much."

"You sound like my dad." I grin up at him, one hand going to my stomach.

I'm grateful for the heat in his eyes when he looks at me. I don't feel very sexy these days, and aside from Apollo's roaming eyes, I haven't gotten much attention from men since it became glaringly obvious that I'm pregnant, despite Gigi's insistence of people with a pregnancy kink.

"I'm not your dad," he mutters as I step onto the concrete decking around the outdoor pool.

"I'm well aware." I look at him over my shoulder, ignoring the other houses at the back of the property.

All the original Cerberus members live on this side of the street, but we're all free to come and go as we please.

He follows me inside when I tug open the door to the indoor pool, the heated water making the air around us warm and humid. Drew doesn't miss the way my clothes begin to cling to my skin. I only pray my hair doesn't frizz even more. If he's going to be coming around more often, showing up unannounced, I may have to start considering how I look. He doesn't seem disappointed when I release his hand and take a step back.

"They're bigger," I whisper, noticing his eyes locked on the front of my shirt.

His tongue snakes out and traces the upper curve of his mouth, and I feel it on my skin, my nipples pebbling despite the warmth surrounding us.

"I bet they're amazing. I mean," he clears his throat, "they were amazing before."

He saw most of me that night, pushing my shirt up around my waist and tugging down my tank top and bra to expose the top of me. He, on the other hand, only moved the pieces of his clothing out of the way necessary to get inside of me. Not seeing all of him was one of my few regrets from that night.

"You wanted to talk?"

His eyes hitch up from the front of my shirt to meet my gaze.

"Yeah, umm." He clutches the back of his neck, turning to start pacing.

I take a seat on one of the loungers, realizing my mistake after I drop down. Hopefully, this conversation doesn't take the same path as the ones before it because if he walks away this time, I'm going to have a hell of a time getting back up on my own.

When his back is to me, I notice him adjust the front of his jeans, and I love having that little bit of power. He's not completely disgusted by me if his body still reacts that way.

"I'm sorry."

"For?" A lot has happened recently, so I don't know exactly what he's referring to.

"For staring at you like that. It's rude."

It's hot, but whatever.

"I didn't want to talk about that."

What a shame.

"I wanted to talk about the baby."

He can't even face me when he brings it up, and I try to strengthen myself, resolving the part of me that hoped he'd come around to accepting his decision to not be involved.

"So you're going to sign over your rights?" I ask when he continues to pace without saying a word.

Nothing like ripping the Band-Aid off, right?

"No." He spins around to face me finally, his handsome face awash with fear. "Is that what you want?"

"No," I answer honestly. "I just figured that's what you decided."

"I want to be involved, Izzy. I want to be a part of his life. I want to be a dad."

I don't know if this is a hasty decision or if he's been hyper focused on it like I have, but I need to know. "Just last week you told me the opposite. Parenting is full time, not something done on a whim."

"It's not a whim." The words are soft where I was expecting anger. "I have—there are a lot of things in play here."

"I know."

"I'm going to prison, but I want to be involved now and if you'll allow it when I get out."

"Okay." He watches my face, his eyes darting between mine like he was expecting an argument.

"However you want that to look, I'm okay with."

"However I want?"

"I know you don't have to give me anything."

"You're the dad."

"I know. It's just..." The pacing starts again.

"Can you sit?" I indicate the lounger beside mine. "You're making me dizzy."

He moves to sit, but the second he's down, his leg begins to bounce.

"Talk to me," I urge. "Tell me your concerns."

"I may not be the same man if I get out of prison."

"When," I clarify.

"Prison is dangerous for cops. I'm only out on bond because the judge was worried I'd end up getting killed in jail."

I swallow thickly, emotions threatening to bubble up.

"Okay." I don't know what else to say. He doesn't seem like he's in the right head space to argue about the path his future is taking, and I don't know enough about his case to argue.

"Like I said, I could come out different. Those situations harden people."

"Do you plan to be a criminal when you get out?"

"No."

"Do you plan to join a gang or something while in prison?"

"Of course not."

"Do you regret what you did?"

"Every damn day," he says without hesitation.

"Why did you do it?"

"There were—" He snaps his mouth closed, his eyes looking anywhere but at me. "Circumstances."

"Ones you don't want to tell me about?" He doesn't speak. "I understand it's an open case."

I plan to leave it at that, but he clutches my hand.

"You died that night."

"Wh-What?"

"The girl in the car looked like you. Her car was similar to yours. I didn't think. I didn't take the time to assess the entire situation. She begged me to help her right before she died. In my head, the girl that took her last breath that night was you."

"Wh-What?" I hear the words, but they can't be true. Tears don't even have the chance to burn the backs of my eyes before they start rolling down my cheeks, leaving hot, angry streaks behind.

"I thought she was you. That man was pissed about his truck being impounded, and I just flipped out."

"You blacked out?"

He shakes his head. "I knew exactly what I was doing. I could easily lie and say I didn't, but I can still feel the impact of my knuckles on his face."

He drops my hand as if his are still tainted with the man's blood.

"You were gone, and he was arguing with Warren about impound fees."

"You killed him for me?"

I don't even know how to feel about such brutal vengeance being committed in my name.

"Maybe? I don't know. I didn't mean for it to end that way. I didn't hit him the first time with the intention of killing him, but once I got started, I couldn't stop. Yours—Megan's words *help me* just echoed in my head."

"M-Megan?"

"I didn't even know her name when I walked up to the wreck that night. It was pure luck. I acted before I even knew."

"I told you my name was Megan." A ragged sob bubbles from my throat. "I caused this."

"No," he snaps, his eyes finding my face when moments ago it seemed like he couldn't even stomach the sight of me. Tears form on his bottom lashes before losing the battle and running down his face. "My actions are my own. Two families lost someone that night, and neither one of them deserved what they got."

He sweeps a thumb over my cheek, and I don't even try to resist turning my face to prolong the contact.

"I thought you lied to me when the information came out. Megan wasn't a college student. She didn't have any aspirations of being a teacher."

"You remembered all of that?"

"I remembered everything." His hand cups my cheek, but my own guilt is preventing me from looking him in the eyes. "She was married. Her husband came to the jail to thank me for killing that man. I wanted to beat him, and that made no sense because the man just lost his wife."

"It's why you were so stunned when you showed up here."

He nods. "I thought I was losing my mind. I was so angry. I was mad at a dead girl for lying, at myself for not trying to hold on to you that night at the diner. I've kicked myself a million times for handling things the way I did. If only I had told you that I wanted to see you again, or convinced you to come home with me that night, things could've been different. Maybe you wouldn't have been on the road that night."

"But I was here. I was safe."

"Yes." He presses his forehead to mine. "You're safe. We're having a baby."

"Everything is fine," I promise him.

When my hands reach up to clasp at his neck, he jerks away, standing from the lounger and turning his back to me.

"Everything isn't fine. I killed a man."

"Because of me." It's going to take a while for me to process this information. "Does your attorney know?"

He shakes his head. "And he won't find out. The reasoning doesn't matter. As a cop, I'm expected to handle situations differently. Emotions aren't supposed to get involved. I was wrong that night, and I'll be punished for it."

"So you're a martyr now?" I snap. "If you explain what happened—"

He spins to face me, resolve on his face rather than the anger I expect. "I'm going to prison. I want to be in the baby's life, but I understand if that's not something you want."

"I want that," I assure him.

"I want to get to know you better. I want to spend the time I have left before my court date getting to know the mother of my child."

"Okay," I agree.

I don't know where this is going to end up leading the three of us, but I know the man standing in front of me is a good man, one any child would be blessed to know, despite the way he sees himself.

Chapter 12

Drew

"Do you want to explain why you've been carrying that same bag of candy around?" Sophia asks, and I do my best to hide my smile.

"I like candy," Izzy says, her eyes darting to mine like we have a secret.

I wink at her, loving the way her cheeks turn pink and how her bright eyes sparkle.

"What's going on?" Sophia asks, sounding confused, and that confirms my suspicions that Izzy hasn't told her best friend what I told her several nights ago.

She doesn't owe me anything, but she understands that what I told her isn't something I want spread around. Something changed between us that night, and it was hard as hell to just press my lips to her temple when we walked back across the street and not wrap my arms around her and beg her to come home with me.

"I'm missing something," Sophia prods.

"Leave them alone," Colton says shifting her weight on his lap so she can't glare at Izzy.

"Can I have one?" Sophia asks, her hand out.

"No." Izzy clutches the bag closer to her chest.

"Is it special candy or something? I like Reese's, too."

"They're just mine."

And they're not going to go away because I've been refilling it each day, noticing how she prefers the cups with the pieces inside of them.

"How are your classes, Izzy," Colton asks and Izzy looks relieved with the distraction.

She grins at her best friend before addressing Colton. "They're good. Much more detailed than undergrad."

"Tell me about it," Sophia muses.

Sophia, I discovered, planned to get her graduate degree. Izzy on the other hand had to shift things around after she found out she was pregnant, not wanting to start a new job only to need a leave of absence. She's been working her butt off in the classes she's taking this semester, knowing if she doesn't get ahead, she's going to struggle once the baby gets here.

We've talked a lot over the last couple of days since I told her my desire to be involved in the baby's life. I wish I could make things easier for her, but she seems to be taking everything in stride and determined to give our child the best life she possibly can.

"The semester just started," Izzy continues, "and I've already written two papers. I had no idea there was so much involved on the administrative side."

Colton nods. "Sophia has been pretty busy too."

With his words, Sophia turns her head and whispers something in his ear. It's clear by the way his face lights up that whatever she told him was sexual in nature, and for the very first time in my life, I'm jealous of another man's relationship. Lawson has Delilah and she's amazing, but I never saw them together and thought that what they have was something I desired myself.

Not until Izzy.

But getting something romantic started between us isn't smart. Our future doesn't resemble that of any of the other couples around here. The Cerberus guys leave for work and return, usually within a couple of weeks. They aren't facing any long-term separations. Wanting a relationship with Izzy is selfish, and not a bridge I'll cross.

"It's why the boys have been over here more than at home," Sophia says, and I look up to realize I've once again gotten lost in my head and missed part of the conversation. "Because it's hard to focus on school while they're smelling up the place."

"Amelia gets pretty active in the mornings," Izzy says about her little sister. "I usually nap when she's most active and get work done when she goes down for her nap. I'll do the same thing when this little guy gets here."

Her words feel like a crushing weight because I know I won't be around to help her with that.

"You're supposed to sleep when the baby sleeps," Simone says as she makes her way across the room, her little boy asleep in her arms. "You'll go insane if you don't."

I grin at the little boy in Simone's arms as they continue their conversation about sleeping habits with newborns. Realization that I'm going to miss all of this hits me like a ten-ton truck. My court date is two weeks before Izzy's due date. I'll be in prison, fighting for my life, surrounded by some of the evilest people in the world by the time my son takes his first breath.

"You okay?" Izzy asks, her hand on my leg, concern marking her pretty face.

"Yeah," I lie because dwelling on something I can't change doesn't make any sense. We both know what's in store for us, and we've been avoiding that specific topic since our conversation by the pool. "Do you need anything? Another root beer?"

"A foot massage," she counters with a smirk.

"I will," I promise. "But that may bring more questions from everyone than answers."

"They're going to ask the questions anyway."

She wiggles, making a move to lift her feet into my lap, but isn't quite able. I bend, lifting her feet to my lap, but the front door opens before I can slip her shoes off.

A team of exhausted looking Cerberus men begin to pile into the room, each one weighed down with huge duffel bags.

Jinx and Rocker head straight for Simone and the baby, wide smiles on their tired faces.

Rivet doesn't even make eye contact with anyone as she arrows toward the hallway leading to the rooms. Cannon got up and walked away fifteen minutes ago, so he must've known how close they were to being home. There's no doubt in my mind what's going to be happening in their room in less than five minutes.

I massage Izzy's calf while we both watch Jinx take River from his mother's arms. He peppers the baby's face with kisses, the little boy waking up from hearing his name with giggles and a scrunched nose, no doubt his daddy's beard tickling him.

I must not be smiling because Izzy's hand covers mine before she claps it and drags it to her stomach.

She's consoling me, letting me know without words that she understands what I'm feeling watching Jinx with his little boy.

"Well, isn't this cozy?"

Izzy frowns when she looks up, and I'm not surprised to see Apollo standing near the edge of the sofa glaring down at my hand on her belly.

"Hi," she says, making no effort to get away from my touch or get up to greet her friend. "Glad you're back safe."

I see his jaw flex, see the irritation in his eyes, and I get it. I honestly do. Izzy is an amazing woman. He knows it just like I do. He knows what he's missing out on, and I feel guilt over that as well.

You're not worthy of her yet. Right now that man is Apollo. Hound's words come back to me, and they may have been true a week ago when he told me that in his truck, but they don't hold the same weight they did then. Although I'm in a different head space, I know Apollo can give her everything I can't.

The man glaring at my proximity to Izzy can be there when the baby is born. He can be around to help her when she needs a nap and the baby won't settle. He can keep her stocked up with Reese's and listen to her when she moans happily with each bite.

But I'm here now, and I promised myself I'd be around until I couldn't be, although not in a romantic sense.

Am I keeping her from him? Am I causing problems between the two people who are destined to be together once I'm no longer in the picture? Maybe I should take a step back? Maybe not being around is what's best for my son? Maybe being here is causing more harm than good?

But fuck my life if I don't feel territorial right now, like I need to hunker down and growl until he walks away. I want to put her behind me and dare the man to keep looking at her, and warn him he's in danger if he tries to touch her.

"Maybe I should go," I say instead because this isn't about me and my feelings. I want her to have the best. I need my son to have the best, and there's no way to cut this situation where I'm the answer.

"Stay," she whispers, her fingers holding my hand tighter to her stomach.

"Go take care of your gear, Apollo." That demand comes from Sophia, and even as nosy as the girl is, she just gained a few brownie points in my eyes.

With an angry huff, his boots carry him away. I keep my eyes on Izzy, assessing her reaction to see if her friend walking away causes her distress. Besides the small frown tugging the corners of her mouth down, I don't see anything else that would cause alarm.

"That man—"

"Enough, Sophia," Colton erupts. "Stay out of it."

"Please," Izzy adds before turning her face up, a new beaming smile there. "Hey, Dad."

"Iz." Hound bends in the middle, pressing a kiss to his daughter's temple. "How was your week?"

"Good. Although I think I've gained ten pounds eating candy."

Her fingers flex against mine, drawing Hound's scrutiny, but instead of him decking me in the face, he simply nods in my direction before crossing the room to where Gigi is wiping Amelia's face.

He didn't growl or yank me up by the collar, which is awesome, but I also feel like it's the closest thing to approval I'll ever get from the man.

Kincaid walks into the clubhouse, a happy but tired look on his face. It lights up when he looks across the room to find Gigi and Amelia.

"I'm waiting for the day he looks at our kids that way," Griffin whispers on the other sofa, his face tucked into Ivy's neck.

Ivy and Gigi, although twins, couldn't be any more different. Griffin, Shadow's son and Cannon's brother spent a little time in jail after some stuff that went down with his platoon while he was in the Marine Corps. I don't know the details, but I know he didn't go to prison.

Griffin is the only child of the original Cerberus guys that went into the Corps and then joined the club in an official capacity. He looks just as tired as all the other guys, but he's also ridiculously in love. I don't think he'd want it any other way. None of the couples surrounding us look like they'd rather be any place else.

Except Apollo when he comes back into the room sans his gear. His eyes dart in our direction before he turns around with a huff and heads to the kitchen. Jinx follows him with a devious smile, drawing the attention of Legend and Thumper, two other Cerberus members who scurry after them like a plan is being put in place. So long as it doesn't have anything to do with Izzy, I don't care what they do.

"Probably planning another orgy," Sophia says with a laugh. "They've been gone for a week so we may be asked to leave soon."

The Cerberus clubhouse has been expanded since the first time I showed up here as a teen, and I know Kincaid has even more plans to add new rooms for team members as the club grows, but we're technically in their space. Other than Cannon and Rivet, who is a member, all other paired-up couples live elsewhere.

"We should go," Colton says as he smacks Sophia's hip lightly to get her to stand up.

"Us too," Izzy says.

"Nope." Gigi steps up to us, her arms wrapped around Hound's waist. "Mom and Dad are keeping Amelia tonight. I want you two to join us for dinner, but I need an hour."

"Two hours," Hound corrects.

Gigi smiles. "I need two hours before you guys come over."

"Come over?" Izzy's brow draws together. "I live there."

"I'd love to join you for dinner," I say. "We'll see you in a couple of hours."

Izzy frowns as she watches her dad walk out of the clubhouse.

"I need to get my own place. So rude."

Sophia leans over to hug her friend. "You really want to be over there while they go at it?"

"Gross." Izzy swats at her laughing friend. "But getting kicked out sucks."

"At least they warned you this time. Remember last time when you—"

Izzy makes a gagging noise that causes several people to chuckle. "Shut up. I'm scarred for life."

"Enjoy your dinner guys," Colton says as he guides Sophia out of the clubhouse.

"She doesn't cook," Izzy whispers when other conversations start up around us.

"I'm sorry?" I look at her in confusion.

"Just a warning if you were thinking you were getting a home-cooked meal. There's a better chance of mac and cheese and chicken nuggets. Gigi doesn't cook."

"She was pulling a casserole out of the oven last night when I left," I remind her.

"Emmalyn made that for us. She's great at reheating, but put a mixing bowl in front of her and the kitchen turns into a science experiment."

"Do you know how to cook?" I ask.

"A little." She grimaces. "I grew up with a chef, so I never really learned."

"A chef?"

"My mom's family has money. My stepdad is wealthy as well. They said their time was better spent on other things than worrying about household chores."

"Were you raised by nannies?" I have no right to argue what her plans are as far as childcare, but I'm curious to know what she plans once the baby gets here.

"They raised me. I didn't have a bad childhood, just one filled with overprotective parents that lied to me for years about who my real dad was. I guess I'm lucky they didn't consider me a household chore."

She smiles, but it doesn't reach her eyes until she lifts my hand and places it right back on her belly.

We settle in again, chatting with those around us as two hours tick by. Apollo, Jinx, and the other guys never come back through from the kitchen.

Chapter 13

Isabella

"That was an eye opening experience," Drew says as we take the stairs that are off the front porch of the clubhouse.

"I swear pheromones are pumped into the ventilation system," I agree.

I would tell him I'm not immune to them either, but I'm sure he's well aware with the way I've been squirming the last half an hour.

"I've seen a lot of stuff." He chuckles. "But that was—"

"Hot?" I ask.

"Very." He clears his throat, his hand at my back but his eyes straight ahead.

"I don't even think they realize how they're acting when they've been away from each other so long. I'm glad Dominic wasn't around."

"So they're like all three together?"

"Yep. A triad I think is what they refer to it as. Jasmine loves them both and is intimate with them both. Max and Tug love her and they love each other."

"It's like threesomes all the time." There's a hint of awe in his voice.

I swat at his chest. "Feel like you're missing out."

"No. I've had more than—" His jaw snaps shut, cheeks flaming. "I don't think it's the same thing."

"Same thing? As in different from the threesomes you've clearly had."

"I was a little wild in college."

"It didn't stop with college," I remind him, pointing to my belly. "That night we had was pretty wild."

"True. We could've had an audience and not even known it."

My feet stumble a little on the gravel, but of course he's there to keep me safe. The warmth of his chest makes my breathing hitch.

"Those guys didn't seem to mind even though they didn't go as far as we did that night."

"They're used to being watched."

"Like as a triad they participate in the orgies Sophia mentioned."

I stop and turn around to face him. "Are you interested in participating? You seem really focused on what they were doing."

"And you weren't?" He huffs. "You squirmed the entire time they were making out."

"I did not." I knew he could tell. Damn it.

"Did too." He brushes a strand of hair from my cheek, tucking it behind my ear. "And I'm not interested, but I haven't seen grown people act like that."

"We're grown."

"I haven't seen people act like that since college."

"College people are grown," I argue.

"Fine." He pulls in a ragged breath. "I've never seen two guys just openly make out the way they were."

"It's hot," I tell him with a shrug.

"So I discovered."

"Considering batting for the other team? You know—" Feeling like Sophia, I snap my mouth closed. I was seconds away from making a joke about hooking up with guys in prison, but that's just wrong. I feel disgusted for the thought even popping into my head.

"What?" he asks, not letting me off the hook.

"They're used to being watched because they go to a sex club in Denver."

"Hale-ish?"

I nearly choke. There are so many things about this man I don't know.

"No, Izzy." He spins me around, his eyes burning into mine. "I've never been. Some of the guys at work used to talk about it. They didn't go to the clubs in Albuquerque because they didn't want to run into people they know or had arrested before. I've never been to a sex club."

"Okay." I've been saying that word a lot lately.

"Are you ready to go inside for mac and cheese and chicken nuggets?" There's humor in his voice as his eyes dart to the front door of my house.

"No." How can he even think about going in there with how keyed up I am right now. "They may not be finished."

"Probably not." He groans, his face close to mine, and I realize his hands are still on my hips from when he spun me around. "This is familiar."

Then I'm lifted, my butt landing on cold metal, and I'm right back where I was the night we met, sitting on the hood of my car with him leaning in close to me.

"Jesus," he pants before pulling away and slamming his back against the car beside me.

"Yeah," I agree.

His hands scrub down his face. "That night was the best sexual experience I've ever had."

His confession feels like a bomb set to detonate between the two of us.

"Is it crazy if I say me too?"

He turns his head to look at me, blue eyes sparkling in the moon light. "Crazy because you were a virgin?"

"I was."

"I know. I just don't know why you never asked me to stop."

I can't look at him when I respond. "I didn't want to stop. It happened just the way I wanted it to."

"On the hood of this car?" There's humor in his tone as he taps the hood with his hand. "That's how you wanted it to happen."

"No. I wanted passion and desire. I wanted an erotic experience because I've always thought that those first times we all see in movies where the guy's always checking in and going slow were boring. I never wanted that."

"You didn't get it either."

Come for me. God, the memory of those words from his lips make cold chills race down my arms.

"I wouldn't change a thing."

"Not even the missing condom?"

"Nope. Not a thing."

"I just forgot. I'd never done that before, but I was so wrapped up in you, that I didn't even think about it. Getting inside of you was the only thing on my mind."

"Okay." The word comes out breathy, much the same way my words did that night.

I ache for him. My skin is on fire without his touch. "Drew."

"Izzy." He drops his head between his shoulders, refusing to look up at me. His hands dig into the front pockets of his jeans.

"Is there a reason we've only had that one night? Do you not want me?"

He snorts, his left hand pulling from his pocket to grip an obvious erection over the fabric.

"Don't be ridiculous."

"Ridiculous is both of us wanting it and yet neither of us are doing anything to get us there."

"I want you." His eyes look up to find mine. "But you deserve better than me."

"We're having a baby."

"And that doesn't give me any rights to your body. You don't owe me that because I forgot to wear a condom the one night we were together."

"It's just sex."

It wouldn't be just sex to me, and I think he knows it.

"Sex complicates everything. You were a virgin that night. I got you pregnant. Things are already complicated. I can't handle much more."

I blow a puff of air out. Knowing what I'm about to say is going to make me sound like a petulant brat, I plan to say it anyway. "But I'm horny."

He chuckles, a sad excuse for a laugh.

"If you won't—"

He spins, shoving between my legs until I feel his thickness against my center.

"If you even open that pretty mouth to tell me that if I won't you'll find someone who can, I'm going to lose my shit, Isabella."

I glare down at him. "I wouldn't do that."

"What were you going to say then, hmm?"

Challenge fills his eyes, but they soften when I shift my hips a little against him.

"I'm going to have to skip dinner and take care of it myself."

His eyes fall to my lips as he groans.

"Somehow that's worse." His hands rub up my thighs, his thumbs circle my belly on either side.

"I don't know what kind of relationships you've been in before, Drew O'Neil, but I'm not the type of woman who will use others to make someone jealous."

"Apollo seems to be doing that easily enough on his own."

"And I've told you I'm only friends with Apollo. Yes, he thinks he wants more from me, but the man wants a happy ending and I don't think he cares how he gets there."

"A happy ending like…" He pulls his hand from my stomach making a crude motion.

"No!" I slap his chest as he laughs, the seriousness of the situation floating away on the cold night air. "He wants to be in love. Wants someone to take care of. Wants someone to come home to. It's not me he wants but the potential my situation has to offer him. He'll get over it soon enough."

"He knows you're amazing. He's not a stupid man. I don't think he's going to go away as easily as you're hoping."

"That's on him. I can't control how the man feels." I swivel my hips one more time. "Can we get back on topic, please?"

"I was hoping you forgot about that," he grumbles.

"Really?" I move again, his erection hitting a part of me that makes me groan. "Doesn't look like you forgot about it."

"Do you know how easy it would be to give into that urge?" He traces my neck with the tip of his nose. "How easily these leggings would tear and how fast I could be inside of you?"

"Show me," I beg.

"I can't."

"Do you need me to beg?"

"It won't even take that, Izzy. We both want it. I'm not going to deny the chemistry we have. Anyone around us can see it, but I don't think it's the best idea."

"Okay." I clear my throat.

He takes a step back, his eyes finding mine before drifting to my mouth. "That easy?"

I could slap the man!

"What do you want me to say? You're back and forth so fast it's giving me whiplash. It's just sex, Drew. If you don't want it or don't want it from me, then just say so."

"You're not listening." He fills the space between us with his large body, that erection right back where it feels so good as his lips flutter over my ear. "I want it. I want it from you. I'm not going to fuck you again on the hood of this damn car."

"In the garage," I bargain, making him chuckle. "In the pool house?"

"Stop," he groans, as he steps away again. "I'm not going to rush, and I'm not going to undress you somewhere where someone else can see your amazing body, but soon."

"Promise?"

"I promise."

"You better keep your word."

"There's very little that could happen that will keep me from experiencing you again, but promise me."

"What?"

"Just sex."

My heart breaks a little, but I still agree. "Just sex."

Chapter 14

Drew

"Thank you," I say to Gigi as she passes me the pizza box.

Izzy was wrong. Her stepmom ordered pizza rather than making mac and cheese and chicken nuggets. Even though Hound spent the last two hours with his wife, he's still reluctant to pull his eyes from her as he eats. I'm just thankful the sexual tension in the room isn't resting on just mine and Izzy's shoulders.

It's just the four of us at the huge dining room table, and I'm kind of disappointed little Amelia isn't around as a distraction.

Conversation is stilted. Even Gigi doesn't seem to have much to say, but that's probably a good thing considering her normal topics of conversation lean toward inappropriate.

The promise I made fifteen minutes ago to Izzy still has my cock half-mast behind my zipper. Yep, right here with her dad in the same room, I can't get myself under control. I blame the dry spell, the one that consequently has been there since that night in the parking lot with Izzy.

The promise. Damn it. I knew I was going to give in. Hell, I wasn't far off from having the tables turned on me where I was the one trying to convince her what a great idea it was. I'm still not opposed to suggesting it after the meal. She may have been given enough time to rethink her position and will decide it's best to decline.

I look over at her to assess where her thoughts are. In my head, I made the promise hoping she'd change her mind as time went on, but with the way she's still squirming in her seat and looking at me with filthy sin in her eyes, I'm guessing that isn't going to happen. Just the sight of her flushed cheeks and the way she continues to swallow is enough to change my breathing pattern, and panting like a lust-filled sex addict at her father's table isn't a very good idea.

"Guess it was lucky you two were outside when the pizza delivery guy showed up," Hound says as he pulls another slice of pizza from the box. His eyes bore into me as if he can read the dirty thoughts in my head. I wish I could say it was enough to put them on hold, but it's not.

"Lucky us," Izzy mutters as she picks a pepperoni off her slice and lifts it to her mouth.

Getting entranced with her lips while sitting three feet from her father is a horrible idea, but it's looking like bad ideas are becoming my thing, something I seem to be making a habit of these days. I lick my lips when her tongue tastes her own.

Is she doing it on purpose? Is her goal to make me lose my mind right here in her father's dining room? If so it's working like a fucking charm.

"I thought you were hungry, Drew. You haven't touched your food." She licks pizza grease from her finger, and somehow the tables have turned.

I charmed her that night, knowing when I first laid eyes on her that walking away without getting a taste was impossible. She was shy and timid. That girl isn't in this room tonight, and if she isn't aware of how her behavior is affecting me, then the world absolutely isn't ready for this woman.

Gigi snorts a laugh at Izzy's teasing. She isn't exactly being subtle, but if I know Gigi well enough just from being around her the last two weeks, she interprets exactly what Izzy is doing.

Hound grunts, accustomed to his wife's silliness, but I know he's uncomfortable with Izzy being a sexual creature. Pregnant or not, no woman should try to seduce a man in front of their father. I'd chastise her for it, but I'm a fool and enjoying it way too much, despite the inconvenient hard-on I'm suffering with right now.

I'm uncomfortable, both mentally and physically, because this has to be the most awkward meal I've ever had, which is saying a ton because I spent four months of meals in jail looking over my shoulder, wondering when I was going to get shanked.

"The food is great," I tell her, focusing on my plate rather than her mouth. I can't just tell everyone at the table I'm reluctant to replace the taste of her skin with pepperoni pizza. "Thanks again for the invite."

Hound nods at me when I make eye contact with him. "I should be the one thanking you since you paid when the guy showed up."

"It's my pleasure."

And it's because of pleasure that I pulled out my wallet to pay just to give us a little more time before we had to go inside. My cock was raging hard and even the scrunch of the guy's face when he pulled up with the food to find me between her legs and ready to break the promise of not fucking her on the hood of her car again didn't flag that fucker at all.

Conversation continues and we somehow manage to keep the serious topics like the baby and my impending prison sentence from coming up. Both subjects are like elephants in the room, things we need to discuss but are all somehow in agreement tonight isn't the time for it.

"I'll help with dishes," I say when the meal is over.

"Nonsense," Gigi counters. "You paid. I'll take care of this."

Izzy passes her plate off to Gigi but doesn't stand. Hound sticks around as well, his eyes burning a hole in the side of my head.

"I was thinking we could walk some of this off."

Izzy nods her head, the look in her eyes making it clear she knows I'm planning to serve up that promise I made. My balls are aching with eager anticipation.

"I think that's a great idea," Izzy agrees quickly.

"Actually..." Hound begins, the pregnant pause making my skin itch. "Drew, I was hoping you could help me with something."

Izzy's face falls, and it would be comical if it weren't for the disagreement going on in my jeans.

"Sure," I tell him with a forced smile.

I don't think the man hates me, but it would be pushing the limit if I refused whatever it is he has in mind.

The man stands, a looming presence over both of us before leaning in to press a swift kiss to Izzy's temple.

"Get some sleep, sweetheart. You have that exam tomorrow."

And that answers any questions I have about how involved he is in her life. If the man knows his grown daughter's school schedule, then he's aware of a lot more than I initially thought.

Thankfully, he leaves the room long enough to tell Gigi what his plans are.

"You look disappointed," I whisper as I round the table and help Izzy to her feet.

"That evident?"

"If you poked those pouty lips out any further, you'd trip on them on the way up the stairs."

"You made me a promise."

"I did," I agree. "And I plan to keep it. Goodnight and good luck on your test tomorrow."

I press my lips to her forehead and immediately step back. Being close to her right now is hard enough. Lingering isn't an option. I walk away, waiting for Hound on the front porch as Izzy heads up to her room.

"Ready?" he says as he steps outside.

"I don't even know what we're doing." I try and fail to hide the disappointment in my voice, but at least with Izzy not close, I've managed to get better control of my erection. The cool night breeze helps as well.

"Come on," he urges, stepping off the porch and heading in the direction of the clubhouse.

My feet itch to run, my head going crazy with thoughts of what's going to happen. Hound is a good man, as is every other man that wears a Cerberus leather cut, but I'm not a club issue. What's happening between Izzy and me is personal. The intimacy of that situation doesn't mean Hound won't use the club to get his point across.

Even with that in my head, I follow the man across the street, knowing the entire club could be over here waiting to kick my ass. When he turns left instead of going inside the clubhouse, it doesn't ease my fears. If an ass kicking is what he thinks I deserve, I'll take it on the chin. I'd be furious if someone put my own daughter in the same position I've put Izzy in.

When it was only sex, before I walked away that night with a heaviness in my chest for doing so, it didn't seem such a bad situation. Getting laid on my lunch break? Sign me up twice.

But things are different now, and not just because we're living so close together and I'm stuck on the property. Izzy is an amazing woman, one I could honestly see spending the rest of my life with if the situation was a little different. Even if she wasn't pregnant with my kid, if I wasn't going to prison, I'd pursue that woman with everything I have.

The Cerberus garage, one Lawson spent most of his time in when we first arrived, is empty. It's not teeming with angry men ready to help their friend seek justice for the devious things I did with Hound's daughter.

"You've been helping Lawson at the shop."

"I have."

Coming home with grease on my hands and rebuilding motorcycles was never my idea of fun, but sitting idle and doing nothing isn't something I'm interested in either. Lawson is paying me to work, and that helps me to feel productive. I'm going to need commissary money for as long as I'm able to stay alive in prison, and that's not a bill I'll allow anyone else to foot.

"Other than working in the shop with him, do you have any other experience with shopwork? Electrical, machinist? That sort of thing?"

"Lawson is the mechanic. I've never had much interest in it."

"That's going to change over the next couple of weeks."

"Okayyy." I drag out the word because I have no idea what the purpose of any of this is.

"You're going to prison." His eyes meet mine. "At least that's my understanding."

He's saying more than he thinks he is. He knows my stance on what happened. He knows what my decision is.

"I am."

He nods before turning back around to point at a machine that looks too complicated to be in an average person's garage.

"I'm going to teach you as much as you can learn. I'll need you to clear your head and focus. It's going to come in handy once you're inside."

"Come in handy?"

"New Mexico offers many different jobs in the system. You'll need to work. Not only will it keep you busy so time goes by faster, but the shop has many options for keeping you safe."

He picks up a tire iron, holding it over his shoulder.

"And by safe, you mean to defend myself?"

"Exactly."

I know what I'm facing in prison. I know inmates will come after me the second they find out who I am and what I did. I can't really blame them. They were raised to hate the police. Some officers join the force for the power it gives them, and although that wasn't my reason for joining, my desire to help people doesn't exactly compute with killing a drunk driver in a rage.

I also know I'll fight back if I have to. I'll defend myself to the death. I have something, a little boy coming in less than six weeks, to live for.

"Let's get started."

We work for hours, leaving me so tired that when we finally cross the street again, I don't have the energy to even look up at Izzy's bedroom window.

Chapter 15

Isabella

"Hey, stranger."

Drew lifts his tired eyes in my direction. "Hey. How are you?"

"I feel like I should be asking you the same thing."

"Exhausted," he sighs, his body melting into the sofa.

"I figured. What time did you get done last night?"

Dad has been keeping him busy in the garage, and when Dad isn't showing him things, the other guys are there ready to pick up the slack.

"Just after two."

"And then to work at eight this morning?"

He gives me a weak smile. "Yeah."

"It's too much. I'll talk to him."

"Don't." He reaches for my arm as if I were fixing to get up and have this discussion with my father right this very second. I couldn't if I wanted. I've been banned from the house for the next couple of hours. Gigi's due date is nearing and apparently they have ideas about how to jump-start her labor, ones they both assured me they didn't think I'd want to hear. I've read the *What to Expect* book. I know what they're over there doing, and it's a disgrace seeing as how every man in the club, sans Apollo, has been cockblocking me since Drew made that promise two weeks ago.

"They're helping me," he assures me.

"I've hardly seen you," I grumble, resigning myself to never having sex again, especially when it seems there isn't a person around that is willing to give us a few minutes alone.

"We have dinner together every night."

"It's not the same. I want—"

He laughs. "I know exactly what you want."

"The guys are gone. Dad is occupied." I waggle my eyebrows suggestively. "Now is a good time."

"Lawson and Delilah have Samson and Camryn over for dinner."

"And? We don't have to go to your house. There are plenty of rooms here at the clubhouse."

"There isn't a single empty room here."

He's right. Apollo, Thumper, and Legend took the remaining rooms several months ago, but I heard discussions about Rivet and Cannon building across the street to clear up another. Cerberus MC is continually growing, and there are plans in place to expand the clubhouse to accommodate more people. We're starting to look like our own little village out here.

"Jinx is hardly ever home these days. He's a mostly clean guy."

"I'm not fucking you on another man's bed, especially one that used his own free time to teach me how to weld last week."

"You could—" I drag my finger down his chest. "Just bend me over it."

He huffs, his head falling back on the sofa as his eyes close. "You're going to kill me by saying stuff like that."

"I'm—"

"Horny," he interrupts. "I know you are. I am, too. If my balls got any bluer, I'd need a trip to the emergency room, but I'm not going to disrespect the men here. They've all been very helpful."

"At cockblocking."

He laughs again.

"What about Apollo's room? You don't even like him." I bite my lip and wait for his reply.

His head rolls forward, a serious look in his eyes. "I don't dislike Apollo. He's a good man. We're not hooking up in his room either."

Guilt swarms my gut because I know if Drew agreed, I would've disrespected my friend that way. It's shameful even suggesting it, but a complete disgrace knowing I would've followed through with it.

"You're right. Bad idea. What about a hotel room?"

"Can't leave the property."

"Maybe you can have Lawson get a connecting room. It would be like at home. He'd even be closer."

"You want my brother and his wife hearing me make you come."

I just want to come, honestly. I scrunch my nose.

"Exactly. Just sit here with me."

"Last time I did that, you fell asleep."

"I'm exhausted," he repeats.

I lean back against the sofa as Drew closes his eyes. I smile when he lifts his hand to my belly.

"How's my boy doing?"

"Moving like crazy all day."

I cover his hand with my own. It's the only touching we do, his hand on my stomach, and I can't help but want more. I want kisses and light brushes. I want whispered promises and intimacy.

It seems Drew is sticking to the promise of just sex, and that may be easier to handle if we were actually getting to have sex. I had more opportunities in high school while living with my mother than I have now as a grown woman. It's left me very frustrated, both mentally and sexually, but moments like this where his fingers are flexing against me are amazing too.

"Everyone is gone," I remind him.

There is literally no one left in the clubhouse, and everyone on the property has already gone back to their own houses.

"There's very little chance of anyone showing up." It takes effort, but I'm able to shift my weight up until I'm straddling his lap. Just the new position has my heart racing and my breaths coming out in a rush. His hands go to my hips, the roundness of my belly an awkward bulge between us.

"Izzy," Drew warns, but he doesn't push me away. His eyes are focused on the front of my sweater. My breasts, even in clothes, have the ability to make him lose his train of thought. I'm not above using them to my advantage right now.

"Shh," I hush him as I lower my mouth to his.

Expecting him to pull away, I gasp in surprise when he grips the back of my neck and crashes his mouth to mine. I don't know if it's the build up to this moment, something that's been weeks in the making, or if it's because we already know this time around what it's like between the two of us when we come together this way.

"Fuck, I want inside of you," he grumbles against my mouth before rolling his tongue against mine.

The kiss is sloppy, heated with passion and missed opportunities, and the echo of his mouth on mine makes me throb.

"I want that. I've wanted that for so long."

I cup his face with both hands, living in this moment, loving the feel of him, the taste of him, the warmth of his body against mine.

"Jinx's room isn't sounding like such an awful idea," he says as he rolls his hips.

I moan in agreement. "Or here. We can just do it here. I won't last long."

"Me either. Fuck, Izzy, move like that again and I won't last long enough to unzip my jeans."

His hands go back to my hips, stilling them when I didn't even realize I was grinding against him.

"So here?" I ask again, desperate for an answer or another solution.

"No. Fuck, no."

"Really?" I whimper. "There's no way I can—"

"The conference room," he suggests. "Get up. We'll go in there."

He helps me with a laugh when I try to scramble off his lap.

"Slow down, baby. We'll get there. Fuck, I didn't want to bend you over a table, but it's looking like that's what's going to happen."

"Okay," I readily agree. I've never been the type to need romance and a soft bed. I was completely okay with how the one and only time I've had sex went down.

I'm light on my feet as he holds my hand across the living room. I'm practically prancing with excitement.

"Shit," he hisses when he opens the door to the conference room.

I haven't been in here many times—the place is practically sacred—but at least it's not one of the guy's bedroom.

"The lights are automatic?"

I shove him further into the room so I can close the doors behind us.

"I don't mind you seeing me naked. I'd never dream of denying you the sight of my boobs. You can't seem to take your eyes off of them in clothes," I tease.

When I rise up on my toes to wrap my arms around his neck, he turns me away from him. I wanted more kissing but if he wants to just bend me over now, I'm okay with that too. I wiggle my ass against the erection straining in his jeans, hissing with need when he grips my chin and angles my head to the side.

"Are you okay with that?"

"Yes," I practically purr, my butt still enticing his hardness. "Anything."

"Fuck, Izzy, not that... *that*."

He turns my head slightly, and there in the damn corner is a camera, the red light blinking to indicate that it's recording.

"Umm." I glare at the offending thing.

"That night we talked near the pool, you told me that Max knows anytime something goes down around here."

"He does." I'm on the verge of tears.

"If the lights are activated by motion sensors, then I'm guessing the camera probably is as well."

"Yeah."

"So we triggered two things when we stepped inside here."

"Probably."

"And Max checks when things are triggered."

"Good chance."

"And with the way your ass is still working against my cock, I'm guessing you're okay with him watching us right now."

I swallow thickly, honestly torn between answers. "He'll probably turn off the feed."

"The light is still blinking, Izzy."

"Maybe he hasn't checked."

"Maybe he's watching and enjoying." His fingers grip my hips but I don't get the feeling he's doing it to stop me. "Maybe he wants a show. They like that sort of thing, don't they? Didn't you tell me they go to that sex club?"

"They do." My mouth is going dry with the rough breaths rushing past my lips.

"Are you willing to risk it? Do you want me to spread you out on the table your dad's club meets at to discuss their business?"

Now that he puts it that way. "Yes."

He laughs, the warm air from his lungs ghosting over my neck.

"I'll do it, Izzy. I'm so fucking hard for you right now, I'll eat your sweet pussy until you come."

"Oh, God," I whimper. I've never had that done before.

"I'll help you to your knees so you can choke on my cock."

Or that.

"I'll fuck you until you scream my name right here. Just say the words."

My eyes are still glued to the camera.

"Maybe we can get Max to give us a copy of the video." His fingers trace down my stomach, coming dangerously close to the waistband of my leggings. "Are you wet for me? Are you dripping with just the thought of my mouth on that pretty little pus—"

My phone rings, a shrill sound that echoes around the room.

Drew clears his throat as he takes a step back. I nearly fall over, having had much of my weight pushed against his body.

"You better get that. It's probably Max telling us to get the hell out of here."

Pulling my phone from my pocket, I answer it with closed eyes. "H-Hello?"

"We're heading to the hospital." My eyes snap open at my dad's voice.

"It's time?"

"Yes. I need you over here if you plan to ride with us."

"I'm on my way."

I hang up the phone, legs still weak form the things Drew told me, but my blood is now filled with a different kind of excitement.

"Gigi's in labor. I'm going to the hospital."

"Okay." He clears his throat, reaching a hand to his jeans to reposition his erection.

"Come with us?"

"That's a really private thing, Iz."

"Just to the hospital. I want you there."

He gives a grin. "Yeah?"

"Please?"

"Of course." He cups my cheek, pressing his lips to my forehead before guiding us out of the conference room.

The cold night air makes me shiver, in part because my leggings are thin, but mostly because my head was so overrun with sexual need, I almost had sex on camera. Dad would kill me if he found out, and that's only if the shame of knowing a video of me like that existed didn't do me in first.

Dad, helping Gigi out of the house, meets us on the porch.

"Drew can you drive us?"

"Of course," he responds, catching the keys with ease when Dad tosses them his way.

"Kincaid and Emmalyn have Amelia, but we told them to keep her at their house until tomorrow," Gigi says between hisses of air.

"Is the pain bad?" I ask as Dad helps her into the back of the SUV.

"Not very pleasant." She gives me a weak smile and I know she's downplaying it to keep my own fear at what I'll soon be facing at bay. "But tolerable. Well worth it in the end."

The entire ride to the hospital I stay turned in my seat, watching Dad help Gigi with her breathing and assuring her everything is going to be fine. I know he's ecstatic for the little boy about to be born, and I'm happy to have a little brother.

That excitement doesn't keep away the knowledge that I'll be doing this on my own, however.

Drew is going to prison, that court date happening before my own due date. He won't be there to drive me to the hospital, to hold my hand while I'm in labor or rub ice chips against my lips. He won't be there to encourage me when I feel like giving up.

By the time we make it to the emergency entrance, my mood has grown somber. I'm stuck in my head about the things I'll be facing soon, and it's taking away from the excitement I should feel about my family expanding.

"You okay?" Drew asks once we're in the waiting room.

"Yeah. Childbirth is scary," I offer as an explanation. There's no sense in making him feel guilty about things he can't control.

We settle into the plastic chairs, waiting for word as other people begin to trickle in. Cannon arrives alone, Rivet being out of town for work. Samson arrives, joined shortly after by Camryn. She's an OB/GYN, but wasn't allowed to deliver Gigi's baby due to her close connection to the family. Camryn's best friend, Charli, has that honor tonight. Lawson and Delilah aren't far behind the others. Ivy waves to all of us before disappearing behind the double doors where her twin sister is in active labor.

"How's your patient?" Delilah asks Camryn.

"She's fine." Camryn, seeing the confused look on my face, tells me that their dinner plans were cut short because she was called into the hospital to help on a case.

Excitement fills the room as we all wait for the news of the newest Cerberus baby to be born. Feet tap, several of the guys pace as if it's their own woman giving birth, and I can't help but smile at the family I've been blessed to be a part of thanks to my dad.

"Did I miss it?" Simone waddles up, one hand under her belly like the weight of it is dragging her down, her other hand pushing a stroller with a sleeping River in it.

"No news yet," Camryn says as she stands and reaches for the other pregnant woman. "You need to sit."

"I'm fin—oh God!" Simone nearly doubles over in pain.

"Can you keep an eye on River?" Camryn asks me. "Looks like we're going to have two babies tonight."

"Rocker is out of town," I remind her, like his absence will slow things down as I stand to take over supervision of River.

"Jinx is too," Cannon says rushing to Camryn's side as if he can help with what comes next.

"I'm calling Khloe and Jasmine," Delilah says as she pulls her phone from her purse.

Khloe, Kid's wife, and Simone have become close friends over the last year. Due to the different situation Simone is in with being in a relationship with Rocker and also River being Jinx's biological son has somehow led to a friendship between her and Jasmine. Maybe it's their unusual relationships that have made way for those connections, but I'm just glad Simone is going to have someone here with her.

"I'll watch River," I say as Camryn begins to lead a still buckled over Simone through the double doors.

"I'm here!" Jasmine rushes in, holding her phone in the air. "Max is going to set up a video conference so Rocker doesn't miss it."

"You're not watching her give birth, you fuckhead," Rocker yells.

"I've seen it all before!" Jinx insists, his voice also echoing around the room from Jasmine's phone.

There's a scuffle coming from the phone making several of the guys standing around laugh.

"I'll settle this while you get her settled," Jasmine assures Camryn. "Take care of her, and I'll be there in a few minutes."

Camryn nods before disappearing with Simone.

"Listen, you two stubborn-headed mules," Jasmine begins, looking down at her phone as she walks away.

"Complete chaos," Drew says as he places his palm on my lower back and looks down at River. The child is still passed out, accustomed to all the action going on.

"Always chaos," I agree.

Chapter 16

Drew

I'd be lying if I said I wasn't going to miss this.

My eyes skate over the room, watching several of the people arguing over who is going to get to meet Hound's new baby first.

It's all done in good fun, no one getting seriously upset on the order.

The idea of family never really crossed my mind. Making up my mind long ago that I didn't want to bring children into this crazy, toxic world, I was happy with only having Lawson, and two brothers don't make a family. Not like the one I'm witnessing now.

I coo down at a smiling River as Delilah playfully referees a game of shortest straw between Cannon and Lawson.

This is family, a group of people not even related, excited for the babies' births. It calms me to know this is what Izzy will have. Although I won't be here, she'll have a group of people who love her to get her through. I take comfort in that knowledge.

"Is he awake?"

I look up to see Jasmine standing nearby.

"He is." I smile down at the sweet little boy.

"Simone is ready to introduce him to his little brother."

Three new little boys—two born and another on the way. This family is growing by leaps and bounds, not a one of them bitter about the growth. Nothing like the time when I was seven and Mom thought she was pregnant again. You'd think she'd been given a fatal cancer diagnosis. She didn't even respond as dismally as she did when that actual cancer diagnosis came several years later.

"He's perfect."

A smile is on my lips before I even look up at Izzy.

"Dark hair like Dad's. This perfect little nose."

"What did they name him?" I ask as I stand, my arms instinctively going around her waist.

"Jameson of course. He's a junior."

"I bet your dad is so proud."

"He can't stop smiling. Gigi is a champ."

I lean forward, ready to press my lips to hers when a throat clears beside me.

"We're going to head out after Delilah gets in a quick visit. Charli came out and told us we need to disburse and come back again tomorrow," Lawson informs everyone.

"Okay," I say, unsure of why he's telling me all this. "So you won't get to meet the little guy tonight?"

"We'll be back in a few hours," he assures me. "I figured you needed a ride home. Izzy are you staying up here?"

Her hand flexes in mine.

"I think I'll go home and get some sleep. I'm exhausted."

Just her words remind me how damn tired I was hours ago at the clubhouse. She's a good distraction, but I don't know how I'm still standing right now.

"Sure." Lawson looks from her back to me, but I ignore whatever he's trying to convey.

The wait isn't long. Delilah comes out grinning as wide as Izzy did, letting everyone know that Gigi is tired and Hound isn't allowing anyone else in the room. I stick close to Izzy on the way out of the hospital, not even bothering to hide the fact that I want her close to me on the elevator. Lawson holds Delilah against his chest, his hand rubbing up and down her back. She's happy, but that doesn't make her pain any less. They want a baby so badly. They're married and in love. They've done everything outdated standards tell them is the right path before starting a family, and yet they haven't had their own dose of good news. It's heartbreaking.

I press my nose to the back of Izzy's head, feeling a little guilty for what I have.

"Do we need to stop anywhere for food?" Lawson asks as we leave the parking lot a few minutes later.

"I'm good," Izzy answers.

"Let's just go home," Delilah says, her eyes focused out the passenger window. "We still have dinner waiting for us."

The ride is silent, spent with Izzy's fingers tracing over my hand and up my arm. It seems like an absent gesture, but she's doing that wiggle she does when she's turned on. I've seen it enough during dinner with her family to know exactly what it means. Despite the activities of the evening, of watching two women go into labor, she hasn't forgotten what was in store for her in the conference room before her dad called.

It doesn't take my head long before its riding shotgun on the very same train she's on.

"I'm going to walk her home," I tell Lawson as I help Izzy out of the back of the quad-cab truck.

"I don't think—" He snaps his mouth closed when Delilah smacks him in the chest. "See you in a few minutes."

"My house is empty," Izzy whispers when we get far enough away from my meddling brother that he can't hear.

"I know."

"Are you walking me over or tucking me in?" Suggestion fills her words, and I'm hard because it takes even less than that to get me there these days.

"Wouldn't want your feet to get cold. Probably need to make sure the blanket covers you fully," I answer as we climb the front steps of her porch.

I'm tapping my fingers against the leg of my jeans as she takes forever to find the right key and get the damn thing in the lock.

By the time the front door is pushed open, I'm a man possessed. No sooner is it pushed closed do I have her pressed against it with my mouth on hers.

"Mmm," she groans when I shift my mouth to lick along her neck.

"Don't mind starting where we left off do you?"

My hands trace down her stomach as I lower my body.

"N-no. Remind me again."

"My mouth on this pretty little pussy." Without delay, I tug down her leggings. "Can you stand?"

"Y-yes," comes her breathless response. I lift one leg over my shoulder, pulling her simple cotton panties to the side. "Maybe?"

"Hold on to me," I urge, my lips an inch from her delicate flesh. "I'll be quick."

"Oh shit!" she screams when I dive in. "Drew!"

Fingers tangle in my hair, and although I'm only seconds into something I want to spend the rest of my life doing, I can already feel the tremble in her legs.

I don't waste energy with filthy words. I don't pull my mouth away to give her a moment of reprieve. I devour, lick, and suck on her until she's pulsing against my mouth, her core playing the most erotic melody against my lips and tongue. Fuck, I kind of regret not doing this in the conference room. Having the video, knowing what her face looks like when she's overcome with passion from my mouth is something I'd love to see.

"D-Drew?"

"Yeah?" I lick at her again, forcing her hips to jerk away, her body too sensitive for more so soon.

"I can't stand much longer."

I'm on my feet in the next instance. "Good thing part two has you on your knees."

I'm going to come the second I feel her breath on my cock. I just know it.

"Help me?"

Her lips are swollen from my mouth, wet and ripe, looking like a crisp apple I want to take a bite from.

With her hands in mine, I help her as she begins to lower herself. Jesus. Am I really going to let this happen? She's going to suck my cock in the entryway of her father's home.

"Izzy, wait." I try to pull her up, but it puts her off balance. She releases my hand, hitting the umbrella stand to the right of the door.

"What's wrong?" she asks, regaining her balance and looking up at me from her knees.

Jesus, fuck. I'm going to hell.

"Nothing. You okay?"

"Perfect," she answers, her eyes drifting from mine to the front of my jeans.

My cock jerks in need.

"May I?" she asks sweetly as I reach for my zipper.

I drop my hands away, Izzy taking that as my answer, and the rasp of my zipper makes my nuts draw up.

"I've never—"

"Shh. It'll be perfect." Literally nothing short of her biting the head off could make this an unpleasurable experience.

"I've watched videos," she whispers as my jeans are tugged open.

I groan when she pulls the elastic band of my boxers down, my cock falling heavily, right in front of her pretty face.

"Tell me if it feels good." Her breath on the damn thing is nearly enough to make me paint her face, but I understand what she's asking. Turning me on, pleasing me, turns her on, and fuck if that isn't the sexiest situation to be in.

"Feels amazing," I grunt when she wraps her tiny hand around the base.

"And this?" Forming a perfect O, she doesn't waste time licking the head before pulling it into her mouth.

Fucking stars. Flashes of light. Is that St. Peter over there, because I'm in fucking heaven.

I nearly fall over when a fist bangs on the front door at Izzy's back.

I have enough wherewithal to push my hand against it when the nob turns.

"Is everything okay?" my asshole of a brother asks from the porch. "I heard a crash."

Izzy giggles, covering that perfect mouth with both of her hands.

"We're fine. I knocked over the umbrella stand." I grind my teeth after explaining, knowing full well I'd be on the porch beating his ass if my dick wasn't out and still inches from Izzy's face.

"Okay," the traitor says. "See you in a minute."

I listen to his boots on the wooden porch as he walks away.

"I need to go," I grunt.

"Stay."

"Can't." Was I really fixing to fuck this girl's throat right here? I want her dad to respect me, and nothing about what we're doing would garner an ounce of that. "But I will tell you I'm tired of being cockblocked."

"You aren't though," Izzy says, her bright hazel eyes blinking up at me as she leans forward and sucks my cockhead right back into her mouth.

"Izzy." I mean for her name to come out like a warning, but it's a plea.

Forgiveness seems to be something I'm asking a lot of these days, and honestly, what's one more thing?

I may have lasted longer than I thought I would, predicting I'd blow the second she touched me, but a handful of plunges into her greedy mouth isn't much better.

"I'm coming," I warn, probably blowing my load before Lawson even has time to make it back to his own yard.

Fuck, what a dismal performance on my part.

For never having given a blow job before, Izzy sure doesn't seem to have a problem swallowing. The grimace on her face makes me chuckle.

"That bad?"

I help her stand, tucking my cock back in my jeans regardless of its objections.

"Not the best."

"Can't be too bad. Let me see."

I take her mouth with mine, ignoring the taste of myself on her tongue. She moans, her arms going back around my body and making it nearly impossible to walk away.

"That's so dirty," she says when I muster enough strength to pull back.

"Can't really be okay with you tasting my cum if I'm not willing to taste it myself."

Her teeth dig into her lower lip.

"I like that sound you make."

"When I come?" I've never really paid much attention.

She nods. "It's like a cross between a grunt and a growl. Very manly. I want to hear it again."

"Soon," I tell her, pressing a kiss to her cheek because her lips would be too much of a temptation. "See you tomorrow."

I don't look back at her when I step outside. Seeing her flushed cheeks under the porch light would leave me explaining to my brother in the morning why I never came home. Hell, he'd probably come right back over here in another five minutes if I didn't leave.

"Have fun?" Lawson asks as soon as I step into the kitchen.

There's no humor in his tone so I ignore him as I pull open the fridge. I don't need a damn thing but a good night's sleep, but I need to keep my hands busy.

"She's a good woman, Drew."

"I know." I drop my head lower, looking inside at all the food but not focusing on anything in particular.

"She deserves better."

"She's a grown woman. What we do isn't anyone's business."

"I'm not talking about what just happened between the two of you."

"Then what?" I ask, standing to my full height to glare at him.

"Does it change anything?"

"In regard to?" I cock an eyebrow at him.

Lawson was always in my business as kids. He took on the fatherly role early on, but he's crossing a line right now.

He sighs, his fingers flexing against the granite of the kitchen island like he's resisting the urge to wrap his hands around my neck for being stubborn.

"Will you fight for yourself? Does being with her mean you're finally going to open your eyes?"

"My eyes are fully open."

"Your eyes have fucking hearts in them right now, and I don't mean from whatever activity you just experienced. You've been watching her, tracking her. You love that girl, and you're still going to walk away from her?"

"I'm not walking away from anyone," I snap, unwilling to even think about the love comment. "I'm going to be dragged away in handcuffs. It's not the fucking same."

"And you have a little boy on the way."

"My dad had a son too. Didn't keep him out of prison."

"You aren't your father, Drew."

"Aren't I? Isn't it better that I'm going to prison before he becomes dependent on me?"

"He needs you. *She* needs you."

"She has an entire family of people to help her."

"Not like you can. If you think you going to prison isn't going to hurt her, then you're a damn fool."

"I'm not trying to hurt anyone." Pain flashes in his eyes, and I know I'm not only leaving my son and Izzy behind. My actions have hurt so many people.

"The attorney says—"

"I killed a man!" I roar, too emotional to worry if Delilah is upstairs sleeping. "I'm not going to stand before a judge and beg him to understand. There is no understanding. There is nothing that will bring that man back or give his family peace. I have to live with that. I have to be punished for that."

"You don't have—"

"Enough!" I swipe my hand through the air. "I'm not having this conversation again. You won't change my mind. *She* won't change my mind."

"Drew."

I walk away, heading right upstairs, but even as exhausted as I know I am, I won't be able to sleep tonight.

Chapter 17

Isabella

"Have you been sleeping?"

"Yes." I lower my eyes, focusing all of my attention on the straw floating in my root beer.

"You're lying. I always know when you're lying." I can feel Sophia's eyes boring into me.

"Sleep doesn't come easy these days. I'm as big as the clubhouse and my feet hurt when I'm not even standing on them."

"You know what will help you sleep. Org—"

"If you say orgasms, I'm going to get up and walk out of here."

"All the way back to the clubhouse? I thought your feet hurt."

A weak smile tugs up the corners of my mouth.

"So, no orgasms then." *Not since that night.* "We can talk about something else then. Thanksgiving is next week. Are you going to make that chocolate pecan pie you make every year or are you going to be too tired?"

I don't even want to think about Thanksgiving. Normally, the holiday is filled with laughter and joy, dozens of people coming together to eat ourselves silly and play cards games.

This year it's just the Thursday before Drew's court hearing. The Monday after the holiday seems like a ridiculous time to have such proceedings. Why not wait until after Christmas? Shouldn't the judge and courtroom staff be using up their saved vacation hours around this time of the year?

"I'm never too tired to make a pie."

"Good. I invited Colton's parents before talking to him about it, and I don't think he wants them there."

"Oh really?" I look up at my smiling best friend. I can get behind talking about anything other than what's been plaguing me for the last couple of weeks.

Drew has managed to avoid me since that night in the entryway. Before, I could tell it was the guys keeping him busy, but he's declined every invite to dinner, saying he doesn't want to intrude since Gigi came home with little Jameson. We haven't spent any real time together, and the time we have spent in the presence of others is stilted and seems like an obligation to him.

Our *just sex* conversation has played over and over in my head, and as many times as I've run it through, I don't recall him mentioning it would only happen once. Hell, if he wants to get technical, we didn't have *actual* sex. His definitions may be different from mine.

"Do you even know what we're talking about?"

"Yes." I watch her face fill with doubt. "Colton isn't happy that you invited his parents to Thanksgiving."

She looks a little shocked, and I'm just glad she hadn't moved the conversation very far forward since I stopped paying attention.

"Did he say why?"

"He thinks his dad has lost his mind. Franklin bought a motorcycle and now Sally is buying t-shirts crude enough to give Cannon a run for his money."

A genuine laugh bubbles out of my throat.

"Sally? Really?"

"Yep." Her eyes widen. "We went to dinner the other day, and she said it was canceled. They've had a dinner every weekend since Colton moved out of the house. I thought Rick was going to cry."

"Why would she cancel dinner?"

"His parents said they were going for a ride on the bike."

"It's freezing outside!"

"Yeah, but that wasn't a concern for them. Colton swears the Cerberus guys are a bad influence on them. He's adamant that peer pressure is making his parents insane."

I laugh again. "Ridiculous."

"And Sally's shirt?" She points to the front of her sweater. "It said *I Love Dirty Old Bikers*."

I snort a laugh. "That's amazing."

"Colton doesn't think so. He put his foot down when Franklin offered to buy Rick a bike."

"That boy is best friends with Landon. Him ending up on a bike is inevitable."

"I know! And when Colton commented on his mom's shirt, Franklin opened his leather jacket showing him his." She points at her chest again. "His said *Motorcycles are like women. It's always best to have two*."

"No." I slap my hand over my mouth. If I've learned anything about people since my dad joined Cerberus, it's to not count anything out with age. "Do you think?"

She gags. "I don't even want to think about it, but it seriously skeeved Colton out. He had a talk with Dad."

"That probably didn't go well. Dominic can't usually be swayed in any direction."

She shrugs. "It didn't go the way Colton wanted it to. Dad listened to him, but he just as quickly reminded him that his parents are grown. He told him that parents are just as unimpressed with what their children do sometimes."

"Oh, crap."

"Yeah."

"So he did hear?"

"Apparently. Thinking about it now, I may not even be able to show my face at Thanksgiving. You may have to bring that pie to the house."

Sophia called me last week and told me that Colton had been working a case that kept him away for the better part of four days. He only came home long enough to shower, eat, and grab a couple naps. She complained about being sexually deprived, and somehow I managed to keep my mouth closed and didn't remind her what deprivation really looked like.

Her parents were visiting when he finally came home. She gave explicit details about what she did to him in the shower, only to walk out of the bathroom with her parents both still sitting in the living room. Apparently, she was so hard up, she forgot they were there.

"I can't believe they didn't get up and walk out."

"Oh, they did. But they just waited until we were done."

I shudder. Dad obviously knows I had sex, but I can't imagine him hearing any part of such exploits. I don't think Dad would sit there and listen. He'd kick Drew's ass. Not that Drew is scrambling in my direction these days.

"You have to remember what he walked in on with Jasmine, Max, and Tug. At least he didn't *see* what was going on between you and Colton."

"Still mortifying."

"Very," I agree. "So what else is going on?"

"Rick and Landon both got accepted to Lindell."

"Two Lindell Lemurs in the family? That's amazing news."

She frowns. "Yes and no. Landon was recruited by the baseball team, a full scholarship to play."

"And Rick?"

"Walk-on, no scholarship for athletics."

"What about academics?"

She cringes. "He's trying, but his grades haven't been that great."

"Are you saying Colton doesn't have a college fund for him?"

"He does, but he never considered Rick would want to go to a university out of state."

"And Rick won't consider New Mexico?"

"And be away from Landon? Not going to happen, but we'll make it work. Dad offered to help with the expenses, but Colton is stubborn and turned it down."

"Of course he did."

"Men," we both mutter, laughing for saying it at the same time.

"So, tell me about Drew."

"What about him?" And that fast my mood takes a nosedive.

She must read the change because her hand clamps over the top of mine. "I'm sorry you're going through this."

"It's hard," I confess. "He won't even talk to me."

"You guys were together at the clubhouse yesterday."

"Ten people were at the clubhouse yesterday," I remind her. "We're in the same room all the time, but we hardly speak."

"He did seem a little distant. Have you tried talking to him?"

"And what should I say, Sophia?"

"We've gone over this."

"And this isn't the same as you urging me to talk to him in the beginning. I thought we were past all the hurt and anger. He wasn't mad about me not seeking him out when I found out I was pregnant. We talked and shared things and we—" I shake my head. I love this girl sitting across from me, but I'm nowhere near as comfortable talking about sex as she is.

"You hooked up and he's ghosted you?"

"We didn't hook up. Not all the way." I sigh. "It doesn't matter. We're not talking anymore. He's in Albuquerque."

"Court?" she snaps. "Why are we here? Is his hearing today?"

"It's just a meeting with his attorney."

"Are you sure?"

Tears burn the backs of my eyes for half a second before they're streaming down my face. "He wouldn't do that, would he? He wouldn't not tell me? He's adamant he's going to prison, Sophia. He wouldn't go to prison without letting me say goodbye, would he?"

"Calm down," she says, pulling her phone out and shooting off a text.

"Who are you texting?"

"Dad. He was going out of town today. I bet he's there with them."

We wait for what seems like hours, but is probably only a few minutes before her phone chimes.

"Look," she says, turning her phone around so I can read the message.

Sophia: Iz is freaking out right now. Is Drew going to prison today?
Dominic: The fool isn't going today.

"You didn't have to tell him I'm freaking out," I mutter, the news from her dad not making me feel much better.

"I wanted him to know how serious it was. I can't have you going into premature labor while everyone is away."

"It wouldn't really be premature. I'm due in three weeks."

Two weeks after Drew's court hearing. Two weeks after my baby's father is getting carried away to prison.

Chapter 18

Drew

"I need to know the details so you'll have a fair trial."

"No. I've told you everything."

"Drew," Lawson hisses. He knows the full truth, but the state of my mind that night should have no bearing on the outcome of the hearing.

"And trial? I said no trial. I'm pleading guilty."

"I set it for trial," the attorney says, his eyes darting past me to either Hound or Dominic. They both decided to tag along today, and what a fun trip down that was.

"Change it."

"It's frowned upon to do that this close."

"It's better than showing up on the day of the hearing and having to discharge an unneeded jury. No fucking trial."

My attorney's jaw flexes, and his eyes once again go over my shoulder.

"Look at me," I seethe. "Are you my attorney or theirs?"

He pulls his glasses from his face, using his handkerchief to wipe at his brow. "Technically, both."

"Is this my case or theirs?" I clarify.

"Yours." He places his glasses back on his face and opens a thick folder in front of him on the table. "Right now, you're not wanting a trial, but may I suggest holding on to the date with the jury pool just in case? Many people change their minds at the prospect of prison the closer they get."

"Please, Drew," my brother begs, and the pain in his voice now is no easier to handle than that night weeks ago after I walked Izzy home.

"I won't change my mind," I say weakly.

Fuck, do they not understand that I don't want to go to prison? I don't want to leave my son to be born with no dad around. I don't want to walk away from whatever I stupidly let build between Izzy and me.

Do they know how hard it's been to distance myself from her these last couple of weeks when all I want to do every time I see her is wrap my arms around her and bury my face in her hair? I want to spend time with her, every second of every day. I want to raise our son together, and maybe in a couple of years, convince her to have more babies with me. I want all of this with her—from her—not because I'm going to prison, but because it's how I see my future.

She's my future.

Correction, she could've been my future had I not lost my head.

"Keep the jury," I say, only to appease my brother. My convictions stay strong.

"Good." The attorney makes a note in his file. "Now with that in mind, the best the state can do is voluntary manslaughter. What happened that night was in the heat of the moment. Now, they may try to argue that as a police officer your head handles things at a quicker pace, but I don't see one person who'd consider..." he flips to another page in the folder, "fourteen feet a distance long enough to come to terms with the death of Mrs. Barnes. So we're going to argue for the lesser offense."

"I knew what I was doing." I look the man in the eye when I say it.

"You attacked him with the intent to kill him?"

"I murdered that man."

"You caused his death," he clarifies. "Murder, in legal terms, carries an entirely different definition. Your offense doesn't even come close to meeting the elements of that crime. The best the state can do is argue it as voluntary."

"I wouldn't have stopped," I confess, and that takes a lot, especially with Izzy's dad and Dominic both in here.

I could've asked them to leave. My attorney urged me to handle this privately, but I knew there were going to be things discussed, things I'd have to say, and having them in here while I say them to the man in the business suit is easier than speaking these words to them directly. I'm a fucking coward.

"If Warren hadn't pulled me off of him, I would've hit his face until my knuckles made it through to the asphalt."

"Tell him why," Lawson urges.

I ignore him.

"What?" Hound asks. "What aren't you saying?"

"I'd like them to leave," I tell my attorney, and I can feel the irritation rolling off of all three of them as chairs scrape across the floor and they make their exit.

"Do you want to tell me what your brother was referring to?"

"Mr. Crampton, I know I'm going to prison."

"Getting off completely isn't going to happen," he sighs. "I think you knew that from the start."

"I'm not asking for release."

"But the way you're talking, it's sounding like you'd rather do the six years that comes with voluntary manslaughter rather than the eighteen months that involuntary carries."

"Six years is the max?"

He nods. "For voluntary. I think we can get it reduced if you let me fight this out in court."

"Six years," I repeat.

As a police officer, I know some sentences are messed up compared to the crimes committed.

"Beating someone to death only gets six years? Doesn't seem like enough."

This entire room is going to be filled with nothing but hot air if this guy doesn't stop sighing from across the table. "Voluntary manslaughter gets six years—things like catching your wife cheating and pulling a gun and shooting them both dead, or a parent catching someone raping their child and they kill the predator."

"Like beating a man to death for killing an innocent woman while he was drunk."

"Exactly."

I raise an eyebrow at him.

"No. You couldn't have known he was going to die. You used your fists not your side arm. We can prove to a jury that if you wanted to kill the man, then you could've shot him."

"I didn't pull my service revolver, Mr. Crampton, because he wasn't a threat to me."

"I can still convince a jury that this was involuntary manslaughter."

"You can't convince me that it was, though, and at the end of the day, that's all that matters to me. I want you to cancel the jury."

"But you said—"

"Cancel the jury, Mr. Crampton, and I'll have you disbarred if you speak of my case with another member of the Cerberus MC."

"Cerberus, huh?"

"Anyone, Mr. Crampton, and that includes my brother, the woman having my baby, and your own damn wife. Do you understand?"

"Mr. O'Neil, I urge you to—"

"I'm not changing my mind today, tomorrow, next week or the Monday morning before court. I'm pleading guilty to voluntary manslaughter."

"Do you want me to ask the state's attorney for the maximum sentence as well?" There's something to be said about a grown, professional man rolling his eyes, but I ignore his frustration.

"Whatever the state is willing to offer is what I'll accept."

And since he's said more than once the state wants voluntary manslaughter and a six-year sentence, I doubt he can change their minds before my court date.

"I think you're making a mistake."

"And as you're well aware, it's my mistake to make."

"And when the other inmates find out you were a cop?"

"I'll cross that bridge when I get there."

"You will die in prison if they know."

I swallow thickly, unable to look him in the eyes, and then I stand up and walk out of his office with my head held high. I don't make eye contact with the three men waiting in the lobby.

Izzy accused me of being a martyr once, but I don't see it that way. I call it integrity. Not many men would take the high road. Not many men would walk away from the chance to fight for a lesser sentence.

I don't want to be like other men. I want to be able to look my son in the eye one day and explain to him what it means to make mistakes and face them head-on. Hopefully, this will be a lesson to him to fight hard at not making such mistakes.

Hopefully, I'll be given the opportunity to meet him some day.

The knowledge that it may never happen sits heavy in my gut, feeling like a solid chunk of concrete by the time we make it back to Farmington.

Chapter 19

Isabella

"I can't wait to dive into that," Lawson says with a wide grin, his eyes gleaming as he looks down at the chocolate pecan pie. "Maybe I should hide it so I don't miss out on getting a piece."

"I made five of them," I tell him, my smile not even getting close to reaching my eyes.

"Still. Didn't you make the same amount last year?" I confirm with a nod. "I didn't score a piece."

"If memory serves, you and Delilah disappeared very shortly after the meal."

He grins even wider. "Worth it."

He playfully nudges my shoulder with his own before crossing the kitchen to ask Delilah if she needs anything.

His wife is wrapped up in holding Simone and Rocker's little boy too much to even lift her head when he approaches.

"Soon," he whispers, pressing his lips to the top of her head.

It's a heartbreaking thing to see two people so in love, so desperate for a child of their own. My hand flutters down the front of my own stomach unbidden.

Life doesn't seem fair some days, and that sad thought stays with me while I busy myself with anything that keeps me from going out into the living room.

Drew is in there. He arrived over an hour ago with Lawson and Delilah, but he's yet to show his face in this part of the clubhouse.

Avoidance seems to be his thing these days. He was distant before his meeting with his attorney a few days ago, but since he's returned, I've only been able to catch glimpses of him. I've become the fool watching from the window when I hear Lawson's truck pull up after they get home from work, waiting to watch Drew climb out with his head down as he crosses the street to enter the Cerberus shop. Dad hasn't mentioned him. Gigi's been too busy with little Jameson to concern herself with my life, which is a blessing. The woman doesn't usually know how to be subtle and having tact isn't something she's ever been accused of.

"Did you make them?" Sophia wraps her arms around me, her fingers settling over my huge stomach.

"Yes. Five of them."

"Won't be enough. Let's hide one so we can binge on it later."

I laugh at her suggestion. "My doctor urged me to cut back on sweets. My weight gain this last month was higher than she liked."

"That sucks." Sophia urges me to turn around.

I can't look at her. I know what her eyes are going to say. It'll be the same thing her mouth has said over phone calls and video messaging from the last couple of weeks. My heightened emotional state can't handle the sadness and crying in front of everyone here isn't a good idea.

I don't want to ruin the holiday's jovial mood.

"How long have you been up?" Soft fingers sweep under my eyes.

I knew I should've applied makeup to cover the dark circles, but I just couldn't be bothered with the effort.

"Since five," I whisper, turning my head to focus on anything else but my best friend's face.

"You're still not sleeping well." It isn't a question. The circles under my eyes are from a greater loss of sleep than one early morning, and she's making it clear that she knows it.

"Still hard to get comfortable," I explain.

"Well," she rubs my belly like it's a genie's lamp, "this little guy will be here soon."

"And you'll get even less sleep," Simone comes in, looking just as frazzled as I feel.

Rocker gives a small smile, his hand in Simone's as they make their way into the kitchen. He looks like he hasn't lost a wink of sleep, but I know better. His ability to survive on very little rest is a side effect of working for Cerberus. At home they have a lot of downtime, but more than once, Dad has talked about going practically twenty-four seven when they're away from work. Once they have a job, they don't rest often until it's done. Due in part because things are time sensitive, but also because the guys are eager to get back to New Mexico where their loved ones are.

"Maybe if Rocker got up and helped a little more often," Sophia hedges, her mouth speaking before she realizes the situation.

Rocker frowns.

"He gets up every single time. We have a system. You wouldn't notice it by looking at his sparkling eyes, though." Simone cups his cheek before pressing a soft kiss to his lips.

"So do I," Jinx adds as he walks in with a squirming River in his arms.

"You could sleep," Rocker argues. "No one is asking you to help with Cooper."

Jinx scoffs like the words are the most ridiculous thing he's ever heard. "We're a team. A family."

Both Rocker and Simone smile.

A team. A family.

I have that in spades, but I still feel alone.

I turn back to the sink, but before I can find something else to keep me busy, Kincaid walks into the room.

"Why are we all standing around? Isn't there food to be eaten?"

More people shuffle into the room, the entire crew making it nearly standing room only.

Arms encircle loved ones, looks go around the room when Kincaid begins to talk about the club and family, and how we've been blessed with new babies, and how he hopes for many more in the next year. He speaks about loyalty and hardship, how we've been blessed. And I feel every word, all of it ringing true in my own mind.

When we bow our heads to pray, I catch a flash of Drew standing near the doorway, several feet of distance between him and Thumper, the newest member of the MC. It's almost as if he's physically there, but his mind and soul are elsewhere. It's clear he doesn't feel like he's a part of the family that Kincaid just spoke of, but it couldn't be any further from the truth.

I lower my head, swiping away a stubborn tear before it can track all the way down my face, praying no one saw it. Sophia crushes that wish when she squeezes my hand, and when I look up, I see Drew watching me, sadness filling his eyes. When the prayer is over and everyone begins to shuffle as they fill their plates, he doesn't come to me, instead taking a step back and leaving the room.

"Why don't you take a seat. I don't want you run over," Dad says as I stand frozen in the middle of the room. "I know what you like. I'll make you a plate."

"I don't feel well." It isn't exactly a lie, but it's not a physical illness dragging me down today. Emotionally, I'm exhausted, and the knowledge that it won't be ending anytime soon seems like a burden I won't survive.

"Because you haven't eaten. Take a seat."

He leaves no room for argument, and since I don't want to explain to my dad why I'm in the middle of my own little pity party, I cross the room and take a seat beside Sophia. She didn't waste any time filling her plate.

"I'm serious about that pie, Iz. Do you see the way everyone is drooling over them as they get their turkey and dressing?"

I chuckle because it seems like the appropriate response at the moment.

"Seriously. Watch."

I look over at the dessert bar, a long table stacked with at least ten variations of sweets, and I'll be damned if she isn't right. Several of the guys look longingly at the table, their eyes directed at the end where my pies sit. Apollo approaches slowly, looking around suspiciously before scooping a piece of the pie right on top of his food.

"No manners," Sophia mutters, but there's humor in her voice. "Rookie."

"He's new. This is the first Thanksgiving, leave him alone."

"There are no real rules in place," Lawson mutters as he takes a seat across from us at the long table.

Delilah shakes her head at the scowl on his face as he watches Apollo walk out of the kitchen to enjoy his meal—and his pie—in the other room.

"I think I'm going to—" Delilah places his hand on Lawson's arm when he makes to stand.

"There's plenty," I assure him.

Both he and Sophia scoff.

"It's just pie."

"The best pie ever," Colton says as he takes a spot on the other side of Sophia.

My friend's head swivels between him and me, a look of betrayal on her face. "Care to explain? It's his first Thanksgiving too."

Colton shoves a huge bite of stuffing and dressing into his mouth, leaving me hanging.

"I've never made a pie for him."

"But," he swallows, "she has made them for the department. I had a slice last year. Amazing."

He kisses his fingers like a chef before diving back into the food on his plate.

"Izzy."

"Sophia," I mock.

"How many pies did you make?"

"There's five on the table." I point in that direction, chuckling when I notice Lawson staring at me like I've personally insulted him.

"How. Many. Did. You. Make?"

I roll my lips between my teeth to keep from laughing, and the fact that my friend is being ridiculous enough to make me laugh actually makes me want to cry.

"Dad took another five to the police station this morning," I confess.

Lawson's fork falls from his hand, his eyes unblinking, the clanking noise as it lands drawing the attention of several other people.

"What?" Sophia snaps.

Colton mouths *sorry* behind her back as she glares at me.

"What's wrong?" Dad asks as he walks up with a plate piled high.

"I can't eat all of that."

"Quit changing the subject," Sophia hisses.

"What's going on?" Dad looks around the table. "Is something wrong?"

"I don't know," Sophia huffs, her arms crossing over her chest. "Is betrayal wrong?"

"One of the worst things a person could do," Lawson adds. Delilah smacks at him, and I don't miss the twitch of his lip. He's fighting a smile.

Sophia? She may never recover.

"They just found out about the pies I made for the police station."

"Isn't it awesome?" Dad says. "She's been sending them down there for the last three years."

Sophia gasps, and I swear if she was wearing pearls, she'd clutch them like an old southern woman seeing someone wearing white after Labor Day.

"Better not mention the banana pudding then, huh?" Dad presses a kiss to my temple before walking away.

"What?" Delilah snaps, her eyes wide now that her favorite treat has been given away as well.

"I made one for here, too."

"I didn't get any last year."

I look from her to Lawson, grinning as he leans down and whispers in her ear. Her cheeks turn pink, and by the time he pulls his head away, she can't look anyone in the eye.

"Oh."

"Yeah, oh," I echo.

"What happened last year?" Colton asks, his eyes darting between the couple opposite of us.

"Well, those two..." Sophia begins, uncaring of Delilah's apparent embarrassment.

I love my friend, but really, she needs to learn how to read the room.

"I also made peanut butter cookies," I interrupt, drawing my friend's attention off of Lawson and Delilah, "with crunchy peanut butter."

Her favorite, even more so than the pie.

"They're at your house?" Hope fills her voice, thinking the treats are safe.

"A few are left." Mostly the ones that came out of the oven a little too crisp or oddly shaped.

"Perfect," she says, appeased enough to finally bring her attention back to the plate of food in front of her.

"That pie?" Lawson asks as Drew steps into the room, the tail end of people making their plates. "Does it have cinnamon in it?"

I shake my head.

"Okay. Good, because Drew's allergic."

Using my fork, I scoop up some mashed potatoes. I'm not the least bit hungry, but I'd rather focus on the meal than any conversation pertaining to Drew O'Neil.

As much as I want to look away, I catch myself glancing up as he moves from one spot to the next, adding food to his plate. My heart breaks a little more when his eyes glance down at the empty spot beside his brother before turning away and walking right out of the room.

Chapter 20

Drew

"How was I supposed to know!" Legend snaps, his face masked with disappointment.

"Literally everyone was talking about them," Thumper says, smacking his friend on the back of the head.

"And the chances of convincing her to make another one?" Legend asks.

"None," Jinx mutters. "She only makes those pies at Thanksgiving."

I don't know if they're purposely carrying on a conversation about fucking pie to annoy me because Izzy made them, or if it's because they're that amazing. I didn't try one. I heard everyone whispering about the damn things, but I felt like I wasn't deserving of anything she took the time to make. I'm in the same boat as Legend, only I've kept my displeasure to myself.

"Hey, Drew, think you can convince—"

Thumper smacks his friend again, and Legend doesn't finish his sentence after they have a silent conversation between the two of them.

I'm pretty sure Isabella Roze Montoya would rather spit on me than talk to me these days. Not that I've tried. Avoiding her hasn't been hard in the physical sense. According to Hound, she's stayed pretty busy with schoolwork, even through the holiday to get ahead. Mentally, it takes everything I have in me to not go to her. I can't even look at her house when I leave Lawson's because I know if I catch a glimpse of her, I'm going to end up at her feet apologizing for being a piece of shit.

Today is like every other Saturday since Hound brought me out to the shop. The place is filled with Cerberus guys, several drinking beer and shooting their mouths off. A couple are focused on tweaking stuff on their bikes, but most are just standing around like they're waiting for something.

I get my answer when Kincaid walks in. One clearing of his throat is all it takes for the guys to snap to attention. Silence fills the room as one by one the guys walk up to me, shaking my hand before walking out of the garage.

Emotions clog my throat, each slap on the back and sad nod sent my direction making tears threaten to fall.

I respect these men, respect the work they do, respect the way they live their lives, respect their integrity. Even Apollo walks up to shake my hand, the look on his face not one of satisfaction that I'll soon be out of his way as I expected.

It takes probably five minutes for the men to shuffle through, leaving me, Lawson, Hound, Kincaid, Dominic, and Lawson's dads Jaxon and Rob in the room. I know Shadow and Kid would be here right now if they weren't working on something in town.

"None of us have any firsthand knowledge of what you're facing."

Kincaid's words aren't meant as an insult, but they still feel like a kick to the gut. Of course these guys don't know what prison is like. They'd never lower themselves so far to end up there.

"But we know the type of man you are," Dominic says.

"You're the type of man willing to do something not many other people are capable of," Jaxon adds.

"A good man," Hound says, his voice hitching at the end.

Jesus Christ. Am I really going to cry in front of these men?

I look up, knowing these guys can tell I'm fighting my emotions.

"I question your actions from that night," Lawson says, his voice filled with the same pain and sorrow sitting heavy on my chest. "But I've never questioned your integrity."

Several grunts of agreement echo around the room.

"Monday may bring a different result than what we're hoping for, so we wanted you to know how we see you. We know the man you really are, Drew O'Neil, and if the worst happens, I want you to know—" Kincaid taps his chest before waving his arm to indicate the other men in the garage. "—we want you to know that we're proud of the man you've become."

I don't open my mouth to argue, simply offering him a nod, the motion a lie because I don't feel the same. I'm not standing here proud. I'm crushed, devastated, and burdened by my choices.

"Thank you," I manage, getting choked up as each one of them walks toward me, taking turns to shake my hand and clap me on the back in that bro-hug way.

Several throats clear numerous times, Lawson having to turn his back to me to get himself under control.

"So," Kincaid claps after a long moment of silence. "Let's go over the skills you've learned the last month or so."

I spend the next couple of hours being tested on mechanics, machines, and even some electrical work as the other guys slowly begin to trickle out of the shop. When I pull off the welding mask, I notice Hound is the only one left in the room.

Despite what he said to me earlier in front of the others, I fully expect him to unleash his true feelings, that he's glad I'm going to be gone, and Izzy is better off without me around.

Ready to agree with him, I frown when he looks at me with such warmth that the tears I managed to somehow hold back earlier, threaten again.

The look is also knowing, as if he's somehow aware of what I've instructed my attorney to do.

"I'm holding out hope for Monday." I nod, unable to tell him the truth about what's going to go down. "But in case it doesn't, I want you to know that provisions have been put in place if you go to prison."

"I don't want any help."

"And I didn't ask. You're the father of my grandchild, and I'll be damned if I'm going to have to tell that little boy that his daddy died in prison."

I keep my mouth closed, all the while wondering if my son would be upset losing a man he never knew.

"You'll have a job that will keep you busy," he continues. "The days will go by faster that way. You'll be protected, but don't go getting involved in anything illegal or any gang shit. When you get home, you'll either have a job here with Cerberus or at Lawson's shop. If you want to get an education in something other than the criminal justice degree you have, we'll make that happen too."

He cocks an eyebrow at me when I open my mouth to argue.

"You will come home, Drew. This is only a bump in the road."

Yeah, a six-year bump in the road. Coming back to a child who doesn't know me and a woman who will hate me may not be an option, despite his belief that it's possible.

"Thank you," I say, honestly grateful that this man would lift a finger to help me even though I didn't ask.

"Now head home."

He walks out of the garage, leaving me standing there like a fool.

Cold November air fills the garage from the open door, and it's the only thing that makes my feet move. I'd stay in here forever if I could, but there are numerous things I need to do before heading to Albuquerque tomorrow.

Keeping my head down like usual, I make my way across the street. I've done this very thing day after day, focusing on my feet rather than the houses in front of me, but something is different tonight. I don't know if it's because this will be the last time I can look up at her house, or what, but my eyes lift, my feet stuttering on the gravel when I see her standing on her front porch.

Cold breaths leave Izzy's mouth in puffs, her slender arms holding a thin blanket around her shoulders, the fabric not big enough to cover her stomach.

Unable to swallow the lump that's been forming in my throat since the first man walked up to me and shook my hand, I have to look away.

Wanting her, needing her in my arms is unfair. The time I spent with her these last couple of months is equally cruel. The hope I see glimmering in her eyes guts me, and I have to walk away.

The house is silent when I enter, and I'm thankful that my older brother isn't standing around waiting for me to get home. The last thing I need right now is another argument about fighting my case.

Filled with familiar things, my room stills seems empty. As I pack my things away in boxes, praying this room will be a nursery by the time I visit again, I'm nothing but a robot. I have no sentimental connection to a single thing in here. The clothes are meaningless, the personal belongings bringing no memories or feelings.

I avoid the window, knowing I can't see her again. My hands shake with fear, terror of what could happen to me in prison regardless of Hound's assurances. My mind races, questions echoing inside asking if I'm doing the right thing.

I strip down to my boxers, knowing tonight may be one of the last times I'll close my eyes knowing I'm safe.

Chapter 21

Isabella

Talk to him. It'll make you feel better.

Those were Sophia's parting words after she left with a container full of crunchy peanut butter cookies on Thursday.

Tonight, two days later, I finally got up the nerve, and he couldn't even stand the sight of me. Dad knew I was waiting when he came home, pressing his lips to my forehead without saying a word. The kind gesture of bringing me a blanket nearly made me sob.

I was able to hold those emotions back until Drew looked up at me before walking away.

My tears have dried, the pain and sorrow transforming into an angry rage I can't recall ever feeling before.

Maybe Drew isn't a good man. What kind of man smiles at a woman, makes them feel comfortable and light on her feet only to turn around and discard her like trash? A good man doesn't make someone fall in love with them only to be disgusted by the sight of them later.

And that's what I feel. It doesn't matter that it's unrequited. It doesn't matter that he doesn't want to even look at me.

I fell in love with him.

It didn't happen overnight.

It started *that night*.

It started with the first smirk, the first wink, the very first words out of his mouth.

I was thinking of getting a burger, but you're making those pancakes sound like they're the best thing you've ever had in your mouth.

The filthy innuendo only served to irritate me even more right now.

His hands, his mouth, that laugh I heard so little of. All of it made me lose myself to him.

Those are things that make my feet move off the porch. Those things are what have me sneaking into Delilah's house like a thief in the night. They're what make me push open his bedroom door without so much as a light tap on the door.

He's made his choices, and although I have to live with them, I sure as hell don't have to take them lying down. I won't be trampled on. I won't be disrespected, and I won't let him go to court without him knowing how much he hurt me, how much I want him to heal me.

The tears are back as I wait for my eyes to adjust to the darkness of his room.

"Izzy?" His voice is raw and broken as he stands.

But I steel my spine, ready to lay all of my pain at his feet.

"You're an assh—"

His lips are on mine, his hand tangling in my hair, and if the warmth of his body against mine didn't feel so good, I might have the strength to push him away.

"We—"

"Shh. No talking."

I nearly open my mouth again to argue, but it's filled with him, his tongue, his moans, all the things we both need to say but can't.

The thin blanket is pushed from my shoulders, pooling at our feet, but his roaming hands wipe away the chills threatening to form. He's everywhere—my neck, my breasts—his warm breath pebbling my nipples. His fingers tangle in my hair, moving my mouth exactly how he wants it.

Skilled hands remove my t-shirt before working my sweats and panties down my legs, and I let him. I let the man who has worked very hard over the last few weeks to break my heart touch me, caress me, make me his.

Because his mouth isn't lying. His body isn't walking away from me or avoiding me when I walk into the room. I'm the center of his world right now, and I feel like the center of his with each nip to my skin, with each lick of that wicked tongue.

He doesn't ask permission when he guides me to his bed. He knows he already has it, the slickness of my desire coating his fingers as he brushes them down my slit.

I moan, a desperate sound, begging him to keep going.

And he does, first burying his face between my legs, licking at me with a combination of aggression and softness as if he can't make up his mind.

His hand is over my lips, silencing my cries when I come, and in the next breath he's hovering above me, his chin glistening, his breaths rushing past moonlit swollen lips.

I press against his chest when he slides his body between my thighs, his intent clear. I resituate my body, lying more on my left side than my back. I want to feel good when we come together again like this, and that would be impossible if I'm lying flat.

A master at adaptation, he doesn't miss a beat, placing my ankle over his shoulder and straddling my other leg.

When he slides into me, it's nothing like that first time. There's no rush, no threat of being caught, no race to the finish line for either of us. When his hips slowly begin to move, gliding into me until he's buried deep before pulling back out, he never takes his eyes from mine.

I see promises in them.

I see a future.

I see apologies for the mistakes he's made.

He begs for forgiveness with his eyes, with the tears rolling down his cheeks.

I nod, knowing I don't have to open my mouth to say the words to let him know he has nothing to be forgiven for.

"Drew," I whimper.

"Shh," he urges, his hips still moving at a maddening pace. "Just this."

"This," I echo.

This is heaven.

This is what I've been dying for.

Not the sex exactly, but the intimacy, the walls down and his true feelings in front of my face.

My own tongue snakes out when he sucks his thumb into his mouth. I know what's coming. He did the same thing that night, but my body isn't ready when he presses the wet finger to my clit. I groan, a low rumble of pleasure, uncaring for the others in the house. There are only two people who exist right now, two souls finally lining up, a love so true no words are even needed to express it.

My body convulses when I orgasm, muscles tightening all over from the sheer force of the pleasure he has given me.

He's not far behind, moaning my name as he spasms inside of me.

Warm, wet lips press to my calf before he pulls away and situates himself at my back, his fingers tracing a heart on my belly. The baby, awake from the activity, moves, rolling around in my stomach as if he knows his daddy is near and he's missed him.

"Drew."

"Shh," he urges again.

Then I feel hot tears on my back, and all I can do is cup my hand over his where his son is saying hi, and I cry a little too.

As I fall asleep, I'm torn between the happiness I feel for him, finally making me understand how he feels and the torment I know I'm going to experience if he goes to prison.

By the time I wake the next morning, Drew is gone, having not bothered to say goodbye, and the house is empty.

Like a fool, it takes me longer than it should that he wasn't confessing his love, but saying his goodbye with his body.

If only I was smart enough at the time to realize it wasn't goodbye for now, but a goodbye forever.

Chapter 22

Drew

"We'll need to reschedule," Mr. Crampton says after shaking my hand in the tiny room reserved for client meetings at the courthouse.

"No," I tell him.

"I wasn't able to get the state to agree to a reduced sentence."

Lawson stiffens beside me. "Reduced sentence? Doesn't the trial have to happen first?"

"There's not going to be a trial," I say without looking my brother in the eye.

"If we go through today, you'll get the full six years."

"I'm awar—"

"Six years?" Lawson yells.

"Law," Jaxon warns. "Calm down."

"Six years?" Lawson seethes, his voice barely lower than before. "I thought he was looking at eighteen months with involuntary manslaughter."

My attorney looks at me for direction. I told him not to speak to anyone about my case, and I'm regretting it now. Explaining this today of all days is harder than I ever thought possible.

"I'm pleading to voluntary manslaughter. It carries a six-year sentence."

"I'm still planning on asking the judge to reduce it." Mr. Crampton gives me a weak smile letting me know the request won't matter.

"Please." Lawson spins me around, and the tears on his face would have the ability to break me if I hadn't done it to myself two days ago. "Drew?"

"You've been an amazing brother. I couldn't ask for a bett—"

"Don't," he snaps, shaking me by my shoulders. "Don't start that shit. I'm not fucking saying goodbye to you."

I snap my mouth closed. I won't say it if he doesn't want to hear it, but it doesn't change anything. If the dream I had last night has the power of prediction, I won't last a week in prison. Holding Izzy Saturday is the only thing that kept me from the grave that night anyway. I never wanted to go to prison, and if she hadn't arrived, there was a good chance my brother's goodbyes would be spoken over my grave instead of here, right now.

"We need to get out there. Judge Slate doesn't take kindly to tardiness."

"Drew," Lawson says one last time, but Kincaid, his dad and Hound urge him from the room.

"Mr. O'Neil?" I turn to face my attorney. "I can ask for an extension. This case has moved very quickly through the system. It's not unheard of to need a delay. I can get a few more months. Maybe revisiting with the state's attorney after the holidays could yield a better result."

"I'm ready today."

If I walk out of this courtroom today, I may never get the nerve back up to reenter.

"You're sure?"

"Yes." The answer is filled with gravel, forcing me to clear my throat. It only makes my attorney frown deeper.

"I've never met a man like you before, Mr. O'Neil."

He doesn't clarify if he thinks I'm a fool or if he commends me, but it doesn't matter either way.

I can't face the people in the crowd. The fact that there's anyone here to witness my downfall makes my stomach turn more than it already was. Other than Hound, Lawson, Kincaid, and Jaxon, I think all the other Cerberus guys stayed back at the clubhouse.

Hound assured me that he'd keep Izzy home, but then he showed up himself at the hotel we stayed at last night. I didn't see her, and I didn't ask. I just pray the man was able to keep that promise to me.

"The judge is going to ask some questions," Mr. Crampton whispers as we walk toward a table to one side of the room. "Pay attention and answer respectfully. There are a lot of people in the crowd."

"Ready to lynch me," I mutter.

"Unlikely. There's a full docket today, cases being cleared before the Christmas holiday. The clerks were stupidly excited when I called to cancel the trial. It cleared up a lot of time to get many other things done." He nods, whispering flat pleasantries to the men standing at the other table in front of the judge's bench. "Now, I'm going to refuse the offer for the reading of the petition, so only those here for you will know what happened. With a plea, it's pretty straight forward. No details are given other than the offense."

"I understand." A blessing in disguise of sorts, I guess.

I imagined standing before a judge and getting sworn in many times, but I was always there to testify against a perpetrator rather than being one. I don't miss the irony of being my father's son, having become a felon before being awarded that opportunity to represent the state in any capacity.

"O'Neil."

I refuse to turn my head toward the voice, just the familiar sound makes my throat seize.

"Mr. O'Neil, that man is wanting to speak with you," my attorney says. "We have just a few moments before the judge arrives though."

I turn my head, but I don't make to move closer. Just the sad look in Warren's eyes is enough to make me regret looking in that direction in the first place.

"I'm sorry," he whispers, his throat working.

I clear my throat once again. The damn thing is going to be raw before this is over with. Looking into the desolate eyes of a man I respected, a man I learned so much from is another load of bricks to carry on my back. He nods before walking away.

"Ready?" I nod at Mr. Crampton as the bailiff asks everyone to stand.

My name along with my case number is verified. Legal jargon is used, and I blame someone having a cold for the sniffle I hear at my back. It has to be someone with a cold, because Hound fucking promised me. I lose track of what the judge is saying as my ears perk up, waiting and hoping to hear a cough or a sneeze, but all that comes is another sniffle.

An elbow hits my arm.

"And how do you plea to the charge of voluntary manslaughter, Mr. O'Neil?" The judge glares at me, making me wonder if he had to ask it twice.

"G—" My voice cracks, and I have to cough. "Guilty, Judge."

"Are you aware, Mr. O'Neil, that entering a guilty plea will absolve the court of any further action on your case? You will not be allowed for an appeal?"

"Y-yes, Judge."

He looks down, signing God knows how many pieces of paper as the court reporter types away, as if doing this so long she already knows what he's going to say when he looks up at me.

He lists off the things he just signed, giving small details about each order before setting his pen down.

"Mr. Crampton, are you and your client prepared to move forward with the punishment phase?"

"The state and I haven't come to an agreement on that, your honor. I would like a rec—"

"That's fine, Mr. Crampton. The court isn't willing to accept a plea agreement as it is."

My pulse pounds. Mr. Crampton was sure this would be the way things would go if we proceeded today, but hearing it from the man with all the power has the ability to make my knees turn to jelly.

Another sniffle, this one getting dangerously close to a sob.

"Are you ready, Mr. O'Neil?"

"Yes."

"Drew, no." The two words are a whisper, a plea of their own.

Tears burn the backs of my eyes. "Yes, Judge."

"Having plead true to the offense of voluntary manslaughter, the court hereby sentences you to six years in the New Mexico State Penitentiary. Five thousand dollars in fines will be assessed."

Sobs at my back, so broken and filled with so much pain, I couldn't look at her if I wanted to.

The threatening tears make themselves known, rolling down my face in hot rivers.

The judge continues to speak, his words drowned out by Izzy's crying. I only catch a few things like, "time served," and "should be more."

I'd openly agree with him, but from the look on the man's face, he wouldn't be impressed with it.

The judge's gavel hitting the bench is the pin in the grenade.

"They're going to take you back and fingerprint you now. There's paperwork you have to sign."

Before I can step away from the table, a bailiff wraps my wrists in cuffs. I hated the feel of them the night of the crash, and I hate them even more so.

"Drew!"

Don't look. Don't look. Don't you fucking look. You had another night with her. Stop being a selfish bastard and walk out of here like you swore you would.

I'm five feet from the door, being escorted by two uniformed jailers when I hear her cry. This one is different, not filled with sorrow and regret but genuine pain. Keeping my face pointed to where I'm heading is impossible.

I expect to find her hazel eyes, red-rimmed with tears, not her bent over in pain, her tiny hands clasping at her belly.

Hound doesn't see me look either. He's too busy trying to figure out what's wrong with his daughter.

"Izzy!" I hiss, turning to go to her, but the men at my sides stop me. "Let me go!"

"Mr. O'Neil!"

"She needs me! Izzy! Is she okay? Let me go. I changed my mind! I want a trial! I want a trial!"

I'd do anything, say anything to go to her right now.

Wood hits wood, that same tool used to help seal my fate echoing around the room, then the judge's booming voice calls out, "Mr. O'Neil, one more word out of you and you'll also be held in contempt of court! You've been convicted of your offense, and your sentence starts now."

I don't say another word. Grunts and hisses are all I can manage as I try to fight my way to her. Jailers swarm me as if they were able to clone themselves with the snap of a finger, and I have to crane my neck to watch Hound and the other guys ushering Izzy out of the courtroom.

Chapter 23

Isabella

"You can," Sophia urges. "You can do this."

My head is shaking, the pain too much to allow for words.

"You can," Gigi insists. "A few more pushes, and you'll get to hold that sweet little boy of yours."

The doctor is between my thighs, also whispering encouragement, but I'm spent. I've been in labor, my water breaking on the way to the hospital, for the last nineteen hours. I'm in Albuquerque, not Farmington where my doctor is. I didn't meet the man at my feet until I arrived. This isn't how it's supposed to be. Babies are supposed to be born when both parents are present.

I know the waiting room is filled with everyone, all of them having driven down when they got word that I went into labor at the sight of Drew being dragged away in handcuffs.

"I need him here," I hiss, unable to catch my breath long enough to push yet another time.

"You can do this," Sophia repeats, avoiding my demand.

She can't reason with me and I know it.

"Look at me," Gigi snaps, her fingers on my chin making it impossible to look anywhere else but her face. "I thought your dad was dead when Amelia was born. This baby is coming whether you help or not. Prolonging it will only cause complications. I know you want Drew here, but that isn't possible. Don't punish your child by being stubborn."

"Gigi!" Sophia whisper-hisses, but my stepmom doesn't even look over at her.

"What's it going to be, Isabella?"

"Another contraction is coming," the nurse advises as I pull my jaw from Gigi's clutches.

The pain in my body is tolerable in thanks to the epidural, but my heart is shattered. I want a do-over. I want the things Drew wished were different that night we met. I shouldn't have walked away. I should've demanded his first name and told him my real one. So many things had to line up in the most tragic way for us to end up this way—for me to be here without him. This should be a celebration, a joyous occasion, but it's marked with regret and bad decisions.

"Push," the doctor orders, and somehow I manage to obey. The contraction ends, and I get a chance to breathe. "And again, Ms. Montoya. You're almost there."

I bear down, using the pain and anger and devastation in my favor. The rest is a blur, my mind filled with all the things that could've been, should've been, the disappointment for things that will never be.

I'm stunned, literally speechless when the nurse hands me my little boy. Tears streak my face, my breath hitching on each inhale more often than not. He's stunningly perfect, eyes squeezed tight, unimpressed with seeing light for the very first time.

"Should he be this quiet?" I ask, concerned because he hasn't cried since they calmed him down right after his birth.

"He's fine," Sophia assures me, her fingers pushing sweat-drenched locks of hair off my face.

I look to Gigi for reassurance. I love my best friend, but she's never experienced birth. Gigi has done it twice.

"He's perfect." Her eyes fall back to the little boy in my arms. "Are you ready for your dad to come in?"

"No," I answer after a long pause. "I just want some time alone."

Taking my meaning, Sophia presses her lips to the top of my head before leaving. Gigi follows her out. The nurses bustle around, cleaning things up and making sure I'm comfortable before giving me a little time alone with my son.

I'm grateful babies are born with no knowledge. Although I want to tell him all I know about his daddy, just thinking of Drew makes me cry, the tears once again going from happy to pained.

A soft knock sounds on the door, and I almost ignore it, but good manners win out. It isn't my dad who sticks his head in when I answer, but Lawson. Delilah isn't even with him, and I understand the significance of him being the first one in. He lost Drew to the prison system yesterday, too.

"I'll come back later if you don't want me here." He scrubs at the back of his neck. "Gigi said you didn't want visitors, but I just couldn't—"

"Stay," I whisper, not wanting to wake the sleeping angel in my arms.

Lawson comes closer to the bed, peering down at the baby but making no move to reach for him. He must sense my unwillingness to hand him over just yet.

"He has your nose," Lawson observes.

"Maybe." I just don't see any of myself in him. I don't see any of Drew either for that matter.

"He's beautifu—" Lawson's words are lost on a sob, and I know he already misses his brother, but he also wants this for himself, wants to stand beside his wife while she holds their own son for the first time.

I keep my eyes on my son, giving him a moment to compose himself.

"Sorry. Shit... I mean crap... I told myself I wouldn't act like this. You're going to be a wonderful mother."

He doesn't say goodbye before spinning to leave the room.

The visitors pile in after that, one after the other all telling me how gorgeous he is, how happy they are he's here. They offer to make meals and babysit, and come over and keep an eye on him so I can rest. I have dozens of people here wanting to help, and yet I've never felt more isolated in my life. Even being under the overprotective thumb of my mom and stepdad growing up didn't make me feel so abandoned.

"We can put him in the crib so you can rest," one nurse says after most of the people filter out with promises to return tomorrow.

I nearly opened my mouth to ask them to stay away. Giving birth is exhausting, and I just want to be alone, but I couldn't tell those smiling faces to get lost. I suffered for weeks while Drew ignored me, so I can't imagine having people around who care could hurt any more than it already does.

"I just want to hold him a little longer."

The nurse nods, but I can see the sympathy in her eyes. It makes me wonder how much everyone is gossiping about me in the waiting room. I didn't exactly let Drew hold onto his pride after being convicted. I think I could've been charged with contempt of court, exactly what the judge threatened him with, if I weren't in labor at the time.

Did he realize his mistake? Regret his decision to plead and not take any offerings of a reduced sentence? How could he want to stay away from us for so long?

He didn't want me there. Dad told me as much, but I couldn't stay away. I wanted to be there to support him, let him know that we'll be here when he's released. I couldn't even let him walk away with dignity. I ruined that moment for him, made it more horrible than it had to be.

"Knock, knock."

I sigh, looking over at the door.

"Most let their knuckles make that sound on the door then wait for someone to tell them it's okay to enter."

My best friend scrunches her brows together. "Those people are losers."

"Or courteous," I counter. "What are you doing here?"

"Why wouldn't I be here? I told you I was coming back."

"It's late. You should be home with Colton."

"He was called into work."

That saddens me. Colton is a homicide detective with the Farmington PD. If he's at work, that means someone died.

"That's sad," I mutter.

"That's life," she says. "Or rather death. Circle of life and all that."

She stands beside the bed, arms out expectantly.

"May I help you?"

"You can hand him over or I can take him. I haven't gotten to hold him yet."

"No one has."

"Hand him over. You need rest."

"You sound like the nurse," I mutter.

"She sounds like a smart woman."

Reluctantly, I allow Sophia to take him from my arms, knowing it would be impossible to hand him over.

"Shh," she coos when he whimpers. "You're fine, sweet boy. Have you decided on a name?"

"Not yet," I lie.

I know what it needs to be, but I'm so raw from everything to share it with anyone else right now.

"You're not alone," she says as she takes a seat on the rollaway bed meant for my spouse or significant other.

"Yes, I am," I say, knowing I can be vulnerable with her and she won't judge me.

"I know you're going to miss him. I know you love him. I know it's going to be hard some days for you to get out of bed and move forward, but you'll do it. You're strong and amazing, but on those days you feel like you can't shoulder any more weight, you have so many people here for you."

"I know." Tears drip down my cheeks, and it's happened so many times the last couple of days, I've stopped worrying with wiping them away.

I have everyone but the one person I need the most.

Chapter 24

Drew

"You're in that busy head of yours again, kid. I warned you about that." Scorpion grunts as he pushes his body up and down in the small space remaining in our cell.

"Yeah," I agree, simply because I can't help it.

My mind is never far from Farmington these days.

I've been here a week, the intake and assignment to this block all a blur. I focused more on those around me than what was actually taking place. I was near pissing myself when I was escorted to the cell with this huge motherfucker in it.

He didn't say a word when the guard dropped me off, and I knew just by the hard look on his face that I wouldn't survive the night.

The door clanked closed beside me, but when I dropped the low-budget supplies I was provided, ready to give as good as I got, he chuckled.

The brute introduced himself to me as Scorpion, disappointed a little when his name didn't mean anything to me.

Before I went to sleep that night, I got the entire story, or what he was willing to share at least. He's in prison with three consecutive life sentences for a triple homicide. As a former cop, I had sized him up pretty quickly and presumed he was in here for a violent offense. His body, hands and arms especially, carried the scars of a man rarely willing to back down from an altercation.

What did shock me was his reasoning for those murders. As the former president of the Renegades MC, Brooks "Scorpion" Hannigan killed three of his own members the night he found out one had been raping his sister. The two others were running a child porn website and were literally making child pornography right under his nose.

That's not even the crazy part. Not only is he Makayla, Dominic's wife's brother, but he's also Jasmine's—the one involved with Max and Tug—biological father.

Scorpion is the protection, one of the *provisions,* Hound told me about two days before I was sentenced. I don't exactly feel safe, and it's only been a week, but there hasn't been a whisper of my offense.

Other than Scorpion, most of the guys on this cell block have ten years or less to serve. Knowing there's light at the end of the tunnel for them means most keep to themselves.

"And what's that?"

I don't bother trying to hide the letter in my hand. The man has four inches and about sixty pounds of muscle on me, which is saying a lot because I'm not exactly a small guy. He could take this from me, and I wouldn't even mutter a word about it.

"A letter from Lawson."

"That's your brother, right?" I nod.

The thing about Scorpion sharing a lot of his story was my story was expected in return. I confessed to beating a man to death, but I left out the fact that I was a first responder to the scene of that accident, letting him believe I was just a random guy who happened upon it. Strangely enough, I did confess that I thought Megan was Izzy, and laid out most of the details and my connection of her and I to Cerberus.

"Any news?" he asks as he climbs back to his feet, his muscles pumped and slick with sweat from his workout.

"Izzy had the baby. They're both doing fine."

"That's good news. I know you were worried about that."

Scorpion stands to the side, not in the least bit shy about whipping out his dick to piss in the shared toilet in our cell.

"And what else did we talk about?"

"Don't say anything about where you keep your stash?"

He chuckles, his head shaking, but I know he doesn't find it very funny that I'm avoiding his real question. He didn't make many rules when I entered into this world, but no bullshitting was one of them. I'd have his protection. He'd guarantee my safety, but if there was a problem he had to know about it. If people were whispering, he had to know about it.

There's nothing in this cell that could get either of us in trouble, but Scorpion has been here for over twenty years. His connections alone in the prison system is how he landed as the only lifer on this block. He literally has nothing to lose. He's also the king of the mountain so to speak, and that power isn't awarded to him just because he's massive and wakes up ready to die every day.

According to him, he runs the biggest contraband business the New Mexico Prison System has ever seen. If it's something available on the outside, he can get it on the inside.

Hell, the man still has women brought to him on occasion and the state conjugal visit program ended over six years ago, plus, he's never been married. His power extends well outside controlling inmates and probably goes as high if not higher than the warden himself.

I struggled with knowing this information when I first arrived, but I'm not a cop on the inside. I'm a felon. Turning a blind eye to guys getting porno mags and cigarettes isn't the same thing as allowing horrific things to happen without me telling someone. Hell, to ensure my own safety, I'm at the point I'm willing to turn a blind eye to just about anything these days.

Scorpion doesn't abide by rape, so the only action the guys are getting on the block are from those willing to whore themselves out in exchange for contraband. Surprisingly, it happens more than I thought.

He runs a tight ship around here, and although prison sucks, it could be worse.

"Seriously, O'Neil. What did we talk about?"

"I remember what we talked about."

"The only way to get through these long-ass days is to cut all ties with those on the outside."

"I know." I want to do that. I want to rip this letter to shreds and never open another one. I've already refused to have a visitor list, something Lawson ripped my ass for in the very letter in my hand.

"Seeing you inside, caged like an animal is selfish. They need to let you do your time in peace."

"Yeah."

"I've been here twenty years, and it feels like I just got here last week."

I huff a humorless laugh. "You're full of shit."

He chuckles again, a throaty sound I've grown used to over the last couple of days. The man isn't afraid to laugh and have a good time, something I haven't managed since I arrived.

"Okay. Maybe like a month then. But seriously, man. You can't survive in here if your head is still on the outside." He kicks at my shoe when I don't look up at him. "Five years, seven months and three weeks right?"

"Right."

"Then worry about those people when you only have months left on your sentence. Did you hear from the foreman?"

"Start work tomorrow."

"Where."

"In the shop."

"You know I got—"

"I won't." I look up at him now. It isn't the first time the man has offered me a job working for him. "Thank you, though."

"Let me know if you change your mind."

I give him a weak smile. He already knows it's never going to change.

"Don't wait up," he says, looking in the metal mirror hanging on the wall.

"What?" I look around. "It's nearly lights out. Where are you going?"

"Gotta date." He winks at me, the door to our cell popping open when he steps close to it as if he owns the device to make it work. He turns back in my direction, his eyes serious. "Cut them off, Drew."

I nod, agreeing with him, knowing I'll follow through, knowing I'll push every person in my life away to make my time in here easier. I'll get the supplies and put pen to paper. I'll rip my own heart out to keep from breaking theirs any further, but it won't get my brother out of my head.

It won't keep Izzy from infiltrating my dreams and making me promises. It won't keep fantasies of a little boy I'm only able to conjure in my imagination from smiling up at me or running to me, trusting me to catch him in my arms.

Cutting them out of my life won't keep the tears off my face every night. It won't keep me from reliving the night I ruined my life over and over because somehow that night is now easier to stomach than memories of the last time I saw Izzy curled over in pain. I definitely can't think about the last night we shared together, how I had to keep shushing her because if she talked then I was going to confess my love for her, and that would only make it harder.

The first letter, the one to Lawson, is easier to write than it should've been, but I blame machismo and hope that he understands my reasoning for sending it. He's a man and as such, he should be able to take a step back and realize he might do the exact same thing if he were faced with the decision to make. Men think more with their heads and less with emotion.

So the next two letters were easy to write as well.

The last letter, the one I dread, stays a blank page for days before I can bring myself to put more on the paper than *Dear Isabella*.

It sits and taunts me when I get back from the machine shop every day. One day, I hid it under my pillow, unable to even stomach the sight of the two words on the top. Scorpion, being the helpful asshole he is, pulled it out and put it right back on top of the tiny desk we share.

My heart is in my throat the day I finally man up enough to write the words that have been playing over and over in my head. On paper, the requests are very formal, my emotions controlled enough to get my point across and not much else.

Inside my head, hell, inside this prison cell, I've never been lower in my life.

Scorpion stands outside the cell, his wide back hiding me from view as other inmates walk by, curious to know why I'm so upset. My sobs should say enough. The way I rage inside that tiny room and tear everything to shreds says what I can't with words. Broken knuckles keep me from the machine shop for several weeks, but Scorpion demands I work in the laundry during the interim. Since the machine folds the clean sheets, I can't really argue.

I don't know how he did it, or what concessions he had to make, but I never got in trouble, never got written up for destroying state property that day in our cell, even though the mattresses had to be replaced.

I was working, every day, waiting for the promise of them fading from one into the next, waiting to look up at the calendar to notice a year had gone by when it only felt like a week. At this point, I'd be happy for a single day and night to feel like less than a century a piece.

Chapter 25

Isabella

I never knew obsession until I held my son in my arms for the first time.

I'm obsessed with his soft, pouty lips.

Obsessed with the tiny whimpers he makes right before he fully wakes up.

Obsessed with the tufts of fine hair on his little head.

I'm even obsessed with his tiny little fingers and toes.

I'm obsessive over spending every minute with him as if he's going to be snatched from my arms at any second.

Obsessive over who gets to hold him and spend time with him.

I'm just infatuated with this little being.

He's asleep now, cradled in my arms because the thought of putting him down is foreign to me.

I can't take my eyes off of him, can't keep my fingers from brushing down his perfect cheek.

Time no longer exists for me. The days fade into nights which eventually give way to another dawn, but realistically, I know it's been three weeks since he was born, three weeks since Drew was dragged away in handcuffs, unable to convince the judge he changed his mind. Three weeks of being a single parent, of pain and heartache, loneliness and wishing things were different.

How did I let myself fall in love with him?

It wasn't supposed to be like this.

From the second I found out I was pregnant, I knew I was going to face parenthood without the help of the father, but he was supposed to stay gone. He wasn't supposed to show up one night as Lawson's brother. He wasn't supposed to open up to me, share things I doubt he's ever told another soul. He sure as hell wasn't supposed to make love to me and then leave.

And it was love. No one can convince me otherwise.

The way he held me close, the way he looked at me when he was inside of me, the way he touched my cheek and made promises with his movements instead of words was a passion I know I'll never feel again with someone else.

I don't want anyone else. I don't think I ever will. If waiting six years for him to come back home is what I need to do, then I'll happily take that on.

The baby takes a shuddering breath before settling again, and I smile down at him. He's going to be in kindergarten by the time his daddy is going to be able to dress him for school or attend a function with his class. He's going to be a walking, talking little miniature version of Drew, having the same eye color and hair just a few shades lighter than mine. We'll miss Drew, but we'll survive. There's always the opportunity for visits and letters.

The time should fly.

I'm not in a position to believe that right now because the last three weeks have dragged on and on, but eventually things will get better. I'll busy my days with taking care of him and working on my graduate classes. I can make it work.

I stare across the room, looking at nothing in particular as I picture what our reunion will be like. He'll take me in his arms and kiss me like he's never going to get to again. I'll be in his arms, nose buried in his neck. Of course there will be tears, probably millions of them, but nothing will be able to keep us apart.

A soft knock on my door draws my eyes.

"Yes?"

Rather than Gigi or my dad, Delilah walks into the room, a faint smile on her lips when she sees the baby. I'm not unhappy to see her, but it still feels like an intrusion, something I've felt each and every time someone comes in here recently.

Then I see her face. It's dry and free of tears, but it's apparent that she's been crying. Her cheeks are flushed, eyes puffy and rimmed in red.

"What's wrong?"

Suddenly I'm on high alert. The guys are at the clubhouse right now, gearing up for a job so I know it's not bad news from the field.

"Delilah, what's wrong?" I snap when she takes a couple of steps closer but doesn't speak.

Horrific thoughts hit me all at once. Drew was terrified he'd be hurt in prison. Inmates don't like cops, and since they can't retaliate against the men and women in uniform who hurt them, they take that anger out on everyone. Cops in prison become surrogates for everything someone in uniform ever did to them or a loved one, some of that anger warranted by the bad apples in the group, but more often criminals hate cops for simply catching them. Their crimes weren't the issue, the arrest and subsequent incarceration is the problem.

"Is it Drew? Is he hurt?" I barely get the words out, sobs clogging my throat.

My hysteria wakes the baby who begins to whine. He's not very appreciative of the tremble in my arms as I hold him closer.

"It's not *that*."

I look up at her, trying to determine if she's sugarcoating the truth, and I find her with her arm out, a letter in her hand.

Fear wraps its cold tentacles around me as I stare at the innocuous envelope, knowing full well it's the equivalent of a bomb, holding something that's going to blow my life and hope to pieces.

I can't take it from her. I can't muster the strength to release my hold on my son long enough to pull the thing from her fingers.

Delilah, knowing that I'm unable, places the letter beside me on the bed before leaning in close enough to kiss the top of the baby's head. She gives my shoulder a squeeze before taking a step back.

"I didn't read it, but I want you to prepare yourself. Lawson got a letter as well, and I don't think yours is going to be much different."

She keeps talking, but her words are drowned out by the pounding of my pulse. It sounds like a marching band in my head, and the noise is loud enough to force my eyes closed. When I open them again, she's gone, my bedroom door once again closed, sealing me off from everyone else.

It's bad news. It has to be. Maybe he isn't hurt. Maybe he isn't in trouble, but the news is bad. If Lawson got a letter and it had the power to make Delilah cry, then opening mine is the last thing I want to do.

I stare down at the thing for hours. The baby wakes, ready to be changed and eat, but I continue to stare down at the letter.

My son has been my only focus since he was born, that attention being an attempt to keep from thinking of Drew. With my eyes on the crinkled envelope still in the same spot Delilah left it on my bed, I don't know how I manage to change the baby's diaper and get him situated at my breast without taking my eyes off of it.

Mid-morning fades into early afternoon, and I find myself still in bed, still waiting for the thing to disappear. It doesn't and I know it won't. It's just sitting there, and I know what's inside of it is going to be painful. The longer it sits, the worse I feel, as if the information inside will change me so fundamentally that it has been seeping toxic fumes into the room.

My legs are weak from sitting cross-legged all day, and I nearly stumble when I climb out of bed to place the baby in the crib on the other side of the room. I'm livid at the power taken from me, that letter nearly making me fall and hurt my son.

Maybe it's acceptance. Maybe it's the protective nature that has been growing every minute since I found out I was pregnant, but I'm livid by the time I cross the room and scoop the letter up from the bed. Only my name is on the front as if it was sent in a single package including Lawson's letter. There's no return address or inmate number, nothing to indicate on the outside who the letter is from.

For a single second, the length of time it takes my eyelashes to flutter, I imagine it being something else, something less poisonous, a letter from my college kicking me out, a ticket from a traffic light camera although I haven't gone anywhere in weeks. Anything but what it actually is.

It's a fool's wish, just the breath someone takes on the prayer that their worst nightmare isn't looking them in the face before getting the horrible news.

Ignoring the paper cut I get from sliding my finger under the flat, I yank the letter from the envelope, letting it fall to the floor at my feet.

Isabella,

I'm sorry.
The first night I met you, I saw a gorgeous girl sitting alone in a diner.

Your lips, the way you indulged in your meal without a single concern for those around you turned me on.

That's what it was. Arousal.

I wanted you, so I made sure to have you before you left.

It was a mistake.

Had I known it was going to end with you getting pregnant, I never would've done it.

I don't want a kid. Even if I did, no child deserves to have the black cloud of a felony convicted father around him.

I don't want a woman in my life because we share a connection I never wanted.

I don't want contact with you.

No letters.

No visits.

No updates.

Nothing.

I don't want you waiting for me nor sitting awake at night wondering if I'm safe or when I'll come home.

Farmington isn't home. It never was, and it won't be where I return when I get out.

You'll never see me again.

I'll never be a father to your baby. You need to find a man that wants to be a dad. It'll never be me.

I shouldn't have led you on, shouldn't have made you care for me.

Because I never cared for you.

You're better off never thinking of me again.

I'm sorry I ever met you. If I had just walked away that night, none of this would've happened.

If I had just walked away that night, I wouldn't have killed that man. I wouldn't have mistaken that girl for you.

My life is ruined.

Just forget about me.

I plan to forget about you.

Drew O'Neil

Blinking doesn't make the words disappear. Flipping the single page doesn't change a thing. Even if the thing went up in flames, the hateful things written there would still be seared into my brain.

Had I known he was going to eventually blame me? It's always been in the back of my head. Even when he touched me, when his lips brushed mine, when he held me in his arms, I knew it would come to this.

The letter flutters to the ground when the baby begins to whimper, and I do the only thing I can. I pull him from his crib, hold him to my chest, and begin the task of getting on with my life. Drew O'Neil doesn't want us? Then that's fine. This little boy will have more love than he can handle, even if his daddy is a lying coward.

Chapter 26

Drew

I fucking told her not to do this.

I was explicit about my demands.

I hold the birth announcement to my chest, somehow hating the damn thing and considering it my most treasured possession.

His date of birth, technically the day after my sentencing, which I consider a small blessing.

He was born weighing seven pounds thirteen ounces and was twenty inches long.

But those facts aren't what makes my eyes burn.

The name at the top—Andrew Keen O'Neil Jr.

She named him after me.

A little boy exists in this world with my DNA and my name, and I told his mother I didn't want him, didn't want her.

I deserve every second of the pain I feel.

Chapter 27

Drew

Drew,

Please find enclosed a picture of Andy.
He has your eyes, and despite only having those two tiny teeth, he also has your smile.
He's taken to eating baby cereal like a champ, although he hates vegetables and seems able to sniff them out when someone is trying to be sneaky and add them to the things he likes.
His favorite toy is a stuffed elephant, and for some reason he enjoys Sam Smith's music over all others.

She doesn't even put her name at the end of the letter.
Andy.
What a ridiculous thing to call a kid. I was adamant growing up that no one called me that, but as I look down at his smiling face, those two little teeth mentioned flashing in his grin, I think it suits him.

Chapter 28

Drew

Drew,

Andy took his first steps yesterday. You can't tell from the picture, but he was moving so fast, he barely stopped in time before running into the wall.
He's trying to keep up with Little Jameson and Little Cooper, so he's doing things a little early for his age.
He's an amazing sleeper, although fall daylight saving time was tougher on him than expected.
He's infatuated with Sophia, smiling anytime she's near.
He loves his granddad's motorcycle and whines to sit on it each time he sees it.
There's a certainty he's going to have tiny little biker boots and a leather jacket under the Christmas tree this year.
He was Chase from Paw Patrol for Halloween.

Once again no name at the bottom. This woman is doing everything I asked her not to do, and somehow it's making things easier, not harder like Scorpion insisted.

I tuck the two pictures—one of him walking across the room and the other of him in his little police dog uniform—away for safe keeping.

It's not lost on me that I'm an incarcerated former cop, and my son dressed up as a police officer for his very first Halloween. Hopefully, he has a shot at being a better man than I am.

Unlike last time, I can't hold back the tears until I'm alone in my cell. Scorpion shakes his head before walking out and leaving me to wallow.

Chapter 29

Drew

Drew,

Andy turned one last week!
Of course the party was Paw Patrol themed.
The little guy is obsessed with all the characters, but Chase is still his favorite.
Other than wearing the frosting, he wasn't interested in the cake.
It was probably too sweet for him.
His hatred for vegetables has turned into loving them.
He has eight teeth and uses them on everything.
He's like a puppy gnawing on anything he can get his hands on.
He's in a nursery setting twice a week for socialization.
He's protective over a little girl there named Avery, won't even let Cooper and Jameson near her.
You can't tell from the picture because he's sitting, but he's very tall for his age. In the seventieth percentile according to his pediatrician.
Not only does he have little boots and a leather jacket under the Christmas tree, but I'm sure Kincaid got him a little helmet to complete the ensemble.
He's spoiled and loved.
One happy little guy.

The picture shakes in my trembling hand. I've come to expect nothing personal about Izzy. She never mentions herself or how she's doing. She's sticking to that demand of my letter, but the updates keep coming on Andy.

The picture isn't a full one, the edge of the right side cut oddly, and I know she was in this picture. Izzy was there, and she cut herself away. She's not a vindictive person, doesn't have a hateful bone in her body, so knowing she did this to keep up what I told her breaks my fucking heart.

But I'm too far in. A year into my sentence with many more to go. Seeing her would make things difficult. Seeing my son hurts and somehow heals all at the same time.

Chapter 30

Drew

Drew,

Please don't worry.
We discovered today that Andy is allergic to peanuts.

Don't worry. He's fine.
His symptoms were swollen eyes and redness as you can see.
He had no respiratory distress.

The picture of my son in the tiniest hospital gown I've ever seen with a plastic medical band around his little wrist is concerning, but it's the tears staining the pages that I know came from his mother that has the ability to break me.

I know the pain that dripped on the paper had nothing to do with the fact that she'll probably never eat her favorite candy again. She was scared, and I know just looking at this picture of Andy in that hospital room made all of those fears come back.

I'm missing all of it, and I love the pictures and updates, but I should be there for both of them. I should've been able to hold her in my arms when she cried for him. I should've been there for all of it.

Chapter 31

Isabella

"That's the wrong foot."

"Mine!"

"Yes, it's your foot."

"Boot!"

"Those are your boots, but they won't be comfortable if you put them on the wrong feet. Let Mommy help you."

"No! Mine!"

"I'm not trying to take them away, Son. I'm just trying to help."

"He's stubborn," Dad says with a light chuckle as he slides past to go into the kitchen.

"He gets that from his daddy." I frown, keeping my eyes on Andy rather than looking up at Lawson. "Drew was always fiercely independent."

"The book I'm reading says to allow them to do things wrong. A little discomfort won't hurt them, and if it bothers them enough, they'll correct the issue themselves," Delilah adds helpfully.

I open my mouth, irritated with everyone offering advice on what to do with my own child, but when I look up, I see a soft, sad smile on her face. She's read hundreds of books about raising kids since she was informed of her infertility problems seven months ago. I know Lawson is concerned for the obsession, but he's hesitant to say anything to her. She's in a very raw place right now and snapping at her when she's only trying to help wouldn't be very kind.

"Momma!" I turn back to Andy and apparently giving him a few extra minutes was exactly what he needed. His boots are on the correct feet and he has a wide-toothed grin on his handsome little face.

"Good job, buddy. Are you ready to go across the street for the Easter egg hunt?"

On long legs, he darts to the door, pulling it open while I grab his basket.

He knows not to open the front door, but that doesn't mean he listens. Like Lawson observed, the boy is insistent on doing things he's told not to. Sixteen months and going on grown, he keeps me on my toes.

"Hi," he whispers, his little nose in the crack allowed by the locking mechanism Dad had to install after he snuck outside two weeks ago.

"Who?" Jameson says, running up and shoving Andy out of the way. "Hi."

"Is it Sophia?" I ask, smiling when Andy squeals.

My son loves his Aunt Sophia, and he's been impatient for the last two hours since she spoke to him on the phone this morning. I don't know if it's the thrill of seeing her or all the candy she promised that's got him so excited. A combination of both, I imagine.

Making sure Jameson's face is no longer in the way, I close the door long enough to unlatch it, but it isn't my best friends smiling face on the other side when I reopen it.

Andy's Easter basket falls to the floor, bright green, fake grass spilling all around my feet.

"Momma, uh oh! Help."

Unaware that I'm losing my mind, Andy moves around my feet, helping pick up the mess and shoving it back into his little Paw Patrol basket.

With a stern face and blue eyes I've tried desperately to forget, Drew stands on my father's porch, arms full of wrapped gifts.

"What's going on?" Lawson asks as he steps into the entry way. "Who is—No way!"

His brother's excitement gives me the chance I need to take a few steps back. I look away, unable to see Lawson wrap his brother in a hug.

"What's going on, baby girl?" Dad asks. "You look like you've seen a ghost."

"Not a ghost," Sophia says as she steps around the hugging brothers. "Just an asshole."

"Sophia!" Delilah snaps.

Sophia shrugs as she steps up in front of me. She knows all about the letter. She knows the man standing out there broke my heart. She knows he wanted nothing to do with his son.

She doesn't know about the pictures and the updates I've been sending every couple of months. She doesn't know that my heart is still a shattered mess, even though I imagine she has figured it out each and every time I refuse to date or look for someone new.

"Well, this is a surprise," Apollo says as he joins the guys on the porch.

"Aww, hell," Sophia mutters. She breaks my line of sight with Drew, bending a little to get on my level. "What do you want me to do? I can tell him to kick bricks? I'll even kick him in the nuts if it's what you need. Just say the word."

I shake my head, not tossing the ideas out entirely, but because I don't know what I need right now. A warning would've been nice, but from the way Lawson is acting, he had no clue his brother was going to show up today.

"I need a minute," I tell her, my eyes going to Andy who seems quite content to drape the fake grass over his head.

If I was cognizant enough, I would pull out my phone and take a picture. He's absolutely adorable, but I can barely get my body to inhale right now.

"Are you okay? Why didn't you tell me he was coming?" Apollo lifts my chin, urging me to look him in the eyes.

"I d-didn't know."

"Can you—" Apollo points down at Andy.

"I've got him," Sophia assures him, and then he guides me from the room.

Knowing the kitchen wouldn't be far enough away, Apollo leads me up the stairs, but even as he closes us into my bedroom, I still can't take a full breath.

"What's he doing here? It's only been a year and a half." He wipes tears I didn't know I had from my face.

"Sixteen months," I correct. "And nine days."

"You've been counting?" He looks disappointed.

"I know how old my son is."

He frowns at the harsh way the words leave my mouth, but I have more important things to worry about than his feelings.

He said he wasn't coming back here. He said he wanted nothing to do with us. So why is he standing on the front porch with presents wrapped in Paw Patrol paper?

"Why would he just show up?"

"I don't know."

"What does he expect? You to just forget the way he treated you?"

He knows about the letter as well. Sophia, as always, had a hard time keeping her thoughts to herself. I only told her, but everyone, and I mean everyone—including my dad—knows what he did, what he wrote in that letter. As determined as I was to do right by my son, it took months for me to finally heal enough to do more than just take care of Andy. I failed my classes for that semester because despite the progress I made in class, I didn't have the energy to take the final exams. I got an ulcer which took months of meds to heal, and only the threat of surgery from my doctor made me care enough to get better. I didn't want to spend weeks in recovery. I didn't want it to be painful to lift my baby.

Drew did more than broke my heart. He drove me to the point of insanity, and although I'm now weaning myself off the postpartum depression medicine, I'll never be able to forgive him. He compromised my ability to take care of Andy, and that's unforgivable.

"I'll go down and tell him he isn't welcome here."

"He's Andy's father."

"He doesn't deserve him. He needs to leave."

"Apollo." Sitting on my bed, I drop my head into my hands. "I can't make rash decisions where my kid is concerned, and he can't be forced out. His brother lives right next door."

I resist the urge to look at my bedroom window—the one directly across from his old one—wondering if he's going to be staying in that same room again. Not knowing has the potential to drive me as mad as the information being confirmed.

"The donation of his DNA doesn't give him the right to show up unannounced with an armful of gifts. Bribing a toddler is disgusting. He hurt you both."

"He's done nothing to hurt Andy, and my heart isn't your concern."

"Wow." He takes a step back, his hands dragging over the top of his head as he glares at me. "You still have feelings for him. He destroyed you, made it impossible for you to get out of bed, Iz. You had to take antidepressants because of him. He's horrible, and you're defending him?"

"Many women have to take antidepressants after childbirth," I remind him. Hell, he's the one who advocated for those damn pills when they came up in a conversation he was butting his nose into. "And he's not a horrible man. My expectations were set too high. That's my issue to deal with and none of your concern."

"So you're just going to let him show up and be daddy?"

"I'm not letting him do anything."

"So you're going to ask him to leave?"

"I'm not doing that either. Drew and I will have to have a conversation, but it's Easter. Andy is excited to hunt eggs, and I'm not dealing with any of it right now."

He looks a little more at ease, but his hands are still clenched, like he doesn't know what to do with the adrenaline filling his blood.

"Let's go then."

I stand, allowing him to wrap me in a hug when I get close enough. His woodsy scent is familiar and calming, and I focus on that instead of the millions of other things trying to gain space in my head. I won't think about Drew's handsome face or the way relief hit me when I first saw him. I'll never let the fantasy that he's come back to sweep me off my feet, to be a daddy, for us to be a family get another second in my mind.

"Maybe he escaped and the police will be here shortly to arrest him?"

I chuckle into Apollo's chest. "That's ridiculous."

"I didn't see any prison tattoos, but that doesn't mean he didn't join a gang."

I almost tell him that Drew would never do that, but the man I thought I knew never existed.

I don't want a woman in my life because we share a connection I never wanted.

Those words, and many more, were in the letter he sent. I've memorized the thing, read it so many times the paper is frail and thin. Each time my mind tries to imagine things differently, I pull that letter out. I read it over and over again until the anger is dripping from my pores, and then I use the fuel to be the best mother I can be.

Chapter 32

Drew

Wanting to cave Apollo's head in when I watch him come down the stairs with his arm around Izzy's waist makes no sense.

I may love her, but I also hurt her. I told her to move on and wasn't even nice about it. It seems she took my advice, and I came here today expecting I'd find exactly what I'm seeing from the doorway. Her going to Apollo, a man that has never been shy about his feelings for her, kept me awake at night, but if she's happy then I'm hap—actually, no. I can't even lie to myself about it. I'm not happy. I'll never be happy without her.

She doesn't make eye contact as she hits the landing at the bottom of the stairs, but a sweet smile forms on her pretty face when she looks down at Andy.

It's been almost impossible not to run to him, scoop him up and hold him to my chest. He doesn't know me. Izzy may not have even told him about me. I was a fool for coming here today unannounced.

"Dada!" Andy yells as he abandons the Easter basket he's been playing with to run to Apollo.

"Hey, buddy." The man scoops up my child with one arm, a move so practiced he doesn't even pull away the one wrapped around Izzy. "Ready to hunt for Easter eggs?"

"Drew."

I don't know what my face looks like, but I'm certain I'm not smiling at the happy little family because Lawson grabs the sleeve of my shirt and pulls me to the side.

She doesn't even look over at me as she leaves, but I can't keep my eyes off of her. I watch her walk away, leaning into his touch until they disappear into the clubhouse across the street.

Gigi walks out next, precious Amelia walking beside her while she's trying to manage a wiggling Jameson in her arms. Hound is taking up the rear.

"Good to see you, Drew." He claps me on the shoulder before turning around to lock his front door.

"Do you want me to put these inside?" I point down at the pile of gifts, some looking a little worn and ragged from having to carrying them on a bus and then a taxi to get here.

"No."

And there goes any hope that he didn't know about the letter I sent Izzy. God, if I could turn back time, I'd do my entire sentence all over again just to rip that thing to shreds instead of dropping it in the mail.

"He's my son," I say weakly, knowing I don't have much of a leg to stand on.

Hound turns back toward me. "And gifts are best given in person, not just dropped off. Will you be joining us across the street?"

I look to Lawson, and as a man who has never really been good at hiding what he's thinking, I turn back to Hound.

"I don't think that's a good idea."

"Okay," Hound says, accepting my refusal. "We'll bring you a plate back."

Lawson doesn't say a word as we stand on the front porch and watch them leave. Amelia is wearing a sweet little dress with decorative flowers at one hip. Gigi is in a nice dress, and it's shocking since I remember her having a preference for leggings. Although, she was pregnant most of the time I was here before my incarceration.

"Wait. Why is he wearing slacks and a tie? Is Easter that big of a deal? I don't remember Cerberus being overly religious."

"Oh, umm." Lawson grips the back of his neck. "Kincaid insisted everyone dress up. They've hired a photographer to take family pictures."

I nod, trying for calm and cool when the news hits me square in the chest. It's another thing I'll miss, another consequence of my actions from nearly two years ago.

"Pictures are good to have," I manage. I have at least a dozen that are absolutely precious to me, so I fully understand. "Where did Delilah go?"

Lawson's wife was here when I arrived, but disappeared shortly after giving me a hug.

"She went across the street to help hide eggs. Come on."

He steps off the porch, making his way toward his house. I grab the presents and follow after him.

"How much of a pain in the ass would it be to catch a ride back into town?"

"Town?" he asks as he makes his way up the steps to his own house.

"Yeah. I got a hotel room."

"You have a perfectly good room here." I swallow painfully.

If the room is still available that means he isn't a father. Delilah didn't get pregnant while I was locked up.

"I think the hotel would be better."

"Before we start arguing about that can you tell me what you're doing here?" He raises a hand to hush me. "And before you get your feelings hurt, I'm not upset. I'm over the fucking moon, but you had a six-year sentence. You're not wearing an orange jumpsuit so I'm guessing you didn't escape."

"I'm not a violent man. My uniform was blue."

"My mistake," he says as he steps inside his house, turning to me to take some of Andy's gifts from my hands. "So, you didn't escape?"

I can't help the laugh that bubbles from my throat. "I didn't escape. I worked my ass off, stayed out of trouble, and I wouldn't put it past Scorpion to have pulled a few strings."

"Still sixteen months isn't six years."

"My meritorious good time combined with my industrial good time earned an early release."

I still feel a little guilty that I was ecstatic when the warden gave me the news. I kept my nose clean, something I was planning to do from day one anyway, and I was able to serve less than a third of my sentence. I didn't argue with them when I got my release date. I also didn't tell anyone I was getting out, hence, the surprise when I showed up unannounced.

I didn't tell anyone because I was terrified I'd get a letter back saying I wasn't welcome. If anyone here was going to tell me to kick bricks and never show my face again, I wanted them to say it to my face.

"Well, I'm glad you're home."

Home.

I can't tell him it doesn't feel like home, but I'd rather be no other place. I don't tell him that I swore to Izzy I wouldn't come back here. I'm not the same man I was when I wrote that letter, but I doubt she'll be open to hearing that from me. I knew what I was doing when I wrote those awful words—those lies.

"I can't just take over part of your house again, but I was hoping you needed some help around the shop, at least while I'm looking for another job."

"I always need help around the shop," he offers. "Did you give your parole officer the hotel address?"

"No parole. I was released free and clear."

He breathes a sigh of relief. "A free man."

One still weighed down by the choices I've made, but yet technically free.

"Yes."

"We want you here."

"Delilah isn't here, and I don't know that she'd appreciate you speaking for her."

"We always planned for you to come back here, Drew."

"Even after writing you and telling you to forget I ever existed?"

I said as many mean things to Lawson as I did to Izzy.

"I knew you were in a bad place both physically and mentally when I received that letter. I took it all with a grain of salt."

"I shouldn't have... I never should've sent those letters."

"Which ones are you referring to? The one to me? Izzy? Hound? Or Apollo?"

I scrub my face with both hands. "All of them."

"I know what was in mine, and I can guess what was in Izzy's because she was a shell of herself for months, but I have no clue what you wrote to Hound. And why would you send Apollo a letter?"

Maybe sending them all in the same package to my brother wasn't the best thing to do. Answering questions about them now isn't going to be fun.

"I broke Izzy's heart, that's if she felt for me what I thought she did."

"You broke her heart," he assures me.

"Apollo's letter was telling him I was stepping aside, and he'd never find another woman as amazing as Izzy. He's a good man, and that's what she needs."

"He is a good man."

He gives me nothing more. He doesn't confirm what I suspected at the sight of them together, at my son calling that man Dada.

"And they're together?"

"They're together all the time."

"Fuck," I hiss. "Can you stop being coy? Are they together *together*?"

He shrugs, the partial lift of his shoulders maddening enough to make me want to spit fire.

"I guess you'll have to ask her that yourself."

Chapter 33

Isabella

"He's not going to last much longer," I observe, my eyes tracking Andy across the yard.

"I don't know how he's still going. I'm exhausted."

I grin at Sophia quickly before turning my eyes back to my son.

"You shouldn't have gotten him Matchbox cars."

"What?" She sweeps her hand to Andy playing with the cars on the patio. "He loves them."

"He does," I agree. "But he's too young for them. The pieces are a choking hazard."

"The only thing that boy puts in his mouth is food."

She's right. He had a bad habit of chewing on things, but after Raider, Lawson's dog, yipped at him for biting his tail, he hasn't chewed on anything else. He's even given up bottles and moved on to sippy cups. He's growing too fast, too soon.

"Still. He'll have to be supervised constantly while he's playing with them."

"I can't believe he doesn't like the blue bunny I brought him."

"If it's not a Paw Patrol plush, he doesn't want it."

"So..."

"No."

"Really? I know you want to talk about it."

It being him, Drew O'Neil.

"I promise. I don't."

"So we're just going to pretend he's not right across the street with more muscles than sense?"

"Yep."

"Izzy. That's not healthy."

"You staying in my business when you have secrets of your own you don't want discussed isn't healthy. Avoidance much?"

"I told you that in confidence."

"I told you about the letter I got in confidence." I don't pull my eyes from my son when she huffs in irritation. "You told everyone."

"I didn't tell everyone. I was talking to *you* about it."

"At the New Year's Eve party where everyone was in attendance."

"It was a long time ago."

"Do you think my dad has forgotten about it, or anyone else for that matter?"

"I don't think it would bother you as much if he were still in prison. So tell me what the issue is."

"There's no issue."

"There is, and I think it's that you still have feelings for him and it's hard to go back to someone if everyone that loves you hates him because he's a complete asshole."

"I don't have feelings for him." Lie number one. "And I don't think people *hate* him."

"They certainly don't like him."

"Lawson certainly was ecstatic to see him."

"That's his brother. Of course he's going to be happy. It's written somewhere that you have to always love your family."

"Do you think they've been in contact?"

"How should I know?" Sophia lifts her soda to her mouth, her eyes on Andy since I told her how strictly he has to be supervised with those small toys. "You know how distant Delilah has been. When I do see her, Drew doesn't come up."

"She's sad," I agree. "It's heartbreaking."

"And that's why I don't want to share my own secrets."

I huff a laugh. "You don't want to admit to your husband you lied to him."

Colton and Sophia got married in a small ceremony last summer here at the clubhouse. She was a gorgeous bride. I was her maid of honor, and Colton's son, Rick, was his best man.

"I didn't exactly lie to him."

"Telling him you're no longer taking the pill—"

"I told him I wasn't on the pill. He still wanted to come in me."

"You told him you had an IUD inserted."

"Details."

"Important details," I clarify.

She worries her top lip with her teeth. "Think he's going to be mad?"

I look across the yard to Colton who is standing and talking with Dominic and Kincaid.

"I think he'll be ecstatic, but the longer you wait, the greater the chances of him being upset. Take it from someone who knows. You won't be able to hide it for long."

"I only took the test yesterday. I wanted to do something special to announce it."

"He should've been there when you took the test."

"He was at work."

"You should've waited."

"He's going to be pissed. He's been planning a trip next fall. I can't go skydiving!"

I laugh, something I haven't been able to manage since Drew showed up several hours ago.

"People shouldn't jump out of perfectly good airplanes anyway," I muse. "He's not going to be mad. What did he tell your dad when Dominic asked about kids?"

"Colton told him that if I want babies, he'll give me a dozen."

"There. See? He won't be mad. Just tell him now. Hey, Colton!"

"What are you doing?" Sophia grabs the arm I'm waving at her husband, pinching me when he starts walking this way.

"What's up?" His grin is wide. He already knows something is up because Sophia acting this way is common, but I'm not going to spill the beans about a shopping spree at Bath & Body Works, or tell him that she dented the bumper on his truck again.

"Sophia, tell your husband what we were talking about."

She glares at me, but I keep my eyes on Andy who is still playing with his cars even though his eyes are starting to droop. His nap was nonexistent, and putting him down this early in the evening means we're going to have a very early morning tomorrow.

"I didn't have the doctor put in an IUD when I went three months ago."

"That right?" I can hear the humor in the man's voice. He knows his wife so very well.

"Yeah, apparently I'm allergic to plastic—"

"The truth," I correct. "You're allergic to the truth not plastic."

"What did you do, little liar?"

"I got pregnant."

"You're pregnant?" The whoop of joy doesn't come out of Colton's mouth but from Lawson who, across the yard, has wrapped his arms around Delilah and is swinging her around in joy.

Cheers go up all over the yard. People are squealing and running to congratulate them. No one sees Colton lift his wife from her chair and kiss her like a man possessed. He's not mad, and if I had to guess, I imagine he knew she didn't get an IUD. He's the one who checks the mail, reading every piece in detail like the detective he is. He's also frugal, so I don't imagine it slipped passed him that her explanation of benefits came from the insurance company and didn't have that procedure listed.

"I think we'll share our amazing news some other time," he whispers against her lips, and somehow knowing Drew is across the street, the sight of them so in love and expanding their family hits me a little harder than seeing them interact so lovingly before.

"You have to be the one to tell my dad," Sophia says with a smile as she rests her head on Colton's chest.

"I don't mind."

"He's going to know you came inside me."

I scrunch my nose. Did she forget that I'm sitting here?

Who am I kidding? She doesn't care.

"I think he knows we have sex," Colton says, the smile never leaving his face.

"He heard you that one time," I remind her. "When you forgot they were in the living room and you jumped his bones."

Colton winks at his wife. "Let's go congratulate Lawson and Delilah."

I stand when they head in that direction, stopping by Andy to scoop him up in my arms. He settles, his head leaning on my shoulder, tiny fist clutching a green truck.

"He's going to fall asleep in the bathtub tonight," Apollo says, joining me on my trek across the yard.

"Probably. I'm going to be up before the sun even thinks about peeking out."

"We're not leaving until Tuesday. I can watch him for you tonight."

I keep my eyes focused ahead. It's not that I don't trust Apollo with Andy, but I haven't spent much time away from him. It makes my skin itch just to think about going home, even if it is just across the street.

"I'll be fine."

"I watched him that night you were too drunk to drive home."

"Sophia drugged me."

"By drugged, you mean kept pouring when you asked her to?"

"I still regret that night."

I went to Sophia's house on my birthday. At her insistence that I not stay home and feel sorry for myself, a few drinks in her living room didn't seem like such a bad idea. Then I woke up half on the sofa, half on the floor with a splitting headache and puke in my hair.

"He was fine."

"I'm not going to use up all my favors just to avoid an early morning."

He stops me in my tracks, turning me to face him. His hand runs down Andy's back.

"It's not a favor. You know I'd drop anything I'm doing to help you out."

"Which Caroline found out when I asked if you'd grab a pack of diapers since you were in town a couple of months ago."

He shrugs.

I lower my voice. "She stopped me in Wal-Mart the next week and took it upon herself to tell me she didn't appreciate getting interrupted during sex." I smack him with my free hand. "Who does that? Who stops in the middle of sex to run an errand?"

His smile is wide. "I told you I'd drop anything to help you out."

"And she broke up with you."

"We weren't even dating, and she left the door unlocked for me after I went back over. You got your diapers she got her—" He winks at me, something that's been easier to accept since he's been acting more like a friend and less like a jilted lover this last year.

Something changed after Drew left. I thought Apollo would push even harder for us to be together after Andy was born, but he's taken on more of the pseudo fun uncle role instead.

"What about Amanda?" I look over his shoulder. His date is grinning up at Jinx like she's already head over heels for the man. "If you don't get over there, Jinx may be the one entertaining her tonight."

He winks again, this one a little more salacious. "That was always part of the plan."

I smack him again. "You guys are gross."

"We're sexual creatures, Izzy. Orgasms are fun. You should try it sometime."

"I do just fine," I mutter, turning around to walk away from him.

"Your own fingers and battery-operated toys have nothing on tongues and cocks, my friend."

This is another newer thing about Apollo. He treats me like one of the guys, a real friend, not some damsel that needs protecting. I mean my dad would probably skin him if he heard what Apollo just said, but it brings a disgusted smile to my face.

"It's going to be a group event if you don't get back over to your date," I warn. "Amanda is eyeing Thumper and Legend like she's ready to take on the entire crew."

He bites his lip, not saying a word, and it makes my eyes widen. "You guys are so bad!"

He presses a kiss to my cheek. "I'll be over in twenty minutes to help you get him tucked into bed."

"You have plans." I indicate the girl who looks like her wildest dreams are coming true right now. "I've got it tonight."

"You know I wouldn't miss it. Besides, she'll have plenty to keep her busy. Probably won't even know I'm gone."

He presses his lips to the back of Andy's sleeping head before walking back across the yard. I watch him as he goes, killing time when I notice a swarm still around Lawson and Delilah. Amanda is a nice enough girl. She works at the post office and was always kind to me when I'd go in to mail the letters to Drew. She never turned her nose up at me when she noticed the prison address and inmate number on the front of the envelope.

I look away when she grins as Apollo wraps his arms around from the back while Thumper still has his hands on her hips. Nothing says thank you for dying for our sins and rising from the dead like an Easter orgy, I guess.

I'm not hating on her. More power to her. Safe, sane, and consensual, right? If that girl wants to be twisted into a pretzel while handling five guys, more power to her.

Personally, I don't even want to think about sex. I don't even want to be flirted with. A cute guy winked at me at the gas station the other day, and it flustered me so much I nearly drove off without paying for my gas. I'm over cute, smirking guys. They're after one thing and one thing only, just like Drew said in his letter. He was using me that night. I was a mistake, one that created the possibility of a lifelong commitment he didn't want.

Now he's back, and I'm terrified he's going to inject himself into our lives and hurt me again, hurt us again.

I paint a fake smile on my face because it's my turn to congratulate Lawson and Delilah on their amazing news.

Chapter 34

Drew

Staying in the house while Lawson and Delilah were across the street with Izzy and Andy was more difficult than that first night in prison when every sound, every thump or grunt from one of the other guys made my eyes widen in fear.

I wanted to be where they were even though I don't belong, even though I trashed any chance at being welcomed.

"You going to sit out here all night or are you just waiting for Apollo to leave?"

I stand when Hound speaks, only partially because I learned early on in prison that difficult conversations don't happen when someone is sitting. It puts me in a weakened position, and even though I highly doubt Hound is here to kick my head in, that doesn't mean he's exactly happy with my reappearance.

"Will it take all night for him to leave?" I hedge, trying to get more information. "Or would it be better to just come out in the morning and watch him walk away?"

I catch his eyes narrowing in the low porch light.

"Are you trying to say that my daughter would disrespect me enough by messing around with someone under my roof?"

"She's grown. Would you even consider it disrespect?"

"Drew," he warns. "Did you disrespect me?"

"I didn't sleep with your daughter in your house, Hound." I take a seat, falling back into the rocking chair on the porch.

He steps around the bushes, joining me in the second one. "You broke her heart."

"I know."

"Are you here to put it back together?"

"Are you here to warn me about trying?"

"Are you always going to answer a question with a question?"

I chuckle. "I doubt she wants anything to do with me."

"You have a baby together."

"Yeah, a kid who is calling another man dada." I'm not even capable of hiding the bitterness in my words, so I don't even try.

"Jameson calls me dada when I come home. He's an observant child. I come home. I kiss my wife. He calls me dada. Apollo spends a lot of time at our house. He comes in, kisses—" I grunt my disproval. "—kisses Izzy on the forehead. He sees what Jameson does, and he does the same. It's more like they're twins than uncle and nephew. You should see them when all the kids get together. Amelia can't keep up even though she's the oldest when those two are joined with River and Cooper."

"So they aren't a couple?"

"If you came across the street for the egg hunt, you'd know that Apollo brought a date."

I nod, hating that I missed it, more that I didn't get to watch my son hobble around and pick up eggs in the yard. Who am I fooling? Seeing Apollo there with someone other than Izzy would've calmed a lot of shit in my head.

"She's still over there, in fact."

"Yet, Apollo is in your house."

"He helps a lot with Andy. You can't fault the man for being around. He's a good man."

I manage enough to nod in agreement, but I don't use any words. I'm too petty to admit that Apollo is a good man out loud. I know he is, that's why I sent him the letter.

"Back to you breaking her heart. What did you tell her in that letter?"

"So many horrible things... unforgivable things." I lean forward, the rocking chair squeaking under my weight as I place my head in my hands.

"Why?"

I shake my head, emotions growing in my chest. It's reminiscent of the way I felt in that courtroom, seconds before the judge sentenced me.

"I'm a fool, an idiot. I wanted her to move on. I didn't want her hurting."

"You hurt her with whatever you wrote her. She was devastated."

I swallow thickly. "I know."

"Do you remember you wrote me a letter as well?"

I can't answer him. I poured my heart out to the man, focusing, at the time, on the bond we forged with hundreds of hours in the shop across the street. He was the father of the girl I loved, but then he was also someone I could look up to, a father figure of my own. I respected him, and in doing so I told him everything in that letter. I wrote about my failings, my disappointments, the love I'll always have for his daughter, about the guilt I felt for not being man enough to be a good dad. All of my fears, my weaknesses, I laid at his feet in that letter.

It looked nothing like the one I sent to Izzy.

"The man that wrote that letter was one of the strongest men I've ever met. There aren't many men willing to hold their heads high and do what you did in that courtroom that day. I don't know that I could've done it."

"Act a fool and nearly get charged with new offenses?"

He chuckles. "I don't think you would've done that if Izzy hadn't been so upset and going into labor."

He has better faith in me than I do. I was seconds away from spinning around and begging for mercy before she cried out in pain the first time.

"Do you still love her?"

"Of course I do. I thought about her every single day since I left."

"Because you love her, Drew, or because you didn't have anything else to focus on? Because there's a difference. The last thing I want is you getting involved with my daughter and then figuring out this isn't a life you want. You have a child involved. I'd never keep you from your son, but that relationship and the one you have with Izzy are separate. There are several scenarios you have to consider here."

I sit up straight and face him.

"You can walk away, forget Izzy and Andy exist, but with that, I'd ask that you sign over your rights, make a clean break and never show your face again. Andy is young now, but he doesn't need some strange man dipping in and out of his life every couple of years making promises only to back out of them."

"I—"

He holds his hand up. "Listen to me. Option two is being involved in his life with absolutely no expectation of having anything but a co-parenting relationship with Isabella, and that needs to be talked about in detail with her so she knows where to place her expectations. With that, it means no flirting, no touching, no kissing, nothing that even resembles romance. You do things with and for Andy only unless it's a group activity.

"The last option would be to work on getting her back because you want a future with her, and that doesn't just happen tomorrow. I can't speak for her, but I know how badly you hurt her. If she even considers building something with you, that's not going to happen anytime soon. She's as stubborn as I am when she's been hurt. I still can't look at her mother without seeing red and wanting to spit fire."

"I want—"

"Do you want option one?"

"Fuck no," I hiss. "I'm not here to manipulate—"

"Then that leaves option two or three. Wait. Maybe it needs to be a combination of those options. I don't think going over there and—"

Noise from Hound's front door draws both of our attention.

Of course, Apollo, being the trained special secret ops whatever guy he is, knows two people are sitting over here. Like he owns the place, he walks toward us with a swagger in his gait that I loathe. He stops in the same spot Hound was standing in when I first noticed him earlier.

"Drew. Glad you're back." He holds out his hand for me to shake, and I look at it like it's going to poison me if I touch it.

"Go on," Hound urges, nudging my shoulder with his hand.

I stand, shaking Apollo's hand, feeling a little better that I'm elevated above him. He squeezes tighter than necessary because he just has to, I guess. He draws me in close as if he's going to tell me a secret, but Hound has great hearing, and it's too quiet out here for anyone to talk and others not hear.

"I didn't take your advice in that cheap shot of a letter you sent me." He squeezes even harder, making me grind my teeth, but I refuse to show weakness by pulling away. "It proved how much you loved her. She loved you just as much, if not more, but break her heart again and I won't even bother hiding your fucking body."

He releases me with a shove before turning around and walking away.

"You wrote him a letter, too?"

I rub at my sore hand with my other one as I retake my seat.

"I wanted Izzy with someone that would treat her right. I knew Apollo wouldn't hurt her."

"He backed off before Christmas that year," Hound explains. "They're very close, but only friends."

"I can't lie and say I'm not glad he didn't listen to my advice."

"Okay. Back to what we were talking about. I have a wife and two kids to take care of. I can't be sitting out here all night."

I smile at the man. He's not brushing me off, but he does have other responsibilities.

"You need to spend time with your son. Izzy isn't going to fight that, but she may not be thrilled about leaving you alone with him. She hardly trusts anyone with that boy, but on the other hand, she may not be able to stomach the sight of you, so you may have some alone time with him. You need to work on a relationship with him before you even consider having one with her. So maybe start with option two and then see if option three is even a possibility."

"And if I go to talk to her tomorrow and she throws her arms around my neck?"

He stands, his laugh boisterous and loud. "Oh, you stupid fool. That's never going to fucking happen. Get some sleep, kid. You have some groveling to do tomorrow."

Chapter 35

Isabella

"And once again, you're not listening to me."

Dad sighs, his jaw ticking as he looks at me. "I never ignore you, and you know it."

"But you argue with everything I say."

"Not everything."

"Most everything," I amend. "I can't do it. I can't just take Andy over there to see him."

Dad hit me with it first thing this morning.

You need to talk to Drew. There's a lot that needs to be discussed.

"Now is not the time to be stubborn."

It's my turn for a flexed jaw.

"You need to do what's right by your son."

"And I'm not arguing the fact that Drew needs to build a relationship with Andy, but I don't have to be there to watch it."

"Andy doesn't know him. He's a stranger. He needs his mother there to let him know it's okay."

"He trusts you as much as he does me. You can take him."

"I'm busy."

"I overheard you tell Gigi you were going to go tinker on your motorcycle. That's not busy."

"Upkeep on my bike is important."

"And can be done at any time."

He sighs again, his chin lifting up as he points his face at the ceiling, as if asking for divine intervention for my stubbornness. He won't find it because I'm not giving in.

Seeing Drew yesterday hurt. I already have to look my son in the face, one that is nearly a mirror of Drew's. Talking with the man who broke my heart is a punishment I'd rather not face any time soon.

"He won't spend time with Andy until he talks to you."

I narrow my eyes. "Did he give that ultimatum?"

"No." Dad sighs once again, the sound becoming so familiar, I can't remember a time when he wasn't a little frustrated with me.

"Is there something I need to know?" I take a step forward. "If you don't trust him to be alone—"

Dad holds his hand up. "This isn't about trust. Drew would never do anything to hurt his son."

"But—"

"Never, Iz. Don't even let your mind go there. He's a good man."

He's a heartbreaker.

I've never thought Drew could hurt Andy, but it's not my child I'm worried about getting hurt. Just the sight of him on the porch yesterday nearly gutted me.

"Okay," I whisper. "But I'm not going to talk to hi—"

There's a knock on the door.

"And there he is now. I'll be in the garage across the street if you need me."

This was a damn setup. I should've been suspicious when Gigi offered to take Andy to nursery school this morning. She's never out of pajamas before noon most days.

I listen as Dad greets the devil on his doorstep.

"Good morning. She's in the living room."

I turn away, unwilling to see him walk into the house, grateful that the wall to the room hides the front door. I can't see him standing in the entryway. He's done it before, one night while he was on his knees while he—

Nope. *Those* thoughts aren't allowed, no matter how starved I am for more than the platonic touches I get from Apollo.

It seems as if an eternity passes by and he still doesn't speak. When I turn around, he's not even in the room. Maybe he left. Maybe I get to avoid this situation just a little while longer, but when I go around the corner, I find him standing in the entryway, his face tilted up, hands shaking at his sides. He's even bouncing back and forth on his feet like he's preparing for battle.

I don't plan to fight, though. Other than discussing his plans to spend time with Andy, we have nothing else to say.

"Drew." Planning for monotone and dry, I'm surprised at how much gravel is in my tone when I speak.

"Izzy." And that breathy sigh from his lips has no damn place in this house. "You look—"

I clasp my arms over my chest and give him a point for maintaining eye contact. I'm in an oversized t-shirt and sweats, but I still feel underdressed. I imagine wearing a parka and snow boots wouldn't make me feel any more prepared for battle.

He clears his throat, his fingers still flexing in and out.

Does he want to touch me?

Is he struggling as much as it looks like he is right now?

If so, good.

I want him to want me. I want him to know what it's like to yearn for something he'll never have. I want him to hurt as much as he hurt me.

I have to look away. Seeing him brings too much back. Seeing him makes me want to run into his arms—after slapping him in the face and calling him an asshole.

Footsteps follow me into the living room, but this room holds memories too. We spent a lot of time watching television and getting to know each other here.

Taking a seat, I look up at him. Waiting for what, I don't know.

In my head, when I let myself fantasize about him coming back, I always saw him clinging to me, begging for forgiveness, and begging me to take him back.

Those fantasies faded rather quickly, in part because he never wrote back when I sent him updates on his son. Hell, I don't even know if he got them. It's possible he trashed them without even opening them.

No, that's not right. The gifts he had in his arms yesterday were covered in Paw Patrol. Either he read the letters or Lawson updated him about what his son likes.

The fantasies of him returning to confess his undying love eventually gave way to anger, an emotion so powerful it bordered on hatred, but hating the father of my child was something I could never bring myself to do. I can't even lie to myself and say I wanted him to stay away forever.

I close my eyes, hating the way my head and heart are battling. Tears threaten and that makes my back stiffen. If I thought I was over him, I was sadly mistaken. He has more power over me than I thought, and that only makes me angrier.

I open my eyes to glare at him. He watches my face, no words coming out of his mouth.

"We have a lot to discuss." I pull my eyes away, focusing on sweeping my hands down my thighs before resting my hands in my lap.

"We do." His voice cracks.

Neither of us speak for long moments, but I track his movement as he takes a seat on the couch. I chose the recliner on purpose. It made it impossible for him to get too close to me.

"Andy doesn't know you," I begin.

"I want to change that. I was—"

I hold my hand up, silencing him like Dad did half a dozen times to me earlier. I take pride in the way his mouth snaps closed.

"I don't think it's smart to just drop him at your house. You need to spend time with him here first." As much as I hate the idea, Dad was right about me needing to be around when they first get to know each other. "He calls Apollo dada, and I don't want you correcting him. I don't want you encouraging him to call you anything but Drew for now."

He nods, and that surprises me. I figured Drew would show up and demand his place in Andy's life, pushing any connections the child made while he was incarcerated out of the way.

"We can start small. Maybe an hour a day."

"Okay," he readily agrees.

"I don't want you bringing him gifts every time you show up. It's like you're trying to buy his love."

"That's not—"

"It's creepy," I interrupt.

"Okay."

His hasty agreement makes me feel like I'm being the biggest bitch in the world, but I don't want my son to get hurt. This man was adamant in his letter that fatherhood wasn't what he wanted. I was a mistake. Andy was a consequence of that mistake, and he wished it never happened. He blamed me for his actions that landed him in prison, and I think that hurt the most because before he was sentenced, he was hellbent on making it right. He was willing to pay for his actions only to turn them around and point those fingers at me.

"And not every day." He frowns at this. "The days he has nursery school he's overly tired and cranky. It would be too much stimulation for him."

"Can I just sit with him on those days?"

I blink over at him. "You just want to sit and watch him?"

I figured he'd want to play and get him riled up, another thing I was going to have to put effort into to calm him down when Drew went back home.

"Well, yeah." He scratches at his cheek like maybe it was a dumb suggestion. "Do you ever just sit and watch him play?"

"All the time."

"I'd like to do that too."

"You coming over here is for him. I don't want you thinking I'm going to carry on a conversation with you. We've said what we need to say."

He frowns again, and I hate that even disappointed, the man is handsome.

The fact is, *we* haven't said anything.

He said what he wanted to say in that awful letter and yet the second he's released, he's here in my face.

"We don't have to talk. I'm here for Andy."

And that declaration feels like a knife to the heart.

"Very good." I stand, indicating that the conversation is over.

"Can I see him? I can keep an eye on him while you work on schoolwork or something."

I search his face. What does he know about how I spent my life while he was gone? I'll be furious if I find out that Lawson or Delilah have been sharing information about me to him.

"When you visit, I'll be in the room." He doesn't look discouraged at all by this information. "I get schoolwork done while he's at nursery school."

"Okay." It's another quick agreement.

"And I should've started that half an hour ago."

He stands, walking toward the front door.

"Thank you," he says as he reaches for the doorknob. "I'm glad you aren't making this difficult. In my head, I was imagining that you wouldn't let me see him. I know I hurt you, and I want—"

"Goodbye, Drew. You can visit with him tomorrow. He wakes up from his afternoon nap about three."

He nods, and I'm thankful he isn't pushing the issue and leaves.

I wish I could say I go right upstairs and get to work on my assignments, but I spend the first hour after he left crying into my damn pillow.

Chapter 36

Drew

"This may not be the best time."

My hope falls the second the words leave Izzy's mouth. Even though I was agreeable with her rules yesterday, I still walked away wondering why she was making it so easy for me to spend time with Andy. Maybe she didn't feel safe refusing me, which is nuts because I've never given her any reason to be fearful.

You went to prison for killing a guy. That's enough, idiot.

"Okay."

My chest constricts. I want to see my son. Legally, I have rights to see him, but if Izzy doesn't want me here, then what can I do short of hiring an attorney and fighting for the right. It would only hurt her even more, and that's not my intention, but I'm not walking away and just forgetting he exists.

Hound's option one, the one where I just leave and sign over my rights will never happen.

I didn't want to have a custody battle for him either. Doing so would obliterate any chance of getting her to love me again.

"Maybe tomorrow?"

"That might be better."

"Okay."

I'm unable to hide my disappointment when I turn to leave.

"Drew." She sighs. "It's just that—"

You hate me, and had time to think about what we agreed to yesterday, and now you're backpedaling.

"Gigi and Dad went to dinner. I have Jamie and Amelia here as well."

I tilt my head, not fully understanding.

"They're like siblings. You're not going to get very much individual time with him if you stay."

"I like kids," I say with a shrug, my chest reinflating at the possibility that all isn't hopeless. "I can hang out with all three of them."

Her eyes narrow, tiny hazel slits looking up at me, and I don't know if she's leery about me unconcerned about being with three children or if it's because I wrote in my letter that I didn't want kids.

Not all of that was false. I never imagined wanting kids, but almost from the very first second I knew she was pregnant with Andy, I knew I wanted to be his dad.

"I don't mind."

"You're sure?"

"The more the merrier."

She steps aside, holding the door open for me, and if I weren't trying to play it cool, I'd jump and clap my heels together in excitement.

That enthusiasm sobers a little when it hits me that I'm going to meet him officially for the first time, not as his dad but as Drew. I'm going to get to see more than his little face peeking through a slit in the open doorway or watch him play with Easter grass like it's the most fascinating thing in the world.

Izzy sweeps her hand in the direction of the kids. All three are in the center of the living room floor with a mess of jumbo building blocks scattered around them. Amelia is working hard on what looks like a castle. The boys seem content to just put them in a pile.

"Andy," Izzy says.

She's close enough to my arm that I can feel the warmth of her body, but when I look over at her, she takes a step away.

"This is Drew. He's your Uncle Lawson's brother."

Well, that introduction puts me right in my place.

She didn't say I'm her friend. There was nothing personal, no link to her at all. Thankfully, Andy is only sixteen months old and not able to understand that by her introduction, I guess it would make me his uncle as well.

I keep my frown to myself. We're doing this at her pace. It's something I agreed to, and I'm just happy to be here.

"What do you have there?"

He looks up at me, his eyes the same color as mine, hair—like mine—an unruly mess. He even has that same cowlick in the front that I battled with throughout high school until I just accepted the stupid thing. A little grin plays on his round face before he turns his attention back to the blocks.

I take a seat on the floor near the kids but make sure to keep some distance. I don't want to take over their space. Just like I told Izzy yesterday, I'm happy to just sit and watch.

Sitting and watching however isn't something the kids are interested in. It takes mere minutes of me being on their level before I have a stack of blocks in my lap and two smiling little boys who think I'm a jungle gym.

Jamie tuckers out first, his little mouth opening on a yawn more than once before he sits on a bean bag on the other side of the room and passes out.

Amelia loses interest in the blocks but finds the cartoon Izzy has playing in the background entertaining.

I follow the sight of the little girl as she crosses the room because she's heading in Izzy's direction. I haven't taken many opportunities to look over at her, but I'd be a fool not to look now. Her eyes are pointed in the direction of the television, but I don't doubt for a second she's paid attention to every word I've said to the kids since I arrived over an hour ago.

A loud grunt and a clatter draws my attention, and I watch with an eyebrow raised as Andy smacks one jumbo block against another.

"Watch," I tell him, gently pulling the block from his little fist.

His head turns, eyes daring mine as I wait for him to pick up another and hit me with it. Lawson mentioned him being fiercely independent, but watching him get angry because he can't figure something out doesn't sit well with me.

"Look." I wave the block until it catches his eye. "Like this."

His eyes follow the block as I press it down to lock with another. He grabs the pair from my hand before ripping them apart again. They're tossed to the side, and I do my best to keep from laughing. He's tall for his age, but compared to my size, he's a tiny little thing. His attitude is much larger than his body.

"Like this," I say, taking another duo of blocks and putting them together.

He snatches those away as well.

I want to ask Izzy if this is what cranky looks like but she was clear that I was here to visit with him and not her.

"See?" I do it again. He snatches them again.

But then it turns into a game. I put two together, he pulls them a part until we're out of blocks within reach because he's tossed them away.

Surprisingly, he crosses the room, gathering the blocks and placing them back in front of me again, smiling as he waits for me to put two together. He's fascinated by it, his laughter the sweetest sound I think I've ever heard, and the game continues for over half an hour.

I couldn't be happier.

Then the front door opens, causing Andy's eyes to dart that direction. I don't turn around because I figure it's Hound and Gigi coming back, but then my son's face lights up.

"Dada!"

Hound explained it the other night. Andy is mimicking what Jamie does when he gets home, but it doesn't make it hurt any less.

"Hey, buddy."

I turn just in time to see another man scoop my son up and wrap him in a hug. Apollo is a good man. I've known it for a while, but knowing that doesn't stop the green irritation of jealousy from trying to make me a bitter man.

I stand, refusing to stay on the floor while Apollo bonds even more with my child.

"Are you playing with Drew?"

Even Apollo doesn't make a mistake and call me his dad. It makes me wonder how many conversations about me have gone on before I showed up today.

"Hey, man." Apollo offers me his hand, and I take it even though it kills me to see Andy's hand flat against the man's chest.

"Hey."

We shake, and I try to stuff down the agitation that he's a better man than me. If the tables were reversed, I might gloat about how another man's kid likes me more than his father. If the tables were turned, I never would've taken a step back from Izzy. I would've made her mine the second I got a chance because I know the quality of woman she is. He's a fool for not jumping when he had the chance because there's no way I'm backing down now.

"It's good to see you." I look over at Izzy. "I guess I better go. Tomorrow?"

"Sure," she answers with a quick nod of her head.

"Bye!" Andy says, his little hand waving when I walk toward the door.

"I'll see you tomorrow, little guy."

My heart is in my throat as I leave. I want to hug him, hold him in my arms, but that will have to come another day.

Chapter 37

Isabella

"Ack. That's nasty." I pull the beetle from Andy's tiny hand. "Don't touch it."

Andy's brow furrows, but he doesn't stay upset for long. His eyes focus on something else.

"That's a butterfly," I tell him. "Isn't it pretty?"

He watches the butterfly fly around, getting excited when it lands on the front porch rail. Then he's on his feet rushing toward it. Thankfully, the thing flies away before he can scoop it up.

"Bye-bye." He waves as the butterfly disappears around the house.

Avery wasn't at the nursery school today, and when I picked him up, he was in rare form. He doesn't exactly get upset and stay that way for long, but he was a little crankier than usual when we got back to the house. Since he loves to be outside, I figured spending some time on the porch would be better than making him feel cooped up indoors.

"Look at these."

Andy turns his nose up at the jumbo building blocks. He doesn't want to play with them unless Drew is here to do it with him. Drew has been making daily visits, even on the days he has nursery school, keeping his word that he'll just sit and observe if Andy isn't interested in interacting, for the last couple of weeks.

He doesn't strike up conversation with me, only speaking to me when he has questions about his son's day. The lack of interaction is killing me, and I hate myself for being a little jealous of the time Andy is getting with him.

Drew hasn't grown bored or made an excuse as to why he can't show up. He's been here. Every. Single. Day. Most days, he simply washes his hands before rushing over, leaving the scent of motorcycles and hardworking man in his wake when he leaves. Those days are the hardest on me, the nights spent recalling his scent while trying to resist fulfilling urges that have compounded since he got out of prison.

Other days, he takes a shower before arriving, and I'm not disappointed in the woodsy scent on those days either.

He's gotten his haircut recently, the floppy curls no longer hiding his bright blue eyes, and the first time I opened the door to him, it was alarming. He stood, waiting for me to step out of the way for a solid two minutes while I just stared at him. Of course he didn't say anything about it, didn't tease me for gawking, because that isn't what we do. He comes to spend time with Andy and then he leaves.

It's exactly what I wanted, and I flipping hate it.

"Doo!" Andy yells, his tiny hands waving in front of him as Lawson pulls up to the front of his house.

Drew's smile is contagious as he sees his son waving at him.

"Doo!" he screeches again when the passenger truck door swings open.

Drew doesn't even bother swinging the door closed before he's rushing across the yard. He swings Andy up in his arms eliciting another squeal from him.

"Hi, Doo!"

Drew nuzzles his neck, making him laugh, and seeing the two of them together like this is what I always wanted. Watching Drew leave and not getting so much as a high five from his son the first couple of days was heart breaking, but he didn't force the issue. After a couple of days, Andy was more comfortable around him, initiating contact and sitting in his lap while Drew read him a book or they played with toys.

Now, Andy waits by the door in the evening saying Doo over and over, waiting for him to arrive.

"Did you have a good day?"

I bite the inside of my cheek, frustrated like I've been every time Drew asks Andy a question he knows the kid can't answer. It forces me to speak to him without him directly talking to me. It's another thing I asked for. He's giving it to me, and it only makes me wish I never opened up my mouth.

"He had a timeout for throwing a toy. Avery was gone today."

He nods, but keeps his eyes on Andy and the child climbs all over him. Drew is careful, keeping both of his hands on him at all times, but it still makes me nervous to watch.

"You can't get upset when your friend is gone, little guy. Avery wouldn't want you in trouble."

Andy settles as he places his palm on Drew's cheek.

"Okay?"

Andy nods, and it's as if he actually is listening to what he's hearing. The little promise to behave makes my heart smile a little.

"Good man. Now, what are we going to play today? I see your blocks up on the porch."

Andy doesn't bother to look back at his toys. Exhausted from misbehaving all day at nursery school, he drops his head to Drew's shoulder and closes his eyes, little feet swinging under Drew's arm.

God, I wish I had a camera ready.

With his eyes closed, Drew leans his head, resting it on top of his son's and it's the most serene I've ever seen the man.

There's no doubt he loves this little boy, and Andy is better for it. Keeping Drew away from him was never my intention. I'd hoped when I sent the updates that he'd change his mind, mostly for Andy, but deep down I knew I was doing it because I couldn't imagine my life without a little part of him in it.

"I'm going to the festival tomorrow," I offer, unsure why I'm bringing it up now. I've been planning to attend since I saw the flyer weeks ago at the grocery store.

"Want me to watch him?" I know he doesn't make the question lightly. Not once has he asked to keep him without me, an issue he could honestly force at any moment. He has just as many rights to our little boy as I do.

"I'm taking him with me. They have a little area for smaller children to play and a petting zoo. Amelia went last year and spent the next month asking about it. Gigi is planning to take Jamie. Simone will be taking River and Cooper."

"I bet he'll have a good time." His eyes find mine for the first time since he stepped out of the truck, his hand rubbing soothing circles on Andy's back.

"I was thinking, I mean... if you wanted to go."

"You want me to meet you there?"

"We could ride together." His head tilts as if I've just spoken a foreign language and he doesn't understand.

"I'm sure Andy would enjoy both of us being there."

"Together? What about Apollo?"

"They're going to be out of town working."

His face falls a little, and I catch the disappointment before he can school his features. I don't correct his assumption that he's a consolation prize, but honestly he isn't. I didn't think of even asking Apollo to go. It just seems like something we would do as a family.

You're co-parenting. We're not a family.

Knowing this makes me frown as well.

"I'd love to go. It may take two of us to keep this guy out of trouble." He rubs his son's back a little longer before walking closer, making to hand him off. "I was hoping to spend a little time with him this evening, but it looks like he's not up for it."

"You could stay."

Jesus, Izzy. Eager much?

"I mean, since he's asleep. You could sit out on the porch with him while he naps."

"Really?" The surprise in his voice makes me feel like a jerk.

"Yeah, I mean, he can't nap long because he won't want to go to bed, and I don't want you to miss out on seeing him."

Drew swallows, his eyes searching mine, and I have to look away. I don't want him to see the vulnerability there. I'm not ready for what it could mean.

Drew follows me across the porch, taking one rocking chair while I sit in the other. We don't speak as he rocks back and forth, his son in his arms, but the silence isn't awkward either.

When Dad gets home twenty minutes later, he pulls Andy from Drew's arms, waking him up with raspberries on his little belly, leaving the two of us sitting on the front porch in silence as the sun sets.

When my stomach growls, Drew stands to leave.

"Thank you for offering me the chance to go tomorrow. What time should I be here?"

"Early. It starts at ten, and I'd like to be there before the crowds swarm."

"I'll be here."

His eyes sweep over my face one more time before he walks away.

It takes everything I have not to call after him and beg him to stay just a few more minutes.

Chapter 38

Drew

I seriously think she's trying to kill me. First it was the sight of her in a cute little sundress, then when I got close enough to grab the diaper bag from her before leaving her house, her perfume hit me in the face. In addition to the flowery scent threatening to make me hard, I have to see her bare shoulder all the while resisting the urge to touch her soft skin.

She's an evil woman, and the crazy part is, I don't think she has a damn clue what she's doing to me. She has no idea how many times since leaving the house that I've wanted to draw her into my side or kiss her perfect lips. Just the brush of her hand when she passed me Andy on our walk into the festival was enough to light me on fire. It's the closest we've been since I got back, and it was enough to make me forgo the plan to only spend time with Andy.

Three weeks is a long enough wait to profess my love for her, right?

The silent walk toward the petting zoo keeps my lips sealed.

She's cordial today, but there isn't a single hint that she wants more than a little help with Andy today. She isn't smiling and laughing. She's not finding a reason to brush against me. If anything, she's been keeping her distance since the second we accidentally touched earlier.

"Can we have two?" Izzy asks the lady selling pebbled food for the animals.

I pull out my wallet to pay for them before she can dig through her purse.

"You don't have to pay for that."

I wink at her. "Sure I do."

Doesn't she understand that I owe her so much? I spent the first sixteen months of my son's life in prison without being able to send so much as a nickel her way. Lawson, with the help of Shadow's expertise, was able to assist me in getting accounts set up for Andy, but Izzy has been refusing any type of support.

At first, the cynical side of me thought that she didn't want me to pay for anything because she didn't want me to have any more leverage if I tried to fight for a court-ordered custody agreement, but Hound assured me that she was just stubborn and wanted to do things on her own. I've been giving that money weekly to Hound. I have no idea what the man uses it for, but he's been supporting Izzy and Andy, so whatever it is goes to help them both. Eventually, the woman is going to have to give in, but it's not something I'm willing to pick a fight over right now. Business at the shop is very good, and Lawson pays me a great wage. I haven't even looked for other jobs because I've realized just how much I like working with my hands.

"The goat is in a mood, so keep an eye on her," the lady warns as she opens the gate for us to walk through.

"Are their eyes always so beady?" Izzy asks, keeping close to the fence while the goats just stare in our direction on the other side of the pen.

Izzy had the right idea about showing up early. We're the only ones at the petting zoo right now, and I'm happy to have this time alone with the two people I love most in this world.

"No goats in Arizona?" She grins.

"Not in the city. I didn't grow up in the country."

"They're harmless," I assure her, but then the goat notices the bag of food in my hand and starts to walk in our direction, her jaw working back and forth like she can already taste the treats we have to offer. I get a flash of teeth, and I'm not scared, but I'm not taking the chance of Andy getting his fingers bitten either.

He's wiggling in my arms, excited for the experience.

"Like this," I tell him, placing a few pebbles in his hand and moving his arm out so the food drops to the ground a few feet away.

The goat, spoiled from being hand-fed for hours on end doesn't look very impressed with having to bend her head down to eat from the ground.

Andy squeals again, his little hand digging into the bag. He makes a little noise, one I've heard him use with Lawson's dog Raider.

"Like this." I show him again how to drop it on the ground. It takes three tries before he gives up on the idea of getting closer to the goat.

Izzy takes pictures. The woman's always taking pictures, and as grateful as I was to get them in prison, I wish she was beside us making these memories as a participant rather than just behind a lens.

"Why don't you hold him? I'll feed the goat and he can pet it."

Her nose scrunches.

"Is that look because you don't want him to touch it, or because you're afraid it'll touch you?"

"Can it be a little of both?"

"Come on," I urge. "You have a gallon of hand sanitizer in the diaper bag. Don't be a baby."

She grins, putting her phone away before holding out her hands to take Andy. Her fingers brush my chest, and at least I'm able to keep from releasing a hiss this time around. When it happened earlier, she asked if she shocked me. I couldn't admit that I was electrified, just not in the way she meant.

"Stand to the back. You can let him down."

"The side," she barters. "Don't those things poop without warning?"

"They're pellets not explosive feces," I tell her with a chuckle.

Her brows furrow again, but at least she's still smiling.

I bend in front of the goat, distracting it with a handful of food as Izzy inches closer with Andy. She hasn't put him down. She's crouched with him sitting on her bent leg, slowly guiding his hand toward the animal.

"Soft, like with Raider," Izzy instructs, then squeals when the goat turns to face them.

I was too busy watching them that I didn't realize the thing had eaten all the food out of my hand.

"I think that's enough," Izzy says, standing with Andy in her arms. "Not much of a petting zoo with only a single goat, but I think that's probably best."

"We have ponies coming later," the woman at the gate says with a forced smile. "The girl with the rabbits has a stomach virus and couldn't make it."

"Too bad," Izzy says. "I could cuddle a rabbit."

"Did it bite you?"

I turn to see Sophia and Colton approaching.

"Thankfully, no."

"So you're planning to eat that yourself?" Sophia points down at the second bag of feed we didn't use. Izzy passes it off to a kid walking up, much to the chagrin of the lady selling the food. I know she was hoping to make another sale, but come on. One goat? She may not get much action around here until the ponies do arrive.

"Drew, good to see you." I shake Colton's hand.

"You working today?"

"The Chief wanted a presence. I'm not technically on the clock, but he's well aware that encouraging us to dress in uniform will keep us busy all day. I'll spend the day telling people where the port-a-potties are like the police department are the ones hosting the event."

"Well, I'm not complaining." Sophia looks her man up and down, eyes waggling comically.

"Oh," I say turning to her. "I hear congratulations are in order."

They were going to announce their news to everyone at Easter, but that was the same day Delilah found out she was pregnant. Having been trying for so long, their celebration took precedence. Sophia and Colton didn't tell anyone that I know of but Rick, Colton's son. Rick posted the news on social media, alerting everyone last week. Lawson mentioned at work a couple days ago that he felt bad they didn't feel like they could share their news. Delilah felt guilty as well. Dominic was livid they kept it to themselves.

Her hand automatically goes to her flat belly. "Thank you."

I clap Colton on the back.

"I was going to go grab a funnel cake," Colton says, making Sophia's eyes light up like he just announced they were going on a three-week beach vacation. "Drew, wanna tag a long?"

I look over at Izzy who is focused on slathering both hers and Andy's hands and arms, clean up to their elbows in hand sanitizer.

"Izzy loves the turkey legs," Sophia offers with a wink.

Colton and I walk away, heading toward the concession area of the festival.

"This place gets crazy at about noon. People wait in line for forever to get some of this stuff. Stay away from the Cajun food stand. They say their stuff is fresh, but I have it on good authority that they buy it frozen."

"Good authority?" I can't help but laugh.

"Rick is working at the grocery store to save for college spending money. He said last week that old man Guidry came in and bought fifty pounds of frozen crawfish."

"The horror," I tease with a grin. "So small-town life is good?"

"The best, but I wouldn't call it a small town. We have a population over forty-five thousand, but I've lived here my entire life and never forget a face. You know how it is."

"I do," I agree. A good memory and recall is what makes a good cop. For once, I don't feel the pain of that loss—like a fist to the chest—like I normally do.

At some point during my prison sentence, I took a step back and evaluated my life. I knew that if I could have any form of relationship with my son and interaction with Izzy, where I worked didn't matter. I no longer wanted to live—or die as it were—for the job. My focus needed to be on my family, and I lucked out with the job at Lawson's shop because he's all about his family as well.

Which reminds me.

"Lawson and Delilah are going to need that room I'm staying in back soon. Got any leads on apartments?"

"Those newer ones out on the interstate aren't bad, but they're not exactly suited for a family."

"Oh." I look over the menu, deciding what I'm in the mood for. "I don't know how much time Andy will be spending with me. Izzy doesn't even leave the room while I'm there."

"Still. There are a couple of houses for rent over on Carl that would be suitable. Plus, you have a few months to decide."

We place our orders, a funnel cake for Sophia and a turkey leg each for Izzy and me.

"What are you doing tonight?" Colton asks as we walk back in the direction we left the girls. "I have a poker game going."

"Sounds illegal," I tease.

"We don't play for real money, but with the way Monahan plays, you'd think the fate of the free world rested on his shoulders."

"The police chief?" He confirms with a nod.

"He's not really all that bad."

"I'm not sure they'd appreciate sharing time with a felon," I mutter, my hope of getting out of the house fading away as quickly as it arrived.

"I want you to come. They won't mind. Seven o'clock if you're interested." He gives me the address as we walk up to the girls.

Izzy looks surprised with the turkey leg, making it clear she didn't hear a word Sophia said while she scrubbed the evil goat germs off our son.

"Thank you," she whispers.

The trade off—one of the turkey legs for Andy—goes smoothly, and she grins around the leg as she sinks her teeth into it. I have to look away. Sophia chuckles when I turn to show Andy some vendor selling silly hats. Clearly she didn't miss my reaction.

Chapter 39

Isabella

"Insanely," I say before licking salt off the back of my hand, "unfair."

"It was a carnival game, Iz." Sophia hands me a shot of tequila, cocking any eyebrow when it doesn't make my face scrunch.

Only the first three caused that reaction. I don't know what number that one was, but I didn't even taste it. It may not be a good thing. It's definitely going to cause problems tomorrow, but right now, I just don't care. Gigi offered to watch Andy when he passed out early from a hard day at the carnival and since I needed a serious distraction, I took her up on the offer.

"Did you not see his back flex? I swear Under Armour should be outlawed. Or at least make guys buy a size bigger than the one they think would work. I could see every muscle." I chew on a lime wedge before looking at my friend. "Every single one."

"So you're into backs."

"I'm into Drew O'Neil," I confess then slap a hand over my mouth. "Just joking. Ha ha?"

She chuckles. "Yeah, ha ha. Funny joke. You're obsessed with that man."

"Am not," I argue. "He just has a great back."

"You spent quite a while staring at his front today as well if I recall correctly."

"You should pay more attention to your own man. He looked lonely today."

She huffs, knowing I'm full of shit. "I can't get enough of him. If anything, he was grateful my focus was elsewhere. I threatened to suck him off at the festival."

"What?" I shake my head. "Where would you even do that? Don't say the port-a-potty. I may actually puke, and that would be a waste of perfectly good tequila."

"No puking," she says. "At least not until morning."

"No puking at all," I counter, but I know if I keep going, it's going to happen anyway. And since I have no plans to stop until my head forgets all about Drew O'Neil and his perfect back, then it looks like I'll be worshipping the porcelain throne come morning, if not sooner.

"In the emergency aid tent."

"What?"

"That's where I threatened to do it."

"Do what?" She's not making any sense.

"You can't even carry on a conversation," she says, but there's a smile on her glowing face.

"Because you're making me drink all alone."

"I'm pregnant, you fool. Here, have another one."

Not bothering to lick and salt my hand, I simply tilt the saltshaker over my mouth and tap the side. The shot is held in front of me.

"You're the best bartender ever." I tilt back the shot and take the lime wedge from her fingers.

"Are we going to talk about Drew?"

"No."

"Really? You don't want to?"

"I can't."

"You can't or you don't want to with me?"

I search her face, my buzzing mind unable to decide which one of her heads to focus on so I look at the wall.

"I don't want to be judged."

"Judged because you have the hots for a good-looking guy?"

"He's not just a good-looking guy, Soph. He's my baby's father."

"I'm well aware." She places her hand over mine when I reach for the saltshaker again. "And we have hardly talked since he got back. I know you're feeling… stuff."

"Stuff?" I snort, an awful sound escaping both my mouth and nose at the same time. "I feel like I should jump his bones. He's so flipping hot. And he smells amazing. It's like woodsy and fresh some days, and others, it's like he rolled around in man."

"Man?"

I wave my hand dismissively. "You know what I mean. He smells like hard work and dedication."

"Didn't know a man could smell like dedication. Is that a new scent by Dior?"

"This!" I point to her. "This is why I didn't want to talk."

She clamps her mouth closed and her hands go up. "I'm just teasing. Tell me about him."

"You don't want to hear it."

"No," she counters with a wide smile, "I really do."

"It's not fair. His back muscles, his scent. The way he's so nice and sweet with Andy. I never expected any of it."

"Because of his letter?"

I glare at her. "He said our son was a mistake, that he wished he'd never met me, Soph."

"He didn't mean it, and you won't be able to convince me otherwise."

"He still wrote that to me. I can't get over that."

"Sounds like you already have."

"I haven't," I lie. "I'll never be able to."

"Not even after looking at his back? He won that unicorn for you today. Andy doesn't like unicorns."

"Neither do I."

"You didn't until you saw it. He heard you squeal with excitement."

"First off, I don't squeal. Secondly, he won it on the first try. What happened to him spending all day trying to get it for me? That's romance, not knocking down all those damn wooden milk jugs on the first throw."

"The man has a good arm," she says with a shrug.

"God, his arms." I fall back on her bed, and the room spins around me. I bet if I focus hard enough, I can imagine myself in a fantasy land where it wouldn't be wrong to be lusting after him. "It's awful that I watch his damn mouth while he's talking to Andy. It's disgusting that I think of the other things that mouth is more than capable of while he's playing with our son."

"Good with his mouth, huh?"

"The best. I mean, my only, but still the best. And then he had the nerve to touch my lower back as we got on the Ferris wheel. What kind of psycho does that?"

"You hated it?"

"Loved it." I roll my head on the mattress to look over at her. "It set my blood on fire. It was either come over here or stay at home and flick my damn bean all night. Do you know how unsatisfying that is?"

"Not lately. My man takes care of me often."

"Good mouth?" I ask.

"The best." She winks at me. "Why don't you just go for it? Tell him to get you off."

"I can't. I don't think he wants a relationship with me." I ignore her scoff. "And I can't just have sex with him. My heart couldn't handle it."

"If you think that man isn't still head over heels for you, you're nuts. And I never said just have sex, but so long as you're being standoffish around him, it's never going to happen. He's waiting for you. He's not going to make a move until he knows it's what you want."

"He hurt me," I whisper.

"I know he did. Will you ever forgive him?"

"Am I fool if I do?"

"I think you already have."

She's right.

He's disproved every word he said in his letter. He spends time with Andy, always smiling. His joy when he's around his son isn't forced or fake. He genuinely loves every second he gets with him. I catch him grinning at me, and despite the hateful words he wrote, I never see it on his face or in his actions.

"He's been giving Dad money to help with Andy."

"As he should."

"I told him I didn't want it, so he went behind my back."

"You can't fault the man for taking care of his son. It's his responsibility and you need to let him."

"Each week, Dad just drops the cash on my bedside table. I just shove it in the drawer and forget about it."

"Silliness. At least put it in an account that gains interest."

I grin at her. "Look at you thinking like an adult. I will."

"I'll remind you tomorrow. You're too drunk to remember. Back to Drew. If you care for him, you need to tell him."

"I'm afraid he's going to hurt me again. It's hard to come back from."

"Honey, you're already there, you just need to take that extra step."

"Everyone knows what he did. Going back to him makes me look weak."

"Not at all." She clasps my hand before lying down beside me, her eyes on my face. "You know I always have my ear to the ground so to speak, and I haven't heard a single bad word about him since he showed back up. Everyone at the clubhouse loves him. Your dad speaks highly of him. No one is going to think poorly of you if you try to work things out with him. Honestly, everyone is expecting it to happen sooner or later."

"Ugh!" I slam my eyes closed. "Did you see the way his fingers curled around that damn ball?"

"No, but it seems like you did. Do you need a few minutes alone to work out your frustrations? I'd say change the sheets when you're done, but Colton and I went at it twice this afternoon and I didn't so..."

"Gross!" I hiss, but I just can't find the strength to climb off the bed.

She laughs. "You're the one who wanted to come in here."

"I wanted to hang out at your house, not lay on cum stains."

"Not my fault you insisted on the bedroom."

"Dillon always stares at me when I see him. You could've told me it was poker night before I left the house."

"Officer Ramshaw is a damn fine catch."

I cringe. The man isn't my type at all, despite having a thing for men in uniform. Apparently, after having *the* man in uniform, no one else measures up.

"I don't want to get drunk in front of a room full of cops."

"Not just cops."

"What?" My eyes widen as glare at her. "Did you invite my dad? Oh God, your dad? Why would you do this to me? I've been drinking!"

"You realize you're grown, right? That you have a kid and are of legal age to consume alcohol?"

"Still, I don't like to do that in front of adults."

"You're an adult," she whispers, but I don't feel like one right now.

I feel like a petulant child who wants a new toy but is being told no. Only the toy is Drew, and I'm the one telling myself no. It's a complicated position to be in.

"Drew is coming."

"What?"

"Drew. Colton invited him."

"You brought me here under false pretenses?"

"Need I remind you that you invited yourself? I didn't know Drew was coming until I told Colton you were on your way."

"You could've called me!" My eyes dart around the room, my drunken brain considering jumping from the window to escape rather than having to go downstairs and face him.

"I didn't want to distract you while you were driving."

"My ass!" I hiss.

He's going to think I'm a terrible mother. My son is at home with my parents while I'm here getting sloshed. Un-fucking-believable.

"He's out there. You're in here. It's no big deal. You don't have to see him unless you want to. Now let's go back to talking about how much you want him."

"I changed my schedule for him."

"You did what now?"

"I rush around all day taking care of everything so I have nothing to do in the evenings, just on the off chance that he'll stay a little longer." I stare up at the ceiling. I've already confessed so many things, I might as well confess them all and get it over with. "I could take some time for myself or get some studying done while he's there, but no. I just sit on the sofa and watch them play. I listen just as hard as Andy does when Drew reads him a story. I nearly asked him to stay last night when he carried him to bed. It was the first time he'd ever been in my room, and God, Soph. I wanted him in my bed so badly."

"Why didn't you?"

"I hadn't shaved my legs in like four days."

She laughs which makes me laugh, and before I know it, we're practically rolling around on the bed like idiots.

"You love him," she says softly once we settle.

"So much."

"You need to tell him."

"I can't."

Chapter 40

Drew

"Hey, man!" Colton seems a little overeager when he opens the front door to see me standing on the porch. "Can I get you a beer?"

"No thanks. I have an early morning with Andy tomorrow."

"Maybe a soda?"

"I'm good."

Instead of directing me to the living room where I hear several guys giving each other shit, he guides me the opposite way toward the kitchen.

"Listen—"

"I can go," I say before he can tell me that the guys aren't exactly happy about my invite.

"What? No—I mean—"

"They don't want me here. I get it. I knew this would be an issue once I got out." I reach out to shake his hand. "No big deal, man, I completely understand."

"What? No." He smacks my hand away. "This has nothing to do with the guys."

"Then why else would you have to separate me from them?"

"It's ah, shit. Sophia invited Izzy over."

A slow smile spreads across my face. "Is Andy here, too?"

"He's at home with Gigi. Listen, they came to the kitchen and grabbed a saltshaker, three limes, and a bottle of tequila then disappeared upstairs."

"Sophia is pregnant. Three limes—shit."

"Yeah. It seems Izzy plans to drink herself stupid tonight."

"And you're just going to let it happen." I move to head toward the stairs but he grabs my arm.

"Sophia would never let her get so drunk that she's in any real danger. Her keys are put away, and she's here for the night. I just didn't want you to be shocked when they come down to raid the fridge during the middle of a hand."

"I'll be fine." I keep my eyes on the stairs as if she's going to glide down them at any moment.

"You sure?"

"Do you want me to leave?"

"Not a chance. I'm hoping you're really good at poker and someone is finally able to beat the chief. He gloats for days after a poker night, and I'd like some peace and quiet at work for once."

He slaps me on the back and I follow him from the room.

Introductions go around the table, and only one guy by the name of Ramshaw looks at me with what I determine is annoyance.

Ignoring him, I let them deal me in, but my focus isn't on the table or the men around it. My head is upstairs, my ears perked up waiting to hear any sound coming from Izzy.

"And boom," Monahan says thirty minutes later. He slaps a full house down on top of the pile of poker chips. "What do you have, kid?"

"Umm?" I cringe when I look down at my hand, getting stares of disbelief when I show them.

"They're not even suited. What were you going for there?"

"That's awful?" another detective by the name of Gaffey snaps. "A pair of threes? You suck at this."

Colton shakes his head as he collects the cards from the table, but there's a knowing look in his eyes. He's well aware of why I can't concentrate on this damn game.

"Good thing we aren't playing with real money," I mutter, looking down at my paltry stack of remaining coins.

"Speak for yourself," Chief Monahan says as he scrapes the chips in his direction and begins to sort them into piles.

"Anyone need another beer?" Ramshaw asks as he stands.

"Bathroom?" I ask Colton as I stand as well.

"Just down the hall—oh wait, I forgot that floor is torn out. Up the stairs, first door on the left."

I hate the idea that all the guys will be coming upstairs when they need to piss. Izzy is up here, and I don't want that Ramshaw guy getting anywhere near her. He either hates me because of my past, or he's seen her. Any single man would be a fool to not look twice. The girl is off-the-charts gorgeous.

I don't think I've seen a better looki—

"Shit," I hiss when I clear the stairs and see her standing there.

I haven't been drinking, but I'd swear she's an apparition, a figment my imagination has conjured. When have I ever gotten so lucky to be thinking about her and she just appears?

"H-hi," I stammer like a grade-school kid running into his crush in the hallway. Even my face is heated.

I lick my dry lips, nearly groaning when her eyes try to track the movement. I would've been able to tell she's drinking even if Colton hadn't told me earlier. She's relying heavily on the wall, and somehow she's lost a shoe. Thankfully, she's wearing sandals with that same damn dress she had on this morning at the festival.

"Hello there." Her teeth dig into her lower lip as her eyes flutter.

I can't tell if she has something in her eyes or if she's flirting. It brings a grin to my face. She's absolutely adorable.

"Funny meeting you here."

"I could say the same for you. Do you come here often?"

I inch closer to her when she goes to move, afraid she's going to fall over. "Are you using cheesy pickup lines on me?"

"Do you want to be picked up?" She winks, or at least I think it's a wink, but both of her eyes flutter closed.

See? Adorable.

"This is my first time here." Although I'm completely sober, I lean against the same wall, a mere two feet from her, and rest my head at the same angle as hers, hoping it will make it easier for her to focus on my face.

"You won me a unicorn today."

"I did. Do you like it?"

"Love it." The words come out breathy, and it's my turn to be enthralled when she licks her lips.

"I just came up to use the bathroom. Are you having fun with your friend?"

"She fell asleep. Pregnancy is exhausting."

"I remember you telling me that. I think napping became a staple in your life."

"We have a baby together."

"We do," I agree. "The most amazing little boy ever."

God, if she keeps staring at my mouth, I can't be responsible for my actions.

"Don't try to go down those stairs alone."

"I'm hungry."

"Let me use the bathroom, and I'll help you."

"Okay."

"Iz, don't try to walk down the stairs. You might fall."

She nods her head in agreement, but when I turn to go into the bathroom, she follows me.

I don't have the chance to even turn on the light before she's crowding me. With my back to the vanity, I have nowhere to go, not that I want to get away from her in the first place.

"I can't believe you just showed up in my life again. Knocking on the door with a pile of gifts."

"Iz, I—"

"Shh." Her fingers smell like tangy tequila and limes when she presses them to my lips. "Looking hotter than I ever remember, muscles pulling your t-shirt tight. It's not fair."

"I didn't do—" I attempt to talk against her fingers but she presses harder. Her body is close, nearly touching mine, and I have to grip the edge of the sink to keep from grabbing her hips and pulling her even closer.

"I can't listen to my heart." She closes the distance, smiling when I groan. "All I can hear is my body, and what it's telling me I need."

"I—" She shuts me up this time with a kiss.

Her tongue, spicy from the alcohol she's been drinking, is the best thing I've ever tasted as it brushes against mine. I'm drunk on her, intoxicated with the whimpers she's forcing me to swallow because she's trying to dive deeper as if her one and only goal is to climb inside of me. Doesn't she know she already lives there? Right in the middle of me, owning every cell of my body.

"Iz," I whisper when she repositions, her lips slick and sliding against mine.

"Want you," she pants, her hand finding mine.

I attempt to tangle our fingers, but she has other plans, moving my hand to the center of her. Her heat is nearly enough to fry my brain, but her decisions aren't her own right now. If I didn't taste tequila on her lips, if she hadn't come here with the intent to get drunk because she couldn't handle spending the day with me, things would be different.

If she were sober, I'd have her in my arms, legs around my waist, my cock reminding her just how good it is between us.

But she's drunk, and her regret in the morning isn't something I think I'd survive.

"Izzy."

"Mmm." Her hips circle, the slickness of her arousal soaking through her thin panties, and I think I've earned hero status when I pull my hand away instead of sliding the silky fabric to the side and giving her exactly what she's begging for.

"Isabella." I pull my hand away.

Her eyes snap open, throat working on a swallow, and I can see the embarrassment trying to creep red and hot on her cheeks.

"Again?" she hisses, and I have to grip her hips to keep her from pulling completely away from me. "If you're rejecting me again, I'll never forgive you this time."

"Iz." I press my mouth to hers, a quick soft kiss to let her know I'm not going anywhere. "I want you. I've never wanted anything more in my life. Feel this?"

I grind my hips against her, the pressure against my cock nearly unbearable.

"Don't ever doubt it again, but you've been drinking, and I can't risk the regret you'll have tomorrow. It'll compromise what I have with Andy, and I can't do that. I can't lose him."

Tell her you don't want to lose her either.

But I can't because it's not like I have her. Right now she may be in my arms, her body demanding things from me, but she mentioned not listening to her heart, and that means she isn't fully on board. Satisfying carnal needs right now isn't the same thing as earning her forgiveness and having her love.

"You really love him," she whispers.

"Of course I do."

"You said you didn't want him."

Her bringing up that stupid fucking letter has the power to break me. "I was in a really dark place. I didn't know if I was going to survive. I was facing six years, and I didn't want yours or Andy's life to suffer because of me. I thought cutting ties would be best for everyone, and it killed me to put those lies on paper."

She looks away, her eyes blinking rapidly. I can't tell if she doesn't believe me or if my truth is just too much for her to handle right now. This isn't a conversation we should be having when she may not remember it in the morning.

"The letters you sent, the pictures, all the updates, I lived for those. Knowing he was doing well kept me alive. It gave me something to live for. Knowing I had a little boy out there with my name made me fight harder, work harder, do whatever I could to get back to him as fast as I could."

"All for Andy."

I press my palm to the back of her head, turning it so she has to look at me. "And you, Iz. For the two of you."

I press my mouth to hers one more time, relishing in the touch of our lips together because I know it may be the very last time.

"If you feel this way, if you still want your body pressed to mine like this, want my lips on you, my mouth tasting every inch of your skin in the morning when you sober up, all you have to do is let me know, but if your heart isn't involved, if you don't want a future with me, then I think it's best we keep things like they are. I won't survive getting another taste and not having all of you."

How I walk away from her, leaving her in the bathroom alone, I'll never know.

Chapter 41

Isabella

"You look like you've had better days." There's humor in Drew's voice, but I don't smile.

Holding my arm up to shield my eyes, I try to see his face, but the sun behind him is too powerful.

"I overindulged," I complain as he shifts on his feet. "Are you coming in?"

"Want me to just plow over you?"

"Plow something," I mutter as I stand to the side.

"What was that?"

"Nothing. Andy is in the playpen in the living room. He's been going like a cyclone since I got home twenty minutes ago. I hope you brought your A game."

"Always."

I close the door behind us.

"Home alone?"

"Dad, Gigi, and the kids went across the street."

I don't exactly hate being here alone with him, but it gives us the opportunity to talk about what happened last night, and despite wanting to have been too drunk to remember, I wasn't. I remember the words, the emotion in his voice, the way his hands felt on me, mouth on mine. All of it. Like it's been seared into my brain.

Although I can remember, I'm not physically able to hash it all out again. I'm exhausted, my mouth still doesn't taste right after brushing my teeth, and Andy seems hellbent on using a week's worth of energy all before naptime.

"If you don't mind, I have some things around the house to take care of."

He watches my face as I run my fingers through my hair.

"Are you avoiding me as a whole or just avoiding what happened last night?"

I blink up at him. "That's rude."

"Really?"

"It's courteous to ignore what people did while they were buzzed."

"Drunk," he corrects.

"Buzzed," I say again. "And it's not that I want to avoid it, but I have a headache, and I'm in desperate need of a shower."

"I'll help Andy use up some of his energy. You go take care of yourself."

Jesus, does he know what saying that does to my body, what I *need* to take care of?

"I'll be upstairs." I point as if the simple words won't compute for him.

I don't look back, but I can feel his eyes on me all the way up to the second level. A masculine chuckle follows me into my room.

Not only do I need a shower, but I have a million other things I've put off doing all week. I flit around my room, thankful my stomach is holding steady and not threatening to revolt, cleaning and straightening. I won't want to have to do this once I'm clean, but it doesn't make the tasks any easier.

Every so often, Andy's giggles float up the stairs, making me smile. Drew's deep voice changes tone as they play, and I realize I've become accustomed to hearing him in this house playing with his son. It's natural, him being around, being a part of both our lives. The shock is that I want this. I want him in the same space. I want to build a life with him.

I rejected the idea outright last night when he said what he said, but the longer I let the idea ruminate, the more I can see us together, raising Andy as a couple and not just two people co-parenting the same amazing little human.

It's still on my mind, the conversation we had in the dark last night, the way he used his words instead of trying to tell me what he felt with his body. He stopped me from climbing him like a tree although he was rock solid, his body ready to give me what I was close to begging him for.

He could've easily lifted me, slid into me.

But he didn't.

Drew O'Neil took the higher road, and as bitter as I was last night, going into Sophia's guest bedroom with an ache between my thighs, I know he made the right call. Having sex last night would've clouded everything else.

Well, despite the headache still teasing the corners of my head, the sexual fog has mostly lifted, and I know I want him, all of him, not just the amazing sex we have together.

As if a weight has been lifted from my shoulders with the realization, I feel lighter on my feet as I head into the bathroom, stripping my clothes off as I go. Since a shower seems like too much work, I run water in the tub, washing my face at the sink while it fills. I pop in my headphones, finding a soft playlist to listen to, no intent to get out of this tub until my mind if fully made up and my headache is gone.

I groan with deep satisfaction as I slip into the water, knowing full well there's only one reason I didn't put bubble bath or salts into the tub.

Before long, my head is spinning, fingers wandering where I knew they would end up, but my own touch has nothing on what the brush of his fingers felt like last night. He made my body come alive even with the numbing effect of the alcohol I consumed. God, what would he feel like right now with me completely sober?

Heaven, that's how because he's touched me before, his reverent fingers exploring, getting me close to the edge.

"Come for me."

His words from over two years ago still have the power to make me shudder.

It doesn't matter how many times I've tried to think of someone—anyone—else while doing this, my brain always settles back on him. Knowing he loves his son, wants more than sex from me, does something to strengthen the fantasies.

My body is humming, legs shaking with an occasional twitch I'm unable to control. A sense of naughtiness washes over me since he's right downstairs, but it also adds a little extra thrill, and my mind takes that and runs with it.

My eyes closed, lips rolling between my teeth as I concentrate on images in my mind that he's watching me, commanding every swirl of my fingers. He's telling me to wait, not yet, and my body obeys as if the words have been whispered in my ear, his breath ghosting over my exposed skin.

My nipples furl, the tease of the lapping water on them like a soft caress. Unbidden, one hand slides up, twisting one slightly, and it has the power to make me moan for him.

"Yes," I pant. "Make me come."

"Jesus."

My eyes snap open, hands rushing up to cover myself. Embarrassment pinks my cheeks, the heat making its way down the tops of my breasts. I could cry right now, watching Drew leaning against the bathroom doorframe. In my head, I wanted him to watch me, wanted his eyes on me, words commanding my moves, but the reality of it leaves me feeling exposed.

I open my mouth to ask him to leave, but I just can't seem to do it.

I know what he saw, know what he heard, and from the way he's biting his lip, I'd guess he isn't exactly upset with any of it. In fact, the bulge in his jeans answers a lot of questions.

"Enjoy the show?" I stand from the tub, water sloshing down my body, and I pause before climbing out because he seems like his eyes need a little time to assess every inch of me.

"Depends on who was in that pretty little head of yours while you were performing."

And God, I was performing, albeit a fantasy that quickly turned into reality.

"And if I said it was you?" I step over the edge of the tub, my feet sinking into the soft bathmat.

He licks his lips as I inch closer.

"You're the most beautiful woman I've ever seen." His hand goes to my cheek and the sexual need is overpowered by more emotions than I can count.

"Drew," I whisper as his lips press to mine.

"I know."

As his kiss deepens, I feel a towel wrap around my damp shoulders, the warmth cocooning me against his chest.

The tears begin to fall in earnest, but he doesn't pull back and ask me what's wrong. Letting go of the past, forgiveness, and hope for the future all hitting me at once is utterly exhausting, but instead of forcing the issue, instead of trying to tease me into the girl that was just in the tub, he carries me across the room and holds me in his arms as I cry.

Chapter 42

Drew

I press my lips to the top of her head when she shifts her weight. She's only been asleep for thirty minutes, and although she probably needs a longer nap, her body, the one trained to take care of a toddler all day, won't allow her much peace right now.

"Have a good nap?" I whisper against her hair.

She shifts and stretches, keeping her body against mine as she lifts her head to look at my face.

She's still in a towel, but I managed to tug a blanket over her back when we laid down. As much as I want her, I enjoyed the weight of her pressed to my chest for the limited time she allowed it. Now the big question is how is she going to react now?

"Where's Andy?" She looks toward the empty crib in the corner.

"Exhausted himself by playing so hard. I came up to tell you he was down for a nap." I point to the baby monitor on her dresser across the room.

I should've called out from the open bedroom door, but my cock told me to investigate the moans I'd heard. Neither he nor I were disappointed, but that doesn't mean it was any less of a violation.

"How long—"

"You've only been resting for about half an hour." I rub my hand up and down her back, wondering how long I'll get her like this before she freaks out and starts pulling away again.

"You held me while I slept?"

"I enjoyed it, but you twitch in your sleep."

She chuckles a little. "We should talk."

I swallow a lump threatening to form. "Yeah, we should."

"Maybe—" She presses her hand to my chest to get up, but I hold her tighter.

"Like this. Talk to me while we're touching."

"I, umm—"

"I'll go first." I clear my throat, wondering how far I can get into this conversation before my emotions start leaking out of my eyes.

"I want you," she says before I can speak again. "I *need* you."

"Do you still love me?" We never said the words to each other, but I could see it in her eyes, feel it in her touch before I went away.

Her breathing goes a little ragged, and I fear I pushed her too far too fast.

"I'm so sorry for distancing myself from you before I left. I regretted it while it was happening. I wrote that letter, and I know it hurt you. I won't deny that was my intent at the time, but it came from a place deep inside of me that didn't want to see you lonely. I thought a little heartache at the beginning would be better than years of pain while I was locked up. Just know that hurting you, shattered me as well. I didn't write it with a smile on my face. It took me weeks to get those thoughts down on paper and by the time I wrote it, I hated myself so much for what I was doing to you."

"Drew."

"No, listen. If you're going to push me away, if you think you can't do this or you just don't want me, I want you to make the decision with all the information, not just some and whatever assumptions you've concocted in that beautiful head of yours."

Did she just hold me a little tighter? God, the possibilities.

"That night we met, I knew something was different about you. At the time I figured it was just attraction, and that turned into the burning chemistry that led us to where we ended up that night, but there was a hole in my chest not long after you left. I chalked it up to great sex, thinking it would fade, but it didn't. I yearned for you, ached to spend more time with you. Then the accident happened and everything went to hell. Then by some miracle, here you were, happy, healthy, carrying my child, and that threw me for another loop. I kept my distance because I knew you could do better, knew you would be better off without a felon in your life. I thought our son could have a better life if I wasn't in it. And all of that may be true." I hold her face until she's looking at me. "Call me selfish, but I don't want you to do better than me. I can't offer you riches and a huge house. I'm probably not going to be able to pay cash for a brand-new truck for Andy when he turns sixteen, but know that I will love you with every inch of my heart if you'll let me."

Tears streak her cheeks, and her eyes flutter when my thumbs sweep them away.

"I don't deserve you, but I want you anyway. I want you and Andy and a family. I want all of it, but if you're not ready, I'll wait however long it takes for you to get there with me. But if you can't, if you don't think it's possible, then I need you to tell me now. So I'll ask again. Isabella Montoya, do you still love me?"

"I f-feel like it's too much."

Is it possible for a broken heart to break even more?

"Like it's too soon. I question whether I'm crazy or listening to the wrong parts of me, but God, Drew, I love you. I want what you want, but this isn't just about me. We have to worry about Andy's well-being and what's best for him."

"You love me?"

"I said more than that," she whispers. "Are you only hearing what you want to hear?"

"I heard you say you love me, and if you love me only half as much as I love you, then everything is going to work out. We made an amazing little boy, Iz, and he's only going to reap the benefits from both of his parents being together."

"Together," she whispers as if the declaration wasn't going to lead us to that point.

"Yeah." I press my lips to hers. "I know there are things I have to make up for, time I lost, and things that may have happened while I was away that I'll have to deal with, but if you tell me you want the entire package, you're stuck with me."

"I want all of it," she says, her mouth hovering over mine, and it makes me question whether or not I'm dreaming. I've only been back several weeks, and right where I'd hoped I'd be the day those prison gates swung open and released me.

"Are you only doing this because you think two parents for Andy are better than one?"

She shakes her head. "No. I want this too."

"Final answer?"

"Will you just kiss me already?"

I don't make her wait for the answer. I cover her mouth with mine and kiss her silly. Then Andy's whimpers come through the baby monitor, putting a stop to where I was nearly willing to take things. That would not be a very fun conversation to have with her dad had they happened to come home. And although my nuts are blue, I'm happy that we were given a little bit of a distraction.

Going down and taking care of our son doesn't stop the saucy looks the little vixen is giving me. Her dad takes one look at the two of us when they get back home, and all he does is slap me on the back like it's a congratulations and walks out of the room.

Chapter 43

Isabella

"You are."

"I am not," I hiss, looking around my room paranoid as if someone can hear what Sophia is saying on the other end of the line.

"It's a dick appointment. Just admit it. You want me to watch Andy for a couple hours so you can get some dick."

"Would you hush! It's lunch."

"Lunch doesn't take four hours. Just admit it's a dick appointment and I'll keep him overnight for you."

"It's not—wait, all night?"

Her knowing chuckle makes me smile.

"Is that a confession?"

"Do you know how hard it is to get time alone with him? It's like Dad knows, and he's purposely cockblocking us."

"I'll watch him… for your dick appointment."

"I—it's just lunch."

"With a side of dick."

"God willing," I mutter.

Drew seems to be fine with spending time with both of us, but I'm going crazy. We've started and stopped so many times over the last week, I think I'm going crazy, and getting off with each other while on the phone late at night isn't the same.

Her laugh comes through the line.

"Glad you think this is funny."

"I'm just happy you two got your heads out of your asses and are finally together. You know if you moved in together, you wouldn't have to schedule time in a hotel."

"That's crazy. Don't you think it's too soon for that?"

"You guys love each other and you have a child together. I'd say that time came a long time ago."

Silence fills the line.

"Iz? No one is going to fault you for following your heart."

She'd said as much the night I was drinking at her house, but I didn't want to listen then. I'm all ears now. We haven't exactly announced that we're together, but we also haven't avoided being seen holding hands and whispering to each other while people are around. I haven't noticed any weird looks, or whispers about me being a fool. Everyone at Cerberus loves Drew.

"I know," I tell her. "And thank you for watching Andy. We'll drop him off soon."

When I get off the phone with her, I check my hair and makeup one last time before heading downstairs. Drew smiles up at me, his eyes roving from the tips of my sandaled feet to my eyes.

"Wow, Iz."

He presses his lips to my forehead when I get close enough.

"What are you wearing under that dress?"

"Nothing," I whisper, smiling inside when a shudder runs through him.

"He's all ready to go," Gigi says as she carries Andy into the room.

"Dad!" our son yelps the second he lays eyes on Drew.

He smiles just as wide as he did the first time four days ago when Andy called him that. The sight of the tears shining in his eyes that day told me I'd made the right decision. We have a lot of pain to overcome, but I wasn't lying when I told Sophia I forgave him long ago.

After both Dad and Apollo showed me the letters he wrote to them, I fully understood what I meant to him. The only thing that makes me pause is knowing all that pain was for nothing. I never stopped loving him, and despite his hateful words, they came from a place of love as well.

"Are you ready to go see Aunt Sophia?" Drew asks, his fingers tickling Andy's ribs.

Our son wiggles in his arms, a laugh so pure and sweet coming from his smiling mouth.

"Have a good time at lunch," Gigi says as we make our way to the door. "Use protection!"

We both shake our heads as we walk out, Drew grumbling something about not being hungry for food as we load Andy up in his truck.

***

"This can't be right," Drew mumbles as he leans forward to look out the windshield. "This is the right address for the restaurant."

With the last right turn, we arrive at the front of a hotel.

His eyes dart in my direction. "Izzy?"

"I mean—" Heat flushes my face. "They have room service."

He licks his lips as if the idea is enticing.

"A hotel room? For four hours?"

"Sophia said she'd keep him all night."

"It's eleven in the morning."

"I got early check-in, but we can go to lunch first if you prefer, I mean, if you want to even stay here."

"Want to?" He scoffs, his hands working the steering wheel until he's parked. "I'm dying to spend a little alone time with you."

We're giggling like two teens about to get into trouble as we make our way inside. Check-in takes longer than I would have liked, but just swinging by and picking up keys would be too long.

"If they have a smart TV, we can finish watching that movie we started last night."

I have no interest in finishing the movie that put me to sleep after ten minutes.

"We can even watch—"

I press my lips to his the second he opens the door. "No TV."

"Okay," he says against my lips, gasping when my fingers immediately reach for the button on his jeans. "Not wasting any time, I see."

"Nope."

My dress comes off over my head, me slipping out of it as I lower to my knees.

"God, this isn't going to last. Don't want to come in your mouth, Izzy."

"Then you better show a little restraint," I tell him, my mouth wrapping around his length the second I free him from his boxers.

"Jesus!" The hissed curse makes me smile, my tongue licking the underside of him.

"Feel good?"

He makes a sound from deep in his chest, his fingers tangling in my hair. Long eyelashes flutter on his cheeks as he looks down at me.

"So fucking good. Do that again."

I do my best not to gag, but fail when I take him deeper. He doesn't seem to mind as his hips rock forward and back several times.

"Seriously, woman. I'm fixing to embarrass myself."

He pops free, his thumb rubbing over my bottom lip.

"I love my cock in your mouth, but I've waited so long for you."

He reaches for me, and I stand as his hands flutter down my sides.

"I can't believe you didn't wear anything under that dress."

Rough fingers tease my nipples, and he seems just fine with taking his time. Each brush, every breath he breathes over my skin ignites different parts of my body that by the time he takes a step back, I'm an inferno, burning up from the inside out.

"I can't believe you're still wearing clothes," I whisper, my fingers teasing the hem of his shirt.

That's all it takes for him to strip, unceremoniously throwing his clothes in all directions.

His cock, thick and proud points at me, and I'm unable to resist wrapping my hands around him. He groans, the sound hitting me right at my center.

"Did you bring condoms?" he asks, his throat working like he's unwilling to go all-in right now if I didn't.

"In my purse."

He attacks the thing, turning back with a smile at the box in his hands. "Twelve? Think it'll be enough?"

"Promises, promises," I say, crooking my finger to draw him closer.

He winks, tossing the full box on the bed before lifting me off my feet. My sandals drop to the floor, leaving us both fully nude and ready for each other. He brushes against my core, the plush head of his cock a tease of epic proportions before he settles me on the bed and hovers over me.

"Wanna make you come." I grab his head before he can start kissing down my throat.

"I will. Please, Drew."

His fingers shake as he opens the box, tearing one foil square from the rest.

"And you're sure about this?"

I look between my legs. I'm glistening, spread open wide, and he's asking this now?

"Yes," I pant. "Please."

He leans over, mouth on mine as his fingers brush over me, testing my readiness. I swallow his groan when he finds his answer.

"Waited so long. Fuck," he moans when he pushes in the first inch. "Every dream, every fantasy. God, I never got it right. So much better than I remember. Jesus, Izzy. Like a fucking glove."

He finds a rhythm, his hips moving with perfect precision as he kisses me.

When we came together like this in his room that one time, I only thought he was speaking with his body. Having heard the words, knowing he loves me makes this time so much better.

"Come for me."

God, those three words from his mouth again.

My fingers dig into his back, urging him on, and before I can open my mouth to say the words, I'm falling apart, coming, the orgasm so strong my body quakes from it.

He groans, his cock spasming inside of me, and holds me tighter, his breathing making rushing sounds in my ears.

"Forever, Iz. I'm going to love you for the rest of my fucking life."

"Same," I manage because my brain hasn't come completely back online. "Ready for round two?"

His laugh echoes off the walls as he rolls over, and after he discards the condom, I'm back against his chest, his fingers tangled in my hair.

"Can we have a serious discussion?"

I smile against his chest but decide to tease him anyway.

"Is this where you break up with me?"

He huffs, knowing I'm not serious.

"This is where I ask you about the future."

"Which part?"

"The part where we live together, where we're a family and where we get to hold each other all night every night. The part where you're on birth control or want another baby and I can fill you with my cum every chance we can get."

I smile. "There's a lot to unpack there."

"I know." He holds me tighter.

"I can get on birth control, but I don't think another kid is a smart idea right now. At least until I finish school."

"Good point."

"And the house together? I was planning to ask you the same thing."

"Really?"

I chuckle at his surprise. "Of course. I can't live with my dad forever, and since you have that stupid no-sex-in-his-house rule, then I think it's best."

"You want to move out just so we can have sex."

"That's not the only reason, but it's one hell of a good one, don't you think?"

He kisses me, his hands holding my face as if he thinks I'm going to disappear. "You're making all of my dreams come true, Isabella."

I smile into the kiss, knowing he's making my dreams come true as well.

Chapter 44

Drew
Months Later

"That's not it. That one." I point to the clear bottle of Pedialyte.

"Unflavored?" Jinx scrunches his nose. "That's gross."

"Maybe she's going to mix something else in it?"

"Maybe Izzy is out of it from being up all night with a sick kid? There's no way she wanted unflavored. That's made for sick dogs or something. Grape is always better. That's what I'm getting for River."

"She asked for the clear."

"Maybe you need to get some of each just in case."

"Probably," I sigh, my hands once again rubbing my tired eyes. "Where do you think the kids got it from?"

Andy, River, Cooper, Amelia and Jamie have all had a stomach virus for the last day and a half. The entire club—all but Apollo because he's a pussy and throws up at just the sound of someone else gagging—has come together to help take care of the kids.

We still haven't gotten any sleep, both Izzy and I staying awake just to watch and make sure our son is going to be okay.

"That freaking satanic nursery school."

I chuckle, exhaustion deep in my bones. "The one at the church?"

He glares at me. "River is spewing like that kid from the *Exorcist*. All of the children have been infected with a demon."

I don't argue with him. Apparently, he hasn't had much sleep either.

"Cooper doesn't even know he's going to be sick. One minute he's fine, wanting to get up and play and the next he's erupting on the bed like a volcano."

I cringe, picturing that exact same thing happening to Izzy and me last night.

"We almost ended up in the hospital last night," I confess.

"For real?"

"We gave Andy a popsicle, just to get fluids in him. Big mistake. He got sick. We thought he was puking up blood."

"Popsicle was red?" I nod. "We did that the first time River got a stomach bug. All three of us freaked out."

"Okay," I say, looking down at the list in his hands. "What else do we need—"

"Daddy!"

We both turn to see a pale-haired boy running in our direction. He hits Jinx's legs, arms up high waving in the air.

"Daddy!"

Jinx picks the kid up, but I've never seen this child in my life. Telling from the look on Jinx's face, he hasn't either.

"Hey, buddy. Where's your momma?" The little boy turns in Jinx's arms and points.

A woman, flustered and breathing hard walks toward us, a little girl on her hip.

"Please, just—" she glances over her shoulder. "Just go along with it."

Jinx nods, but his eyes stay over her shoulder for a second as another man approaches slowly.

"Hey, honey," the woman says enthusiastically, moving her head to press her lips to Jinx's cheek.

Jinx, being the dirty dog he is, turns his head, meeting her lips instead. I may be delusional from lack of sleep, but I swear I see him slip her some tongue. The woman continues to cling to him, going so far as to lift up on her toes when he makes to pull away.

When they do finally split apart, Jinx wraps his arms around her waist. They'd look like an all-American perfect couple, her in her sleek looking business suit, two kids, one boy, one girl, if it weren't for Jinx's unkempt beard and leather cut.

"How was your day, gorgeous?" He whispers low to her ear as the other man finally makes it to us.

"Reagan?"

"Oh! Brian? Is that you?"

The other man frowns.

"Meet my husband—"

"Miles Alexander," Jinx says, giving his real name instead of his club one, pulling his arm from around the woman's back to shake the stranger's hand

"Brian Wakefield. Reagan, you have kids?"

"*We* have kids," Jinx answers, resituating the kid better on his hip.

"With a biker?" Brian asks stupidly. "I bet your dad loves that."

"It was nice seeing you, Brian, but we need to get back home. The kids aren't feeling well." As if to prove her statement, she points to the basket filled with soups, juices and Pedialyte.

"Yeah, okay." He runs his hand over the back of his neck before finally walking away.

"What's for dinner, sweetheart?" Jinx's question is a purr, and the innuendo is so thick around us, I feel like I'm interrupting something.

"I… umm… I'm so sorry about that. You know how exes are. Come on Elijah. We need to go."

The little boy wiggles to get down, but he turns to wave before falling in step with his mother. "Bye, Daddy!"

Stunned we watch them walk away.

"Who the fuck was that?" I ask. "Do you know that woman?"

"Never seen her before in my life, but for real, man, I'm already in fucking love."

I shake my head, pulling two of each flavor of the electrolyte drink from the shelf and dropping them in the shopping cart. Jinx is still staring off in the distance like he's waiting for her to reappear.

Jinx

Copyright

Jinx: Cerberus MC Book 16
Copyright © 2021 Marie James
Editing by Marie James Betas & Ms. K Edits
EBooks are not transferrable. All rights are reserved. No part of this book may be used or reproduced in any manner without written permission, except in the case of brief quotations embodied in critical articles and reviews. The unauthorized reproduction or distribution of this copyrighted work is illegal. No part of this book may be scanned, uploaded, or distributed via the Internet or any other means, electronic or print, without the publisher's permission.
This book is a work of fiction. The names, characters, places, and incidents are products of the writer's imagination or have been used fictitiously and are not to be construed as real. Any resemblance to persons, living or dead, actual events, locale, or organizations is entirely coincidental.

Synopsis

Fake relationships have no place in an adult's life.
Until they do.
It was one kiss.
One trick to convince her ex she's in a happy relationship.
One kiss is all it took.
Captivated isn't a strong enough word.
Haunted is a little closer.
Obsessed fits the bill.
I'm obsessed with Reagan Dunn.
Only Reagan isn't looking for that happy relationship.
Until she needs me to pretend again.
Pretending is perfect.
Pretending gets me closer.
It gives me the opportunity to prove that we are the perfect combination.

Chapter 1

Jinx

"You don't have to pull that weapon out of your arsenal," I tease, but River's bottom lip continues to wobble as fresh tears roll down his cheeks. "It's okay."

Before I can carry the little guy to the bathroom, he starts to gag again. At least this time, we make it to the toilet before he gets sick again. I pat his little back, doing my best to ignore the stench of vomit on my clothes.

He sobs as he pukes. It isn't the first time he has suffered from a stomach virus, but he doesn't seem to remember being like this before. I know he's very confused about what's going on. He only wants to watch television and eat breakfast, but he can't keep anything down.

"Incoming!"

River seems to be finished—thank goodness—so I pull him out of the way just in time for Drew to hang his son, Andy, over the toilet.

I grin as he turns his head, gagging at the sounds his son makes.

"Where are they hiding all of it?" Drew complains before gagging once again.

"At least it's only—" My mouth snaps shut when River's stomach gurgles. "Oh hell."

"Is that—?"

I nod. "Things are about to get worse."

Both boys are still in diapers—River closer to being potty trained than Andy, who is nine months younger—which I guess is a good thing, but that only applies if they hold up to what's about to happen.

Andy whimpers, spit dripping from his chin, and I wet two washrags, handing one off to Drew after ringing them out in the sink. We wipe the boys' faces, and I force myself to think back to the good times when my son wasn't sick, when making sure I tire him out with games and fun activities before bed was all I had to worry about.

No one talks about these times, the hours spent worrying about illness and showering in cold water because those helping had already encountered their dose of toddler puke and got to clean up first. No one talks about the cramps in your arms from rubbing whimpering little backs, or irritated skin from scrubbing your child's breakfast out of the living room carpet. People keep all of that a secret because who would want to have children if it was spoken of? I'd never wish away my son, but fuck, this is the worst.

"I need help," Drew says, but he's not complaining, merely admitting defeat. "Come on, big guy. Let's go find Mommy."

River blinks up at me, tears staining his chubby face.

"You'll be okay," I promise, but at the same time I wonder if I will be.

River's eyes dart to my shirt before looking back up at me. He points, his little nose scrunching up.

"Yeah, buddy. I know. I'll get cleaned up soon."

"How's he doing?" I sigh in relief at the sound of Simone's voice from the doorway.

"I'd say better, but I thought that twenty minutes ago. On a side note, chicken nuggets were a bad idea."

She sighs, and I know that sound. I'm very familiar with her irritation today. Normally, she's pretty laid back, but we're all exhausted, and her ability to let things slide vanished about three hours ago.

"Saltines and flat lemon-lime soda," she sighs, holding her hands out for me to pass River to her.

"I know," I grumble. "But he wanted chicken nuggets."

"Who's the adult?" Her eyes betray her snarkiness, still shining even though they're puffy.

"Today is one of the times I wish I wasn't," I say as I pull my soiled t-shirt over my head. "I need to shower. Did you leave me any hot water this time?"

I honestly feel like we should all be wearing hazmat suits because showering four times a day is absurd.

"There was some left when I got out, but Callum was still in the shower."

I frown at the mention of my best friend, Rocker. Even though he and Simone have been together for a while, they're incapable of keeping their hands to themselves. If they showered together, then the chances of getting even lukewarm water are minimal.

"We're in the middle of a crisis," I hiss, but feel no real animosity. "What's that?"

Simone covers the fresh red mark on her neck before I can even point to it.

"Stress relief," she mutters, a small smile playing on her lips.

"And what about me?" I tease, my eyebrows jumping suggestively as I unzip my jeans and drop them to the floor.

Once upon a time, Simone, Rocker, and I had a wild night of drunken debauchery. That's how River came to be. It was a hard-fought battle, but Simone and Rocker ended up together, and I get to be a dad without the true headache of baby-momma drama. We all live together, and since it's all he's known, River hasn't blinked an eye at having one mom and two dads. I'm sure there will be questions later on as he gets older, but for now, everything is perfect. Well, as perfect as things can be in the middle of a stomach virus episode.

"What about you?" Simone asks, her eyes staying on mine despite the fact that I'm standing in the middle of the bathroom in nothing but my boxers.

"I'm stressed."

"Okayyy." She rubs River's back as he drops his exhausted head to her shoulder.

"How about a little stress relief?" My eyebrows start working again, but she's unfazed.

"Are you trying to entice my woman?" Rocker says, his head popping up over her shoulder.

"Are you worried?"

"Not in the least," he says as his arms circle around both her and River. He presses a soft kiss to the top of my son's head, and God, I'm the luckiest man in the world.

Having a friend who loves your child is great. Having a friend that loves your child like he's his own? That's a joy not many people get to experience. I know Rocker would lay down his life for River, and I'd do the same for their other son, Cooper.

"You say that, but she won't stop staring at my—" I point to my dick, unwilling to say the word in front of River despite the tiny snores coming from him.

Simone cocks a disinterested eyebrow, her eyes darting to my waist when I shove my boxers to my ankles. My dick doesn't even twitch, and I know it's because I'm exhausted. Simone is Rocker's woman, but she's drop-dead gorgeous. Normally—although I'd never cross that line again, unless they begged—I'd be aroused with any attention. There's been too much going on for my dick to even take notice of her perusal. We're both drained—my cock and me.

"Would you stop staring at it," I complain. "You're making me feel inferior."

Rocker chuckles before pressing a kiss to Simone's forehead and walking away.

"Drew is going to go to the store. I gave him a list but wanted to see if there's anything you want added to it."

"Tell him to wait a few minutes, and I'll go with him."

Her eyes narrow, and I know it's impossible to pull one over on her, but I need a fucking break. I've been puked on twice already, and it's not even noon. If she gets shower sex and orgasms, the least I can have is an hour away from gagging noises. Plus, I hear River's stomach grumble. I know what's coming. I'm going to avoid that shitty situation as much as possible.

"Didn't you say that Gigi was coming over with Amelia and Jamie?" I ask as I pull back the shower curtain and turn on the water, thanking every deity in the universe for the warmth cascading over my hand.

"I think they're going to quarantine at home," she answers as I step over the tub ledge, groaning in relief as the water sluices down my body.

"Just tell him I'll go with him."

She sighs but eventually agrees before walking out of the bathroom.

My shower is quick because I wouldn't put it past her to rush Drew out the front door, so I'm stuck here in misery with her and Rocker.

My hair is still damp when I walk into the living room with my socks and shoes hanging from my fingertips. Drew is still here, but he gives me a look that tells me to hurry the hell up before one or more of the kids get sick again.

"How's Cooper doing?" I ask as I plop down on the sofa to put my shoes on.

"So far so good," Rocker says as he hands River a lidded cup. "But it's going to happen."

"We were talking about all staying here until they're better, then going next door while this house is cleaned," Simone says.

"That sounds like a plan. We have plenty of room." Izzy, Drew's woman, gives me a weak smile as I agree.

"You ready?" Drew asks as he inches toward the door.

"You have the list?" Izzy asks, and Drew holds up his phone.

"I got it. Just text if you can remember anything else."

Drew presses a kiss to Izzy's forehead, and as much as I know he's ready for a break, he looks as equally concerned with leaving them here while we head to the store.

I ruffle River's hair as he stares glossy-eyed at the television before I walk out the front door. Drew offers to drive, and I don't argue. Maybe I can get a little nap on the way.

Chapter 2

Reagan

"We're only here to get something for dinner," I warn when I look in the rearview mirror and my son's eyes light up at seeing the grocery store.

"Juice!" he says with a wide smile.

"And juice," I mumble, gearing up to shop with two kids.

I want to get in and get out, but that's always an impossibility with kids who think they need to touch everything in the store. Mom normally helps, watching them when I have to run errands, but she had an appointment this afternoon. I'm grateful for the help I get with Elijah and Katie. Some single mothers don't ever get a break. I'm able to go to work without the worry of daycare expenses because my mother keeps them.

"One juice," I bargain as I slide out of the car and go to Katie's side first. If I pulled Elijah out of his booster seat, my three-year-old son would dart off. I've had to chase him down enough to learn from experience. Now getting him inside and strapped into a shopping cart will be the challenge. The child wants to be free to explore, and of course wraps his little arms around every snack that comes in his line of sight. I thought boys ate a bunch when they got older, but this kid is already a bottomless pit.

"Straight into a cart," I tell Elijah as I re-adjust my one-year-old on my hip before unbuckling him. I wait for the nod of agreement, but I know better. He's only placating me.

I grip his little hand as he jumps down out of my car, holding tight so the little escape artist can't get away.

He's anxious to get inside, and I let him drag me in that direction. Even playing at the park after my half day of work didn't use a fraction of his endless energy.

"Wait," I urge as he tugs harder, trying to pull me away from the line of shopping carts near the front door.

"Reagan?"

I freeze at the sound of a voice I never thought I'd hear again. I refuse to turn around. If I ignore him, maybe he'll just disappear. I was never good enough for Brian Wakefield. It didn't matter that we were both in law school, or that my grades were better than his by a full letter. His family had more money, more opportunities to offer him. I came from a lower middle-class family and fought tooth and nail to get a scholarship to college. He had the world handed to him, uninterested that the free time I had after studying was spent working so I didn't have to go into debt. He thought he owned my time then, and will no doubt have the same attitude now.

In an effort to get away faster, I release Elijah's hand to place Katie in the front part of the shopping cart. Of course, my son seizes the opportunity to run away.

"Elijah!" I hiss, shuffling after him.

I can't waste a second loading Katie into the cart, so I hitch her up on my hip and take after him.

"Daddy!" he yells, and I have to sigh.

He's done this—running up to a strange man in public—three other times in the last couple of weeks. I didn't know not having a father figure in his life would cause problems so early, but here we are.

"Daddy!"

I look up at the guy, wondering if he's going to be an asshole like the last one was, but this guy doesn't cringe away like my son has a disease.

Bright hazel eyes look down at Elijah as my son lifts his arms up. Without pause, the dark-haired man scoops him up and expertly places him on his hip.

"Reagan?"

Shit! In my effort to chase down my escapee, I somehow managed to forget all about Brian.

The leather-cut-wearing man smiles as I approach, and I have a decision to make. Do I apologize for my kid, or do I do something crazy to make Brian get the hint that I don't want to speak with him?

"Please, just—" I glance over my shoulder to see Brian closing in fast. "Just go along with it."

He looks behind me and must catch my meaning because he gives me the faintest nod.

I'm a little floored with how handsome he is. As far as fake daddies go, Elijah couldn't have picked a better subject.

"Hey, honey," I say, trying to get into character as I brush my lips against his cheek.

Instead of my lips hitting his cheek, his mouth meets mine. He doesn't stop there. With my son in his arms and Katie propped on my hip, this guy urges my mouth open. My eyes widen in utter surprise when his tongue swipes mine.

Did I just moan?

God, I must be starved for a man's attention because I don't pull away. If anything, I take a half step closer as he teases my mouth with expert precision. I lift up on my toes, needing more when he pulls his mouth away.

Five seconds and I'm a breathless mess. It isn't until he's smiling down at me that I realize I've wrapped my free arm around his waist, and I'm holding him tight.

He groans, teeth scraping over his wet bottom lip, and I don't know if it's in irritation or approval, but it sobers me a little.

Before I can pull completely away and apologize, the man wraps his arm around me, effectively pulling me into him. We each have a kid on opposite hips when Brian inches closer. Confusion draws his brows in before he speaks.

"How was your day, gorgeous?" the stranger asks, his warm breath ghosting over my ear that sends a shiver over my entire body, igniting hormones I've managed to ignore for quite some time.

"Reagan?"

I swallow. "Oh! Brian? Is that you?"

My old flame frowns, his eyes darting up to the man I just locked lips with.

"Meet my husband—"

"Miles Alexander," the guy says, not missing a beat.

He pulls his arm from behind my waist and offers his hand to Brian. I miss the warmth of him immediately.

"Brian Wakefield," he says with a hint of disbelief. "Reagan, you have kids?"

"*We* have kids," Miles answers as he readjusts a wiggling Elijah on his hip.

"With a biker?" Brian asks stupidly, as if the man in question isn't standing right in front of him. Leave it to this jerk to dismiss anyone he doesn't deem worthy of his attention. It seems nothing has changed in the four years since I saw him last. "I bet your dad loves that."

The mention of my father angers me. Brian was such a huge part of my life in college, but there's no reason he should know that my dad died a couple of years ago. His lack of intel makes me hate him a little more than I already did.

"It was nice seeing you, Brian, but we need to get back home. The kids aren't feeling well." Without giving Brian any further explanation to his rude questions, I point to the basket filled with soups, juices, and Pedialyte in front of Miles's friend.

"Yeah, okay." Brian runs his hand over the back of his neck, looking like he wants to keep interrogating me, but eventually he walks away.

"What's for dinner, sweetheart?" Miles purrs in my ear, and until this second, I didn't realize he stepped in even closer to me.

His nearness speaks of intimacy, but my cheeks flame with embarrassment. Never in my life have I walked up to a stranger to speak with him, much less kissed a man I didn't at least have a brief conversation with.

"I... umm... I'm so sorry about that. You know how exes are. Come on, Elijah. We need to go."

Anxious to get his promised juice, Elijah wiggles to get down. I grab his little hand as soon as his feet hit the floor, unwilling to let him get away from me again. Knowing my son, he'll pull the same stunt with the next guy he sees, and if Brian is still in the store, there's a chance he'll see my indiscriminate son call another man daddy. Wouldn't my ex just love that?

Before we get too far away, Elijah turns back to face Miles, waving with his free hand. "Bye, Daddy!"

I can't stay in this store. I can't run the risk of running into Miles or Brian down another aisle. One awkward situation today is enough.

"Juice!" Elijah insists as we head out the front door.

"Let's get chicken nuggets. I'll get you a juice, too."

Elijah is ecstatic with the offer, jumping into the car and trying to help with his seatbelt the second I get the door open.

Thankfully, Farmington is just big enough that I may never have to see the man again.

I've heard stories around town of men in the Cerberus MC, but I've never actually spoken to one of them. The descriptions I've overheard various women talking about don't do them justice. The guy Miles was with wasn't wearing a leather cut indicating he's in the club, but even that guy is very good looking.

As I place Katie in her car seat, I make a mental note to ask my best friend, Cassie, if she knows anything about them, although I don't think I'll ever be able to face the man again after what I just did.

Despite the heat in my face from my actions, I can't seem to keep the smile from my lips as I drive across town and get the nuggets and juice I promised Elijah.

Chapter 3

Jinx

"If we came the other day, we'd already be through all of this," I say to Simone as I lift River from his car seat.

"And like I said before leaving the house, a stomach virus isn't a reason to go to urgent care. He's been able to drink and eat."

"He pukes everything up," I counter, my eyes darting to the bag beside the car seat. I've been puked on so much, I've prepared by bringing a change of clothes in case the little volcano erupts again.

"I think they're just trading it between each other now," she explains.

"And that's your reasoning why Rocker is groaning in bed like he's dying?"

"You mean what you were doing yesterday?"

I can't meet her eyes as I cradle River's little head against my shoulder, urging him to go back to sleep.

Yeah, I got sick as a dog yesterday, and if the kids feel half as bad as I did, then urgent care was probably the best way to go. I was miserable, but at least I didn't puke on myself. I can't say the same for the fella in my arms.

"How are you not sick?" I ask as I pull open the door to the office building for her.

She shrugs. "I'm sure it's coming. I doubt I'll be able to escape unscathed."

"Holy shit," I mutter when I open the door leading to the pediatrician's office. "The entire town is here."

"I'll get him checked in," Simone mutters on a sigh, knowing that we're in for a long wait even though we have an appointment.

I want to ask everyone in here if their kids go to that Mother's Day out program at the church because I'm sure that's where our kids picked up this disgusting virus, but they all look as exhausted as I feel. One kid is gagging into a blue plastic bag on the far side of the room, and although there's an empty chair on the other side of his mother, I opt to stand.

I don't have as sensitive a stomach as Drew does, but I'm still not a hundred percent after my own encounter with whatever this virus is.

Swaying side to side when River grumbles in his sleep, I rub small circles on his back to soothe him. He was fine yesterday, but then he woke up again this morning and puked in his bed. We're all miserable, but he turned his nose up at crackers and lemon-lime soda, and we knew it was time for a doctor's visit.

"Surprisingly, they're on schedule," Simone says as she approaches me. "I bet they're going to tell us the same thing I told you. It just has to run its course."

"He's miserable," I remind her. "I don't like seeing him sick."

"None of us do."

She places her hand on the back of his head, and I know she's checking for a fever. She may pretend to be exasperated with Rocker's and my concern about the sick kids, but she's just as worried. The little guy has been sick since last Thursday. Today is Monday and enough is enough.

"I'm most worried about dehydration since he's refusing to drink."

I nod in agreement. I'd rather deal with puke than dry heaving as a man and as a father.

My eyes dart around the room, taking in the other sick kids, needing to see if any of them seem to be sicker than River. They all look miserable, their parents as equally tired, but then I see a woman I never thought I'd lay eyes on again.

Reagan, the woman from the grocery store is across the room, her glaring eyes locked on me like just the sight of me makes her want to cause bodily harm. It isn't until her gaze shifts that I realize Simone's head is leaned on my shoulder.

It isn't sexual. We have a sick kid, but I can see how this looks to an outsider. Why I care what this strange woman thinks about the two of us standing here together is beyond me, but I do. The need to explain fills my blood with urgency.

The relationship Simone, Rocker, and I have is unconventional, and although no one at the clubhouse batted an eye with how we co-parent River, people in the outside world probably wouldn't understand. Co-parenting is one thing, but living in the same house? Having conceived my son in a drunken threesome? Yeah, those details raise questions.

"Can you take him?" I ask Simone, but she waits too long to respond. "I'll be right back."

I carry River across the room, not able to lose a second of time to hand him to her.

"Hey."

Reagan continues to glare at me.

"We're not—that's not my wife. I mean. I don't have a wife. She's River's mom." I point to the sick child in my arms as if she wouldn't have seen him until he's mentioned. "He's my son, though. It's a complicated situation, but I'd like to explain how—"

Her head tilts, but the anger doesn't leave her face.

"I don't care what you have going on in your personal life," she hisses, her eyes dropping to the sleeping little girl in her lap, annoyed further that I may be the cause for her to wake her child. "You got us sick."

Now that I take a better look, I can tell her eyes are tired. She's no longer wearing a business casual suit like she was two days ago in the grocery store, but leggings and a loose shirt look great on her too.

I open my mouth to tell her such, but Elijah draws my attention.

"Daddy?" He looks green around the gills, and I instantly know that he has the same thing River has. "I don't feel good."

"I'm so sorry, buddy." I don't reach for him, although I'd like to rub his back like I've been doing for River. Him running up to me in the grocery store is different from me initiating contact with a child.

"He's sick because of you."

"I wasn't sick," I argue, but I know better. I started feeling bad not three hours after that grocery trip. "Besides, you approached me."

"You kissed me," she snaps, her eyes darting around her to make sure she isn't drawing attention.

She is. Or should I say, I am, but I'm used to the attention the leather cut garners when I'm out in public.

"You kissed me," I counter.

"I was going to kiss your cheek. You're the one who went full-on tongue."

"You weren't complaining when you lifted up on your toes and wrapped your arm around me."

She falls silent, her cheeks pinking a little.

"It was a great kiss."

"A germ-infected kiss. One that I passed on to my kids."

"I'm sorry I got you sick. Let me make it up to you." I have nine inches I'm willing to offer that has the power to make her forget about all her troubles. "Once the kids are better, of course."

Her eyes narrow as if the suggestion is beyond ridiculous, but she doesn't turn the offer down.

"Do they go to the program at the church?" I ask, able to drop the subject for now.

"No," she answers but offers no further information.

"So that guy—"

"Elijah and Katie Dunn?"

Reagan's eyes flash with relief as the kids' names are called, but I can't tell if it's because she's been waiting a while or if she's just happy to get rid of me.

My hand brushes her arm as she stands, urging Elijah to hop down from the seat he's been occupying.

"I'm sorry I got you sick. I meant what I said about making it up to you."

"I bet," she says as she ushers Elijah toward the nurse standing just outside the door leading to the back of the doctor's office.

I follow her until she disappears on the other side, mouth hanging open.

"Trying to pick women up at the pediatrician's office? That's got to be a new one," Simone says as she drops down into the seat Reagan just left.

"That's the girl from the grocery store," I inform her. Drew had told everyone the story with a wide grin on his face the second we got back to the house.

After she walked away, I stupidly confessed that I didn't know her, but there was a good chance I was already in love with her. I'm not, of course. I don't do love.

Sex.

I do sex, and I do it very well, but there's just something about that woman. If she thinks playing hard to get is a deterrent, then she's thinking wrong. I love a challenge, and although she may be holding back, I swallowed her moan at the grocery store when her lips were plastered against mine. She was just as shocked as I was by the connection, and that alone is worth exploring.

"Really?" Simone asks. "That woman?"

"Yeah," I say, looking over at her. "Why do you say it like that?"

"I get why you helped her at the store, but you approached her just now like you're interested in seeing her again."

"Maybe I am."

"She has two kids, Jinx."

"Well aware."

"You said you'd never date a woman with kids."

"I have a kid." I point to our sleeping son for emphasis.

"Still. You said you don't date women with children."

That used to be a rule, and I said that to her when Rocker was worried I was going to try to hook up with Simone before they made things official. Then it was something I lived by. Kids got in the way when I was trying to bang their moms. Kids got up in the middle of the night. Kids left toys on the floor, which sometimes made sneaking out of the house difficult. Nothing wakes a woman up like a man stepping on a fucking Lego in the middle of the living room floor.

I've had my fair share of women with kids, and very seldomly did I enjoy the aftermath. Women with kids have expectations, ones I've never been interested in fulfilling.

"I don't date."

She frowns. "Then leave her alone."

See? She's got a man, but she still knows what women with children want.

Leave her alone?

Not a chance. I lost all ability to move on when her lips met mine. Add in her slick tongue against mine, and I was a goner before I even had a choice.

Chapter 4

Reagan

"A stomach virus," the doctor says.

I've always used this doctor for my kids, but his less than enthusiastic diagnosis leaves me wondering if keeping my kids here as patients is best.

"I've seen over eighty kids in the last week with the same thing," he says, and my nose scrunches.

Man, now I understand his lackluster approach.

"What can I do?"

"Push fluids as much as you can. Crackers and dry toast until they feel like eating more."

"So, exactly what I was doing before?"

He nods before letting his eyes drop back down to the folder in his hands.

"If Katie goes more than six hours without a wet diaper, then give us a call back, but they should both be fine in a day or so. Make sure to clean the house thoroughly more than once during the course of the illness to prevent recontamination. I've had several families that keep passing it back and forth."

"Okay," I answer, thankful for the job that provides health insurance. "Sorry for wasting your time."

He looks up at me, frowning. "You aren't wasting my time. I completely understand wanting to get help when your kids don't feel well. I wish there was something I can give to get them better faster, but this is just one of those things."

Just one of those things.

I've heard that more than once in my life. Hell, I've said it often enough myself.

Getting pregnant and the baby's father wanting nothing to do with the child. *It's just one of those things.*

Getting pregnant a second time only for that baby's father to confess to being gay, although ecstatic to co-parent a child with me. *It's just one of those things.*

Although that was a different situation than the first, and I think I'll always feel a little twinge of irritation for being the girl Shane tried to be straight with that one night when he was questioning everything about his life. I don't know how to feel about being the one that made him realize he wasn't bi-sexual but one hundred percent gay.

It's just one of those things.

I give the doctor a small smile as I wake Elijah up so we can leave. I feel anxious, hoping to see Miles one last time on the way out of the office, but I also pray he isn't anywhere around. Seeing him walk into the doctor's office with a woman hit me harder than it ever should have. We kissed to get Brian to leave me alone, and that was it. Thinking about him numerous times over the last forty-eight hours was something I chalked up to having been single for so long. Of course, he'd come to mind. The kiss was mind-blowing but feeling some sort of ownership over him from our brief interaction and hating that woman I saw him with isn't my place.

He tried to explain she wasn't his wife, but people have kids all the time without being married. I have two kids of my own to prove the point.

It's complicated. Those were his words, and they can encompass a million things.

Things I don't have the energy to even think about.

Thankfully—or regretfully depending on which emotion I decide to go with— Miles is nowhere to be seen as I make my co-pay and leave the office.

Taking the stairs would be the fastest, but I opt for the elevator despite only being on the second floor. Elijah is in a bad mood, and it's understandable considering how sick he's been for the last day and a half. I accused Miles of getting us sick, but I've felt fine. I know it's more likely they picked the virus up at the park, but I was angry at seeing him and wanted to make him feel guilty. It has backfired, of course, because he was so nice. He didn't have any obligation to walk up to us and explain why he so readily kissed me like he was starving.

I sigh again, mildly thankful that Elijah is too worn out to run away from me as we exit the building. At the same time, I wish he was his happy, wild, and free self. I hate when my kids are sick, more so when I have to miss work because my mother is willing to watch them when they're healthy but draws the line at dealing with vomit.

Elijah crawls inside the car and doesn't give me grief when I buckle him in his seat. I know he's ready to go back home and get into bed. Katie grumbles a little, waking slightly when I put her in her seat, and as I climb behind the wheel, I pray we can make it home without either of them getting sick.

I know something is wrong the instant I back out of the parking spot, but I ignore the mild wobble of the car. My car is old. I've had it since high school, and there's always something or other going wrong with it. By the time I make it to the stop sign, I know it's a flat. I want to cry. Hot tears burn the backs of my eyes, but I check the rearview mirror, making sure no one is behind me and park to the far side of the parking lot.

They say when it rains it pours, and right now buckets are falling on my head despite the sun glaring from above.

"Mommy?" Elijah whispers when I put the car in park, leaving the air conditioner on so they don't get overheated.

"The car has a flat," I explain. "I'll be right back."

"I help," he offers, and it pulls a small smile from my lips.

"Thanks, buddy, but I got it. Just rest and we'll be home soon."

His eyes flutter closed again, eyelashes resting against his pink cheeks.

Katie is back asleep, but I crack the passenger side window in case one of them gets sick again.

After popping the trunk, I climb out, a whispered prayer on my lips that I remembered to get a full-sized tire the last time this happened. I nearly ran the tread off the donut my car came with last year, but for the life of me, I can't remember buying a replacement tire like I vowed to do.

The bad luck continues as I push open the trunk and pull the bottom flap away. That same damn donut is there, and if my misfortune continues like I get the feeling it will, the damn thing will be flat. The last thing I need to spend half my day on is waiting for a tow truck. It's times like this I miss my dad. Before, I could call him, and he'd come running. I was never an obligation to him. He wouldn't sigh and ask me what I needed when I called, the way my mother does. She helps me out of obligation not love. If my dad were still alive, I wouldn't have a donut in my trunk. He would've replaced it the last time I used it.

I clear my throat to keep the tears of self-pity away and pull out the things I'll need.

I'm a strong independent woman, not because I want to be, but because I've been forced into this situation. My mother would say it's of my own making, and that's true to a point, but having a man right now would be nice.

"Need some help?"

I startle at the question, dropping the tire iron at my feet, just barely missing the tip of my shoe.

"What is your problem?" I snap, turning around to face Miles. "Why are you everywhere?"

He hitches his thumb over his shoulder. "Just got finished at the doctor's office. You looked like you could use some help."

I reach for the tire iron at the same time he does, only he's faster. He grins, tapping the metal on the palm of his left hand like he knew I was about to use it as a weapon against him.

"I'm sure your son's mother is ecstatic about being stuck in a car with a sick child while you help me."

He grins even wider. "She's going home to her sick man and her other child. I'm on my bike."

Of course, the biker would ride his bike to the pediatrician. Can't cage a wild animal after all.

I cringe with the stereotype bouncing around in my head. It's not fair to judge him so quickly, but I'm tired and irritated, and everything that could go wrong today has. I keep taking the hits, and there's no end in sight.

"I'm fine. I can change a tire on my own."

"*Can* doesn't mean you have to," he says as he nudges me out of the way so he can pull the donut from the trunk. "You'll need to get a new tire soon."

The thing bounces on the asphalt, and I breathe a sigh of relief that it isn't flat.

I don't agree with him, because in a way it's like admitting defeat. I keep my mouth closed, arms crossed over my chest like I'm put out by his presence, as if I wasn't just thinking that a man to help me would be a blessing.

I have no idea why I'm so irritated with him. Maybe it's because his kiss has been on constant replay in my head for days. Maybe because my eyes can't help but wander down his strong back when he folds over to pull the tiny jack from the trunk. Maybe because his hands are so sure as he situates under the car and lifts the backside of my car with an ease I know I would've struggled with.

"Like I was trying to explain inside, Simone isn't my woman. Our son was conceived during our one night together."

"And was she dating her man then?"

I'm in no position to judge. I know what people think of me being a single parent to two kids with different dads. Imagine what they would think if they knew both of them were conceived during one-night stands?

"She wasn't, and you may not want to hear this, but he was there."

I gawk at him when he looks up at me.

"It was an umm… a group thing."

A group thing?

Jesus, what have I walked into?

"Sounds like fun." I snap my mouth closed immediately when the words come out because they don't escape with cynicism but actual longing. Jesus, do I honestly want two men to ravish me? Maybe. I've never been in a situation like that. Hell, I get into enough trouble with a single man at a time.

He winks at me, and it makes my skin tingle. Or crawl. I haven't decided which yet.

"It was a great night, and now I have a son, but there was nothing more than that night between us."

"Sounds like it would be complicated."

He laughs, a warm embracing sound. "It may seem that way, but her man is my best friend."

"And that makes things less complicated?" I scoff.

"Actually, yes. I think co-parenting my son with a man that loves his mother and loves him as much as I do is the best thing ever."

He busies himself with my tire, and I let my eyes drift away. I'm going to keep saying weird things if I don't focus on something other than his sure hands and his rippling arm muscles.

"We all live together." My eyes snap back to him. "In the same house."

This man is telling me to my face that he once had a sexual experience with that woman and hasn't touched her since. I don't believe him. What man spends time inside of a woman and stays in close proximity and doesn't want to do it again?

"And I know what you're thinking, but I'm telling you, there's been nothing since that night. She's happy with Rocker, but we're still a family, you know?"

I don't know. Jeremiah couldn't get away from me fast enough when I told him I was pregnant with Elijah, and although Shane and his fiancé Martin are involved with Katie and thankfully Elijah, I wouldn't call us a true family. Shane never offered to let me live with them, and I would've turned him down if he had. Living there after knowing him in a sexual way would be way too weird.

The only family I have is my mother, and most days she makes that seem like a burden rather than a blessing.

"I'm glad it works for you." My foot begins to tap, and I have to physically make it stop. I don't want to seem ungrateful, but I'm dying to get away from him if only because he makes me nervous. I can't stop thinking about his mouth on mine, and the last thing I want disclosed to him is how much I want to kiss him again. The man has a complicated life with his baby momma and best friend. Besides, he was doing me a favor not trying to entice me to date him.

He's fast and efficient, and before I know it, he's putting the tire iron and jack back in my trunk. A quick peek inside the car lets me know that both kids are still sleeping, and thankfully there's an absence of puke in there.

"Let me help you," he says when he closes the trunk.

"You've been a great help." I shift my weight from one foot to the other, unsure why I'm suddenly nervous as I gain his full attention. "I better get them home. I've been lucky to avoid vomit in the car thus far."

"Let me come home with you."

Heat races up my spine at the suggestion.

"If I got you sick, let me help with the kids. I'm an expert at heating up chicken noodle soup."

His grin is contagious, and I find myself smiling back at him.

Wouldn't my mother just love for me to show up at the house with a man wearing a leather cut. I'm sure every curtain in the neighborhood would be pulled back at the roar of his motorcycle as he parked it on the street in front of my house.

"You look tired, too. Let me help you."

"That's very sweet of you," I hedge.

"I'm not a weirdo."

"You just always kiss women who need rescuing in the grocery store?"

"Only one so far, but I can't say that I'm disappointed."

"I need to go," I rush out as I step around him toward the driver's side door of my car. "Thank you for your help."

"Reagan."

I don't stop when he calls my name.

I also don't make it home without Elijah waking up and puking.

See? If it weren't for bad luck, I wouldn't have any luck at all.

Chapter 5

Jinx

"How did it go?" Simone asks when I get back to the house.

"She had a flat," I say, still mildly irritated that Reagan seemed to want to escape the second I was done changing her tire.

"I know she had a flat." Simone swats at me playfully. "I mean, did you ask her out?"

"I didn't." She didn't give me the chance.

"Rookie," she says with a giggle.

"I asked her if I could go to her house."

Simone drops the wooden spoon she was holding. "You did what?"

I shrug. "She said I got her and the kids sick. I offered to go home with her to help."

She turns to face me fully. "And in your head, you thought offering to go home with a woman you don't know would work?"

A slow smile spreads across my face. "She's not the first woman I asked to go home with."

"But you're not at a bar, you idiot, and she's a mother with two kids. She's not going to say yes to something like that."

"She needed help."

"And for all she knows, you could be a psycho."

"What are you two arguing about?" Rocker asks as he shuffles into the kitchen looking like death warmed over.

"Jinx tried to pick up that woman from the grocery store at the pediatrician's office," Drew says, making me realize he's in the room.

I turn to glare at him. He simply smiles before turning his attention back down to the cookbook on the kitchen bar top in front of him.

"What are you even doing in here?" I ask him.

"We're making homemade chicken noodle soup," Drew answers.

"I'm making chicken noodle soup," Simone clarifies. "Drew is giving me ingredient measurements."

"You know how to read?" I tease.

"My cellmate taught me in prison," he says without missing a beat, and my eyes dart to Rocker.

Drew has been opening up to us more recently, but he rarely talks about the time he spent in prison.

Rocker nods in approval.

"Good thing," my best friend says. "I'm starving."

"You need crackers and flat soda," Simone says as she turns back to the stove.

"I'm a man. I need real food."

"You were crying like a baby earlier," Drew reminds him.

"And you haven't gotten sick, yet. Just wait, asshole. You'll want your back rubbed when you throw up ten times, too."

"Three times," Simone corrects. "Men are such babies."

"And women have better immune systems, apparently," Rocker mutters, frowning when Simone turns her head away when he tries to kiss her.

"We just aren't so ready to spread germs like you guys are. Go sit down. I'll get you some crackers."

Drew pats the stool beside him, but Rocker sneers in his direction. That stool is on the far side of the kitchen, and there's no way he's going to sit that far from his woman. It's like they're attached at the hip. I don't envy the fucker at all for being so dependent on her. Sad sap.

"I think we're coming to the end of it," Drew says, his nose still stuck in the cookbook. "Andy hasn't puked all day. Did you add the carrots?"

Simone passes Rocker a sleeve of saltines, and the man glares down at them like they're inherently evil.

"Not yet. I'm still working on the stock." She goes back to the stove. "So, she shot you down, huh?"

I groan. Just when I thought the conversation about Reagan was over, she asks again. Leave it to the woman to circle right back without missing a beat. Women are the reason men lose every argument. Men are like squirrels, easily distracted. Women have the ability to file things in their heads like a damn online database.

"She didn't seem too keen about me going to her house," I mumble.

In truth, she got out of there as fast as she possibly could. Her escape would've been comical if I hadn't been left standing in the parking lot watching the direction she left long after she disappeared.

"Your charm is broken," Rocker says, sounding a little smug as he tries to open the pack of crackers.

"She's not a girl at a bar," Simone repeats.

"She's very pretty," Drew says.

"Who do you have a crush on now?" Izzy asks as she walks into the room. "Andy just puked again."

"Spoke too soon," Simone says, her nose scrunching. We've been dealing with sick kids for what seems like an eternity and there doesn't seem to be an end in sight.

"I was saying the girl at the grocery store is pretty. Jinx got shot down again today at the doctor's office."

"She works at the doctor's office?" Izzy settles in Drew's lap when he slides the bar stool out a little.

God, I'm surrounded by happy couples. I thought I was getting away from most of that when I moved out of the clubhouse, but I guess not.

"She was there with her sick kids," Simone explains. "Jinx tried to go home with her."

Izzy's eyes widen. The woman may have a child, but she's not very experienced when it comes to casual anything. As in, not experienced at all. She and Drew hooked up the night they met. It was her first time, and she got pregnant. They've been through hell to get where they are now, but she was never with anyone other than him. At least that's what I've gathered from snooping in on conversations around the clubhouse when everyone gets together.

They moved in next door shortly after she and Drew made things official. She and Simone got close, and now we're always over at each other's houses.

"You tried to pick up a woman with two sick kids?" Izzy sounds disappointed in me.

"I offered to help her with the kids," I hedge. "She blamed me for getting them sick."

"And by helping, you were going to—"

"Help," I interrupt before Rocker can accuse me of something more sinister than cleaning and making lunch.

"Yeah. Okay," he says with a weak laugh.

I would throw something at his head if he wasn't able to read me like a book. I mean, I would make lunch and help clean, but sick kids rest a lot. Reagan looked tired, and she did say she passed the virus on to her kids from me, but she didn't look like she was still sick. What grownups do when the kids are sleeping is no one's business.

"You're thinking about it right now!" Simone accuses, the wooden spoon in her hand pointed in my direction. "Like I said at the doctor's office. Leave that woman alone."

"You don't date women with kids," Rocker says, parroting his woman's words from earlier like he was in the room when she said it instead of at home crying like a tit bag.

"She's very pretty," Drew says again like it explains everything.

I point at him. "See! She's not pretty. She's absolutely stunning, and I'd be a fool to just walk away."

"It's not walking away when she shoots you down," Rocker says with a smile that has more meaning than teasing.

He may be able to read me like a book, but that ability goes both ways. I know what he's thinking. He's assuming I've gotten bitten by the same damn love bug he has where Simone is concerned.

"She's different." What I feel when I see her is different.

Hell yeah, I want to get the woman naked, but I also want to wrap my arms around her and hold her to my chest. I don't see myself spending my entire life with any one woman, but I wouldn't mind visiting her more than once.

"Stop," Simone says with more authority than I've heard from her in a while. "Don't fuck with single moms."

Rocker raises his eyebrows at her insistence. The woman has never been a single mom, but I know she had a lot of doubts when she first got pregnant. She didn't know if she was going to end up with one of us or alone, and that seems to have done some damage, even though we tried to assure her she was going to be taken care of.

"It's possible she's already in a relationship," Izzy offers. "Maybe that's why she turned you down."

"You didn't see the way the woman kissed him back at the store," Drew says. "I thought she was going to climb him like a tree."

"Being in a relationship and being satisfied are two different things," Simone says, causing Rocker to snap his eyes back to her once again. "Not me, babe. You know you keep me very satisfied."

A slow smile spreads across my best friend's face, and I know he's willing to get her naked right now just to prove his skills, sick or not.

"Down boy," I mutter, smacking him on the shoulder and making the cracker in between his fingers fall to the floor. "You've got nothing to prove. I hear your prowess through the walls nightly."

Simone winks at her man before turning back to the stove as Rocker grunts as he bends over to pick the cracker up and toss it in the trash.

"She's a great kisser," I confess, and maybe that's why I can't get her off my mind.

I've kissed more women than I can count. I don't sleep with everyone my lips come into contact with. Sometimes a good make-out session is enough, but Reagan's lips made every other woman pale in comparison. Or maybe it was because she shocked me by coming up and begging me to play along while she tried to avoid her ex.

Who knows?

What I do know is that without answers, I'm never going to stop thinking about her.

The only problem is, those two occurrences, at the store and again today at the doctor's office were happenstance. I may never see the woman again.

Chapter 6

Reagan

I ignore the queasiness making my stomach roil as I swipe mascara on my lashes. I blame pure exhaustion on feeling so drained. Taking care of two sick kids will do that to a person.

"You're sure they're better?" Mom asks when I leave my room and enter the kitchen.

"Neither one has thrown up in the last twenty-four hours," I explain. "They're fine. Just tired from being sick for the last couple of days. They may not have their appetites back, so maybe a light breakfast and lunch."

"I know how to take care of kids, Reagan. You survived, didn't you?"

"Thank you for not killing me," I tell her only half-joking as I gather my purse and car keys.

My mother mumbles something I don't bother to pay attention to as I walk out of the house. The fresh, morning air doesn't help to settle my stomach, and I know I should call in sick. It's obvious I have that stupid virus, but I've also missed two days of work. I can't afford to miss another one.

I absently think about the donut still on my car as I drive to work. I should feel ashamed, but I haven't had time between taking care of Elijah and Katie to get another one. Work is only a few miles away, and if this one goes flat, I'll just freaking walk. Making a plan in my head to use my lunch break to run to the tire shop, I feel better about the decision. If only I physically felt better as I pull up to work.

I wave to one of the girls that works at the office adjoining ours before unlocking the door and heading to the small kitchen area. I gag at the smell of the coffee as I set a new pot on to brew and manage to escape without heaving all over the countertop.

I'm flushed, feeling overheated and cold all at the same time as I settle at my desk and open my emails. I want to cry at the sight of the long list marked urgent. It seems nothing gets done around here when I'm gone, and although I've worked here for almost two years, I still feel guilty for missing work. My boss has a way of making her employees feel like burdens. Even asking for earned time off is an assault on my nervous system.

I don't regret my kids, and if could guarantee I'd end up with the same exact ones I have now, I would've waited, at least until I finished law school instead of having to drop out to support Elijah before finishing my first year. The plan was always to go back. I want to be an attorney, but then Katie happened, and my plans were once again derailed.

I work in a law office but being a lawyer and working for one as a paralegal isn't the same. It's all of the stress, all of the work, and a fraction of the pay. You could say I'm a *little* bitter, and you'd only be off by a lot. I wake every morning wishing my life different, easier. Wishing I could do more for my kids. Wishing I had the money to move out of my mother's house. Wishing I could afford legitimate daycare where my kids didn't just sit in front of the television all day.

Wishing. Wishing. Wishing.

Life never goes to plan for anyone, but mine has been altered epically with my choices.

Two kids and a dead-end job with no prospects of things getting better, I'm going to blame not feeling well on my internal pity party. I'm normally not such a fatalist. Usually, I can find the good in every situation, but today just isn't going to be one of those days. Today, I'm going to struggle to keep water down, and my attitude in check.

I give my boss a weak smile when she saunters in, nose in the air, forehead scrunched as she approaches.

"Reagan?"

"Yes, ma'am?" I swallow, trying to force down the bubble of nausea in my throat.

"You look unwell."

"I'm a little tired. The kids—"

"I think it's rude."

"To have kids?"

I shouldn't question her. Normally, I'd just smile and get back to work. I may hate my job, but it does come with health insurance. There aren't many places around town that have benefit packages.

"To come to work with the intent to get all the others in the office sick."

"That wasn't my—" I bite back the words.

I don't want to get anyone else sick but missing another day of pay isn't something I can afford. I've missed two already and it might as well be three with what my co-pay cost me at the doctor's office on Monday.

"Go home."

"But—" She waves her hand to silence me.

"Don't come back until you're well."

She doesn't leave room for an argument as she heads to her office. Her door snaps closed, leaving me staring after her with the threat of tears burning hotly behind my eyes. I gather my purse and keys, seconds away from walking out of the door when my phone rings.

I answer, praying she changed her mind, but all I get is a snapped order to bring her a cup of coffee before leaving. For a woman so worried about germs, I'm surprised she's insisting I touch something that's going near her mouth.

I make the coffee, barely avoiding the urge to lick the rim of her cup just to be petty and leave the office before she can give me more tasks. I know she's not going to count a second of the time I spent at the office today, and I may not make much, but I draw the line at working for free.

Going home and crawling back in bed would be in my best interest, but I know that won't happen. I'm sick, and most people would give me a reprieve, but my mother isn't one of them. The second I step through the front door, my mom will hand off the kids. I shouldn't be irritated by that. They're my kids after all, but I just need a break, a few minutes to wallow.

I end up at the park, watching people use the walking trail before the sun gets too hot to bear being outside. The car is smothering, and since the motor burned up in the electric windows, I stand outside of my car, head tilted back as I try to enjoy the fresh air.

A dog yips nearby, happily chasing after a ball tossed by its owner. Two women power walk, arms pumping back and forth as they gossip with smiles on their faces. A mother with two small children laughs as the kids run around the play area. From this vantage point, life is good. People are happy and enjoying life.

My stomach turns again, and I take slow, deep breaths to ward off the queasiness. It helps some, but I know I'm going to puke before the end of the day. I know I'll probably feel better after I do, but I hate getting that sick. I'll put it off as long as I can.

Turning to get back into my car to head home, the roar of motorcycles draws my attention to the main road. Three bikes come into view long seconds after the sound hits my ears, and it makes me smile thinking of Miles's offer to help me with my sick kids. Those machines are so loud and dangerous, but what a thrill it would be to feel the wind in my hair and sun on my skin.

The black leather cuts are unmistakable even from a distance, but it isn't until the guys are less than a block away, that I realize one of the guys is actually Miles. Even with my stomach turning, I can't keep a small smile off my lips. I've never looked at a man on a bike and thought he looked sexy, but there's no denying I'm thinking it now. Maybe it's because I sort of know him, or because I've seen his bright smile. Maybe it's because I know how talented his tongue is against mine.

Maybe I've lost my damn mind and the germs invading my body have somehow gotten into my brain.

Something is going on because I can't pull my eyes from him or his strong hands on the handlebars, and his thick thighs showcased in tight jeans. God, I'm desperate, and if Cassie were here, she'd laugh at my gawking.

The guy in the front lifts his fingers for a wave, and all I can do is continue to stare like a weirdo. Then Miles notices me, a grin spreading across his handsome face. He gives me a little more enthusiastic wave, but he never slows. He doesn't whip into the park parking lot to speak to me, and I feel like it's a missed opportunity, one I brought on myself for running away both times we've spoken to each other.

Not long after the roar of their machines fade, I climb in my car and head back home. Maybe I can convince the kids to lie down for an early nap so I can get some rest as well.

My phone chimes with an email, and needing one more minute alone before going inside, I check it. I know it's work related. I get no other texts, but the second I open the damn thing, I regret it.

My boss has sent a mass email welcoming a new attorney to the firm. Normally that wouldn't be a big deal. She's known for using brand-new lawyers for some of the simpler cases. She gets cheap labor—all the while charging clients her premium hourly rate—and the attorneys get experience to fill in their resumes with.

It's the name of the attorney that makes me cringe. Brian Wakefield.

Of course, she hired Brian because my life at the office isn't miserable enough already.

I wouldn't be surprised if lightning struck the house at this point because that would just be the icing on this shit cake of a day.

It isn't until I get inside, doing my best to ignore the snide comments from my mother, and get the kids settled in my bed for a nap that I realize this is so much worse than just running into an ex at work. I lied to that man, something that normally wouldn't bother me. I don't owe him a damn thing, but I get the feeling that telling him I'm married is going to come back and bite me in the ass. At a minimum, it's going to make me look pitiful and desperate. At a maximum, he's going to find a way to use it against me which may lead to me leaving my job. I know I'm completely expendable at work. My boss is a user, never taking into account the hard work several of us do around there. As far she's concerned, she can hire someone off the street to do my job and be just fine. What she doesn't take into account is that the other people in the office will take up my slack if only to keep her off their backs.

God, why does my life have to suck so hard?

It only gets worse when a secondary email comes through announcing a welcome-to-the-firm party with the insistence that everyone is required to attend. I'll show up alone, and my secret will be revealed. I might as well start looking for a new job now.

Chapter 7

Jinx

"And what do you think?" Thumper asks as he walks by and slaps me on the back.

"I'm always down." I smile, but don't feel the internal joy my facial expression is trying to convey.

"This guy is a beast," Rocker praises. "His recovery time is practically non-existent."

Most people would find it weird that your best friend is well aware of your sexual prowess, but that's just how things are around here.

"And Kincaid doesn't have a problem with it?" Apollo asks.

Rocker chuckles at the little ass-kisser. "Kincaid's fine with it."

"And Simone?" Apollo challenges.

Rocker holds his hands up by his ears. "I'm not going to participate. I won't even be at the clubhouse."

"What are you assholes talking about?" Legend asks as he enters the clubhouse kitchen.

"Planning another party," Max answers with a wicked grin.

"You mean an orgy?" Legend corrects as he grabs a grape from the bowl in the center of the table and pops it into his grinning mouth. "I'm down. Tonight?"

"Wait. You attend the orgies?" Apollo looks perplexed. "And is Jasmine okay with—"

Tug growls at the fool.

"We like to watch and be watched," Max says as he places a calming hand on Tug's thigh. "No one touches her but us."

I have to say it was a little weird the first time I walked into the living room and saw Kincaid's niece riding Tug's fat cock and had to do a double take when Max walked up and shoved his dick in Tug's mouth, but those guys are a part of the club. It was made clear very early on that the clubhouse is welcoming to any and all sexualities. Everyone had the right to say no, and everyone had the right to get up and walk away if they saw something they didn't like. So long as the activities are safe and consensual they were approved.

A lot of the guys that are paired up don't attend, and Kincaid and the other original members stay very far away when we plan these parties, but we're testosterone, adrenaline-filled men. Fucking and fighting is what we do best, so when we aren't working, the parties are the best thing for us.

I want the party. I *need* the party.

I think having a little clubhouse fun will be what finally makes me able to get Reagan out of my head.

Seeing her yesterday standing outside of her car at the park made me miserable. I couldn't stop and talk to her. Not only would the guys give me shit and call me a pussy, but we were heading across town to finalize some supplies we ordered from a local business. I was working, but I'm sure it looked to her like I was giving her the cold shoulder. She isn't interested anyway, and that's been a harder pill to swallow than anything else.

Maybe it makes me an asshole to get upset when a woman turns me down seeing as how it never happens, but I'll eventually accept it. This party may be exactly what I need to start the process.

"So where do the women come from?" Apollo asks, drawing my attention off Reagan and back onto the room.

"What?" I ask. "They're from around town."

"Hmm. Okay."

Tug chuckles. "Did you think they're ordered online or something?"

Max laughs, bringing a smile to my face.

"No," Apollo huffs, making it abundantly clear that he had that train of thought in some fashion.

"They're women not appetizers to a Door Dash order," Rocker adds.

"And everyone just fucks in the living room?"

"Jesus," Rocker huffs. "No one will force you to pull your dick out in public."

"You're making it a bigger deal than it has to be," Max says. "It's just fun. If you don't want to get dirty in the living room, take a girl to your room."

Thumper is quiet as the conversation continues, and that's a little out of character for him. I can't tell if he's nervous about the party or if he's sitting back and taking in all the details. The guy is normally jovial, the center of attention and quick to make everyone laugh. Right now, he's a little subdued.

My phone rings before I can ask him if something's wrong, and I'm smiling for a totally different reason.

"Excuse me," I tell the guys as I stand and walk out of the room. "Hey, kid."

"Kid? Did you forget I'm a grown man?"

"You'll always be a kid to me, Kalen. What's going on in your little slice of heaven?"

"I got the job!"

His excitement is palpable even all the way from Texas.

My younger brother Kalen is my complete opposite. Whereas I couldn't get out of Lindell fast enough, he never wanted to leave. I enjoyed my time growing up in the sleepy little town, but I always had bigger dreams than the place could provide.

My parents promised that after seeing the world through my travels with the Marine Corps that I'd come back and settle down there, but they couldn't have been more wrong. I don't think I'll ever be free of the bug that urges me to experience life one Cerberus mission at a time. My body demands the thrills and the danger. My morals and upbringing insist on helping others and bringing bad guys to justice. Cerberus offers all of that. Plus, my son is here, and he's someone I'll never walk away from.

"That's awesome, man. When do you start?"

"Beginning of the next semester."

"Teaching math?"

"Yep," he confirms "I'm now a nerdy college professor."

"At Lindell University, no less." I almost open my mouth to ask why he doesn't want to live a life bigger than our hometown, but I remind myself that not everyone wants the same things in life.

"Mom wants you to come home for a celebratory dinner."

"I have things going on here," I lie.

I'm sure there wouldn't be an issue with me going home for a few days. I would like to see my family, but at the same time, I'm never eager to be bombarded with a million questions, all of them rolling into why don't you just come home.

"Roxie moved, man. You don't have to worry about her anymore."

I huff a humorless laugh. I haven't thought about my high school girlfriend in years. Yeah, she broke my teenage heart, and I guess I can be thankful for that because it was the catalyst that got me here, but she was never meant to be a fixture in my life.

Kalen must take my silence as a need to change the subject. "How's River?"

"He's fine," I say, wanting to guide the conversation away from home more than anything because next he'll start the guilt trip about how Mom misses her grandson. I gear up to tell him that the road works both ways. "You know, two of the kids from here are attending Lindell. They're freshmen."

"Which sport?" he asks, and I sigh in relief that he doesn't press the issue about River.

"Baseball. Landon Andrews is there on a scholarship and Rick Matthews is a walk-on." I say, knowing Kid would like eyes and ears on his only son. "Maybe keep an eye on them?"

"Sure thing," he agrees. "What else is going on in your life? Haven't heard from you in a while."

He's right. I know I should call more often, and a familiar guilt begins to settle in my gut.

"Nothing really. Just sitting around waiting for news of a new job."

"No parties?"

"What do you mean?" I ask, well aware of what he's referring to.

"The umm... you know..."

"Orgies?"

A reluctant laugh spills from his mouth. "Yeah."

"We're planning one for this weekend. Wanna fly in for it?"

The offer isn't real. Other than the women—and men if one of the guys wants to scratch an itch—outsiders aren't allowed.

"No!" he snaps. "I would never do something so—"

"Perverse?"

"Scandalous," he whispers although I'm pretty sure he's alone. He wouldn't have the courage to ask if he were around other people.

Different lives indeed.

"You don't have casual sex?" I tease, certain his cheeks are flushed, and the tips of his ears are turning red.

"I do… I mean I have, but not like in a group setting."

"Your college years sound boring."

A quick laugh is his only answer.

"Forget I asked."

"Is that code for *can you video record it for me*?"

Silence.

"Kalen?"

"I'm just trying to be a part of your life, man."

The guilt I was trying to avoid hits me in the fucking chest. "I'll see what I can do about planning a trip, but you and Mom need to understand that with River and I comes Simone, Rocker, and Cooper."

"Your family."

"Yes."

"Mom loves kids," he sighs, and it's immediately clear why he needs me to visit.

"She still hassling you about getting married?"

"Every time I see her. It doesn't help that I made out with Beth a couple weeks ago."

"Crazy Beth?"

"Yeah."

"Is she stalking you?"

"I wouldn't call it stalking, but she has registered the two of us for wedding gifts."

"What have I always told you?"

"Don't dip my wick in crazy, but that's the thing, Miles, I didn't even sleep with her. A few drunken kisses, and the woman has lost her mind."

"It's that Alexander charm," I tease. "Gets them every time."

Plus, he's an eligible bachelor in a small town. Limited selection tends to make even less than perfect people attractive. It's the low supply and high demand factor. Everyone is in a frenzy to scoop up whatever they can.

"Yeah, I guess. Hey. Adam just got here. Think about coming for a visit, will you?"

"I will," I promise, honestly wondering if Rocker and Simone would be welcome in Lindell. The townspeople are very nice, but what we have is outrageously unorthodox to people who seldomly travel outside of a hundred-mile radius of the town.

We say our goodbyes, and I head back into the kitchen. The conversation has transformed from the party to motorcycles, and this is one safe conversation I can talk about all day.

Reagan only enters my mind a dozen times, and that's an improvement over the hundred I thought about her yesterday.

See? Things are already starting to look up.

Chapter 8

Reagan

"You're sure you're okay with this?"

Shane tilts his head to the side, his eyes sparkling. "Of course. He's her family which makes him my family."

Shane and I have a very flexible custody agreement, but when I drop Katie off, he insists that Elijah be allowed to stay as well. At first, I was hesitant. Elijah's father didn't want anything to do with him, and I found it hard to believe that there were people in the world that would love my kid when they were under no obligation to do so. It became very clear from the beginning that Shane only had the best of intentions where Elijah was concerned.

We were friends before that one night as lovers, and I knew he always wanted a house full of kids.

Katie squeals when she sees Shane, her little fingers flexing open and closed until he takes her from me.

"They're better?" he asks, and I know it's out of concern for the kids rather than fear of contaminating his home.

"They are and thank you for dropping off the Pedialyte and chicken soup."

"Of course," Martin, Shane's fiancé, says as he bends to pick Elijah up. "Are you feeling better?"

"Daddy!" Elijah screams, throwing his arms around Martin's neck.

The man's eyes widen as he looks to Shane before looking at me.

"He's been doing that to everyone. Strangers even," I explain. "I have no idea why."

"I kind of love it," Martin whispers, his hand rubbing circles on Elijah's back as he drinks in every second of the hug.

Then it's over, and my son is wiggling to get down. He's never one to be caged very long.

"Are you going out tonight?" Shane asks, turning from the front door and walking deeper into his house. "You look amazing."

I follow because even though I frequently desire a break from parenting, it's never easy to just drop them off and leave, knowing it'll be nearly two full days before I see them again.

"Cassie was invited to a party." I shrug. "I figured it would be nice to get out of the house."

I've been trapped at home all week, first with the kids being sick, and then two days of feeling bad myself. It's time to get away from my mother.

Martin chuckles as his eyes find Shane's.

"What?"

"What, what?"

"That look. What does that look mean?"

"There was no look," Shane says but then they do it again.

"That look!"

"Cassie was invited to a party? Do you know what you're getting yourself into?"

"No clue, but I'm hoping it's not some sort of wine tasting. I freaking hate wine."

They both chuckle. "Just be safe?"

"Always," I say, closing the distance between us and pressing my lips to the back of Katie's head. "See you on Sunday. Elijah, come say goodbye."

My son squeals as he runs up to me and wraps his arms around my legs. "Love you!"

Much to his annoyance, I pick him up and give him a big hug. "Be good for Uncle Shane and Uncle Martin. Be nice to Katie."

He gives me a serious nod before wiggling to get down. I give them all a quick wave before heading out to my car. Since my mother hates Cassie—she's too wild for someone in her mid-twenties—we made plans to meet in the parking lot of the very same grocery store I lost my mind at this past weekend.

She's late, but Cassie is always late, so it doesn't bother me to sit in my car and have a few blessed moments of silence. If I lived alone instead of with my cynical mother, I'd much prefer to go home, put on some pajamas and stare at mindless television all night. Going out is never a desire, although I do have fun with my best friend when she is able to convince me to let loose. Tonight will be no different. I just have to get in the groove so to speak.

Cassie flashes me a grin as she pulls up beside me. Embarrassingly, I have to open my door to hear her when she starts talking.

"Get in the car!"

"I thought I was driving." Cassie is as wild as my mother thinks she is, and that means I always drive. I don't have to get drunk to have a good time, but Cassie doesn't have fun unless it involves frequent damage to her liver.

"Not tonight."

"Cass," I sigh. "I have kids."

"And I love your kids, but you're free tonight."

"So, you aren't planning on drinking?"

A slow, mischievous grin tugs up one corner of her mouth. "You can drive us back if you think I've had too much to drink."

Translation—you're driving us home tonight.

I climb out of the car, taking the opportunity because it means I'll be crashing at her house tonight. All the time I can get away from Mom the better.

"And where are we going?" I ask, standing near the passenger side door of her car while she gathers junk and tosses it in the backseat. She's worse than my messy kids, knowing full well she wanted to drive but made no strides in preparing for it.

"You'll see."

"If we end up at another frat party—"

"That was one time."

"One time too many." With the seat clear, I drop down and put my seatbelt on.

"That guy was hot," she argues as she pulls away from the grocery store.

"He was a child."

"He was twenty-one."

"He was a freshman," I remind her.

"He was drinking. You could've pretended he was older."

I scoff at her ridiculousness.

"He was legal, old enough to make you come."

"He grabbed his junk all night while staring at me. I'd wager money he doesn't even know what a clit is."

"So, you're saying you need a man with more experience?"

Why does her question make Miles's smiling face come to mind? The things that guy could do with his tongue; I have no doubt he'd have bedroom skills.

"I just need a little room to breathe. Where are we going?"

"How are the kids? Feeling better?"

"And changing the subject so suddenly isn't at all suspicious."

"You normally talk about the kids every second of every day. Now you're suspicious when I bring them up?"

"You call them crotch goblins."

"I say it with love. What's got you so wound up?"

"Besides missing a week of work and dealing with puke for three days straight?"

Her nose scrunches.

"Brian is in town."

"Brian, Brian. As in college boyfriend, douchebag Brian?"

"That's the one, and it gets even worse. He's been hired as the new attorney at Hollow and Beck."

"Are you—"

"Am I what? Pissed? I'm not very happy about it."

"I was going to ask if you were thinking about getting back with him."

"Gross, Cassie. No. Never in a million years. The guy is a total dick."

"He was good looking though. Is he ugly now?"

I take a minute to formulate my answer. I stopped finding Brian good looking when I saw his true colors in college, but I guess from the outside looking in, he's handsome. "He's okay."

"How was he in bed?"

"Mediocre, but after catching him watching himself in the mirror while we were having sex, that dropped several notches."

"Mirrors are hot."

"He wasn't watching *us*. He was watching himself. Flexing his muscles in weird ways."

"Yeah that's not good. At least you had prior notice. You can prepare yourself before seeing him for the first time."

"About that..." I look over at her. "I saw him at the grocery store Saturday."

A slow smile spreads across her face, the lights from her dashboard glinting in her eyes. "And you fucked and ran?"

"No. Jesus, why do you always think I jump into bed with random people?"

"He's not random, and I'm feeling a little judged for my sexual freedom."

"Stay free my friend. I have kids. I don't have the luxury of casual sex. There's just no time for it."

"You have a full hour for lunch."

"That I use to eat. Do you want to hear the story or not?"

"Of course. Go on."

"Before the kids got sick, we went to the grocery store."

"Riveting story." I watch her eyes roll in the dim light, and if I weren't in desperate need to tell someone about the man I met, her response would be enough to make me clamp my mouth closed like a petulant child refusing to open their mouth for a spoonful of peas.

"Would you stop?"

Cassie laughs, and I know she's only teasing me. How we're still friends when our lives are so completely different, I'll never understand.

"I did something stupid. Brian called my name, and you remember I told you Elijah has been running up to random men and calling them daddy?"

She nods. "I told you to have him do that to the old men at the country club. It's the best place to find a sugar daddy."

I sigh. "He did that in the grocery store, only this man didn't cringe away like Elijah was covered in slime. He scooped my son up like he was part of his own family."

"And that was stupid?"

"No. When I walked up to him, knowing Brian was right behind me, I told him to play along and then I kissed him. Well, I went to kiss him on the cheek, but he turned his face. Instead of a peck on the lips like I was anticipating, this man full-on stuck his tongue in my mouth."

"Did you slap him?"

My cheeks heat. "I kissed him back and let me tell you it was the hottest kiss of my entire life."

"Did you get his phone number? A guy that likes kids and is a great kisser? Sounds like a love match if I've ever heard of one."

"I didn't have the chance. I was so embarrassed, and then Brian came up asking all these questions like am I married and why am I messing around with a biker? He spoke to me like the man and his friend weren't standing right there. I was more embarrassed with Brian's horrible behavior than I was at forcing a stranger to kiss me."

"Did you say biker?"

"Yeah, he was one of those Cerberus guys, Miles?"

Her brow scrunches.

"Do you know him?"

"What's his road name?"

"His what? I don't know."

"You didn't ask?"

"I was too busy apologizing for my behavior and running away."

"And if you saw him again? Would you jump his bones and go for the second-best kiss of your life?"

"No." Because I'm pretty sure the kisses would only get better. "I saw him again at the doctor's office. I'm almost certain he got all of us sick. If anything, I'd hold out my hand and demand he pay me back for a week of lost wages."

"Really? You'd do that?"

"In a heartbeat."

Truth is, I'd probably stammer over my words trying to apologize for jetting away from him after he changed my tire like I was an ungrateful woman who expected him to get his hands dirty for me.

"But back to Brian. The firm is having a party for him, and all of the lies are going to come to light. I never should've approached that man. I was a coward."

"Just ask the guy to pretend to be your husband."

An incredulous laugh bubbles out of my throat. "Not a chance. I'll probably never see him again."

She's silent for a long moment before speaking. "You know where he works, Reagan. Just go ask him."

To her there's a simple solution, but not only does telling one lie end up turning into several more, the man makes me absolutely weak in the knees. Just thoughts of that kiss we shared makes my belly flip flop. The last time I got tingles even close to that was with Jeremiah, and he couldn't get out of town fast enough after finding out I was pregnant.

"I can't just show up and ask the man for a favor like that." He also rode right past me while I was at the park the other day and didn't stop. He wouldn't be interested in helping me. I wounded his pride when I turned down his offer to help with my sick kids, but I'm no fool. I know what he was hoping for. I'll focus on my fantasies of him being the perfect man—all information obtained from one kiss—rather than letting in the truth that he's a guy who just wants to get me naked and leave before the sun comes up the next day. I've had enough of that sort of drama in my life, and I have no intention of seeking it out again.

I may not be actively dating but settling down with a man that loves me and my kids will always be my end goal. One-night stands and casual sex isn't even on my radar.

"You never know," Cassie says as she heads out of town. "The opportunity to ask may just pop up."

When I ask her once again where we're going, she just smiles and says, "You'll see."

Chapter 9

Jinx

"That one's mine," Apollo says with a beer-drunk smile.

"You don't have to claim every woman that walks in the front door," I remind him. "There's plenty to go around."

"And it looks like you'll have your pick if you don't seem so eager," Max says, but his eyes stay locked on Tug and Jasmine.

The pair are across the room, hips close, hands wandering as they dance to a song playing from the stereo. It's like watching fully clothed sex, and I can admit I'm not immune to the sight of them.

I've always liked watching people as they interact. I wouldn't call what they're doing a mating dance because they love each other, but the promise of sex is rolling off of them.

"God, they make me so fucking hard," Max grumbles as he shifts in his seat before turning his beer bottle up to his lips.

"Would you punch me in the throat if I agreed?"

He turns his head, giving me a slow smile. "Do you really think I'd get upset that they turn you on?"

I shrug.

"We love it when people watch us, that people are envious of what we have. I'm ecstatic that we have the opportunity to play here instead of having to drive to Denver. We get to go home at the end of the night rather than facing that long-ass drive. It's fucking perfect." He licks the mouth of his beer bottle, and I'm almost certain he doesn't even know he's doing it.

I've always identified as a straight man, never had any desire to mess around with another dude. And maybe it's the alcohol flowing through my blood, but the sight of his mouth teasing that bottle makes me stand up and take notice.

I blame the pheromones floating in the air for my body's reaction. Or maybe it's the lust in his eyes and knowing that it won't be long before the three of them pile together in front of everyone and fuck like they'll never get the chance to again.

Watching people fucking and being involved in numerous threesomes myself isn't a new idea for me. Seeing three people completely dedicated to each other in every aspect of their lives getting it on? That's a fucking scorching sight.

Women are looking our way, each one trying to decide who they want to get naked with tonight, but I'm nearly resolved with waiting for Tug, Jasmine, and Max's show. I could easily stroke myself to completion just listening to their groans and commands. It wouldn't matter if Jasmine was taking both dicks or getting spit-roasted or if one of the guys bent over to take a cock. I've seen them in all sorts of combinations, and each one is equally as hot as the next.

"Would you be offended if I sat right here and pulled my dick out?" Max asks without pulling his eyes from the dancing pair.

"I could ask the same question," I say, using the heel of my hand to press down on my erection.

His laugh is low and heated.

"We don't share."

"I know you don't. Still hot as fuck to watch."

"That's the entire point. Here, hold this." He pushes his empty beer bottle against my chest before standing.

"I can't believe Dominic doesn't care that his daughter is—"

"What?" I snap, my focus on Thumper.

"So free," he says, and then I notice his eyes on them as Max tangles himself around the other two. "Most men would lose their shit knowing their daughter was sleeping with two men."

"She's in love with two men. That's a huge difference," Apollo clarifies.

"He wants her to be happy, and I doubt it would matter if she was happy being one of the other girls who is here just for a night of fun. We don't get a pass to do this ourselves while judging the women who do the very same. The double standard is bullshit," I say to no one in particular.

"Here, here," Legend says, taking a second to pull his face from a woman's bare tits to join the conversation. The woman grins at him before slipping off his lap and heading toward the open bar.

"I'm not the only one who noticed that there are like three girls available to every guy, right?" Apollo asks, his face lit up with joy.

"These parties used to be bigger. There were more guys around, but everyone went and fell in love," I say, but it isn't a complaint. I'm not upset at all for my brothers finding the loves of their lives. If anything, I'm probably a little jealous.

Rocker is at home with Simone, probably curled up on the couch or already getting down and dirty themselves.

All of the guys have healthy sex lives, and just because it's with the same woman every night doesn't make it any less incredible.

"That's Cassie," Legend says with a nudge to Apollo so hard it shakes me on the other side of him. "She's really into tag team."

Apollo looks across the room, but I keep my eyes on Max's wandering hands as he strokes the front of Tug's jeans while lowering his head to suck on Jasmine's nipple.

"How the hell do you know that? I thought this was your first party. I knew you guys were fucking lying four months ago when I went back home for a week." Apollo sounds like an annoyed child who just discovered that his parents ordered pizza while he was staying the night at his grandparents' and was forced to eat brussel sprouts and wild salmon.

"We didn't," Legend says. "I met her at *Jake's*. She already had two guys from out of town lined up and was looking for a third."

Apollo's eyes narrow, and it's clear that he doesn't fully believe him.

"And you just fucked her with two dudes you didn't know?"

"Jealous?" Legend teases Apollo. "I'll fuck her with you, too. Don't get all upset about it."

"Fuck," Thumper groans, and I nod in agreement.

He's watching the scene on the makeshift dance floor that's got me enthralled.

"Almost as good as participating, isn't it?"

He grunts his approval, and the rough sound is laced with the same carnal need I'm feeling.

"Does it make me a little gay?" he asks when both Max and Jasmine sink to their knees and take turns deep throating Tug's cock.

"Wanna suck my cock to verify?"

When he doesn't answer, my head slowly rolls on the back of the couch to look over at him. He's not even paying me any attention. His eyes are locked on the triad across the room.

"Makes me wish the music wasn't playing so loud. There's nothing that gets me hotter than the noises people make when they're turned on."

"Right?" I agree lazily. "She stops breathing when she comes. The absence of that sound nearly made me cream my jeans like a teenager the first time I witnessed it."

"I'll leave you old perverts to it," Apollo says as he stands. "Legend? Want to introduce me to your friend?"

I grin at the younger guys. Thumper is older than those two even though he's one of the newest guys to the club. He spent twelve years in the Corps before joining Cerberus.

My eyes follow the pair across the room as they approach Cassie. She's been to a couple of parties before, and although I've never had an experience with her, Rocker used to rave about how wild she is in bed. He's a one-woman man, now, however.

My eyes don't fall on Cassie, but her timid friend. Pink cheeks under familiar gray eyes dart around the room. Instead of looking at the women or the triad messing around on the dance floor, it's as if she's trying to look anywhere but where the action is happening. She's uncomfortable, but also intrigued. I can see it in the quick peeks she tries to hide under long lashes when she drops her gaze to the floor. It's a combination I can work with. Sometimes, as illustrated by the way Thumper and I are feeling right now, watching is just as good as participating.

"She caught your eye," Thumper says lazily. "Better go before Apollo tries for a group thing."

Just the thought has me on my feet. I put my beer bottle and the one Max handed to me, that I was still holding onto for some reason, on the side table and cross the room.

"Hey," I say when I approach, resisting the urge to brush my fingers along the color in her cheeks.

I want my hands all over this woman. I want her under me. I want those sounds Thumper was just talking about panted against my fucking neck when I slide into her for the very first time, but I won't touch her without knowing for certain it's what she wants. Cerberus men are walking horndogs, but we don't take things we aren't given permission to have, and that includes liberties with a woman's body. Just being in this clubhouse doesn't mean she's given anyone the go-ahead to move in and conquer. We have one woman that shows up and never messes with the guys, and I've spent more than one evening watching her watch everyone else as she uses her long, skillful fingers to get herself off.

"I... umm..."

"Wait," Cassie says with a horribly fake curiosity. "You two know each other?"

Reagan grumbles something about her friend being an asshole.

"We can go outside if you're uncomfortable in here," I offer.

Her eyes dart back to the front door, but she doesn't make a move to head in that direction.

"Or you can stay. Want to join me on the sofa?" I hitch a finger over my shoulder, and her eyes widen when she looks in that direction.

"They're umm... busy."

I turn to see Thumper with his eyes glued to a woman giving him a striptease.

"They won't mind."

"You're here to unwind," Cassie says.

"You said this was a party, not a—"

Cassie cups her hand to her ear. "There's music playing. Drinks are over there and free. People are dancing. It's a party."

Reagan's eyes dart to Tug and gang, and I nearly groan when her teeth dig into her bottom lip.

"Cassie, why don't you go have some fun? I'll keep your friend occupied."

"Ask him," Cassie insists before walking away.

Legend and Apollo follow after her like needy puppies.

"Ask me what?"

"Nothing," she says too quickly for me to believe her.

"Want a drink?"

"I'm driving."

"Want to leave?"

"I'm stuck here until Cassie is ready to go."

"She normally stays the night."

"And you know this how?" The spark of jealousy in her voice has the potential to make my cock harder than the scene playing out on the dance floor.

"She's attended more than one party here."

"And woke up in your bed?"

I shake my head. "Women don't sleep in my bed at these parties."

"I see." Her eyes fall to her hands.

"No, I don't mean I keep them up all night. If I'm going to fuck someone at one of these parties, we do it out in the open. It's part of the thrill, you know?"

"I don't know, actually."

"Something you want to experience?"

"No. I don't think that's—"

"No one here will judge you, and no one will touch you if it isn't something you want."

"And those three? That woman wants those two men?"

I know who she's referring to, but I look over my shoulder anyway.

Jasmine is on her knees servicing both of her men's cocks. Wetness drips down her chin, and the way her fingers are dancing over her clit tells everyone in the room she's in heaven. Maybe Reagan is as new to this sort of scene as she seems.

"They're all in a relationship together. They literally all three sleep in the same bed every night."

"They both love her?" A sadness marks her eyes, and it makes me wonder how one woman could get two dedicated men whereas she probably doesn't have one in her life. I don't think she'd be here if she was still in a relationship with her children's father.

"They all three love each other. It's a triad not a threesome. If you wait long enough... Oh, see?"

Tug and Max lock lips, each one with a hand on the other man while their other ones tangle in Jasmine's hair.

"Wow." The word comes out on a breathless rush.

"Fucking hot, isn't it?"

She clears her throat and is looking away by the time I'm able to pull my eyes off the way Max rubs his thumb over Jasmine's lips when she releases his cock.

"I'm not into group sex."

"Have you ever tried it?" She shakes her head, cheeks as red as tomatoes at this point. "Then how do you know?"

"It just doesn't appeal to me."

"And your panties aren't wet from watching them?"

"Being turned on at watching it and wanting to do it myself are two different things."

"So, you are turned on?" I can't help the words coming out on a growl.

God, this woman fucking does things to me.

"Is that what you're into? Group sex and exhibitionism?"

She already knows how River was conceived, so I change tactics. She seems more curious than appalled.

"I wouldn't want to share you with a single soul in this room. I wouldn't want them looking at you when my mouth tastes every inch of your skin. I don't want them to hear the moan you would make when I slip inside of you for the first time, or the filthy words you're going to say when I pinch your clit right before you come."

Her breath hitches as her eyes find mine. "You're so sure of yourself."

"Wanna put it to the test?"

"I thought this was a regular party."

"This is a regular clubhouse party."

"I didn't know I was coming here, and by the time I realized it, Cassie wouldn't take me back to my car."

"I'll take you back. I've only had one beer."

"I can't leave without her."

"Can't or won't? She's a big girl. Like I said, she doesn't leave until morning time."

"I knew she was a little wild, but she never mentioned biker orgies before."

"What have you heard about Cerberus?"

"Not much," she answers. "Nothing bad."

"Have you ever heard about wild sex parties and group fucking?" She shakes her head. "There's a reason for that. We're not bad guys. We do a lot of good, but we also like to fuck and have fun. We have a reputation to protect. The only people allowed here are ones we can trust. Cassie has proven her trust, even if that meant keeping secrets from you. By bringing you here, she's trusting you with our reputation. Can Cerberus trust you, Reagan? Or do you feel the same way about dirty bikers that your ex does?"

Her brows narrow, forming a crease on her forehead. "I don't have a problem with anyone or have any judgments about what they do for fun."

"I believe you," I tell her honestly, and it has more to do with her embarrassment over the way that dickhead acted in the grocery store than her words right now. Actions do speak louder than words.

"I'm just not comfortable with…" She waves her hand to encompass the entire room.

"People seeing you turned on?"

"Y-yes."

"We don't have to stay out here. There's an empty room if you want to just grab a drink and talk."

"You live here?"

"I don't. I live with Rocker and Simone across town."

"But you three aren't like," she angles her head toward the moaning across the room, "them?"

"What happened with Simone only happened once," I say again, because it feels like she needs the reassurance even though all we've shared is a kiss.

"You want to sleep with me?"

"Only if you want to sleep with me."

"Way to avoid the question," she mutters.

"Listen." I crook my finger under her chin. "All you have to do is say the word, and I'll fuck you better than you've ever been fucked in your life, but I'm not an animal powered by my dick. If you just want to hang out, then that's what we'll do. If you want to stay out here and watch, I'll join you. If you want someplace more private and away from the moans and sex-scented air, I'll find a place for us to go. We can sit on the front porch or go out to the garage. The ball is in your court, Reagan."

Chapter 10

Reagan

"So? A drink?"

I nod, feeling heat rush up my arm when Miles takes my hand and begins to guide me across the room.

"I see you convinced her to stay, Jinx," Cassie says from near the pool table when she notices us walking hand in hand. "Treat my friend right."

Cassie winks at me before bending over the table and lining up the cue. She's a sex kitten on her best day, but tonight she's in her true form. Having men fawn over her puts her in her true happy place.

"Does she—you know what, never mind." There are just some things I don't think I want to know about my friend.

"Alcohol, soda, beer, or water?"

"Whiskey and coke," I say without thinking much about it. If I was at a bar, that's what I'd order. Just one though, because I'm driving. "Jinx?"

"Yeah, babe?" he says as he pours two drinks.

"No." I laugh. "Your name is Jinx? And don't call me babe. It's impersonal and creepy."

"Okay." He chuckles. "Noted. My road name is Jinx, and before you ask, it's because I had the worst luck as a kid and teen. It took years in the Marine Corps before my bad luck changed."

My eyes dart around the room. Other than the two guys with that one woman, I count three other guys. No one is wearing one of those leather cuts, so I'm only assuming they're employed by Cerberus.

"You're curious? Just point."

"I'm not pointing at people while they're getting busy."

"That one," Jinx says angling his head to the guy being sucked off by the woman while she's also getting banged doggie style. "That's Max. Just his regular name. He works IT here. The guy raw dogging her is Tug. Apparently, he used to jack off a lot."

"And the two with my friend?"

"Aw, well those two aren't as fun. Apollo, the one staring at her ass, liked space or some shit. The other one is Legend."

"So, he's great in bed?" It's an honest conclusion to draw.

"He wishes. I mean I don't know, but his name stuck with him from the Corps. He came in all scrawny, but his attitude was like that of a beast. His drill sergeant saw things in him no one else did. Called him a legend one day and it stuck. At first it was used to taunt and tease, but when his body grew into his attitude, he was unstoppable."

"That's actually a great story."

"Grinch is the one getting his cock sucked over there."

My cheeks heat even further, but I give the guy he's indicating a cursory look before dropping them to the drink he hands me. He smiles down at me before clinking his glass to mine. I take a sip, nearly gagging on the drink that's more whiskey than anything else.

"Oh, shit, sorry." He swaps our glasses. "Gave you mine by accident."

"And it wasn't to try to get me drunk?"

"Do you think you'll ever stop thinking the worst of me?"

"You mean all men?" I wink at him, but there's a burn of truth in my words.

Even Shane, a man I would consider a friend, hurt me. I don't begrudge him a happiness that as a woman I'd never be able to give him, but I want someone who will be there for me like Martin is with him and vice versa. I'm not a wild child like Cassie. I want to eventually settle down.

"I guess I'll just have to prove to you that I'm not an asshole."

I take another sip of my drink, smiling that he got the mixture just perfect.

"And him?" I indicate the man sitting on the sofa.

He's got his dick out, stroking a strong hand up and down it, but it doesn't make me as embarrassed as the three going to town in the middle of the room, so I'm not as quick to pull my eyes away. The woman that was dancing in front of him not long ago is spread out on the couch with another woman licking between her legs.

Now that I have to pull my eyes from.

"That's Thumper. Rumor is, he fucks like a rabbit."

"Quick and done?"

"As in all the time, but oddly enough, I haven't seen him have sex with a single woman since he came here."

"Maybe he doesn't like to do it in front of people," I suggest.

"Maybe he does come quick. I mean, look. The man has his cock out. I don't think he's shy."

"Maybe." I quickly agree because before I can say another word, ropes of cum splatter his chest. "Jesus."

"Turn you on?"

I huff. "It's hard not to be with everything going on."

"We can still find someplace quiet," he offers, and I get the vibe that it's more for my comfort than a desire to get me alone so he can press his luck.

"That may be best," I whisper when the girls separate and inch toward the mess on Thumper's chest with their tongues out.

Jinx takes the drink from my hand before setting it and his on the counter, and then my hand is in his once more as he leads me out of the room and down a dark hallway.

Before I can blink, we're closed inside of a spacious room. He flips the overhead light on, and it adds to my comfort.

"The guys don't spend much time sitting in their rooms. I apologize that there aren't any chairs." He crosses the room and falls to his back on the bed, hands locked behind his head.

I focus on the dresser instead of the way his muscles pull the fabric of his t-shirt.

"Comfortable?" I manage to ask when the movement of him crossing his ankles draws my attention.

Are his jeans custom made because dammit they fit him perfectly.

"Very." He pats the bed beside him. "Why don't you join me?"

"I'm not the type of woman who crawls into bed with a man she doesn't know." I bring my forearm to my mouth to try to hide my yawn.

"Doesn't know? Have you already forgotten we're married with two kids? Come here."

He holds his arms open, and I'm glad he's teasing me about the way I acted in the grocery store. It's like the elephant in the room, that and his confession from earlier that he wants to fuck me silly. I'm glad we can focus on what I did instead of what he wants to do.

My skin heats as I debate my choices, but if I dig deep and listen to my own voice in my head, instead of the words I think my mother would use right now, I want to crawl in the bed with this man, if only to feel his warmth along my side.

"I'm not fucking you."

He bites his lip to keep from smiling. "Can I eat your pussy?"

I flush again. "I didn't shave."

"Pussy wouldn't grow hair if it wasn't meant to be there."

He winks. The man actually winks at me.

"No oral," I hiss on a laugh.

"Fingers?" He pulls his hand from behind his head and waves them at me.

"No."

"Wanna stay fully clothed and dry hump like teens?"

"I want to take a nap."

"It's bedtime, Reagan. Come on."

"No hanky-panky," I warn as I step closer and kick off my shoes.

"Does that include jacking off after you fall asleep?"

"Are you really that hard up?"

He grins wider. "I'll keep my hands to myself."

"By jacking off." My eyes dart to his cock.

"Keep eyeballing my dick, and I won't be able to wait until you fall asleep."

"Maybe you should take care of it and then come back." I crawl up the bed on the empty side.

"Keep letting your shirt hang down like that, and I'll just come in my jeans."

I laugh, but don't make an effort to tug up the neck of my shirt.

"You seriously don't have to stay in here with me. Just lock the door on your way out." I yawn again, letting my eyes fall closed when he doesn't make a move to touch me.

Why do I feel so safe with this man?

"I'm right where I want to be."

"I ruined your orgy."

"Nothing is ruined, Reagan."

My breaths slow as silence fills the room.

"Just turn off the light when you leave." It doesn't bother me now, but if I manage to fall asleep and wake with the lights on, my entire sleep cycle will be ruined.

The bed moves, but I don't open my eyes to watch him leave. I also know I'm not going to be able to sleep with questions about what the man is doing and with whom as I lie here. Darkness falls over the room, but instead of the door opening and closing, a lock is flipped into place a few seconds before the bed dips once again.

"How are my son and daughter doing?"

I smile in the darkness. "They're better. I got sick. Missed an entire week of work."

"Where do you work?"

"I'm a paralegal at Hollow and Beck." I fight another yawn and lose. "I've been there almost two years."

"Do you like it?"

"Hate it," I mutter. "Should've been an attorney."

"Still time, Reagan."

"Two kids, Jinx."

"Call me Miles."

"Two kids, Miles," I repeat, pulling a soft laugh from him.

"Can I hold you?"

I swallow before deciding on an answer. "Thought you were going to jack off."

"I was teasing, but you give the word—"

I roll over and swat his chest, or what I think is his chest until, my fingers grace over his chin.

"Shit. I'm so sorry."

"Didn't think I was into violent women, but I'm willing to try anything for you."

I huff another laugh and settle my head on his shoulder. An arm goes around my back, and I nearly sigh in pleasure. Physical touch from a man is something I've apparently been starved for, and I'm shocked at the ease I feel when I settle against him fully.

"How long has it been since you've been held?"

"Too long," I confess, praying my emotions stay locked down tight.

Finding a man that wants to sleep with me isn't hard. I'm decently attractive. I have decent genes, although my body will never be the same after two kids.

It's finding a man that's okay with just this, intimacy without sex that's been a chore my entire life.

"Sleep well, Reagan."

I feel the ghost of his lips on the top of my head as his strong heartbeat lulls me to sleep.

Chapter 11

Jinx

Maybe it's the slam of a door down the hall that jolts me awake, or maybe it's my body's insistent urge to rut against Reagan. No matter the cause, I'm wide awake far earlier than I want to be.

I wouldn't trade last night for anything. Having her on my chest, her warm breath tickling the hairs on my chest is perfection, but interrupted sleep sucks. If I were holding her in my arms at home...

I barely refrain from chuckling. If we were home, I would've been up the second the sun threatened to peek above the horizon. River is a morning person, and while most days I am too, I don't want this moment to end.

My eyes are still closed, arms wrapped firmly around this woman when a devilish female squeal sounds in the hallway. It's followed by the sound of a slap, then a low moan.

"Keep it up, and you'll be right back in that bed," Legend growls.

I realize Reagan is awake, yet unmoving when she smiles against my chest.

"Is the party still going?" she mumbles, some of her words lost against my skin.

"Probably," I whisper, needing to cling to this moment just a while longer.

"You're poking me." She proves her point by rolling her hips in a devious way that makes me want to flip her on her back and poke her harder, deeper, poking her until she's breathless, moaning my name and coming on my dick.

But she laid some ground rules last night, and I know if I ever want to see her again, I need to respect them. I wouldn't take anything she wasn't offering, but I can be very convincing when challenged. I don't, however, want her to leave here with regrets, despite knowing she'd enjoy herself in the moment.

"Yeah. Morning wood," I agree, but it's so much more than that.

In due time, I mentally remind myself.

"You held me all night."

"I did."

"Thank you."

Her appreciation over something so simple makes me take pause. I want to know everything about her—all her desires, her fears. I want her life story, the good and the bad, but most importantly I want the names of the men she's had in her life that would deny her something so elementary.

"We could stay like this all weekend," I offer.

"Mmm." She snuggles deeper, not purposely trying to entice my cock, but just the scent of her skin is enough to get that bastard excited and ready for action.

The silence is heavy around us, and normally I'd just bask in it, but a million questions burn inside of me. She'll be leaving soon, and although the night was amazing, I want more out of it. Not just sex. He wants that, too, but it can wait.

"Tell me about him."

"Who?" she asks, her voice still weak from sleep.

"That dickhead in the store."

I feel her swallow against me. "I'm sorry he was so rude."

"Don't apologize for assholes, Reagan. That man is responsible for himself. Is he Katie's father?"

She stiffens, her fingers curling against my skin in a very unflattering way. It's as if she wants to claw at me rather than caress. My cock, the opportunist that he is, doesn't distinguish the difference.

"And you just immediately assume that I have two different baby daddies?"

"I presumed if he was the father of both, he wouldn't have been so surprised to see you with two kids, and conceiving a second child with the man while him being unaware of the first either makes you a magician or him a complete fucking idiot."

She swallows again. "Brian isn't the father of either of my children. Brian is just a jerk that I dated my first year in law school."

"You loved him?"

"I thought I could love him. I loved the idea of him, loved that he was so attentive to me when we first started dating. I later learned that he was controlling rather than protective."

"Hindsight."

"Exactly. His family is rich, so he didn't understand that I had to work while going to school. It didn't matter that he filled his time away from me with any woman willing to strip down for him. He said I was the problem in the relationship."

"He broke up with you?"

"I broke up with him." Her words make me hold her a little tighter.

I don't do it because I get the impression she's still hurting over the decision, but because I know many women put up with a load of shit for the security a man with money can offer.

"If he's any good at math, he'll probably start to wonder if Elijah is his."

"Got pregnant with him shortly after the breakup?"

"Within weeks. What Jeremiah and I had was casual. I figured I couldn't get my heart broken if I wasn't in a committed relationship, but you know how it goes."

"I don't. Tell me."

"Maybe it's a woman thing or maybe it's just a me thing, but I have a hard time separating sex and feelings. Despite not wanting to care for Jeremiah, sleeping with him ended up shifting things that way. I was such a fool. He lavished me in attention whereas Brian would withhold affection as punishment when I did something to upset him. I freaked out when I found out I was pregnant. I mean, a kid changes everything, you know? But I wasn't terrified to tell him."

She pauses, and I know the rest of the story isn't going to end in butterflies and rainbows.

"He wasn't happy?" She shakes her head against my chest.

"He was livid. The guy who showed me so much attention turned into a cold man I didn't recognize. He blamed me for trapping him. Said he wanted nothing to do with a baby."

"Sounds like a douche."

"A total douche," she agrees. "I had to drop out of law school and come crawling back to my parents' house because working part-time wasn't possible. I still had a plan though. I was going to go back to school, eventually. Then after a few drinks one night, I thought sleeping with one of my friends was the best idea ever."

"Katie's father?"

She nods. "Shane is a great guy. He's involved in both kids' lives. That's where they stayed last night."

"But you aren't together?" What man would be crazy enough to let this woman go?

"He's engaged, and I'm happy for him and Martin. That night—"

"Martina?" I ask, thinking I heard her wrong.

A breathy chuckle escapes her mouth, the warmth of it on my chest nearly enough to make me lose my train of thought.

"Martin. You heard correctly. Shane was struggling with his sexuality. Apparently, I was the test that made him realize exactly who he was. He's happy now."

"Sounds like a douche, too," I mutter.

She pushes against me, raising her head to look into my eyes.

"He's a good man. Should he have handled things differently or at least took the time to use a condom? Maybe, but without him I wouldn't have her, and I don't regret my kids one bit."

I smile up at her. "I know all about surprises and how split-second choices can change your entire world. I'm not judging you, Reagan. Come back down here."

I press my hand against her back, urging her to lie back on my chest, but she resists.

"Something else is bothering you."

"It's stupid." She pushes more until she's no longer touching my body.

"Try me," I say, sitting up as she slides her legs off the bed and plants her feet on the floor.

"Brian finished law school. He's not from here, and I was hoping that seeing him at the grocery store that day was just him passing through or something, but it turns out he's been hired by my law firm."

"So, you're going to have to see him every day?"

"Unfortunately."

"Do you think he's going to be trouble? I can get a couple of the guys together, prove to him just how fucking dirty bikers can be."

She laughs but there's no humor in the sound.

"Just give me the word." God, what I wouldn't trade for ten minutes alone with him.

"That's probably not wise, but he's going to know."

"Know what?"

She looks over her shoulder at me, eyes sad but resigned.

"He'll know that I lied. He'll find out I'm not really married. I'm going to be so embarrassed when he finds out, and if he's the same Brian that he was years ago—and with the way he acted at the store, I suspect he is—he's going to gossip like an old lady around a quilting circle."

"You're afraid of rumors?"

She sighs again, and I'm beginning to hate the uneasy rush of breaths from her lips. If she's going to be puffing air, I'd prefer she do it because my lips and my touch made her that way, not frustration from an ex rolling into town and making trouble for her.

"How would he know? Do you think my name would come up in conversation at work?"

"Knowing him? Without a doubt. He'll try to make me look bad, something he did before we ever broke up. He's such a jerk. An elitist asshole who needs to feel superior to everyone else. If he thinks I'm happy, he'll do whatever he can to ruin it."

"The offer still stands. Most people like that balk when faced with an actual threat."

"He'd probably sue."

"Cerberus has better attorneys than he could ever hope to be."

"And your legal team takes cases to defend a woman you just met?"

"My wife," I correct with a smile. "And our two children."

She gives me a sad smile.

"So, he's going to be working with you. He may say some backhanded shit, but you'll get through it. I'm still getting to know you, but I get the feeling that you're a strong woman."

"I wish I never lied."

"We shared a fan-fucking-tastic kiss because of that lie," I remind her.

"It was great," she muses. "But not only am I going to look pitiful when I show up to his welcome-to-the-firm party alone, it's going to give him ammunition to cut me down."

"Don't go to the party alone." I shrug. It's the easiest solution.

"Are you offering to go?" she asks with a scoff and a quick roll of her eyes.

"I'd love to. Thank you for asking."

"I didn't exactly ask."

"You don't have to. If my wife is going to a party where her asshole ex is, then I'm going too."

She stands from the side of the bed and turns around to fully face me. I resist the need to spread my legs, grip her hips, and urge her to stand closer. I don't, however, have the power to not look at her tits. I'm only so strong, and it seems this woman has the power to weaken me at every step.

"And pretend to be my husband? From the outside that may seem like a great plan, but my coworkers know I'm not married."

"Do you talk to them about your home life?"

"No," she answers. "I keep to myself."

"So how do they know for a fact? It'll work. Tell me where and when, and I'll be there."

"It's next week at the country club."

"Fancy. Saturday?" She nods. "If I'm not at work, then I'll be there."

"Wearing your leather cut?"

"Do you want me to be the big bad biker?"

Her eyes rake down me, a motion so lewd it makes me want to dirty her up a little.

"Take a shower with me."

She takes a step back instead of coming closer like I'd hoped she would.

"One kiss, and you're begging me to get naked?"

I stand, closing the distance between us. "Will two kisses make you change your mind?"

She covers my mouth with her hand as I lower my head closer. "Married couples don't do morning-breath kisses, do they?"

I smile against her palm. "You'll find that I'm not like most men."

"I'm not getting naked with you."

"Showering with clothes on is silly."

She bites her lip to keep from smiling.

"There are new toothbrushes in the bathroom. You may not want to shower with me, but if my breath doesn't stink, are you willing to kiss me?"

She doesn't answer one way or the other, but giddiness still fills my blood when she walks toward the bathroom with a smirk on her pretty face.

Chapter 12

Reagan

I look at Miles's face in the mirror and give him a foamy smile. His eyes dart to my lips, and it does nothing to ease the tension circling around us.

It's not weirdness that makes me want to divert his attention but a cloud of sexual tension that feels almost tangible in the small bathroom. Half of his front is close enough to my back while we both brush our teeth that I can feel the warmth of him. If he knew how close I was to accepting his offer to shower together, he probably would've pushed the issue a little more.

But he seems to be a gentleman, as much of a gentleman one can remain with his erection brushing against me as he scrubs his teeth.

I hold my hair back as I bend to spit and rinse my mouth, and the man takes the opportunity to grip my hip with his free hand as if I need help to maintain my balance. I cock an eyebrow at him when I stand back to full height. He ignores me, and his hand doesn't move. It stays there while he spits and rinses, and while he tosses both of our toothbrushes in the trash.

"Have you made up your mind?" he asks as he uses his grip to urge me to turn so he can look into my face instead of at my reflection.

"What decision was I supposed to be considering?"

Both of his hands are on my waist, and I may even assist him when he lifts me to sit on the counter. I don't want the man straining his back after all.

"Kissing."

"I like kissing," I tease.

"We had a great kiss."

"We did."

"It was too short, cut off too soon."

"It was appropriate for the setting."

"There's no one around, no ex-boyfriend you're trying to make jealous."

"Jealous?" I hiss, my anger spiking. "I wasn't trying—"

His lips are on mine, his body pressed against me between my splayed legs.

"I know," he whispers against my lips. "But I like the fire in your eyes when you're a little irritated."

He swallows my next argument as well, kissing me so long I'm nearly unable to remember my name much less the reason I was going to snap at him.

"Your mouth," he pants against my lips.

"Mmm."

His fingers tangle in my hair, and although my mind is grateful he isn't going in for the kill, so to speak, my nipples burn with the need to be touched. The butterflies this man gives me are swarming in my gut. I won't even mention what happens down below when he grips my hair, not to the point of searing pain, but just enough of a yank to angle my head a little.

His kiss dives deeper, and my hands roam down his back, an effort to memorize every rigid muscle straining against the fabric of his shirt.

Jesus, this man is deadly. If his mouth is capable of making me whimper with just a kiss, I can only imagine what that skilled tongue of his can do elsewhere.

My thighs flex, squeezing him to me, and then he's lifting my leg, hitching it high on his hips as he rolls his body against mine. There's no jerkiness or tremor to the movement, just fluidity that has me seconds from begging him to strip me down.

I smile up at him, feeling flushed all over when he pulls away.

"We have to stop."

"We don't," I argue, my hands moving from his back to caress his chest.

His eyes roll a little before he's able to refocus them on my face. His lips are cherry red, wet, and more enticing than a steak to a starving man. I want to feast on them for hours. I want them all over every inch of my body, as he'd promised last night. My hormones are in overdrive, and I don't see them calming anytime soon.

What I was hesitant about last night, I know I'm ready for this morning.

"Your phone was ringing."

That puts a halt to things. No one calls but my mother when she's annoyed with my kids, and Shane when something is wrong.

Miles steps back without hesitation when I press my hands to his abdomen. *Jesus, are those muscles real?*

I shake my head as I walk out of the bathroom, realizing how steamy we made it in there when the cool air of the room hits my flushed face. A text sounds from my phone before I can reach it.

"Martin isn't feeling well," I tell Miles after reading the text. "I need to go grab the kids."

"That same nasty stomach virus?"

"The one you gave us?" I smile at him as I shoot off a text to Shane before slinging my phone into my back pocket.

"I'm not exactly up to date on virology, but I think most viruses have a longer incubation time than twenty-four hours. I thought you said the kids were better."

"They are."

"Then they didn't get them sick. Do either of them work at the satanic nursery school?"

He'd asked me about the program at the church when we saw each other at the doctor's office, but I didn't think anything of it.

"Do you hate the church or the program?"

"Neither," he answers as he steps closer. I don't hesitate to lift my arms to his shoulders when he pulls me closer. "I hate germs. I was sick as a dog."

"I have to go," I remind him when his mouth lowers to mine once again.

This kiss is slower, feeling more like a promise of more rather than a desperation to satisfy a need.

He smiles softly, his tongue licking at his lips like he can't get enough of my taste.

We exchange phone numbers with his promise to keep me up to date about whether he'll be able to make the party, but we don't make plans to see each other again before then.

Finding Cassie is easy. She's in the kitchen drinking coffee when we make it out of the bedroom. Her cheeks are flushed, eyes tired from a night of what appears to be wild fun, but instead of pressing her mouth to one of the guys like Miles does to me, she gives them a wave before walking out of the room.

I wave to Miles as Cassie drives away, all the while wondering if I'm going to regret last night. We didn't do anything scandalous, but that's probably more of a problem than if we would've ended up naked in bed together. My heart clenches when she pulls on to the road because missing him already can't be good for my heart.

"Have a fun night?"

"The best," I answer truthfully without giving her any further details.

***

"What kind of example does this set for your daughter?" Mom snaps the second I walk in the front door.

Elijah scurries away, no doubt to make sure no one touched his toys while he was gone.

"My daughter was at her father's house last night. For all she knows, I slept in my own bed," I mutter, hating that the day is going to end up in more bitter arguments with her judging every move I make.

You'd think I'd be used to it by now, but I'm not.

I place Katie in her highchair and move around the kitchen to make her something to eat.

Happiness fills my daughter's eyes when I hand her a cup of watered-down juice. If only everyone could get as excited as she is right now, the world would be a much better place.

"Being loose is what landed you in this situation in the first place."

I grip the box of cereal so hard the sides cave in, but I keep my mouth closed.

For the briefest of seconds, I let her get into my head, and I begin to feel bad about last night, but then I remember that nothing happened other than Miles holding me while I slept and kissing.

Still, the accusations have the power to drag my mood right into the ground. Was staying with him and the endorphin rush it gave me worth the misery of being on the receiving end of her words? Was a night spent in comfortable companionship with a man I may never truly know, enough to be able to not have any regrets?

Several deep, calming breaths later, I resume getting a snack for Katie.

My mother huffs, clearly not amused by my refusal to take her bait.

"Did you hear me, Reagan?"

"How could I not? You're practically yelling."

"So, what do you have to say for yourself?"

"I don't have to explain my actions, Mother. I'm an adult."

"An adult that still lives with her mother," she snips. "An adult that continues to make bad choices that I have to pay for."

"You're paying for my mistakes?" I hiss, cringing when Katie's eyes begin to well with tears at the angry tone in my voice.

"I swear, Reagan, if you get knocked up again, the man better marry you. I'm not putting my life on hold to raise another one of your kids."

I cough in an effort to stop my throat from closing up from emotion, but it's no use.

My mother, satisfied that she's hurt me once again, walks away mumbling about me being an ungrateful child.

I brush Katie's soft hair away from her face before bending down and kissing the top of her hair.

"I'll never see you as a burden," I whisper to her, all the more ready to get out of this toxic house.

My kids don't need to be raised around a woman who only views them as a mistake I made and a burden on her life.

Mom acts as if I don't use nearly all of my paycheck on bills. If I were living here free of charge, I would've had the ability to move out long ago.

Chapter 13

Jinx

"How many?" Thumper asks as he pulls his mask over his face.

"Last count registered seven, but there could easily be more," Max says, his voice coming in through the video feed on the computer. "The walls in the basement area are too thick to get an accurate heat reading."

"We have intel that says these guys are very physical with their girls. As you all know, most of these traffickers want to protect their commodities. These guys are a little different. These women are mere products to them, and at the rate they've been turning over stock, they have no problem disposing of the ones they consider useless," Shadow says, his disembodied voice also back at the clubhouse with Max.

Legend nods, taking everything in as a few of the other guys grumble their distaste.

"There were fourteen bodies in that grave, but it wouldn't surprise me to find similar locations around the actual property. The ground has been dug up in numerous locations," Hound informs from us the front of the room. "This mission is going to take a little more time. We were called in by the Guadalajara police because they're getting too much push back from the community."

"Because these fuckers aren't taking girls from their homes, but from the surrounding areas," Griffin mutters.

"Yes," Hound agrees. "And they're afraid that if feathers are ruffled too much, then they'll change tactics and go for the closer targets."

"There's going to be a lot of recovery, and not just from the compound. Many families are going to get the worst news they'll ever hear in the next couple of days, but even knowing that, I need you to be safe. Don't let your emotions get the best of you," Kincaid adds as he looks up from a folder in front of him.

"What's the direction on arrest?" Rocker asks as he cracks his knuckles.

Everyone in the room perks up, waiting for the answer.

"We're letting God sort these fuckers out," Kincaid responds, and it brings a whoop of exhilaration from everyone in the group but Thumper.

He stands to the side silent, as his eyes make a circuit of the room.

Maybe he thinks we're all psychos, but there are some of us here that have been doing this long enough to know that the men that run these sex trafficking rings have the ability to get out of jail, eventually. There's been more than one situation where the direction was to arrest and release to the local police only to be back to bust up another ring they're involved in mere months later.

Putting every last one of them in the ground is the best way to ensure that they can never hurt another person again.

"A head's up," Shadow says, and several guys groan.

Those words are never good.

"Thermal readings indicate children in the compound."

I growl. I've never been okay with kids being in situations like the one we're about to face, but after becoming a father, I'm doubly homicidal where kids are involved.

"The traffickers' kids or are they—"

"We don't know," Shadow interrupts before Tug is forced to ask fully. "We don't have any reports of children being taken in a hundred-mile radius of the place, but we know how it is."

How it is, is beyond fucked up. In some circles, the kids are a hotter commodity than women of legal age. There are a lot of sick perverts in the world, and it's not unheard of for us to raid a place and find kids from different countries or children that have been moved from one location to the next to be used by sickos that have predilections for that sort of shit.

My blood is boiling by the time we make our final preparations and load up in the blacked-out SUVs.

Dawn is still a couple of hours away, but the normal sleepiness that would settle inside of me at this time of day isn't around. We're all focused on the job, ready to face the devil for our misdeeds if the day ends like that for us.

What's the old cadence from boot camp? *Ready to fight, ready to kill. Ready to die but never will.*

That's very fitting, and it may seem irrational to be willing to fight for someone else's family while I have one back at home—a son that needs his father, a son that has the potential to lose both of the men in his life on the same day—but I'd want someone willing to do the same for River if it ever came down to it.

He'd know his father is gone because he was helping put a stop to some of the evil in the world. That's a pride I can take to the grave with a smile.

"Everyone comes home," Kincaid says, his authoritative voice seeping into my head from the comm system in my headset.

We all nod without speaking. Words are no longer necessary as we pull up to the compound that is stupidly not even protected by the high stone fences we normally encounter. There isn't even razor wire around the house, but we won't take the lack of protection to mean they aren't armed to the teeth because we know they are. Men like the ones we're minutes away from meeting with gunfire may be quick to rid themselves of women they deem useless, but they will protect the ones they've kept with everything they have.

Comms are silent as we file out of the vehicles. Night vision goggles make it easy to see the hand movements from my team leader. We split three ways, each team taking a different entrance. Until technology is available to prevent incidents from friendly fire, we have to be diligent not to injure someone from Cerberus, but all piling through the front door isn't safe either. Not only does it give the perps a chance to escape, but it also makes us easier targets.

I read the hand movements easily as Hound instructs us on our next move, and as we breech the side door to the compound, gunfire is muffled by my earplugs. The commands given and enemy body counts coming through the comms are still easily decipherable, and it becomes clear very quickly that the count was way off. We passed seven insurgents by five men already, and the count keeps rising.

I call out one of my own as I drop a man rushing toward us with a knife like he has nothing to lose, before patting Thumper's back to let him know we need to move ahead. We descend the stairs into the basement with as much caution as a couple of guys in full-body gear can do, but this is still one of the most dangerous positions to be in. Not only will the guys down here have time to prepare for an attack, but they also have a slight advantage and knowledge of the layout.

We use flashbangs on a regular basis but try to avoid using them in the places we know the victims are being held. They've been through enough trauma, and we try our best not to further that as much as we can.

A bullet flies past my head, embedding into the wall, and we have no choice. Thumper, the trained killer that he is, pulls the flashbang off his belt and tosses it toward the enemy fire. Several men yell, alerting their friends of what's going to happen, but before the guys can duck and cover, we take five down. From their reactions, I'm sure they thought we were about to hit them with a grenade, but I can't smile at their stupidity because the scene in the room is stomach-turning.

From what I can see, there are no adults down here besides the dead men lying on the floor.

Children. There's nothing but children. Dirty-faced kids that will never be the same after experiencing the horrors most people can only imagine.

I swallow down bile as it tries to force its way up my throat. There will be time for all of that later. We have a job to do.

One man twitches, his leg scraping along the concrete floor.

Thumper unleashes his entire magazine into him before dropping it to the floor and shoving another one into his rifle. Any other time, I wouldn't have a problem with it. I don't have an issue with the guy getting filled with lead. Hell, if I could resuscitate him and do it all over again, I'd repeat the ritual until there were no longer any bullets left in the world, but the children down here are already terrified. I place a hand on Thumper's arm, ignoring the tremble in them like I'd hope he'd do for me if the roles were reversed.

What it must look like for two men to come down the stairs and kill six men while dressed in solid black with their faces covered by masks. Terror fills their eyes as I take a step closer to them.

"Rivet," I hiss into the comm when two of the kids scurry away. "When it's clear up—"

"I'm on my way," she answers.

We don't pawn these jobs off on our only female member because we feel like this is a woman's job. We're beyond grateful to have her as part of the team—one because she's fucking awesome, but two because the women we encounter and in horrible cases like this, the kids are more comfortable around women. I wouldn't bat an eye if Kincaid brought in an entire roster of female commandos. It may be exactly what the team needs.

"What do you have?" Kincaid asks.

"From my count..." I pause as I try my best to get a head count. "Eleven."

"Women?"

"It's all children," I clarify. "Only kids down here."

"Only kids mean that the shallow grave we found across town doesn't belong to this group. They wouldn't change their operation so drastically," Shadow says, and I'm grateful the children can't hear the comms because cussing and promises to kill every man that gets involved in shit like this—traffickers and patrons alike—fills my headset.

I nod in agreement as Thumper walks across the room and kicks each one of the guys on the ground. I know he's looking for another reason to pull his trigger.

Rivet joins us a moment later, speaking softly in Spanish she's picked up since coming to work for Cerberus. She assures the kids they're going to be alright, but the level of abuse they've suffered for God only knows how long doesn't allow them to believe it. Several fight when we try to get them to leave the basement.

"They have four rooms upstairs," Hound hisses when I finally make it out of the basement and into the kitchen. "I've never seen such disgusting shit. Little fucking torture tables."

"Sick motherfuckers," I snap. "Do we get to burn this place to the fucking ground?"

"In due time," Kincaid answers. "We need to gather as much intel as we can."

We get to work collecting all paperwork and ledgers kept by these guys. We seize every receipt, taking pictures of every tag we can find that may help us in locating the next compound. Cerberus used to take only paid jobs, locating those people that were abducted in high-profile cases, but somewhere along the way, things shifted. We always help where we can when we get a call like we did about this one from the Guadalajara police, but more often, we do independent jobs, ones we discover through information obtained from places we raid.

We may have been called in by the police for this job, but there's a very good chance that our next one will be from a lead we gather here today.

"Did you see this shit?" Rocker asks as he flips the child-sized torture table over.

"Prideful motherfuckers," I hiss, taking a picture of the company's logo on the underside of the table.

Not only is the table a custom piece, but the manufacturer included their name and stateside address. What may have meant to be a method of marketing could easily be their downfall. I'd like to see what kind of explanation they come up with for making child-sized things like this.

"Did you check the cross?"

Rocker shakes his head as he heads over there, searching the back for another tag.

"Same fucking company," he hisses as he snaps a picture.

We relay the information to Kincaid. "I'll contact the National Center on Sexual Exploitation, but I think I'll also give Deacon Black a call. He may be able to move things along a little faster."

Rocker nods at me with the news. The NCOSE does a lot of good, but Deacon has a way of circumventing the system and breaking through more red tape than any other organization I know of. Blackbridge Security is filled with a wealth of great men, and they've helped us on more than one occasion when the ring we needed to take down was too large for Cerberus to handle alone.

"The—ah, fuck, guys." Rocker and I both freeze at the sound of Tug's emotional voice coming through our comms. "The graves, man. Fuck. All fucking kids."

I was hyped to get this job done and get back to Reagan, and I've dealt with some shit on this job, but after today, I don't think I'll ever be the same.

Chapter 14

Reagan

I'd call it nerves making my hands shake, but I think anxiety is a better descriptor.

I've somehow managed to avoid Brian all week at the office. He's been too busy trying to make himself look good in my boss's eyes to concern himself with the ex sitting at the front desk.

I know tonight will change things. He's been unable to keep from darting his eyes in my direction all damn night, and with every sip from his constantly refilled whiskey glass, I know I won't escape unscathed. He'll open that stupid mouth of his in front of people, many from the community and not just the people who work at the law firm. He'll ask about my husband or make some remark about how I spend my time slumming it with the dregs of society, both lies of course.

I'm not married to Miles. Hell, I haven't heard from him all week after I texted Monday morning to give him the exact time of the party. He replied back that he'd try to make it, but he was heading out of town for work. I haven't heard from him since.

Also, Cerberus is far from the dregs of society. I should know. I work in the legal system. Despite their parties, and the things they do to have fun and unwind, they're respectful men.

Granted, I know Miles wanted to do some *very* disrespectful things to me, but I wouldn't have complained about one second of it.

I take a long, slow breath. Thinking about the man who isn't here will only make me want to escape faster than I already do, which is saying a lot because I've been eyeing the exit since I got here.

Studiously avoiding the side of the room Brian is on means I'm constantly moving as he works the room like a seasoned politician. These skills are either innate to him or taught to him by his father, a state legislator, at an early age. His smiles are easy, convincing even to those that don't know any better. He's an all-American man, quick to tell a joke that easily disguises his hatred for all things that don't land solidly in his idea of a perfect world, one that's easily white, male, and rich.

He disgusts me. I'm disgusted with myself for ever thinking I could love a man like that. College, especially law school is geared toward making people more aware of the world they live in. Many graduate with ideals the complete opposite of what they had when they entered the program. Brian hasn't changed an ounce.

I take a glass of champagne from a server as he passes by with a full tray, vowing to only drink half since I tossed back the first glass within minutes of arriving.

I feign interest in the fabric of my dress rather than socializing, counting down the minutes until I've been here long enough that it wouldn't be considered rude to leave. I didn't want to be here in the first place, but even more so now since it's clear Miles isn't coming. I try not to feel disappointment even as it settles low in my stomach, mixing with the alcohol there like the final ingredient required for an explosion. My heightened agitation doesn't bode well for my reputation if Brian tries to approach me with disdain or his chauvinistic attitude. It's bad enough watching him work the room like a movie star. If only these people knew he was probably gathering information to use against them later.

I place my half-consumed glass on an empty table, head filled with plans to go to Cassie's place after leaving here. The kids are back at Shane and Martin's. I dropped them off to apologize for cutting their time short last weekend. I'm grateful for their help, but my mood from not hearing from Miles, knowing it meant he wasn't going to be here tonight made me want to remind them that I didn't get a reprieve when I was sick earlier in the week. I know it was safer for them to be away from them while they were sick. It would mean cutting the recurrence of illness down, but as a mother, I don't get those luxuries.

Besides, Shane is Katie's father, and although I'm grateful for his love for including Elijah in everything they do, he's her damned father. He's supposed to take care of her.

I sigh, eyeballing the glass of champagne I set aside and trying to calculate if finishing it off would really impair my ability to make it to Cassie's unscathed. I don't want to risk it, and that annoys me all over again.

"Such a sour face on the prettiest woman in the room."

A wide smile is on my face before I can even turn around and face him.

"Sorry I'm late, sweetheart. Busy day at work."

And in front of God and country, Miles pulls me to his chest and plants his mouth right on mine. If being a single mother with two kids isn't scandalous enough, then the kiss he lands on my lips seals the deal.

I groan, my fingers tangling in his suit jacket.

Wait, what?

I pull back, smiling wide as I look down at his clothes.

"A suit?"

He snaps one side of the lapel. The dark jacket fits him like a glove and holy hell does the man wear it well.

"Do I look okay?"

"Totally fuckable," I answer without thinking.

My eyes widen as I cup a hand over my mouth, but he doesn't seem taken aback at all.

"I hear the bathrooms here are very clean," he whispers as his fingers wander down my bare shoulder.

I choke on a laugh, but the sound still escapes louder than I'd like. Miles nods at the people who look our way, but I only have eyes for him.

"One more kiss?" he asks as he clasps both of my hands and pulls me closer.

He's kissing me before I can make my choice, and I groan against his mouth. This is the one I would've made even if he'd let me choose.

When he backs away, he pulls my left hand to his mouth and kisses my palm.

"What the hell?" I snap, noticing the ring sparkling on my finger.

"Do you really think I'd let my wife walk around without letting everyone around know that she's mine?"

His grin is vibrant, but the sight of jewelry on that finger makes my hand shake in his.

"Don't freak out."

"I'm not," I argue.

"You are." He kisses my palm once again, refusing to believe my lie. "Maybe a dance would calm your nerves."

Soft music is playing, but everyone is standing around chatting. "No one else is dancing."

"Then we'll be the envy of everyone here."

He leads me to an area big enough to dance in without hitting people, never pulling his hand from mine.

"You didn't text this week," I whisper when he drags me against his body.

My fingers trail down the silky material covering his back as he presses his cheek to mine.

"Work keeps me busy when I'm away. Did you miss me?"

"Immensely," I confess.

"I missed you, too. How are my kids?"

"Shouldn't a married man always know about his kids?"

I freeze in his arms, but Miles is leading and doesn't let me stop moving.

"Always a pleasure to see you, Bruce," Miles says with little to no inflection in his tone.

"It's Brian," the man at my back snaps, the whiskey he's consumed nearly enough to make him break his good-guy façade. He clears his throat. "Reagan, are you enjoying your evening?"

"I was," I mutter, trying to turn around and face him, but Miles holds me tighter.

"I've been away for work and would like a little quiet time alone with my wife. So, if you don't mind?"

Brian must not step back because the nastiness in the air that always seems to follow him doesn't dissipate.

"Wife? Are you referring to Reagan or the other woman you have a child with?"

Miles doesn't miss a beat. Where my feet stutter, waiting for everyone in the room to home in on this conversation, the man holding me is as calm as can be.

"We're very proud of our blended family, Brian. As a man brought on board at Hollow and Beck, a firm that deals mostly with family law, you should know that family is very important to your boss."

My boss couldn't give a rat's ass about people's families, but parents fighting over kids pay very well. It's actually disgusting if you think about it, which I don't have time to do.

I don't know Miles well enough to guarantee that he doesn't cast me aside long enough to punch Brian in his face. Hell, Brian could be reason enough for the man in front of me to walk away altogether.

"And I guess all of the men at the Cerberus compound are just as pragmatic in their beliefs?"

"Well, we all do value family, and we're quick to agree that the more people involved in raising a child the better. The resource of family isn't limited to only those involved in creating a child."

The entire time he's speaking with Brian, Miles is moving his feet and forcing me to do the same.

"And do you take off your wedding ring when you fuck the whores at the compound?"

I press my face into Miles's chest. He's had great answers, but if he spouts off some bullshit about me joining in or enjoying others as they watch, I may murder the man.

"Why are you so concerned about my bedroom business?" he asks instead. "And although I'm well aware of the brief interlude you had many years ago with Reagan, you need to get over her as she's clearly done with you."

"Get over her?" he scoffs. "She's a—"

And just like I predicted, I'm set aside, the quick action making Brian drop whatever he was going to say.

"Miles," I plead as he approaches my ex.

But Miles doesn't lift his fist. He doesn't even raise his voice as he steps to within a foot of Brian. I see the flash of a ring on Mile's left hand as he reaches up and pretends to brush lint of Brian's jacket.

"If you open your mouth to utter one more foul word about my wife, I'll put you in a shallow grave." This threat is made with a smile on his face so wide it would look like the two are old friends from anyone looking at them.

Brian however looks like he's moments away from shitting his very expensive pants.

"Do you understand?"

Brian doesn't answer verbally or nod his head, but Miles must see something in his eyes that he's satisfied with because he takes a step back.

"It was nice chatting, Brian," Miles says loud enough for those that stopped talking long enough to watch what was happening. "I'm going to have one last dance with my wife before we head home. I've missed her, and the kids are anxious to see their daddy."

Daddy. Not father like someone as pretentious as Brian and many of the others around here would say. I find that I kind of love it. It's like a great big fuck you to all of those standing around that have ever complained about the minor annoyances their children have ever been.

Unafraid of the man swallowing thickly, Miles turns back around to face me, pulling me once again to his chest as he urges my hips to move with his.

"How are you so wonderful?"

He shrugs his shoulders under my hands that have settled there. "I grew up with amazing parents."

"You're wearing a wedding ring?"

"As every married man should," he says simply. "I never take it off."

I hide my smile in his chest as he presses a kiss to the top of my head.

I'd be a fool to think I've heard the last of Brian. His pride won't allow him to walk away without having the final word, but I know he won't force the issue tonight. That confrontation will more than likely come Monday morning at the office, but since that's over thirty-six hours away, I opt to bask in Miles's woodsy scent and the movement of his body against mine instead of worrying about it right now.

Chapter 15

Jinx

"I swear I won't keep you up all night," I vow as I walk out of the country club with my hand in Reagan's.

"Only half the night?" she asks playfully.

I wink at her, trying to keep her mood light. She's acting like nothing is wrong, but I know that confrontation half an hour ago is still on her mind. I've met a lot of assholes in my life, ones that are inherently evil, but it's the slick fuckers like Brian Wakefield that sometimes have the ability to do the most damage.

"I have to get the kids early from Shane's. They have some sort of brunch to go to."

"But you're free tonight?" I hedge. "I don't bite."

She chuckles, a sound that makes my blood run a few degrees hotter than normal. "Why do I get the distinct feeling that is a lie?"

"I don't bite hard," I amend.

She smiles wider.

"More like nibbling." I prove it to her by pulling her even closer and sinking my teeth into her shoulder.

She groans, her head angling further away so I have even better access.

"I'd be happy just to hold you again."

"And what does your cock think of that idea?"

She presses against me, rolling her hips against my straining length as if I need proof that I'm always hard for her.

"My cock doesn't rule my life."

"Too bad," she whispers.

I pull back, eyes wide. "Are you planning to take advantage of me, Mrs. Alexander?"

"Alex—Oh I see what you did. Your last name? Next, you'll be insisting it's my marital duty to lie on my back and spread my legs for you."

Even though there's a lot to unpack with that statement, I keep things light. "You're more than welcome to get on top. I've also been told that bending over the edge of the bed is a lovely position. And even if those don't appeal to you, Mrs. Alexander, then I can let you decide if you'd rather be the six or the nine. Lady's choice because I'm a gentleman."

"So generous," she says, and I can tell she's trying to keep a straight face. "I'd love to come home with you."

Would pumping the air with my fist right now be too over the top?

"Really?" She nods.

"I'll follow you."

"You can ride with me."

"I'd prefer to drive."

"Your car is safe here."

"Where everyone from the office can see it deserted? Would a married couple who live in the same home leave one behind?"

Damn she's got a good point. "Very analytic and forward thinking of you."

"I was going to be an attorney."

"Will be an attorney," I correct, and I know it's the wrong thing to say when her face falls.

"Maybe it's too late. I don't want to disrupt your household."

"They're heavy sleepers. Just scream into the pillow when you come."

"We're not having sex tonight," she warns, but there's a glint in her eyes that holds the promise of possibility.

"And I don't have to have sex with you to make you scream my name." I press a quick kiss to her lips before she can object. "I'm in that SUV. Can't wait to see you again."

I walk her to her car before heading to mine, and I watch her headlights the entire way to my house wondering if she's going to change her mind before arriving and drive off in a different direction.

"Big house," she says as she walks up the driveway.

"Home sweet home. Come on."

I grab her hand, using my free one to enter the pass code on the doorknob to gain entry. She stays close when I reset the alarm.

As quietly as we can, we climb the stairs to my room. I swear my heart is beating so loudly in my chest that Rocker is going to come out of his room and want to know who's playing drums, but the house stays quiet.

"Rocker and Simone have the downstairs room," I explain when we finally make it to my room. "The boys are down there as well. It works best for Simone when we're gone for work."

"So, this is yours then?"

Of all the things she could focus on, she picks up the teddy bear wearing a Marine Corps dress blues uniform.

"That's River's."

"You let him sleep in here with you?" She hugs the bear to her chest and smiles because it's such a mother thing to do.

"I'm a sucker for his little pouty lip, and the kid learned from an early age what a pushover I am."

"I bet you're a great dad." With care, she places the bear back on my bed.

"I try to be. Is Shane a good dad?"

"He is. They also treat Elijah like their own son, and that's amazing."

"They sound like great guys."

She gives me a small smile.

"Did you love him? Shane?"

"No. Like I explained last week, he was a friend, and I guess I love him in that way, but it was never a romantic love."

"Scratching an itch then?"

"Something like that."

"I didn't mean to upset you," I say, stepping closer when her eyes insist on looking anywhere but at me.

"I'm fine."

"Says every woman who isn't fine at all."

"We don't have to talk about our lives." She presses her hand to my chest, and I cover it with my own. "Didn't you promise to hold me?"

"I did," I say, giving her what she needs by dropping the subject and not delving any deeper even though I want to tell her all about my life as much as I want to learn about every aspect of hers.

I close the distance between us, using my knowledge of women's clothes to easily find the zipper of her dress along her side.

"Wh-what are you doing?"

"Naked holding," I whisper against her neck.

"M-Miles."

"Okay, not naked. You can keep your panties on."

She chuckles, but the soft laugh fades away as I slip her dress over her shoulders. I step back, taking her in as the dress falls to my bedroom floor.

"God, you're beautiful."

I stop her hands before they can cover the exposed skin between her bra and her panties.

"Don't."

"This is awkward."

"There's not one awkward thing about any of this other than—" I reach my hand into my slacks and situate my cock better. The cut of these damn things doesn't really allow for a comfortable erection. "There, that's better. Where were we?"

"You were going to find something for me to sleep in."

"I thought we decided you were sleeping in my arms."

Her eyes dart away, and I can't have that, so I gently pinch her chin between my thumb and forefinger and direct her gaze back to me.

"What's wrong?"

"You're," she swallows, "all muscle and I'm... this."

"Absolutely gorgeous? Radiant and sexy as hell?"

"Covered in stretch marks and jiggly," she counters.

"Stop," I whisper, my hands going to her hips. "Boys worry about shit like that. A man knows the battle you fought for those. Growing babies from an egg and a single sperm is a fucking miracle, Reagan. Your body is perfect."

I press my lips to hers, relieved when she kisses me back.

"I promised no sex. I'm going to respect your wishes."

"I take it back," she pants against my mouth as her hands reach for the buckle on my leather belt. "Sex sounds amazing."

"So fucking tempting, but I'm a man of my word."

"Chivalry is dead, Miles. I don't want chivalry."

"What do you want?"

I'd give this woman the world if I were able to clasp it in my hand and wrap a bow around it for her.

"You promised so many things. How can I pick only one?"

"You want it all?" She nods vigorously. "And no regrets tomorrow?"

"Is this when you tell me you won't call after tonight?"

I pull away and look down at her.

"I can handle it if that's the case, but I'd like to know in advance."

"Maybe this was a bad idea."

She swallows as I step away, her hands shaking as she bends down to grab her dress off the floor.

"What are you doing?"

"L-leaving." Her voice cracks, and it nearly splits me open.

"I don't want you to leave. I don't mean you being here is a bad idea, Reagan, but if you're already thinking that I just want sex, want to fuck you and then walk away, then I don't want sex on the table right now."

"But I thought—"

I cup her cheek and force her eyes to mine. "Quit fucking thinking. Quit comparing me to the men you've been with in the past. I'm nothing like them. No matter what we do tonight, I'm going to call you tomorrow. Even if you walk out of here and change your mind about seeing me, I'm probably going to harass you until you do. I'm going to send you flowers, and text you goodnight. The last thing I want to do is fuck you and forget you. I couldn't forget you if I tried."

I use my thumb to sweep away a tear as it begins to glide down her cheek.

"Do you hear me?"

"Yes," she whispers.

"Do you want to leave?" She shakes her head as she lets her dress fall from her fingers back to the floor.

"Do you want something else to wear?"

I kiss her when she shakes her head again. The woman steals my breath as her arms go around my back.

She squeaks in surprise when I lift her off the floor and lay her on my bed.

"Can I make you come?"

"Please," she pants against my lips. "I need you inside of me."

"Not tonight, but I promise it'll be worth it."

Her eyelids lower halfway as I climb off the bed and begin to strip out of my clothes. It's not a strip tease, my movements are very economical, but her eyes drink me in as if it's the most erotic thing in the world. God, she's great for my ego.

"You're sure about this?"

"So sure. Come here."

She's still in her underwear, so I keep my boxers up even though I'm leaving nothing to the imagination with the way I'm straining against them.

Then I cover her like a blanket. Feeling the warmth of her body against my bare skin for the very first time is an out-of-this-world experience, so enticing I wish I could forget it just to do it again and again.

"Open," I urge, pressing against the inside of one thigh.

When her legs spread and I sink against her, I groan in relief. How have I gone my entire life without this?

Her hips roll. Two layers of fabric is all that separate us, and it's the best torture I've ever experienced. I don't have much control in going slow. Other than my high school girlfriend when we were both virgins, I've always been in a rush to get what my body was demanding, but even with her, I fought like hell to hold back. It's nothing compared to the restraint I'm attempting right now.

I'm fighting—and losing—that battle again tonight.

"Feels so good."

She swallows my grunt of agreement.

"Miles, please."

"I love to hear you beg. Tell me what you need."

I pull my mouth from hers, smiling when her cheeks flush in embarrassment.

"Okay, don't tell me. Just tell me if I'm going too far."

She nods, whimpering when I pull back, leaning my ass on my calves to look down at her.

"Pull your panties to the side." She looks away, but her fingers do my bidding, revealing pink slickness.

"Look at what you do to me." I run my hand down my stomach, ab muscles flexing with power before looping my thumb in my boxers and tugging until my cock springs free.

Her teeth dig into her bottom lip, eyes glassy with desire.

"So fucking hard for you. Your pussy is already wet for me. Can I touch it?"

She licks at her lips as she nods, and I want to glide my dick along that fucking tongue coating it with the release already drawing my nuts up. We'll get to that point eventually, but tonight is about her. Well, *mostly* about her.

I dip my thumb a fraction of an inch into her wetness before moving it back up to her clit. It's swollen and hot, and I'm sure she can feel her own pulse of need in it. My mouth hangs lax as I work her with slow circles, hating that it's a finger and not my tongue giving her pleasure.

"Feel good?"

"So good."

Her hips move in opposite circles to my thumb, and I can't believe how close she is already. A pussy this pretty should be worshipped every day, and I make a vow right this very second that I'll do exactly that if she'll allow it.

"I'm not going to enter you," I promise as I pull my thumb away and circle my hand around my cock. "I just want to rub you. Is that okay?"

"Please."

I press the tip between the thickest set of lips I've ever seen, begging my body to give me more than a handful of strokes before betraying me. She mentioned last week that she didn't shave, but her pussy is bare tonight, and God, so fucking warm that my glide against her is unimpeded.

"Miles!" she hisses when I press forward, the underside of my cock sliding easily along her clit.

I keep my promise, not inching inside of her like my body is begging me to do, but I watch in awe as I rub the length of my cock over her most sensitive area.

"Feel good?" I ask again.

"You're going to make me come," she warns, and thank fuck, because even though this doesn't come close to some of the freaky shit I've done in the past, this is hands down the most erotic thing I've ever experienced—my cock sliding against her, and I know it's more her than the actual action.

Jesus, this woman is going to ruin me.

"Do you need it? Is your body begging you to take my cock?" My eyes stay on hers; my cock still moving back and forth along her slit. "I want to do this to you while you're standing. I want to stroke my cock between your thighs and nestle right up against this gorgeous cunt. I want to come all over your panties, and have you pull them back up, walking around the rest of the day with my cum keeping you wet for hours. God, Reagan. I want to see it dripping off your skin—hot, fat drops falling from this pretty pink pussy of yours."

She groans with my teasing. "Just a little harder. Just. Oh, God, *that's it*."

Her back arches, making it nearly impossible not to slide inside of her, but I manage. *Barely*.

"Fuck, Reagan. Watch us."

The pulse of her orgasm is so strong, it vibrates against me, and before her body even settles against the bed, I'm jetting ropes of cum onto her stomach. I want to go back for more. My body is desperate to slide back between her slick lips and spend the rest of my life there, but I know how dangerous that would be.

Sleepy eyes blink up at me as perfect pink lips form a satisfied smile.

"I made a mess on you."

"I'm not complaining. Plus, with all that dirty talk, I figured you'd like me messy."

"You willing to sleep with my cum coating your skin?"

Her nose scrunches, and a husky laugh slips out from my throat. "Let me get something to clean you up."

Clean up turns into another hour-long make-out session, but we both decide not to take things any further tonight. Some wouldn't call taking what we did tonight slow, but it's a turtle's speed compared to how I normally am. When Reagan sighs against me, locked in my embrace, I discover that I really like slow with this girl.

The moonlight glints off the ring I put on her finger earlier, and I find myself smiling down at it, liking the look of it on her slender finger.

Chapter 16

Reagan

I'm a realist. I don't live in a fantasy world where my days and nights are filled with happiness and cloudless skies. I've experienced too much in life to let my head get tangled up in unobtainable dreams.

But waking up alone in Miles's bed still makes my heart clench a little.

He would've stopped last night had I uttered a whisper of unease. I know he would have, but that doesn't mean that the man wasn't using lines on me to get what he wanted. He wouldn't be the first man to trap me into a sense of security in order to get off.

If I wasn't in a second-floor bedroom, I'd consider climbing out the damn window. The voices coming from somewhere else in the house means I'm going to run into someone on my way out. God, why does the morning after have to be so awkward?

We didn't go all the way, but this is no less of a walk of shame than it would've been if we had.

Messy hair? Yep.

Same dress from last night? Of course.

A little shame swimming in my gut? More than I'd like to admit.

Smelling like sex? That's an affirmative.

I pull on my dress. It was perfect last night for a party at the country club, perfect for a slow dance with a man I can't get out of my head, but this morning the low neckline and mid-thigh length are completely unacceptable.

Rifling through his dresser for a pair of sweats that will only fall down my legs would be going a little too far.

Tugging the dress over my head, I zip it up, refusing to let my mind wander to Miles and how easily he found the zipper last night without having to search for it.

With a deep breath in through my nose, I close my eyes and steel myself to what's coming, then I leave the room. I paid no attention to the layout of the house last night when we arrived, so following the voices is the only thing I can do. I may want to slip out without a word, but I'm also not that type of person. I may never see him again after today, but I'll be damned if I'm going to sneak out without seeing him one last time.

I knew Miles wouldn't be alone. The chances of the man holding a conversation with himself were a ridiculous thing to consider in the first place, but the sight of another man and Simone, the woman I saw with him at the doctor's office, still makes me jolt to a stop just inside a very large, modern kitchen.

Simone sighs when she sees me, and it makes me question everything Miles told me. He swore there was nothing going on between them, and I'm no expert on reading people's facial expressions, but this woman isn't even trying to hide the disappointment swimming in her eyes.

"Really?" the woman snaps as she waves her arm in my direction, and although it seems she's angry, her voice holds a note more reminiscent of exhaustion, probably from being put in this situation over and over, than real anger. "We have a baby together, Jinx. How many times are you going to bring a woman into our home? I thought after the last time—"

"Stop!" Jinx snaps—I can't even picture him as Miles in my head right now. He isn't a man I have a serious crush on. He's a biker with a well-earned reputation for sleeping with as many women as he can get under him. "Not this time."

The other man chuckles, but he doesn't say a word.

I freeze, worried about my safety when Jinx walks up and wraps his arms around me. I don't know where to look. Do I keep my eyes on her? I've realized Jinx is a complete asshole, but I don't think he'd get violent with me. The woman across the room on the other hand? She may not have any restraint.

"Really?" Simone says, but this time there isn't the hint of the irritation and exhaustion she had earlier as a smile begins to spread across her face. "I don't need to scare this one off?"

"No," Jinx says.

"What's going on?" I manage, my face hot with the embarrassment of being the center of a situation I don't understand.

Jinx doesn't answer, and it's clear he's not exactly comfortable right now.

"I'm Rocker. Callum if you prefer," the other man says as he approaches with his hand out.

I take it as to not be rude but drop it after a single pump of my hand. Jinx is still plastered to my side, and there's too much going on for my brain to realize until now that he needs to step back. When I wiggle my shoulder to get him to release me, he only holds me tighter.

"The asshole clinging to you like a baby koala is well... an asshole," the man says as if it explains everything.

"Reformed asshole," Jinx clarifies.

"We have this whole thing where he pretends we're all together to scare women off the morning after."

I swallow because that's honestly horrible. It may be a fun time for them, but as the woman standing here after spending the night with him, I don't find it the least bit funny.

"That's—"

"Awful," Simone says as she scrunches her nose up.

"In my defense—"

"There is no defense for it," Rocker says, interrupting his friend.

"I always tell them the score. I don't lie to them, and I didn't lie to you last night. This isn't the same."

I can't even look at him. When I drop my eyes to the floor, I feel a finger hitch under my chin. His hazel eyes soften as they look down at me, and I easily get lost in them like a stubborn woman who is either under some sort of spell or so desperate for him to be different from every other man in existence.

"I have a past that I can't change, but this—you—aren't them. You're different. I'm different because of you." Before I can argue, swoon, or even agree, Jinx turns his head and jabs a finger in the direction of the other two people in the room witnessing this moment. "Neither of you say a word."

I look over at them, expecting to find eyes rolling and annoyance at the lines he's feeding me, but they both have looks of utter disbelief on their faces. Rocker's mouth is even hanging open an inch as he slow blinks at us as if he's unsure of what he's actually witnessing.

It tells me that this is something Jinx hasn't done before.

"Why are they so shocked?" I whisper.

"Umm, because we never thought we'd see the day," Simone whispers as well, as if normal tones will ruin the moment. "Oh, Jinx."

"My little boy is all grown up," Rocker teases, and I can't fight the smile threatening to form.

"They're idiots," Miles—because I can admit when I read a situation wrong—grumbles. "Would you like a cup of coffee?"

"I really need to go."

"It's still early. Just one cup?"

"I'll get it," Simone offers, but then Rocker steps close to her.

"I'll get it."

"My woman, jackasses. I'll get it," Miles argues.

Both of his friends smile and step out of the way, but then Miles freezes. Comically, his head goes from the soft hand Rocker placed on Simone's stomach and back up to their faces half a dozen times before he speaks. "Really?"

Simone grins even wider, and if a person could look like a proud strutting animal, then that's exactly what Rocker looks like right now.

"My symptoms were hidden because of that nasty stomach virus," Simone says a second before Miles shoves Rocker out of the way and wraps his arms around her in a hug.

The jovial mood is contagious as I watch the three of them celebrate the good news. Then a little jealousy settles in because this is how the news of a pregnancy should be celebrated. Not even Shane took the news of me being pregnant with Katie like this. He was shocked, terrified even, and it took months before he could smile about it.

"Get off my woman," Rocker growls after Miles swings a squealing Simone around in a circle.

Miles releases her and steps back, clapping his friend on the shoulder. "I'm stoked for you guys, and also a little worried."

"Worried?" Simone smacks at him. "There's no need to be worried."

"The way you guys are going, there's eventually going to be so many kids in this house that I'm going to be forced to move out." I hear both the tease in his voice and a hint of fear.

"We'd never do that," Simone whispers, picking up on the fear.

"The house next door is for sale," Rockers says with a chuckle. He's a man, so I guess he can be forgiven for not catching on to his friend's anxiety over the situation. "We can take down the fence on that side just like we're planning to do with Drew and Izzy's side. We'll live like polygamists with one huge, connected backyard."

Chapter 17

Jinx

I agree with Rocker's suggestion, smiling as much as I can. Them having another baby is amazing news. Babies are a blessing, every one of them, but I can't help but feel like I'm being left out. Not like out of their bed, but they're moving forward, and I'm going to be getting in the way at some point.

Maybe we were fools to think that all of us living together for River's benefit was something that would work forever. Nothing has changed yet. I still get up at night to help with Cooper, just like I did with my own son. I treat him no differently, and I know this new baby would be no exception.

But they may not feel that way. They've never hinted that I need to leave. Even now Rocker is joking, but I still search his eyes, trying to find a hint of truth in them that he wants me gone. I come up empty, but it has already planted a seed of doubt right in the center of my chest. I know living someplace else wouldn't stop me from spending as much time with my son as I want. I know the door will never be locked. I know if I did consider moving next door that the only thing that would change would be where I crash for the night.

I know all of this, but the threat of change leaves me jittery.

Reagan opens her arms when I cross the room to her.

"I remember those days," Simone says as she turns toward the coffee pot, making me realize I forgot I was on a mission when I noticed Rocker's hand on her stomach.

Funny that I felt a little discomfort and my first instinct was to turn back around and seek Reagan.

But I won't second guess it. I was being truthful when I told her I wanted to call and send flowers and spend time with her, but I didn't realize I would seek her embrace for comfort so quickly.

I know Rocker and Simone are shocked that I stopped the little game we've played more times than I'd like to admit. It wasn't until I saw the pain and disappointment in Reagan's eyes that I realized what a shitty move it was. Rocker was right in calling me an asshole, and now I have the urge to seek out every one-night stand I've had and apologize for being a complete dickhead.

"Here you go," Simone says, offering a steaming cup of coffee to Reagan. "Seems he can't leave your arms long enough to make it himself, even though he just threw a temper tantrum over doing just that."

"Thank you," Reagan says. "Are all the kids better?"

Rocker groans, and I laugh when Simone smacks him across the stomach.

"Yes. Even the big man-babies are better. That nasty virus had everyone miserable for over a week," Simone answers as Rocker rubs his abs like she actually injured him. I have no doubt he'll manage to convince her to kiss it and make it better before the day is out. "You have two kids?"

"Yes. A three-year-old boy and a year-old little girl. Elijah and Katie."

"Drew told us the story about how you two met," Rocker confesses. "It was hilarious."

Reagan drops her eyes to her coffee. "Not one of my finest moments."

"Forget that noise," Simone says with a chuckle. "Did Jinx tell you he was smitten from that very first moment?"

I clear my throat, smiling down at Reagan with a shrug when she looks up at me. I won't deny it. I couldn't even lie if I wanted to. God, I think I'm obsessed with her pink cheeks. I run my thumb down one, and as she blinks up at me, I wonder if she's willing to skip coffee and let me wake her up in other ways. I open my mouth to ask if she forgot something in my room, but my asshole friends can read me like a book, and they take pleasure in getting on my nerves.

"We're all going to the park later. Want to join us?" Simone asks.

"I'd love that. The kids stay home with my mom while I work, so they don't get much interaction with other kids."

"We're not sending River and Cooper back to nursery school. Izzy, she lives next door, isn't sending Andy back either. I've almost got Gigi convinced not to send Amelia and Jamie back. I figure they can get enough interaction with them all together that they won't miss out on anything," Simone continues.

My fingers trail down Reagan's back as she sips her coffee and carries on a conversation with Rocker and Simone as if she's known them for years. I frown when she looks at the clock on the far wall and declares that she has to leave. She and Simone quickly finalize plans for the park, agreeing to meet there later in the day before I walk her out.

I flip Rocker off when he makes kissing noises on our way out of the house.

"I like your friends," Reagan says as we get to her car.

"They're pretty great. I hate that you have to leave."

"Will you be at the park later?" She bites her lip as if it took a lot to ask me that question.

"I have work," I explain, wishing that I could be there to hang out with her.

"I guess hanging out with my kids is a little too soon."

Just like I've done numerous times before, I hook my finger under her chin, angling her face up to mine. "I want to be there. I want to hang out with you and your kids. I don't just want you in the darkness, Reagan."

"Okay." The response is soft as she looks at my face.

"I'll try to make it, but I don't know how long I'll be at the clubhouse." I press my mouth to hers in a brief kiss. "Answer the phone when I call."

She nods her agreement before lifting up on her toes to kiss me again. I fucking love that she isn't afraid to go after what she wants.

"Be safe."

I watch her walk away before going back inside the house. I avoid the kitchen, knowing what I'm going to face in there and head straight to the living room. Cooper is in his swing, happily batting at the zoo animals hanging from his mobile while River's eyes are glued to a cartoon on the television. I scoop my son up and blow on his belly. His giggles fill me with a joy I never thought I'd crave.

"Reagan seems nice," Rocker says as he enters the room.

"She is."

"Too nice to be toyed with," Simone adds, her warning as clear as day.

"I'm not toying with her," I say as I lower River back to the couch.

"So, you've changed?"

"Or you've finally found a woman that doesn't make you want to do more than—," Rocker coughs to fill in the blank, offering a different option to Simone's declaration.

"Maybe it's a little of both. She's amazing." They're both grinning at me when I look at them.

"You're in love." Simone clutches her chest, and if she were any other woman, I'd feel like she's mocking me. Her smile isn't just on her lips, but in her eyes as well.

"Not in love," I counter. "But definitely falling quickly."

Many men may feel like complete fools saying something like that so soon, but I'm a man who has always been able to accept what's happening to me. I saw real love growing up. Hell, I see it in my best friend's eyes every day. I witness it with several of the men at the clubhouse.

And I know I see hints of it when I look in the mirror. Reagan Dunn has me wrapped around her pretty little finger, and I don't think she even knows it.

Speaking of fingers. I glance down at the band on my left hand. I put it on last night before meeting her at the party. It was a ruse, a ploy to make others believe the lie she admitted to regretting. I should probably take it off, but for some reason it just feels right being there.

"Something you need to tell us?" Rocker asks when he notices what's trapped my attention.

"I wanted people to believe we were married last night at her party," I explain.

"Party's over. Take it off," Simone says.

They both laugh when I drop my left hand and flip them the bird with my right, thankful that my back is to the kids so they can't see it.

"You have fifteen minutes to be ready. We have to debrief at nine," I mutter as I leave the room.

I'm not even mad at the squeal from Simone's mouth that tells me we're going to be late if they have anything to do with it.

***

"Eventually, Kincaid is going to be pissed at us being late," I grumble as I park my SUV outside the clubhouse.

"I bet half the guys aren't even here yet," Rocker argues. "We were gone for nearly a week. Kincaid understands why we're late."

"Why *you* were late," I clarify.

"And if Reagan didn't have somewhere to be, you'd still be at home wrapped around her."

I can't really argue with him, so I don't even try. Climbing out of bed before she woke up was the only reason she made it to grab the kids on time. If she had woken up and rolled her body against mine, I would've been lost in trying to recreate the sounds she made last night when she was spread open for me.

Rocker chuckles when I groan.

"Hard to walk away, isn't it?"

"The fucking worst, man."

"We heard you guys last night."

"We tried not to be loud when we got there. At least we didn't wake up the kids. That fourth stair still creaks. I'll take another look at it when—"

"Not when you guys got there. We *heard* you."

"From downstairs?" I ask with suspicion. Is this man just wanting me to talk about what we did last night? "Get real. I wasn't that loud."

"But she was. I felt the urge to come upstairs and give you a high five."

"I'm not talking about this with you."

He laughs like that response was his goal all along.

"And that's how I know you more than just like her."

I climb out of the SUV, unwilling to share that part of Reagan with him.

"That moan echoed around the entire house. I—" I don't know how my hands ended up gripping his shirt or how I managed to slam him against the grill of my vehicle, but here we are.

"Don't," I warn, but instead of aggression, the man just laughs in my face.

He got exactly what he was going for, and I played right into his fucking hands. He's still laughing when I pull my hands away and take a step back.

"Don't stop on our account," Max says as he walks closer.

"For real," Tug adds. "A little aggression always makes my cock hard."

I scoff as I face the men.

"Does Simone play with you guys? I bet—" Rocker growls, cutting Max's sentence in half.

It's my turn to laugh. "Not as much fun when you're on the other side of it, huh?"

"What?" Max asks with a smile on his face and his hands in surrender by his ears. "You've watched us."

"Not my kink, man," Rocker huffs, but there's no real animosity in his words. We both know these guys are only giving us a hard time. "Jinx is in love with the girl from the grocery store."

I glare at my friend, only mildly irritated that he turned the tables on me.

"The pretty one that came to the party with Cassie?"

A grin spreads across my face. "I didn't think you guys were paying attention to anything but each other."

"We always know what's going on," Tug responds as we make it up the front stairs to the clubhouse and walk inside. "I could be sucking his cock while Jasmine—"

"While my daughter does what, Tug?"

The four of us snap our heads in Dominic's direction.

"She made the best French toast this morning," Max answers without missing a beat. "She said it was the same recipe that Makayla used when she was younger. I have to say, I think she's holding out on us as far as the cooking goes."

"She had us convinced she doesn't cook at all, but two weeks ago, she made a pozole recipe that was nothing less than a miracle," Tug continues.

"That's my mother's recipe," Dominic says with a nostalgic smile. "Did she use chicken or pork?"

And just like that, these two deviants have avoided getting their faces punched.

I walk into the huge conference room, stomach grumbling with the talk of food.

Thumper looks up at me, darkening the screen of his phone and shoving it in his pocket. I'd smile and joke about him hiding some hot chick in fear that Legend would get a whiff and start sniffing around, but he doesn't look pleased at all.

"Something wrong?" I ask, taken aback when a wide smile—a completely different look than the one he had when I first walked in—covers his face.

The grin he's giving me is the one we all know. Thumper is a lot of fun, always quick to tell a joke or make people laugh, but I'd be a fool to think his life is all happiness and cheap thrills. We've seen too much in our line of work to smile all the time. I look at him closely because I'm beginning to wonder which man is the real him—this smiling man or the one that was frowning moments ago.

"Life is great, man. What's this I hear about the girl from the grocery store?"

Chapter 18

Reagan

I don't know if the smile on my face as I drive home with the kids is because of the mood back at Shane's house—the kids were laughing and playing when I arrived—or if it's because of memories from last night and this morning with Miles.

I decide it's a combination of both because I'm at a point this morning where I don't have to choose. For the first time, almost all aspects of my life things are fantastic. I have two amazing kids, and if I allow myself to believe everything that's come out of Miles's mouth, a pretty great guy that I'm getting to know.

My mood sours the second I get the kids out of the car and enter my mother's house. Only this time it isn't her scowling face and well-aimed nasty words that drag my mood out of the clouds and right back down to the ground.

That award goes to the man sitting at the dining room table.

"What are you doing here?" I snap the second I see Brian sitting there with a cup of coffee in front of him.

I'm quick to notice it's half-empty, and no longer has steam billowing from the top, indicating he's been here for a while.

"Don't be rude, Reagan. Brian came by to visit because he's concerned about you."

I don't pull my eyes away from my ex to glare at my mother. I feel like I'm being ambushed, and despite my mother's ability to hurt me, Brian is the greater of the two threats right now.

"Concerned?" I scoff.

Brian doesn't have the ability to have concern for anything other than himself. When we were dating, he was quick to remark on what he would call my frugal upbringing. I was always a few notches beneath him, and more than once he hinted that I should be grateful that a man like him would be interested in a girl like me. He's worried about the man I've been spending time with, yet he was the one that was slumming back in college. I'd find the entire situation ironic if my hands weren't trembling with rage.

"Go put your things in your room," I tell Elijah as I situate Katie in her high chair.

Elijah runs out of the room, obeying on the first request. I consider him lucky to not have to be around the vileness that's floating in the air around the two at the table, wishing Katie was old enough to entertain herself while this situation plays out.

"Brian tells me that he's met your husband," Mom says with mock surprise in her voice. I can sense the judgment without even looking at her face to verify. "He was quite shocked when I told him that you aren't married."

If I could get away with knocking the smirk off his face, I'd smack him twice for the way he's looking at me.

"Is that why you're here?" I ask Brian, ignoring my mother as best I can. "To get the final word? It seems a little petty for a grown man, an attorney no less, to worry about the goings on in his ex-girlfriend's life."

"Brian is worried for you. He tells me that the man you've been lying about being married to is one of those bikers from just outside of town."

Brian leans back in his seat. He hasn't said a word since I arrived, and he really doesn't need to. Whatever they discussed before I got home is enough to turn my life upside down, and the slight tilt of his head tells me that was his intent all along.

"Do you have nothing better to do?" I shake my head in confusion, because I seriously don't understand why he's so hell-bent on sticking his nose in my life right now. "I thought you were always too important to worry yourself with my family."

More than once the man refused to come home with me and meet my parents. He had better things to do, like bang his way through the freshman dorm.

"You know I don't tolerate liars in this house, Reagan. It's a sin. And you're still wearing a fake ring?"

I clutch my left hand in my right as if she hasn't already seen the damn thing. I knew I should've taken it off before coming home, but I wanted to hold on to the fantasy just a little while longer.

"Putting on a ring when you aren't married is bad luck." Leave it to my hypocritical mother to tangle superstition with biblical wrongs nearly in the same breath.

"My personal life isn't either of your concern."

"The hell it isn't!" my mother snaps, her fist pounding on the table in front of her so hard Brian's coffee cup rattles against the saucer.

I barely manage to choke back a laugh. We aren't people who use cups and matching saucers. I have no damn idea where she even pulled the pair from.

"Did you think I'd just sit idly by and let you get tangled up with some criminal? I'd never let something like that happen to my grandbabies."

Three deep breaths don't even begin to calm the anger racing through my blood. Without a word, I pull Katie, who begins to grumble from sitting there and not having a snack put in front of her, from the high chair. I leave the room and head to my bedroom, pulling my cell phone from my purse.

I don't know why I call him, but Miles is the first person on my mind as I close the bedroom door.

He told me he had to work, so I'm surprised when he answers on the second ring.

"Hey," he says in that smoky tone that would make me feel a certain kind of way if it weren't for this morning's events.

"You aren't going to get into trouble for answering at work, are you?"

"Still waiting on a few guys to get here. Are you missing me?"

More than I think I'm ready to admit.

"I don't have Simone's phone number."

"If you wanna know my secrets, all you have to do is ask."

I wish I could smile at the teasing in his tone, but I just can't manage it.

"I have to cancel the park playdate."

"Did something happen?" He's quick to switch gears, and my eyes burn with the concern he's showing.

"It's nothing. I just—"

"I don't want to start whatever this is between us with lies, baby. Please don't."

Baby. Jesus, this man.

"Lies are the problem," I mutter, thinking back to the grocery store.

"Listen to me, Reagan—" The sound of a chair scraping fills the line as well as a couple guys teasing about already being in the doghouse, but it only takes seconds for silence to return. "I haven't lied about a single thing. Tell me what's going on, so I can fix it."

If only it were as easy as he makes it seem.

"Not your lies. *My* lies. Brian is here. He's sitting—"

"Are you in danger? Where are the kids?"

"We're fine, but he told Mom about you. He knows I was lying."

"Is he refusing to leave?"

"I didn't ask him. I can't."

"The hell you can't, Reagan."

"This isn't my house, something my mother reminds me of daily."

"Get the kids ready."

"Excuse me?"

"I'm coming to get you. Get the kids ready."

"That won't go over well," I warn.

"Do you want to stay there with him?"

"Of course not."

"Then get the kids ready, Reagan. I'm on my way."

His command left no room for argument, and I spend the next five minutes making sure the diaper bag is packed adequately, tossing in a couple changes of clothes and supplies for more than a trip to the park would require.

By the time I have Elijah and Katie ready, there's a knock at the door.

I rush in that direction to open it, wondering why I didn't tell him I'd just meet him somewhere. Mom is standing in the entryway, the door already open, and the look on her face is one of pure disgust. But it isn't Miles on the front stoop but Simone and another woman.

"Ah!" Simone says with a wide smile and concern on her pretty face. "There she is. It was nice to meet you, Mrs. Dunn."

My mom doesn't take the hint and step out of the way. I ignore the masculine chuckle from the dining room. I won't give Brian one more second of my time. I don't even know why he's still here. He did the damage he was aiming for. He should already be across town ruining someone else's life.

"Are you ready?" Simone asks, her eyes meeting mine. "The kids are anxious to get to the park."

Elijah squeals with the word, but the friend with Simone stops him before he can fly past her.

Ignoring my mother, I move past her on the front porch, and it becomes very clear that my mother wasn't scowling at the women on the porch.

Jinx is standing outside of his SUV at the end of the driveway, but he's not the only one there. Like a show of force, there are several other vehicles lined up with people I don't recognize. I count at least five leather cuts outside my house.

I ignore Mom calling my name as I walk away from the house.

Chapter 19

Jinx

"Daddy!" Elijah screams the second he sees me, and I barely have time to bend down before he's rocketing himself in my arms.

When his little arms squeeze me around the neck, I blame the dust in the air for the burn in my eyes.

"Are you ready for the park?" He nods his head vigorously. "Let me introduce you to my son."

River squeals in excitement at seeing a boy close to his own age when I pull open the back passenger door. "Friend!"

"River, this is Elijah."

They chatter, a conversation that's so all over the place, I can't keep up as I buckle Elijah into the booster seat I got out of Simone's car earlier.

When I turn back around, Reagan is standing right there, her face a combination of emotions that I plan to completely unpack later.

"Hey there, sweet girl," I say to Katie, tickling under her chubby chin until she buries her smiling face in Reagan's neck. "Hey, baby."

I want to look at the man standing on her mother's porch in the eyes as I lower my head to kiss this woman, but he doesn't deserve the attention. I'll be able to prove my possession over her soon enough.

Her eyes shine bright when I take a step back.

"Unlock your car so I can get her car seat. Cooper's is too big for her."

"You brought all these people," she says as she digs into the purse on her hip to find her keys. "I wouldn't be surprised if my mother has a stroke."

"I'll introduce you to all of them when we get to the park." She hands me her keys, making me realize that her car doesn't have a fob that unlocks it, and I hate that she has to struggle with two kids and use a regular key to unlock it.

I pass Simone who doesn't even have to be asked to go stand by Reagan as I walk up the driveway. I nod at Mrs. Dunn and that fuckhead Brian before unlocking the car and pulling the infant seat from the back. Manners would have me walking to her mother and introducing myself, but from the way I've heard Reagan talk about the woman, it wouldn't be well received. Since I'm not a man who likes to waste his time, I don't.

It only takes a minute to get the car seat locked in beside Elijah, and Reagan hands Katie off to me. The little girl beams up at me as I get the straps over her shoulders and everything clicked into place.

I manage to grab the passenger side door handle before Reagan can open it.

"I know you said chivalry is dead, but don't make me look like a complete asshole in front of your mom."

She gives me a weak smile as she climbs inside, and although there's a part of me that tells me not to press my luck, I ignore it and kiss her again.

I cup her face in my hands. "Are you okay?"

"I am now," she says, but I can't help but notice that she refuses to look back in the direction of the house.

I glare at Brian as I walk around the front of the SUV to get into the driver's side, and at least the man has the common sense to cower a little. He's probably intimidated by the group I have with me but worrying about a group of men would be a mistake on his part. When I deal with Brian Wakefield, it's going to be man-to-man.

"I never expected this," Reagan says once we get to the park for the kids to play.

We've settled in at one of the picnic tables off to the side of the play area.

"Does it upset you?"

"That my knight in shining armor came to pick me up for a playdate with an army?" She grins, her eyes on Elijah as he tests the perimeter boundaries the other men in the park have set. Kincaid grins as the child stops in his tracks and looks up at the MC president before turning back around and running to the slide. "I'm not upset."

"Good."

"Is this all for me?" She waves her hand to indicate the guys standing just outside the pea-gravel play area.

"Would you be impressed if I said yes?"

She shakes her head, amused with my antics. "I wouldn't believe you."

"You're worth it," I tell her, hoping she's in the right headspace to actually believe it for the truth it is. "But no. Kincaid is here because he's Amelia's and Jamie's grandfather. Hound is here because he's their dad. That's Drew and Izzy. Hound is Izzy's dad. Drew is Andy's dad."

"I may need to write this all down."

"You'll learn, eventually."

"And the other guys?" she asks, pointing to the small group standing near the swings, ready and waiting for the kids to go over there and demand to be pushed.

I point each of them out. "That's Delilah, Lawson, Griffin, and Ivy. As you can see, Ivy and Gigi are twins. Griffin is with Ivy. Delilah is with Lawson."

"And those two?"

I grin at Itchy and Snatch. One is at the top of the slide helping kids, and Snatch is at the bottom catching them as they come down.

"The one at the top is Itchy. He and Snatch, the guy at the bottom, are married. They adopted Samson, the guy over there and Delilah. They're twins. Lawson is Snatch's son."

"But you said Delilah and Lawson are together?"

I smile at her. "I guess they're technically stepbrother and stepsister, but Lawson was raised by his mom. Snatch didn't even know about Lawson until after she passed. He was practically grown by then."

Her smile grows.

"Cannon," I point to the other side of the park, "is dating Rivet. He's Shadow's youngest son and Griffin's brother. She's Cerberus, but I'm guessing you knew that from her cut."

"And those three?"

"You probably recognize Legend, Apollo, Thumper, and Grinch from the clubhouse. They're the only single Cerberus guys left."

She gives me a weird look.

"I'm not single, baby. I have you."

She looks away, but her eyes are shining with glee.

"We're a pretty big family," I add, watching Simone hold Katie on her lap in the center of the merry-go-round as Rocker spins it slowly. The little girl giggles, the sound traveling back to us on the breeze. "We all take that very seriously. That's why there are so many here today. Our kids are the most precious thing we have, and we keep them protected. Kincaid is throwing around the idea of having a park built on the property."

Her face grows serious. "That's kind of isolating."

"We don't see it that way. Have you noticed how many people have pulled into the parking lot only to turn around and leave? We don't mean to be, but we're an intimidating group. We don't want people to feel like they can't come and play, but those folks are doing what they feel they have to do to protect their own kids. We do a lot of community involvement stuff, but people are still a little apprehensive to approach us outside of those situations."

"I didn't even notice your cut at first when I saw you in the grocery store. I just knew I had to do something to get Brian off my back."

"My good looks drew you in." She laughs, and I love hearing the sound so soon after her upsetting phone call earlier. "Why me and not Drew?"

Her cheeks pink, and I resist the urge to touch the blush. "I said I didn't notice your cut, not that I didn't notice your handsome face."

"So, I'm better looking than Drew?"

"Would you stop?" she says, smacking her hand against my chest.

I grab it and hold it there, keeping my eyes on hers because I know the kids are well looked after with everyone around.

Her face falls as she points her attention to me.

"Something is bothering you."

"I just—" She shakes her head.

"Tell me."

"It's not—I don't want to bother you with things that aren't your problem."

"If it involves you, it involves me."

"You speak as if you've already made your mind up about me."

"Was there ever a choice? What kind of husband would I be if I didn't do my best to keep my wife happy? Tell me so I can fix it."

She sighs, her eyes dropping to her hand against my chest, and I don't know if she's looking at the ring still there or something else.

"I appreciate you showing up to get me, but I think it's going to make things worse at home. I wanted to get away in that moment, but I have to go back and face her, eventually. I've always planned to move out, but I'm so far away from that happening that it's best to not rock the boat while I'm still in it, you know?"

I lift her hand to my lips and press a kiss against the tips of her fingers.

"She watches the kids for me when I work. I wouldn't be surprised if she refuses to keep doing that after today."

"I can help with that."

We both look up to see Simone standing there with Katie. The little girl squeals when she sees us, but she moves her arms in my direction when Reagan reaches out to get her.

Simone grumbles about me being a lady's man as she passes Katie to me.

"Help with what?" I ask as I settle Katie between my legs and hand her a stuffed toy from the diaper bag Reagan brought with her.

"The childcare situation." I grin at my friend, knowing where this is going. The only question is will Reagan be amenable. "We're keeping the kids home, as you know. It wouldn't be a problem for you to bring Elijah and Katie over every morning."

Or just stay the night with them there with us.

"I couldn't," Reagan argues.

"We'd be happy to have them," Simone replies.

"I—it's not—" She looks away. "I don't pay my mom. I mean, I pay most of the bills, but I don't give her cash for watching them. I don't make enough at work to afford childcare."

I can hear the emotion in her voice. She isn't upset admitting that her mother helps her with the kids. It's not knowing what she's going to do going forward that's beginning to freak her out.

"I wasn't offering because we're trying to make a buck off you, Reagan." Simone takes a seat on the far side of us, taking Reagan's hand in hers. "You need someone you trust with your kids—I mean, I hope you trust me—and we're staying home with River, Cooper, and Andy. It just makes sense."

"I couldn't burden anyone else with my problems. It's not—"

"Burden?" Simone snaps, and then she clamps her mouth closed for a brief second while taking a long breath through her nose. "Your kids aren't burdens, and I'd like to slap anyone who has ever made you feel like they are. Let me ask you this, do you like that idiot beside you?"

I grin when Reagan looks in my direction. "Maybe a little."

"Good, then that's all that's required. I'll see you Monday morning. Just make sure to write up a list with allergies and emergency numbers." Simone pats Reagan's hand like the decision has been made and arguments against it will not be tolerated before standing and going to help Rocker with the kids on the jungle gym.

"Me for one," I whisper as I lean in close to her neck, pressing a soft kiss there, "thinks starting my days with seeing you will make things easier. Knowing I get to see you in the morning and in the evening every day will make the time that you're gone a little more bearable."

She leans her head against mine but doesn't speak. During the rest of the time spent at the park, she doesn't bring the topic up again.

And when I drop her off hours later, she doesn't confirm that she'll see me on Monday morning.

I drive away not knowing where her head is at, and it kills me.

Chapter 20

Reagan

Yesterday was the absolute worst. Not the time spent at the park but the aftermath of leaving with my mother so angry.

If I had imagined that my mother would've reacted the way she actually did, I probably never would've come home. At first, I thought I never should've left, but I had a great time at the park. I can really see myself spending more time with Miles and all of his friends—no, his family as he called them.

The way they respect each other was reminiscent of how things were when my father was still alive. My mother was much more tolerable back then.

Just as I suspected, she gave me an ultimatum—either I stop seeing that biker or find someone else to watch my kids. I'm only surprised that she didn't insist that I move out, but as I get Elijah and Katie ready for the day, I get the feeling it's coming sooner rather than later.

"You're really going through with this?" she asks when I place Katie in her playpen before tending to my son.

"Can you go find your shoes?" I ask him, waiting until he leaves the room to address my mother. "I'm not doing anything, Mom. You're the one who said that I needed to find alternate daycare."

"I said you needed to stop seeing that man or find someone else to watch them."

I place the packed diaper bag by the front door. "I guess you know my answer to that."

"What kind of mother chooses a man over her kids?"

I spin around to face her. "I'm not choosing him over them. I'm choosing him over you."

Her eyes widen as if she can't believe the backbone I've seemed to grow overnight. It leaves her speechless.

"Mommy!" Elijah runs back into the room waving a shoe in each hand.

"How about Mommy helps you find two that match?"

He squeals in delight as he turns and runs back toward our shared room. I don't think my mother would physically harm Katie, but I rush to find matching shoes for Elijah, opting to put them on his feet in the living room rather than while we're still in the bedroom.

"I think you're making a mistake," Mom says as I lift Katie out of the playpen.

"And I think you're judging a man you don't know."

"He rides a motorcycle. He lives at the clubhouse. I know I'm no spring chicken, but I've heard rumors about what goes on there."

She'd died an early death if she knew anything of value, but I know she's referring to the whisperings from people who don't have a damn clue. Like Miles told me that night, the people allowed there can be trusted. They aren't running around town and gossiping about their parties.

"Miles doesn't live at the clubhouse, and it wouldn't matter if he did. I'd tell you to get to know the man before you judge him, but that ship has sailed. You're wrong for that, and you're even more wrong for believing a word that came out of Brian's mouth yesterday morning."

"Brian is a successful man," she argues as I grab my car keys and lift the diaper bag strap to my shoulder.

"Brian cheated on me more times than I can count. I was never good enough for him. If you think even for a second that he was here because he's concerned for me, then you're more of a fool than I thought. He survives in chaos, Mom. That's all yesterday was."

"He wants to give you a better life."

I glare at her, knowing he never said such a thing to her, but she's horrible at reading people.

"Even if that were true, I'd never even consider it."

Elijah must sense the mood. It's not like we're even trying to hide it at this point. He walks to the car slowly, waiting patiently for me to open the back driver's side door so he can crawl across the seat to get in his car seat. I don't look at my mom as I strap Katie in, but she's still standing on the porch glaring at us when I go around to Elijah's side and do the same for him.

My mood is absolute trash as I make my way across town to Simone's house, but I manage to let some of my troubles go when I walk inside the house to find Miles galloping around the living room on his hands and knees while River squeals.

"Faster, horsey, faster!"

"They have ponies, Mommy!" Elijah doesn't pause before running across the room and jumping on Miles's back right behind River.

"You know those boys are going to insist I do that when the guys leave," Simone says as she joins me. "I might be able to do one at a time but look at that overachiever."

I can't seem to take my eyes off of the man, and as much as I want to touch him and kiss him, I'm just as content to watch him play with the boys. He smiles up at me, winking in my direction as he makes a circuit of the room.

"Let me get her in the high chair," Simone says as she reaches for Katie. "Any allergies?"

"None that we know of. I haven't given her peanut butter yet, though."

"We're a nut free house. Little Andy is allergic. So, no worries there. Come on, sweet girl. I made oatmeal. Do you like bananas?"

I smile after Simone until grunting, galloping, and neighing draw my attention back to the spectacle in the living room.

"This pony is tired," Miles says, sounding a little breathless.

River climbs down first, tugging on Elijah when my son seems quite content to keeping riding. After another trip around the room, Elijah notices the pile of toys in the corner, and Miles is quickly forgotten.

He flops over on his back, head turned in my direction as he breathes hard.

"The kids keep me fit."

I scoff. "I don't see how playing a horse gets those abs, but please share your secrets."

The man looks toward the boys, and after finding them playing contently with a set of huge building blocks, he looks back at me. With a slow hand, he tugs up the hem of his shirt. "These abs?"

"You're so bad," I say, laughing.

"You have no idea," he says as he stands and makes his way to me. "Do you have a few minutes before you have to go?"

"I have no time at all," I tell him. I could probably spend five more minutes here and still be safe, but I also know five minutes isn't close to being long enough for whatever he's suggesting.

"Mmm." He nuzzles my neck, easily having the ability to make work a distant memory. "Maybe you'll have more time when you get off work."

"I have no plans this evening."

"I'll just have to make some for us then."

It takes seven minutes for me to pull myself away from him, forcing me to race to work.

Luck is on my side because I hit every green light, and traffic is clear near the school. Finding Brian already standing in the small kitchen at the office when I arrive makes me wish I never even had to get out of bed this morning.

I turn around to leave, planning to grab a cup of coffee when he vacates the kitchen and goes back to his office, but he snaps out my name.

I grind my teeth together as I turn to face him. I know the fake smile on my face resembles more of a sneer, but he's an attorney here. I have to get along with him. Hell, I have to work for him. If he needs something, it's our dynamic that I'm supposed to get it for him. I hate being put in this position, and plan to use my lunch break looking for another place to work. Being here with him daily just isn't plausible. I'll go crazy by the end of the week. I'm certain of it.

"Did you have a nice weekend?" he asks. To anyone else around, he'd seem like a man just making small talk, but the two other people in the kitchen don't know he showed up at my house and turned my life upside down.

Okay, maybe that's giving him a little too much credit. What is going on with my mom was always coming to a boil. She would've had the same opinion of Miles if she saw him on the street without this asshole filling her head with all sorts of shit, but at least if she met Miles on my terms, I would've had a better ability to handle the narrative.

"It was fine," I say through gritted teeth.

"I heard you were cavorting with a group of bikers at the park," he says just as Mr. Hollow walks in.

Aaron Hollow founded this law firm, and I have great respect for the man, but he's also inching up on eighty. It would be too much to expect him to have a better attitude about the men in Miles's club than Brian does.

"The Cerberus guys?" Mr. Hollow asks.

"Yep," Brian says with another satisfied grin on his face. "Reagan here fancies herself married to one of them."

Mr. Hollow looks my way with one bushy eyebrow raised in question.

"I'm dating Miles Alexander. We're not married."

"Miles?" Mr. Hollow asks. "Which one is he?"

"Jinx," I say barely over a whisper when Brian chuckles.

"I like him," Mr. Hollow says, shocking us both. "He helped my daughter once at the gas station. You know the one down on Main that got those new pumps? She couldn't figure it out, and he helped. Refused the tip she tried to give him. Those Cerberus men are stand-up guys. Did you know that they raised over eleven thousand dollars a couple months ago at the fundraiser in the park? Did you see the new equipment on the playground at the elementary school? That's in huge part due to those guys."

"Really?" I ask with a wide smile on my face. I ignore Brian as he leaves the room muttering about getting back to work.

"Yes, and don't let anyone tell you differently. My old friend, Dr. Davison—God rest his soul—worked with those guys for years and years. He never had a bad word to say about any of them. I think people just don't know how to act around them, but I've never had any trouble." Mr. Hollow looks over my shoulder before locking me in his gaze. "Brian Wakefield is an asshole, dear. Don't listen to a word he says. He's not going to last long around here."

He pats my shoulder with a shaky hand before walking out of the kitchen.

My day just got better, and it gets ten times better when I make it to my desk and realize that we only have to work a half day due to the construction crew that's coming in to retile the bathroom floor.

Best Monday ever.

Chapter 21

Jinx

I grab a towel from the counter and dry my hands as I go to answer the knock at the door, but it isn't a delivery guy with yet another online purchase package. It's so much better.

"You don't have to knock," I say as I step to the side and let Reagan enter the house.

"This isn't my home."

It could be.

"Yeah, but your kids are here. Well, I mean your kids would be here if they weren't riding around town while Simone tries to get Cooper to calm down and go to sleep. The boy fights a nap like no one's business." I press a kiss to her lips before closing the front door. "Not that I'm complaining, but aren't workdays usually until five or so?"

"It's a half day. We had some scheduled construction work in the office. My kids are gone?"

"Riding around. I could lie and tell you that they'll be back shortly, but sometimes it takes well over an hour before Cooper falls asleep." I reach for my phone in my back pocket. "They just left a few minutes ago. I can call Simone and have her come back."

She blinks up at me.

"Or we can find something else to do until they get back."

Her cheeks flush. "Were you cooking?"

I look down at the dish towel in my hands. "I was washing the lunch dishes."

She cocks an eyebrow.

"What? Men do dishes."

"Where's Rocker?"

"With Simone."

"She doesn't work?"

"She worked at the bank for a while but took part-time hours after Cooper was born. She turned in her notice around Christmas. I've never seen Rocker so happy. I think he wants to keep her home and pregnant the rest of their lives."

"And how does she feel about that?"

I can tell in her tone that the idea doesn't interest her at all.

"Simone worked because it's what she always had to do. She was on her own for a long time. Her first husband was a piece of shit, and she—"

Her eyes widen. "She's *that* Simone. The one who had to—"

"He attacked her, Reagan," I rush to explain. I know people have a lot of opinions and very little information where Simone's situation is concerned. "She had no other choice."

Her hand presses to my chest. "I never had any doubt. Is she okay? I mean, even though he was a horrible man, I can't imagine being put in that position."

"It was years ago, but yeah. I think she's good. Rocker treats her like the queen she is, and I don't think she hates being here full time. She loves kids. She wouldn't have offered to watch Elijah and Katie if she didn't. Izzy was here with Andy, but she took him home for his nap. He doesn't fight sleep like Cooper does."

I grab her hand before carrying the towel back into the kitchen. I release her as I head to the fridge. "Did you eat lunch? I can heat up some macaroni and little smokies. It's what we had."

"We're alone in this big house and you want to eat macaroni?"

I pull my head from the fridge and thank fuck for the cool air from the inside, because I look back to find her with the same look on her face that she had when she watched me strip down to my boxers the other night. My body responds immediately.

"There's only one thing I could imagine eating right now."

She shifts her weight on her feet as I close the refrigerator door and make my way closer to her.

"Are you sure?" I ask because the desire in her eyes make it very clear what she has in mind to occupy our time while Simone and Rocker are out riding around with the kids.

She nods. It's one tiny dip of her head, but it's all the permission I need.

My mouth finds hers, the fingers on one hand gripping the back of her neck while the other presses low against her back to drag her against me.

I drink her whimpers down, rolling my hips to prove to her what my body thinks of her idea.

As much as I don't want to waste a second getting inside of her, I know I can't lay her out on the kitchen island. She must be just as anxious because her legs wrap around me the second I lift her.

I regret the need to pull my mouth from hers as I carry her up the stairs to my room, but I can't say I'm disappointed when her lips meet my neck. Groaning with a tighter grip on her ass, I kick my bedroom door closed. I refuse to pull my hands from her, but I'm not concerned about being walked in on. We do have boundaries in this house, and it only took Simone walking in on me once to keep her from making the mistake a second time.

"Need you naked," I breathe against her mouth.

"You have to put me down for that to happen," she returns when I don't make a move to lower her feet to the floor.

She nips my lip when I smile against her mouth.

I run my teeth over the mild sting and shift my weight, indicating I'm going to release her. I don't want her even an inch from me, but things are going to get out of control and be over before I get the chance to worship her if we keep going at this pace. I don't have all day like I'd hope, but I know I have more than the five minutes my body is indicating.

"Let me," I say as I grab her hands before she can get the second button on her blouse open.

First, I push the navy blazer from her shoulders, taking another long moment to fold it in half and drape it on the dresser.

I know this woman wants me, but I don't want her embarrassed and wrinkled when she leaves. She still has to face her mother when she gets home. My eyes lock onto my working fingers as I unbutton her shirt, revealing the tops of her breasts. They heave up and down with her rapid breathing, and I'm able to elicit a gasp when the backs of my hands brush against her nipples in my efforts to get her naked.

"I like how easily you blush." I trail my finger down her breastbone to indicate the pinkness there.

"You're going too slow," she complains, bringing a smile to my face.

"Don't be impatient." I lower my mouth to hers as I pull her shirt off.

Fuck, I want slow, but my hands and body have a different idea. Deft fingers tease her nipple over the top of her bra, and although she looks amazing in it, I hate the damned thing right now.

As impatient as I accused her of being, she further proves my point when she unclasps the thing and shoves it down.

"Slow," I hiss against her lips teasingly.

But then she presses her palms to my chest, and I heed the warning.

I lick my lips, needing a little more of her taste as I take a step back and look down at her.

"I don't want to be treated like I'm fragile. I don't want slow."

"No?" She shakes her head. "I want to worship your body. I want to spend hours getting to know every single inch of you."

"I want to feel alive."

"And this does nothing to make you feel that way?" I pinch one nipple, pulling a sound that's half gasp, half moan from her lips.

"I want to be fucked." Her cheeks turn a darker pink, bordering on red, but her eyes stay locked with mine.

"And I want to fuck you."

"Are you purposely toying with me?"

I grin, but don't say a word. My shy girl is riling herself up, and I know I'm going to be the luckiest man in the fucking world when she finally snaps.

"Are you afraid of taking what you want?"

Her eyes narrow, and I know I'm skating a very thin line right now. I pull my t-shirt over my head and drop it to the floor. Her eyes lose focus for a brief second as her mouth hangs open a fraction of an inch.

"Are you refusing to give me what I want?"

"Not in the slightest. I like that you're desperate for me."

"My body is aching for you, and you're making jokes."

"Anticipation is an amazing thing, Reagan. We don't have to rush."

"I want to get to the good stuff."

"This is part of the good stuff, baby. If it wasn't, your tongue wouldn't be hanging out of your mouth like that." I unbutton and pull down the zipper on my jeans.

My cock throbs in relief to have a little more room.

"I don't know that I've ever seen someone so turned on for me," she whispers, her eyes locked on my middle.

"I was this turned on the other night. I'm always hard for you like this."

"And this?" she asks as she takes a step closer and runs her finger over the tip of me. I still have my boxers on, but it does nothing to desensitize the touch. "This wetness?"

"Fuck, woman, are you trying to kill me?"

She lifts up on to her tiptoes, as close to my ear as she can manage with our height differences. "I'm wet for you, too."

If I thought for a damned moment I was in control of this situation, it shatters that very second. I growl as I reach for the zipper on her very proper slacks, reminding myself over and over that ripping her clothes would be rude.

The slacks survive, the fabric on her panties do not.

"You ripped them," she says with shock, but I don't think she's complaining.

"You were taking too long to get them off."

"You didn't give me a chance."

"I'll fuck you in your heels later, but they have to go for now." I point to the shoes on her feet hindering the removal of her pants. "Off. Now."

Her smile is devious as she kicks her shoes off and then works on getting her slacks off. I don't waste another second shoving my jeans and boxers down and out of the way.

"You make my mouth water," she whispers when we're finally naked. "Let me—"

I stop her before she can act out her intentions. My cock is leaking double time with the slight dip of her body indicating that she wants to take me in her mouth. My cock jerks, kicking violently between us at the denial of hitting the back of her throat.

"Next time," I promise. "If I remember correctly, I mentioned tasting you downstairs."

She shakes her head as her arms reach up and circle my neck. "If I can't taste you, then you can't taste me."

"That's how it's going to be?"

"If I'm anything, it's fair. I recall you saying it was lady's choice. I pick the nine. Get on the bed and be the six."

I lift her in my arms, loving the way my cock feels against the soft skin of her stomach as I carry her the rest of the way across the room and lay her out on my bed.

"I'll come the second your lips touch me. We have to wait. I'll come down your throat some other time."

"You're convinced I swallow," she teases.

"You're too greedy not to."

She buries her face in my neck, moaning my name when I roll my hips against her. This is the best type of torture.

"Please, Miles."

"You need me?"

"Yes."

"And you're sure?"

"Yes," she pants, her fingers digging into the meat of my ass as she tries to bring me closer.

We're locked together, both knowing that the only way I can get closer is to get inside of her.

"I need to get you ready," I whisper against her mouth.

"I'm already there. Touch me."

I slide a hand between the two of us, blaming the vibration in my fingers on need rather than the fear that I'm going to somehow fuck this up, and I don't mean the sex. If anything, that's one thing I know I'll get right. I worry that I'll say something or act a certain way she won't like that will make her walk away.

But then my fingers find her slick and hot, her moan of pleasure at the slightest brush against her clit make my lower abdomen tighten.

"See?" she groans. "So ready."

"Fuck, baby. We may have to do this twice," I say as I shift my hips back, lining my cock up. "A million times even."

The first dip into her pussy makes my eyes roll back. Yep, I'm going to embarrass myself, but as I sink another inch deeper, I can't even concern myself with the aftermath.

"Miles, no!"

I stop, my hips stilling but not pulling back.

"What's wr—"

"Condom." Her fingers tremble against my stomach. "You have to wear protection."

"Motherfucker," I hiss as I slide out of her heat.

She turns her head to the side, no longer looking as needy as she was just moments ago. "I'm sorry. I just—"

"Reagan," I say, turning her head so she'll look at me. "I freaked because I forgot, not because you said I need to wear one. I just got so lost in you. I'm sorry, I wasn't even thinking. Do you still want to do this?"

"Are you nuts? Of course. Quit wasting time."

I huff a laugh as I reach into the bedside table for a rubber. I have it on my cock, and I'm repositioned in record time.

"You ready?"

She rolls her perfect hips against me. "Yes."

"You sure?" I tease her with my cock, running it up and down her slit much like I did the other night.

Even the tension from nearly taking her bare and the time it took to get the condom on hasn't helped with the threat of coming too fast.

"If you don't stop teasing me—oh, damn, that's good."

"Think I can get you off like this?" I bite my lip as I push my cock through her slick lips.

"Y-yes. You know you can, but Miles..." My name is a plea on her lips.

"This?" I moan as I slide my cock inside of her. "You need this?"

Her back arches, neck exposed as her head tilts back. "Yes."

The single word sounds like it's built of a thousand letters as I find the end of her.

And then there's no room for words as I pull back and slide back in. She didn't want slow, but she doesn't seem upset with the speed I've chosen. But goddamn, she's going to kill me.

I reposition myself, much the same way I did the first time I got to see her pretty pussy. I lean back with her thighs splayed open; legs hitched over mine with her ass a few inches off the bed. I know it gives me the ability to angle my cock up and hit that delicate spot inside of her, and fuck if I don't need all the help I can get right now.

I sweep my thumb over her clit.

"Jesus, look at you. Such a greedy pussy." Her body swallows me, gripping like a fist along my shaft, reluctant to let me go when I pull out. "How close are you?"

Her head shakes back and forth, but her mouth forms no words, then I feel her flutter along my length.

"Fuck, fuck, fuck," I chant, leaving my leaned-back position and pressing forward.

I slam inside of her over and over and over as she pulses out her orgasm.

"Fuck, Reagan. You're making me come." The words meet my release halfway through, and my cock shudders inside of her.

The sounds of our breathing are loud in the quiet room.

"I've never come so quickly in my entire life," I confess. She smiles up at me, her eyes hazy and still clouded with desire.

"Me either. Now kiss me."

I comply, kissing her until we hear the sounds of Simone and Rocker getting back with the kids. We steal a couple more minutes together because I can tell by their whispers that the kids are asleep.

Not counting the day my son was born, I think this has got to be the best day of my life.

Chapter 22

Reagan

I've never had an addictive personality. Yes, I've been guilty of thinking I've fallen for a guy way too soon, but that was infatuation, an ideal rather than actual emotion. Those were a rush of endorphins and mild insanity. I've never known true love, and I'm not even close to thinking that about Miles. Well, I *try* not to let my mind go there.

But I know I'm miserable when I don't see him. I know my mood this week has been off because he's out of town for work.

I can't even deny how the man makes me feel, both in my chest with just the thought of him and also when he's around. We've tried to sneak as much time together as we can the last three weeks, but it's not even close to enough. My blood literally heats when I see him, and let me say, it's difficult to make it through the day after seeing him each morning. I spend the entirety of my day squirming in my desk chair in anticipation of the couple of minutes we may get to steal when I go to pick the kids up.

This week has been misery, but I still have a smile on my face as I walk into the house. Katie squeals at the sight of me, her arms waving wildly, little legs kicking so hard they threaten to knock her over onto the blanket in the middle of the living room floor.

Elijah? That child doesn't even notice me. He's too busy playing with the other boys and Amelia.

"How was work?" Simone asks when she walks back into the living room. She sets Cooper down with the other boys before going to the kitchen. "Something to drink?"

"Work was long. Most of the attorneys were in court because it's docket day, so I didn't have to deal with Brian, but those are also the worst days. We're always running around like chickens with our heads cut off because despite our best efforts, they never have everything they need. How were the kids?"

"Perfect," she says with a smile. "As always. We're having pot roast for dinner. Can you stay?"

"No. I'd rather go home and hang out with my mother."

She laughs as she pulls down a glass from the cabinet. "Things aren't better at home?"

"She's trying to freeze me out," I explain with a quick shrug. "I honestly think she believes it's a punishment. The last week and a half have been some of the best days I've had since moving in with her."

Simone and I have grown close over the last couple of weeks. She's the type of woman who draws you in. She's kind and helpful. She never judges, and she gives some of the best advice I've ever heard. I think her life experiences have granted her the ability to think outside of the box.

"It won't be long before you're able to get out of there," she says as she places a glass of ice water in front of me.

I nod, giving her a weak smile. We talk about everything, but her watching the kids for me still makes me feel bad. I can't confess that I'm no closer than I was. Her keeping Katie and Elijah is a huge weight off my shoulders, but it hasn't changed a single thing financially because my mother didn't take money for watching them. She expected help with the bills. I'm still paying those bills, and I'm stuck between a rock and a hard place because the second I stop paying, the expectation is that I leave. That allows no time to save.

I've looked for a new job, but there's just not much available around town. People here keep the better paying jobs knowing there aren't many. Besides, Brian has laid off bothering me for the most part after Mr. Hollow's declaration about the Cerberus MC a few weeks ago. I doubt he's done harassing me forever, but he's kept to himself mostly since then.

"Do you know when they'll be back?" I ask.

The question has been on my mind since I kissed Jinx goodbye on Saturday, but I've kept it locked in my head rather than letting it escape my lips.

I frown when Simone smiles at me.

"What?"

"I was wondering how long it was going to take you to ask."

"Don't tease me," I mumble as I drop my gaze to the glass in front of me.

"You're falling for him," she says instead of answering my question.

"And you know that because I'm curious about when he gets back? Maybe I just miss his bedroom skills."

"I have no doubt that's part of it." She winks at me, and I wonder how long it'll take before I'm fully comfortable knowing she's had him in that way. "But it's more than that."

"I'm—" Denying it doesn't feel right, so I don't say it. "I miss him."

"You know he's never dated. As long as I've known him, he's never been this way."

"What way?"

"He's never had women over in the daytime for starters."

"My kids are here," I argue.

"And he paces the floor like an expectant father when you're running a few minutes late. Last week when you had to stop for gas, you remember finding him climbing into his vehicle?" I nod. "We weren't out of milk, Reagan. He was going to go look for you."

"He could've texted."

"And if you were driving, that would put you in danger. He'd never do that. He cares about you, and I know you find that hard to believe."

"I don't question that he likes me," I mutter.

"And I don't mean him specifically. I don't know your entire story, but I'm good at reading people. You have a lot of issues where men are concerned." She holds up a hand to stop me when I open my mouth. "And I get it. I totally do. I've had a lifetime of bullshit to deal with, but I also know a good thing when I see it. I also know you're waiting for the other shoe to drop."

"Is it that obvious?" I release a light chuckle even though I feel like I'm under a microscope right now. The scrutiny sets my nerves on fire, and not in a good way.

"Jinx doesn't have the best track record with women. I know you knew that the first time you walked in this kitchen after you stayed here that first night, but he's different with you. I've never seen him so caught up before."

I swallow. I've felt like the only woman in the world when I'm with him, but it's nice to hear coming from someone who knows him so well.

"He never wanted a family. Boasted more than once about his disinterest in dating someone with kids, but he was made to be a dad. You've seen him with the kids. The man is amazing."

"He never wanted kids?" This seems to be the part I'm getting stuck on despite her having said so much more.

She shakes her head. "He didn't know he wanted kids."

In my experience, men are so quick to change their minds.

"I see."

"Not *I see*," Simone says as she crosses the kitchen to stand directly in front of me. "He's different because of River. He's different because of you."

I nod to appease her, but my mind is racing.

"I need to get home," I tell her as I stand.

Maybe it's him being gone. Maybe it's the information I just got. Maybe it's more of my own damage, but I can't stay here a second longer.

"Reagan," Simone says as I leave the kitchen to gather the kids. "I'm not trying to scare you off. If anything, I'm trying to reassure you that what you have with Jinx is real. He cares about you."

"I know. I just forgot I made plans with Cassie," I lie. "I'll see you in the morning."

Elijah grumbles his complaints as I usher him out of the house, but he doesn't give me too much of a hard time. I think I moved too fast, jumped in too soon. Now my kids are staying five days a week at his house. I'm probably overreacting, probably thinking too far ahead, and that's classic Reagan, jumping to conclusions. Only this time instead of thinking of a future with this man, my head seems hell-bent on urging me to run.

It's now that I realize just how much I've allowed myself to think of us being more than a little fun.

Yes, he's made declarations about wanting to see me and spend time with me. Yes, he's gotten what most men shoot for before disappearing. He isn't gone, but my heart is telling me to tread lightly. God, it's going to hurt so much when he decides he's had enough of me.

I drive around for over an hour, but by the time I make it back home, I've decided I'm going to ride this wave as long as I can. I'll keep my heart out of it. Well, at least the parts he doesn't already own, and maybe I'll survive him when it's over.

A pipe dream for sure.

Chapter 23

Jinx

"I was expecting a bigger smile," I tell her with a teasing grin.

I could've just called her on the phone, but the allure of seeing her on video was just too enticing.

"And you said before that work keeps you too busy to call and text."

I frown. "That was last time. We have a little more freedom this trip."

"I'm just surprised to see you."

"And that makes you sad?"

"I'm not sad. It's just—It's nothing."

"If something is wrong, tell me so I can—"

"Fix it," she says, and the tone sets me on edge.

"What's going on?" I haven't seen her for over a week, and the distance before was making me anxious. Knowing she's upset over something and I'm a thousand miles away is borderline unbearable. God, I've got it bad for this woman.

"Nothing, I'm just—I miss you."

I give her a weak smile. "You'd tell me if that fucker Brian was still bothering you, wouldn't you?"

She nods, her eyes darting across the room.

"Are the kids still awake?"

"No. They've been asleep for a while."

"Did I wake you? The time differences always fuck with me."

"What time is it there?"

I give her a weak smile.

"Oh, right. You can't tell me because I might be able to locate you."

"I'd rather be there with you."

She nods, refusing to look at the camera.

"Reagan." Her name is a plea on my lips.

"Hold on." Her phone camera points to the ceiling for a long moment before she picks it up again. "I had to get headphones. I don't want to wake the kids. Katie has been so whiny the last two days. I think she's cutting more teeth."

"I'm sorry I'm not there."

I watch her throat work on a swallow.

"Baby, look at me." Her eyes are drawn to the screen, and even through video it's not hard to see the emotions swimming there. "If you're having a hard time with the kids, Simone is more than willing to help."

"I'm able to take care of my own kids, Miles."

"I'm not saying—I wasn't implying you're incapable. Everyone needs help every once in a while."

She gives me a weak smile. "I'm doing okay. I'm sorry. I'm just tired."

I'd offer to let her go, but I'm a selfish bastard.

"I miss you." Her voice is low as if she's pained with admitting it.

"God, I fucking miss you, too."

"Where are you? Is that a shower curtain?"

I look behind me and chuckle. "I'm hiding out in the bathroom. Rocker is on the phone with Simone, and they're well, he needed a few minutes alone."

Her head tilts, and the smile I've been waiting on since she answered the call is growing on her face. "Really? Then shouldn't he be the one in the bathroom?"

"He'd do what he's doing right now with me right in the room. The man has no qualms about pulling his dick out in front of me."

"Wow," she mutters. "You guys are closer than I thought."

I decide to avoid that topic of conversation because I know she isn't one hundred percent comfortable with my wild sexual history involving Rocker. We've shared too many women, and even though that isn't something that will ever happen again because he's with Simone, I'm not going to rub it in her face.

"I needed some time to myself, as well," I remind her.

"Watching him jack off turns you on?" The question is asked in a teasing tone, and when she bites her lip, my cock thickens in my sweats.

"Not particularly."

"So, your cock isn't hard?"

"My cock is hard, but that's because I'm looking at you, not because my best friend can't go twenty-four hours without reminding Simone that he has a dick."

"Show me," she whispers.

"That Rocker has a dick? I may have been wild in the past, baby, but I'm not even a little okay with showing you his cock," I tease.

"*Your* cock," she specifies. "Show me your cock."

I don't hesitate to lower the camera, slowly trailing it down my bare stomach to the front of my sweats. I pause before hooking my thumb in the waistband and pulling it down. She makes a sound that settles in my nuts when it springs free.

"What would you have me do if I were there?"

I angle the camera back so I can see the desire pooling in her eyes, but I'm met with a blacked-out screen.

"You turned the camera off?"

"I turned the lights off," she clarifies. "I already feel like a pervert."

"A pervert? You've seen my cock before, Reagan. Show me those tits."

"I can't," she whispers. "I don't want to wake the kids. You'll just have to listen to the sound of my voice."

She groans after a brief sound of fabric rustling.

"Are you touching yourself?" My hand is already reaching for my dick, and I groan in return when my rough hand wraps around it.

"Yes," comes her breathy response.

"If I were there, I'd swipe my tongue straight up the center of you. God, I love that you're keeping that perfect pussy wet for me. Dip your fingers inside. Can you feel how needy you are for my cock?"

I stroke faster, hating that I can't see a thing she's doing but knowing just the sounds she's making is going to be enough. I'm a damned fool for this woman, and I'm loving every torturous second of it.

"I miss your touch. Miss your fingers right here."

"Where, baby? Tell me where you want my fingers."

"In my pussy. Fuck, Miles. It's so hot. The tips of my fingers are burning up."

I groan again with need. "Yeah? I bet you're drenched."

"Soaked. I'm going to have to change my sheets. Mmm."

"Pinch your clit, just the way you like me to," I urge, my hand clamping the head of my cock to keep me from coming.

"Miles!" she hisses, her voice louder than I know she wants.

"That's it, baby. Make my pussy come. I'm going to devour you the next time I set eyes on you."

A low breathless whimper hits my ear, and I'm done, shooting ropes of cum on the floor in the next breath.

"I can't wait to see you again," I confess.

"Miss my pussy?" Her tone is lighthearted, but there's an undercurrent of something else there, as well.

"I miss everything about you, Reagan. I miss the way you look at me, the way you absently hold my hand without even thinking about it. I miss the way your breath feels on my neck when we have to say goodbye in the evenings. I miss sitting on the couch together and watching the kids play. I miss all of it."

"And my pussy?" The unease is gone now with my assurances.

"And your pussy," I agree. "And your tits. And that sexy as fuck mouth of yours. I miss your hands."

"I hate that you're gone for so long."

"I'll be home soon," I promise.

She yawns, and as much as I want to stay on the phone with her all night, I know she has work in the morning.

"Get some rest, baby."

"Think of me?"

"Couldn't stop if I tried."

"Good night, Miles."

"Good night, baby."

The video call ends, and as good as the orgasm made me feel, I'm left feeling a little out of sorts as I clean up the mess I made. I don't know how to prove to the woman how infatuated I am with her, and maybe that's the problem. I'm only letting myself get so deep where she's concerned. When I realized I was falling for her, I started to pull back just a little. I'm an idiot to think she wouldn't notice.

I didn't want to bombard her with my feelings. If I had it my way, the woman and her kids would be living in the house with us. I hate knowing she goes home to a spiteful mother. I hate watching her climb into her car and drive away. I hate that she goes to work and has to face a vile man that wants to ruin her life because he likes to see others suffer.

And it scares me.

No.

It *terrifies* me.

"We're a sad damn pair," Rocker mutters when I leave the bathroom. "Have you told her you love her yet?"

"No," I say instead of denying the emotion. I press my fingers to my chest. "Is that what this is?"

He laughs. "Yeah, man. Are you going to tell her, or are you going to fuck things up because it freaks you out?"

"Does it make me an asshole if I say I haven't decided yet?"

He watches me as I climb into the empty queen bed next to his. "That depends."

"On?"

"Are you afraid to say it because you think it's too soon or because you feel like it would trap you into something you don't know for sure that you want?"

"I don't have one foot out the door if that's what you're thinking."

"Can you see yourself spending the rest of your life with her?"

I stay silent. I've stopped myself each time I've begun to picture that kind of future with Reagan, not because I don't want it but because I don't know if it's something she wants. I realized not long ago that going all-in, no matter how much we could both want it, doesn't guarantee a happily ever after. There are a lot of cogs in this machine, and any one piece could break and ruin us. I don't know if I'll survive her.

"Then you don't say it until you're sure, but I'll warn you, Miles—" I know he's serious when he doesn't use my road name. "She's not like the women you pick up from the bar. Her kids are involved. If you break her heart, you break theirs."

His words are a slap to the face. I don't think about walking away from her. I picture her leaving, and it makes me realize I'll lose three people I care about, not just one.

As I fall asleep, I know without a doubt that her heart is safe. It's mine that I'm worried about.

Reagan

I scrunch my nose at Cassie. We haven't really seen each other since that party at the Cerberus clubhouse, and she just won't stop talking about what she's done there. It's like now that I know about their parties, the floodgates have opened.

"Don't look at me like that. It was fun."

"I have no doubt it was fun, and I'm glad you had a good time. What I don't understand is why you feel like you need to tell me about sleeping with both of them at the same time."

"Well," she huffs with fake indignation. "Don't judge me for it."

I chuckle. "I'm not judging, and you know it."

"I just needed to tell someone," she says with a shrug as she parks her car outside of *Jake's*.

"Lucky me," I mutter with a smile.

"And you and Jinx?"

"Miles," I correct. "We're good."

At least I think we're good. We've talked the last couple of nights, but he's never said when he was going to be home. I knew better than to ask. Simone has said more than once that she doesn't get any more information than I do. He isn't being sneaky, but there are rules when he's working. I need to respect that, and I'm doing my best.

I just didn't know I was going to miss him as much as I have. When Cassie called and wanted to go out for a few drinks tonight, I didn't even consider saying no. The kids are at Shane's for the weekend and staying home with Mom is something I've been avoiding since the day I showed up and Brian was there.

"Just good?" Cassie turns in her seat to look at me, a wide smile on her face. When her eyebrows waggle, I know she wants details.

"No," I tell her. "I'm not talking about it with you."

"But I told you all my details," she whines.

"Because you're an oversharer. It wasn't tit for tat."

What I won't confess so soon is that things are different between Miles and me. She's having fun with guys who are only having fun. Despite wanting to put some distance between the two of us, I haven't been able to do that with him, not even with him gone.

If I'm thinking, it's about him. If I'm smiling, it's because of him most times.

"Tell me about that smile."

I force my lips into a flat line.

"Girl, you got it bad."

"Are we getting a drink or what?" I ask, avoiding the subject and climbing out of the car.

Her huff of annoyance is swallowed by the music coming from the bar. But I know by the determined look in her eyes as we go inside that the topic isn't over. Maybe she's trying to live vicariously through me, but as I watch her greet several guys with quick waves, I don't see a hint of displeasure on her face.

People are different. I know this, but I can't imagine spending my life without someone by my side. That desperation was part of why I didn't want to get so close to Miles. I want him more than I could ever explain out loud, but at the same time, I'm trying hard not to *need* him. Yeah, my body is desperate for him, and I need him in that way, but I don't want to have to depend on him for my smiles or my happiness. I need to be strong on my own without relying on him for my own happiness.

"Miles is a wild man. I haven't experienced his abilities." She laughs when I glare at her, and she holds her hands up. "And I never will. I like sex, but I have my own limits. I'd never touch your man, Reagan. Like I was saying, I've heard some fucking stories, and I'm going to get them out of you, eventually."

"If you've already heard what he's capable of, then why do you need to hear it again from me?"

I look around the room, eyeing every woman here, wondering if they've been in his bed.

"Because he's different with you."

Simone has said as much, but Cassie doesn't live with the man. She has no basis for that declaration.

"The guys said so."

"The guys?"

"From the clubhouse. It was out of character for him to disappear with you that night. If he's going to fuck a woman at one of those parties, he does it out in the open."

"We didn't sleep together that night," I mutter as I try to flag down the bartender. If we're going to jump right back into this subject, I need a damn drink. The heat of the bar and humid air from it being so busy is already making my stomach churn.

"And that's different, too. I hear you stayed the night at his house, and yes, before you ask, the guys told me that, too."

"Sounds like you're hanging out with a bunch of damn busybodies," I snap, my cheeks growing flushed and not in a good way. After what I faced that next morning in his kitchen, I know for a fact I wasn't the first woman to stay the night with him. My interaction with Rocker and Simone may have been different, but I wasn't the first.

For some reason, my head decides to focus on that part rather than the many times I've been over there since. I know in my soul I would've been back over there even if my kids weren't staying with Simone but acknowledging that seems like too far of a stretch.

I grumble, hating that I can't just accept that the man likes me, that he wants to be with me. I keep going back and forth, and I'm beginning to hate myself for it. I look up at the bartender as if he holds the solution to my troubles in his very hand.

"Whiskey and coke," I tell him.

"Just a coke for me," Cassie says, shrugging when I snap my eyes in her direction. "You seem like you're going to need more than just one drink, babe."

My stomach continues to turn as we wait for our drinks.

"I didn't mean to upset you," she says when the guy walks away to make our drinks. "I was trying to prove that the guy is hot for you."

Hot for me is great, but I know I need more than chemistry and sexual need. Hot doesn't indicate a future. Hot doesn't protect my heart from getting hurt. Good sex solves a lot of problems, but it won't even touch the things I need out of life to feel whole.

And there I go again, needing to depend on someone else for my own completion.

"Want me to start a tab, Cass?" the bartender asks when he places the glasses in front of us.

"Sure thing," she says, keeping her eyes on me instead of looking his way. "I can see your mind working, Reagan, and I'm a good friend so I'm going to tell you like it is."

Here we go. She's started more than one conversation with those words, the last time being when I found out I was pregnant with Katie. Shane had confessed his sexuality, and I was left unable to argue. I couldn't open my mouth to beg him to give us a chance even though I didn't love him that way. I couldn't discount who he was as a person for my own gain.

"Jinx—Miles—is a good man. Honestly, all of the Cerberus guys are. They're an elite breed of men. He's stable, both mentally and financially. I say if you can get your claws into him, dig deep and hold on. And before you tell me to stop sounding like a fucking gold digger, I'm going to stop you." I snap my mouth closed. "I'm not saying use him. I'm telling you that if you're in love with him, and he's in love with you, get out of your own damn way and let it happen. You'll never find another man as dedicated to you as him. You're a lucky girl."

"Is that regret I hear in your tone," I mutter as I bring my glass to my lips and take a sip. I cringe because it tastes off. I look down at the glass in confusion.

"Bite your damn tongue, woman. I don't want nor need a man. You're different though, and that's not an insult. It's not a bad thing. We're just made different. You want to settle down and live a boring life. I haven't even begun to have fun yet."

I smile when she winks at me, but my stomach is threatening to revolt.

"Excuse me," I tell her as I place my drink on the bar. "Be right back."

I know what's wrong before I can even shove open the heavy door to the bathroom, and when I lose the contents of my stomach and rinse my mouth, all I see is fear in my watery eyes.

How many times can I possibly fuck up before I learn my damn lesson?

Chapter 25

Jinx

I pace the length of the entryway and back. Over and over and over.

I texted Reagan that I was home, and all but demanded that she come over. I spoke with her yesterday before she went out with Cassie, so I know that Shane and Martin have the kids. She's got a free night, and it's been over a week since I've had my hands on her. My body is humming with need, every ounce of me anxious to see her.

She replied that she was coming, but it's been much longer than the five minutes it takes to get from her house to mine. I'm reaching for my keys when a soft knock hits the front door. I tug it open with a smile, reaching for her in the next breath.

"I fucking missed you." She squeaks when I hug her too hard, but I don't make a move to step back and give her space. We've had a thousand miles of space, and I'm over it.

I've been excited to get home from work before. What we do is very dangerous. I've even been excited to find someone to hook up with. After that night with Simone and finding out that she was pregnant with River, I vowed to never have sex with someone I couldn't track down later, and that put a stop to the random chicks in different countries. Plus, all the guys seem anxious to get home to their women, so we haven't been sticking around any longer than we have to.

This is the second trip since I started dating Reagan, and the absolute worst. The first time, we'd only shared a few kisses. After knowing what her skin feels like against mine, I've been itching to feel it again.

"It's good to see you, too," she says with a weird pat to my back.

"Is something wrong?"

"Nope, but you're crushing me." She takes a step back when I let her go. "Where is everyone?"

"Kids are asleep. If we stick around down here much longer, you're going to become very aware of what Rocker and Simone are up to."

She chuckles, but the humor doesn't reach her pretty eyes.

"Do you want a snack? Something to eat?"

Her eyes dart in the direction of the kitchen, but she shakes her head. My palm finds her cheek, and I nearly lose it when she leans into the touch.

"Would it be rude if I just wanted to go upstairs?"

"Are you using me for my cock, Reagan?" I tease.

Her eyes dart to my waist, and I do nothing to hide just how hard I am for her already.

"I like your mouth, too."

That sounds like a yes if I ever heard one, and I swing her up in my arms and race up the stairs with her.

"You're going to make me sick," she says, and although I doubt it's possible, I slow my steps, placing her as gently on my bed as I can manage. She still bounces once, and her laughter this time covers her entire face.

"You missed me, huh?"

"How could you tell?"

"I blinked and you're half-naked," she says.

"Like a magician," I say. "Get naked."

I step out of my sweats, leaving them in a pile on my floor and prowl toward her.

Her shirt clears her head, and she discards it with just as much care as I showed with my own clothes.

"I love this bra," I say, my fingers tracing over the thin strap. "Now, get rid of it."

"Eager, aren't you?"

"And you seem determined to drive me crazy."

She laughs again when I press on her shoulders, making her fall back on the bed. I tug her leggings down, not taking a second to appreciate the matching panties she's wearing.

"And this, fuck, baby, this drives me insane."

My mouth is on her, tongue splitting her open to find the exact center of her in the next second. God, she fucking tastes like everything magical in life. She's lost to the pleasure because when I reach up to grab her breast, she still hasn't pulled the damn bra off. I waste no time pushing the cup up and finding her nipple.

"Miles," she gasps, making me smile against her for the briefest of moments before I dive back in. I need her to come and fast. We have all night, but this first time isn't going to last. I'll always take care of her first, and when she pulses with a scream against my mouth in less than two minutes, I want to beat my damn chest with my fists.

I breathe her in one last time, looking up at her gorgeous face. Her mouth is hanging open as she struggles to calm her breathing. Her eyelashes are resting against her pink cheeks.

She's fucking perfect.

My cock flexes, reminding me that it's his turn, and it takes seconds to grab a condom and get ready to dive into her.

"Over," I insist, using my hands on her hips to flip her to her stomach. "Fuck, baby."

She positions herself on her knees, her back arched so her breasts are pressed to my bed, as I take a handful of her ass cheek.

"You wouldn't believe me if I told you, you have the perfect ass."

The whole goddamned thing is a sight for sore eyes.

Unable to resist, I lower my mouth down and lick her drenched pussy from the back, breathing heavy against her skin.

"Miles, I need your cock."

Who am I to deny the woman what she desires?

"Hard. Fuck me hard," she insists when I get into position, so I do.

I slam into her, only keeping her from flying away from me with the firm grip I have on her hips.

I don't stop. I piston into her like I'll never get the chance again. And thank fuck I spent my first orgasm of the day in the shower before texting her that I was home. It's the only thing that prevents me from coming in under a minute.

"Fuck, just like that. Rock back into it, baby. Let me hear you."

"Oh God," she whimpers.

"Reagan, fuck, Reagan. Jesus, baby. Are you close?" So, I may have made it past a minute, but I'll be damned if I'm going to see the positive side of two. I reach around her, smiling when my fingers run into hers already working herself over.

Perfect, so damned perfect.

"Take it," I hiss. "That's it. Come all over my cock."

I fuck her through the orgasm, my fingers so tight on her hips that I'm sure to leave bruises behind. She doesn't seem to mind as she rides out her release. I want to fill this woman with my cum, but that isn't a conversation we've had. My mind flashes back to our first night in the room, and I'm a slave to my need when I pull out, rip the condom off, and jet cum all over her back.

I swipe the tip on her ass cheek, and just look at the mess I made on her skin. All I really want to do is slide right back inside of her and keep going. My cock doesn't show any threat of softening soon. I've been away too long for that to be an issue.

"That was so good," she says, her eyes finding mine over her shoulder.

"I can get another condom," I tell her.

"Okay," she agrees, but then she turns her head, and I hear her yawn.

"You're tired. Let me get something to clean you up."

I would offer her my shower, but I'm a sicko and I want her smelling like me.

"I thought we were going to have sex again," she complains as she settles against my chest after I used a wet washcloth on her back.

"Maybe in the morning," I tell her as I pull her closer to my side. "Let's get some sleep."

When her breathing evens out in minutes, I know I made the right choice. I fall asleep thinking that we have plenty of time for round two when we wake up.

But when I open my eyes to the sunlight streaming into the room, I do it alone. She isn't in the house, and when I text her after discovering her gone, her response is a simple *I had to go home.*

She gives me nothing else, leaving me wondering what in the hell I did wrong to make her leave.

Chapter 26

Reagan

I left him long before the sun came up Sunday morning, and I wish I could say I did so with my head held high, but there were tears streaking down my face before I even made it to my car.

Sunday was spent most the same way until I had to pick up the kids.

Miles texted a few times, concerned, but I told him I just had a lot to do.

Dropping them off this morning was hard, but he wasn't there. I knew picking them up was going to mean facing him, but he wasn't there then either. I turned down Simone's offer for a chat, saying that I had plans with Cassie. Truthfully, I do have plans with Cassie, but I didn't want to linger around in fear of running into him.

I know I need to have a conversation with Miles, but I don't know how to approach him when I'm having trouble wrapping my head around what our situation has turned into.

"Just start from the beginning," Cassie says after I walk into her apartment and make sure the kids are settled in front of the television.

"I'm pregnant," I blurt.

Cassie doesn't gasp or get a pained expression on her face. She smiles like I've told her I've won an all-expense-paid trip to the Caribbean.

"And it's Jin—Miles's baby?"

"Of course, it is."

"Don't get defensive. I had to ask."

"And yet you're smiling like a damn fool."

"I can't believe you're not. This is great news."

I huff, falling back on the couch with irritation. "Great news? Please explain to me how getting knocked up for a third time by a third guy is good news."

"It's not just any guy. It's Miles. He's Cerberus."

"I know he's Cerberus, Cass," I growl. "That has nothing to do with—You know what? This was a mistake. I'm just gonna go back—"

"You're not going anywhere," she snaps, grabbing my arm before I can stand.

"I don't have time for this." In truth, I'm exhausted, but that's early pregnancy for you, I guess.

"You'll make time because I'm your best friend. If you came here expecting me to react like your mother and berate you for getting pregnant by a man that cares for you, then you're barking up the wrong damn tree. You're not even in the right forest, honey."

"He's going to hate me."

"He won't."

"He will. I know what the first words out of his mouth are going to be."

"Yeah? And what will that be?"

"Is it mine?"

"I'll cut his nuts off personally if he says that."

"We used a condom every damn time. Except—"

"Condoms aren't a hundred percent effective, and except what?"

"He umm, the first time, he forgot, but he didn't even go all the way inside."

"Four percent," she mutters. "That's why I always insist on a condom before a cock gets anywhere near my pu—"

I smack her arm and point at my kids. "Seriously? And four percent?"

She clears her throat. "Four out of a hundred percent. Those are the statistics with getting pregnant from pre-ejaculate."

I huff a humorless laugh. Hearing her use such a technical term is so out of character for her.

"Four percent? Really?"

She shrugs. "I know a lot of stuff like that because I'm hell-bent on not having kids."

"And I'm a fool for not knowing about the four percent. I guess I should be more educated. If I had known, I would've—"

"Would've what? Taken Plan B?" She cocks her head to the side.

"Maybe."

"How long ago was it?"

"Nearly a month ago."

"Too late for that. There are other options."

"Cassie. I couldn't."

She nods. "I know."

"It's nothing against—"

"You don't have to explain yourself. So, what's the plan?"

"I have to tell him."

"Of course, you do. When is that going to happen?"

I want to fling myself on the floor and throw a temper tantrum like a child, but I know it probably wouldn't make me feel better. It would just be wasted energy, and I don't have any to spare these days.

"I don't know. I'm still trying to wrap my head around being so stupid… again."

"Again. This is nothing like the other times. He is nothing like the other guys."

"Shane isn't a bad guy," I argue.

"But he's gay, so he doesn't count. Miles isn't Jeremiah. Honestly, if I were ready to settle down, one of my top picks would be a Cerberus man."

"And which one exactly?" I ask, needing a minute to get the attention off of me.

She shrugs. "Any available one. They're all hot as hell, and they fuck like maniacs. Well, I haven't had Thumper yet, but I'm working on that."

I can't help the laugh that escapes my throat. My best friend is wild as hell, and I love her for it.

"You know, Simone was a bartender at *Jake's* when she met Rocker and look at her now. After getting pregnant, that man bought her that big house. I heard she quit her job at the bank. Worse things could happen than getting pregnant by one of those guys."

"And Miles is the father of that baby," I remind her. It isn't a secret, so I doubt she's forgotten it.

"And Rocker is with her. They have a second child."

"And another on the way," I add.

"See? That's a woman who knows how to keep a man."

"By burdening him with children?"

"You've spent a lot of time with them. Does Rocker seem burdened by her?" He's blissfully happy. "Not in the least."

"Then Jinx—sorry, Miles—isn't going to be either. He cares for you."

"Because I get to leave every day. He has no real obligation to me, Cassie. This could fu—mess everything up."

She waves in the direction of my kids as if to remind me once they get a little time in front of the television, the rest of the world disappears for them.

"This could push him away."

"I think you're going to be floored with his reaction. I don't see him being even the slightest bit upset over the news. Don't let your expectation of how he's going to react cloud what really happens."

"You make it sound like I sabotage myself. Jeremiah couldn't get out of town fast enough. It took less than forty-eight hours to change his phone number, and—"

"And Shane likes men. You didn't turn him gay, and as I've said more than once, it's fucked up what he did. Why do you think I only speak to him when I'm forced to?"

"You should forgive him," I mutter.

"You forgave him. That's as good as it's going to get."

I give her a weak smile. "Do you really think Miles is going to be happy?"

Her jaw flexes before she answers. "How about I'll kill him if he isn't?"

I shake my head, amused at her fierce protective nature.

"We'd have to go on the run from the Cerberus guys. Get new identities." She flips her hair over her shoulder. "But I always thought my parents should've named me something a little more exotic. What do you think of Lucia Nicole?"

"I think both you and Lucia are nuts," I mutter, but my spirits are lifted a little, and I know that was her intent.

"Do you love him?"

This question stops me cold.

"If you don't, then that could change things."

"I think so, but I thought I loved Brian."

"Miles is nothing like Brian," she snaps. "Don't even compare the two."

"I know he's not, but—"

"No buts. Nothing alike."

"My point is that I thought I loved Brian, and then I quickly realized I didn't. I was coming to that realization long before I found out he was dicking every girl who was willing. What if I find out that I don't love Miles?"

"How is that going to make him any less willing to be a father to—oh? I see what you're asking."

"We're not a package deal. I can accept that, but I also don't want to lead him on."

"I think the only thing you can do is act relative to what you feel now, and if those things start to change, then your conversation would be different. I know I don't know shit about love, but I think you should give it a shot if that's what you're feeling right now. I don't see Miles walking away from you and a baby."

"I'm scared."

"I know, and you should be to a point. I heard going from two kids to three kids is complete and utter chaos."

I huff again. "And how do you know that?"

She shrugs. "Research. I was messing around with a guy who had a history of triplets in his family. Reading all that craziness is what kept me from going all the way with him."

"Even with condoms?"

"I mean, I sucked him off, and he eats pu—kitty like a champ, but I wasn't willing to risk carrying three little devil spawns in my womb."

"I like kitties!" Elijah says, his eyes wide and hopeful when I look over at him.

"Yeah?" I ask, smiling. "Aunt Cassie was just talking about getting a little kitty. Would you like to have a kitty to visit when you come over?"

Elijah springs to his feet as my son runs up to her with pleading eyes.

"An orange kitty, Aunt Cassie!"

I'm going to kill you, she mouths, but then she proceeds to ask him more questions about a cat.

My friend may not want her own kids, but she's an amazing woman. I love her. My kids love her. I couldn't ask for a better person in my corner.

And just for a few minutes, I'm able to forget that my life may be imploding soon.

On the drive home, I realize that I've done this on my own twice before, and despite her insistence that three kids are utter chaos, she must not understand that my life is already crazy.

What's one more person to love?

Chapter 27

Jinx

"You're acting weird."

I don't bother looking toward Simone after she makes her observation.

"Not more than usual," Rocker adds.

I flip them both the bird as I make a pass toward the kitchen.

"Does he always pace like that?" Rocker asks loud enough for me to hear.

"Only on the weekdays."

"Didn't you tell me that Reagan wasn't coming today?"

I stop dead in my tracks and glare at them. "What?"

Simone shrugs with a half-smile as she lifts her cup of coffee to her mouth.

I narrow my eyes at her, agitated with wasted time. "Why wouldn't you tell me that? Where is she?"

Simone frowns. "I figured she'd tell you about Elijah's dentist appointment. Wait. She didn't?"

Rocker doesn't cut a joke as I continue to stand there, and I know his lack of response is because of the look on my face.

I have no idea what happened while I was gone for work, but since coming back, she's been distant. She took off Sunday morning after an amazing night together. Work kept me away yesterday, and her texts have all been short, bordering on the edge of cold.

"Did something happen while we were away?"

Simone places her coffee cup down. "Not that I know of."

"And she hasn't been acting weird?"

"Yesterday she seemed a little rushed to get out of here, but she said she had plans with Cassie. I didn't think anything of it."

I pull out my phone and call her, but after several rings, it goes to voicemail. I shoot her a text and pocket my phone, unable to just stand here and wait for her to respond.

"Where are you going?" Rocker asks when I grab my keys and wallet from the console table by the front door. "Maybe she just needs some time to think."

"And would you wait around and do nothing while Simone was stuck in her head?"

Rocker looks to his woman before answering. "I did wait."

"And looking back now?"

A slow grin spreads across his face. "I would've been right by her side the entire time."

They both get that lovestruck look in their eyes, so I leave before I witness something I don't want to see.

The quick pass by her house reveals her car is already gone, but there's only one children's dentist in town. The drive is spent with my fingers tapping on the steering wheel and my mind racing, trying to figure out what I did wrong or what could've happened that would have her pulling away. I don't think she'd let that douche Brian get between us, but I know she has a tendency to let others' words drag her down.

Instead of making a plan to kill the asshole, I concentrate on driving and taking slow breaths. Other than Simone, I've never felt more territorial over a woman before, but the possessiveness I have for my son's mother is completely different from what I feel for Reagan.

I sigh in relief when I see Reagan's car in the parking lot, but I still want to kick something when I climb out of my SUV to greet her only to find her struggling.

Doesn't she know she no longer has to struggle?

"I thought we were a team," she says to Elijah with a frustrated tone in her voice. "We're in this together, buddy, but you have to meet me halfway."

"No!" Elijah snaps.

"You have to have your teeth cleaned." She sighs.

"I don't—Daddy!"

Reagan freezes still bent over as she attempts to coax Elijah from the car. Katie squeals in delight at seeing me, and it brightens the light inside my chest.

"Hey, baby girl." I take her little hand when she holds it out to me. "Is big brother acting out?"

"No!" Elijah says as Reagan stands to face me.

"Hey," I say when her eyes find mine. "Why didn't you tell me you had an appointment?"

She shrugs, her eyes darting away. She's frustrated. That's easy to see, but she also looks exhausted. There are dark circles under her eyes, and she's on the verge of tears.

"Come here," I whisper, pulling her to my chest with one arm around her waist and the other comforting Katie as she tries to wiggle away. "Let me get him, and we can go inside together."

She doesn't agree verbally, but at least she steps out of the way so I can grab Elijah.

"Do you know how lucky you are?" I ask as I bend down and unclip the straps of his booster seat. "The dentist has video games, and when you're done, all the good little pirates get to raid the treasure chest."

Elijah looks up at me, skepticism on his round little face.

"Last time I was here," I continue as I lift him from his seat, "they had slime and slinkies. I'm pretty sure I even saw a couple of whistles."

Reagan mumbles something about noisy things being just what she needs, and I bite back a smile.

"If you pick a whistle, it has to stay at my house though, okay?"

Elijah nods with enthusiasm as I turn to face Reagan with a wide smile. She doesn't look very impressed that I was able to get him out of the car without a struggle.

"What's wrong?" I ask, reaching up to cup her face. She allows it, but only for a second before turning toward the building.

"We're going to be late."

I'm able to catch up to her before she can pull the door open on her own, and I'm sure even people we don't know could look in our direction and feel the frostiness that's rolling off of her. It's clear there's a conversation we need to have, but I know this isn't the time or the place.

I'm anxious as she signs both kids in. There are a million ways I can think of to put her in a better mood, and not one of them is appropriate in front of children. I pretend to play the video game attached to the wall with Elijah, and I'm thankful he's only three and easy to impress because our avatars are just running around in circles. He's thrilled however, playing so loudly I have to remind him twice to lower his excitement.

I keep half of my attention on her as she finishes at the front desk and takes a seat opposite of us. The waiting area isn't very crowded, but I can feel the attention of others on me.

"Look, Daddy!" Elijah tugs the sleeve of my shirt before pointing to the screen.

"That's awesome," I praise.

"I'd like to call him daddy," I hear one of the moms in the room mumble.

Reagan cuts her eyes in the direction of the voice, but she doesn't look impressed.

She must know I can't control how other people act or what they say, and God, I wish Elijah was just a little older. I'd grill him to find out why she's in such a terrible mood.

"Ugh," she groans. "Can you take her?"

Reagan snaps to her feet, holding Katie out for me. The second the little girl is in my arms, she darts toward the bathroom.

"Has Mommy been feeling bad?" I ask Elijah, but the question falls on deaf ears because the little Lego guy is too entertaining to allow for any outside interruptions.

"Do you feel bad?" I ask Katie as she reaches up to tug on my hair.

I press my lips to her forehead and then her cheek to test her temperature, but she feels fine.

"So hot," another voice whispers.

I turn all of my attention back to Elijah as I bounce Katie on my lap.

It's long minutes before Reagan comes out of the bathroom, and her face is even more flushed than when she darted away. It's clear she's sick, and that explains so much. I wouldn't be in the best of moods either if I were in her place.

I hand over my controller to another kid that has walked up and go to my girl.

"Are you okay?" I ask. "Do you have that virus again?"

"I think so," she mutters, but it's in the way she refuses to look at me that betrays her lie.

"It's not a virus," I whisper, my pulse pounding, heart kicking up as a smile forms on my face. "Reagan?"

She turns her head, finally looking in my direction.

"You're pregnant?"

Tears well in her eyes.

"You're pregnant?"

She swallows, and one tiny dip of her head is all it takes to get me on my feet. I pick her up with a cry of utter happiness and swing her around. Katie laughs, enjoying the spin, but Reagan just looks greener when I finally put her back down.

I lean down to press my lips to hers, but she covers her mouth before I can.

"I just got sick," she explains.

I press my lips to her forehead instead.

This changes everything.

Literally everything will be different, and I'm beyond fucking thrilled.

It's not planned but I've found that some surprises are the best damn thing that can ever happen to a man.

Even the woman that mutters, *"Three kids? Stay off her already,"* doesn't dampen my mood.

Chapter 28

Reagan

"Listen," Jinx says, taking my hand once we're outside of the vehicle, preventing me from going inside the building. "I know you're scared."

"I'm not scared," I say, my voice a snap of attitude. "I've done this twice before, remember?"

He frowns, his fingers pushing away a lock of hair that has caught the breeze. His warm hand on my cheek has the power to make me break, and sheer will is all that keeps the floodgates from opening up.

"Look at me," he whispers.

God, I want to give him everything. I'm happy about this baby, and right now he is too, but that thrill will fade for him soon enough. I can't use the way he is with Simone as an example. His best friend loves that woman. I'm an outsider. I'm not someone he's forced to be around constantly. It would be very easy for him to put a lifetime of distance between us.

His obligation to me compared to Simone isn't even close to being similar.

He presses his lips to mine, and the kiss is almost soft enough to make me think that things will be okay, that he's different from Jeremiah. That he's not going to drop some life-altering bomb in my lap like Shane did.

"I'm beyond fucking ecstatic to be doing this with you," he says against my mouth, his warm breath skating over my wet lips. "You know that, right?"

I nod because he's said as much over the last two weeks while we've been waiting for a doctor's appointment to confirm the pregnancy. I've taken several at-home tests, so I know I am, but this is just the next step.

He hasn't once questioned paternity, and it makes me wonder if he's just as knowledgeable about that four percent as Cassie is.

He doesn't look at me and frown. If he's glancing my way, his handsome face is always smiling, and it provides some comfort, but I know the thrill will wear off. Honestly, I'd rather it be sooner rather than later. The last thing I want is him around for the entire pregnancy and then declaring it to be too much after the baby gets here.

"We're going to be late," I tell him as hot tears burn the back of my eyes.

"They always run a little behind. Are you feeling queasy?"

"I'm okay," I tell him and at least that's the truth. I haven't gotten sick for the last week and a half, and as much as it should be a relief, it has me worried more than anything.

He angles my head so he can look me in the eye.

"You're not alone."

I want to hiss out some smartass remark about how I'm well aware because he insisted on being here, but I keep my mouth closed. I don't know when I turned into such a bitter, hateful person, but I seem to be settling into the role with ease these days. I sort of hate myself for it, but self-recrimination isn't new for me either.

"Baby, please." He leans his forehead against mine, uncaring of the people walking to and from their cars.

This hard man, uncaring of what people think, comforting me is nearly enough to let me sink against him, nearly enough for me to knock down that final wall and give him everything. God, do I want to lay my problems and doubts and fears right at his feet like he's asked me to more than once. I want to hand it all over. I want to get a full night's sleep without tossing and turning because my mind won't turn off. I want to walk through life feeling his assurances with every ounce of my being. I want all of his words to be true, but experience tells me to proceed with caution, because as much as this situation looks and feels different from when I got pregnant with Elijah and then again with Katie, my luck never holds out. I feel in my gut that things won't end well with us, and I have to protect myself from that pain.

I squeeze his hand and press a kiss to his lips, giving him a small smile when he pulls his face away from mine.

"We're going to be late."

His cheek twitches, and I know he wants to say something, but he doesn't. Miles guides me through the front door and to the doctor's office. I should probably beam at the looks we get. Even women here with their significant others dart their appreciative eyes in our—well, *his*—direction. He is a sight this morning in very-well-fitting dark jeans and a t-shirt that hugs every inch of him from the waist up.

Danger and warnings of caution just seem to roll off of him even when he smiles and dips his head in greeting when he catches people staring.

"Reagan Dunn," he tells the woman at the front desk when I can't seem to open my mouth to answer when she asks my name.

I may possibly be losing my mind, but I feel like my world has turned into a tunnel, and the only thing I can focus on is the weird pattern on the carpet.

Miles snaps me out of my trance as we sit down on the far side of the room.

"I'd like to think I know everything about you, baby, but I can't fill this out. Your social security number never came up in conversation."

I huff a laugh, hoping he doesn't read too much into it as I take the clipboard from him. I spend the next ten minutes completing paperwork, going slowly so I won't have to speak with him. He's antsy beside me, and I don't know if he's anxious to be here or if he's responding to my mood. I won't be able to go much longer before I'm going to have to answer his questions, but at least that won't be right now.

I have to pull out my phone to get the exact date of my last period. I hazard a glance at Miles's face when I pull up the app, but he doesn't seem annoyed or suspicious. I can't believe he's never asked. How many times has he been told he's going to be a dad for him to be so calm and trusting?

We're called back just as I'm dropping off the paperwork at the front desk, and I think I'm going to go back alone, but the heat of Miles's body is against my back in an instant. His hand on my hip as we follow the nurse should be comforting. I feel like a total asshole. Cassie told me last week that if I don't chill out, I'm going to ruin this. She accused me of sabotaging what I have with him and even went so far as to tell me not to come crying to her if I push him away. She claims I'm the one to blame if he backs away, not him.

It's one of the many things that have kept me up at night.

Like a gentleman, Miles averts his attention to a picture on the wall while the nurse checks my weight before taking my hand when I step off the scale.

The wait in the room isn't long, before we hear a soft knock on the door. A very gorgeous woman walks in, but my focus is on Miles as his eyes grow bright and a wide smile spreads his face.

"I'm Dr. Charli Hunter," the woman says as she walks in and heads straight to the sink to wash her hands. "I was looking at your chart, and although you're here for a pregnancy confirmation, I see you missed your annual appointment."

I cringe, already knowing what's coming.

"I meant to reschedule," I begin, but stop when she gives me a soft smile.

She seems nice enough, and I probably wouldn't have an issue with her if it wasn't for the grin on Miles's handsome, stupid face.

"We can do that today. You provided the nursing staff with a urine sample?"

"Not yet," I answer, and then follow her out of the room.

"Right in there. There are instructions on how to collect a clean sample on the back of the door."

I hurry through my business, certain that I'll find Dr. Hunter in the room flirting with Miles, but he's in there alone.

"She said to put that gown on." He points to the folded cloth in the middle of the paper-covered exam table.

"Could you wait in the waiting area?"

"I've seen it all before, Reagan."

"Have you? From the way you were eyeballing that doctor, it seems you've seen quite a bit," I hiss, my fingers fumbling with the gown as I yank it from the table. I bite back more comments as I start to strip.

"What?" he asks, but he doesn't seem upset that I lost my temper. "Charli?"

"First name basis, huh?" I turn my back to him. He may have seen it all already, but that doesn't make me any more comfortable stripping down in front of him while I'm angry.

"Reagan." I nearly sob when he stands, pressing himself against my back. "She's married. To her boss, actually."

"And I'm sure that would stop you. You seem awfully familiar with her. Are there any women you haven't fucked in this town?"

He spins me around to face him, and I have to look away when his deft fingers find the front clasp of my bra. "She's Camryn's best friend. Samson, you saw him at the park, remember? That's Camryn's guy. I know Charli through him. I've never slept with the woman."

His warm lips dip down and brush over my shoulder, and I'm seconds away from telling him this isn't the time or place to get handsy, but then I feel the gown sliding up my arms.

"Are you hungry? Is that the issue? I promise to get you as many snacks as you want." He presses his lips to mine, his eyes shining with humor.

"Y-you never slept with her?" He shakes his head, his hands running up and down my arms like I'm a scared animal that needs to be comforted. "Never seen her naked?"

"No, Reagan. Never. Don't want to either. You, on the other hand..." His eyes dart to the front of my gown, and my body responds in a way that's going to be embarrassingly obvious when the doctor gets back in here to do my exam.

"I'm sorry," I apologize. "I'm just all out of whack, I guess."

"It's the hormones," he says with a wide smile.

The teasing tone makes me want to slap him, but I chuckle instead because my moods are all over the place.

"You don't have to stay in here while she does this," I mutter as I climb on the bed, the paper crinkling under my weight.

"Do you honestly think I'm going to miss the only chance I may ever get to see another woman finger you?"

My eyes widen as I glare at him.

The man just smiles wider, and my cheeks have to be fire engine red when Dr. Hunter knocks on the door before entering.

Chapter 29

Jinx

"So?" Rocker asks the second I get back home.

I've smiled so much since I dropped Reagan back off at work, my face is starting to hurt. I still keep grinning of course.

"The in-office test confirmed the pregnancy, but it's still too early for an ultrasound."

"Jesus, man," Rocker says as he shakes my hand for a brief second before pulling me in for a hug. "Did you ever think this would be our lives?"

"No," I tell him as I take a step back. "But I can't say I'm upset."

"Maybe it's twins and we'll be caught up."

"I'm already ahead, fucker." I playfully shove him out of the way so I can grab a drink from the fridge.

"How do you figure?"

"I have River."

"I'm counting River, too."

"I know you are, and I'm counting Elijah and Katie. She's mine, and they're mine." I give him a shrug. "This new baby makes four for me and only three for you."

"You're excited."

"Fucking ecstatic, man."

"You're claiming her kids, so what's your next step?"

This is a hard question. I completely understand her bad mood. Simone had them regularly, but it feels like it's something more than just her body's physical response to growing a baby.

My smile fades away. "I don't know. I know what I want to do."

"And what's that?" he asks when I don't offer up any details.

"I want her to move in with me." I'll give him credit for not flinching. I mean, technically, we have room now, but it's going to get really tight with two new babies coming into the household.

"Do you think she's ready for that?"

"We're having a baby, Rocker."

"That's not an answer. Maybe she doesn't want to live here."

"I was thinking seriously about that house next door, but it needs a lot of work."

He sighs with a shake of his head. "You know every man working for Cerberus will be willing to help get it ready. They did with this place, and all we had to offer in exchange is free beer and hot pizza when the day was done."

I nod in agreement. A dozen men working on this place when we first bought it meant the work was done in record time.

"But that's not where your apprehension is, is it?"

"Not all of it. Every time I bring up the future, she shuts down or changes the subject altogether."

"It's a conversation you need to have."

"I fucking know that." I've told myself I'll catch her in a better mood, but she always seems so sullen and withdrawn when we're together.

She's fine with letting me hold her so long as we don't have to talk, but we haven't been intimate since that night I got back after being gone for over a week.

"She's just been distant, and I don't want to put even more space in between us."

"I hate to be the one to bring it up—"

"Then don't," I snap.

"Are you saying you haven't considered—"

"I said don't, and I fucking mean it. That baby is mine. I know it is."

Rocker doesn't know Reagan. She's not the type to sleep around. Even his words don't have the ability to plant a seed of doubt in my head. That's how sure of her I am.

He holds his hands up. "Okay, man, but even if she doesn't want to talk about what's going to happen, you need to sit her down and have that conversation, anyway."

"And that's it? That's not it. What are you thinking?"

"You said to not say anything."

I could choke him right now. "Say it."

"She has two kids already, Jinx. Have you considered that she isn't as ecstatic about being pregnant again?"

"Simone has two kids and is over the moon about the new one coming," I counter. They could have a dozen kids, and each one would be a welcomed surprise because every baby is a blessing. What scared me when I was younger no longer even registers as fear where kids are concerned. Not one negative thing came into my head when I figured out what was going on with Reagan at the kids' dentist office.

"And Simone is in a stable relationship," he argues, and it's like a slap to the face.

"We're fucking stable."

"Are you sure? And even if *you* are so sure, does she believe it's stable?"

"We're good. We don't argue or anything." I won't tell him about the accusation she threw at me earlier in the doctor's office, but it's not because I'm in denial. I just know she's a little agitated, and that has to do with pregnancy hormones.

"You don't argue, or you don't *talk*? You know there's a massive difference when it comes to women." His eyes search my face, and I don't know what he finds, but it makes him frown. "She could be pissed, could be running a million scenarios through her head, and you'd never know it. You have to get her to speak."

"Are you pushing this so hard because you want me out of the house?"

"What? We're talking about your relationship with Reagan not the damn house next door."

"But if things work out with us then I'm expected to leave?"

His mouth falls open as he shakes his head in clear confusion. "What? No. Why are you turning this back on me? We love having you here, Jinx. Would four more people moving in make things super tight, yeah, but that doesn't mean we can't make it work. What concerns me is that you say you're happy, but you don't seem happy. You say your relationship is good, but then you say she's pulling away from you. I'm just trying to help."

"I hate the idea of moving away from River."

"No one's asking you to."

"But staying here with four adults and six kids?"

"Chaos," Rocker says with a quick laugh. "But we can manage chaos."

"I don't think Reagan will be as keen on the idea, especially not after leaving her mother's house. I think she's going to want privacy."

"If you do what she wants, and it's something you're not interested in, that's going to cause problems down the road. If you're concerned about your role with River, that's never going to change. I was serious about linking the backyards. You're welcome in this house as if it's your own. That's not going to change. If you want a baby monitor next door if you move, then that's doable, too. We're not pushing you out, and we support you no matter what your decision is."

"I appreciate that."

"And if she doesn't mind living with all of us, then we can always buy a bigger house." He leans in closer like he has a secret to share. "Because I'll tell you right now, the babies aren't going to stop coming. We'll have a football team here before you know it."

I laugh at the wink he shoots me.

"And what does Simone have to say about it?"

"I think, yes! Yes! Yes! Was her response when I asked."

"And you tell me to talk to my woman. Maybe don't ask serious questions when your head is between her legs."

"Mind your business," he mutters, but there's no real agitation in his shining eyes.

"Moving out does mean we don't have to listen to you guys fucking all the time."

He raises his can of soda in a salute of agreement before taking a drink.

"She's coming over tonight," I inform him. "Shane and Martin are going to see family, and they're taking the kids with them. Reagan said she normally tags along, but she has to work. I'll talk to her."

He claps me on the back before leaving the room. I'd ask where he's disappearing to, but he hasn't seen Simone in thirty minutes, so there's no doubt in my mind he's going to hunt for her. I'd be doing the exact same thing if Reagan wasn't at work.

Chapter 30

Reagan

"What was that for?" I ask when Miles pulls his mouth from mine.

I barely made it in the front door before he pressed his lips to mine, dipped me low, and kissed the hell out of me.

"I missed you," he whispers, his hot tongue skating over his lips as if he's still searching for my taste there.

"Are we alone?" I run a hand up his chest, intent in my eyes.

He pulls my hand from his chest as he walks us deeper into the house. "We are."

"Then why are we standing here instead of heading to your room?"

He scoops me up like a bride and hauls ass through the house. He doesn't toss me on the bed like I expect. He places me down gently before covering his body with mine.

One kiss leads to another and another, and before I know it, I'm breathless and begging for him to strip me naked. It's been too long since he was inside of me last, and that time was spent with me lost in my own head about my fear over telling him about the baby.

Something changed at the doctor's office earlier. My bad mood, the sour one I've been holding onto for days, faded away, leaving me with a little light of hope inside me.

All day at work, I thought about him and this baby, and realized Cassie is right. I'm the one holding back. I'm the one already preparing for things between us to end, and I hate it. He hasn't shown any sign of ending what we have. He had one hell of a chance to do that when I confirmed I was pregnant after he made such a huge deal about it at the dentist's office. He's done nothing but smile and act excited about the surprise.

"Please, Miles. I need you," I pant when his hands only seem to want to glide down my arms and my back instead of undressing me and touching me in all of my needy places.

"We have all night," he says against the skin of my neck.

"But I need you now."

"I think—" He clears his throat as he pulls away.

Instead of reaching for the hem of my shirt when he grips my wrists, tugging me into a sitting position, he takes a seat beside me.

"We need to talk."

That good mood I was in disappears like warm breaths on a cold night, leaving me as equally lost and frigid.

"I see."

"Do you always do that? I only ask because I need to know how to handle your moods."

"*That*?" I snap. "What exactly is the *that* you're referring to?"

I cross my arms over my chest, shoving down the urge to run out of here and never look back. We're going to have a child together, and as much as I want to leave, I know I can't run from him forever.

"Do you always go to the worst-case scenario in your head?"

"It's protected me in the past," I grumble unsure if I'm overreacting or not.

"You don't need protection from me, Reagan. I pray one day you'll actually believe it."

"*We need to talk* has never yielded positive results for me in the past."

"And it doesn't for most people, but this isn't one of those situations."

I nod, still not sure what's coming.

"We're having a baby."

"We are."

"I'm so fucking happy we're having a baby, Reagan." His hand finds mine, dragging it to his lap.

If he's ignoring his erection, then I guess it's only fair that I ignore it as well.

"Are you?"

"What?" I snap my head up to look at him.

"We're going to get to that, baby. I promise, but talk to me. Are you happy about having another baby?"

"I'm scared," I confess.

"Of what?"

I doubt my initial response of *everything* will be enough. "This is my third baby. You're the third father."

"So, this is a moral issue for you? People have no room to judge. Every time someone has sex, they run the risk of pregnancy."

"I'm not—that's not the entire issue."

"Would it help if I told you that I'm the last?"

I tilt my head. "The last?"

"I want to be the last man that gets you pregnant."

Oh, he's going to be. I've already decided that after this I'm getting my tubes tied.

"This is my last baby," I confirm.

He gives me a slow grin. "If that's what you want, but that's not what I mean. I want to be with you, Reagan. Not just because you're pregnant but because I care about you. I'd give you ten more babies if that's what you want."

"Let's not get carried away," I say with a chuckle, but my cheeks heat.

This is definitely not what I expected when he said we needed to talk.

"You're it for me."

"Are you talking about getting a vasectomy because that's a big choice too? When you get married, she may want—"

He presses his fingers to my mouth, getting lost for a second in the sight of my lips when they part on an inhale.

"Are you trying to divorce me already, baby?"

My finger feels empty. The ring he gave me is at home, and I've been meaning to give it back to him. Okay, so maybe I've purposely been forgetting it.

"I know this was a surprise, Miles, but I don't think you need to make drastic decisions based off of me. Most women don't end up pregnant practically every time they have sex. Maybe I'm just extremely fertile."

"And maybe I have super sperm. Getting you pregnant with precum should be considered a talent." He winks at me, and his words set me a little at ease. It helps me to realize he's never going to accuse me of trapping him or getting pregnant by someone else.

"But seriously, don't get a vasec—"

"Now I know why Rocker does it," he mutters.

"What?" I shake my head. "I'm not following."

"Because you're not listening. You're locked in your head, trying to figure out what I'm going to say next instead of actually hearing what I'm trying to tell you. Off," he says as he lifts the bottom hem of my shirt.

He tosses it to the floor before unsnapping my bra and pulling it from my body.

"What are you—"

"Hush. I have things to say, and I need you to actually absorb them. Now stand."

I obey absentmindedly, and then my leggings are shoved down.

"Fucking shoes," he grumbles as he pulls them and my socks off my feet. "This just won't do."

And then my panties are around my ankles.

"On the bed. Legs spread as wide as you can manage."

I must not move fast enough because he has me where he wants me in the next breath. The leggings and panties are pulled from the remaining foot they were tangled on and he's standing at the end of the bed.

"Are you ready to listen?"

"I hear better when you're naked," I tease.

"Fucking figures. I hate when he's right."

"Rocker? Why are we talking about Rocker?"

"Just... hold on." He pulls his shirt over his head, and his fingers are opening the zipper on his jeans before his shirt flutters all the way to the floor.

He's in a rush, and the sight of him makes my body light on fire. We've never had a problem with this part. The chemistry between us doesn't allow for any misgivings or doubts, but sex is only a fraction of what a relationship is supposed to be, an important one, but a fraction, nonetheless.

"Are you listening?"

I nod, my eyes focused on the eager erection jutting from his hips.

"Reagan?"

"Hmm?"

"Reagan!"

I snap my eyes up to his. "Listen."

"I am," I tell him as I draw my brows together. "You really want to talk?"

"And I need you to listen."

I swallow thickly before sweeping my tongue out.

He groans, and the sound makes me spread my legs even further.

I catch his gaze between my legs, and my fingers begin to wander at his attention.

"I'm listening," I tease now that he's the one enthralled.

"Stop touching my pussy."

"*Your* pussy?"

"You heard me, Reagan. Hands by your hips."

My clit throbs when I pull my fingers away.

He crawls up the bed, his lips trailing up my bent leg. Then his fingers are exactly where I need them. My head presses into the pillow as a low groan escapes my lips. Jesus, it feels like it's been years since he has touched me.

"Listening?"

I give my head a vigorous nod.

"I'm not getting a vasectomy."

"Okay," I say on a breathless whimper.

"I want you to move in with me."

I squeak in surprise at his words but then his fingers find that perfect little spot inside of me.

"Is that a yes?"

"Wh-what?" I manage.

"Move in with me."

My body seizes. "Yes."

"Yes?"

"Yes! Yes! Yes!"

Every muscle in my body tightens as I begin to clench around him. The orgasm lasts forever, fluttering tiny muscles inside of me for what feels like an eternity. When I float back down to earth, I find Miles with his chin just above my clit, fingers resting lightly on my lower belly.

"Did I just agree to move in with you?"

His smile grows, spreading across his entire face. "Yeah. You did. Not planning to change your mind, are you?"

His fingers begin to drift lower, and I grab them. It's just too soon for another, especially after how hard my release was.

"Are you sure?"

"I've never been surer about anything before in my life, Reagan. We're having a baby. I want to be with you every second of the day."

"How do Simone and Rocker feel about me moving my brood in here?"

"Two kids aren't a brood, but I was looking at the house next door."

I watch his face. "And moving away without River?"

He seems content with his decision when he opens his mouth to respond. "It's not away. Just next door. Granted, I'm sure we'll spend a lot of time here and them at our place, but I'm not going to miss anything."

"What will the rent be?" I ask.

"Doesn't matter."

"It does to me," I argue.

"It'll be a mortgage, and it's not your concern."

"I'm not living with you free of charge. I'm not like that. I need—"

"You need to worry about growing my baby and nothing else."

"You sound like a caveman," I mutter.

We can have this conversation at a later time, I guess.

"I don't have a bone through my nose, but I have one elsewhere."

I laugh at his stupidity. Well, until he sits up on his knees and his cock hangs heavy between us.

"You're pregnant."

"I am," I say with a whimper when he strokes his cock over my sensitive clit.

"Do you have an issue with this?" he asks as he dips the head against my slit.

"No. Do you?"

His only answer is sinking into me bare, and I forget all words for the rest of the night.

Chapter 31

Reagan

"Did you get the package?" Cassie asks with excitement in her voice.

"Package?" I ask as I look at my face in the visor mirror. I don't normally eat in my car, but the atmosphere in the office today was off, and I'm in too good of a mood to let anyone drag me down.

"I had it delivered to the new house. Online it says delivered."

"We live like ten minutes apart. Was there a reason you couldn't just bring it to me?"

"I ordered it online. I didn't buy it then ship it. That would be stupid."

"And having it shipped to a house under construction is smart planning?"

I snap the visor closed, content that there's nothing on my face before I head back into the second half of my workday.

"Just ask Miles when you see him this evening."

"Miles is out of town for work."

"Then Simone."

"Simone doesn't live next door."

She sighs. "Are you purposely trying to get on my nerves?"

"Only because you're so easily annoyed."

"Find the package and call me before you open it. I want to hear your surprise."

"You could see my surprise if you hand delivered it."

"Reagan, stop!" She laughs.

"I'll find the package. I'll video call you so you can see and hear my surprise, but right now I have to go back into work."

"Love you."

"Love you, too."

I realize just how easy those words fall from my lips. It also makes me feel a little off considering Miles asked me to move in and we've been making plans to head in that direction for the last three weeks, but we've never said those words to each other.

He purchased the house on a quick sale, but there's so much that has to be done, it'll be awhile before we can move in. Our excitement hasn't ended since the day he asked. My doubts have finally begun to slip away, replaced with excitement for this new chapter in my life.

"You seem happy," Angela says as I walk into the women's restroom at the office.

"It's a good day," I say as she leaves the restroom.

My joy is gone the second I lower my clothes and sit on the toilet.

My eyes tear up at the sight of the blood on my panties, and I'm borderline sobbing when I wipe and find more. I clean up as best I can with shaking hands.

When I leave the stall, I stare at my reflection for a long moment, but I can't seem to muster any hope or an explanation other than the tragedy I'm facing.

It takes three attempts to dial the number to the doctor's office, and the hold they place me on lasts a lifetime.

"I'm sorry, ma'am, but Dr. Hunter is in surgery. I'm a nurse in the office. Maybe I can help you."

"I'm bleeding," I sob.

"How far along are you?"

"Ten weeks."

"Spotting during the first trimester is fairly common. If—"

"This is my third pregnancy. I never had that with my first two."

"I know you're scared."

I wait for her to offer advice or urge me to come to the office, but she doesn't.

"Let me check your file. Give me one moment please."

The elevator music that plays while I'm on hold is cheery and enough to drive me insane.

"As I said, ma'am, Dr. Hunter is in surgery. Is it heavy or spotting?"

Isn't a little still too much?

"Sp-spotting," I answer, tears still rolling in fat drops down my face.

"If it gets heavier, I want you to come into the office."

"And now? What do I do now?"

"Lie down for a while. Drink plenty of fluids."

I don't even have the grace to thank her for her time before I hang up on her. I also don't tell a soul what's going on as I head to my desk. I need to leave and do what the nurse instructed, but today is a docket day and we are incredibly busy. I have no doubt I'd lose my job. Mr. Hollow hasn't been feeling well recently and hasn't been in the office for the last week and a half. The other half of the firm's partnership wouldn't bat an eye at telling me to go right back to work.

As I submit paperwork and clear files off my desk, I find that I can't concentrate. I don't know anyone that would be able to, but before I can tell the other paralegal in the office what's going on, my phone rings.

"Hello?" I ask not recognizing the number.

My heart races thinking there's something wrong with Elijah or Katie.

"Reagan?"

"Yes?"

"This is Charli. Dr. Hunter. I'm sorry I missed your call. Tell me what's going on."

I give her all the information I have, uncaring that the other people in the office are openly staring at me as I lose my shit on the phone.

"Are you okay to drive?"

"I think so."

"I want you to come to the office."

"The nurse said this is common."

If she's freaking out, I'm going to freak out more.

"And you're upset. So, let's see if we can get some answers to calm your nerves."

I agree, and without saying anything, I leave the office. I don't remember a second of the drive and thank heavens traffic was light, and it's only a couple miles away.

They wave me back the second I show my face at the front desk.

"Dr. Hunter is in with a patient, but she's ordered a sonogram. Head right in there and Leslie will get you started."

I follow the point of the nurse's finger, meeting a smiling Leslie who instructs me on what I need to do for a vaginal ultrasound.

I warn her of the blood, but she just gives me a weak smile, telling me that there are disposable pads I can use under me in the cabinet. After situating the puppy pad looking thing under my hips and inserting the tip of the ultrasound wand inside, I have to lay there and wait. The seconds seem to tick by forever, but I know it's only been a couple of minutes when Leslie walks back in.

"Ready?"

I give her a nod as she reaches a gloved hand under the blanket covering my legs. I stare at the ceiling, doing my best to fight back tears. I don't want to look, but eventually I can't not look.

The image on the screen is so different from the ones I've seen before. I've never had a sonogram before sixteen weeks, so looking and not seeing a baby freaks me out.

"It's okay, right?"

"Just looking."

Leslie doesn't say another word for five minutes.

"Just tell me," I urge.

She gives a soft smile, one that's decidedly more somber than the one she had when I first walked in. "Let me get Dr. Hunter."

The wait while she's gone is excruciating.

"Hi, Reagan. Let me take a look here."

Dr. Hunter doesn't reinsert the wand. She looks at the series of images Leslie saved in her machine before turning to me with her lips in a flat line.

"There's no baby?" I ask, my voice so weak I'm not even sure she heard me.

"The embryo—"

"The baby," I snap in correction.

"Nothing developed in the gestational sac. It's what we call a blighted ovum."

"I'm ten weeks. Maybe it's too soon," I argue. "It's just too soon."

I snap my eyes back toward the screen that shows nothing. There's nothing there.

"I'd like to get blood work today, and then blood work tomorrow. I'm going to monitor your hCG levels before I make a decision about what we need to do going forward."

"I haven't had any symptoms for weeks," I mutter.

Dr. Hunter leaves the room, and Leslie follows her out.

My chin quivers uncontrollably as I redress.

As a mother, I fell in love with this baby the second I threw up at the damn bar. I was scared, terrified what I'd do but I never, for a second, didn't love it, and I won't stop doing it now. I hold my head high as I walk to the front desk to pay my co-pay. I'm not giving up on him.

My hope doesn't fade as I go to the lab for bloodwork, but when Miles calls later that night, I can't bring myself to answer his call. I can't tell him because if there's a chance that the doctor is right, it's going to split our world right down the middle.

I've finally been able to accept that I love this man, and this has the potential to rip all of that right out from under me.

Chapter 32

Jinx

"The room rental doesn't cover the hole you're about to walk into the carpet. Can't you sit down for a minute?"

I'd growl at Rocker for being an asshole if I had the ability to pull my nose from my phone.

"What's going on?" he asks when the pacing and my fingers working over the screen don't stop.

"Reagan isn't texting me back," I mutter.

"It's a little early there for a mutual spank session," Legend teases.

I glare at the asshole. "Why are you in here anyway?"

He rolls his lips between his teeth to keep from laughing, but then his face sobers when he realizes I'm not in the mood for jokes or games.

"Tough crowd," he mutters before leaving the room.

I try to call her once again, but after six rings, it goes right to voicemail, just like it has the last three times I've called.

"Have you given her enough time to respond?"

"Yes."

"Really? Because Simone says six minutes isn't enough time. I'm told I can't freak out for at least forty-five."

"I haven't spoken with her all afternoon." I look at the time in the top corner of the screen. "It's after seven there."

Me: I swear, woman, if you don't let me know you're okay, I'm going to send Max over there.

Those blessed three little dots pop up, and at first, I'm relieved, then the doubt starts to set in. She's been happy. We've been making plans, and even though I drew the line at starting a Pinterest account so she can show me things she likes about houses, I'm fully involved and paying attention when she sends links and pictures of stuff. We're making plans, but I should've guessed that leaving again for work was going to cause another problem. The last time, I deduced, was because she found out she was pregnant, and she was freaking out with how to tell me.

This time? Who fucking knows?
Reagan: I'm trying to get the kids to bed.
Me: Wish I was there.
Reagan: When do you get home?
Me: Not for a few days.
Reagan: I'll see you when you get home.

Did she not read the damn text correctly? I told her days. If she thinks she can avoid me for days, then she's clearly lost her damn mind.

"You'll break it if you keep squeezing it like that," Rocker says, and I nearly punch him in the nose when he goes to take the phone away from me. "What did she say?"

"She's putting the kids to bed," I mutter, pocketing my phone.

She responded finally, and that helps my nerves some, but I don't think I'll be able to handle it if she shuts me out every time I have to leave for work. It's not one of the things we talked about. News of the baby kind of took over everything else, and now that I've bought the house next door to Rocker's, we've moved to focusing on that.

"She's crazy," Rocker says.

"Do you want a broken nose because I won't even apologize, no matter how fucking angry Simone gets at me for messing up your handsome face."

"You think I'm handsome?" he asks, hand swiping down his smiling face.

I growl, and he gives me a fake shiver of terror.

"I don't mean like normal crazy. She's pregnant crazy."

I continue to glare at him because the clarification doesn't make what he said any better.

"Hormones, man. I'll call you a liar if you ever tell Simone I said this, but they're fucking nuts when they're pregnant."

"Simone was fine with River and Cooper," I remind him.

"Simone was good at hiding her crazy. They hyper-focus on things and get distracted. Don't you remember us finding Simone in the floor of the nursery with clothes scattered all around her?"

I shake my head.

"That day she was crying in the middle of the room. She had five more pairs of baby pants and no shirts that matched. She'd been there for over an hour. How could you not remember that?"

"Was that the day you sent me to Target to get shirts?"

"And you brought back seven instead of five, and we had to hide the extra two until we could get matching pants for them? Yes, that damn day. Like I said. Pregnant women are nuts."

"Reagan seems upset. She's just—"

"A little off?" I nod. "Pregnancy brain, man. It's not just for forgetting things. Everything is registered on an apocalyptic scale when they're pregnant. Just nod your head and smile, man. That's all you can do."

"I can't fix the problem if she doesn't talk to me and tell me what's wrong," I argue.

"And there's a good chance there isn't anything you can really fix." He slaps me on the back. "Just give her extra attention when you get home. Do your best to anticipate her needs, and if all else fails, make her come. That always works with Simone."

I comb both of my hands through my hair in frustration. "I fucking hate being away so long."

"We all do, but we have a job to do. Now, let's go grab something to eat before bed. We have a hell of a day tomorrow."

"Don't forget your fucking wallet this time," I hiss, smiling as he laughs and turns back to the bedside table to get his wallet.

I've fallen for that one too many times. The guy isn't broke, but he's not forgetful either. I know he's keeping a running tally of how many times I end up paying for his meal before I walk out and leave him to try to barter doing the damn dishes instead of getting arrested.

I step outside of the hotel room to see Thumper leaned up against the wall with his back to me and his phone to his ear.

"I'm telling you there's nothing," he hisses, clearly upset. "You're looking for something that isn't there."

There's a pause, and I know I shouldn't be eavesdropping in this man's phone conversation, but there's also been something off with him for the last six weeks.

"Then it's bad intel. I'm fucking trying. I've already—"

"I know you'd never leave me there alone," Rocker says with a laugh as he walks outside of the hotel room.

Thumper spins around, guilt clear in his eyes as he meets mine.

"I gotta go," he snaps into the phone before ending his call. "Hey, guys. Heading to dinner?"

"Yeah," Rocker says as he tucks his wallet into the back pocket of his jeans. "Wanna join us?"

"Naw. I already ate."

My eyes follow him as he disappears around the end of the hallway.

"Have you noticed him acting weird?" I ask when we leave the hotel.

The walk to the restaurant is only a couple of blocks, so we don't bother with one of the vehicles.

"Who?"

"Thumper. He's just been off."

"We all have our moments. This job can be lonely even with all the guys around. Plus, everyone is *off* to you these days. Quit reading shit where there's isn't anything to be found."

"Has he ever mentioned having family?"

Rocker shrugs. "Fuck, Jinx. I don't know. I don't get in the habit of grilling everyone."

"I didn't ask about grilling him, but he hasn't mentioned anyone to me."

"You were in the Corps just like the rest of us. You know there are guys out there that aren't up for sharing all their business. He was special ops. He's not going to open his mouth and blab his business like a fucking sorority sister."

"And you haven't noticed how his demeanor has changed? When he first got to Cerberus, he was all smiles and laughter. Now he's secretive and quiet most of the time."

"Are you sure you aren't projecting your issues with Reagan on someone else?" I shove him through the door of the restaurant, and he laughs at me. "See? She makes you violent."

"You're a real asshole, you know that, right?"

"Guilty as charged." He takes a ridiculous bow in front of me. "But seriously, if you have concerns, shoot it up the chain. Leave it at Hound's feet. It's why he gets paid so fucking much."

"Maybe I will."

"Do you also want to sit alone? You seem to have an entire pity party surrounding you. I don't know if there will be room for me at the table."

I smile at the hostess as she greets us.

We drop the subject, somehow managing to speak only about sports and gossip at the clubhouse. As if in silent agreement, we don't open our mouths to talk about things that are bothering us. We don't talk about our hormone-crazed women or my concerns over Thumper. We don't mention the fact that there's a good chance there's asbestos in the flooring at the house I just bought.

But even after a lighthearted meal filled with laughter and jokes, I don't feel any better when I crash against the itchy sheets of the hotel bed an hour later. I'm stuck in bed listening to Rocker saying dirty things into his phone in the bathroom, all the while my goodnight text goes unanswered.

Chapter 33

Reagan

I can't keep my leg from bouncing up and down as I wait at the doctor's office. I had blood work drawn today before heading into work, and now that it's my lunch break, I'm back to speak with the doctor. I'm trying to prepare myself for bad news because if everything was fine, they'd tell me over the phone, right?

I wouldn't have to come in and speak with her if she was wrong yesterday. I want to run, to ignore the news she has to deliver. I want to put my head in the sand and make it all go away. Losing this baby would be a tragedy because it means I'll lose Miles as well. Without this child, he has no reason to stay, no reason to stick around.

I've practically chewed a hole in my lip by the time I'm called back.

"I wish I had good news for you, Reagan, but the blood work shows a drop in your hCG from yesterday."

"It's only one day." I swallow down the need to cry. "Maybe I just need more time."

"It was already incredibly low. My concern is infection."

"I don't understand."

"The gestational sac is still in your uterus, and it's been there all this time. There's a higher concern for sepsis if we can't get it to pass."

Pass? She makes it sound like the part of my body that's supposed to be nurturing a growing child is a gallstone.

I nod, somehow understanding what she's saying while still remaining confused.

"I hate to have to give this news, and before you can ask or beat yourself up, nothing you did caused this. Sex, work, stress, strenuous exercise—nothing like that caused this. There was something wrong with the egg or the sperm or both from the onset of conception."

"That doesn't make me feel any less guilty." A tear rolls down my cheek, and for a moment, I hate that she's the bearer of such bad news so often that a tissue appears in my line of vision before I can even ask for it.

I take it, shredding it in my trembling hands before I can even get it to my eyes.

I'm broken and so angry. I want to curl into a ball and cry, but at the same time I want to swipe everything off the counter and rage about life not being fair.

I do neither.

I sit there, crying as silently as possible, waiting to hear her sigh in frustration because she needs to get on with her day.

"What happens next?"

"I'm going to write you a prescription."

I nod, knowing I need something strong to keep me from losing my mind.

"It will help you pass the sac and hopefully prevent the need for a D&C."

I look up at her, my eyesight bleary with my tears, but I can't manage to form a sentence even with a million things running through my head.

"You'll need to take it with food. Wear a heavy-flow pad, and you'll need to make sure you pass the sac, Reagan. I can't stress that part enough. If you don't in the next forty-eight hours, I need you to let me know so we can schedule the D&C." She rubs my back, and although I don't know this woman, it's comforting.

Until it isn't.

I shrug her hand away because it's just too much. I don't feel like I deserve comfort. She says it's not my fault, but I can't keep my mind from swimming through every single moment since that night with Miles. I analyze what I did, what I didn't do. Even as recent as yesterday, I didn't go home and lie down like the nurse instructed me to do.

Shame has me asking her to use a different pharmacy than the one I normally use. She gives me a sad nod and agrees.

As I leave the office, I wonder how I can stay on my feet and keep my legs moving me toward my car when my heart is utterly broken. People glance at me, whispering to others as tears streak down my face, but I don't have the energy to dash them away.

I sit in my car so long, I get a text message that my prescription is ready all the way across town. The drive is silent, the radio powered off, and I feel numb by the time I pull through the drive-thru to get the prescription.

I'm on autopilot for the next couple of hours.

I make arrangements for the kids to stay with Shane for the next two days. The paperwork that came with the medication warned of abdominal pain, but I can't imagine anything worse than how I feel right now. I deserve every ounce of pain in the world.

Simone tries to coax me into explaining what's wrong when I grab the kids, but she doesn't continue to pry. I lie and assure her everything is fine, refusing to think about what I'm going to do with the kids next week. I'll never be able to bring them back here, not after Miles finds out what I've done. I stop just short of falling into her arms. I can't lose it now. Elijah and Katie don't have the capacity to understand what's going on, and honestly, I don't have it in me to admit out loud just how big of a failure I am.

Shane and Martin are both home, and somehow their schedules line up for them to be off the next two days. I don't give them details, and they don't ask questions either. Maybe it's the sheer devastation in my eyes that keeps their mouths snapped closed.

Another miracle happens in that Mom isn't home when I get back. I force soup down my throat, and I hope the five bites I was able to choke down is enough.

It takes me over an hour to convince myself that the doctor is right, and this is something I have to do before I'm able to take the damn pill.

After popping it in my mouth and swallowing, all I can manage is curling up into a ball and sobbing. The tears renew when Miles's name flashes on my phone. I hit ignore, knowing he'd be here to comfort me through this only for him to slowly drift away over time.

Just when I had something amazing in my life, karma or fate or whatever force that is tasked with making sure I'm not happy caught up with me.

Chapter 34

Jinx

"I don't know." Simone sighs into the phone. "The kids are here, so she has to be at work. I haven't seen her smile in days, Jinx. She drops the kids off and picks them up, but she's withdrawn. I don't know what's going on, and she won't talk to me."

"Thanks," I snap, hating that Simone is catching some of my attitude. "Sorry."

"Don't worry about me. Go figure out what's going on. I just hate that I can't help."

The entire drive from the airport back to the clubhouse I'm a nervous wreck. Hell, I've been a nervous wreck for the last five days. Reagan hasn't returned a text or answered a call in three days. I haven't heard anything from her since those vague, short messages she sent about getting the kids ready for bed.

I don't waste time when Shadow pulls up outside of the clubhouse, and I'm grateful we always debrief the morning after we get home because I'd be in trouble if we did it immediately upon arrival. Nothing could keep me from going to her right now.

I breathe a sigh of irritated relief at seeing her car parked outside of the firm. I know Simone wouldn't lie to me about her dropping the kids off, but even knowing it didn't settle my nerves.

My eyes find her the second I pull open the door, but her head is angled down as she reads something on her desk.

"Reagan?"

She freezes at the sound of my voice, and when her head lifts, eyes finding mine, she isn't smiling. There's no happiness in her eyes at the sight of me after spending a week and a half away. It makes my heart skip a beat. The sparkling joy and suggestive mischief that's normally in her eyes are absent.

"Can we talk?" I do my best to swallow down the lump forming in my throat before it suffocates me.

"I'm working, Miles."

She looks away, the shadows under her hallowed eyes darker than I've ever seen before.

"Reagan, please," I say a little louder.

I don't care that I'm drawing the attention of others in the office. Leaving without finding out what the fuck is going on isn't an option.

"Five minutes of your time, Reagan." Her eyes snap up to mine, but I see resignation not anger, and that's worse than anything. The lump grows bigger, and a hum of fear settles inside of me. I haven't felt this kind of terror since my days in the Marine Corps. It's that same tingle, the threat of death, the heaviness in the air just before tragedy strikes.

"Is there something I can help you with?"

I keep my eyes locked on Reagan, not bothering to look at the woman who has approached us.

"I just need a few minutes, Mrs. Beck." I take a step back, not realizing I was crowded over her, as Reagan stands. I follow her out of the building and around to the side of the office.

"You need to talk to me," I snap the second we're out of earshot. My words are low, hissed through clenched teeth. "Ignoring me for days is unacceptable."

She keeps her back to me, arms crossed over her chest. I want to spin her around, force her to face me. If she's going to leave me, I refuse to allow her to do that like a coward. But I can't touch her right now. I'd never hurt her, but I have a swath of emotions boiling inside of me, and I don't want to take the chance.

"Talk to me!" I hiss again.

I'd think she was frozen if it wasn't for the slight tremble in her shoulders.

"You're pregnant with my fucking baby! You don't get to just shut me out!"

This gets her attention.

"I'm not pregnant with your baby!" she screams as she spins around.

I watch, mouth hanging open as tears fall from her eyes.

My first thought is that she's been lying to me, that she's pregnant with another man's baby, but in my bones, I know that isn't what's going on.

"I was at the doctor's office with you, Reagan. It's my baby. Why are you doing this? Why are you trying to push me away? I'm nothing like those other two assholes. I'm—" The next thought hits me in the gut, burning through me like I've swallowed acid. "Did you—did you terminate the pregnancy?"

I'd had concerns over that when I first found out because she was so withdrawn and sad, but I was sure we'd overcome that. When I left for work, she was happy. We were making plans. God, I left knowing our futures were going to be together.

A heavy weight begins to crush me because fuck, it's her body, and that makes it her choice, but I don't know that I'll be able to move past it. I would've been heartbroken had she said that's what she wanted right at the beginning, but there's no coming back from this happening after we discussed fucking names. Hell, we argued over whether we wanted a boy or a girl.

"Reagan?"

Her eyes are dropped to her hands.

"Please, tell me you didn't."

She shakes her head, but her sobs are too strong to speak.

I step closer to her, but stay a few inches from actually touching her, terrified that I'll collapse under my own pain if I feel the heat of her skin against mine. My throat is dry, my eyes stealing all that liquid.

"Reagan?"

"I l-lost the baby." Her head continues to shake as if she can't believe the words coming out of her mouth. "The d-doctor said there was never really a baby. The s-sac was e-empty."

My own head begins to shake, but it doesn't help. My chest caves in, somehow now emptier than it was just moments ago when her hands cover her lower abdomen.

"But how is that possible? I loved the baby." Her eyes look up at me. "I love the baby, so how could it have never been a baby?"

"Reagan," I whisper, holding my hands out and stepping closer. "Oh, baby."

She takes a step back when I inch closer to her. "But it's gone, and now you're going to hate me, and I don't think I can handle looking at you and seeing you look at me in a way different from how you used to. I just can't. I can't even look at myself. Dr. Hunter said there's nothing that could've been done, but I know I ate something or maybe it was that sip of alcohol at *Jake's* or not getting enough sleep. Maybe it was—"

"Baby," I whisper just before pulling her to my chest.

"I wanted our baby. I would never—"

"Shh. I know. I know." My hand rubbing her back doesn't feel like enough.

Sobs wrack her shoulders as her hot tears dampen my shirt. I dash away my own tears before lifting her in my arms.

"I have work," she says when I carry her to my SUV.

"It's fine," I say as I urge her into the passenger seat, hating that the house is miles away.

I don't want to release her, but I know she doesn't want to be seen like this by anyone.

I know I break several traffic laws on the drive back to my house, but thankfully I make it there without getting pulled over by one of Farmington's finest. She's withdrawn again by the time we make it into the driveway, but tears are still pouring from her eyes, breath hitching with every other inhale.

I carry her into the house, ignoring the chaos of the kids playing in the living room.

Simone gives the sight of me holding her in my arms one look before nodding and going to tend to Elijah who has seen his mother upset and begins to ask what's wrong.

"Let Miles help her," Simone cajoles as I carry her up the stairs, taking them two at a time.

"I shouldn't be here," she says when I lower her to the bed and pull her heels off.

"This is exactly where you should be," I whisper as I situate her on my bed and crawl in beside her. "Let me hold you."

And I do. For hours. I know she's exhausted. Emotional trauma is more strenuous to the body than physical stress could ever be, and she's been struggling with this for days, probably since before those last texts she sent.

My heart is broken, and it just continues to break as her body refuses to give in to the sleep it so desperately needs.

"Shh," I soothe, my hand continuing to rub circles on her trembling back. "Sleep, baby. I've got you."

It's another hour before she fully relaxes against me, and it isn't until I know for certain that she's asleep that I let my own tears fall in earnest.

Chapter 35

Reagan

I've been asleep for hours. The sun has fallen below the horizon, tinting the room in soft shades of light, and as much as I need to get out of this bed and go find Elijah and Katie, I allow myself a few silent minutes.

I just can't pull myself from his arms, knowing it could be the very last time I'm encircled in them.

I'm not surprised by his reaction. Not that his mind automatically went to my having terminated the pregnancy or the comfort he showed once I admitted to the miscarriage. I should've lied and told him that I did do it on purpose. At least he would hate me now instead of later.

And he's going to hate me. What man wants to be with a woman that can carry two other men's babies but not his own? The sense of failure I felt before he showed up at the office has multiplied tenfold.

I spend the next couple of minutes trying to distance myself from all of it. I need space from the loss, space from him, space from the comfort he's offering because I know it's going to shift. He may not openly despise me today, but the time is coming.

I spent the better part of a week after he found out about the baby trying to build the courage to tell him that I loved him, and now I'm grateful I never said those words out loud. Hearing him saying them back only for him to deny them later would be too much on top of everything else.

I've had days to cry silently at night since I found that spot of blood. Days to accept the direction my life is heading. Days to wrap my head around losing him.

It hasn't been nearly enough.

But regardless of my inability to strengthen myself against what's coming, I know I have to steel my spine. I can't curl into a ball while the rest of the world fades away. I have Elijah and Katie to worry about. They need me, and it's not fair to give them less than what they deserve.

Rejection is coming. The other shoe is finally dropping, and I'm a damn fool for ever letting myself think that this wasn't the direction things were heading. I shouldn't have ever let myself believe in a happily ever after with him. I fought against it, kept that fact in the back of my head.

Even now I struggle to let it resurface, and I blame the pain I saw in his eyes when I told him the news for the struggle I'm having now. I know I need to pull away. Staying or begging him to not toss me aside won't help in the long run. If anything, it will only make the end more bitter.

He flexes against me when I try to pull away, then his soft, warm lips meet my forehead, making me wonder if he was ever asleep to begin with.

"Tell me what you need," he whispers against my hair as his hold on me strengthens.

I need things to be okay.

I need my baby back.

I need him to look at me with love and adoration the way he did before he left for work eleven days ago.

"I need time," I whisper. "Space."

"Reagan," he mutters. "Baby."

Maybe being the one to end things will make it better. Maybe it'll help me to heal faster.

I won't survive watching him try to hold on only to let me go in the end.

Men don't stay.

I guess I should count my blessings that he has stuck around as long as he has, but the outcome was always going to be the same.

"I don't want to let you get out of this bed."

And I don't want that either.

"I need to check on the kids."

He opens his arms when I push against him the second time, and I turn my head toward the bedroom door because looking at his handsome face would just be too hard.

"Reagan?"

Without turning fully toward him, I angle my head over my shoulder to indicate I'm listening.

"We're going to be okay, baby. I promise."

I nod, the agreement a lie I feel in the deepest parts of me.

I head to his en suite to wash my face before facing my children. I've done my best not to let them see or sense my pain over the last couple of days. I know Elijah is going to have questions. I heard him upset when Miles carried me inside the house earlier, and I justify the lies I know I'm going to tell him because he's just too young to know such bad things exist in the world.

I don't look toward the bed and the man still lying there when I leave the room.

Simone, once again, doesn't pry. She hands me my keys, telling me that my car is in the driveway. And somehow, I make it out of the house without having to face him again.

He doesn't come down the stairs to find me, and when I pull out of the driveway to head back to my mother's house, I give the house one last look.

It's already starting.

Chapter 36

Jinx

I never came out of my room last night when Reagan left. Doing so would end with me on my knees begging her not to leave the house.

She told me she needed time and space. I think that's the last thing that's going to help her heal, but I have to respect her wishes.

I woke up this morning a little less of myself than I was when I fell asleep, but I also woke up determined. I can't change what happened, but I can make things better for us going forward. That's why I was ripping out water-stained sheetrock in the house I bought, long before the sun came up.

Three hours in, the sun is beating through the open windows, making me wish I'd started this project months ago before the New Mexico sun was hot enough to threaten to melt the skin from my bones. I don't think being completely splayed open at this point could make me hurt much more than I already do.

I smack the forked end of the hammer into another place in the sheetrock before pulling it toward me to make the hole bigger.

"Hey, man!"

I take a long breath before turning to face my jovial best friend.

"Getting started a little early, aren't you? We all agreed to help. There's no sense in doing it all alone."

"Couldn't sleep," I grunt as I swing the hammer again.

The reverberation isn't as satisfying as I imagined it would be when I rolled out of bed this morning and hustled over here.

"And it seems you don't want anyone else to sleep either," he jokes.

I laugh, but it's only skin deep.

I look at my friend, and his smiling face makes me feel even more dead inside.

"You're not going to be able to help in slippers," I mutter as I drop the hammer to the floor and use my hands to pull pieces of the broken sheetrock from the studs.

"Well, I don't think they make steel-toe slippers."

"I wouldn't want to exist in a world where they do."

"I just came to show you this."

A black-and-white picture pops in front of my eyes.

"Wow," I say with as little emotion as I can, dropping the debris and palming the image.

The threat of tears burn in my nose and behind my eyes. I'm man enough to admit I cried like a baby last night. I was hurting. I'm still hurting.

And for fucked-up reasons I can't understand, the sight of the sonogram image in my hand makes me hurt even more.

"Congrats, man."

I pass it back to him before the pain takes over and I end up crumpling the precious thing.

"I mean, I expected a little more enthusiasm, but I guess when you see Reagan's—"

"There won't be." I clear my throat when the words escape on a pained breath. "She lost the baby."

"Fuck," Rocker grunts. "I'm so fucking sorry."

I shake off his hand when he places it in the center of my back.

"Sorry. I just—"

"Naw, don't worry about it."

Silence fills the air around us, and I can only image how uncomfortable he must feel right now. It's not my intention, but I also don't have it in me to worry about his feelings right now.

"I'm happy for you guys, but—"

"I umm... it's... just don't worry about us."

I hate that I can't celebrate his joy with him right now. I hate that I'm questioning why us. I hate the bitterness inside of me that can't be as happy for them as I should be. God, I would never want anyone to go through this. I wouldn't wish it on anyone, and I don't want it for myself either.

I blame no one. No matter how much Reagan blames herself, I don't. If she said the doctor advised her that there was nothing that could've been done, then I believe her. I know these things happen, but why did it have to happen to us?

Bitterness is sour on my tongue, making me feel like a piece of shit.

Despite what Reagan told me, I can't help but wonder if things would've been different if I had insisted she move her and the kids in with me weeks ago. Her mother is a source of so much of her stress. She hates her job even though she hasn't said anything about Brian bothering her for weeks. I let her stay in those overly trying situations and look where we are.

"This is why she wasn't texting you?"

"Yeah," I mutter with my fists against the wall. My head hangs low between my shoulders. "She blames herself."

"There's no blame."

"I know, but I'll never convince her of it. Hell, I can't help the blame I'm placing on my own fucking shoulders."

"And you need to keep busy?"

I nod. "I'm not avoiding the situation. I can't get it out of my head, but if I can get this house ready and get all of us moved in, it'll help make things better."

"It's going to take time to heal, Miles. It won't happen overnight." He sighs, but it isn't laced with frustration. "Fuck, man. I don't even know what to say, and that makes me a complete asshole."

"No," I argue. "I didn't know what to say to her. She said she needed space and time, and I just let her walk out."

"You're giving her what she needs."

"What she says she needs," I clarify. "I want her in my arms. If she's going to cry, I want those tears burning my skin. I don't want her facing that shit alone, lost in her head where she's questioning everything."

"You can't force her to be here."

"I can't go against her wishes."

"Then you need to set a deadline. Make your mind up just how much time, just how much space you're going to give her, and when it passes, then you step up and make her see what's right in front of her."

"She's already pulling away. Fuck, if I haven't fallen in love with the woman, only to end up losing her." I choke on my words.

I sink to the floor as my legs give out. We've both lost so much already. I don't know that I'll survive if I lose her, too.

I don't fight or try to pull away when Rocker sinks to the floor beside me. His strong arms wrap around my shoulders, and I lose it, sobbing out all the pain that shows no sign of relenting.

Chapter 37

Reagan

"Good morning," I tell her when she opens the door.

I struggled with the decision to bring them today, but Mom made it easy seeing as she was gone from the house by the time I got them ready.

I'm exhausted with everything going on including still needing to find a new job and a place for the kids to go during the day.

"Come here," she says, stepping into me and wrapping me in a hug before I can argue.

I lean into her, taking all the comfort she's willing to offer. My eyes burn, but they haven't stopped for days. I somehow manage to keep my tears from falling.

"I'm not going to ask questions," she says as she continues to hold me. "But please know that I'm here if you need someone to talk to."

"Thank you," I whisper as she steps back. "They haven't eaten breakfast."

"Good," she says with a smile. "I made cinnamon rolls."

"Elijah will love you forever."

I'm able to leave without getting choked up but the care she's showing me without knowing what's going on is more than I could ever ask for.

The friendship that I formed with her in the last couple of months is just one more thing I'm going to lose.

Work starts slow, office staff and attorneys filtering in slowly, but it's expected on a Monday morning. No one is as punctual as I am. I know that fact goes overlooked by most and met with disdain by others who think I'm just sucking up.

The day passes slowly, my mind adrift on anything but my job. Lunch comes and goes with me unable to stomach the thought of food. I feel like a zombie wandering through life with no direction. I'm numb and vibrating with pent-up energy all at the same time. It's a weird place to be.

The energy I've managed to muster begins to flag in the middle of the afternoon, and although I know I'm going to regret it when I attempt to get some sleep tonight, I can't resist the draw of the coffee pot in the office kitchen. My fingers tap out a somber tune on the countertop as I wait for the slow drip, drip, drip of caffeine.

"Oh, Reagan. I'm surprised to see you here."

I grind my teeth at the sound of Brian's voice. Work has kept him busy for weeks, and normally I'd be on the lookout for him. I've managed to avoid having to utter a word to him outside of the things my job requires, but I guess that luck just ran out.

"I'm here every day, Brian," I mutter, keeping my eyes on the coffee pot that seems to be purposely punishing me by working so slowly.

"You took off Friday. Just jumped in the car with that biker without a word."

I do my best to ignore him, but he seems hell-bent on invading my space. I take a step to the side, facing him with my back to the countertop. I cross my arms over my chest.

"It wasn't very professional. I know Old Man Hollow may have a positive opinion of those bikers, but I assure you that Mrs. Beck does not hold them in the same regard."

"Yeah? And how would you know that?"

A slow, menacing smile tugs up the corners of his mouth. "She told me as much at dinner that night."

I huff a humorless laugh. I'm not one bit surprised that he'd go so far as to try to get in her good graces. He's a snake always out for himself.

"And then we talked about it again Saturday morning."

The implication makes me cringe. She's old enough to be his mother, but that doesn't bother me either. To each their own, but the woman is married.

"Yeah? I can't imagine that Mr. Beck would be okay with that."

I nearly sigh in relief at the coffee pot hissing out its final push of coffee, indicating that I'm only a minute away from escaping this tiny kitchen. There isn't enough room for Brian, me, and his overly large ego.

"He was out of town. She was lonely."

I grab a cup from the cabinet and pour myself a cup of coffee before facing him again.

"This is Farmington, Brian. Sleeping with your boss isn't going to get you anywhere."

"But leaving work early is sure to get you fired."

"Why?" I snap.

"Isn't it obvious? You can't just come and go as you please, Reagan. This is a place of business."

"Not that, you fucking idiot," I seethe as I tell myself that throwing hot coffee in his face will land me in jail. "Why are you like this? Why are you so determined to cause problems for me? Did you think after seeing me that I would just get little hearts in my eyes and want you back?"

His laugh makes me see red. "Wow, Reagan. You're so full of yourself. You aren't even a blip on my radar. Why would you be? What man wants a single mother with two kids? One that lies about being married to try to cover the fact that she's a whore that sleeps with everyone? You can't even have the grace to get pregnant by one man. You did it with two."

Three, I think as my lower lip begins to quiver.

The man really knows where to dig to extract the most pain. He must be a beast in the courtroom.

"I hate you," I snap, but he blocks my path when I try to step around him.

"No," he practically yells. "And I've told you that I'm not interested in what you're offering. Keep asking, and I'll report you."

I look at him in confusion, but when he steps aside, I know why he said it. I can't even make eye contact with the office manager as I rush out of the kitchen and back to my desk.

He's done it. He's issued the final blow. I'm not even surprised when I'm called to Mrs. Beck's office at four. I'm not shocked at all when she asks me to step inside and shut her door. I'm not even stunned to see my personnel file on her desk, her manicured fingernails tapping against it.

"Have a seat, Reagan."

"Is there a reason to draw this out? I'm fired, right?"

She frowns, the wrinkles around her mouth becoming more pronounced.

"We haven't reached that stage yet. There are procedures in place for situations such as this."

"And what exactly is this situation?"

"Another employee in the office has filed a sexual harassment complaint against you."

I scoff. "Brian?"

"For legal reasons and to protect the rights of the other employee, I'm not at liberty to divulge that information."

"He wasn't so protective of your right to privacy when he was in the kitchen earlier, bragging about how he's sleeping with the boss."

Her eyes dart to the side before they harden in my direction. I'm great at context clues, so I didn't even need her confirmation, but now that I have it, I'm even more disgusted.

"Don't worry about proper procedure on how to get me fired, Mrs. Beck. I quit, and if you have any further questions about the case you're trying to build against me, go through my attorney."

"And," she says with an obnoxious tilt to her head, "who might that be?"

"Mr. Hollow of course."

"That's not possible," she snaps, her back straightening. "You can't retain an attorney from this office. It's a conflict of interest."

"Only for those still working here when the case goes to court."

I leave her office to the sound of her huffing in anger. I grab my things from my desk, including all the personal effects that have accumulated over the years.

As I walk out of the door, I hear her snap out Brian's name.

I get into my car with the pride of knowing that Brian set out to ruin my life, and if I had to wager, the man will also be unemployed by the end of the day. Mrs. Beck isn't going to risk a lawsuit against me, and I know she'll highly suggest Brian doesn't either. She doesn't want all of her dirty little secrets coming to light. What she didn't know is that crawling into bed with Brian Wakefield was the biggest mistake of her life. I can only hope as I drive away from the office that she'll become his focus now. I've had enough of Brian Wakefield to last a lifetime.

Chapter 38

Jinx

"What's wrong?" I ask stupidly when I open the door to Reagan standing on the front porch.

There is so much wrong, but after the conversation I had with Rocker this morning, I know what I have to do.

Laying it all out at her feet is the most I can do. If she doesn't want me after that, then I have to accept it.

Hell, what am I even thinking? I don't have to accept shit. I won't let her push me away because she's hurting. I won't let her throw something so special away because she can't wrap her head around the fact that I'm nothing like the assholes she's dated in the past.

"The kids aren't here?"

"They're at the park."

"Okay. I'll go get them from there."

"No."

The single word stops her in her tracks before she can turn to leave.

"We have to talk about this."

She tries to look away from me, but I don't allow it.

"You're hurting," I say, my voice soft. "I'm hurting, too."

"Miles." Tears form in her eyes, threatening to spill over.

Doesn't she know that I'm here to catch them? Doesn't she know that I want—no I need—to be the one she leans on when's she's sad or upset?

Then it hits me. I've never told her exactly how I feel. I've been focused on showing her through actions how much I care for her.

"I love you, Reagan Dunn, and I'm not—"

"What?" Her eyes widen, but her chin quivers instead of her mouth turning up in a smile.

"I love you."

"Please don't do this. It's only going to make it harder."

"Are you leaving me?"

"I have to before—" The tears break free, falling too fast for me to wipe them all away. "Before you leave me."

"Baby," I whisper, my hand cupping her cheek. "I'm never leaving you."

"You will," she argues.

"Then I dare you to stay until that happens." She shakes her head slightly but doesn't pull from my touch. "And you'll be waiting forever, Reagan. I'm not going any damn place."

"I lost our baby."

"We lost a baby, and I won't let it rip us apart."

"I feel so broken," she whimpers.

I pull her to my chest. "Then I'll hold you until you're put back together."

"Please don't hurt me more, Miles. I'd never survive it."

"Baby," I breathe against her hair. "Never. You're fucking stuck with me."

"I love you, too."

I hold her tighter as my own tears dribble down my cheeks.

***

"We're going to have to face everyone eventually," Reagan mutters against my chest.

Exhaustion overtook both of us after our confessions in the entryway. We landed in my bed, tangled in each other's arms and napped for an hour. I feel like I could sleep for several days, but my body is on high alert where she's concerned. Once I felt her breathing change, I was wide awake.

"Rocker knows. That means Simone knows. She's not going to hold it against us for taking a little time for ourselves."

She snuggles tighter to my side as my fingers begin to sift through her hair.

"I want you here with me always. I don't want to wait until the house next door is ready. I need you to think—"

"Okay."

"Okay?" She nods, her smile sweet against the bare skin of my chest. "You get that I'm asking you to never leave, right?"

"I know, and you're going to get more of your wish than you realize. For a while at least."

"I'm not complaining."

I hitch a finger under her chin and tilt her mouth up so I can kiss it. The action is soft and sweet, somehow passionate without it turning into sexual need.

But then it does. I blame the fact that we've managed to close the distance between us, the emotional more than the physical, but mostly it's the way she moans into my mouth.

"Mommy! Daddy!" Elijah screams as he rushes into the room so fast, I'm sure the doorknob just went through the wall.

He tries to fling himself on the bed, but it's a little too high. Reagan turns to watch as he scrambles quickly up and throws himself on top of us.

"Sorry," Simone says, sticking her head in the door. "I tried to stop him. He's so fast. Come on, Elijah. Let's give them a little time alone."

"Daddy," Elijah says with his tiny hand on my cheek. "Mommy has been sad."

"Has she?"

He nods. "Fis it."

I chuckle at the mispronunciation.

"I'm fixing it, buddy. We're taking a nap. Wanna take one with us?"

His eyes dart between Reagan and me.

Without another word, he lays his head on my chest, his little eyes fluttering closed.

Simone smiles, slowly backing out of the room and closing the door behind her.

"Is it bad that I love it when he calls me daddy?"

"I think it's sweet," Reagan says softly as she rubs her son's back. "I was afraid it would bother you."

"Never," I promise. "I mean, I don't know how to handle it if Katie does it."

"We'll cross that bridge when we get there."

"I love you so very much." I press my lips to her forehead.

"I'm the luckiest woman in the world."

"I consider myself pretty lucky, too."

With her in my arms and Elijah snoring softly on my chest, I can't imagine any other place I'd want to be.

Chapter 39

Reagan

"And this?" Izzy asks, holding up a lamp.

"The living room. Maybe on that far table?"

It's been months since our loss. It still hurts. I still find myself sinking low with thoughts of what happened, but Miles has been there every step of the way.

He's never faltered. Never made me doubt the words he makes sure I hear from his mouth every single day since he first said them.

"Where does this go?"

"The kitchen," I tell Shane.

"Really?" He looks down at the box in his hands as he draws closer. "It's marked with three X's."

"That means it's bad for the kids. It's either cleaning supplies or alcohol."

"Not where I thought that was going, but okay."

I laugh as he walks away.

"Need some help?" Instead of taking the box from my hands, Miles wraps his arms around my waist before pressing his nose into my shoulder.

"I can handle it."

"You seem ready to throw the entire box in the trash."

"I just want to get my hands on the psycho who thought it was a good idea to use so much tape on the damn thing."

"What's in it?"

I tilt the box to read the side. Miles must read it too because he laughs.

"I think you were tired when you packed it. You said books were more valuable than gold before using nearly an entire roll of tape on it. Here."

He produces a knife, first cutting through the tape on the sides before going for the top.

"You cut one of my books, and they'll never find your body," I warn.

"Who will keep you warm at night?"

"My anger will keep me nice and toasty."

He steps to the side and uses great care to get the flaps of the box open.

"Why are you opening this? The bookcases won't be here until next week."

"I needed to smell them." I give him a shrug as I lean in close to do exactly that.

"Weird, woman," he mutters.

I smack at him. "Go help bring more boxes in."

"I thought we were going to have a hard time filling this house, but we may run out of room soon," he says as he watches several guys come in the front door with their arms full.

"You told me to find what we needed. As it turns out, that was just about everything."

"You accepted the challenge and ran with it." He winks before heading back out to grab more furniture.

I work diligently for the next hour. All the Cerberus guys showed up to help and made fast work of getting everything into the house. Miles insisted on putting most of the furniture together himself even though several of the guys offered. He finally conceded and told them to come back tomorrow afternoon.

"Are you purposely running our helpers off," I complain, my body tired from getting up early and working all day.

"I wanted to be alone."

"And you forgot we have two children?"

He's the one who started calling them that, and the day I first heard it was when I gave myself fully to him. It wasn't until that moment that I realized I was still keeping tiny pieces for myself. I was terrified to lose him, willing to walk away first to avoid any more pain, and God, am I grateful every single day I wake in his arms that he refused to let it happen.

I didn't need time or space. I only needed him.

"Shane offered to take them, but they were so tired from the busy day, they were already in their room asleep."

He presses himself to my back, arms circled around me, and we just stand there and look over the mess in the living room.

"Simone is going to keep an eye on them tonight. She said Elijah was a little upset. Someone promised him a camping trip tonight."

I laugh. "No, I told him his bed wasn't put together, and he'd get to sleep on a pallet like he would if he went camping."

"That's not what the kid heard."

"Think any little fairies will sneak in here tonight and clean this mess up while we're sleeping?"

I giggle when he spins me around to face him. "You think we're getting any sleep tonight?"

"Look around you." I point to the bare windows. "I may have gotten a little turned on watching people get it on at that clubhouse party, but I'm not giving the neighbors a show myself."

"Gigi and Izzy hung the curtains in our room. Haven't you been up there?"

I shake my head, angling it a little to the side when his warm lips meet the skin there. "I've been down here unpacking and directing traffic all day."

The next thing I know, I'm swept up in his arms.

"If you drop me, I'll never forgive you."

"Have you not seen my muscles?"

I trail a finger down one flexed bicep. "You have very sexy muscles."

He pauses halfway up the stairs to press his lips to mine.

"If you keep saying such salacious things to me, I'm going to bend you over on the stairs and fuck you silly."

I bite my lip. What? Is he expecting me to object?

"Looking at me like that will also get you into trouble."

I blink up at him as innocently as I can manage, but the growl that rumbles from his chest tells me that he isn't reading purity in my eyes.

My eyes drop to his mouth, and it sets him into motion.

"I wanted you to see what the girls did for us today," he says as he uses the tip of his boot to nudge open the bedroom door, "but it's going to have to wait."

"What they did?" I ask in confusion, spinning my head around to look at the room after he uses his shoulder to flip the light on. "Oh, Miles!"

"Nope," he snaps. "I warned you."

I look over his shoulder as he heads into our bathroom. "They even hung the pictures!"

"Yes. It's all very lovely," he says as he lowers my feet to the ground. "Now get naked."

I laugh when he wraps his arm around my waist to prevent me from going back to take in the room.

"We need a shower. Strip."

I don't move fast enough, obviously, because he begins to help me.

I glare at him when my shirt gets tangled on my head. "Buttons, you weirdo."

My words are muffled behind the fabric covering my face.

"Who the fuck puts buttons on a t-shirt?" he complains as he pushes the fabric down before working the offensive things open.

"American Eagle," I mutter.

"And this is the worst invention ever." His fingers go to the front zipper of my sports bra. "Ah, better."

"Don't do that!" I hiss, smacking at his face when he goes to lower his mouth to one nipple. "I'm all sweaty and gross."

"Would you leave me if I told you I'm willing to eat week old pizza off your ass?"

I scrunch my nose, and he laughs, a gravelly sound that makes me wonder if he's joking or not.

"Mmm. Still delicious." He presses kisses to my sternum on his way to the other breast. "Never wear that thing again."

"I figured I was going to be running up and down the stairs all day. Had I not worn it, my boobs would be too sore to enjoy—ah, I love your teeth."

He kisses away the bites before raising his mouth to mine.

"I'm enjoying all of this, but please know I won't be returning the favor. I know how hard you worked today, and I draw the line at—" I point to my mouth then the crotch of his jeans.

"There's only one place I want my cock right now, Reagan."

I wave my hand in front of him in question.

"Not even close."

"Yet, we're just standing here talking."

"You're talking," he clarifies. "I'm enjoying the view."

"Yeah?" He nods, and I'm so thankful for this man.

I laugh every single day with him, and he doesn't freak out when sometimes that laughter turns to tears. Those days are fewer and farther apart with each day that passes.

His fingers begin to work his clothes off as I continue to strip to the skin in front of him.

Although he's ready for me, standing tall, proud, and thick, he makes no overtures in the shower. He doesn't miss an opportunity to trace a nipple or slide his fingers against my slit, but he doesn't lift me or urge me to bend over either.

It seems the first time we make love in our new house, he wants it to be in our bed. I know neither of us has forgotten, but I'm not counting the time he fucked me last week when they delivered the new washer and dryer. A little conversation about the spin cycle turned into me moaning and not needing the machine to even be plugged in to come on his cock.

"You're thinking super dirty thoughts," he whispers as we towel off in the steam-filled bathroom.

"I'm always thinking dirty thoughts," I remind him. "Are you thinking clean thoughts?"

"That's not even possible when you're near." He hangs his towel on the towel rack that also got hung today.

I'm going to have to get the girls a gift basket or something. They did an amazing job up here today.

"Do you want your blow dryer?"

"I don't have the energy to even worry about it," I tell him as I wrap my wet hair in a microfiber towel.

That's all he needs to hear, because the second I lift my head and secure the towel on the top of my head, I'm back in his arms.

"How much are you looking forward to foreplay?" he whispers as he carries me out of the bathroom and places me in the center of the bed.

His cock is hard between us, pressing rigidly against my stomach.

"I'm ready for you," I tell him. "I'm so keyed up right now."

"You're sure? I don't want you to feel left out."

"I'm never left out." A smile spreads across my face, because I'll never walk away from a chance to tease him. "Well, except that one time."

His teeth dig into his bottom lip. "It happened once, and you're the one who bounced on my dick like a pogo stick saying all that nasty stuff to me. I got overly excited."

"Mhmm," I agree.

"And I hadn't seen you for two weeks."

"I remember."

"And I think I more than made it up to you."

"I think you still owe me."

"A debt I'm willing to pay right now." His hips move back and then forward.

I moan my pleasure when he spears into me.

"God, you're fucking perfect. Open wider for me, baby."

My legs fall open on his command, my body needing everything he's offering.

"Not yet," he says when my fingers start to wander down my body.

"But I want to come."

"And you will, baby, but I want it to be together."

I whimper, my body right there on the edge, but this man can play me like an instrument. He knows just what to do and how to keep me on edge.

"If you hold back just a little, then I can come twice," I barter.

"Oh, you're going to come far more than that tonight."

I arch my back with his promise, lifting my breasts up so they can't be ignored. His mouth trails kisses down my sternum. His tongue snakes out to taste. The man worships my body, and when he whispers, "Now," against my skin. I explode, coming down just in time to feel him pulse his release deep inside of me.

He asked once, the first time we made love after our loss if I wanted him to wear a condom. He understood without further conversation with a simple shake of my head what I was willing to give him. It hasn't been brought up since.

We both want a baby together. I don't face that possibility with the fear I was once strangled with.

It hasn't happened yet, but we'll be over the moon if it does. Pushing down the worry that we'll have another loss is always in the back of my mind, but I know I have him no matter what.

I'm done with pushing him away, done with waiting for the other shoe to drop. Done with thinking I don't deserve happiness.

I only fill our lives with happiness and joy, with time with Elijah and Katie. We find pleasure in each other and our friends, and when he's gone, I now have an entire team of women to rely on.

I'm no longer alone in a crowded room. Miles Alexander brought me into the light, and I have to say, I love the feel of the sun on my face.

Chapter 40

Jinx

"Did you try this one?" I ask Rocker, holding up a bottle of the IPA that Apollo brought back from his visit home.

"Is it any good?" my best friend asks.

I shake my head, my nose scrunching up.

"What?" Apollo snaps as he comes running into the kitchen. "That's the best stuff ever. Try it. It's hoppy and light all at the same time."

"I'll stick to this," Rocker says, backing away as he lifts his regular beer to his lips.

"That hippie shit is never going to pass in this clubhouse," Dominic adds.

"It tastes like sweaty balls," Tug complains as he places the bottle he just sipped from on the counter.

"You would know," Max tells him with a wink, making me spit my beer across the floor. "I like it."

Wow, Reagan mouths from the other side of the room.

"You know the rules," Dominic growls, but there's a tiny grin playing on his lips as he leaves the room.

"What's that about?" Reagan asks when I step up closer to her.

"Dominic is Jasmine's father, remember?"

"And Jas—Oh! Yeah. Okay." She buries her face in my neck, and I know it's to hide her embarrassment, but I'll take any touch she offers up. "So, what's the rule?"

"They can't talk about sexual things in front of him."

"I don't blame him," she says with a quick laugh. "I still can't look any of them in the eye."

I hold her tighter, still unable to get enough of this woman. We've been together for months and fully in our new house for two weeks, but this is the first time she's come back to the clubhouse. People seem to gravitate to our house or Rocker's next door because it's just easier to come to the people with kids than having to pack half a house to go somewhere else.

There's no special reason we're here. Kincaid just thought it had been too long since we all got together.

"Have you met Colton's son, Rick, yet?" I ask as I guide her out of the kitchen and into the common area.

"Not yet."

"And Kid's son, Landon?" She shakes her head. "I'll introduce you to them later."

"I remember you telling me they're best friends."

I look across the room, finding that the boys are as far away from each other as possible without one being outside.

"I'm not getting in the middle of whatever the hell is going on. Probably fighting over some girl from college."

"Why do you keep looking around the room? Are you expecting someone else?"

I shake my head. "Just counting."

"Okayyy."

"Have none of the girls explained the Cerberus curse?"

She looks up at me, a wry smile on her face. "I don't believe in curses."

"We didn't put two and two together for a long time, but Cannon pointed out last year that after someone in Cerberus finds the love of their life," I squeeze her closer to my side, "the next time we all get together, some sort of drama takes place. It's going to happen today."

"Maybe there's just an increased chance for drama when so many people get together," she suggests. "What happened last time?"

If this was a sitcom, I'd scratch my head as I thought back, but for the life of me I can't even remember. Izzy and Drew were the last ones to get together.

"I met you."

"At the grocery store. See? Your curse doesn't even hold water."

"I sure hope so. Apollo, Legend, and Thumper are the only single men left. Hey, where's—"

"Conference room, now!" Kincaid snaps the second he flies through the front door. Shadow follows behind him with a snarl on his lips, and I know this is going to be bad.

"Go sit with Simone, baby." I press a kiss to the top of her head and file in behind Rocker as he passes.

Kincaid is vibrating with rage as he stands at the front of the room waiting for all of us to take our seats.

"Is that everyone?" Shadow asks as he looks around the room.

"We're waiting on Thumper," I say as I pull out my phone. "I'll shoot him a text."

"Don't," Kincaid snaps, his eyes boring a hot hole in my face. "Thumper is no longer on the team."

If his anger before didn't get our attention, that news does.

"Fuck," Apollo mutters. "Is he dead?"

My hands begin to shake. We risk our lives every day when we're gone and working, but to lose a brother at home would be tragic.

"He's going to fucking wish he was," Shadow mutters, but then glances at Kincaid without saying another word.

A silent conversation passes between them before our president speaks again.

"Shadow just discovered some pretty fucked-up news."

I knew I shouldn't have listened to Rocker when I voiced my concern about Thumper's change in behavior. I just pushed it out of my mind that same day because I was struggling with the distance Reagan was putting between the two of us. By the time I got home, we were dealing with our loss, and Thumper was back to his regular happy self. I even felt bad for questioning his loyalty. We all go through shit, and I was an asshole for wanting to get into his business as a deflection of my own.

"Fucking lay it out, Prez, because I'm losing my shit over here," Scooter insists.

"Thumper was recommended to us by a friend," Kincaid begins. "I was told that Edward 'Thumper' Jones was a perfect fit for the team."

"Who fucking told you?" Tug hisses as he cracks his knuckles.

"It doesn't matter. The guy who made the recommendation was duped as well."

"So what? He wasn't in the Corps? He's excellent in the field. Maybe—"

"His time in the service was cut short because of a dishonorable discharge," Shadow interrupts. "But that's not the topic of discussion right now."

"His real name is Javier Nolasco. From what we have gathered, he was born in the US, but he has family ties to El Salvador," Kincaid continues.

"Is he ashamed of his family? Why would he lie?" Rocker asks, because like me, he just can't wrap his head around where this is going.

"Javier Nolasco is the leader of a sex trafficking ring in El Salvador."

The screen behind him activates, and every jaw at the fucking table drops as a series of images flash.

"As you can see, he's right in the fucking thick of it," Kincaid hisses.

"That motherfucker," Tug grunts, and it's received by several other explicit agreements.

"One of our worst enemies has broken bread with my fucking family. He spent time with my grandkids." Kincaid begins to shake and despite the size of the table we're sitting around, it looks like he's ready to lift the edge and flip the damned thing over.

"We're tightening security here. It's going to be close quarters. After everyone is cleared, we're going to close ranks." No one bats an eye that our president is saying we're all going to need to be vetted all over again. "Those that live in town are going to have to get closer to the clubhouse. Anyone that sees that as a problem will be out."

No one argues.

"Shadow and Max will work on getting everyone cleared. In the meantime, I want mouths closed. I don't give a shit what your loved ones ask. I don't even want excuses made. If anyone asks about Thumper, your jaws are locked. Do you understand?"

We all nod in agreement.

"We suspect that he was trying to get a read on how the club operates in an effort to prevent infiltration at one of his own places, but we can't be too sure. We have no idea what type of information he obtained while he was here," Shadow adds.

"And the plan?" I ask, feeling guilty that this all could've come to light earlier had I trusted my gut instinct.

"We're going after Javier Nolasco with every fucking thing we've got. We won't rest until I burn that fucker's world to the ground."

Cerberus MC continues with Thumper next!

**Newest Series
Cerberus MC
Gatlinburg, TN Chapter**
Hemlock: Cerberus TN Book 1
Ace: Cerberus TN Book 2

Standalones
Crowd Pleaser
Macon
We Said Forever
More Than a Memory

Cole Brothers Series
Love Me Like That
Teach Me Like That

Blackbridge Security
Hostile Territory
Shot in the Dark
Contingency Plan
Truth Be Told
Calculated Risk
Heroic Measures
Sleight of Hand
Controlled Burn
Cease Fire
Crossing Borders

Cerberus MC

Kincaid: Cerberus MC Book 1
Kid: Cerberus MC Book 2
Shadow: Cerberus MC Book 3
Dominic: Cerberus MC Book 4
Snatch: Cerberus MC Book 5
Lawson: Cerberus MC Book 6
Hound: Cerberus MC Book 7
Griffin: Cerberus MC Book 8
Samson: Cerberus MC Book 9
Tug: Cerberus MC Book 10
Scooter: Cerberus MC Book 11
Cannon: Cerberus MC Book 12
Rocker: Cerberus MC Book 13
Colton: Cerberus MC Book 14
Drew: Cerberus MC Book 15
Jinx: Cerberus MC Book 16
Thumper: Cerberus MC Book 17
Apollo: Cerberus MC Book 18
Legend: Cerberus MC Book 19
Grinch: Cerberus MC Book 20
Harley: Cerberus MC Book 21
A Very Cerberus Christmas
Landon: Cerberus MC Book 22
Spade: Cerberus MC Book 23
Aro: Cerberus MC Book 24
Boomer: Cerberus MC Book 25
Ugly: Cerberus MC Book 26
Bishop: Cerberus MC Book 27
Legacy: Cerberus MC Book 28
Stormy: Cerberus MC Book 29
Oracle: Cerberus MC Book 30
Newton: Cerberus MC Book 31

Ravens Ruin MC

Prequel: Desperate Beginnings
Book 1: Sins of the Father
Book 2: Luck of the Devil
Book 3: Dancing with the Devil

MM Romance
Grinder
Taunting Tony

Westover Prep Series
(bully/enemies to lovers romance)
One-Eighty
Catch Twenty-Two

Lindell
Back Against the Wall
Easier Said than Done
With a Grain of Salt

Made in the USA
Columbia, SC
30 June 2024